ON WINGS OF DARK MAGIC—

A shrill keening filled the air, rising swiftly in intensity, and suddenly they appeared—gargoyles, those creatures out of nightmare visions, the ancient guardians of Horlach's gate!

Leathery, scabrous wings beat violently, the creatures smote wildly with talons, teeth, and barbed tails. The Venturers blurred in a vision of fury. Swords struck, rebounded.

As one of the creatures flew at me, I could sense Kaedric choosing his first victim. Yet even as his sorcerous fires ate at the gargoyle's heart, I felt a terrifying foreboding of doom, a fear all too soon confirmed as Kaedric's spell was turned against all of us by Horlach's sorcerous trap. . . .

TALES OF THE TAORMIN

"There seems to be no limit to what a skillful and creative writer can do."   —*Kliatt*

"Ms. Franklin writes with a richness of detail and a grandeur of vision that exercises one's imagination to the fullest. Fresh and original in her work, this gifted author is making a real name for herself among science fiction fans."   *Rave Reviews*

"The world of FIRE GET is complex, richly populated, and intriguing . . . characters come alive . . . vividly evocative . .. filled with real people who have intricate and interrelated histories."
                                                      —*American Fantasy*

TALES OF THE TAORMIN

FIRE GET
FIRE LORD

Cheryl J. Franklin

DAW BOOKS, INC.

DONALD A. WOLLHEIM, FOUNDER

375 Hudson Street, New York, NY 10014

ELIZABETH R. WOLLHEIM

SHEILA E. GILBERT

PUBLISHERS

http://www.dawbooks.com

First printing, January 2005
1 2 3 4 5 6 7 8 9

DAW TRADEMARK REGISTERED
U.S. PAT. OFF. AND FOREIGN COUNTRIES
—MARCA REGISTRADA
HECHO EN U.S.A.

PRINTED IN THE U.S.A.

FIRE GET

To Dr. Walter S. Cascell,
who always understood so much more than
communication engineering,
but never quite mastered levitation.

I
THE SPARK

Chapter 1

Year of Serii—8983
Ixaxis, Serii

The ferry approached. The priest who waited at the dock had watched it journey the breadth of the narrow strait. The dawn was chill, but the clouds were high, and the island loomed sharply in the midst of the choppy sea. Occasionally, the priest darted a brief glance at the dark, incurious boy who squatted near the dock's land-edge. The boy was small and excessively thin; he tossed a glinting dagger from hand to hand with idle expertise.

Churning water tossed the ferry roughly against the dock. The dock shook, and the priest jerked to regain his footing. The dour ferryman placidly secured his craft.

A short woman, bundled against the damp, disembarked, pulling a limp scarf from graying, disheveled curls. Disgruntled, she muttered, "I despise boats." She stared coldly at the priest. "I did not think members of your calling cared to associate personally with our guild."

The priest answered evenly, "I bring you a candidate."

"Would you then sacrifice a member of your flock to us? That is what your sort calls heresy, is it not?"

"No calling is immune from folly," said the priest. "I recognize the difference between those who might follow my vocation and one who must follow yours." He gestured toward the boy, who maintained a sullen disregard of the conferees.

The woman frowned disapprovingly at both the boy and the

wickedly honed blade he sported. "Have I been dragged across the sea at this appalling hour to salvage an unsavory urchin? Your letter indicated life-threatening urgency, not some holy man's mission of charity." She grimaced with distaste. "What makes you think this mudlark has the makings of a wizard?"

The priest answered very softly. "He destroyed the city of Ven."

"Ven was destroyed by fire."

"Ven was destroyed by this boy's anger."

The woman looked sharply at the priest. She turned a pensive gaze upon the boy and walked deliberately across the dock. The boy did not acknowledge her. "I am Mistress Marga," she said. "What is your name, boy?"

The knife spun from the boy's hand. He caught it deftly, held it before him, and studied the blade closely. He looked up at the wizardess and studied her with the same emotionless intensity he had bestowed upon the knife.

The woman returned the boy's stare, noting with greater interest the startling impact of clear blue eyes as cold as frost looming in the emaciated face. They seemed to penetrate deeply and with purpose instead of shying from her as expected of a lad of such wretched background. She shivered, absurdly uneasy for one who could cow the highest Lords of Serii.

The boy rose abruptly to his feet, and she realized how very young he was to be so hard. Deliberately disparaging, she said, "The priest seems to think you have sorcerer's blood in you. Did you concoct that fable to avoid religious conversion?" As the boy did not answer, she continued caustically. "It was a novel but foolish deception." She turned away from the boy and began the return walk to the waiting ferry.

The priest warily watched both wizardess and boy. The boy closed his eyes tightly, clenching his fingers around the dagger as he pointed it toward the woman's back. The woman stopped, and the priest smiled slightly at the brief shock displayed on the wizardess' countenance. The woman turned again to the boy, who lowered his arm, seemingly against his will, and dropped the knife to the rocky earth. The boy's eyes pursued the knife. He regarded the wizardess from lowered lids.

"It appears you were right, priest," said the wizardess thoughtfully. "He is a revert. Does he know his parents?"

"Only his mother, and she is dead."

"A pity," said the woman. "Both his parents must have been latents."

The priest nodded vague comprehension. "Will you take him then?"

"As your letter so aptly stated, priest, we have little choice. A Power like that is far too dangerous to let grow untrained. Yes, we will take him. I think you have brought me far more trouble than a miserably early morning boat ride." She called to the boy. "I am cold and hungry for my breakfast, and I do not intend to wait for you all day." She acknowledged the priest curtly, "Father Medwyn," and marched determinedly to the ferry.

With a slow, peculiarly graceful act of caution, the boy recovered his dagger. He hesitated, then crossed to the priest and paused. The holy man raised his hand in blessing. The boy neither spoke nor varied expression, but he waited until the priest had completed the prayer before stepping lightly onto the rocking ferry.

The ferryman released his craft and maneuvered it into the returning current. The priest watched the ferry as it journeyed back to the island which owned it. He saw it meet the far shore, though he could no longer discern its passengers. He seemed disappointed, as if some expected event had not transpired entirely as he had hoped, but he smiled ruefully and began to turn away.

A light beamed across the water, and the priest raised his eyes. It was a clear and golden beam, and it sped from the far dock to the water at the feet of the priest. The priest smiled broadly. "Thank you, my son," he whispered.

Chapter 2

The cliffs were steep and chalky. They crumbled at the gentlest touch, and their shards littered the narrow beach. They gave the island an insubstantial semblance which was deceptive. The chalk coated the island in filmy layers, but the foundations were built of solid adamant.

The ferryman had not lingered at the dusty white beach. He had deposited his passengers and continued toward the cove which lay on the island's leeward side. The craft bobbed and disappeared around a bend of unkindly shore.

"Come along, boy," commanded Mistress Marga. She walked with assurance toward the cliff and seemed to vanish within a fold of rock. The boy watched quietly. Since debarking, he had made only a single move, a slight shrug which had sent lightning across the channel he had just traversed. He had frowned then, as if regretting an impulsive gesture.

He crossed the rough sand carefully, suspiciously studying the cliffs which dominated his view of the legendary island. He stared closely at the wrinkled steps which had been carved from the stone. There was a smooth plane of darker rock beside them. He stepped through it.

Mistress Marga faced him. She nodded slightly at his appearance, but she gave no other sign of acknowledgment. She had bypassed the simpler tests which she had planned, choosing instead the difficulty of the unexpected. She had known full wizards to take the stairs regularly without ever noting the door embedded in energy's illusions. She wished for a moment that she had allowed the boy to precede her. The hint her disappearance gave might have been unnecessary, and now she would not know. She reminded herself not to underestimate the boy's Power on the basis of his origins. Not every major Power had risen from the ranks of Serii's nobility.

She led the boy through the gently luminous lower halls of Ixaxis. The ways were seldom traveled; few students knew of their existence, for very few recent students had descried the spell-hidden entrance. The Powers of Ixaxis had waned since Ceallagh's days.

Mistress Marga opened the wrought-gold doors of a small cubicle and waited for the boy to join her. The boy stiffened. The wizardess observed the hesitation which might have signaled fear, and she filed the reaction carefully in her mind. The boy entered, but he remained tensely defensive from the moment she closed the doors until their reopening in the Ixaxin school's lower storage chamber. She could feel his Power waiting, and she gathered her own Power, an act of caution which she knew her fellow instructors would deride as absurd.

"This way, boy," she ordered. She knew the name by which the priest had called him, but she would not use it until the boy gave it. The priest—she had disregarded most of his letter as superstitious exaggeration. She would reread it with greater respect.

The boy was absorbing the abundance of wonders in his new surroundings, and Marga slowed slightly to allow his observations. He would be questioned later to discover their extent and perspective. He could not have known much of art or any fine craftsmanship in the slums of Ven.

She took him directly to the Headmaster's office, and bid him wait in the tiny entry. The boy was guarded there from any possibility of escaping, and she thought he knew it. Such perception ought to have been impossible without extensive training.

"He is a major Power, Vald," argued Marga to the white-haired Headmaster. "He would totally disrupt a novice class."

"Really, Marga, it is unlikely he can even read. How can we possibly place him at a senior level? It would be utterly unfair to him—

as well as to the other students who have worked toward that status for years."

"Senior status is not a matter of prestige. It is a gauge of developed Power, and some of our students could bear a reminder of that distinction."

"I am sorry, Marga," said Master Vald with finality. "He goes into the novice class. When he is ready for advancement, he may petition for the testing like any other student."

"At least meet with him."

Master Vald sighed. Mistress Marga could be a very difficult and obstinate woman, but she was a gifted teacher. "Very well, Marga. Bring the boy here, but please recall that I have a class to teach in a few minutes."

"Did I ever forget a class, Vald?"

"Not one of your own."

Marga sniffed. She opened the office door and beckoned to the boy, who appeared not to have moved at all. "This is Master Vald. He is the Headmaster. He will direct your studies according to your capacity and development."

"What is your name, boy?" asked Master Vald, and the boy gave no answer. Master Vald looked at Marga with considerable exasperation. "There is little purpose in your coming here, boy, if you do not intend to answer the simplest question. To be accepted for full Ixaxis training is a high honor. If you prefer not to accept our teaching, we shall bind your Power and return you to the life you left. Now, do you wish to be schooled with us?"

For a breath's moment, there was no response, and Mistress Marga grimly wondered what Master Vald would do if no answer came. She knew that the implied threat of returning the boy was hollow. They could not bind a major Power. They must train or eliminate, while they were still able, any Power which threatened Serii. That was the life and purpose of Ixaxis, but the mandated alternative to training had been unnecessary for millennia.

The boy's clear blue eyes narrowed in an inspection too knowing for an ignorant slum-child. He is proud, this boy, thought Master Vald with disapproval. "I wish to be schooled, Master Vald," said the boy in a careful emulation of Master Vald's clipped accent.

Days ago he knew only the incomprehensible Ven patois, thought Marga. It is remarkable that he even understands us, but already he has begun to copy us. I told Father Medwyn that he was a revert. I only half believed it, but he is; he truly is. He has the Power, the intelligence, the tenacity of life of a Sorcerer King. Lords help us if he has as well their unscrupulous, egotistical cruelty.

"Very well, boy," said Master Vald, "we shall accept you as an Ixaxin novice. Mistress Marga will take you to the Hall of Novitiates."

"Master Vald," acknowledged Marga with the half-bow of Ixaxin respect. She disagreed with the Headmaster's placement of the boy, but Master Vald had handled the interview well. The boy did not demur from following Mistress Marga in either bow or exit from the Headmaster's office.

"This is Hrgh, boy," said Marga. "He is one of our senior students, and he will be your class proctor."

Hrgh smiled as engagingly and insincerely as only a Dolr'han of Liin could manage. He was not allowed to use his title as long as he was a student, but no one could mistake the finely chiseled features and the perfect self-assurance of Serii's highest House. "You are from Ven?" asked Hrgh, and his voice was a smoothly perfect instrument of charm befitting the heir of Liin.

The younger boy stiffened very slightly at the question, and he granted it only a minimal nod. Marga grunted. The boy was determined to be difficult; perhaps Master Vald was correct in keeping him with the novitiate. "Explain our rules to him, Hrgh," said Marga. "Assign him quarters and a student's robe, and introduce him to his instructor."

"I know the proper sequence, Mistress Marga," returned Hrgh with a touch of condescension.

"As you know the proper respect due a scholar," rebuked Marga. Arrogance was a Dolr'han failing, and Marga enjoyed reminding the young Lord Hrgh that Ixaxin status was a function of merit rather than family birthright. Sorcerous Power was inherited, but its correct application demanded incessant work. Marga reconsidered: it will be difficult to teach that lesson to this boy of Ven who does so much without effort. She noted then that the boy was displeased by her censure of Hrgh. So, he is still vulnerable to certain types of Power, she thought with sharpened interest.

"You did not complete the introductions, Mistress Marga," said Hrgh in a grudgingly deferential tone.

"The boy has given us no name, Hrgh," responded Marga. She felt some reluctance over leaving the boy in Hrgh's care, but Hrgh was very capable. Hrgh was the strongest Power they had, though he was still some years away from scholar status. Marga closed the door behind her and felt the release of a flood of pent up tension of which she had been unaware. This waif shall not succeed in frightening me again, she asserted, and because she was Marga, her resolve became fact.

That old woman has no sense of her station, thought Hrgh, and look at this miserable specimen she has brought me: a nameless slum dweller. "As you give no name," said Hrgh indifferently, "I shall call you Venkarel. That means Ven-no-name in the ancient language of Liin. You are cognizant of Liin, I trust."

The boy looked uncertain. It made an ordinary child of him for the moment. He shook his head, and his dark hair fell across his crystalline eyes.

"You are not a very communicative sort, are you?" demanded Hrgh. "Liin is only the First House of Serii and the wealthiest, most influential domain in the Seriin Alliance."

"The King lives in Tulea," proffered the boy tentatively.

"You do speak. How comforting. I naturally exclude His Majesty from comparison. However, I must say that Tulea is only one city rather than a true domain. I cannot expect you to appreciate the difference, of course, but I assure you that Liin has no peer. These will be your quarters." Hrgh opened the shuttered door of a stark room which was little more than an alcove in the warren of the novices' dormitory. Hrgh pressed his hand to a recess where a lock would normally be found. The recess began to glow with pale gold. "I have marked it: Venkarel. It will be your place of sleep and your place of study during your years in the novitiate. You will eat in the common area with the other novices."

"Where are they?" asked the boy with his first show of interest.

"At class, of course. This is a school."

"Why are you not at class?"

"I am senior level, you impertinent serf, and novices do not question the higher ranks."

The boy dropped his lids lower over his blue eyes. "I am sorry, my lord Dolr'han," he said very humbly, but there was a flash of Power which Hrgh did not detect.

"We do not use titles here," said Hrgh, but the boy's servility pleased him. Hrgh did not consider the incongruity of a boy who knew nothing of Liin recognizing Liin's ruling family and its heir. Hrgh did not consider the strangeness of his own decision to cultivate this boy, this Venkarel, as a member of a Dolr'han's select group of followers.

Chapter 3

The Venkarel sat alone in his assigned room. He wore the gray robe of an Ixaxin student, and there were books on his desk: elementary texts which were his to read. He had mastered these and others in the library's privacy, but he would not yet admit to greater knowledge than his instructor had demanded. The other novices bemoaned the weight of work, but the Venkarel distrusted their complaints. This learning was so simple; these people appeared to give so many things without demand for payment. The Venkarel suspected entrapment, though he had not defined its form. He trusted none of these people save Hrgh. The Venkarel did not himself understand why he made this exception, but he did not question it yet; Hrgh had ensorcelled him well.

The Venkarel had learned survival in the slums of Ven, and his teachers had not been gentle. He knew the ways of treachery. He knew no other way to live. He had followed the priest, because only the priest had dared come to him after the terrible fire, the fire which had eaten his world. He had followed, because he had not known how to live in a world suddenly bereft of enemies. He felt comfortable here, though this place was very strange, because here he could find enemies again. He thought he understood the rules. The strong survived, though strength was measured differently on Ixaxis. Here, he was strong.

The Venkarel had categorized his fellow novices as either conspirators in deception or idiots. He had known their kind: Deev and Ag had been the same. The Venkarel regretted the comparison as he thought of it, for it recalled the blood, the fire and the madness.

Hrgh was the only Ixaxin who had gained any measure of the Venkarel's confidence. Hrgh was the only member of senior level whom the Venkarel had met. The Venkarel's conclusion seemed to him as obvious as Zerus' essential postulates of wizardry, which the Venkarel had recently learned: it was clearly necessary to become a member of the senior level.

"What is this?" demanded Master Vald, reluctantly focusing his eyes on yet another of the seemingly endless documents which crossed his desk. He stared at the latest for only a moment. "Master Helmar," remonstrated the Headmaster, "This is a student's test paper. I am not here to review individual examinations."

Master Helmar shuffled unhappily. He was a timid man who little resembled the common conception of a wizard. "I thought you might wish to see this one, sir," he said hesitantly. "It is—not usual."

With a sigh of irritated contempt for underconfident instructors who distrusted their own judgments, Master Vald gave the paper his attention. His eyes narrowed. "These results indicate a perfect score."

"Yes, Master Vald." Master Helmar continued apologetically, "I have tried to discover an error in my assessment, sir, or some irregularity in the boy's responses."

"There is no such thing as cheating on an Ixaxin test, Master Helmar. You know that," mused Vald, distracted now from the chronically uncomfortable instructor. The test results certainly appeared authentic. "I thought we had no strong candidates for senior level this term? How did this student's progress escape notice?"

"He seemed ordinary, sir."

"Helmar, I have never known a perfect score to be accomplished before. This student is clearly not ordinary. I hope you have not misjudged your other pupils so badly."

"He was in my class only three weeks, sir," responded Helmar defensively. "I had little time to gauge his abilities properly."

Master Vald stiffened, and his Power flared into the instinctive shield against danger. "What is this boy's name?" asked Vald cautiously.

Master Helmar answered with equal care, "He is called Venkarel, sir."

"Indeed." Master Vald was not pleased. Marga would gloat. "Send for Mistress Marga, Helmar. Tell her we have a new student for her senior level class." She has shown such fascination with the boy, thought Vald sourly; let her try to manage him.

Mistress Marga enjoyed her small triumph over the Headmaster. It was pleasing to have one's judgment vindicated, and it did not hurt one's standing either. Naturally, Marga did not reveal that she had herself questioned her initial assessment of the Venkarel's abilities. The boy's performance in the novice class had been far from outstanding. Marga had begun to doubt her instincts, but the Venkarel was her student now, and she could substantiate her first analysis. She was pleased, but she was greatly disturbed.

When he was aware of observation, the Venkarel held closely to the average pace of the other seniors. In the private sessions, Marga worked the Venkarel more severely than any other pupil of her long career, though she did not reveal how far and fast she pushed him, lest the boy realize how he was betraying himself. His advancement to senior level had accrued little notice because he was not a novice long enough to be known. He had begun to gain some acceptance because he seemed harmlessly mediocre and Hrgh approved of him. Perhaps acceptance was his only purpose in deception; it would be a common enough motive.

Still, pondered Marga uneasily, he does not try to cultivate friends. It is as if he plays a game against us, and only he knows the rules. I must teach him Ceallagh's laws of restraint before he grows beyond me. I have never had a more urgent task, for he learns so quickly on his own. He sees and remembers everything. I must mold him, or we will have another Horlach, and we have no Ceallagh and Tul to defeat him. I must make an Ixaxin of him.

How did they hold him so long in Ven? Father Medwyn said he was a slave; no wonder the boy rebelled. Lord Gides dur Ven deserved death for allowing such depth of crime to grow in his domain, but his folly cost many innocents as well. The boy's Power must have been dormant until the day of fire, or the cost might have been even greater. Thank the lords that the priest had sense enough to bring the boy to us.

I am nearly tempted to ask the priest to come here again. The

Venkarel gave some trust to Father Medwyn, whereas he has given none to us. No, the boy does follow Hrgh. Most of the students do; it is the Dolr'han Power, and it is potent. Perhaps I ought to be glad that any of us can influence the Venkarel. I just wish it were another. Hrgh is so fully a Dolr'han. He expects to replace Alobar as Infortiare in a few years, though he knows the Lord of Ixaxis cannot also be the Lord of Liin. Hrgh will not like to learn what I intend for the Venkarel.

Marga extinguished the oil lamp beside her desk; Ixaxis had older lamps which gave cleaner light, but she disliked using that which she could never understand. The moon struck the waves below her window. She wished uselessly that the present Infortiare were a stronger man or at least a stronger wizard. She wished that she might call him from Tulea. An Infortiare ought certainly to be strong enough to remain Ixaxin after less than a century in the King's castle, but Alobar had become Tulean and wholly mortal in his perspective. He has even grown old, she thought, though he has known fewer years than I have. He is a kind, old man, and he is useless to us.

A single wizardess ought not try to decide the future of Serii without her liege's will or knowledge. If I am wrong, if the boy is truly no more than a minor sorcerer made precocious by life-threatening circumstances, then I shall look the fool. I shall lose my status and any chance at a seat on the Ixaxin Council, and I shall have nothing. As a wizardess who has acted independently of her liege lord, I may find my Power bound from me as well.

Marga began to pace, then seated herself with deliberation. Ruing the Venkarel's appearance in her previously well-ordered life achieved nothing. The Venkarel was an aberration, and she would have preferred that he not exist; but he had come, and she could only do as she deemed necessary. She knew that she was tampering with Ceallagh's laws, with the King's will, and with the age-old stability of Serii and her world. That was the problem with aberrations: they were contagious. Marga knew that the Venkerel would make of her an aberration as well, but she would teach him to the limits of her capacity and his. She twisted the fine gold chain which marked her as an Ixaxin scholar, and she did that which she had not done since the vicar of Cuira drove her father from the church on the basis of Marga's Power: she prayed.

II
THE TINDER

Chapter 1

Year of Serii—8988
Ixaxis, Serii

The young man with the grass-stained tunic twisted her fingers with his broad hand. "Dad and Ma are at their duties, and the cottage is empty this hour, Ericka," he said coaxingly.

"Quietly, Jhobl," answered Ericka, a young woman whose attractions did not extend above her neck. "The children will hear you."

"I thought you said they never listened to you."

"They are my charges, Jhobl. I cannot just leave them when I wish."

"They play in their own garden, Ericka, and they will be the happier to be without a watchdog for a while. They get little enough time to enjoy themselves as children ought." Jhobl planted a surreptitious kiss on Ericka's neck, and she giggled her delight. "Let them play their games," wheedled Jhobl with another kiss, "while we play ours."

The amorous pair started guiltily when the little girl approached. She was a tiny, solemn thing with hair a shade of gold just shy of white and gray eyes too large for her face. "I cannot find Dayn, Mistress Ericka," she said.

The governess dropped her arms from Jhobl hurriedly, straightening herself into something of a dignified demeanor. She assumed her most authoritative manner. "Now, Rhianna, he was here only a moment ago. Were you not playing together?" she asked patiently.

"Yes, Mistress Ericka."

"And what were you playing at?"

"Dayn hid from me, and I was to search for him."

"Then, Rhianna, it would be unfair of me to find him for you. You know how your father feels about fairness."

"It is not cheating to ask for help," protested the little girl seriously.

"Do not argue with me, Rhianna," said Ericka sternly.

"Yes, Mistress Ericka," said the child again.

"Very well then. Finish your game honestly, and do not come back here until you have done so."

"Yes, Mistress Ericka." The little girl looked troubled, but she curtsied carefully and returned to her search.

"That should take care of them for an hour at least," said Jhobl admiringly, "since the little Lord Dayn will not want to be found. You are a clever one, Ericka." The woman smiled with satisfaction at his praise.

The two of them started toward the neat brick cottage which housed the head gardener of Tyntagel Keep and his family. Ericka stopped suddenly and looked back at the grove of oaks to which she had consigned her charges. "Nothing will happen to them," said Jhobl heartily. "Come along, and quit worrying."

Ericka creased her brow as she responded, "Dayn will be all right, I suppose."

"And so will Rhianna. She is a tough little thing, after all."

Ericka shook her head as she answered, "As if I did not know it. A swat sends other children into tears, but I could nearly kill that one, and she would take no notice."

"Then what bothers you, Ericka?" demanded Jhobl with burgeoning exasperation. He had worked long at this conquest of Mistress Ericka, and he did not enjoy delaying for His Lordship's offspring.

"She is up to something," answered the woman slowly.

"Children are always up to something, Ericka, but they survive it."

"She is not an ordinary child, Jhobl."

"Just what does that mean? You think she is another such as her mother?"

"Jhobl!" exclaimed Ericka with shock. "You should not even say such things in jest."

"Well, is that not what you meant?"

"I never did!" protested Ericka vehemently. Jhobl smiled winningly, and Ericka relaxed. "You are a one," she chided with restored good humor. "All right, I suppose old Baerod's get can tend to themselves a while." Jhobl laughed with her, and she yielded to his insistence, following him through the cottage gate.

Beneath the mottled, oaken canopy they had left, a very small girl watched the day grow darker. She had tired of the game her brother played at her expense, and she was frightened of being alone. She feared her governess almost as much as she feared her father, so she would not leave the wood until her brother had been found. Frantically, she wondered where he hid, thrusting her thoughts against the trees. The leaves sighed in the gathering dusk.

"You could not have seen me, Rani," argued a very displeased young boy moments later, still dubious of his sister's ability to discover his fine hiding place. "I was much too high in the tree. You watched me hide," he accused.

"I did not," protested his sister.

"You did. You cheated, and I shall tell Mistress Ericka."

"It is not cheating to ask for help," insisted the little girl uncertainly.

"There was no one here to help, you stupid baby." The boy grumbled, "Why did I have to have a stupid baby sister anyway?"

Relieved that her brother had not contradicted her view of the game's rules, the little girl continued stubbornly, "I asked the oak, and she told me where you were."

Her brother looked at her with exasperation. He started to sneer at his sister's set face. His dark eyes grew wide. "You used sorcery," he whispered with dawning horror. His voice grew louder with panic. "You *are* a sorceress. Get away from me!" he shouted. He pushed the little girl, and she fell, bewildered. She was only four and not yet learned in Tyntagellian prejudice. Her brother was seven; he raced to his father's keep to report the abomination he had found. Lord Dayn did not play with his younger sister again.

Chapter 2

Year of Serii—9001

The tutor was a pale man with the flaccid, boneless appearance of inactivity. His brow bulged and rose to a balding dome. His colorless eyes were prominent above an insignificant nose. He shifted stiffly, moving his hands as does one who is insecure in his position.

The girl whom he addressed was young, but she was old enough to discomfit the pallid tutor for more cause than the whispered stories about her heritage. She had known many other tutors, and her gaze could invariably rob the pale man of his assurance. She made him sense that she had heard all that he could tell her many times.

"Even the least daughter of Tyntagel's Lord must attend the responsibility of her position, Lady Rhianna," said the tutor in his high, irregular drone. "You are accorded the rights befitting a member of a Seriin First House. Your father, Lord Baerod," the tutor stumbled over the name, "expects that you duly uphold the honor of that privilege. You should serve the more gladly, knowing that you are a burden to him."

The girl, whose hair was fallow silk, studied her tutor with deep, gray eyes. She knew that the pale man lacked the strength to hold his position long. He creaked with anxiety each time he lectured her, and her father did not tolerate such inadequate behavior. She returned to her desk with a fluid motion; her tutor watched, and his head jerked nervously after her, following the sunlight's dance across the girl's frail form. He felt, as always, peculiarly awed by her obedience of his command.

The dark and ugly woman who occupied the classroom corner observed the man's reaction with disapproval. She fingered a talisman, a twisted thing which might once have been a living creature, and glared at the girl with venomous hatred. The woman resolved to bespeak the girl's father that night and recommend the tutor's dismissal.

Chapter 3

Year of Serii—9007

"She is past old enough, Baerod," insisted Lady Altha. "If you do not arrange her marriage soon, it will be admission to all of Serii that you consider your daughter a sorceress."

The Lord of Tyntagel rhythmically tapped the finger on which the onyx signet of his station glinted. He was infuriated with his cousin, and he scowled. *No wonder the Esmarians returned her so promptly after her husband's death*, he thought; *her tongue could sear a wizard. But she is right in this. I cannot pretend that Rhianna is fully mortal if I refuse to see her properly wedded.*

"She would bear children," he argued, more to himself than to his cousin, "and they would perpetuate her Power."

Lady Altha wagged her bony head. "Not necessarily. She is your daughter as well as Eleni's. Why you had to take up with that Alvenhamish witch, I shall never understand. You already had three children from Darya, and there were countless suitable women if you felt you had to wed again. You could hardly have made a worse choice, short of marrying an Ixaxin."

"That is enough, Altha," ordered Lord Baerod fiercely, and Lady Altha grew petulantly silent. *Altha manages the household well*, thought Baerod, *but at times she is as much trouble as Rhianna.*

Tyntagel's liege lord paced the length of his darkly paneled office. *Lady Altha is correct: Rhianna is a liability. Lord Brant has already approached me, and I cannot postpone an answer indefinitely. If I* approve her betrothal to Brant's son, I shall be defying Seriin law, because Rhianna is unquestionably a sorceress. If I admit that Rhianna is a sorceress, I shall be admitting guilt of keeping her from Ixaxin testing, and the Infortiare will strip me of my authority. If I refuse to arrange her marriage out of deference to Ceallagh's ancient laws, I shall be making a mockery of all I have done and said against Ixaxin rule. Brant will never join our effort to depose the Infortiare if I admit that I fear my own daughter's Power. I can contribute little to our effort if I lose Tyntagel,

Our need for allies is immediate. Venkarel is already restoring the old Ixaxin authority with the King, and we must stop him before we have another Horlach in our midst. We need every weapon we can muster, and we are so unprepared. We were so sure that Hrgh would replace Alobar. Who could have guessed that Ixaxis had raised such a devil as Venkarel? Who would have imagined that even Ixaxis could be so mad as to let a revert live? We were lazy, and now we must fight against time. We must stop Venkarel before he realizes his ambitions, before King Astorn becomes fully the Infortiare's puppet, before we are bowed again beneath a Sorcerer King. We must stir every force of mortal Serii against Ixaxis before it is too late.

We have lost Hrgh, but he was always a tainted tool. Lord Borgor is doing well in Tulea; as Adjutant, he may be able to keep the King's Council from Venkarel's grasp, and Borgor's wife has much influence with the royal family. We have warned the other members of the Seriin Alliance. Our agents are spreading throughout Serii. We must enlist all true Lords of Serii—even those whose kin are Ixaxins—if we are to counter the Lord of Ixaxis.

We must be ready to combat Venkarel when he returns from Ardasia. We have little more than a year in which to prepare. He is foolish to leave Tulea at such a time, but he makes too few mistakes. We must not hesitate to use his absence from the court. We must be united against him before he returns.

Rhianna is a liability, but she can gain us Lord Brant and Niveal. Brant will ask few questions about her; he will be glad of any dowried bride for a son who battered his first wife to death. If we delay the actual marriage, Brant will be too deeply involved in our cause to leave us when he realizes what Rhianna is. Tyntagel will lose Niveal's trade, but we shall have Niveal's aid against Venkarel.

Perhaps I can negotiate with Morgh Dolr'han for compensating trade arrangements; Liin has as much at stake in this war as I have.

"Send a missive to Niveal, Master Evram," commanded the Lord of Tyntagel. "Inform Lord Brant that I should like to discuss further his suggestion regarding alliance of our Houses. Invite him to Tyntagel at his earliest convenience."

"Yes, my lord," answered the young man with deference, but Master Evram's eyes were worried.

Chapter 4

Shadows fell heavily across the forest rim, and the weathered castle stone glowed with the burnished gold of dusk. From beneath my darkling oaks, I could see the keep clearly, but I fancied it a distant thing, like an etching in a frame. It held that ordered world in which I had no proper part, though it had been my home for all the years of my life.

The dark of spring's slow evening deepened. Above me misty stars appeared, shy precursors of bejeweled night. I had tarried overlong outside the keep; I would merit the scathing bite of censure for my tardy return. I laughed silently, and a mouse scurried in startlement. My father could impart very real reprisals for disobedience, but he seldom accorded me his direct attention. And I no longer feared scolding from any lesser authority, not after years of daily lectures from family and tutors alike.

Interminable education had successfully impressed upon me the duties of my position. The obligations of obedience never waned, but my formal schooling had ended. The end of my studies came unexpectedly, though I had been educated to an extent which amounted to absurdity for a Seriin noblewoman, and the sudden conclusion left me dangling uncertainly. I had detested Master Chiarge, my final tutor, though he had displayed no more callous cruelty or excess than his numerous predecessors, but I almost rued his departure now, a month removed from him in memory. Freedom of time let me realize my dearth of future plans.

It was an empty feeling which clutched me, a void which refused to be filled by the normal concerns of a Seriin noblewoman. I could match my sister's skills in those arts, such as needlecraft and music, considered requisite for any nobleman's wife, but few visitors to my father's keep approved of sorcerous blood. I had been educated more fully than either of my brothers, though they would each occupy governing positions in which the knowledge might better be applied. I had amassed considerable quantities of useless lore (I could recite a thousand years of rulers for every country in the Seriin Alliance), but the haphazard learning of a peasant child would have served me more practically. The indefinite duties of a patrician spinster had replaced the relentless regimen which my father had heretofore dictated, and I needed to believe that a more active design awaited me.

The oak beside me reached deeply into the earth, exuding a more substantial reality than thoughts of my present circumstances. His spirit calmed the uncertain tenor of my mind, and I leaned against his bole in contentment. The blight which had threatened him was fully cleansed from leaf and limb, and I knew I had wrought one thing well during this otherwise useless period of freedom.

My mother had named me for the legendary Lady of Dwaelin Wood. I had often wondered if my mother's Power had told her that I would bear Rhianna's gift to heal and hold the wild things of the land, or if she merely chose a name common among her people. I could bespeak and understand the simpler lives. It was the trait which had estranged me from my own kind.

I scarcely remembered any camaraderie with a member of my own family. My brother Dayn, always the least intolerant of my kin, had once given me a measure of grudging, childish friendship. I was four years old, and he had thought me brave, for I did not cry at the expertly inflicted thrashings bestowed by our governess, Mistress Ericka. His approval was as marginal as one might expect of a boy afflicted by his younger sister's perpetual company. Even that little had lasted only a season.

Mistress Ericka was the only governess I had shared with any of my siblings. After her dismissal, a new governess had arrived, but

I was not among her charges. A hard-faced nurse of solid peasant stock appeared to tend me and guard the other children from me. I never heard the nurse's name, for she was a superstitious woman; she wore about her neck a prominent amulet of rancid tallow and animal hide such as demons purportedly shun. There were other governesses and tutors for my education, but the nameless nurse had watched me almost incessantly until a year ago, when she had vanished as wordlessly as she had come.

I had disliked the eternal suspicion which had covered that nurse's face like a mask, but she had been a fixture no more annoying than summer midges. By the time I realized that my virtual imprisonment was unusual, I had accepted it. My father had proscribed Ixaxis testing for me, but I learned that his decision defied Seriin law only after I had been taught to abhor the Power which Ixaxis schooling would have fostered in me. My father's overriding hatred of wizards, their Ixaxin guild, and their Lord, the Infortiare, had produced odd gaps in my education, but I had no ambition to become a wizardess. A legion of tutors had instructed me to distrust Ixaxis, to despise the Infortiare, and to loathe my own abilities. Having once, years ago, suggested that the contributions of Lord Ceallagh dur Ixaxis to the foundations of Serii equaled those of King Tul, I was unlikely ever to repeat the crime; the memory of cold porridge and daily beatings for a month did not fade quickly. I acknowledged Tyntagellian histories with all their obvious gaps and inconsistencies, because it was my liege-father's will that I do so.

The last remembrance of sunlight left the sky, and the keep spread darkly against the planes of evening's violet hills. The keep was a squat and angular structure which had grown by haphazard, boxy appendages for too many centuries. It might have been lovely once, the two original towers lifting the eyes from the central structure to the proud, distant heights of the Mountains of Mindar; the greatest loveliness remaining rose from the groves of oaks which huddled near the keep's encircling walls. Only the oaks had withstood the warping of Tyntagel dreams into iron of stark contour. Dour Tyntagel prospered, but my father's rule held nothing of dreams.

I sank my heart and mind into the warmth of the oak, my great friend who had stood a sturdy bastion for so many lifetimes of mage and mortal both, hoping to forfend a fit of that familiar bitterness which had hovered too closely of late. I thought forcibly of my sister, Yldana, who had wed Lord Amgor dur Amlach and gone with him to the King's court in Tulea. I thought of my brother Balev, who occupied himself in the exalted matters appropriate to the heir of Tyntagel; his spiritless, tedious wife, Nadira, had recently borne him a second daughter of exemplary normalcy. Dayn served presently as a captain in King Astorn's army, and in a year he would assume the dynastic functions of his rank.

Envy in my soul had long ago grown stale and sere. I could not conform to my family's pattern, but I could walk in the Tyntagel woods in companionship with the gentle ones therein. I could not rue the gift which gave me such friends. I faced the evening wryly receptive. I had stayed the dragons of despondency for another day. I plucked persistent leaves from my long tweed skirts and sought the bare earth path to my father's gate.

Chapter 5

I hastened, belatedly concerned by the certainty of repercussions if I were discovered in my late return to the keep. I had allowed just sufficient time to assume some delicately impractical dinner attire and the aspect, which fooled no one, of a decorous lady who had whiled away the afternoon in suitable passivity. Intently contemplating my possible punishment, I failed to notice Evram's approach.

"You have been avoiding me, Rani," he called. I had nearly reached the isolated stairs which led to the keep's back passages, and I debated whether I could attain them before Evram reached me. He anticipated me, as he often did, crossing to me in a bound and pinning me with his arm.

"Let me go, Evram," I pleaded. "I shall be late as it is."

"A few more moments will not harm, or does the lady of Tyntagel grow too grand to associate with her father's secretary?"

"Your status in this keep outshines my own, Master Evram. It is you who risk contamination by speaking to the Tyntagel sorceress."

Evram reached his fingers to the nape of my neck in a soft caress. He whispered reassuringly, "You are not a sorceress, Rani. I shall not believe it of you, whatever others may say."

"I am my mother's child, Evram, and I must go." I tried to pull free gently.

"Only if you promise to meet me after supper."

"You know that I cannot. I must read to my great-aunt until she tires of it, and by then you will be home and the keep will be locked against you."

"Lady Retl has the grippe, and she will want no company tonight. We may not have another such opportunity. Meet me in the garden house, Rani."

His hand moved tentatively, and I moved decisively away from him. "I thought you had agreed not to think of me thus, Evram."

"I agreed to give you time, but I shall not wait like Nimal until your father has wed you to some Seriin lord whom you do not love."

I answered austerely, for kinder words would not dissuade Evram. "You are presumptuous, Master Evram." He released me, for the force of my denial hurt him. I had never before used the voice of my rank against him. "I am sorry, Evram," I said sincerely.

"You are Lord Baerod's daughter after all," returned Evram bitterly. It was a cruelly knowing insult; I had upset Evram badly. He gave me a stiffly formal bow. "I have behaved improperly, my lady," he said with excessive, hollow contrition. "Please accept my apology."

He did not raise his face to me, and I spoke to his chestnut brown hair. "In the future, Master Evram, I trust you will recall that I *am* your liege's daughter." He darted at me an unhappy glance which I refused to acknowledge. I breathed a sigh of sympathy only when he had gone. Evram felt betrayed. I had rejoiced once that Evram did not shun me for my sorcery, but I had sorrowfully concluded that stubborn illusion was the true recipient of his love. Evram refused to connect me with what he considered an irredeemable sin; he refused to believe that I could speak with a tree.

I concentrated more firmly on passing unnoticed through the maze of corridors which I had trod for years. An uneasy aspect of my tainted abilities, evading notice was a gift I used seldom and guiltily. I attained my room without further interruption, but I touched my chamber door to find disquiet, familiar and inescapable. There is no privacy in Tyntagel Keep, I thought ruefully. I turned my face toward the worn, silver tile floor in resignation. Lady Altha's presence in my somber chamber did not augur well for me. She disliked me intensely and only grudgingly accepted me in what she viewed as her personal domain.

Lady Altha's sharp profile, an uncomfortable medley of prominent nose and jutting chin, promised malevolence with every angle
of taut rigidity. She whirled toward me, emitting the peculiar
crackle of a flounce of stiffened black silk and crinoline. Her dull
umber eyes reflected neither light nor kindly emotion. I ought to
have grown immune to her tirades; I bore them better than most by
dint of practice, but the heat of her tongue could still occasionally
wound me.

Lady Altha sputtered in her haste to express disgust. "You have
no more responsibility in you than a selfish child, Rhianna. You
might at least show consideration for your father, whose absurdly
excessive generosity toward you defies all bounds of sense. The
debt you owe that saintly man is altogether unrepayable. How you
have the nerve to keep him waiting astonishes me. It will not establish a favorable first impression for Lord Brant, I assure you. Do
quit dawdling, and try to present yourself decently. You look as if
you have been wallowing with the swine—or the swineherd."
The hard-packed Tyntagel soil on which I had sat did not cling,
and the swineherd was a boy of ten who shook as if palsied each
time he saw me near. Lady Altha was not exhibiting her best vi-
tuperative form. I could only conclude that my father had perturbed her with a rare imperative.

She thrust at me an extravagant gown of pale gray sea-silk,
finely embroidered and fitted, and I accepted it with meek dismay.
Warily silent, I fumbled with laces and clasps meant to enclose my
sister's more substantial frame. I recalled certain of Evram's words
from an alarming new perspective.

Lady Altha maintained her shrill scoldings as she draped me
with an absurd excess of pearls and silver filigree, berating me as
usual for circumstances I did not control. "You have no concept of
your duties, Rhianna. By your age, Yldana had received offers from
every significant House of Serii—including Liin. It takes more than
a First House heritage to attract a Dolr'han." I restrained a reminder that the extolled Lord of Liin had conspicuously omitted
the rite of marriage from his offers to my sister. "If you had only inherited a little more from your father!" grumbled Lady Altha disparagingly.

Lady Altha's diatribe did not waver as she swept me from my
room; our footsteps beat aching echoes in my ears. "You might

show some gratitude for your father's considerable efforts. Niveal is an important House, and Lord Grisk has a very promising future, despite those ridiculous stories about Lady Tilla's death. Personally, I cannot imagine why Lord Brant would consider you for his son. You are scarcely a prize, even with the substantial dowry your father has offered and the influence of a First House lineage as your portion. Your father's labors must have been monumental." Lady Altha gave me a last inspection, a despairing shake of her head, and a muttered sigh of exasperation before she thrust me through the arching portal of my father's hall of office.

It was a vast room with dark oaken vaults and sparse, severe furnishings. It was the hall of Tyntagel Keep which outsiders most often encountered, and it did not cast a promising light on Tyntagellian hospitality. Tyntagel acknowledged an emphatic allegiance to King Astorn and a fierce pride in having likewise served Serii since the reign of King Tul, but we had grown socially isolated from Serii's myriad of other peoples, and not just because of the forbidding mountains and canyons that surrounded us.

I knew such terror at entering my father's office that my very blood and marrow seemed to crawl. I entered with that appearance of icy calm which alone bespeaks me as my father's child. My feet tapped evenly across the marble. I walked directly, straying not even by glance, to the cluster of straight-backed chairs which constituted my father's sole concession to visitors' comforts.

I curtsied, a deep if marginally willing obeisance. "Your pardon, my Lord Father, for my tardy arrival. I regret my inability to have obeyed your summons more promptly." I spoke the words precisely, but my mind was furiously fitting to the lanky, white-haired man seated at my father's side the name which Lady Altha had supplied: Brant, Lord of Niveal.

"We shall assess your absence later, Rhianna," answered my father bleakly. "We have more salient matters to discuss at present." Black eyes flashed dire displeasure, but my father's tones flowed with formal courtesy before our guest. "As you may be aware," he continued smoothly, "Lord Brant's second son, Lord Grisk, recently suffered the loss of his chosen wife. The grievous bereavement proved compensatingly fortuitous, since Lady Tilla had produced no heirs in three years of marriage. Lord Grisk will wait the customary year before remarrying; the necessary agreements for your betrothal, however, may be established in advance without impropriety."

"Hamley cannot alone fill all the cradles of Seriin nobility," interrupted Lord Brant in raspy tones of pleasure at his uninspired witticism. "And by-blows only serve to fill a wench's purse." My disciplined father allowed himself only a brief closure of eyes against Lord Brant's coarsely distasteful practicality; Niveal's proffered bonding evidently entailed much value. Lord Brant croaked with impolitic humor, "Tilla was a pretty thing, but delicate beauties make better mistresses than wives. I ought never to have let Grisk sway my choice the first time. Pick a wife for strength, I told him; pleasure is easily found." Niveal's ruling lord laughed heartily.

My father tented his fingers carefully. The quavering light from the amber sconces struck the black onyx of his signet. "You will be wed at year's end following Lord Grisk's mourning, Rhianna," said my father crisply. "The marriage will take place in Tulea, since Lord Grisk currently represents his father and Niveal on the King's Council. You will depart for Tulea with the next spring's first caravan."

With a modicum of asperity which I wryly recognized as injudicious, I remarked, "I must gratefully assume, my Lord Father, that it was my antithetical semblance to the lovely Lady Tilla which first recommended me as a suitable bride for Niveal's matrimonial prodigy. Naturally, my heritage imparts its own special value."

Lord Brant obliviously deflected the storm of my father's anger. "I trust, Baerod, that the girl is stronger than she appears. She has a rather spindly look about her. It would not do to have another as brittle as the last."

My father rhythmically tapped the finger on which his signet shone, a certain sign of his rage. His placid response testified impressively to the level of his self-control. "Rhianna may appear fragile," he said persuasively, "but even her brothers, whom you know to be strong men both, cannot surpass her claim to endurance of health."

"I suppose appearance would be misleading in a sorceress' brat," mused Lord Brant. He tugged at his lapels, garish brocade offenses on an otherwise innocuous velvet coat. "The girl did not inherit her mother's other tendencies, I trust?" he asked bluntly. I cringed at thought of kinship with a man so tactlessly blind to his counterpart's notorious point of sensitivity.

My father glanced at me bitterly. "Rhianna has scarcely more actual Power than I have." Lord Brant nodded approval of the response. I could have cited a legion of dissenters to my father's affirmation, but I did not press myself to give argument under the circumstances. My audience with the Lord of Tyntagel had ended. I would receive no further words, no verbal picture of my intended husband, and certainly no request for my opinion. A clock chimed dolorously as my father dismissed me.

I closed the oaken door and leaned against it heavily, wishing that the wood still held the reassuring pulse of life. My father had refused to apprise Ixaxis of a potential wizardess, but that he would further discard law and tradition in ordering a sorceress to unwilling marriage appalled and shocked me. I realized now that Evram had attempted an indirect warning, but I had gauged his hints by his own refusal to believe me a sorceress. That my father, who too well comprehended the truth, would disregard it was a contingency I had never considered. I could not argue with my liege's command, and I could not comply. I needed another choice; I needed words of calm advice. Evram might listen, but I could not expect him to counter any order my father might give. My father was Lord of Tyntagel, Evram's liege and my own. It was my father's right and duty to command our lives. Momentarily pushed beyond the bounds of sanity, I careened into the only course I could accept.

Chapter 6

Having never previously contemplated rebellion, the plans which I formulated in the ensuing panic-laced hour lacked much in rational substance. I could think only of the trees, my Tyntagel oaks who had never betrayed me. I only wished that I might lose myself among them, discarding duty and its concomitant suffering.

My liege-father's world had used me badly, and there was a forgotten forest not so many leagues from Tyntagel. The heart of the ancient realms of the Sorcerer Kings had been deserted, save for Alvenhame, since the fall of Horlach. They lay northeast of Tyntagel, and the Dwaelin Wood lay still among them. I opened *A Geographical History of Ancient Serii* and stared at the words:

> "During the early years of the Sorcerer Kings' Era, the tract of land known as the Dwaelin Wood was the domain of a lesser Sorceress Queen who used the name Rhianna. Her province lay in the botanical sciences, an area of research which in her later years absorbed her full attention. The human element apparently did not interest her, an aberration which probably preserved her from the covetous designs of her fellow sorcerers, who were at that time obsessed with the conquest and subjugation of mortal realms.
>
> "Rhianna's history is of note chiefly because of its antiq-

uity. Rhianna belonged to the third generation of sorcerers. She is one of the earliest sorceresses of whom any specific history remains, since most records of the early sorcerers were obliterated in their long, mutual struggles for supremacy. Horlach's origins preceded her, but not even names can be definitely associated with other sorcerers prior to the seventeenth generation and the clan of Marbruk.

"Rhianna did not partake of the policies of territorial expansion popular among most of the Sorcerer Kings, but she was equally notorious in her inhospitality to visitors. She eliminated trespassers in her realm as brutally as Horlach did, though she occasionally made exception for individuals she considered of value to her experiments. She imported seedlings and soil samples from throughout the ancient world, and those who brought them to her were generally well repaid, if they survived the sorceress' characteristically erratic temper.

"Rhianna's Dwaelin Wood was by all accounts a remarkable, living artwork. Those who did survive encounters with Rhianna acknowledged universally that her domain had no equal for beauty in its natural form. After her death, the Dwaelin Wood gradually returned to a state of wilderness, but Rhianna's impact persists to this day in the hybrids of her creation."

My nerves shrieked to escape my liege-father's will without delay, but I clung to colder caution; a pre-prandial disappearance would draw needlessly prompt attention to my intent. I joined the household as silently, as calmly as ever did a lady of that House, and I took my appointed place at the long, narrow table. The chairs which customarily separated me from Lady Altha had been removed; Lady Retl supped in her room, and Dayn patrolled against brigands, guarding the northern reach from Hamley to Lake Evin. Balev, heir and dark foil to our father's fierce iron gray, conversed with Lord Brant. Nadira, her red-gold hair tightly curled, minced primly to the seat between her husband and Niveal's Lord.

Those cousins who closely served my father entered: Lord Denor, tall, gray-haired and cadaverous beside his smug and lumpish wife, Lady Wylla; Lord Lachren with Lady Havia, the pair of them too haughty and affected to take notice of me though I sat across from them. My elderly great-uncle, Lord Praetor, arrived in typically querulous mood. He sat beside me and began, as he invariably did, to accuse me of maliciously crowding him.

They chattered normally, their voices discordant against the musicians' softly throbbing lutes. My family observed no change within me. They could not doubt my compliance with my liege's command, for the way of rebellion had been lost with Serii's birth. Not one among my kin had ever sought to learn to read my moods, as I had theirs.

I must have eaten, for I drew no comment, but I could never recall any portion of that meal. When at last my father's rising signaled dismissal, I rose and followed Lady Altha, but I lingered in the dim corner of the upper hall while my family dispersed. I stared at the flickering candles with fixed calm, and I waited.

When an hour of silence had wrapped the keep in chimeric calm, I moved cautiously toward the kitchens. A few indistinct murmurs spilled from the servants' rooms adjacent to the narrow ways I walked, but the access to the pantry which I sought was clear. I gathered journey cakes, flint, a knife, and potent herbs. When I had completed my pilfering, I crept up the steep back stairs to my room.

An owl screeched against the night, but the keep had grown still with sleep. I donned an often patched skirt and tunic, topped them with a heavy woolen cloak, and gathered my chosen supplies into a coarse twill bag. The garments I selected had once belonged to a governess of congenial disposition and regrettably short tenure. Had my family remarked them, they would long ago have been discarded as ill-suited to a lady of high rank, but the things were durable and far more serviceable than the finer garb I possessed. Few critical eyes would espy me in such an outfit.

I took little, for I owned nothing. My father held first title to all the possessions of Tyntagel, and he had never troubled to gift me with anything but my sister's excess. I carefully stowed in their case the pearls which I had worn at supper; I wished no accusation of thievery to follow me. I cast a single glance at my room: the gilt ceiling chased with a tortuous, abstract design which had given me many childhood nightmares; the bed curtained with musty, stifling draperies of burgundy velvet; and the cold, unyielding floor inset with rose marble of unimaginative geometric pattern. The room held memories, but few were good. I locked fast the gilt-encrusted door behind me, a gesture less purposeful than symbolic.

It was absurdly easy to desert my life's home. I knew every back stair and hidden alcove. I knew the trees too well to be daunted by the purportedly impregnable inner wall which encompassed Tyntagel Keep. The outer wall was a more formidable barrier, for it had been built to withstand the flow of madness following Horlach's demise, but I thought myself a shadow and passed before the guards unseen. No Ixaxin wizardess was I. Still, I knew a few small tricks, and the Power which condemned me would suffice for my escape. I dashed to shelter under the forest eave as if pursued by all the hideous gargoyles of Horlach's creation, bidding mental farewells to my precious oaks.

I did experience qualms at the prospect of deliberately tapping my sorcerous Power, but I rationalized determinedly against my Tyntagellian training. The Infortiare was Serii's highest ranking subject, and Ixaxis was heeded throughout the Alliance. The first Infortiare, Lord Ceallagh, had yielded the crown of Serii to the mortal Tul with the understanding that Ixaxis would restrict its own rule to ensuring the honorable application of sorcery. I refused to recall my father's contention that Lord Venkarel sought to restore sorcerous autocracy. I concentrated on the belief that Serii as a whole did not share Tyntagel's prejudice against the bearers of Power. Tyntagel abhorred sorcery, disavowed the influence of wizardry, but supported a kingship and kingdom founded by Ixaxin intervention. The dichotomy had always disturbed me; now, I savored it.

I moved with such haste as I was able to maintain, stumbling through the night up the rocky, weed-held tracks across Tyntagel's treacherous boreal rim. There existed no proper roads through the mountainous barricade of Tyntagel's northern boundary, but Mindar's hills held many passes for a single traveler: steep, narrow and winding ways. The trees and shrubs guided my steps from harm, for I should otherwise have stumbled again and again. Taut nerves denied me sleep for three days after my precipitous departure, and the leagues of my treason stretched behind me.

If my father were to keep the disgrace and my escape at all hid-

den, it would be many days before discreet searchers could eliminate the most likely, southern routes. Such trackers as would eventually descry the proper path would not overtake more than faded
traces of my passing. I did not need to travel quickly; I need only
endure.

The hills of Tyntagel's north marked a drastic change of clime
and contour with their ridges. The lush southern slopes I knew; the
northern tracks were hard and dry, robbed of soil and moisture by
the wind which swept endlessly from the barren plains. There were
rivulets, trickles of water cradled between the rocks, fingers of
springs which fell from moister heights, but they were paltry
things compared to the water-rich Tyntagel streams. Such water as
touched the northeastern front of Mindar's lesser heights had worn
narrow paths through glassy rock. Of growth and life, the lands
were largely barren, defying even sorcerous empathy to find better
sustenance than the plain meal cakes I carried.

I turned northeasterly to travel across terrain increasingly
rugged but less devoid of life. I merely skirted the Mountains of
Mindar, but even the least of their abundant, jagged peaks and
treacherous scarps are not kind to unwary strangers. It was a lonely
land and a strange one, but the first days' desolation gradually
yielded to a more serious season of spring. My progress east
brought glimpses of the ancient valleys, the heights of King Horlach's erstwhile domain and the verdure of Rhianna's gardens. I
curled each night in comfortless, rocky hollows, but nearby trees
gave me solace.

My life did not resettle graciously. As I calmed from my initial,
panicked flight, guilt drove sly talons into me as I gradually realized what I had wrought. A Seriin lady of a First House, albeit less
pampered than most of my class, I had in an evening discarded all
that I had ever known. The world at large was not my father's park
that I ought to greet it blithely and familiarly, as visions of the
Dwaelin Wood too readily inclined me to do. A most trepid adventuress, my aspirations demanded much of Dwaelin Wood.

Chapter 7

If I had heeded the advice of Seriin history, I would have held obediently to my liege's dictates. I would never have trespassed on the shunned lands. There was cause for the desertion of those rich domains. The example of Alvenhame might have warned me: I knew that the people of Alvenhame incessantly recruited mercenaries to patrol their borders. I knew that brigands roamed the old domains unfettered by Seriin law, because there were reportedly older evils that patrolled better than any King's soldier. I knew that predators such as dyrcats throve in the lands north of Tyntagel, though they were found nowhere else in our world.

I could guide a dyrcat's mind. I could evade the brigands as I had evaded the guards of Tyntagel. I hated the guilt of my flight, and I did not savor the losses it incurred, but I did not initially fear. I had never believed in the ineradicable impact of the Sorcerer Kings. I began to learn.

I felt the darkness of oily evil before my eyes beheld its source. It was Brak Lake; I knew the name from many atlases, and I knew its history. Sorcerer King Horlach had coveted the land and the people who lived beside the thriving lake in an era long past. Horlach had wrung the hope from the people, and he had wracked the rich life from the teeming waters. The lake should have shimmered with activity, but it had been stained to a lifeless void which spoke more damningly of sorcerous Power than all the texts of my father's keep.

I wished for Evram's comforting kindness or even Lady Altha's spite. The few trees struggling to survive near Brak Lake were stunted not only in their limbs but in their souls as well. I reached to them as I would to the woods of Tyntagel, but no soft answers did I find. The spirits were within my touch, but they would not respond, and I did not press them. I could cure a tree of blight but not of madness.

I shivered, ragged with icy exhaustion and fear. Brak Lake was the stuff of dark legends. It lay as far beyond my understanding as the Sorcerer King Horlach himself. I felt condemned by my own paltry Power and was desperate to reach Dwaelin Wood. Brak Lake gave me warning, but I did not heed it.

When I first sensed the Dwaelin Wood, my eagerness fanned hope within me. Under the spell of my wishful thoughts, I became almost blissful, despite my ceaseless fatigue and the recognition of my losses. Only one note jarred: having expected to find no dwelling-place of man so near the forgotten realms, the burg I discerned beyond the Friejid River disturbed me. A league from its walls, I could feel the breath of it spilling unsavory air. With every instinct warning me to avoid the place, I carefully detoured around it. Any lingering fear, I banished with the thought that even the lawless reportedly shunned Dwaelin Wood.

For that night I refused to dwell on matters grave and bleak. There was a meadow at my feet; a gently rolling slope, it led from a steep, stark hillside to lush and thriving verdure. The granite boulder sheltering me was covered with emerald, mossy growth. Frail golden blossoms dusted the craggy sides and spilled across my grassy bed. The evening was cool, but spring had come to keep the winter at bay. Dwaelin Wood spread before me, and I rejoiced.

I had never held hope for freedom in my old life. I'd spent too many hollow years knowing only my father's iron walls and will. A priest I once heard speak gave rise to a briefly cherished notion that I might one day escape, but the pathway of faith had been forbidden me because of my sorcery. Near Dwaelin Wood, I felt that I had found that hope again.

I needed hope in any form. By flight, I had forsaken duty to my liege. I had confounded his agreements with Niveal, for my father could not indefinitely conceal my absence from Lord Brant. My sire would see my act as a maliciously conceived rebellion designed to denigrate his noble name. It was a crime of betrayal, and I knew it too well.

Two sparrows lit upon a dusty twig, rousing me from dangerous reverie. Their tiny thoughts were filled with flirting and the finding of choice seeds: familiar things and balm to a troubled heart. The solemn strangeness eased.

Chapter 8

"**T**he rose silk is adequate," drawled the young woman who clearly commanded the attention of the room. "But this," she added with a sniff of distaste for a bolt of pale blue, "is impossible."

"Lady Yldana," pleaded the unhappy merchant, "You did request its making. It was a very expensive investment, which I financed only on the understanding of your assured purchase."

"Your financial woes do not concern me, Master Thesto," said the woman with a pout of displeasure. "I could not possibly wear anything so dreadful."

Master Thesto turned ashen, torn between his great loss of invested gold and the troublesome customer whom he very much wished to cultivate. He searched the room for allies but found few candidates. The Lord of Tyntagel showed no interest; he was rapt in a study of his own, having attended only to humor his eldest daughter. The old peasant woman wrapped in hideous talismans caused Master Thesto to shudder, and he hastened his survey onward to the old woman's charge, where he paused with a gleam of inspiration. Master Thesto was still a stranger to Tyntagel.

He smiled as winningly as his oily face allowed. "Perhaps it would suit the Lady Rhianna," he suggested hopefully. The pale gold girl whom he addressed looked at him with startlement.

Lady Yldana frowned at the merchant, and he cringed as he realized that he had erred, though he knew not how seriously he had jeopardized his hard-won standing as a vendor to the ruling family of Tyntagel. His abjection saved him; Lady Yldana laughed, her humor now piqued. "What an inspired idea, Master Thesto," she mocked. "That faded pallor does rather resemble Rhianna's coloring. They merit one another. Buy the lot, Alhda," she added to a servant, who returned to her mistress a nod of humble compliance.

Yldana smiled at her sister's downturned eyes. "Are you not pleased, Rhianna?" When her sister did not respond, Yldana tutted, "Surely you are not concerned by the loss of any beau who sees you in Master Thesto's dreadful creation? Dear little sister, you have no beaux to be bothered by it. Is it not an inspired arrangement?" She shed delighted radiance upon the room. The Lord of Tyntagel nodded absent agreement with his dark-haired daughter's whim. The face of Master Thesto reflected a man too bewildered to be pleased by the solution of his dilemma.

Year of Serii—9007
Dwaelin Wood, Serii

As a child I used to watch my sister, so secure in her hold of our father's heart and mind. It had always seemed to me that Yldana owned without effort the gift of molding her surroundings to her whim. Her beauty was indomitable, but it was a quality less simple than flawlessness of feature which graced my sister. I could not, as I watched her in our youngest days, imagine any circumstance finding Yldana in less than perfect control. Yet in my initial days in Dwaelin Wood, I often wondered how Yldana would have fared beneath the ancient intertwining limbs, whose leaves whispered enmity with every dry and papery word.

Very different from my precious friends in the dells of Tyntagel, the giants of Dwaelin Wood bred uneasy fears, contagion from their own suspicious lot. Age had brewed in a bitter cauldron the lost beauties of Rhianna's domain, and my pretty dreams were quickly consumed. The Dwaelin Wood hated, and it used its hatred cannily. The trees tolerated my presence with disdainful resignation, because I greeted them with my mind, and they knew I harbored no intent to harm. They had outlived every history Serii could recall. I was a dust-mote in their view; I was a transitory thing.

I had not found the haven I sought, but still my days in Dwaelin Wood passed gracefully at first. I had no strict preceptor waiting to strike me at a hinted lapse of concentration. I had no need to fear the next summons to my father's office, wondering what new infractions I had wrought and what punishment I should incur. I need not tremble because I had perhaps forgotten some duty to my kin. There were no sidelong glances of suspicion as I walked, no superstitious whispers to surround me like a net. The Dwaelin Wood misliked me, but it was impartial distaste for all humanity, a distinction which made Dwaelin Wood significantly easier to bear.

I had found a cavern, a welcome gift to one accustomed to a roof of substantial stone. I had entered the cavern eagerly, for the disturbances of too many recent, restless nights lurked fresh in my memory. It was the feral odor which recalled caution, though the strength of life-force ought to have rung warning within me. My eyes could determine nothing in the dimness, but the sound of breathing came from more than the gentle wind. I retreated carefully, hoping that the dyrcat's languor would outweigh curiosity.

I stared upward through the tightly meshed leaves of aloof giants; Dwaelin Wood's incessant duskiness would soon bow to true night. When I slept beneath an open sky, I felt a vulnerable sense of unease. But Dwaelin's relentless canopy had not lessened my yearning for night-shelter.

I tried to set aside the mingled nervousness and unnatural, almost voluptuous euphoria which the prospect of using my treacherous Power stirred in me; a dyrcat owned Power of its own, enough to stun its prey, enough perhaps to overcome a minor sorceress. I was tired and made impatient by disappointment, else I might have merely sought a safer shelter. Without considering my full intent, I retraced my steps to the cavern entrance.

The dyrcat had awakened, or my Power had made me more able to perceive his watchful regard. He crouched, awaiting me, his sinuous tail twitching very slightly, his golden eyes irresistibly brilliant. He was an enormous specimen, fully as long as a tall man's height, and his silken, shadow-colored fur cloaked the rippling sinews of a prosperous hunter. I met his gaze, and I reached for his mind.

The tantalizing scent of prey, the eagerness for blood spurting

fresh between great, fanged jaws: the violence of the dyrcat's instincts shook me. I had seldom touched the mind of any creature
more deadly than a hunt-hound, and I little liked the frenzied sensation of seeing myself as a succulent meal. The dyrcat clenched his
muscles to spring, commanding me to abide and submit. I turned
the thought against him, and it was he who could not move. Bewilderment invaded the killer's feverish passions, and I used his
confusion to lighten the burden of my strained mental hold.

I struck fire from a flint and set it to a candle. The dyrcat blinked
and dropped his head like a startled kitten. I circled him at a distance, exploring his lair; nothing gentle lurked in the vicious consciousness which struggled in him, locked from action by my own
will. The cavern was vaster than I had hoped. Broken stalactites and
rust-colored stains suggested that it had not always been so dry a
refuge, but any moisture had long ago left it. The limestone network
intrigued me with its castles and curtains, especially where it sequestered a tiny portion of the cavern with an access far too narrow
for a dyrcat's frame. Within the sanctum stirred a draft, yielded by
a crevice from deep and winding earth-wrapped ways; the draft reduced the dyrcat's musky scent to a tolerable annoyance.

However sable sleek and splendid, a dyrcat is not one whom I
would ordinarily select as neighbor, but known danger can from
unknown grant reprieve. Brigands and the hints of ancient evil at
Brak Lake posed sufficient menace to warrant precaution. Yet even
as I claimed the inner cavern, I felt no great certainty that the dyrcat would be so readily controlled a second time.

I released my grip on the dyrcat with a certain wariness, but, to
my relief, the dyrcat seemed at least as leery of me. He tested his
returned mobility, spared the cave in which I cowered some suspicious glances, and thenceforth accorded me only watchful circum-
spection. I never trusted his disinterest sufficiently to pass within
easy reach of his huge, curved claws, but I did eventually grow less
frantically restrictive in the holds I exerted over him. We eyed each
other cautiously, the dyrcat and I, but necessity bred a grudging
tolerance.

Furnished with a carefully gathered bed of bracken, my dim
dwelling was no more austere than many a chamber of my father's
keep, and I found its character in many ways more desirable.
Though crudely hewn, my cavern was securely private as no cas-

tle's room would be. I derived the boon of nearly absolute protection not only from my dubious neighbor, the dyrcat, but also from the aged trees. No one entered Dwaelin Wood unnoticed by its leafy denizens. Their perceptions granted me warning; their choice of paranoic solitude ensured my sanctuary.

I persistently affirmed that even a stark and hungry life offered better comfort than any Niveallan existence. Had I been cleverer in the ways of bending favor, I might have avoided both contingencies, but I could not emulate Yldana. Her gifts gave her the human world. Mine gave only survival, a quality which did not greatly enhance the charm of a noblewoman, a species supposedly too fragile for any exertion greater than a courtly dance.

Mere survival demanded too little of me, and I lacked even a tithe from my father's library to make any solitude bearable. I, who had always been content to be alone, learned from Dwaelin Wood what suffering true loneliness could bring. Melancholy pondering began to plague me, and I gained no solace from my surroundings. Despite the variety of flora in the vicinity of my chosen dwelling, study of unresponsive life was an insufficient substitute for acrid memory. The dyrcat discouraged other animals; I could hardly seek rapport with dyrcat-prey while maintaining even a scant link with the savage dyrcat himself.

In desperation, I stretched my Power toward those in whom the dyrcat had no interest. I found a blossom of a deep blue sheen as luminous as the polished metal of a warrior's bright sword; it flourished on a vine of cunning persistence and lush beauty. I could not doubt that it owed life to my namesake, for its thoughts burned more clearly than many mammals', but it shunned me. The tantalizing brevity of rapport augmented my frustration, until I was nearly mad with hurt and aggravation. I threw my Power and my soul into the grasp of Dwaelin Wood, and that voracious essence absorbed me.

I did not dream nor think beyond the day, each one of which was like the next and the previous. I had tied thick wrappings around my mind, and I did not notice time's passage. Blossoms died, and green faded to summer's tired hue. Summer waned, but I did not recognize the difference, noticing nothing beyond my tiny world of food and sleep and simple studies of my home territory. I was not a lady of Tyntagel; I was a creature of the Dwaelin Wood who knew no other life—until one day as I was gathering columbine, I saw the Venturers.

They had camped beside a clear and leaping rill. There were three men: two were rough and knife-edged warriors indistinguishable from others whom I had seen pass. I might have disregarded those two, evading them as I had the others who had strayed through Dwaelin's grasp. I might have ignored them all, had I not heard the third man speak.

Language, I had forgotten; it stretched itself along old paths within my mind. "How could you have dwelt in Alvenhame for two years without sampling Alvenhamish brandy, Master Hamar?" The man spoke tauntingly. He was handsome; Yldana would have sought his sole attention. With that thought, I realized: I have a sister; I am Rhianna dur Tyntagel, and I have lost four months to the Dwaelin Wood.

"Alvenhame does not pay its soldiers so well as that, Master Ineuil," growled the larger of the warrior pair.

The handsome man grinned. "There are ways of remedying that circumstance," he said suggestively.

"That is why we are here," said the third member of the party. He stammered in a harsh accent which nearly defeated my newly awakened comprehension.

"So you are," mused Master Ineuil. He was fairer in coloring than the Tyntagel norm, but I could detect in his aspect no flaw more serious than a vague suspicion of indolence. He bore a sword but no armor, nor was his visage scarred as those of the professional soldiers he accompanied. "Venture can be a highly profitable trade."

"You have already recruited us, Master Ineuil," said the first warrior. "You need not continue to parade the benefits of our choice." The warrior stood and stretched the thews of his arms; he was undoubtedly the largest man I had ever seen.

"I merely make conversation, Master Hamar," answered Master Ineuil blandly. "We could return to a discussion of Alvenhamish brandy, if you prefer."

"Which only you have sampled," muttered Master Hamar.

"Or perhaps Master Gart could regale us with some morsels of personal history," suggested Master Ineuil cheerfully. He turned his face expectantly to the shorter of the two warriors, a grizzled man whose features were as blunt and knobby as an aged oak and as ruddy as mahogany.

"I am not much for story-telling, Master Ineuil," responded Master Gart shyly.

"A scintillating fellow like you?" scoffed Master Ineuil. "You must have scores of romantic conquests to recount." It was an unlikely accusation, given the most cursory inspection of Master Gart.

"Leave him be," warned Master Hamar to the impudent Master Ineuil, "or I may test those sword skills we discussed on you."

"He meant no harm, Hamar," interposed Master Gart.

"Certainly not!" exclaimed Master Ineuil with widened green eyes. "I have only respect for both of you. Should I have otherwise selected you two out of all Alvenhame's mercenaries?"

Master Hamar, only partially mollified, said, "I hope you fight better than you lie, Master Ineuil."

"My talents are manifold, I assure you," answered the fair man with excessive solemnity.

He would have proceeded, but Master Hamar grunted, "No more tales of your exploits, Master Ineuil. We have already heard your opinions of Bethii, Pithlii, Ardasia, and Mahl, not to mention your extended discussions of Serii's diversity of trollops. We have had no quiet since we joined with you, and I am past ready for a rest from talk."

"That is not a very sociable attitude, Master Hamar," commented Master Ineuil, but he did allow the conversation to lapse.

I had listened with a shameless fascination. Venturers had become less common than in Serii's early days, and I had encountered only one other prior to that day in Dwaelin Wood. There had once existed, in that era after Horlach's defeat, both more cause and more incentive for the Venture calling. I had studied the strictures of Venture, the artifice created by Lord Ceallagh to cleanse a newly freed Serii of King Horlach's more hazardous mementos. The first Infortiare had designed the Venture concept to give hope to those in need of a new beginning, but a Venture was only to be undertaken for a truly important cause, and the Venture code was strict. A pledged Venturer could not leave his quest until it was fulfilled, not though years passed and age thinned the hopes of youth. Release could be granted by the Venture Leader, whose rule over his party was absolute, but reprieve was seldom offered save for direst infirmity; the Venture Leader must justify any release to the Infortiare himself. The rewards of Venture might be great, but the risks grew accordingly.

A man had once arrived in Tyntagel, the grayest, thinnest man whom I had ever seen. He was the last survivor of a Venturing band, enslaved by a vow he had made thirty years before to follow a hopeless path. He ought to have been bitter, I had thought. Yldana had derided the folly of his self-imposed affliction; Balev and Dayn had proclaimed the man a certain criminal deserving of any suffering he accrued. The stringy little man in shabby clothes had looked at my brothers, Tyntagel's proud young lordlings, at Yldana already womanly in figure and hypnotic in her effect, and he had smiled with gentle eyes in which laughter danced.

I never knew the nature of the quest nor why he came to Tyntagel. Whence he journeyed and where he later went were shrouded from my knowing, but I had in cameo fashion glimpsed a man whose purpose gave him life. Perhaps he was flotsam in an absolute sense, but he mattered and he knew his worth.

After four months in Dwaelin Wood, I was sufficiently lost and lonely, riven even from the harsh stability of my father's dominance, to have followed an Ardasian trader to Caruil. If I could have borne to dwell lifelong in silent contemplation of the Dwaelin Wood's ways, I might have found some shade of contentment in the end, but if loneliness grants any boon, it is the gift of freedom. The Venturers had unwittingly brought my latent restlessness to light.

Even the thought of pursuing the trio I had encountered was at least as mad as my initial flight from Tyntagel. I knew nothing of the Venture goal; I knew nothing of the three sworn unto it, save that they were strong and secure even amid the chorus of enmity ringing against them from every tree and leaf, and I had seen no other trespassers display like confidence. I lacked the courage to bespeak the men, fleeing instead to my small shelter as if the Venturers could offer me harm though they could not even detect me. Still, I kept their presence in my mind.

Even as I did battle with myself, I gathered my few possessions, bestowing a blessing upon the stony hollow which had served me well. I had discarded my familiar life once; this second upheaval was easier by far. The dyrcat would be glad at my departure, and he would not be alone in his relief.

Chapter 9

For some few days, unseen and silent, I trailed the Venturers' twisted path. In my cowardice, I observed them from the shadows, unknown to them save as a rustle of sighing wind. I did not fear them physically; I had learned enough of shadow-weaving in my Dwaelin stay to make evasion simple, and they did seem to be men with some measure of honor. It was a derisive refusal of my offer to join them that I feared. I chided myself for my procrastination, but I could not summon sufficient nerve to risk a confrontation.

Still, I eavesdropped fervently, striving to fathom the motive of the Venturers. They spoke sparingly, almost cryptically, of their quest, confounding both my curiosity and my expectations. I did gain a cautious respect for their skills, and I realized that these Venturers were very far removed from the impoverished visitor to Tyntagel.

They formed an odd trio: only Master Gart at all resembled my preconceptions of a suitable Venturer. Master Ineuil was too undefinable: a chiaroscuro of contrasts. Master Hamar was too filled with anger, hating the world's greater part and suspect of the rest; in Master Gart he seemed to have some faith, but hard, I suspected, had been the earning. The warrior pair evinced the camaraderie of long acquaintance, but toward him they called Ineuil they displayed a marked reserve. The restraint was not reciprocated, but

Master Ineuil, I thought (more rightly than I knew), was one whose easy manner revealed little of honest sentiment.

Gart was the steady one, quick of hand but much slower of wit than the effervescent Master Ineuil, who loved to taunt him. Master Gart, even of temper and reliable, muted Master Hamar's outbursts like sound cotton wool. The ravages of a warrior's lot had deprived Master Gart of half an ear. Stolid stability wreathed Master Gart, and I found him likable, though his appeal was rather akin to that of a friendly mastiff.

I could not find any like appeal in Master Hamar. His unreasonable sullenness nearly discouraged my interest in the Venture a dozen times, though it was easy to appreciate his value to such a cause. Master Hamar's was the simple force of massive strength. I saw him lift from the trio's path a fallen limb of enormous substance and weight, and it caused him no apparent whit of effort. He sparred frequently with Master Gart, and each played his weapon skillfully. It seemed to me a dangerous game with potent arms, but no serious blood was drawn. Both were expert, and each knew the other's measure well.

Master Ineuil, the rogue who loved to banter (he often pursued a monologue if no audience would cooperate), fitted the role of Venturer least of all. He seemed uncommonly literate for a mercenary, yet freely extolled the rewards of judicious thievery. He appeared to be widely traveled, as were the others, but Master Ineuil's accounts betrayed a familiarity with a circle of affluence far exceeding a successful mercenary's comfortable prosperity. I might have named him thief; he broadly hinted as much, and Master Hamar often gave him the label. But a thief whose larceny results in significant wealth does not assume a Venture's rigors. Master Ineuil possessed a scoundrel's perspective, a courtier's tongue, and (by his own declaration) too much charm for his own good. I could not adequately explain him.

The three were strangers to me, but I trailed them faithfully from Dwaelin Wood, mentally fashioning them into the main fixtures of the narrow world I had inflicted upon myself. The Dwaelin Wood sped them on their way, since their goal was departure for the village Anx. The name of their destination was not familiar to me, but the most likely prospect for its location did not please me greatly. I had espied one settlement along Dwaelin Wood's southern border. To anticipate the existence of another would prod coincidence overly far.

When I could no longer pretend that the Venturers intended any more palatable goal, I sat upon a granite block and engaged myself in serious debate. I had no reason to follow the Venturers, but I had quite as little reason for any other course of action. I had grown confident in my ability to shield myself from view, and entering Anx would not bind me irrevocably to a Venture. A dram of curiosity added its weight; I rose and ran to trail the Venturers into Anx on a dry summer evening.

The field was sere grass which crackled as we crossed it. The soil was stony and brittle, though the Friejid River tossed the glare of summer light nearby. The leaden wall rose sheer before us, and there were men at the gate who bore arms of deadly uniformity. The men wore many coats and colors, and they eyed the Venturers carefully. The Venturers returned these gazes with a confidence I envied. I trailed the Venturers closely through the studded steel gate, feeling more secure in the three men's proximity. Two strides beyond the wall, the air was thickly yellow, and I turned around to justify my senses, for I had seen no change of atmosphere until I stepped within it.

A sudden pulsation of black netting rose from the soil inches before me. It soared above me, circling over me, and covered the city. As I stared, a small brown sparrow, unwilling trespassor, flew at the barrier and fell, a sorrowful mass of fused and blackened feathers. Some of the men near the gate laughed and pointed. A skeletal creature which might have been a man crawled from the lee of the wall, snatched the fallen bird and tore at it with his teeth. The watchers laughed more heartily.

The Venturers had nearly escaped me in my distraction. They were entering an alleyway which exuded a vile stench. Ineuil made an uncomplimentary allusion to sewer-raised rabble, but he kept his comments short and subdued. A heavy grunt oozed from the smoky haze, and blood spattered the ground as a man slumped against a dirty building. His murderer ransacked his belongings, while onlookers walked indifferently away.

"Anx has lost none of its charm," said Ineuil carelessly.

"Nor its contempt for the unwary, Master Thief," answered Hamar. "Look to yourself and not to the dead."

The Venturers spoke little after that exchange. They fought once but briefly, dispatching a trio of attackers who sprang upon them from a crumbled doorway. "It is fortunate that Anxians seldom cooperate well," commented Ineuil as he wiped and sheathed his bloodied sword.

We spiraled through the vicious, layered city, each stratum of which had been built on the bones of more ancient, sunken structures. The upper layers were most heavily trafficked, but they had crumbled in places, and the Venturers took occasional stairs to the lower flame-lit tunnels, weaving between moldering edifices until clear upper passages could be found. There was death everywhere around me, and it was greeted imperturbably as a natural phenomenon by those I saw. I had seen death before, having too often tended the sorely ill to have avoided it, but I had never witnessed callous murder. It surrounded me in Anx. I should have minded the slayings more had the victims not seemed as foul as the predators.

The Venturers took lodging within an Anxian inn, the likes of which would pale the meanest hovel of ill-repute in Tyntagel to seeming gentle splendor. Loud curses rang from it, filth encrusted it, and the creatures who filled it were the lowest villains. In the first minutes following the Venturers' arrival, I witnessed two murders, one rape and at least a dozen thefts. It was a busy and prosperous inn.

The Venturers supped together in the common room, but with nightfall they separated. Ineuil, in company with a woman of incredibly crimson hair, climbed the stairs to the room which he had taken. Gart and Hamar joined a sallow man who boasted an unsurpassed knowledge of local gambling establishments; the three of them strutted out the inn's door, and I remained, forlornly confused, a prim ghost in the midst of vile chaos.

I passed the night in the common room, evading sleep lest my shield of shadow fail and the Venturers escape me. With dawn, I hoped the Venturers would take their leave of Anx, but morning passed and they did not even emerge from their respective chambers. By the hour of their evening appearance, I was wholly weary and disgusted with their choice of lodgings. I followed them hopefully to another inn where they merely drank and took their dubious pleasures as they had done the previous night. The woman who accompanied Ineuil the second night was a buxom brunette.

I would have left the city then, my interest in the Venturers vanquished by the unwholesome air of Anx. I could have passed the outer barricade of Anx as I had done on entering; I had become more shadow than substance. It was the web of force which daunted me, the web which had destroyed a tiny sparrow, the web which completely encompassed the city. Tyntagellian lore decried such imprisoning barriers of energies perpetuated by sorcery, though the secret of their creation had mercifully been lost with the fall of the Sorcerer Kings. The simpler versions prevented unwanted traffic either one way or both; the more complex systems eliminated the interloper. To those who lacked the requisite key, all accounts acknowledged the barriers impregnable.

Reft of viable alternatives, I dwelt in Anx, cowering in attics or other, lesser holes. It was neither a comfortable existence nor a secure one, for I knew myself vulnerable to the first Anxian who might find me. The weak and unwary did not long survive in Anx's maw; their discarded corpses fed a pyre in the city's central square. It was the vile stench and smoke of that fire which perpetually polluted the air, but the citizens disregarded the atmosphere as completely as they did the unfortunate contributors to its source. There were always new victims, for Anx held wealth for the greedy and freedom for the iniquitous.

I could travel freely within Anx, so long as I maintained my somewhat ghostly status. It was an odd sensation, intoxicating in its way to one so otherwise helpless among Anx's murderous crew. Had I possessed their prevalent penchant for larceny, I could readily have established a highly profitable career. I grew quite adept at stealing meals. I might as easily have taken costlier items without qualms toward the disreputable owners whose right to such goods were as dubious as mine. The notion was mildly entertaining, though it hardly consoled me for my imprisonment within the city. All the wealth of Serii, Bethii and Mahl, a considerable percentage of which seemed destined to materialize in Anx, offered little enticement to a captive specter.

It was remarkably disconcerting to walk the world entirely unperceived by one's fellow beings, however distasteful those beings might be. The trees of Dwaelin had known my presence; I had no like reassurance in Anx. I played foolish pranks to assert my continued existence in the world. To steal a gambler's drink and trade it with another's provoked strong reaction among the violent tempers of Anx. I found it perversely comforting to realize that the Lady Rhianna an Baerod yn Eleni dur Tyntagel had at least retained her ability to irritate.

I watched those who regularly trafficked to and from the city, though it meant trespassing in territory which terrified me. Each trafficker bore a key: a disc of pewter hue, smooth as moonlight and covered by a tracery of ebon lines. Each key permitted passage of one traveler alone, and only once could it be used, for passage returned it to its source. I tried to steal one, but they were more closely guarded than any mundane treasure. The keys were sold for enormous price and distributed just prior to the purchaser's departure from a central cache, itself impenetrably barriered. Whatever ruffian band (currently a renegade crew of Caruillan pirates) controlled the single central key could command the city and virtually inexhaustible wealth. The privilege tended to be transitory; there was always a new band, larger or stronger than the last.

I had tried my new skills at thieving, but I could not steal a key. I could have stolen the price, but I dared not reveal myself long enough to make the purchase. For all my searching for a method of escape, I remained entrapped.

I returned to shadow the Venturers in simple hope that they, who had in a manner brought me, might lead me from the cage. Any latent craving for human company I might have felt in Dwaelin Wood had diminished rapidly under the influence of Anx, but desperation for departure's means gave me a far stronger motive. I trailed them again, but the Venturers had settled themselves as if for a long stay. Masters Gart and Hamar fought incessantly when they did not drink or gamble, calmly dispatching those who sought to rob them and maiming many an injudicious instigator of petty quarrels. Ineuil's sword did not idle, but he appeared more cheerfully determined to sample every moderately attractive harlot in the town. I was naive, and the behavior shocked me; yet, as I compared the Venturers to others whom I saw in Anx, I could not wholly condemn them. The Venturers did not inflict meaningless brutalities as did the other inmates of the town; they wrought no harm maliciously, though their obvious abilities instilled in jealous Anxian moguls a careful and cunning respect. The Venturers puz-

zled and annoyed me with their lingering: indulgence in the plen-
tiful vices of Anx constituted an unlikely quest. Being personally
eager to exit Anx and having little else to occupy my mind, I wondered irritably what the Venturers awaited. Despite their steady attendance to Anxian pleasures, there was a measure of impatience
in all three men.

I came near to bespeaking them, but I had formulated no fit
words of approach. The Venturers would quite reasonably doubt
the intentions of a fleeing lady of Tyntagel in the unlikely ambience
of a thieves' burg. I had concocted a more palatably appropriate
history, one which would possibly justify my interest in a Venture,
but I was still loathe to assume a sorceress' cloak with such feeble
abilities as I possessed.

Little enough did I know of sorcery, formal study of which had
been anathema in Tyntagel. I knew the tales perverted by Tyntagellian prejudice. I knew that sorcerous practitioners' Power ranged
from the trickery of mere charlatans to the unimaginable gifts of
the Infortiare. As for the gauging of such abilities, I could not even
assess my own. I had known from the moment I chose to trail the
Venturers that it was sorcery I must exploit to join them, but I took
no comfort from this decision.

III

THE SPARK
(PART 2)

Year of Serii—9003
Liin Keep, Liin, Serii

"Even you cannot challenge the decision of the Ixaxin Council, Hrgh," implored Lord Arineuil earnestly. "I like their choice no better than you do, but this is not the way to combat it."

"I am challenging Venkarel—not the Ixaxin Council," declared Lord Hrgh Dolr'han with the full, regal confidence of his birthright. "Venkarel has deluded the Council, thanks to that besotted old woman, Marga, but there can be no deception in a true trial of Power. I am the Infortiare in the eyes of Serii. Mine is the strongest Power of our time. I *will be* the Lord of Ixaxis."

"Then let the King decree it, Hrgh. The King's Council is even now pressing Ixaxin to reconsider its selection. Let them complete what they have begun, and you will be Infortiare without need for this farce of challenge."

"Farce?" demanded Lord Hrgh fiercely. "Arineuil, I want all Serii to know that I am Infortiare by right of Power. I want Ixaxis to know, and I want Venkarel to know." Hrgh's silver eyes grew feverishly bright. "I befriended that treacherous scrub, Arineuil. I will not see him take that which is mine. I will not see him use Serii as he used me."

Lord Arineuil shook his head with exasperation. "He is using you still, Hrgh. If he defeats you in this trial of Power, the King himself will be unable to depose him."

Lord Hrgh regarded his friend with contempt. "You actually believe his lies and trickery. Arineuil, I know Venkarel."

"And I do not?" retorted Lord Arineuil dur Ven. "Venkarel decimated my family's domain before he even began his wizard's training. You will not defeat him, Hrgh."

"I know my Power, Lord Arineuil, and I am a Dolr'han."

"You are a man blinded by arrogance."

"And you, Arineuil, are an impertinent fool."

"Venkarel will defeat you, Hrgh," insisted Arineuil wearily.

"Then curry *his* favor," sneered Hrgh, "instead of wasting my time." Lord Hrgh stomped from the room, a richly golden hall of the fabulous Liin Keep.

Lord Arineuil watched his friend with frustrated anger. "You are the fool, Hrgh. Venkarel will defeat you, if only because you underestimate him. He will conquer you, and there will be no one left who can defy him."

Something dark laughed unheard.

IV
THE KINDLING

Chapter 1

Hindsight often strips illusion from the truth, but the chaos of my final full day in Anx long defied my paths of reason. The answers which I thought I sought, I found. Never had more confusion of emotion burned my mind.

I rose that day at dawn. It was a somber time, but such slanting early light as crept through mountain passes could better penetrate the smoky shroud which hovered over Anx than later, stronger daylight, which yielded only a yellowing stain. Beyond the window cracks of my attic domain, I saw a whispered hint of rose suffuse the sky. Beyond my black-webbed cage loveliness still lived.

A severed shriek pierced gentle thoughts. Anx inflicted unpleasant punishment on those who dared relax their guard. I shook the dust from my draggled skirts, a poor substitute for a proper cleaning. I stepped gingerly down the treacherous stairs of the building which currently claimed the title of inn, dodged sleeping forms huddled in the lower halls, appropriated the remnants of a loaf of bread, and quietly passed outside. There was a crumbled ledge on which some yellow lichens grew; aside from man, those lichens alone made willing home in Anx. As nearly mindless as living things could be, no better comrades had I found of late than those pitiful symbionts.

I gnawed the gritty bread, a sorry substance, poorly leavened and impure. I had thrown away so much of life that I no longer knew what lay beyond my hand's reach. I gazed upon the western gate of Anx as if my sight alone could bear me beyond the imprisoning veil. I wore a glum mood when I observed that most contradictory Venturer, Master Ineuil, who, since his arrival in Anx, had not hitherto shown himself before midday. He, too, scanned the western gate, and more restless did he seem than I had previously beheld him.

I roamed the city aimlessly throughout the morning, but always when I strayed near the western gate I found Master Ineuil waiting and watching. Once I came upon him as Masters Hamar and Gart approached his side. The three conferred briefly. Hamar gestured impatiently toward the gate; Gart glowered. Ineuil shook his head irritably, turning his back in curt dismissal. Gart and Hamar continued on their way with no good humor.

Not until dusk did I find Master Ineuil absent from his point of vigil. The oddness of his behavior had revived my curiosity. For want of better goal, I resolved to investigate the Venturers' evening occupations, though I expected no extraordinary discoveries. I began my search idly, peering into all the sordid holes which the three had recently frequented. I sought them from inn to tavern, until the hour grew late and my interest devolved into mere obstinacy. I explored every odd pocket, persistently hunting through even the most noisome quarters. With keening nerves, I searched the alley haunts of murderers, the hives of wretches too cunning to die but too weak to prosper, and the bars and brothels of the veriest villains. Whether by chance or by a force more needful and obscure, I finally discovered a darksome tavern hidden beneath the snarl of the city's more trafficked strata.

A sign, begrimed to near illegibility, proclaimed the tavern's name to be Ceallagh's Crown. The tavern's sour ambience defied any connection to that conqueror of King Horlach, and I smiled wryly at the irony. I was mildly impressed that any Anxian had considered honoring history's hero, but the inappropriate application of his name typified the Anxian mentality. Lord Ceallagh had established Serii's governing duality of King and Infortiare by rejecting kingship and its crown. I refused to credit any Anxian with the subtlety of sarcasm.

Ceallagh's Crown boasted a few rough tables and was dimly lit by a single, flickering lamp near the entrance. The tavern keeper appeared no more sullen than others of his kind. The filth and stench were not excessive by the standards of Anx. Considering its environs, Ceallagh's Crown appeared to be a reasonably whole-some establishment.

As I crossed the tavern's threshold, I summarily revised my opinion of Ceallagh's Crown. As sudden and intense as the impact of a blinding flame to the dark-accustomed eye, a sudden flaring attacked that part of me which understood the trees, and I reeled beneath a wave of bitter pain.

With breathtaking abruptness, the fire vanished. The tavern resumed its ordinary appearance. The few customers speaking softly amongst themselves betrayed no evidence of disturbed awareness. No sign existed of any aberration, save the echo of a dully beating rhythm which drummed still within my veins. Suddenly I feared that madness had evoked the terrible burning in my blood. Had I lost my understanding of reality within Tyntagel's gray stone walls? Was all that I thought had passed only the product of delirium?

Suddenly I saw the trio I sought. The lamp which should have burned near them had been shattered, and a hazy darkness shrouded the corner in which they sat. I had not previously seen the two men who accompanied the Venturers. One of the unfamiliar pair was a small man, gray-haired and robed in priestly garb. I found a clergyman's presence incredible in those surroundings, but it was the other of the pair who attracted my attention, though for no cause as obvious as a holy calling. The second stranger occupied the corner chair, flanked by Gart and Hamar on one side, Ineuil and the priest on the other. He was dark of hair, angular and excessively lean, and he wore a cloak of severest black at odds with Anx's gaudy norm, making him difficult to perceive clearly in the lightless room. His eyes glinted with the pale, frozen blue of winter's ice, and from dark depths he watched me. His eyes pinned me, a frightened butterfly beating frantic, helpless wings. I wrapped myself more tightly in the shadows of the room, hoping desperately that coincidence alone bound that sharp, cold inspection of me.

Bleak humor twitched the corner of an uncompromising mouth, set in a face too carefully controlled to contain any softness of purpose. It was not at all comfortable to find laughing at me a man to whom I ought to have been entirely beyond detection. I wanted to escape his gaze, but I feared to leave even more than I feared to remain. My ability to elude notice was my only hope of preservation in a singularly hazardous environment. If I remained for other reason than attempting to extract an explanation of his perception, I did not acknowledge it at the time. I breathed deeply to still my trembling and drew near the table where the Venturers had assembled.

The three whom I had followed leaned forward to catch the quiet words of the gray-haired priest. I listened closely, stilling my pulse to read the silence. "The Taormin is a powerful instrument, too potent for any mortal's hand, however well-intentioned."

"If it grants such enormous Power," asked Master Ineuil sardonically, "how do you suggest we approach and take it? After exerting such effort to acquire the thing himself, Hrgh is not about to relinquish it at our request. Do the brethren of Benthen Abbey profess some special knowledge of the trinket which they have guarded so long?"

"We should not be so foolish as to seek such knowledge, Master Ineuil," chided the priest. With a pause and a glance at Gart and Hamar, the priest elaborated, "The Taormin is one of the few relics of the evil days still in existence, and it implacably resists destruction. We of the Abbey have been its custodians, its jailers in a very real sense, for untold ages, though few among us have understood the nature of that which we guarded. None of us knows more of it than that which I have just told you. Our calling denies the sort of Power the Taormin gives; that is why it was originally given into our keeping, and that is why the abbacy of Benthen is a deceptive honor. Hrgh's ambition blinds him to the danger he courts. The longer he holds it, the more secure the Taormin's grasp of his mind will be."

"It is not we who have delayed matters so long," muttered Hamar ungraciously.

The cold-eyed one had not ceased to study me, but now he turned a quizzical eyebrow to Hamar and spoke. "I comprehend the inherent urgency of the situation far more clearly than do you, Master Hamar. Any delays were entirely unavoidable. If you think that I have treated the matter too lightly, let me reassure you: I should not be here at all were the potential dangers not vastly more serious than even Abbot Medwyn appreciates."

"You are enormously reassuring, Kaedric," said Ineuil sarcastically.

"I am pleased that you find me so," countered the one called Kaedric sharply. "According to every known account, the Taormin binds to itself those who use it as surely as it is itself bound to the heinous image of its late master. I am not particularly eager to contend with Hrgh, but he is a far more palatable hazard than that which he may unwittingly release." The speaker exchanged an unfathomable glance with Master Ineuil and leaned back in his rough chair with the exaggerated ease of a confident predator. "I do not think you would care to encounter either obstacle without my assistance."

Gart grumbled an unintelligible comment. Hamar glowered, sullenly unresponsive. The priest shifted uncomfortably, watching Kaedric with concern. Master Ineuil looked amused, but he clenched his hands more tightly than before.

Abbot Medwyn broke the ominous silence, selecting his words with obvious care. "Alone of us, Master Kaedric is equipped to counter Hrgh. I called this Venture against Master Kaedric's intention to pursue the Taormin alone. I have not wavered in my reasoning: the world has many dangers and many means through which to counter them. I freely acknowledge, however, the incomparable value of Master Kaedric's expertise in a matter of this sort. I have named him Venture Leader, and I shall follow him. Any who would join us shall obey his word as law until the Venture's end. Agree, or go your ways now."

Stillness ensued until Ineuil responded. "We knew and accepted the Venture's terms before we journeyed here, Abbot. You have few enough followers as it is; very few are mad enough to follow one wizard into another's lair, however crucial the cause or substantial the reward. Do not tempt those who do support you into desertion."

"So be it," decreed Master Kaedric. The cold blue eyes returned to me as he continued, "The Venture is called and we are oathbound unto it. I suggest that we acquaint ourselves with our rapt audience before proceeding further."

His comment elicited some bewilderment from the other Venturers and roused terror in me. Master Ineuil recovered first, remarking speculatively, "So I was right about the shadow. I thought

I felt it in Dwaelin Wood, but my talent for that sort of thing is small."

Kaedric's gaze mocked me, his derision perversely strengthening me with angry defiance, though I had never shuddered more acutely before my father's direst temper. I summoned my sire's stark calm, since my maternal gifts had forsaken me. I willed release of my insubstantial cloak and, unshielded, stepped into the dusky light of Ceallagh's Crown. Master Ineuil laughed, Master Gart snorted, and Master Hamar sneered in disgust. The abbot covered a startled smile and darted a puzzled glance at Master Kaedric, who continued to regard me without expression.

Master Ineuil inclined his head toward me, remarking, "Had I suspected the loveliness of our shadow, I should have been less concerned with eluding her and more determined to seek closer acquaintance."

A flush of embarrassment threatened me; I was unaccustomed to receiving pretty speeches even in mockery. Master Kaedric commented dryly, "Having displayed such keen interest in our business, perhaps the lady will condescend to share with us her name and purpose."

Since I so clearly merited the allegation of guilty intrusion, my anger immediately directed itself toward my accuser. It was quite unjust of me but useful, since it reinforced my nerve. "My name is Rani," I said calmly, avoiding a precise truth which might connect me with a nobly born lady of Tyntagel. "I should like to join your Venture," I continued, gratified by the astonishment my words caused while at the same time horrified as I realized what I had offered.

Master Ineuil appeared to find my declaration exquisitely humorous, but Master Kaedric remained unresponsive. I wished the light were better, that I might more easily read the implacable planes of the wizard's face. The wizard inquired soberly, "And what skill, Mistress Rani, do you offer as aid to our quest?"

I answered with far more surety than I felt, "I have some ability as a sorceress. Obviously, I could not have survived long in Anx without a certain measure of Power." Having launched myself on rash impulse I had no intention of retreating.

Master Kaedric answered idly, "The blindness of the many will not avail you where we are bound."

"I have other gifts," I responded coldly. "If your Venture is vital, can you justifiably reject any proffered assistance?"

"A demon's aid is not a boon," snarled Hamar with disgust, reminding me of my Great-Uncle Praetor with his chronically unpleasant disposition.

"She does not much look like a demon to me," drawled Ineuil contemplatively. "On the other hand," he added with an uncharitable inspection of my tired raiment, "She does not appear to be a very prosperous sorceress."

"Power does not discriminate between pauper's robes and prince's silks, as you of all people ought to have realized by now, Master Ineuil," answered Master Kaedric harshly, darting forth an unexpected flash of fierce anger, the first emotion he had shown.

Master Ineuil's green eyes narrowed, but he shrugged and grinned. "She obviously does have other gifts which I personally find infinitely more intriguing."

"She brings trouble," said Master Hamar menacingly, and the warrior giant rose to threaten me. Master Gart, who had so far observed the proceedings in silent detachment, grabbed futilely at Hamar's arm, as Hamar clenched his powerful fingers on my shoulder. I winced, but I made no struggle for release; it would have availed nothing. I hoped that Master Hamar wished to cow me rather than inflict serious harm, although Master Kaedric had already intimidated me so greatly as to make Master Hamar's endeavor superfluous.

"Sit down, Hamar. We do not need the notoriety of a public spectacle," suggested Master Kaedric calmly, but his quiet words effected that which Gart's force had not. Hamar released me, reluctantly obeying the cool voice with its tones of authority. Master Kaedric continued without pause, considering me with deceptive mildness, "The only traits which Mistress Rani has so far exhibited are impetuosity and foolhardiness, which characteristics unfortunately do not constitute capital crimes. If she endangers us, I shall eliminate her myself." The impersonal promise frightened me a great deal more than Hamar's violent demonstration.

Master Kaedric's words subdued the warrior's explosive temper, though Master Hamar continued to eye me with suspicion, and Master Gart watched Hamar closely. The priest, Abbot Medwyn, suddenly seemed fascinated by the table boards. Master

Ineuil leaned back with an unreadable grimace. The tavern keeper and a few remaining customers occupied themselves with their own affairs; Ceallagh's Crown would sanction violence as indifferently as any other Anxian establishment.

With a glance at Master Kaedric, Abbot Medwyn intervened. "Mistress Rani," said the abbot kindly, "we appreciate your offer of aid, but ours is not a mission to be lightly assumed. I carry a share of Master Kaedric's responsibility for the safety of the Venture members, and I cannot condone your impulsive offer."

"Sir Abbot, my offer is sincere," I retorted very bravely for one ready to expire from fear. "That it may be impulsive and unwisely offered does not mitigate the value of my help. You would gauge the measure of my worth to you? There is no tree nor flower, no bird nor other small one of this world with whom I cannot speak. The gift is not so illustrious as skills which others of your party may bring, but it has merit." I was making rather free assumptions regarding the goals and limitations of those to whom I spoke.

"I say let her join us," inserted Ineuil cheerfully. "None of us truly knows what dangers we face. As Master Kaedric so gently reminds us, our chiefly needed attribute is sorcery." Master Ineuil grinned at me with rather excessive familiarity, an impertinence hardly complainable under the circumstances.

"She already causes argument," groaned Hamar dolefully. "A woman on a Venture!"

To my considerable surprise, Master Gart came to my support. "Women have often Ventured, Hamar. A sorceress belongs not to the common sort of your knowing."

"Mistress Rani could prove useful," drawled Ineuil, the perfect polish of his speech more noticeable by contrast with Master Gart's. "She has already trailed us from Dwaelin Wood to Anx, the one no more kindly disposed than the other toward incautious trespass. Southern Dwaelin is not a place in which I should care to linger alone."

"We are not heading for the Dwaelin Wood," commented Master Kaedric. "Its selective hospitality bears little relevance in Mindar's passes."

I answered him quickly, hoping to forestall another spate of objections to my person, "Even darkest passes are not devoid of those lesser voices which it is often well to heed. I seek no profit of your

Venture; I wish no burden of my welfare bestowed upon you." I hesitated, recalling a nuance of Venture law recounted by that long ago wanderer through my father's land. The Venture Leader's cold eyes probed me, and I tore my gaze from them with an effort which grew painful. I spoke to the abbot, a far less disquieting audience. I plunged myself into insane commitment. "Sir Abbot, I offer to serve your Venture without demands. So long as I uphold the Venture law, you cannot refuse my aid."

"Mistress Rani understands Venture law well," piped Ineuil mischievously. "She cannot be forbidden from our ranks on the basis of hazard to her person, if she accepts the hazard freely. I, for one, rejoice in our good fortune."

Abbot Medwyn glanced uncertainly at Master Kaedric. The wizard watched me fixedly, but he acidly remarked, "When one calls a Venture, one cannot quibble with its inconveniences. You would not have me go alone, Medwyn." Inserting a dark look at the irrepressibly grinning Ineuil, Master Kaedric continued, "I should not stand in the way of such a marked determination as Mistress Rani's, but it would be remiss of me to omit a pertinent caveat. I have sown death before, and I shall not hesitate to sacrifice life again for this Venture's cause. The acceptance of Venture binding-without-demands frees the Venture Leader of any responsibility for the claimant's welfare. Be assured, Mistress Rani, that my attention to Venture law will be no less punctilious than your own."

I met his stare, which pierced to heart's blood. His eyes are cold, I thought, only because they hold no slightest touch of green or gold or amber to counter the pallid blue. It is a physical oddity, attractive as such, and it tells nothing of temperament or trait. It should not hold me; he could not bind me by a gaze. I could walk from the tavern now and leave him to fading memory. There would arise another route from Anx; perhaps Master Ineuil or Master Gart would buy me a key if I stole the price. I need not follow this wizard, a man more dangerous than any Anxian cutthroat.

Abbot Medwyn said softly, alternately contemplating Master Kaedric and myself from a well of old regret which I could not credit to my own plight, "Mistress Rani, you are forcing us to contribute to your destruction. Please, reconsider your offer."

I answered very coolly, "I am quite satisfied with the conditions of the binding as they stand." Oddly enough, it was true. At the last affirmation of my unlikely decision, even my doubt had ebbed to leave me remote and empty. I certainly did not court the solicitude of these strangers, having known only indifferent contempt from my own kin. The concept of danger was too distant to trouble me, and I felt a breath of purpose which defied the fear the wizard roused in me.

"We reserved departure keys only for five," interrupted Hamar, persistently determined to thwart me. "It is late now to obtain another by morning. Are we to lose another day because this street-witch insists on joining us? I warrant all she wants is a departure key anyway." I squirmed inwardly; Master Hamar came uncomfortably near to the truth.

Reasoning in a tone of bland innocence, Master Ineuil insisted, "Hamar, even you cannot deny that there exist far easier ways for a comely young woman to obtain an Anxian departure key than enlisting in a Venture." Master Hamar laughed, but he did cease his objections. I studiously avoided blushing; if I were to play the role of intrepid adventuress, I could scarcely afford the misplaced sensibilities of a sheltered Tyntagellian maiden.

Gart offered helpfully, "Perhaps she has a key already," and expectant looks of varying sympathies met me.

"I have no key," I confessed awkwardly, "but I can supply the price."

Master Kaedric, an unlikely savior, terminated the discussion with an impatient gesture. "Departure keys are the least of our concerns. If we are to leave at dawn, we ought not spend the night in pointless debate. Meet at the eastern gate." He rose, unfurling his narrow height from the tavern's close corner. He was nearly as tall as Master Hamar, though the wizard was very much leaner. He loomed over me as he passed, giving me a momentary, dispassionate glance. He flicked a substantial spate of gleaming coins at the tavern keeper in parting; on the scale of Anxian bribes, it was a mildly impressive sum.

With the Venture Leader's departure, the sustaining energies of defiance and fear fled from me. I was suddenly too drained and exhausted to care for anything but sleep's blessed release. I did not even realize that I had again engulfed myself in shadow, until Master Ineuil bowed sweepingly in my general direction, saying, "If you are yet with us, fair Shadow Lady, then let me bid thee a pleasant repose. I do hope you will honor us with your more substantial presence in the morning. I find it difficult to confer meaningfully with a ghost." Master Hamar commented on the speech with a stream of imaginative invective which perturbed Master Ineuil not at all. I did not wait to hear more, glad even of the smoky stink of Anxian air after the tavern's stifling miasma.

I had found the key to my cage, but its price was strange and dear. I had sworn blind obedience to an unwilling and enigmatic leader who avowed he would not hesitate to see me murdered. I had no clear concept of the nature of the obligations I had assumed. At the least, I should be constrained to share the company of four men of very dubious gentility and a priest who appeared unlikely to adopt the role of proper chaperon. That the prospect would have horrified any of my transitory governesses, served only slightly to console me.

I was utterly frightened, knowing how tentative was the Power which I had offered to the Venture's cause. Yet I still anticipated the morning with a rare eagerness which I could in no way justify. I fell asleep reciting every name of folly I knew.

Chapter 2

Morning neared slowly; its frosty gray gave hint of the coming winter, though autumn had barely begun. I awoke shivering but grateful for the brisk air which fed my energies. In the lesser dark of predawn, I gathered my few possessions and moved quietly down the stairs. I had maintained a precautionary supply of foodstuffs, albeit through methods unorthodox for a young lady of scrupulous upbringing. I headed directly for the eastern gate, snatching a hurried and meager breakfast en route. My state of mind was not conducive to a hearty appetite.

Like so many Seriin cities of ancient origin, the plan of Anx followed a series of concentric circles pierced by spokes of major roads. Though marred by later layers, Anx remained largely symmetrical, but of the eleven roads which emanated from its hub, only the northern five had been maintained beyond the city's central district. The eastern gate crossed the road which was least traveled of the five, for it led into the inhospitable realms of the Mountains of Mindar.

I arrived at the gate early, moving swiftly through deserted streets. Not even the token Anxian guards were evident that chill morning. A single figure stood before the barrier I hoped to cross. The man was dimly visible; yet, he was unmistakably the Venture Leader, Master Kaedric.

Reluctant to share that solitary vigil, I lingered in the alleyways to await the rest of the company. I was not so distant, I suspected, that Master Kaedric's uncomfortably acute perceptions would be genuinely defeated. I trusted rather that his distaste for me would lead him to ignore me, physical separation merely easing the task. I selected a convenient wall to which some traces of plaster tenaciously clung, propped myself against it, and watched for the remaining Venturers.

Idle waiting breeds anxiety, but it was not long before Masters Gart and Hamar made their appearance. Abbot Medwyn arrived very soon thereafter. I tarried briefly, suffering some last qualms. A pallid, timid wraith, I joined the four men. Engrossed in their own preparations and discussions, they gave me no apparent notice. I was still uncertain as to whether they would indeed supply my escape from Anx. I stood awkwardly beside the group, imbued with a feeling of displacement. I studied the stained and sandy soil with a care of attention it did not merit.

Master Ineuil arrived last and unabashedly late, though the sun had yet to lift above the city's smoky pall. He called out an airy greeting, firmly directed toward me. "Exquisite lady, if you but knew how greatly I dreaded to find you had forsaken us, you would surely weep in pity of the desperate night I have spent." I had observed Master Ineuil quite long enough to assess accurately the degree of his desperation. I took appropriately little stock in his flattery, but I responded with a smile, despite myself cheered by the small attention.

Master Hamar muttered unpleasantly, "If Master Ineuil managed to remember the departure keys amid his suffering, perhaps we can get on our way."

Ineuil shook his head plaintively. "Master Hamar, you are a man of no faith. You ought to take lessons in the subject from the good Abbot Medwyn here. I, fortunately, require no such instruction. My faith is so supremely developed that I do not even question our Venture Leader's ability to make five keys suffice for six people. I trust you are suitably impressed by my piety."

"You are a conscienceless heathen, Ineuil," rebuked the abbot mildly.

"Master Ineuil might impress me more," suggested Master Kaedric dryly, "if he offered to pass the barrier keyless himself. It is he who is so singularly enchanted with Mistress Rani."

Master Ineuil chuckled mirthlessly. "You would enjoy that, Kaedric. It would revive fond childhood memories, no doubt." Abbot Medwyn shook his head, while Gart and Hamar exchanged dubious stares in echo of my own puzzlement.

"Distribute the keys," demanded Master Kaedric curtly.

Ineuil murmured blandly, "As Our Leader commands," and handed keys to Abbot Medwyn, Gart and Hamar. Ineuil seemed to weigh the last two keys, each wrapped in a gaudy silken fragment of antiquity. That which his left hand held he gave to me. The protecting fabric fell free in my hand. The disc revealed glowed subtly silver, its smooth surface fiercely cold. Almost immediately, the surface warmed, and the characteristic tracery of black appeared.

I raised my head just as Abbot Medwyn, key held high before him, vanished through the web. Gart and Hamar were already lost to sight. Ineuil still studied the key he held; Kaedric examined the barrier. Each ignored the other outwardly, but one of them hated, and I could not determine which or what. I feared for both of them without knowing why, and I nearly yielded the precious key in my hand so as to alleviate that angry, inexplicable tension.

Instead I grasped my key before me as Abbot Medwyn had done. I breathed a silent plea, closed my eyes, and stepped through the wall of my prison. Beyond a slight disorientation, I felt only the flight of the key from my hand. I opened my eyes, turning to verify my escape. The enclosing net of Anx was nowhere evident, though I carefully scanned the space where I knew it to exist. The air rippled vaguely as Master Ineuil penetrated the wall; the disc he bore shimmered and disappeared. The Venture Leader joined us beyond the deadly barricade with an admirable nonchalance for one who had carried no protective key.

"If you did not need a key, Kaedric," said Ineuil, "You might have told me before I wasted the price." He added with a gallant flourish, "Not to sound ungracious to Mistress Rani."

"If you can wade through a stream, Master Ineuil, why would you ever bother with a bridge?" The wizard spoke scathingly, and his ice-blue eyes held anger. There is deadly bitterness between these two, I thought, and I wondered what manner of man I had so rashly agreed to follow. Watching Hamar exchange cryptic whispers with Gart, I decided I was not alone in my uneasy conclusions.

Chapter 3

I felt a very ragtag piece of chaff on my first day from Anx, but freedom from the loathsome hole made the morning hours glorious. I followed the Venturers absently, caring only that the sky above me shone clear blue once again. I was free of Anx, free of my father's rule, and free of the aimless solitude to which rebellion had led me. The Venture carried me, and I rejoiced to feel again a focus of allegiance. Only when we turned to climb from the gently sloping valley into the mountains themselves did the demands of the enforced march begin to claw at my pleasure.

The road from the eastern gate of Anx dwindled quickly into a primitive path, ill-defined and uneven. My glance strayed northward to the black-green stain of Dwaelin Wood, a wistful tingle briefly reminding me of my discarded fantasy of Rhianna's realm renewed. We journeyed southeast along the foothills' edge, but the highest and most awesome of the Mindar peaks, menacing bastions with long and jagged shadows, loomed above us. My increasing aversion to the lofty passes did not derive from any lack of grandeur; the view sprawled in as majestic a beauty as any vista I had ever seen, dwindling the heights of Tyntagel's horizons into paltry hillocks. I could have enjoyed the view keenly from a less intimate perspective.

I stumbled over a rough stone, painfully recalled from inattentiveness. I had again fallen behind the others, and I hurried to narrow the gap. My normal stride could not match the pace set by Master Kaedric, but I knew better than to protest. Interloper that I was, I could scarcely complain about unchivalrous behavior.

As we trod a level stretch of path in midmorning, Master Ineuil dropped back to bespeak me. "What brought a lovely sorceress to live in the Dwaelin Wood?" he asked curiously.

I answered tersely, shy of individual conversation with this confident rogue whom I had for some time studied unseen, "I am fond of trees."

"Dwaelin Wood does have enough of those." Master Ineuil regarded me doubtfully and shook his head. "What a dismal waste of a comely woman. Mind you, I have known women who ought to be consigned to a lightless corner, but you, Mistress Rani, are not among them."

"I think you cannot be very selective to say so, but it is a kind compliment and I thank you."

"Truth is easy praise: shall I earn gratitude for calling the iris the eye of heaven?" he demanded lavishly. With bland disregard for accuracy, he added, "The thanks I merit are from the world for having extracted you from hiding." He emphasized his words by reaching his arm about me in a more than comradely fashion.

I was severely flustered but determined not to show it. Master Ineuil's interest might have pleased me under other circumstances, but the thought of spending an indefinite term of Venture fending off his advances alarmed me. "Have you not enjoyed enough conquests of late?" I asked with asperity as I stepped away from him.

"Mistress Rani, you have been observing me in Anx as well as Dwaelin Wood! I never had a woman join a Venture for me before. It is a rather stimulating approach. We must arrange some privacy to further the idea."

"I shall dislike to disappoint you, Master Ineuil," I began.

He interrupted me volubly, "If you tell me that you did not join the Venture for my irresistibly appealing company, I shall be utterly devastated, and my agony will land squarely upon your conscience. You will impart disservice to yourself and to the Venture, and that would not be in keeping with your Venture oath."

"You have a fascinating perspective on Venture code, but I doubt that Abbot Medwyn would support it," I said with more hope than belief.

"Holy men have such limited notions," complained Ineuil piteously. He had let his arm drop willingly, but he still walked closer to me than I found comfortable.

Master Kaedric glanced back at us. Cold eyes appraising, he called to Ineuil, and the fair-haired scoundrel left my side with a grimace and a shrug. The Venture Leader murmured to him some words I could not hear, and I walked alone for the remainder of the day. Master Ineuil cast me a few bright grins over his shoulder, but he did not defy the obvious decree of Master Kaedric.

Master Kaedric gave no more direct indication that he knew I followed his troop, but Master Ineuil was not the only one he warned away from me. Master Gart paused once with a shy consideration to aid me up a treacherous incline, but Master Kaedric's immediate censure of the action made any further courtesies unlikely. Master Gart's unexpected and incongruous kindness pleased me rather more than Ineuil's insincere praise, but I held no quarrel with the Venture Leader's relentless policy. I had known myself unwelcome from the outset, and if I were ostracized from the company proper, I should not need to learn as quickly their individual ways; nor should I risk revealing myself. As the day lengthened, however, and my struggle to keep Master Kaedric's pace grew more daunting, I did begin to wonder what Venture-sworn duties would entail upon a Venturess deserted by her fellows.

We had traveled with minimal halts more vertical miles than I liked to consider, and I had lost count of the repetitive ridges which now separated us from Anx. The miles did not daunt the professional soldiers, Hamar and Gart, and Ineuil complained only of boredom. The venerable abbot did not complain at all, but his steps began to falter near evening, a weakening for which I silently thanked him. The forbidding Master Kaedric displayed a concern for the holy man as for no other among us.

The Venturers speedily made camp with no need for any aid from me. Even Master Ineuil executed his tasks with silent intensity, no frivolous jocularity in evidence that night. The chosen site did not inspire cheer: towering, ashen crags on three sides and a spindly pine were the sole relief from stony stringency. I established myself near the pine, somewhat removed from the rest of the party; ancient and weary, the tree's serene tenacity solaced my ragged nerves.

I would have gladly assisted the others, but Master Kaedric's terse commands assured me that my feeble efforts only interfered. So, pursuing the voiceless whispers of the wild, I wandered from the camp to gather such produce as the vicinity offered: angelica, burdock and monarda I added to my own herbal stores; I amassed truffles and sweet apples as a timid offering.

Other foraging than mine had stocked the Venturers' larder, but the Venturers appeared to be more practical than imaginative in their acquisitions. I dropped my contribution before the fire where they gathered. Abbot Medwyn, at least, seemed pleased by the addition to the meal.

I was not so entranced by the eating of charred rabbit that I would ask to join the men in supper, especially when I had felt the buck's death cry, but the fire tempted me sorely. My woolen cloak was warm but did not cover me completely. I debated only a moment. The cold did not suffice to overcome that most worthless commodity, pride. I withdrew wordlessly from the circle of warmth and ate my few bites of Anxian cheese in the solitary company of the tired pine, which at least did not despise me.

I was nearly asleep, yielding mindlessly to my exhaustion, when I received the first recognition of my status as a Venturess: Master Gart summoned me to a sentry shift. I winced at thought of my lost sleep. I had safely passed many nights relying solely on the warning of the wild things, but no danger more heinous than my father's trackers had sought me. I had brought the Venture duties on myself; the thought gave me little consolation. Rubbing tired eyes, I followed Master Gart to the fire. At least I should for a while enjoy warmth.

The Venture Leader was delineating to Abbot Medwyn a scheme of rotational guard duty which I privately considered pointless. I did not even try to pursue the logic of the thing, though its careful complexities might have intrigued me in days of more monotonous Tyntagel tutelage. I heeded the points of immediate interest, resolving to face each duty as it arose. For the first night, Master Gart and I should take initial watch; Ineuil and Hamar would assume the second, and Master Kaedric with Abbot Medwyn would see the night to its end. I sighed and forced myself more fully awake. It would be another three hours before I could seek sleep, and the prospect depressed me.

Had the night brought an army of Caruillan raiders leaping from the dark and brandishing swords, I doubt I could have roused sufficiently to give the warning. Fortunately, my first night as sentry passed quietly. A single curious predator impinged upon my awareness, and he was wary enough to avoid a near approach.

Master Gart studiously polished his blade, though any whisper of wind brought him stiffly alert. I watched the puckered scars scattered across his blunt hands as he honed his sword. It was a guardsman's weapon, the hilt embossed with the worn crest of an unfamiliar House.

"Did you serve that household?" I asked with a nod at the blazoned metal.

Gart smiled shyly. "From the day I could hold a weapon until my thirtieth year. My parents and my sister serve it still."

"Why did you leave?" I asked, genuinely curious. Few family guardsmen left that secure service for a mercenary's uncertain destiny.

"His Lordship cannot support all of his servants' children," said Gart a bit defensively, and I thought the answer had the air of a tired quote. The parting had been accepted with obedient grace, but it had not been welcomed.

"I do not recognize the crest. Is it a Seriin House?" I asked to distract him from his memories of regret.

"It belongs to the House of Coprak dur Sashchlya of Mahl," responded Gart proudly. It was not the name of any major holding, but it might have been Tul dur Tulea for the glow of importance which Gart accorded it. I decided that Lord Coprak had been a fool to dispense with such a persistently loyal adherent, but I bowed my head as if suitably impressed.

"Do you know Master Hamar from Mahl, then?" I asked.

"Hamar is Caruillan," answered Gart. He added hurriedly, "But he does not hold with piracy. He was fleeing the agents of Blood-Talon Cor when I met him in Pithlii. Seven of them were attacking him when we met. I beheaded two of the scum, and Hamar and I have fought together ever since." Gart grinned fondly. I blinked, baffled for a response. The piratical King Cor of Caruil and his murderous affairs were very remote from my frame of reference.

Neither Gart nor I excelled at conversation in such total absence of common perspective, but we lapsed into a surprisingly comfortable silence. I might have been an ordinary daughter of a keep, seated at my father's own gate, the grizzled warrior at my side a retainer whom I had known from birth. The Venture and its ancillary duty of nightwatch began to seem less onerous, but I was no less glad to see the shift end.

I awoke to the throbbing protest of muscles driven too strenuously on the previous day. I rose awkwardly, hobbling painfully as I tried to coax my abused legs into motion. The camp was astir; I left it to lave icy water into sleep-filled eyes as hastily as stiff muscles would permit. I half expected to find that the Venturers had departed when I returned.

The day progressed at winter's pace, awful with the tedium of discomfort. My previous difficulty in matching the Venturers' speed was magnified tenfold, and Master Kaedric's edict against me held wholly unbroken. I ached and bit back tears of frustration and hurt. The Venturers paused at midday, but I feared to sit overlong lest I be unable to coerce my body again into movement. I spent the time resentfully watching the men enjoy their ease and resolving that I should not again let pride keep me from sharing any meager luxuries available: the warmth of a fire or the sustenance of a substantial meal. I should not again yield the greatest portion of my provender to men who neither needed it nor even gave any thanks for it. If twilight ever came again, as I had begun to think unlikely, I determined that I should have a proper supper and a pot of primrose tea, coat my most miserable limbs with wintergreen liniment, and let the trees do my guarding for me.

With every trudging step, I asked myself how I could have brought myself to such a pass, my initial, overwhelming joy at escaping Anx long since vanquished by physical discomfort. I lacked the requisite will for a hermit's life, as my brief stint in Dwaelin Wood had too ably proven. The years spent in study at my father's house no longer seemed so dreary a life, but by running away, I had surely eradicated that as a possibility. The traditional destiny of marriage might have made an acceptable life had it not implied constraint still more rigid than my father's rule; I lacked the perspective to be by nature a suitable wife to any proper Seriin lord, and I could not wish to commit to a life of meek, obedient and mindless hypocrisy. I knew no trade, save for the marginal one of sorceress. With no great glee, I cycled to the conclusion that Venturing was perhaps not the worst of roles for me.

The day did end, of course, though by midafternoon I had perforce retreated in mind to that distant corner out of which my claims to endurance rose. I moved rigidly and automatically, but I did not lose sight of the Venturers. By evening, I felt a meanspirited dearth of charity toward them, which fortified my nerve if not my good sense. When the camp had been settled for supper, I approached the fireside where the men were gathered. Master Kaedric was quite engrossed in scribbling odd symbols in the sandy soil with the tip of a highly polished dagger. The other men chatted idly as they dined on a stew of twice-charred meat and some assorted tubers which I had collected during the day. The trees whispered, and I took strength. I served myself and seated myself carefully. Not one of the Venturers protested. Master Ineuil looked from the abstracted Venture Leader to me and winked broadly. Abbot Medwyn shared my tea. It had been remarkably easy.

Another first shift as sentry, which I thought a less equitable arrangement than Master Kaedric's abstruse scheme ought to have produced, again deferred my sleep. Forbidden from rest and painfully stiff, I was not a particularly sociable companion, even solaced by food and warmth. The prospect of fending Master Ineuil's irrelevant and suggestive prattle through my current blur of fatigue did not lighten my mood. I winced as I sat beside him, my legs reluctant to bend according to my wish.

Master Ineuil tutted and wagged his head. "One might almost suspect, Mistress Rani, that the privilege of my company does not entice you so much as your slumber."

"Your perception is keen," I answered less graciously than I might had my legs and spirit ached less feverishly.

He sighed heavily. "How shall we ever extend our relationship if you insist on disliking me?" he asked wistfully.

His regret sounded deeply sincere: I nearly protested with admission of inability actually to dislike him. I stopped the words, reminding myself of the lessons of observation. I felt wryly flattered, but I had no intention of becoming another conquest. My answer turned sardonic. "Under the circumstances, we seem destined to a certain furtherance of acquaintance, like it or otherwise."

"Only if we use our time together to greatest effect. The travails of travel do not optimize conversational opportunity. Aside from which, my lovely sorceress, our Venture Leader is tediously determined to keep us apart. You cannot have failed to perceive the heinous nature of his scheme of rotational guard duty?" Master Ineuil's tone of horror was quite affecting, as was the innocent widening of his leaf-green eyes. "You and I, lovely Sorceress Rani, shall not again share a sentry shift for over a week."

With a notable lack of sympathy, I suggested, "The only heinous aspect to Master Kaedric's scheme is its monumental complexity. If you have deciphered it sufficiently to predict beyond a week, I am indeed impressed."

Master Ineuil beamed, his green eyes glinting delight. "We progress already, dear sorceress. I have impressed you." He leaned closer to me, his voice sinking to a throaty whisper. "Our lives are linked by fate, my Rani. We were bound when you stepped from the shadow into my life."

The man was quite impossible. He had spouted a very similar speech at least a dozen times in Anx, and it sounded all the more ridiculous now that I was the recipient. "Really," was my only comment.

He straightened, dropping the pose of seducer with uncomplimentary alacrity. "A bit much? You are right, of course. Excessive exposure to the Anxian environment has deprived me of subtlety. I shall endeavor to improve." His conversation veered abruptly. "Regarding a less innocuous purveyor of subtlety: I do hope Our Leader's disdain for chivalry does not prejudice you against the rest of us. Kaedric can be excessively difficult, but it is generally prudent to heed his stronger stances."

"I did rather force myself upon the Venture," I conceded weakly, resisting the temptation to glance toward the dark huddles where the other Venture members slept.

"A fortuitous circumstance for me, fair sorceress, though I am not quite sure just why you did it." Ineuil eyed me curiously. "I wonder if you know how much of a risk you take in countering our Master Kaedric."

"I had not really considered the matter," I lied.

"You ought never to underestimate a wizard, my Rani. The most insignificant of actions can mask monsters. Ixaxin training is partly to blame; it breeds tortuous thinking. But those who seek the training think oddly to begin."

"You imply that Master Kaedric was trained on Ixaxis. He is a full wizard then." I was ingenuously intrigued, though the revelation merely confirmed the obvious.

Master Ineuil disregarded my comments, though I was sure he heard them well enough. He pursued his own thoughts airily. "Complexity can marvelously disguise simple truths: consider Kaedric's infamous scheme of watch. It ensures that each pair of us six shares duty at least one sixth of the time, and the number of turns at each shift is evenly distributed among us through a thirty-six day cycle. Each of us, however, is paired with precisely one other Venturer exactly one-third of the time, weighting the shifts rather substantially. The emphasized pairings are notable: Kaedric with Gart, myself with Hamar, and you with Abbot Medwyn. Do you not find it fascinating?"

"Hardly," I answered with what I hoped was a quelling lack of enthusiasm. I did not want to contemplate Master Kaedric; the wizard had already lodged too firmly in my mind.

Master Ineuil remained undaunted. "You are not intrigued by the fact that our Venture Leader has concentrated the two (if you will forgive me) apparently weakest members of the party? It tells me that Kaedric sees more in either you or Abbot Medwyn than might be expected, and I think I know the abbot well enough to discount him for the stronger role in this case."

"It tells me that your logic is as convoluted as Master Kaedric's."

"My lovely one, you are unkind. Kaedric delights in twisting puzzles to obscure purposes. My interest lies solely in the motivational reasoning of a man I am sworn to follow for the nonce."

I nodded vaguely, determinedly refusing greater interest. Without encouragement, Master Ineuil's prattle grew less consequential, though it persisted for most of the three hours. I began to appreciate Hamar's protest against incessant talk. Exhaustion gradually frayed my attention to the point of ignoring my fellow sentry. I struggled just enough to heed the trees and to force my eyes to retain their focus, but energy to squander in absorbing the erratic irrelevancies of Master Ineuil's chatter departed me. I remembered, however, and pondered, when at last I had earned my rest, the thought that Master Kaedric might not consider me as entirely insignificant to the Venture as he pretended. Master Ineuil's speculations refused to be dislodged; he had activated in me an irrationally insistent interest of my own in Master Kaedric's mode of reasoning.

Chapter 4

I had lived a thoroughly ordered life until my rebellion against my father's choice, and the Venture had restored a comfortable dearth of freedom which revived in me old habits of study. I began to sort the Venturers into niches in my mind, as if I were matching stockings rather than men of mutable dispositions. Swayed by my own conclusions, my theories of these men became my reality. I did not presume any claim to friendship with the five, but the Venturers of my visions grew familiar, and my history held few fonder human connections to dislodge them.

These were hard, disparate men, alike only in acceptance of cruel beauty or fair cruelty. Gart persisted in shy reticence; Hamar glowered in silent distrust. Abbot Medwyn was a man who combined in rare counterpoint faith with placid pragmatism; he barely spoke to me, though he could be quite gregarious with the others. Ineuil talked endlessly, but he very seldom conversed, and nonsense dominated his speech. Kaedric's reserve was unyielding. Each man told me astonishingly little.

It was by Gart that I felt most nearly accepted, despite Master Ineuil's persistent effluence of praise. That Gart's attitude toward me suggested the timid deference of a vassal toward his Lady did nothing to promote companionship, however. Master Gart belonged to that most class-conscious breed of peasantry to whom the least measure of literacy bespeaks authority. Only with his long companion, Hamar, was he entirely at ease; the two of them proudly proclaimed a common heritage of low birth.

I could not doubt the depth of friendship between Hamar and Gart, but I could not fathom it. Hamar suffered perpetual anger, the sort which rises from festered sorrow, and it did not make him pleasant company. I pitied Hamar for the pain which obviously goaded him, but my sympathy ebbed with proximity. Restrained by soldierly discipline, he had not openly threatened me since Anx, but his hatred blared forth at me. The dour features of his bald head stiffened at every sighting of me; his suspicious glare pursued me as certainly as the wardings of the old peasant woman who had held my childhood in strict custody. It was not the Tyntagellian sort of prejudice which filled Hamar, for it did not extend to Master Kaedric, but it was no less pervasive. Watch duty with Master Hamar was a grueling ordeal of mutual distrust.

Abbot Medwyn accorded me little more confidence than did Hamar. The abbot was vastly more tolerant of sorcery than any priest of my prior acquaintance, but he would speak to me only sparingly. He did not hide his disapproval of my presence. He took his Venture very seriously, and he viewed my jointure as irresponsible whim. He was not chronically somber as are so many of his years and calling; Ineuil drew as much laughter as censure from the abbot, and the laughter showed less reluctance in the issuance. But the Abbot of Benthen Abbey bore a heavy weight of worry where the Venture was concerned.

Master Ineuil still defied my efforts to categorize satisfactorily. Apparently a very capable warrior when necessity could overcome indolence, he lightly professed himself to be both trickster and thief, and his eclectic education had not excluded a sampling of the mage's art, though his actual Power was more minimal than my own. He clearly enjoyed the role of irresponsible scapegrace, but I began to suspect a very shrewd manipulator hid behind the pose.

There remained the Venture Leader, the wizard who effected minor wonders with casual indifference: lighting a fire with a glance or exploding a nutshell rather than cracking it in the ordinary way. If I had ever visualized a Sorcerer King, his aspect would have much resembled Master Kaedric; any staunch Tyntagellian

would have placed him immediately. Saturnine and cynical, remotely merciless and coldly impersonal, he fulfilled the very image
of the remorseless men and women who had tyrannized the ancient world. I had been taught to despise wizards. I wished I could
despise Master Kaedric half as much as I feared him.

Chapter 5

Whether by misfortune or some malicious humor of the Venture Leader, my first watch, my first solitary confrontation with Master Kaedric was scheduled for the night's final shift. Nervous fear forbade me more than fitful sleep as I counted the hours before me. I surrendered to insomnia's inevitable victory when the second shift was little more than half over. I arose, intending to give benefit of those elusive minutes of sleep to Abbot Medwyn or Master Gart. Too late for unobserved retreat, I found Master Kaedric surveying the nightscape alone.

"You will regret your lack of rest, Mistress Rani," he murmured with disinterest.

I answered tartly, too afflicted with nervousness to restrain my tongue. "By your own words, Venture Leader, my well-being concerns myself alone. The prospect of lost sleep does not seem to have deterred you."

"Ineuil's injudicious wit is contaminating you. It is not an endearing characteristic."

"I have never believed in hypocritical propitiation," I said, achieving an admirably scathing tone which doubtless failed to hide my reluctance to approach the wizard closely.

"An admirable policy, but a hazardous one if misallocated. Do you intend to assume sentry duty, or were you planning a surreptitious exit from our Venture? I shall willingly release you from your oath."

It was a weighty and generous offer, though the Venture Leader would unquestionably prefer to see me go. I had been freed from Anx; I could pursue my own path unencumbered. Instead of making such a sensible choice, I responded loftily, "I may yet be of use to you, Master Kaedric."

He shrugged indifference. "Then you may as well take your post. Or perhaps you see better through basalt." He acknowledged the overhang which slanted across the entrance to the cave wherein we had made camp. I had welcomed the shelter earlier, for the rain fell softly outside, and the cave was dry and warmly defended against the wind. I had not considered how close to Kaedric I would have to stay because of the narrow access.

I braced myself with the thought that an adept wizard could bespell me quite as well from five feet as from five inches, if he were so inclined. I could hardly expect to contribute anything to the Venture if I were going to be daunted by the prospect of sitting near the Venture Leader. I was stubbornly determined to be of value; it may have been a form of atonement for my dereliction of filial duty. I seated myself with what grace I could manage, taking excessive care to avoid any wisp of contact with the Venture Leader.

He leaned against a fold of polished rock siding, long legs drawn close and crossed after the manner of street dwellers. His cloak was rough, and his fingers tugged restlessly at the collar. He had walked in the rain, for the sheen of it caused his thick hair to cling tightly to itself rather than to stray errantly as was its wont. Ineuil was the more handsome, for Master Kaedric's lines had been drawn too acutely, but the wizard had a graceful strength and eyes which were inescapable.

The rain fell, dimpling the pool which had gathered beyond the cavern access. I watched it carefully. I reached for the thoughts of the trees, but my mind was too troubled to hold the contact long. The dark, cloud-filled sky roiled before me, for the cave opened onto a ledge which had been lifted boldly from the mountain's smooth skin of soil. The clouds thinned, and an aureole of hidden moonlight softened them, but the world a few paces from my face remained a blurred and featureless shadow. I drew my feet more tightly beneath me to keep them from the splatter of the rain, and I clasped my arms about me firmly for warmth.

I spoke randomly, my throat tight with discomfort. "Am I so

predictable that you dismissed both Abbot Medwyn and Master Gart in anticipation of my early arrival?"

"I felt the need for some solitary contemplation."

"I should be pleased to leave you to it, Master Kaedric."

"I never doubted that," he responded dryly, a hush above the rain. He added with his distinctive precision, an exactitude of enunciation which seemed to shield another accent, "But a Venture Leader ought to know something of his followers, and you do appear boundlessly determined to follow." An odd sensation of sitting/standing, meeting the gaze of wintry/fiery eyes in both a gloomy cave and a glittering emptiness tantalized me. Kaedric asked quietly, "What drives you so confoundedly to pursue this quest? Our goal means nothing to you. I doubt you could even tell me what it is."

I answered faintly, "I was not aware that a Venturer's motives demanded scrutiny," hoping that the Venture Leader would desist from questioning me as I tried to consolidate the doubling of image through which I saw him.

"Some degree of explanation could ease your position. Master Hamar, for example, considers you a dubious ally indeed. He distrusts women in any case, and your mysterious appearance among us does little to calm his suspicions."

"It is difficult to defend against irrational prejudice."

"Granted. But you must admit that you are an atypical Venturess, Mistress Rani."

"Then I have found a Venture well suited to me," I retorted.

"Others among us have strong motives regarding the Venture goal itself, a factor which compensates for much that would be otherwise unlikely." An arrhythmic rustle from a ragged copse below us drew his attention. The veil between the images I saw of him thinned. I listened closely to the whisper of fading leaves; something breathed in the rainy night. The air constricted around it heatedly. A darkness slipped beyond dead rock, and I lost the thing's touch.

Kaedric relaxed imperceptibly, releasing the thought which had lashed our watcher into flight. I could feel the pulse of the wizard's Power, a singularly disconcerting sensation which disturbed me far more than the prospect of any nearby prowlers. Unreasonably embarrassed, I blushed as if discovered in some intimate secret.

I found clear blue eyes assessing me curiously. "You are not only an unlikely Venturess, Mistress Rani. You are a very singular sorceress as well."

I disliked the direction the conversation was taking toward my sorcerous claims. "There was something in the copse which the trees found unfamiliar," I countered unnecessarily.

"That 'something' has been studying us for some hours, but for the moment it seems to have accepted my suggestion to depart. Our observer did not distress you; I did. For an apparently educated sorceress, you react remarkably like some credulous child equating wizardry with atrocity."

"I am not fond of sorcery, Master Kaedric, but that makes me no less a sorceress," I stated sharply, wondering helplessly what form of ignorance I had betrayed.

"I am not questioning the existence of your Power," remarked Master Kaedric evenly. He regarded me with a keen attention which I refused to confront. "Your doubt of my ability to recognize it does intrigue me, however. Is it my Power or your own which you question, I wonder?"

"Since you persist in denying my value to the Venture, it should hardly surprise you if I suspected you of a lack of perception," I answered haughtily, speaking rudely out of a sudden suspicion that I could thereby best dispel the Venture Leader's interest.

For some moments, he kept silent. He watched the night, but I felt him studying me closely. Rain touched the earth in a delicate patter. The whispers of the woods had dimmed, lost in the glare of the Power beside me. I tried to reach the mind of an owl, but I could not sufficiently escape the man.

"If you were a whit less transparently ingenuous," he said after the minutes had stretched achingly, "I should doubt you as fervently as does Master Hamar, despite the rather reliable evidence of my perceptions."

I straightened deliberately, forcing my eyes to meet those of the Venture Leader, the clear blue mirrorlike in reflected fire-glow. I repeated stiffly, "I may yet be of use to you, Master Kaedric."

"That is a paltry reason to risk life and soul."

"It suffices me, for I do not risk so much." I continued more bitterly than I had intended, "Durability takes no more account of worth than does the gift of Power."

"Power respects nothing," stated Kaedric flatly. "But even a wizard is bound by a physical shell. Are you so certain of your 'durability' that you would care to test it against a full wizard's Power?" He whispered dangerously, "Are you so sure that you would care to test your strength against me, for instance? With the Taormin in his hands, Hrgh's Power may not be so different from mine. You ought to know what that kind of Power can inflict before you taunt it."

The beat of his Power grew as he spoke, pounding through me until it began to rule the throb of my heart and lifeblood. The rhythm shifted, and the pulsation burned. "Have you ever seen a man afire from within?" demanded Master Kaedric softly. His words held a fever-bright intensity which was almost seductive. "The skin begins to shrivel as the moisture leaves it, and the eyes wither. He cannot scream aloud, for the fire steals his voice. He falls and writhes, but the flame cannot be extinguished, because his own life energy turns inward to help consume its host. It is not a death I should recommend. Is that what you wish to face, Mistress Rani?"

"We each face what we must, Master Kaedric," I answered firmly, trying to deny the tightening pain. I had dreaded Master Kaedric's dissuasion so deeply that its unpleasant arrival actually eased my fear. After the years of my father's tutelage, I could distinguish sincere attack from intimidation, even when the weapon wore a radically different guise. The Venture Leader controlled his Power carefully; I found myself certain that he would cause me no more serious harm now than he had in the Anxian tavern, and the game he played annoyed me.

He ceased his onslaught. An ill-fortuned rodent cried death as the talons of the owl tore its flesh. The mingled hunger and suffering pierced me more deeply for the rawness of my wracked senses. I clenched my arms tightly in misery, forced on myself a rigid control, and spoke with angry hauteur. "You remind me, Master Kaedric, of a bully who tortures small creatures so as to reassure himself of his own superiority."

Kaedric watched me a moment closely, then turned away and commented, "I have roused terror in far more stalwart individuals than yourself, Mistress Rani, but the reaction is not generally an urge to provoke me further. I do find your behavior a trifle eccentric." He startled me with soft laughter, and he grinned fleetingly, for a brief instant disarmingly approachable. "If you detect any un-natural disturbances around us, I trust you will inform me," he continued. "You do appear to be highly empathic toward certain life forms. With brigands and less palatable foes roaming these mountains, no warning system can be too complete."

I glanced perplexedly at the man beside me, seeking evidence of mockery. Impenetrable reserve resumed, he studied the cloud-covered sky. A lock of velvet-black hair obscured his eyes from my sidelong view, and the smooth, hard line of his jaw revealed nothing.

Chapter 6

The next days followed closely the pattern of those first, save that my aches turned dully permanent and my feet turned raw with blisters. The gray and rocky way we trod changed minimally, but the verdant carpet of Dwaelin Wood seemed to withdraw ever farther below us. A few tenacious pines and the scions of a hardy breed of lusterless shrub clung to barren stone. An occasional bird or skittering rodent would acknowledge me briefly, but they were cautious of the company I kept. I understood their wariness; comprehension did not console me for loss of their companionship.

We traveled for another fortnight before the validity of Master Kaedric's cautionings became manifest. We had departed from the established trail to reach our goal in the heart of the Mountains of Mindar. The way had grown steadily more difficult and unpredictable, but this should hopefully deter the marauding bands which so frequently preyed upon each other in the relatively halcyon lowlands. Ineuil and Gart had one night reported the approach of a pair of would-be robbers, but the glint of polished steel had sufficed to discourage the interlopers. Whatever creature had watched us at the cavern camp had not appeared again. Anx had fallen miles behind us, and my mind had grown easier in the far more peaceful wilderness.

Our rate of progress had deteriorated, impeded by sliding rocks and thorny shrubs. Retraced steps abraded tempers. Both Gart and Hamar freely cursed every uncooperative stone; Ineuil darted verbal barbs with indiscriminate liberality; Abbot Medwyn grew unwontedly quiet, save for some suppressed mutterings of a less than pious air. Kaedric grew grimmer, scowled often, and spoke scarcely at all. My own lot having improved significantly from the first, unnecessarily ghastly days beyond Anx, I savored a slightly vindicative sense of justice in the current distress of my companions.

We had been following the third in a series of narrow, apparently unassailable canyons for over an hour. The last ended, as had the others, at the base of a daunting arete. As he had done twice before, Kaedric climbed the accessible base of the barricade, examining its crevices for a means to mount or circumvent the obstacle. I mentally applauded his indomitable persistence, but I did not follow the others to the canyon's end. I was confident that they would soon return as they had come. I sat on a boulder to wait, massaging my right ankle, for I had wrenched it earlier in the day.

I let my mind roam to my surroundings. A few birds pecked grubs from a rotting log. A mouse snatched a seed with greedy glee. A cluster of columbine touched tentative roots to a stony crack. I pictured my sister's horrified distaste for my present circumstances, my brothers' disapproval of my fellow journeyers, and my father's angry disdain. Lady Altha would have shrieked very shrilly of the improprieties of my surroundings. By now, the plans for my journey to Tulea would have been well advanced; I should have been suffering the attentions of a dozen dressmakers in preparation for my presentation to Lord Grisk dur Niveal. I sighed, content despite soreness and fatigue.

The sun warmed me, and I became for the instant heartily glad of the Venture I had chosen to pursue. Master Kaedric did accuse me justly: I had only the dimmest notion of our goal. I enjoyed the Venture as a surreal interlude, detached from any reality I understood. I did not fret at the delays which racked the others, because I had forgotten the future and the past.

Suddenly daydreams, bruised toes and aching muscles were all forgotten. The wild things, leafed and furred and feathered, cried resounding terror. I think I screamed in echo, but I never heard my own cry. I heard an ominous twang, saw a feathered shaft strike the stone a breath away from Kaedric, felt the rush of hurtling arrows as the Venturers scrambled for cover. I willed myself less than a shadow in starlight, pressed flat against the cliff, and prayed that stony solidity might protect me.

I could see Hamar's hunched shoulder protruding from cover, but the other Venturers had vanished from my view. I scanned the opposite heights for the source of the attack; I found a hollow and a solid, hidden ridge. I felt the force of willful violence now, a score of murderous predators gloating on the effectiveness of their trap. They had grown silent following the initial flurry of assault. They awaited some betraying movement from their quarry, and they were patient with the self-confidence of assured success. They outnumbered us badly, and they held as well the advantage of position. I breathed raggedly; dust had caught in my throat, and tears gathered as I stifled a cough.

The air rose, distorted, from the canyon, and the cool clarity of autumn warped into currents of summer-hot heat. The scene before me had subtly shifted. The atmosphere suffocated; the cliff face against which I leaned turned searing. The heat above me became yet more intense. Clattering stones and scattered oaths signified an unwilling departure of the attackers.

Master Kaedric reappeared, leaping deftly down an inadequate stair of boulders to the level of the sand. With an imperious gesture, he summoned the other Venturers and waved them toward the canyon egress. I merged with them as they reached me, still enshadowed by my fear, in time to hear Kaedric whisper sharply to the party, "A slight scorch will not long deter our friends from pursuit. We need a more defensible position, preferably one less riddled with well-armed thieves."

"There was a place not far back which might suit," offered Ineuil after a moment's consideration. Kaedric nodded approval, and Ineuil added irritably, "You nearly cooked us back there, O Venture Leader. Could you be a little more selective in your next attack?"

Kaedric answered distractedly, "Next time I shall be pleased to practice on you, Master Ineuil." Gart shouted warning as an enormous ruffian in greasy furs and motley bits of rust-flecked armor leaped before us. I jumped back, feeling exceptionally useless, as Hamar parried a weighty axe blow. From pocked cliffs before and above us, a dozen more of the brigands appeared. The constricted space between the canyon walls prevented them from reaping full

advantage of their greater numbers, but the same feature of landscape held us firmly caged.

The thieves jeered and taunted, aware of their advantages and
apparently undaunted by their brief setback at the canyon's end.
Even the downing of several of their own by the swords of Hamar,
Gart and Ineuil did not seem to deter them. The villains now visible on the upper ledge, a group more prosperously attired than
their fellows in the forefront of the attack, cheered the carnage
below them as if enjoying a highly entertaining spectacle. The delight of the men remote from the fray—and at least one woman
whom I could see beside them—ebbed considerably when a knife
spun from Kaedric's hand to catch the neck of one of their number.
The injured man sagged, blood spattering freely over his tasteless
finery; his fellows retreated to safer cover, leaving him to howl his
death. The robber band had underestimated their prey.

I had tended wounds in Tyntagel, eased a soldier's death, and
cleansed the stump of a farmer's leg severed to prevent the spread
of black infection. I had not known the dreadful wrack of deliberate killing; the spread of death in that nameless canyon furthered
the education begun in Anx. Blood-drenched earth and dismembered, dying men sent me reeling with nausea. That those who suffered were both my enemies and murderous thieves did not
alleviate my horror. Masters Gart and Hamar tallied their victims
with emotionless zeal; Ineuil mocked his prey, darted deadly, agile
thrusts, and danced away from steely retaliation. Shadowed as I
was amid the hail of blows, I nearly lost a hand to one of Ineuil's
fluid brandishes.

Kaedric stood guard before a calm but very somber Abbot
Medwyn. Save for that first knife cast, the Venture Leader had used
no obvious weapon. The brigands did not approach the remote
pair. Though Kaedric gazed afar as if oblivious, at his feet an un-
bloodied corpse shriveled, pallid and mindlessly contorted.

More attackers joined the battle, and the Venturers slew less easily. With a shouted command in a vaguely recognizable Mahlite di-
alect, Kaedric consigned the abbot's defense to Master Gart and
climbed to a rough outcrop just below the bandits' ledge. His position made him a prominent target, but none of our assailants
seemed inclined to press him, however much their chiefs (safely
ensconced behind stout barricades of boulders) might urge it.

The glances of the brigands began to stray uncertainly to the man silhouetted against the beige and umber strata. I watched him also: I could feel around me all the life-beats save his, which should have pulsed most potently. Though clearly visible, Master Kaedric's withdrawal was far more complete than mine. The air around him rippled slowly, faster, searingly bright. Spirals shivered, fire flew, and a reedy wail of agony rose from the canyon walls. Some of the brigands fell; others scrambled madly. Swords and axes, pikes and daggers dropped forgotten, rattling dismally. A shrill scream seemed to tear sound from the very stone and cast it at reverberating mountain walls.

The fallen men blackened and burned to curling cinders. A few men struggled and crawled blindly, even as their flesh fused and melted from bones already crumbling. Ineuil began to seek the lingerers, ending their torment with quick sword thrusts; Gart and Hamar joined him in his task, and Abbot Medwyn knelt to pray above the dying. I saw Kaedric, and his eyes had filled with fire, though it may have been an image visible to me alone. I shut my own eyes tightly but could not seal away the sounds and scents. The slaughter filled my mind, until I was nearly as mad as the thieves who begged to die.

Chapter 7

When my mind cleared, miles had been lost. I followed Abbot Medwyn docilely, trailing the other Venturers and treading carefully along the ridge which had previously daunted our efforts to reach it. A wisp of smoke and a glimpse of leaping flame marked the battlefield behind us. I averted my eyes from the site of carnage and from the dark figure of the man who led us.

"Are you returned to us, Mistress Rani?" asked Abbot Medwyn solicitously.

I gazed blankly a moment at the robed man who walked beside me, then answered heavily, "Thank you, Abbot, I am quite recovered now."

"I am most pleased to hear it. Sorcerous self-healing still disconcerts me." He loosed the cowl from his head as he nodded. He continued briskly, "I may need to raid your herbal stores this evening. Master Hamar took a slash across the ribs: not a deep wound, but it may infect."

"I have myrrh and echinacea."

"Between us we have a rather satisfactory pharmacopoeia, Mistress Rani. Would you also have some yellow jessamine?"

Uncomprehendingly, I responded, "Yellow jessamine is a bit beyond my abilities, Sir Abbot. That is a rather odd request for a soldier's wounds."

"Kaedric does not wage ordinary war," he answered, and my

memory-wracked soul agreed with a shudder. Abbot Medwyn looked troubled. "Ixaxins use yellow jessamine as a restorative after intensive energy expenditure. Kaedric dislikes the practice, but it has just occurred to me that the herb might be of value. Well, I ought to have thought of it before I left the Abbey." He raise his eyes to me and smiled. "Are you surprised that a priest has studied wizards' lore?"

"I suppose I ought to be surprised at nothing just now; my emotions are worn raw. But, yes, I find it strange." I continued heatedly, "I find it strange that you, a holy man, traffic with anyone who works such destruction as Master Kaedric has done. I find it strange that you can still show such concern for him. I realize that he saved our lives, but surely even murderous thieves do not deserve such death as that. How can you condone it?"

"I do not condone it, nor, I think, does Kaedric. I only dimly understand it, and that little has taken many years, much patience, and a large measure of friendship. As you are a sorceress, the reasons should be more clear to you, but I suppose your Power is nearly as far from Kaedric's as mine. Be thankful for that lack, Mistress Rani. There is no comfort in a gift of that magnitude." Personally I found little comfort in Abbot Medwyn's explanations but I did not speak more. My own prejudice haunted me enough.

We halted early that night, though we traveled several miles before a suitably defensible site could be found. Exhaustion's palpable presence gripped us. We had no sooner established camp than Master Kaedric wordlessly left us. Abbot Medwyn moved his arm slightly in the traditional plea of protection, murmured a soft prayer, and returned to the tending of Hamar's wound.

"I hope you pray for the unfortunates whom Our Leader has yet to meet," scoffed Ineuil. "Those we left are a little past salvation." He winced as the cold astringency of the salve which I was applying to his arm penetrated.

Gart issued a disgruntled chuckle, and Hamar grumbled, "I never mind a few added scars, but I like to feel some purpose in their earning. We might as well have stayed in Anx. This Venture is one wizard and four bits of extraneous baggage." With a scowl at me, he added, "And a fifth bit which is most extraneous of all."

"Kaedric is notoriously effective," commented Ineuil acidly.

"But he could have saved us all some trouble by exercising a shade more promptitude." He winced again. "Mistress Rani's gentle ministrations do brighten the situation, however." Hamar snorted in disgust.

"None of you knows whereof you speak," chided Abbot Medwyn, "if you believe that Kaedric does not need us. It is for Kaedric that I pray."

"You may as well pray for the devil, Abbot," said Ineuil. "The two are not such distant kin." His acrid comment received no argument. Even Abbot Medwyn merely bowed his head more diligently to his task.

I shared the second watch that night with Master Ineuil. Irritating though he could often be, I felt easier on that occasion for the distraction he provided. "Fair Mistress Rani, do you not think my wounds deserve some further care?" he asked very seriously. He extended his finely muscled forearm for my inspection. "I feel some definite concern for this one."

Humoring him, I examined the gash; it was a shallow score, probably uncomfortable but clean. "I doubt your survival hangs in the balance, Master Ineuil."

"I shall arrange a more needful injury if it will gain me your tender ministrations."

"The exchange seems scarcely equitable," I responded, provoked to laughter despite myself and the day's memories. My mirth shattered as a long firelight-cast shadow crossed me.

"You have always had the most inconvenient sense of timing, Kaedric," said Ineuil sourly. "Do you never sleep?"

"Do you never tire of testing me?" snapped the wizard with an abrupt and angry clenching of his long fingers. The two men measured each other, and Ineuil gave a brief, humorless laugh.

"Just once, Kaedric, I should like to be able to meet you on a par. In fact, I should like to see anyone meet you in a truly even contest."

"There is no such thing as a truly even contest in this world," said Kaedric mockingly. "Someone inevitably loses." The wizard turned to me. "Mistress Rani, you share a certain rapport with creatures of the wild. How well can you control the exchange of information?"

I answered him reluctantly, as if reciting by rote a lesson to one of my more daunting and demanding tutors, "Most life forms communicate on a level of primary emotions. I can impart more complex messages, but the effectiveness of the reception depends upon the individual's mode of thinking. If the pattern is sufficiently similar to my own, I can generally emulate it and force comprehension."

"We require a guide. I suggest that you make an effort to find one." The cold-eyed wizard spun immediately away, striding determinedly toward the darkness. He had allowed me no opportunity to demur.

"Welcome to the Venture, Mistress Rani," gibed Ineuil. "You wanted to be useful, I believe."

Frustration tensed me, inadequacy clawing my heart. Take care what you wish, Rhianna, especially in a wizard's hearing. "Master Ineuil, I do not even know our destination. How can I possibly convey instructions to a guide?"

"A sorceress should never permit impossibilities to daunt her," he scolded. "Witness Our Leader's example. However, in this circumstance, perhaps you would permit a mere, primitive mortal to help. We are headed for the castle of the late and unlamented Sorcerer King Horlach, though I rather think that time has reduced the castle to a few moldy, underground chambers. I cannot imagine why Hrgh would choose to inhabit the beastly ruin—he used to be inordinately fastidious—but I apparently misjudged him in a number of ways."

"You know the man we seek?" I asked, unreasonably startled.

"So I thought, but I underestimated his ambition."

"And one should never underestimate a wizard," I said slowly, remembering Ineuil's previous warning.

"Nor the ambition of a Dolr'han dur Liin. I was guilty on both accounts."

"Lord Hrgh Dolr'han dur Liin," I voiced mechanically.

The young jet-haired woman emerged from the carriage, resplendent in emerald velvet and soft ermine. She greeted her dour father with a light embrace and a teasingly secretive smile. She tossed an irritated order at a laggardly servitor and took her father's arm as they entered the looming keep. The keep was gray, and its Lord was iron, but the raven-haired daughter shed warm brilliance on both. Neither father nor daughter observed the pale-haired girl who watched them from the upper stair.

"You look well, Yldana,". said the middle-aged woman who greeted the noble Lord and his daughter in the great hall of Tyntagel Keep. "Did you journey smoothly?"

The young woman negligently dropped her cloak in a servant's hands as she answered, "The journey was odious, as always, Lady Altha." Smiling again, she added, "But my stay in Tulea was very satisfactory."

"You found Lord Amgor's kin to your liking?" asked Lord Baerod with a proud inspection of his beautiful daughter.

Yldana gave a slight shrug. "They are Amlachians, Father, and Amgor adores me. Amgor was a bit of a bore about it all, actually. However, Amgor may not be the only Seriin lord aspiring to a match with Tyntagel." She tilted her head and regarded her father through long lashes. "I do think Lord Hrgh Dolr'han took quite an interest in me, as well."

Lady Altha's flat brown eyes nearly gleamed. "The heir of Liin! Baerod, imagine it: your daughter the Lady of Liin."

The expression of the Lord of Tyntagel had grown stoic. "Lord Hrgh is a wizard, Yldana," he said tonelessly.

A faint frown flickered across the young woman's face. "I did not say that I intended to marry him, father." Her enthusiasm returned. "But he is charming and very handsome."

"And he is a Dolr'han, Baerod," added Lady Altha firmly. Lord Baerod glared at his cousin, and Lady Altha bit back her praise of Liin, saying only, "One must make allowances for a Dolr'han."

Yldana wheedled coaxingly, "Lord Hrgh is not like other wizards, Father. I know that you will approve him when you meet. Uncle Dhavod did."

"You have not invited Lord Hrgh here?" demanded Lord Baerod, but his words were not harsh.

Yldana gave a horrified moue. "Father, I would not. Hrgh has not spoken to me formally, as yet." She twirled in a delicate dance across the parquet as she headed for the stair. "But if he were to request permission to visit, I could hardly refuse, could I, Father? One does not say no to a Dolr'han!" She tossed a kiss to her father from the banister. She brushed past her younger sister. "Should you not be at study of something, Rhianna?" she murmured disinterestedly as she passed.

"Welcome home, Yldana," answered the younger girl wryly.

"Baerod," insisted Lady Altha sternly, "Liin is the wealthiest domain in Serii. You could not deny that to Yldana."

Lord Baerod spoke grimly. "Lord Hrgh may well relinquish the heirship of Liin if Alobar dies."

"Then you would be father-in-law to the Infortiare, and you could work directly against Ixaxis instead of playing these fruitless games of yours."

"You wag your tongue too freely, Altha," said Tyntagel's Lord. His cousin was silenced, but she smirked complacently at his back.

The Dolr'han request for Yldana's hand never arrived. Yldana had shielded her disappointment, citing the impossibility of taking a wizard for husband. It was a transparent ploy. The Dolr'han mystique, strongly abetted by Liin's wealth, could have easily surmounted the force of even Tyntagellian prejudice.

Lord Alobar had died little more than a year later, when Yldana was already affianced to Lord Amgor. No one had doubted that Lord Hrgh Dolr'han dur Liin would replace Alobar as Infortiare. Lord Hrgh had actually yielded his heirdom to his younger brother, Lord Gorng, in anticipation of the Ixaxin Council's official announcement. Hrgh's renunciation proved premature: Ixaxis selected the unknown Venkarel over the paragon of Liin.

Lord Hrgh and most of Serii had roared with the outrage of injustice, and Lord Hrgh had challenged Lord Venkarel to a contest of Power. To the stunned elation of Hrgh's supporters, Lord Venkarel accepted Hrgh's challenge. Shock encompassed Serii when the Dolr'han was defeated. Yldana, who cared nothing for the politics involved, had cheered the defeat of the man who had spurned her. It was the only time I ever heard our father reproach her severely.

I began to theorize aloud. "When Lord Hrgh could not become Infortiare by his own Power, he sought another means. He stole this thing, the Taormin, so as to oust Lord Venkarel." Ineuil raised an eyebrow but did not contradict me. I shook my head. "But surely Lord Hrgh cannot expect Ixaxis to accept him as Infortiare under such conditions."

"In theory, the Taormin could exterminate Ixaxis and everything else we know—if anyone knew how to use it. It was the secret of Horlach's success over his competitors, and the Ixaxins are not what they were when Ceallagh led them in Horlach's defeat. However, I doubt that Hrgh has thought beyond trouncing Venkarel. Overconfidence and hatred of Venkarel drove Hrgh to tackle the Taormin. If it were not such a stupid move, I might laud it."

"You supported Lord Hrgh's challenge."

"I supported Hrgh—not his insane challenge. I certainly did not support Venkarel," hissed Ineuil with abrupt vehemence. "Venkarel is a cold-blooded, calculating bastard who happens to have more Power in his fingertip than any other wizard or wizardess born of the past hundred generations. The challenge was a farce from its issuance."

"Lord Hrgh evidently thought otherwise."

"Hrgh could not accept the fact that a whore's son could ever better a Dolr'han. The tragic irony was that popular demand would have persuaded Ixaxis to replace Venkarel in a short time. Venkarel's selection was a marginal thing at best."

"Until the challenge sealed it."

Ineuil nodded thoughtfully. "Venkarel felled a Dolr'han with all of Tulea as witness, and there could be no further question as to Venkarel's superiority of Power. By Ceallagh's laws, the strongest wizard at the time of selection is Infortiare. Hrgh's punishment was far worse than official banishment from Tulea and Ixaxis; nothing can recompense a Dolr'han for loss of pride."

"You still prefer Lord Hrgh to Lord Venkarel, but you have joined a Venture which favors Lord Venkarel over Lord Hrgh."

"I personally despise Venkarel, but he is as clever as a fiend and certainly far more knowledgeable about wizardry than I. If Venkarel fears the Taormin, then Hrgh's attempt to use it is suicidal insanity."

"Lord Venkarel must have his own followers. Why employ someone who hates him?"

"The challenge was in some ways an expensive indulgence on Venkarel's part as well as on Hrgh's. The feelings against Ixaxis have been mounting steadily ever since."

"Is that an answer?" I asked. Ineuil shrugged. I digested his previous spate of information. "Master Kaedric directly serves Lord Venkarel," I concluded.

After a moment's pause, Ineuil answered, "Unquestionably." He cocked his head, "I must remember not to underestimate sorceresses either."

Chapter 8

I woke myself in the early dawn so as to essay compliance with the wizard's pointed suggestion to seek a guide. Somnolent night still cloaked many of the Mountains' tenants, but I issued wisps of thought to test each tentative touch. I could quickly eliminate those of stationary or overly sedentary habit, as well as those unable to maintain a steady focus of mind. Less surely, I discarded those whose gentle timidity I dared not risk to Master Kaedric's menacing presence. I nearly despaired before I found the one I sought.

When the stars faded fully, I rose and crossed to the wizard. Deliberately, I emulated that austere formality which he could so eloquently project, as I said, "I have found a guide, Venture Leader. We shall proceed according to your command." I was fey with success, intoxicated by the distant touch of the Nighthawk, and still enough myself to delight in the quick, startled flicker of Master Kaedric's eyes. I was only marginally aware of Master Gart's curious stare.

I should have been less eager to comply with the Venture Leader's wishes had I realized the means by which he would command his Venture's guide; I had yet to learn the lesson which Ineuil consistently reiterated. The wizard channeled his instructions to the Nighthawk directly into my mind, and the shock shattered my precarious control. My own panic at Master Kaedric's touch nearly exceeded that of the bird, and, together, the Nighthawk and I fled the mental flame on wings which beat through the dashing winds.

We were unfettered by leaden limbs, and the tortured lands could not hinder our flight. The Mountains of Mindar extended to the ends of our universe, their minutiae clear to our sight. We soared and darted, rushing upward to plummet swiftly through roaring air, veering from impact a breath away from earth.

Pain gripped my arms, and my unsteady legs supported me again on the barren rock of the Venturers' camp. Long fingers, brutally tight, encircled my wrists. I debated desperately the odds of escaping those hard, slender digits, but Master Kaedric abruptly released me. I rubbed my wrists with grateful relief.

"Your Power exceeds your control to a dangerous degree, Mistress Rani," said Kaedric coldly. "I trust you managed to absorb the sense of our goal, at least." I returned the wizard's stare, uneasily aware that my new certainty of destination was not of my own devising. The bitter flavor of decayed Power formed an unmistakable lodestone to Horlach's ruined home, and Master Kaedric had implanted the cognizance of it within me. "We must retrace the last mile," I said in answer.

The Nighthawk's aid speeded our passage considerably. Each night I gathered the image of local geography from my nocturnal partner and conveyed it to Master Kaedric in the morning. Practice enabled me to transfer the visions to a terrestrial frame of reference without effort, though the first few days had kept me wavering with disorientation. Such obstacles as escaped the Nighthawk's aerial view were few and minor. We encountered no further human intervention; the few survivors (whom Master Kaedric asserted did exist) of our prior contest had evidently spread the warning.

Master Kaedric had developed the habit of departing each evening from the rest of the company. Never social, he had grown yet more aloof since the attack in the canyon. Abbot Medwyn fretted at the Venture Leader's absences, but even the abbot conversed more freely when Kaedric was gone from us.

The moon was rising, but it was timid still of the waning sunlight. The fire crept along the scarred bark of an old log, trying to blaze into warmth. The two men coaxed the flame that it might be ready for the return of their companions. They were disparate men, oddly united.

Ineuil asked with dark, bleak insistence, "Why did you call this Venture, Abbot?"

Abbot Medwyn retorted with uncharacteristic sharpness, "Why did you join it, Ineuil?"

"You know why I joined it," snapped Ineuil. "Hrgh must be stopped in his madness, but I would rather not see Hrgh left to *him*." Ineuil jerked his head toward the wooded path which Kaedric had earlier taken. "Gart and Hamar joined in honest intent to aid your Venture, because they did not know whom they would need to serve. Mistress Rani's reasons are suspiciously obscure, but yours are the more so. You have favored that damned wizard for years, even defying your church on his behalf, but you know what he is as well as I do. He does not need us to aid him in recovering the Taormin; if it can be done, he can do it alone. So why are we here, Abbot? Is this another Ixaxin game?"

Shaking his gray head adamantly, Abbot Medwyn replied, "Whatever you may believe, Ineuil, I called this Venture because I deemed that in this Kaedric wished help, though he would never ask it. When I told him that Hrgh had taken the Taormin, he was afraid, Ineuil. I had not otherwise seen true fear in him during all the years that I have known him."

Ineuil pursed his lips and contemplated the holy man. "That might increase my respect for the Taormin. It does not tell me how we who are not heir to the Immortals' gifts can contribute to the recovery of the thing."

"Tul aided Ceallagh."

"Did he?" demanded Ineuil. Abbot Medwyn stiffened slightly at the blasphemy of doubt. "Oh, I know the story well enough," continued Ineuil impatiently, "And I much prefer to serve a mortal kingship rather than an Ixaxin thearchy. But I never understood just what Till did that was so outstanding in the battle against Horlach. Ceallagh led the attack. Ceallagh defeated Horlach—with some help from the Ixaxin Circle. Tul generously accepted the glory of kingship. Explain to me, Abbot, how the great Tul contributed to the foundations of Seriin freedom, and perhaps I shall find a clue to the role you expect us to take."

Abbot Medwyn waited for Ineuil to complete his outburst.

When Ineuil halted expectantly, the abbot said simply, "Tul maintained Ceallagh's humanity."

Ineuil pondered the abbot for several moments. He finally said in a velvet voice, "You do not assign easy tasks, Abbot Medwyn."

"It is a task at which I have long labored myself."

"Are you his friend or his conscience, Abbot Medwyn?" asked Ineuil carefully.

Abbot Medwyn gave a slight, unhappy shrug. "The two may well be the same." He turned his eyes upward to the moon's growing glow. "I feared him the day I met him, a half-starved waif amid the ashes of a dying city. I had no greater love for sorcery than others of my church, but he was a boy in desperate need, and I had no choice but to help him. I have not regretted it, but I have never ceased to fear his Power."

"You are not alone in that," said Ineuil with a grimace.

Abbot Medwyn smiled wanly. "No. I think even his fellow Ixaxins fear him. What must it be like to be instantly feared by everyone you meet?"

"Do not try to stir any pity for him in me, Abbot," said Ineuil darkly.

The abbot signed. "You have little cause to love him, I know. He would not welcome—nor even understand—pity in any case, but it does seem a lonely life."

"Ixaxins have each other. If you are so concerned for him, why did you deliberately omit other wizards from this Venture?"

Abbot Medwyn shifted uncomfortably. "I do not understand wizards, Ineuil, but they seem to interact unpredictably with their own kind." The abbot frowned. "They cooperate in the ordered Circles of Ixaxis, but they suffer still the characteristic which kept the Sorcerer Kings in constant conflict. The Infortiare is the only Lord of Serii who traditionally retains no retinue in Tulea, and I think that there is reason for that custom."

"Abbot Medwyn," remarked Ineuil cynically, "I think you distrust Kaedric as much as I do."

"I distrust what he has the potential to become. With the added influence of the Taormin. . . ." Abbot Medwyn left the sentence dangling. "Until that infernal challenge, Hrgh was far more sanely 'mortal' than Kaedric has ever been."

"I certainly shall not argue that point. You are a devious man,

Abbot Medwyn. You called this Venture so as to surround Kaedric with enough 'mortal' influence to counter his darker instincts when we find Hrgh and the Taormin. Is that why our sorceress' presence displeases you so?"

"My efforts to dissuade Mistress Rani were not altogether on her behalf," admitted the abbot slowly.

Ineuil mused, "Mistress Rani seems unlikely to affect Kaedric in any respect, since he disdains to acknowledge her." Abbot Medwyn did not answer, and Ineuil persisted pointedly, "Or do you think Our Leader shows her a trifle too much contempt? She is only a minor sorceress, of course, but Kaedric has always tended toward inverted snobberies, if anything."

Abbot Medwyn weighed his answer as he spoke. "I think Kaedric fears to contaminate her, which only enhances my concern."

"She is rather an innocent, but she seems well enough able to care for herself."

"Ineuil, you have at times felt Kaedric's Power as I have. It is a very disturbing sensation even to one who is essentially immune to sorcerous exchange."

"So Mistress Rani endangers herself by accompanying us; that is not a novel notion. I cannot believe that a minor sorceress could present a reciprocal hazard to Our Leader." A rustle announced Master Hamar. "I fear, Abbot Medwyn, that you will never appear upon my roster of great chefs," said Ineuil, transitioning to innocuous topics without hesitation.

Chapter 9

My isolated state had not diminished with the passing days of Venture, but the Nighthawk's tenuous acceptance cheered my spirit. As the days of rapport extended, the Nighthawk came to know me and to greet me after his fashion. He led us much deeper into the Mountains' grip than his traditional territory allowed, a strongly generous act of trust which shamed me, because I should have forced his sacrifice, albeit reluctantly, had Master Kaedric so demanded.

Reliant on my little Nighthawk for companionship as well as guidance, I felt sorely rent by his desertion. He departed abruptly, his joyous antics in the waning night breaking into a desperate dart for his homeland. No cajolery would return him; no pleading would he heed. The distance stretched between us, and the surety of contact ebbed. I could have forced him back to me, but I could not bear the hurt of his struggle against my bond. With more regret than I had spared for my lifetime's home, I let fall the tie between us.

I informed Master Kaedric tersely of the loss. Expecting displeasure and orders to seek a substitute, I found his indifference grating; I wondered acridly if my Nighthawk's selfless aid had been of so little value. The wizard said only, "Horlach's influence still unsettles the neighborhood. Our path henceforth should be fairly clear." He dismissed me from his notice, fixedly studying a narrow cleft which we would likely near by nightfall. I watched for a moment the wind-rippled cloak of a man who was utterly removed from my understanding. I resolved never to fall into the trap of sympathy for him; then, I wondered why the notion even occurred to me.

We reached the narrow pass with late afternoon. Red stone walls loomed above us, blocking from view the nether trail, which I had seen angle downward from the Nighthawk's vantage. Just prior to his desertion, the Nighthawk's gaze had chanced across a verdant dell beyond the twisted pass. I hoped that we might find the wood by eventide, for the prolonged confinement in a realm of sterile stone chafed my soul severely.

The paucity of native voices did not strike me until we entered the cleft itself. Those lives which I could feel all rose behind me; from beyond the lengthy passage came nothing. I wondered if the green oasis were illusion born of my own craving, but the detail of its recollected image dissuaded me. I became uneasy, nervous of confinement between the towering escarpment walls, anxious to escape their clutch, but fearful of the silence beyond.

My disquiet eclipsed normal reluctance, and I hastened forward to gain the wizard's side. Ineuil raised a brow, but he moved to let me pass without comment. The Venture Leader looked down at me with mild surprise, and I steeled myself to bespeak him. I whispered, for I hesitated to disturb the ochoco unnecessarily. "The area we are approaching is wrong, Master Kaedric."

He inquired tonelessly, "Is that a navigational opinion or an aesthetic judgment?"

"The direction is correct, but I ought to detect something beyond this fissure. I saw—the Nighthawk saw—a wooded hollow not far ahead. I cannot sense it."

Kaedric slowed his pace minutely. "That was where the bird left you?" he asked.

"He saw the dell, but he never reached it." The wizard frowned, and his consideration of my words appeased my pride but did nothing to ease my tension.

"I wish I could reassure you, Mistress Rani, but Horlach's legacy persists in uncomfortable ways. You have at least reassured me that my own nerves have not yet grown fully unreliable."

I shook my head, more to dispel the thought that Master

Kaedric shared my uneasiness than to disagree. "Yet you intend to continue on this route?" I asked.

"Would you prefer to spend the night in this unnatural corridor? We have come too far to return before dark." I could only continue to shake my head helplessly, and Kaedric nearly smiled, but it was not a mirthful expression. "Whatever awaits us must be faced eventually," he said. "Perhaps I am become claustrophobic, but I prefer to proceed without delay. If you have a persuasive alternative, I am not adverse to hearing it."

"We might be better for some rest," I offered tentatively, but it was procrastination, and I knew it as well as did the man beside me.

Kaedric did halt us long enough for a vote. The party chose to continue, but we moved more cautiously. The Venture Leader's unprecedented willingness to defer to the consensus of opinion quenched any levity among us.

The trail began its descent. Red stone turned black at the passage's end, smooth obsidian pillars marking the terminus as if it were a gate of doom. "Your guide has dismal taste, Mistress Rani," complained Ineuil. "Remind me not to let you choose our next place of assignation."

"It is the entrance to Horlach's estate," said Kaedric soberly. "Horlach was not notoriously sympathetic to the wishes of amorists."

Kaedric passed through the pillars, and in a moment we had all joined him. The land looked little different from that which we had left on entering the corridor, barren rock and dusty gravel comprising the bulk of the scenery. Mountains' shadow had held it obscurely dark until we stood within the exiting alcove's midst. I felt foolish over my fears. Though I still could not sense the lives of the green hollow I now could see, the scent of distant blossoms reached me and somewhat salved my distress.

A shrill keening filled the air, rising without direction and growing quickly to stark intensity. A sour wind struck me, and I discovered the justification of my concern. The gargoyles appeared, the ancient guardians of Horlach's gate. I had read their description, and for a space of seconds I could only stare at them, disavowing their existence in my own time and space.

Leathery, scabrous wings beating violently, the creatures smote wildly with talons, teeth and barbed tails. Their bodies were bloated, taut membranes encrusted with livid veins. The Venturers blurred in a vision of fury. Swords struck, rebounded. One sword blow pierced its target, puncturing the monster and deflating it with a rush of yellow ichor. Red blood mingled with the viscous, oily issue; the gargoyle had raked Gart's back in its fall.

I had shadowed, but one of the beasts flew directly at me, unhampered by my effort to hide. It tore at the flesh of my upraised arm, craning its maw toward the blood it drew. The vile thing repulsed me; its stench choked me; but I stretched my mind to restrain it in the only defense I knew. I had thought the dyrcat unsettling, but the gargoyle of Horlach spawned horror. With effort, I could hold my attacker a pace away from me, but I could do no more to influence it, nor could I in any way aid my fellow travelers.

Ineuil, Gart and Hamar slashed fiercely, and the ichor flowed, spreading across the ground in slimy puddles. Such damage as the Venturers wrought slowed the attack but did not halt it. Hamar lopped the head from one gargoyle only to find the body as menacing as before. The gargoyles could be downed, but there appeared to be no way to kill them short of total butchery. I could see Abbot Medwyn beating randomly at the creatures with his staff; his efforts seemed no less effective than the sword thrusts. The gargoyles persisted in slow dominance.

I sensed it immediately when Kaedric chose a victim: the creature I was containing shared its counterpart's knowledge. The gargoyles evinced no dismay at the flame eating their comrade's heart; the prospect stimulated them to eager frenzy. I felt a foreboding which Master Kaedric evidently shared, for he abruptly curtailed his assault, but the process of destruction proceeded on its own momentum. Inner fluids boiling, the gargoyle exploded in a scattering of scorching gobbets. A few tiny particles hit me, though I stood farthest from the source, and they delved through fabric and clung to skin. I could feel the sharp bite of acid pinpricks which would not be dislodged. They etched trails of remorseless burning. Horlach's guardians had been well designed to discourage sorcerous attack.

I scanned the Venturers with little hope. Hamar had slowed, his prior wound reopened and bleeding now profusely. A hurtling gargoyle knocked Gart to the stained earth as I watched. Kaedric snatched Gart's sword and used it to ward the gargoyles from the soldier's immobile form. The wizard wielded the sword like one more accustomed to the closeness of dagger play; I felt irrelevant surprise that he had ever bothered to hone a blade skill at all. Already, the wizard had modified his Power's attack to a slower, more effective form. I did not doubt that the wizard would preserve his own life against even Horlach's gargoyles; I did begin to despair that the Venture Leader's Power would extend that preservation to the rest of us.

Ineuil's shoulder had been badly torn. Even Kaedric had been marked; beading scratches crossed his finely boned hands. Abbot Medwyn, curiously enough, showed fewest ravages of all. His long staff struck his assailants most often on their whipping tails, but those gargoyles about him had begun to grow sluggish in their movements.

My grip on my attacker weakened, and others of its kind began to hover nearer. I let go my futile shadowing, and my hold firmed again to preserve me. Soon, however, another gargoyle swept before me, focusing on me murky orange eyes of spite which waited for the inevitable failure of my Power. I comprehended my poor, lost Nighthawk's panic as I watched defenselessly; jagged talons ripped my arm from wrist to neck.

I sank hopelessly to the blood-spattered earth. The gargoyle which had raked me churned the dust about me with its beating wings. Abbot Medwyn's staff struck the thing's tail heavily above the daggered tip, and the gargoyle crumpled in slow, almost dignified defeat. I heard the abbot cry aloud his elated discovery of the creatures' weakness, and I considered the unpriestly nature of the shouted advice as I tumbled into oblivion.

I revived marginally to see Ineuil fell a last remaining gargoyle by severing its whipping tail at the base. Kaedric and Hamar gathered Gart between them. Ineuil limped heavily on a flesh-shredded leg. Abbot Medwyn collected his pack and my own, dropped mine wearily, and beckoned me to follow. I dragged myself in his wake, reclaiming my supplies with a struggle. A sorely tattered band, we stumbled down the incline to the valley of green. By a crystal rill bedecked with bejeweled fern, I slumped exhausted.

Chapter 10

My eyes opened to a sun-blessed view of leafy boughs and cerulean sky. Reassured, I let my eyelids droop once more. I greeted the trees, and they responded warmly. It puzzled me that I did not know these ash and alder; I thought I knew each tree of Tyntagel. The oddity did not concern me greatly; no more than did the prospect of my father's anger when he learned that his daughter had slept in the grove like a common vagabond.

"At last my sorceress awakes," said Ineuil, recalling me to the present. "But if she does not soon reopen her lovely eyes, I shall take drastic steps to assure myself of her recovery. Perhaps a kiss — such always seems effective in romantic sagas."

"If you try it, Master Ineuil, I shall give you over to a dyrcat I know, and he has a most unpleasant temperament," I answered lazily, reluctant yet to relinquish my drowsy peace.

"I remember now why I have never pursued sorceresses. Perhaps I shall leave you to Kaedric after all. It would serve him right."

"Where is Master Kaedric?" I asked, suddenly awake.

"Wandering somewhere conveniently distant, I hope. Abbot Medwyn is over that way a bit," he said with a vague wave of his arm, "ladling some ghastly broth into Hamar and Gart. I, fortunately, have been declared cured and no longer in need of such unpalatable measures."

"How long have I slept?"

"Three days and nights, by my reckoning, though I confess I lost some time myself. Those ugly beasties apparently list poisoned fangs among their attractions. Abbot Medwyn has had a busy time of it, tending us all."

"I must offer help to him," I said briskly, shaking dust from my skirts and observing a need for serious mending before long. My arm, which had been laid open by the gargoyle, had sealed with only a trace of a scar. I felt astonishingly well. "Will you direct me, Master Ineuil, or shall I find the camp myself?"

"You are a singleminded wench," sighed Ineuil. "Very well, I shall direct you, but I think your choice displays a lack of discernment. I appreciate your company far more than will those you seek to aid."

"I did not join this Venture to amuse you, Master Ineuil."

"The fact did not escape my notice. There should be a law against beautiful women who have no trace of romance in their souls."

"What did you say about never pursuing a sorceress? I do believe you would flirt with any woman you met, be she blushing maiden or toothless hag."

"At least credit me with some selectivity. I am actually quite particular as to the women I cultivate."

"When you are granted unlimited choices," I amended.

"Quantity does help, I admit. But I promise you, Mistress Rani, if some day I find you in the midst of Serii's fairest, I shall still seek your company over the rest. And I trust that you will regret every aspersion you have cast upon my character." Ineuil pointed at a clearing dimly visible through the trees. "Our temporary home lies yonder. You may detect the aroma of the abbot's brew: rather reminiscent of moldering eggs, I think."

"It is pungent. How did I manage to escape its benefits until now?"

"Kaedric's idea it was, though I wish I could take credit for the results. Our Leader insisted that your ailments would be best served by solitary repose. Abbot Medwyn patched your more obvious wounds and trusted the rest to wizard's judgment." I could not protest Master Kaedric's cavalier abandonment in light of the successful outcome, but I was pleased to maintain annoyance with the Venture Leader on any pretext. I did dislike the thought of having spent three days in isolated oblivion amid a Sorcerer King's haunted domain.

We found the clearing deserted, though Abbot Medwyn's despised tonic simmered above a low fire. Ineuil led me to a shallow cave hidden beneath a curtain of fern. The light diffused through leafy green lent a strange distortion of color, but the wanness of Master Gart was due to a more serious cause. Abbot Medwyn bent beside him, inspecting Gart's bandaged brow and the puckered streaks which spread to the warrior's jaw. Hamar cut short a joke— a stale and most improper one which I had heard my brothers tell—as I entered, and his broad grin turned sullen and suspicious. Gart, however, brightened.

"Master Ineuil," warned the abbot, "if you have awakened Mistress Rani prematurely, you had best look to your excuses before Kaedric returns."

"Why does everyone doubt my intentions?" bemoaned Ineuil. "Having Mistress Rani's own interests in mind, I appointed myself the guardian of her recovery—a position which Our Leader neglected to fill—and I receive nothing but ingratitude and censure. This situation could become entirely demoralizing." He stalked from the cavern, flicking a dangling fern from his path.

"Sir Abbot, I awoke quite on my own," I protested. "Please do not blame Master Ineuil on that account."

"He has plenty of other accounts for blame," quipped Gart with an effort. His wounds stiffened his face, but he managed a lopsided smile.

"Do hold still, Master Gart," scolded Abbot Medwyn, readjusting a dressing on Gart's neck which I had not previously seen. "If I did not censure Master Ineuil regularly, Mistress Rani, he might be forced to realize that he is not nearly as irredeemable as he pretends, and the prospect would devastate him."

"If you please, Abbot," interrupted Hamar. "I could heal a lot faster if this woman would leave us to some peace." Abbot Medwyn frowned, and Hamar continued, "Did no one notice that the gargoyles heeded only her? Even Master Kaedric could not control them so well. Does no one else find that an unlikely circumstance? Mistress Rani's Power seems to be peculiarly constrained to her own welfare—and perhaps that of Lord Hrgh Dolr'han. Lord

Hrgh's supporters do include a number of ladies, I have heard, and this wandering sorceress is a mite too knowledgeable for my taste. Were you disappointed that the gargoyles did not finish us, mistress, or are you just playing with us until your liege lord comes?"

"I am not your enemy, Master Hamar," I retorted, shaken less by Hamar's outrageous allegations than by the lack of protest from Abbot Medwyn and Master Gart. "If you have need of me, Abbot Medwyn, I shall be no more distant than the rill."

My contentment dissipated, I strayed farther than I had indicated to Abbot Medwyn. I sought forgetfulness in the hearts of the woodland dwellers, for there was an ease of security in this place, but Hamar's words rankled. The grain of truth in his accusations could easily coat the whole with credibility, but it was too late to be honest about my name and origin, even had I wished it. I could sympathize with Ineuil's protest of injustice.

I encountered Ineuil near the glade where I had awakened. He was engrossed in casting seed cases in a pond. He scowled at me terribly, saying, "If you have come to make amends with me, Mistress Rani, you may as well return whence you came. I am not yet done sulking."

"Master Ineuil," I demanded, "do you concur with Master Hamar's assessment of me as villainess?" I was sincerely anxious for the answer, though I was unsure why I had developed such a concern for the Venturers' opinion.

Ineuil promptly dropped his querulous pose. "Hamar has been at you again, has he? You ought not to mind him so much, Rani. He has been venting his anger on the feminine gender for years because of some Caruillan woman who once treated him foully. There is no personal malice involved. Anyway, one cannot generally please everyone, and four out of five is an admirable average."

"You vastly exaggerate my popularity, but I appreciate the lie. I am sorry if I seemed ungrateful for your attention earlier."

"You really are depressed," he said sympathetically. "Come, sit and tell me your woes. We shall console each other from the doldrums, which are probably just an after-effect of the gargoyles' poison. What nonsense did Hamar spout at you?"

I sat as commanded, wanting very much to be consoled. "He suggested that I served Lord Hrgh and conspired toward the gargoyles' attack."

"You would have to be a rather incompetent spy to perpetrate an attack which harmed you as much as any other. Is that all that concerns you?"

"Abbot Medwyn and Master Gart seem to share his suspicions."

"I find that difficult to believe."

Hesitantly, I whispered, "I have not been entirely truthful as to my personal history."

"I had not noticed that you even gave one, but we are none of us in a position to quibble with that sort of deception."

I looked at him curiously. "No, I suppose you are not." Ineuil had always seemed misplaced in a Venture, and he admitted to acquaintance with Lord Hrgh. Master Kaedric's solitary wandering could easily foster sinister implications to a mind so inclined, and it was not difficult to credit the wizard with devious motives. "Master Hamar knows none of you save Master Gart," I said, feeling perversely better for the thought.

"We are a dubious lot, all of us, so you may as well accept the stigma of association and expect to find yourself suspected of wicked schemes. Proper young Seriin women do not join Ventures, do not travel the countryside unchaperoned, and certainly do not practice sorcery (not openly, at least)."

"Having committed so many improprieties, I ought to be a jaded sophisticate by now. Instead, I come seeking reassurance like a toddler with a skinned knee." I smiled at him somewhat shyly "You are kind to give it to me. I am not very practiced in the art of friendship; I am not sure I know how to return it well."

"You are making me feel like a cad. Mistress Rani, I always have ulterior motives. I think we had better return to the camp before I utterly disillusion you." He smiled at me almost sadly, and I thought it the sincerest gesture I had seen him make.

We walked under autumn's green and golden boughs, and I finally concluded that the besotted women of Anx had more cause for their choice of favorite than fair features and sly charm. Ineuil was blatantly faithless, but he could instill the delight of self-contentment through his attention. Naiveté abetted my feelings; no man save Evram had ever courted me, and Evram's image had already faded from my mind. I certainly did not count Lord Grisk, my deserted bridegroom, as a suitor. Ineuil did not prate extravagant tributes that afternoon. He was more silent, more clearly troubled, and I liked him far better than I had thought I ever should.

The Venture party remained in the dell for another two weeks, awaiting the return of Master Gart's strength. We should have waited longer had Master Gart's remarkable constitution not so well supported the abbot's cures. I passed much of the time with Ineuil, listening to his tales of far lands and fabulous escapades. Half of his stories glared obviously false; the others glimmered with doubtful excess; but they entertained. Master Kaedric had declared our dell to be a haven of security, a boon of the land's ancient tenants to counter the bane of the gargoyles at the gate. None of us wished to disbelieve the wizard's assertion.

I saw Master Kaedric only once in all those days. I came upon him in the wood; he studied the ripples of a stream as they danced across their flowing mirror. He held in his hand a gold medallion of intricate design suspended on a fine gold chain, and he moved it restlessly so that its reflection in the water returned white flame. He did not look up at me, but he stilled his hand and clutched the gold from my sight with an intensity of subjugated violence. He vanished from my mind, leaving a gaping cold where subdued fire had been. He wore a dangerous mood, and I escaped him hastily.

Chapter 11

It was difficult to leave the vale and reinvade the desolation which surrounded it, but Abbot Medwyn's potions having restored Master Gart, Master Kaedric returned to us impatient for departure. The leaving affected me oddly; I seemed to awaken from a many-months' dream and find myself, the once sheltered lady of Tyntagel, on the verge of a battlefield which soon would run with disaster. Beyond the dale and its soothing assurance of tree and flower, a mounting trepidation began to haunt me with nightmarish chimeras of gargoyles, slaughtered brigands, and concocted visions of a man whom my sister had once adored and a wizard whom I feared to fathom.

Dust swirled beneath my feet. The sky was gray with heavy clouds, but no moisture had reached the powdery earth. Blue clay and black mica striated the ocher stone which seemed to grow from the path, a startling contrast in color alien to Tyntagellian geology. I clasped my cloak tightly against the chill.

A week's span from the healing glen, Hamar, who had been journeying several paces ahead, halted and stared at the sheer mountain face before him. The path widened where he stood, and cracked planes of white stone gave evidence of crumbled paving. On the broad cliff which had drawn Hamar's attention, black bands of metallic sheen framed a precisely inset door. The surface of the door had been marred by the years and vandals, but delicate traceries hinted at a wonder of workmanship.

"Another legacy of old King Horlach?" suggested Ineuil.

Kaedric did not answer but approached the door and gingerly positioned his fingers on a faintly etched diadem. The surface shimmered slightly, the patterns became clearer. Kaedric traced the length of a spiral, and a section of the door receded from a rather orthodox lock and hasp.

"Have you retained your flair for unsolicited entrance, Master Ineuil?" asked Kaedric.

"I would not relinquish such a useful skill, but I am not particularly eager to exercise it here. Horlach's surviving unpleasantries may not be restricted to his gatekeepers."

"We are seeking Horlach's dwellings, unless you have suddenly reinterpreted Hrgh's words to you," said Kaedric sardonically. "This could be an alternate access."

The dark man and the fair exchanged a look which held no fondness. Kaedric stepped back, and Ineuil bent to examine the lock. Moments later, the door smoothly swung wide.

"By the privilege of your rank, Venture Leader," said Ineuil with a mocking bow, "yours is the honor of entering first."

Kaedric twisted his lips in a dangerous smile. He took a torch from his pack, ignited it with a glance, and entered the dark recess. Abbot Medwyn followed him closely; the rest of us lagged only briefly.

A massive chamber burned as bright as moonlight with reflections of Kaedric's torch. I caught my breath in awe, nearly colliding with Gart in my distraction. Only the square of dim sunlight from the doorway broke the illusion of a perfect sphere, polished floor mirroring a ceiling of lucent tapestries. Wrought of delicate inlays, a garden bore glowing azure and yellow-gold blossoms on vines which spun to a crystalline midnight sky. Snowy water lilies clustered at our feet; our own reflections wavered in translucent depths.

"No gargoyles and no Lord Hrgh," sighed the practical Gart.

"Gart, you have no sense of artistic appreciation," said Ineuil.

"He is correct, however," said Kaedric solemnly. "My hopes are proven as groundless as Master Ineuil's concern."

"Evening is near. We could make camp here," suggested Hamar.

"I should rather not accept Horlach's hospitality unnecessarily, despite the exquisiteness of the accommodations," answered Kaedric.

"Nimal's home was never Horlach's," protested Abbot Medwyn.

"You are a romantic, Medwyn," remarked Kaedric tolerantly. "If Nimal of Castor did exist, he was entirely Horlach's tool—gifted but abysmally corrupt. If this was his home, it is as tainted as any other of Horlach's possessions."

"Nimal of Castor," mused Ineuil. "As I recall, he was a sculptor who killed his ladylove and then spent the rest of his life slaving for Horlach in misguided atonement. I do not recollect any stories about his home."

"It was the home he built for the Lady Varina dur Castor," said Abbot Medwyn. "He surpassed all his other efforts in its creation, but it was never used."

"He loved the Lady Varina, the youngest daughter of his liege lord," I remembered softly, "And she returned his love, but she obeyed the dictates of her father and wed a man of her own rank. Nimal perceived the act as betrayal and slew her."

Abbot Medwyn nodded. "He built a home for her, unable to believe in the death which he had caused. Some versions of the legend say that Varina's spirit forgave Nimal his brief madness and awaits him in the hall he built for her, until such time as Nimal forgives himself and joins her."

"And some say that Lady Varina offended King Horlach," interjected Master Kaedric, "inspiring Nimal to play the paid assassin, destroying a woman who loved and trusted him, so as to reap a very lucrative commission."

"I find the versions of both the romantic and the cynic unbearably depressing," said Ineuil. He added to the room at large, "With all due apologies to any lingering ghosts, participation in this accursed Venture depresses me quite enough." He strolled out of the door.

I could not impugn Ineuil's assessment of the melancholy saga, but it was a story I had always perversely cherished. Abbot Medwyn's rendition accorded with the one I preferred to accept. Though thought of Lady Varina's selfless observation of duty now pricked me with guilt, I still felt most clearly the Lady's unembittered hope amid the pathos.

Rapt with introspection, I scarcely noticed that I had picked up Varina's stone. I thrust it deep within my pocket and did not rediscover it until late evening. Smoothly whorled and milky white, the stone extolled the same miraculous workmanship as the chamber we had found. As glowed the chamber's stars, so the gem's soft radiance spread fragile firelight across my fingers. I felt an empathy with the stone, which was an unlikely fancy; I could not envision my besotted Evram in the role of the intense artisan, Nimal, and I had singularly failed to comply with duty according to Varina's example. I found Kaedric regarding me oddly. Defensively, I clutched my find, shielding it from view as he had previously hidden a medallion of gold from me.

"I did not intend to snatch it from you," said Kaedric slowly. "The Lady gifts whom she will."

"I thought you disbelieved such legends, Master Kaedric," I said, strangely struck by the wizard's incongruous comment. "Your rendition of the story earlier hardly accords with a generous specter."

"I dispute the heroism of a man who murdered the woman he purportedly loved. I meant no disparagement of the Lady Varina. Her boundless devotion has always awed me." With the causticness to which I had grown more accustomed, Kaedric proceeded, "Does that admission fail to conform to your preconceptions of a wizard's perfect lack of mortal feeling? Forgive me, I shall endeavor to maintain a more circumspect profile."

"Master Kaedric," I answered carefully, "I have never met a wizard before. I can only gauge a wizard's perspective by the references I know."

"You were never tested as a potential wizardess," he stated flatly.

"No." I elaborated with imperfect honesty, "My Power is very restricted in its nature." I omitted mentioning that my father would have forbidden me the opportunity of such testing had I held the Power of Ceallagh.

"Power may be potent though it is not broad in kind. You are strong enough to have held a gargoyle." He tilted his head as he spoke, and firelight caught the momentarily revealed gold of the chain concealed about his neck.

"I do not create fires with my mind," I returned a little brusquely.

Kaedric answered with brittle glass tones, "Do not use me in judgment of all Ixaxins." His vision had turned beyond me, and I thought I felt a thousand people cry.

Warm with discomfiture despite the evening chill, I forced a neutral tone. "On which side of the Ixaxin norm do you fall, Master Kaedric?" I clung tightly to cool nacre.

His steady, cold gaze returned to me. He responded sardonically, "So far as I can discern, I am very much the worst of the extant species."

"You exclude the Infortiare—and Lord Hrgh," I whispered, not knowing why I felt the need to lower my voice. The other Venturers seemed to have retreated to some small, unreal world very far away from us two.

"No," answered Kaedric, as I had known he would. I pressed Varina's stone tightly to still my disquiet.

The rain, which for days had threatened us, at last fulfilled its intent. Torrents turned the clinging dust to clay which only grudgingly relinquished my every step. Cold and wholly wretched, I recalled warm evenings at the hearthside in Tyntagel with a wistfulness which ignored the less pleasant aspects of the remembered times. Even a night's rest brought scant relief. The minimal shelter of an exposed cliffside made sleep elusive at best. Hamar often glared at me accusingly, as if to blame me for the ire of the elements which impeded our progress. In my drenched and bedraggled condition, I presented a singularly unprepossessing candidate for the minion of a Dolr'han. I thought bleakly that if Master Hamar could detect in my pitiful mien more of menace than of rabbity fear, he had a gift of imagination unsurpassed in history.

Trudging in endless misery, head bowed before whipping rain and sleet, my mind and body grew numb to the surrounding world. Days blurred into dreary nights, and I walked in a dripping cloud, mechanically following the shadowy shapes before me. The stinging which spattered my hand only slowly penetrated my private fog. I brushed at the hand absently, but a network of crimson beads dotted my skin. Rain streaked the blood, and I recognized the cause with a sigh. Trackers from the northern moors of Tyntagel often complained of the pestilence of tsiljieks. Less tenacious kin of leeches, tsiljieks presented no real danger, but I found their presence unpleasantly appropriate to the dismal shards of Horlach's domain. I wrapped my scarf more protectively about my head, striving determinedly to ignore the spreading prickle of punctured arms and ankles.

The tsiljieks did not plague us alone. Eely tendons writhed unseen in the mud and periodically snatched at unwary feet. Gart
persistently tried to capture one. He never succeeded, and I was
just as glad. The tsiljieks, the unseen serpents and the reek of decay
had united in my mind to discourage our trespass, and I had no
wish to give further form to our foe.

The rain ebbed at length, yielding to the icy pall of winter. The
terrain grew hard, frozen and slick. Mud, affixed to my skirts,
dragged at my steps. Silver-white rime dusted stone and limbs of
winter-sleeping shrubs, and the wilds were silent to my mind. The
season of stillness had begun its soft intrusion, and Tyntagel oaks
were miles and months lost. I watched the five men and felt alone.

Chapter 12

Newborn snow cloaked that morning, my last as a Venturess. It was the new year's first day, and it entered gently. The cold had increased, but I had slept soundly, and the stark wintry beauty revived my flagging spirits. The Mountains of Mindar towered above us and around us, freed at last of confining clouds and splendid in their dominance. We did not travel long beneath their spell that morning. Amid a shattered tumble of finely wrought stone, the arched entrance to Horlach's subterranean palace still stood in somber invitation.

They came from under, over, through the stony, pock-marked ruins: near-men, once-men. Their leprous flesh clung in tattered strings to twisted limbs. From rims of blood-colored pulp peered appallingly human eyes. Horlach had infected them, and they could not die. Hacked and hewn by the Venturers, they could not use their strength effectively, but even dismembered pieces continued their writhing attack. The anguish of eons tore my soul with barbed claws. The things cried in my mind, sibilant proof that these had been Sorcerer Kings and Queens, conquered by Horlach and condemned by their own inability to forsake life.

Royal limbs littered the snow. An undead queen grabbed a severed hand and pressed it to the stump of her arm; the flesh melted, fused and joined under the gaze of her warped Power. She jerked a sword from an undead torso and rushed at Hamar with a rapturous whine. Hamar countered her blow easily and severed her body at the waist with a sword-swipe of enormous force. Hamar grinned as he slashed at her dangling breasts; he laughed at her now feeble efforts to wield her sword against him. He turned to another attacker and forgot her.

The undead fought with potent blades of fear and dread, yet I found them pathetic. Their physical efforts could not compete with the agile strength of live opponents, their Power could focus only on extending their own tormented existences, and they were too mindless even to know that they battled to protect a Sorcerer King who had been vanquished millennia ago. Gart and Hamar fought the pitiful guards with the same zeal as in their Anxian competitions, an enthusiasm of sport which they had not shown against living opponents. The exhilaration of the two warriors sickened me more than the creatures they destroyed. It revealed the depths of Hamar's bitterness, roused by legitimate female prey, and such hatred ought never to be unfettered; I understood that Gart merely empathized with his friend's rare delight, but I would never again be able to see Gart unclouded by that grisly conflict. The shy warrior of Mahl, who had in a manner charmed me, ceased from that moment to exist in my mind.

We reached the arch, and Ineuil exercised his skill on the rusty lock of an iron gate. The grate of reluctant metal told his success. Kaedric called to Gart and Hamar. With a final lunge, Gart tumbled through the gate. Hamar delayed, continuing to savor the torment of another fallen sorcerer Queen. Kaedric called again, insistently now. Hamar turned from his victim reluctantly and did not initially see the arm which reached for him. He sliced it free with a curse, momentarily distracted. The mangled queen reassembled her stringy strength and with her other arm drove her sword through Hamar's back. The warrior looked puzzled. He fell, and the deathless swarmed upon him, but I knew he was already beyond knowing.

Gart screamed denial. The rare sport had turned as viciously real and as sorcerously evil as Horlach's memory. Gart raised his sword and poised to leap against the murderers of his friend. "Leave them," commanded Kaedric sternly. Gart struggled against the Venture Leader's will, but the warrior could not but join us beyond the gate, bidden by implacable eyes of blue ice and the Power within them. Ineuil slammed fast the gate, sealing us from all but a faint filtering of the sun.

"Bloody, pious Ixaxin," growled Gart unevenly, leaning against the crumbling wall and glaring at Kaedric with fixed hatred. Gart's anger had mastered his stutter: "You spend our lives like copper kelni on your sorcerers' quarrels, and you do not even care enough to see if Hamar lives."

"Hamar is dead, Gart," said Ineuil wearily.

Gart spared Ineuil a look of venom. "And you pander for them, Master Incuil." Gart returned to Kaedric. "You may live for a dozen of my lifespans, Master Kaedric, and you may be able to destroy Serii with a thought, but you are no more human than those mindless monsters outside and certainly no more worthy."

"Kindly save the moralizing for a more opportune occasion, Master Gart," commented Kaedric coldly. "As a warrior, you ought to be more seasoned to death than to bewail it this way." The wizard was inspecting the dark corridor leading from the alcove in which we stood. "Hrgh has apparently renewed a portion of the lighting system," he said, dismissing any concern over the loss of one of his followers. A dim, unwholesome glow snaked down the visible hall. Kaedric entered the corridor purposefully.

Abbot Medwyn regarded the Venture Leader's back with pained distaste. Ineuil said soberly, "Your purpose in Venture fails, Abbot Medwyn."

The abbot frowned mournfully and took Gart by the arm. "There is nothing more we can do here, Gart," said the abbot. "We must continue." The warrior complied meekly, his furor spent, his eyes tortured.

I trailed the solemn and diminished company through a labyrinth of dark passages. The lighting was sporadic and capricious, and the footing was often treacherous. The Venture Leader led us without pause down the long and broken stairs, and we followed him, using the touch of cold walls where other guidance failed. We pressed deeply into the mountain. I counted six hundred and thirty steps before I stopped trying to keep track. The granular texture of eroded walls sanded the skin from my fingers, but it lent a measure of security in the darker regions. At one wholly lightless point, a glutinous smear, quivering and repellant to the touch, encouraged me to rely more heavily on other than the tactile sense.

Though I disliked doing it, I found that I could sense Master Kaedric quite clearly with a modicum of concentration, and the discovery did smooth my progress.

The ages had not treated kindly the palatial residence of the mightiest Sorcerer King. Throughout the lower levels, we encountered very few chambers of any residual glory; none compared with the cavern of Nimal, though much of Nimal's artistry must once have graced Horlach's castle as well. I grew increasingly doubtful that Lord Hrgh could have made of the ruins any retreat acceptable to a Dolr'han dur Liin.

We passed at length beneath a pillared arch, and found ourselves treading on a black marble floor. Silver mist suspended sourceless above us emitted a light unlike the bilious glow of the other halls. The mist illuminated, but it also concealed. Only when we stood at the hall's end, did the next chamber grow clear to view. The room gleamed brightly gold, unmeasurably vast, and mirror-burnished. The spell-cast curtain which surrounded it refracted images and confused the eye. I could see clearly only the emblem repeated on every facet: infinity's symbol entwined with the initial of Horlach, the crest of a Sorcerer King.

I heard the voice before I saw the man: a voice of persuasive refinement which befitted a lord of Serii's First House. "You disappoint me, Arineuil," said Lord Hrgh with the sorrow of trust betrayed. "You least of all did I expect to see surrender to the Venkarel. Even if our long friendship could not withstand his Power, I should have thought the memory of your murdered kin would have preserved you from his tainted alliance."

Woodenly, Ineuil responded, "I have not forgotten the atrocities of the past, Hrgh, but if my concern for you could not outweigh a futile vendetta, then I should indeed be no true friend."

"So," sighed Lord Hrgh. "He has convinced you that he preserves my welfare by your aid." The curtain across the portal dissipated, and I saw the noble lord of Liin, and he was indeed as fair to see as any prince of legend. Solemn gray eyes regarded Ineuil from a strongly molded face of classic design. A narrow circlet of gold bound auburn hair, and golden raiment added to the aureole of majesty. Enthroned upon a time-worn bench, Lord Hrgh Dolr'han dur Liin could well have been a king giving judgment on his vassals. I knew whence Yldana's yearning for Lord Hrgh had grown, but despite the Power and compassion flowing from the shining man, I felt a chill.

Lord Hrgh spoke again, and his voice rang proudly, tragically. "You have been clever, Venkarel. The good Abbot Medwyn you ensorcelled long ago, and now you take my greatest friend and ally. Did you tell them of the Taormin? Did you tell them that I took it to preserve it from your grasp?"

"I have no need for the Taormin, Hrgh. But if I did wish to take and use it, the decision would not be subject to your veto. I am the Infortiare, Hrgh. I did not seek the post which you so coveted, but that choice belonged to neither of us."

"You err, Venkarel," said Hrgh. "You defeated me once by trickery, but I shall not repeat my incautious faith in the honor of an upstart scrub. Dismiss your followers, Venkarel. I would not see these misguided innocents further victimized."

Watching and listening I felt myself to be viewing a history which had passed long before my birth. Abbot Medwyn chanted a toneless benediction, closely watching Master Gart the while. Gart's loyalties at that moment must certainly have merited the abbot's question, but the warrior stood stoic and still. Ineuil had turned away from the proceedings, wrapped in his own despondent conflict.

I studied Kaedric, a hard, dark silhouette, thin and worn. The golden Lord Hrgh made a far more credible picture of Serii's highest Lord. Kaedric advanced through the portal, and the curtain which had vanished flared again, blurring the two opponents.

"Pray well, Abbot Medwyn," said Lord Hrgh. "The soul of Lord Venkarel bears a heavy burden of iniquity." I felt the bolt of Power which Hrgh flung against Kaedric; the sensation came dimly distant through the shield of the translucent curtain. Kaedric parried it easily.

"You have grown lazy, Hrgh," said Kaedric. "Any Ixaxin novice could strike more cleanly."

"Do not lecture me on a subject I mastered while you slept in the sties of Ven," shouted Lord Hrgh angrily. I heard Kaedric form a mirthless laugh and stop it aborning. The ever-shifting curtain froze to clarity. Lord Hrgh with a smile of sly cunning brought forth from his robes a pod of amber filigree which glowed with milky yellow light. The color warmed and whirled; it ran to Hrgh, engulfing his face and his hands. Fire sprang from Kaedric, brilliant blue and tightly focused. It struck Hrgh but swirled about him and sank into the brightening pod. The energy of the Dolr'han flared outward, the yellow light expanding in a fiery sphere. Streaks of burning darkness filled it. Across the marble floor spread a smoldering trail of sulfureous ash. The yellow light touched Kaedric and shattered in a shower of blinding sparks. Then the room became flame, blue-hot and burning umber, and the only vision I had came as fire in my mind.

The voice of Lord Hrgh crackled with Power. "Submit to me, Venkarel. You cannot defeat the Lord of the Taormin." I heard Ineuil cry out to Hrgh. A virulent bolt shot from the hand of the Lord of Liin, and Ineuil crumpled. "Thus shall I crush you also, Venkarel, unless you accept my rightful dominion."

"You will not use me as you have used Hrgh," answered Kaedric.

"Bravo, Lord Venkarel. You recognize your true foe. You will make an admirable tool, far better than this feeble fool who fancied himself a sorcerer. It is a pity to damage you as I must. This era of yours seems to lack any other Powers of interest." The darkness in the yellow fire redoubled, and blue dimmed to pale silver-gray as Kaedric suffered the blow of the Sorcerer King.

If I had thought, I would have fled. Nothing held me, unnoticed as I was where I clung to the carven wall. Kaedric had called me impetuous and foolish. As I had touched an ailing oak of Tyntagel, I reached out my will to Kaedric, Venkarel, and I restored him.

I screamed at the corrosion of fire which filled me. Shock at my intervention stemmed the battle for a pulsing instant. The darkness twisted within Lord Hrgh Dolr'han recoiled, then burst forth in anxious seeking for the intruder. In that moment of distraction, Kaedric's Power swirled anew. Locked in a realm of charred anguish, I knew relief as the darkness left its search for me and turned again to its attacker.

I drew within me Kaedric's pain, though I felt my own blood boiling. I no longer tried to help him: I could not block the channel which I had opened. My strength seeped from me, and all my memories were lost in a maelstrom of flame and horror, ageless death and the countless victims of a timeless hunger. Identities shifted, distorted and merged, a confusion of sorcerers, wizards and madmen, wicked, woeful and wise men whose destinies crossed in the Taormin. Tides swelled, pulsed and tried to tear apart the tangle, even as the Taormin sought to swallow us in its grasp. Three of us fought, resisted and reinforced the shatterer: Horlach, Kaedric and Rhianna. As a splinter of glass flies free from a broken whole, I spun from infinity to unconsciousness.

V
THE FIRE

Chapter 1

Year of Serii—9008
Benthen Abbey, Serii

The blanket was coarse, the pillow hard, but the smooth linen smelled of fresh spring herbs. I stretched lazy muscles and opened eyes heavy lidded with long sleep. Focus came unwillingly: white-washed walls, beam-crossed ceiling, a dark wood bench polished by age. Pale sunlight fell from a large embrasure overlooking the pallet on which I lay.

An effort to rise brought a wave of dizziness. I fell back to the cot, weak and spent, daunted in the endeavor to review my surroundings better. I considered the strong beams above me and concluded that sleep enticed me more than exploration.

I drifted into a somnolent state which was not quite sleep, and the world therein was afire. The flesh melted from me in blackened streams, leaving me raw and vulnerable and lost. I thrust my spirit forward and opened my eyes. Placid brown eyes returned my gaze from a round, beatific face. The face smiled, so I smiled in response.

The cherub moved away, gathered an armful of linens from the dark wood bench, and left the room through a narrow doorway. An elderly man took her place beside me; a rough brown cowl covered his head. I beat at my sluggish mind and found a name which seemed to fit him. "Abbot Medwyn," I whispered, enormously pleased by my own cleverness.

I slept and woke and gained with each awakening a little more of strength and surety. The fire dreams became less fierce, though they did not fully leave me. The cherub often returned to tend me; Abbot Medwyn came less frequently. Neither spoke aloud, though they conveyed some thoughts by simple gestures.

From the window of my cell, I could view a portion of the abbey gardens: orderly rows of budding beans and marrows carefully tended by silent figures in dull brown robes. I watched their labors in the gentle sunlight, and I was very glad when my cherub gave me a robe of my own and led me to work beside the peaceful, diligent gardeners. Each man and woman kept to silence, and I gave no thought to another way after my single whispering of Abbot Medwyn's name. I learned the few signs by which to make known the nominal needs of simple living. I strengthened slowly, and I grew to health.

The garden stalks burgeoned; blossoms furled their lacy fingers and brought forth their swelling fruits. I watched the dawns with the abbey sisters in the silence of morning prayer. I came to know the bells which called us. I knew the sisters with whom I lived by their eyes and their clever hands, but they were nameless, as was I.

I was contented. Our abbot was gentle and good. We worked long, but we had laughter, though we had no words. Only the troubling of my sleep concerned me still; in sleep, I was alone and unsolaced. With the night-fire and fear came a myriad of shattered fragments: great oaks, gray walls, and eyes of blue ice. I began to see visions of Abbot Medwyn in grimmer settings than the pale of Benthen Abbey, and none would give me comfort in this one question. As the weeks of halcyon springtime passed, the faces of my dreams began to dominate as well my waking hours, and I clung to the peaceful present with increasing desperation.

Evening of a day of storm: an hour had distanced the thundrous rumbles which echoed in the abbey halls. Lightning's ferocious crackle had filled the afternoon, but only the intermittent glare of distant glory touched Benthen Abbey now. The violence of the storm had stirred my inner dreams to frenzy, and I worked with frantic energy to exorcise my restless specters.

Abbot Medwyn summoned me as I completed the polishing of a row of dedicatory plaques. I followed him to his office, second foremost of the rooms which faced the abbey gates and separated the men's halls from the women's. He closed the door and bade me sit upon one of the two straight-backed chairs.

Abbot Medwyn contemplated me over interlaced fingers. "You have been with us for nearly four months, Rhianna," he said. The sound of speech startled me, but response in kind seemed suitable.

"I can recall no more than half that time. I must have been very ill."

"You needed much healing, Rhianna, but you have recovered your strength of body. Your brother, Lord Dayn, has come to take you home to Tyntagel."

For Abbot Medwyn's sake, I tried to understand. I tried to remember a brother and a home outside the abbey. "Is it very far?" I asked.

Shaking his head, Abbot Medwyn pushed a parcel toward me. "These things are yours, Rhianna."

Gingerly, I pulled aside the fold of linen wrapping: a woolen skirt, a cloak and tunic, worn and heavily patched; amid them, a stone of a curious milky-white. I clasped the stone slowly and let my fingers trace the polished whorls. I heard the distant thunder, and the seconds passed. Memory heeded my summons reluctantly. Each fragment of its return eroded my illusory peace. I continued to hope that Abbot Medwyn might dismiss me before my shell of healing serenity cracked, but he did not relent.

"As you fell," said Abbot Medwyn, "Kaedric took the Taormin from Lord Hrgh, who fled into Horlach's maze with a tormented cry quite inconsistent with his previous poise. Kaedric transported us here. He used the Taormin; ask me not how. I wish he had not used the foul device, but it did preserve your life and Ineuil's as well against a questionable alternative."

"You sent for my brother. How much has he been told of how I came here?"

"We sent word to your family only that you were ill and under our care. Kaedric told me your name and kinship before he left."

I did not remark the plainness of the latter comment to my mind. I had acquired new memories along with my own: seemingly senseless images, but I knew them to include Ixaxis and Ven. I presumed without much happiness that the man from whom the images came had accrued some share of my history in exchange.

"I ought to see Dayn. My brothers do dislike waiting." I searched the abbot's eyes. "If I asked to remain here in the abbey, I think you would refuse me. Have I been so unsatisfactory an oblate?"

"I should welcome you to our order, Rhianna, if you truly wished the vows and were not already committed to another path."

"My father has committed me to marriage against my choice."

Abbot Medwyn blinked. "It was not of marriage that I spoke, though that estate does conflict with our vows. Benthen Abbey may not accept a practitioner of wizardry."

"I am not a wizardess, Abbot Medwyn."

"The Infortiare disagrees. Your brother is in the anteroom."

I regarded the door which led to the outermost chamber of the abbey, the anteroom which was reserved for occasional visitors. I pictured my brother pacing in distaste for his current duty. Poor Dayn always incurred the undesirable tasks which Balev and our father shunned.

I had not seen Dayn for nearly two years; that last meeting had consisted of a single formal dinner held during his brief soldier's leave in Tyntagel Keep. He had looked very fine in the crimson uniform of a royal officer, but he had already talked eagerly of the end of his term of service. He wore nobleman's finery now, though an empty scabbard hung at his side; he reached abortively for the missing sword, as if its unaccustomed absence (abbey rules forbade the gear of warfare) distressed him. Poor Dayn—he needed no further unhappiness beyond the prospect of seeing me again. He had not faced me squarely during the twenty years since some leap of logic, intuition, or the sudden coalescence of scattered observations gave him recognition of my sorcerous nature. At six years of age, Dayn had seen in me what no one else had dared observe. I wondered how Dayn would react to the truth of my recent illness.

Dayn mumbled my name; he lacked still the ability to speak easily in my presence. Our reunion was predictably stilted: a formal exchange of the most minimal of greetings. It was Abbot Medwyn who told me that Dayn had married Lady Liya dur Cam not long after I had left Tyntagel. I had not even been informed of the engagement, though it had been formalized months before my leaving.

I told Dayn no more regarding my own immediate past than he

had already heard from Abbot Medwyn, and Dayn certainly did not press me for further information. He made only one disapproving reference to my precipitous departure, muttering dully, "You never could make anything easy, could you?" Dayn had always been the most tolerant of my kin.

Chapter 2

We left Benthen Abbey the next morning. I relinquished to the abbey my share of the Venture reward and the few belongings, save Varina's stone, which I had carried for so many leagues. Dayn had brought me a trunk of clothing packed for me by his wife. I ought to have felt appreciative of her consideration, but I could not even summon enough emotion to regret deeply my leaving the abbey.

I spent the next few days bouncing uncomfortably in a carriage, while my brother rode freely beside the cumbersome entourage which confined me. The only gladness of my state was solitude; my father had not seen fit to equip the company with any female escort. I had resolved to wallow in self-pity, but I could not sufficiently overcome my feeling of resignation.

Tyntagel Keep was just as I remembered. The oak which I had healed before my flight sported new leaves and added stature. I wanted to reach it, but I had strayed too far, and I feared to examine the extent of the metamorphosis. Not one of my family appeared to greet my return. A servant took my trunk but made no offer to assist me from the carriage. Dayn vanished toward the stables, leaving his sour lackey to ensure my cooperation in returning to my ancestors' home.

The second housemaid of the east wing met us in the entry hall and led me to my room. Her name was Rosal. She was very young and often forgetful of her position's proper restraint, even with the Tyntagel sorceress. She had frequently spoken to me in the past, and I had enjoyed her unconscious trespasses. She acknowledged me now only as much as minimally necessary.

My room had not been touched. Dust covered it thickly, and the familiar musty smell had gained in measure. I shook the counterpane, dislodging a spider which scampered under the door. The spider's escape came more easily than would mine; Rosal had locked the door as she left, taking the room's only key.

I counted the folds on the heavy curtains, pressing them with my fingers to feel their familiar texture of soft velvet worn in irregular patches. My window overlooked the narrow road which wove through the village by a route which darted erratically from dwelling to dwelling. Tiny figures traveled it, proceeding with their daily affairs as they had always done. I could name them by their places and paths without need to see their features. They did not change. Each knew his role and followed it from birth.

My own role had been molded tightly around me, and my liege-father would hold me to it. A year's delay had been requested for the propriety of Lord Grisk's bereavement; my intermediate absence could have been kept unnoticed beyond Tyntagel Keep. Any inquiries henceforth could be countered by the vague account of illness and a time of religious retreat. I felt much like the toy which returns invariably to its initial position, no matter how many tumbles it takes.

I had returned to incarceration. Even if I did escape again, I had no practical goal. My horror of espousal to Lord Grisk dur Niveal had not wavered, but my impulsive endeavor to elude it had brought me only greater anguish.

I felt another compulsion now: to seek him whom I had known as Master Kaedric. I dreaded another encounter, fearing to revitalize that terrible fire which my mind could barely contain, but I needed to find him. I needed explanations which only Lord Venkarel could supply, and I needed to understand the change he had wrought in me. Master Kaedric—Lord Venkarel—would not seek me; he had left me to Benthen Abbey. I could not expect another chance meeting, since the Infortiare was generally a most inaccessible personage. The Tower of the Infortiare adjoined the King's castle in Tulea; a Tyntagellian lady inhabiting a hall of that castle stood a much better chance of meeting the Infortiare than would a Tyntagellian runaway. If my father still wished me to travel to Tulea for Lord Grisk's inspection, I would comply.

Rosal brought my meals to my room, removed the remains, and never spoke or relented enough to smile. The punishment did not disturb me. The silence of Benthen Abbey had been deeper, and I knew that the present confinement would pass. I was far too haunted by misplaced, spinning thoughts to fret at the flow of a few days. I was haunted by the shades of another's life. I tatted careful laces and waited while the sun cycled and my mind's fragmentary memories firmed.

"You were careless, Fylla," said the plump woman, a blowsy blossom rank with the attendant smell of stale roses. "You should have come to me before you had the child."

The woman thus addressed was badly worn, her face was pinched, and the smoldering beauty she had always owned had paled with recent abuse. She was ravaged, this woman who had been known as ageless among her peers in a career of notoriously short tenure. She looked a curse at the child, the spindly boy of three or four or five, who had vanquished her. She hated him. She pleaded, "Ora, I can still bring in customers. I was your best draw. You told me that."

"Look at yourself, Fylla. My customers want more than a worn-out skeleton."

"Ora," cried the desperate Fylla, "Just let me stay a week. It'll be worth your while. If not, you can still send me out."

"No more, Fylla," declared Mistress Ora with impatience. She patted her stiffly curled, yellow hair. "Go to Doshk. He may take you."

Fylla's wide blue eyes shone contempt. "Me in Doshk's sty? I'd as soon bed a maggot's meal as the slime he caters to."

"Don't be so choosy, Fylla. You can't afford it. Get out."

The black-haired whore, who had once commanded the highest prices on Ven's waterfront, faced Mistress Ora with pathetic dignity. Ora prospered, but she was old, and Fylla felt a sneering pride at being young. Youth was all that remained to Fylla, and even it was a fostered self-deception; Fylla's birth had preceded Mistress Ora's by thirty years.

Pushing her slight, dark-haired son roughly before her, Fylla emerged onto the foggy street. Her heel caught on a wooden plank rougher than the rest, and she stumbled. Tears stung her eyes, for she used never to trip; she had been beautiful and dancer-graceful and far too fine for the wretches who now comprised her dwindling clientele. Her son regarded her with sorrow from eyes of startling blue.

"Damn you, Kaedric," she muttered, but the boy continued to trail her steps dutifully. She had always been careful, but still the boy had come. She had wanted to abort him, but the burning fever had come to her each time she tried, and then it was too late. He was born, and his eyes were clear and knowing, and she could not leave him, though she despised herself for the weakness.

Her steps slowed at a grimy inn. Two men who entered it eyed her with initial interest, until the fog broke enough to show how weak and colorless she had grown. They veered away; she would have scorned them and their diseased bodies, but their rejection hurt. She stared at the inn for several minutes. The child seated himself placidly at her feet.

A man very fat but strong and cruel appeared at the doorway of the inn. He searched the fog, and he saw the woman. He bared stained teeth. "Why, Mistress Fylla, have you come to pay your respects to me? You're not so haughty now, are you?"

Fylla stiffened, but she smiled in shadow of her old enticements, a stretching of lips which had been seared dry and cracked by her long fevers. "I was wrong about you, Doshk. You have established yourself well."

"Better than you've done," he answered.

"I've had some hard times of late, I admit, but I could still bring you more profits than you have ever seen."

"You're done, Fylla, and you know it." He smeared greasy hands across his apron. An outburst of shouts rocked the inn, and Doshk turned to the door with a snarl.

"Doshk," called the woman, her pride defeated by long strain and hunger. Doshk yelled through his inn, and the fracas quieted to the normal, steady roar. "Doshk," repeated Fylla, "You'll want to replace Gella."

"I can buy a bony carcass from the butcher, Fylla. I don't need to hire one."

Growing frantic, Fylla said, "Then buy the boy, Doshk. He's strong, and he'll have my looks. He'll fetch you good prices in a few years."

With a snicker begun, Doshk paused. Fylla had commanded great prices before the boy's birth, and the child did have the promise of his mother's remarkable coloring and fine features. "He's no use to me yet," muttered Doshk. "Bring him back in a few years, and we'll talk again."

"Keep your worthless bargains, Doshk," said the woman cuttingly, but she knew a breath's relief.

Doshk had not done with her. "Five kesni for him, Fylla. It's a fair offer, and you need it."

"Fifteen, Doshk, and a night's room and board," said the woman starkly. She would not look at her son.

"Five or nothing, Fylla. I don't need another mouth to feed, and the boy is useless as yet."

Fylla wrung her slender hands and felt the bite of hunger. "I can sell the boy elsewhere, Doshk." She wished she could believe it. Even as she spoke, she waited with dread for the fever to start. It had not troubled her since that outflow of fury in which she had actually struck the boy, but she continually expected its return. Fylla did not know how well she had wrought the binding of her son's Power.

Doshk delved into a deep pocket, fumbling with the coins therein. He withdrew seven small pieces of iron and displayed them on his pasty palm. "You can eat for a week on this, Fylla, and maybe you'll get some customers if you're not half-starved."

Fylla snatched at the coins. Doshk let them fall and laughed at the woman's desperate scramble to claim them. One coin rolled to the boy; he gathered it carefully and offered it to his mother. She hesitated only an instant before she jerked the coin from the boy's hand. She left him with his hand outstretched. Doshk kicked him roughly, and the boy struck the gravelly gutter with a soft whimper. Doshk kicked him again.

A weasel-faced young man detached himself from the inn's shadow and pursued the diminished Fylla. She was unwary with distraction and perceived the man only when his scabbed arm encircled her. She screamed as the knife flashed. The man pried the seven coins from her clenched fingers, while blood pooled at her throat.

Fylla's son shuddered. Doshk grabbed his arm and dragged him within the inn.

I dreamed of Fylla for fourteen nights, and every dream ended in a pool of her seeping blood and her son's unshed tears. I was bitterly weary when the fifteenth sun enflamed the morning sky. A tentative knock rattled a bit of broken gilt-work on my chamber door. I folded away the laces which would never be completed within my somber, steadfast once-home. I was glad that Lady Altha still shunned me; hers was not a face I should ever miss. Lady Liya was much pleasanter company, and I craved distraction from the vivid death of a waterfront whore.

I had met Liya once when her family passed some days with us during an excursion they made to Tulea. She still resembled a diminutive doll, tiny and energetic, though maturity had endowed her generously. She could not have been more than nineteen, but I could anticipate Lady Altha's reaction to the potential usurper. Liya would not be dominated as easily as Balev's wife, Nadira.

"Good morning, Rhianna," she announced brightly. "I bring you a gift," she added, handing me the key to my room with a conspiratorial grin. She surveyed my shadowy room with distaste. "What a ghastly way to welcome you home after your illness. Dear me, has anyone even told you that we are now sisters?"

"Dayn did mention your marriage. I do apologize for my inability to attend," I said wryly.

"Well, you are hardly responsible for your illness, are you?" she asked with a touch of authentic curiosity. She would have been unobservant indeed if she had not found flaw in the ruse of long indisposition.

I digressed deliberately, "Have you been acquainted with the prospective disposition of my future?"

"I have been told to advise you in the selection of gowns which will suitably impress your future husband. I am officially ignorant of any specific arrangements," she intoned very seriously. "However," she continued with a wink, "Lord Baerod and Lord Brant dur Niveal have exchanged a number of recent communiques, and some members of the Tyntagel household will travel to the King's court very soon; regrettably, I am not yet listed among those fortunates. I believe Lord Grisk dur Niveal, Niveal's court representative, currently requires a wife."

I laughed with her, genuinely light of heart as I had not been for far too long. I had retained more uncertainty of my journey to Tulea than I had acknowledged to myself. I could consider my next steps when I reached King Astorn's court.

Liya said dreamily, "Of course, there are a great many eligible young men at court other than Lord Grisk. With such a cache from which to choose, one might possibly discover some more appealing alternatives. You would not actually consider Lord Grisk, would you, Rhianna?" she asked with sudden concern. She blushed as she said, "I realize he is your father's choice, but he has been connected with some rather unpleasant rumors."

"If Lord Grisk found me too unappealing for consideration, I should not feel greatly slighted."

Liya's smile reappeared. "I *am* glad, but you should not rely too heavily on displeasing him. You are quite attractive in an ethereal way. I do wish I had your trick of looking at a person as if you saw all sorts of things the rest of us could never comprehend. It gives you such an elusive, mysterious quality. Everything I think or feel is plain for the world to see. I am afraid Dayn will grow bored with my predictability."

"I certainly should not recommend emulating me if you wish to retain Dayn's favor," I disclaimed fervently.

"Oh, come, Dayn does not dislike you so. He may find you a little daunting, but then you are very like your father." Privately I disagreed with appalled incredulity but made no comment. With a rush of remembrance, Liya reached the purpose of her visit. "Your father!" she exclaimed, clapping her delicate hands. "Your father has ordered the dressmaker here this noon. I was told to fetch you for the fitting. We had best hurry, or we shall both reap a wainload of trouble."

Chapter 3

Fabrics finer than any I had ever worn, flurries of conferring seamstresses turning and twisting me like a mindless doll, and Liya coordinating the gradual amassment of an astonishing assortment of laden trunks: the elaborate preparations for my journey to Tulea contrasted sharply with my previous, spontaneous departure. I was assigned a very elegant and opinionated personal maid named Tamar, who experimented endlessly with arrangements of my hair and various ensembles of jewels and other accessories. Her dispassionate attention made me feel more than ever an inanimate object. When Liya and Tamar deemed me suitable, I was paraded before the elders of the Tyntagel household, none of whom I had seen in nearly a year. My father nodded curtly.

The travel caravan began assembling the subsequent day. Liya gushed with delight when told that she and Dayn would join the caravan, which, I learned to greater puzzlement and disquiet, would include my father as well. Liya bubbled with the gaiety of projected activity. Dayn regarded his wife with the tolerance of devotion, but he did not echo her enthusiasm. Some cause beyond a daughter's betrothal spurred my father's decision to travel to Tulea, and it had sobered Dayn to a point even Liya could not reach.

"Rani," I heard, and the name stirred fear and hope, but it was Evram who called me. He seemed paler and plumper than I had seen him last, or perhaps it was only by comparison with a handsome scoundrel/thief and a man whose gaze was ice and flame.

"My father will be displeased if he observes you with me, Evram," I said with a slightly forced smile. "But I am glad to see you well."

"Rani, how could you leave without telling me? I worried for you."

"You would not have allowed me to go, as I thought I must."

Evram bobbed his head nervously, trying to conceal the glances of concern he threw at my father, as yet absorbed in issuing final orders to Balev before our departure. "You ought to have come to me, Rani. I would gladly have taken you to Benthen Abbey if you had asked it. I shall take you from here now if you wish it. I know the guards. They will help us to escape."

"Dear Evram," I sighed sadly. I was certain that Evram did not actually believe that his influence over the Tyntagellian guard outweighed my father's, but it was an offer the more gallant for the uncharacteristic lie. "Please forget me, Evram. I am less than ever what you wish to believe me."

Evram interrupted me, a thing he had never done before. "Rani, I dislike to see anyone treated this way. I offer to help you as a friend." He looked again toward my father, and he shuffled nervously. "I suppose no one told you. I married Mistress Terrell, your niece's governess, last month."

Evram's expression was woebegone and embarrassed. I was relieved and sorry, gladful and hurt. I hardly knew Evram, I realized. I had discounted him as no more than infatuation's foolish victim. He had been my friend, perhaps my only human friend, and I had not repaid his friendship well. My realization came late. "I am pleased for you, Evram. Mistress Terrell is a fine and intelligent woman."

"And a suitable choice for a shopkeeper's son," said Evram with the grin I remembered fondly. He sobered quickly. "Terrell will meet us at my father's shop. I have a cousin in Amlach who will help me start anew. We can smuggle you from the coach as you pass through the oak wood. It is dark there, and we are less likely to be observed. I can take you to Benthen or to another abbey where you are not known, if that is what you wish."

"Evram, I could not allow you to make such sacrifice for me, and there is no need for it. I travel to Tulea of my own volition. I am done with fleeing. Go back to your wife, Evram, and tell her that she need not follow you into exile."

Evram hesitated, and I pressed his hand, fleetingly ruing the loss of old dreams. "You are a kind and good man, Evram."

"We shall always be here if you need us," promised Evram slowly. "We are not important people, my lady, but we are your friends."

"Friends are always important, Evram." But there are deeper, less tangible bonds, Evram, and they demand precedence. They steal me from this gentle world of yours which I have only begun to appreciate, now that I must lose it.

We journeyed slowly, encumbered by a ridiculous train of wagons and carriages. Since Liya rode with Dayn, I was left with the dismal company of Tamar. I offered no objection to the arrangements, since I had resolved to maintain my passive role as far as possible, but the exchange of poor company for the solitude to which I had become accustomed did not improve my temper. Tamar doubtless reciprocated my sentiments, but she at least received payment for her trouble. I gazed sightlessly out the carriage window at the mountains we circled, lost in hurtful memories not my own, and many days vanished.

The road to Tulea stretched wide and well tended, but steep downgrades on either side betrayed the city's origins as a citadel of defense. Traffic thronged along the Seriin capital's single formal access, and our massive caravan congested the street to an inconceivable degree. Since the road had been carved from the ridge of Tul Mountain specifically to confine traffickers to a limited stream, such an unexpected addition to the normal wayfarers as a noble's entourage brought travel to a virtual halt. We spent a full two hours in the final approach to the city's gates; only within a furlong from the gates did the city come into view, sheltered as it was in the arms of Tul Mountain.

Tulea surpassed the most fluent descriptions. She was the heart-jewel of Serii and the home of kings. Gazing down at the distant glint of silver sea, the city rose in tiers to the white crown which dominated the view, the castle of the heirs of Tul. No solemn gray Tyntagellian walls served Tulea; pastel circles faded to pale tints as the buildings progressed up the mountain. In the narrow streets vendors crowed, gay in brightly colored stalls. Wealthy nobles in sea-silk and gold, merchants of countless wares, and tattered, tired travelers from every Seriin city mingled in Tulea's terraces. Wily young rascals darted everywhere underfoot, testing the attention and the patience of their elders. The chaos and the clamor fascinated me, but the castle drew my attention above all else: reminder of the central force of the Seriin realm, King Astorn, the heir of Tul.

I did not at first observe the edifice which loomed above the castle. It was a tower carved from the dark mountain stone, and the grander dwelling of the King made the tower seem stark and insignificant. The base of the tower clung to the mountain; the mountain wall retreated from the tower's continuing height, and a black bar seemed to bind the tower to the castle's upper floor. I had read the tower's description; it was Ceallagh's Tower, the tower of the Infortiare of Serii. I rubbed at the muscles of my neck; they were tight and aching.

We passed through the terraces of the commoners with their layered homes of abutting walls. We continued through the lower terrace of the lesser nobles with its grand manors and elaborate formal gardens carved in green and red and yellow. The bulk of the caravan left us as we reached the level of the royal terrace; the baggage was carried along the servants' path to the Halls of Serii's First Houses. We drove through the finely wrought gates, and the lines of liveried guards parted to let us pass.

Miraculous as it appeared as a diadem above the Tulean populace, the King's castle did not reveal its true enormity and overwhelming opulence until viewed from the King's terrace itself. Fanciful forms, each intricately carved and inlaid with precious ores, adorned the facades of the various Halls as well as the central castle proper. Spires, deceptively delicate, pirouetted and rose from vast gardens to the hub of Tulea, the home of Tul and his many generations of descendants. In Tyntagel, I had never felt the impact of a First House kinship; the King's castle burdened me with a sudden sense of awe that I belonged to a House of such history. I wondered how the royal family members withstood the formidable rivalry of their own edifice, the stunning culmination of inspired centuries.

The individual Halls belonged externally to the overall castle theme of magnificence; within, they bore the imprint of the families to which they owed title. In the Hall of Tyntagel, tapestries and heavy velvet hangings created a familiar stifling sensation, defying the silver and light of the Hall's exterior. The entry was smaller, the stair rose straight instead of curving as in Tyntagel Keep, the salon opened onto a dim inner courtyard, but it was withal the home of my family. I wondered if the same oppressive atmosphere pervaded much of the castle's inner realm; it would be a bitterly disappointing irony.

My uncle, Lord Dhavod, greeted us. He was a solid man of middling years who had never learned to smile. His wife, the Lady Ezirae, fluttered at his side. Ezirae invariably fluttered. Though in her fluffy and frivolous way, Ezirae at times projected the charm of utterly naive simplicity, she was a tediously silly woman. I often wondered how my humorless uncle tolerated her at all.

An excruciatingly correct maidservant entered the hall to announce Lady Yldana duri Amlach with a rigid curtsy. Yldana swept into the room in a wave of pale green silk, immediately commanding the attention of everyone present, eclipsing even the flurry of fuss attending the arrival of Tyntagel's liege lord. Even Liya seemed dimmed by my sister, who had not changed from my memory's glistening picture. Yldana needed no sorcery to bewitch; she drew adulation as irresistibly and implacably as a magnet draws iron.

"I do wish you had given me greater warning of your coming, Father," she cooed sweetly. "I should have prepared a more fitting reception."

"You are a worthy daughter," said our father, his dark eyes softening and his brow for the moment smooth. He bent to kiss Yldana's proffered cheek. "My business in Tulea, however, will allow me little time for social indulgence."

"Nonetheless, Father, you must not expect to devote all of your time to work. I simply will not allow it. Dayn's new wife will label us slavish." Yldana smiled enchantingly at Liya. Liya beamed, and I observed ruefully that my sister had made yet another conquest. "Of course, we must all strive diligently to impress the young lord of Niveal. We do not want our Rhianna to die a spinster." I winced inwardly; Yldana had retained her taste for mockery. I had truly come home.

Chapter 4

We were not spared even a day's reprieve to recover from our journey. My first evening in Tulea included as honored guests both Lord Brant dur Niveal and his son, Lord Grisk. I submitted to Tamar's ministrations, acutely disinterested in the prospect of meeting the man intended as my husband. I was far more intent upon the view from my chamber window of the Infortiare's Tower. I shivered when I looked upon it, but my eyes would not leave it.

My father had never before watched me with such concern nor scrutinized me so carefully as he did that evening. I welcomed Lord Brant politely and nodded a correct acknowledgment at the introduction of his son. I allowed myself a secret smile, for Lord Grisk barely glanced at me before turning his attention to Yldana, whose husband had remained conveniently absent.

Less openly dissolute than my prejudicial antipathy had led me to expect, Lord Grisk might have appeared well-favored to one more receptive than I. He was a strongly muscled man of a type which appeals to many women. The years had not yet displayed the stain of dissipation on his features, and the faint vulgar imprint which I descried could well have been due to my own bias. The only appeal he held for me was his total disdain of my existence.

Supper, always an uncomfortable meal, was rife with schemes and crossed purposes. Yldana deftly directed Lord Grisk toward me, to the obvious approval of both our father and Lord Brant, but Yldana's condescending efforts merely effected a transferal of Grisk's attentions to a discomfited Liya. Lacking Yldana's sophisticated defenses, Liya cast pleading glances at Dayn, who was occupied in a heated discussion with Uncle Dhavod regarding the Infortiare's recent edict against nobles who refused cooperation with required Ixaxin testing. No rescue came for Liya, since only she and I realized her plight; Lord Grisk included me marginally in the conversation, enough to satisfy the peripheral interest of the other members of the party without actually deigning to notice me. As the evening progressed, Liya suffered so obviously that I almost regretted my inability (and lamentable unwillingness) to distract Lord Grisk. One whispered comment from Lord Grisk upset her particularly; I could not hear it, but Liya blushed furiously and excused herself from the table on a hurried pretext of malaise.

Lord Grisk did not appear displeased with himself, though Liya had escaped him. He turned to me, the poor third choice, as he chortled, "Your sister-in-law has led a sheltered life, Lady Rhianna, but she is pert enough that a short time in Tulea should serve to educate her. You had best learn by her example."

"Since I shall not be troubled by personal experience with amorous suitors," I finished for him coldly. "Vows of marital fidelity do not concern you, I gather."

"A pretty woman unattended is an invitation, Rhianna. Fools like Dayn and Amgor marry the enticers but neglect to watch them; they should expect the consequences."

"Whereas you intend to marry a dull wife and enjoy illicitly the more enticing wives of others."

Grisk rubbed the ruddy fringe of his moustache. "You will learn to curb that sharp tongue, Rhianna, but I think we understand each other. You will get a husband—a good catch at that—and I will get heirs I know are mine."

"We are not formally betrothed, Lord Grisk. You are presumptuous."

"I am practical. The formalities await us, but I see no reason to pretend that we shall not eventually wed."

"You discount my own opinion of the matter."

Incredulity stole across Grisk's features before he laughed. "Play coy, if it amuses you. We both know that agreements between our domains have already been made."

"Agreements change."

"That is for our liege-fathers to decide."

His words silenced me, for that I could not dispute.

Liya remained unwontedly subdued the next morning. Dayn's humor seemed no grimmer than it had been since our arrival; I decided that Liya had not told him of Lord Grisk's offense. Fatigue etched hollows beneath her eyes, and I thought the aftermath of journeying alone could not account for it. Liya had enjoyed the privilege of riding much of the way, and she had shown no signs of strain on the previous day. I mentally berated Dayn for his insensitive obliviousness, but I did not feel able to intervene actively.

Yldana waltzed into our midst, the morning sunshine catching fire in her dark hair. "It really is too fortunate," she announced airily. "My dear friend, the Lady Veiga duri Sandoral, has agreed to invite Tyntagel Hall to a little gathering in the castle gardens this very afternoon. It will all be very rustic and informal, you understand, but it will be a terrifically important event. Veiga is the wife of the King's Adjutant, after all." Liya brightened at the news, and Ezirae positively oozed enthusiasm, but Liya's happiness ebbed when Yldana told me pointedly that Lord Grisk would also attend.

My father greeted Yldana's invitation by cordially and firmly declining on behalf of the men of our family, alluding to various urgent matters of nebulous nature. Dayn showed some trace of disappointment, but he pressed his wife to enjoy herself in his absence, a bit of generosity which poor Liya could not graciously refuse. Since Amgor also occupied himself in less frivolous pastimes, the party which Yldana eventually led in her gauzy gaiety consisted of Liya, Ezirae and myself.

Extending across the shady lawns which formed one of the castle's numerous parks, Lady Veiga's elaborately catered event bore little of the rustic feeling which Yldana had described, but I was still eager to participate. I had savored little sunshine since Benthen Abbey. Restored recollections had dimmed the days of gold in those gardens, and I gladly revived memories of the time in that haven to supplant the dark visions which I now more clearly recalled.

Seated demurely between Ezirae and Liya, I pretended to a fascination with Ezirae's embroidery of a blossom which the living flora wholly eclipsed. The dreadful Grisk had appeared all too promptly. He fawned alternately upon Yldana and Liya, uttering coarse drolleries with an impertinent familiarity which Yldana carelessly disregarded while Liya stammered uncertain replies. I think Liya barely understood half of his references; I recognized only a little more by observing my sister's amused responses. Ezirae embroidered in apparently blithe ignorance of the scandalous behavior enacted beside her.

Glowing in sheer coral, Yldana made less effort to discourage Grisk than she had done the previous night. "Lord Grisk," she teased, "you should not squander your attentions on respectable married ladies. Rhianna's finer qualities will become evident to you only if you apply yourself diligently to the study."

"Married ladies can be most educational," said Grisk slyly.

Yldana's perfect lips formed a response, but her lazy glance sharpened abruptly on a point somewhere behind me. Both Ezirae and Liya turned in a blatant show of curiosity which I refused to emulate, but I was equally intrigued by the focus of my sister's rapt gaze. Ezirae fairly squeaked with excitement as she whispered effusively across me to Liya. "Yldana must be absolutely seething. I am sure she did not know Lord Arineuil had returned. It was quite bad enough that he left without a word to her, but now he shows up after a year or more without a bit of notice." The name teased me, but Ezirae's avid interest in the progress of one of Yldana's conquests disconcerted me. I had not thought Ezirae so careless of propriety—even for the sake of the thrilling gossip on which she thrived. "We heard he left on family business," she continued, "But there is little enough family left in the line of Ven, and Lord Arineuil never showed any interest in business before. It was undoubtedly," nodded Ezirae knowingly, "a Woman."

"Lord Arineuil has a simply scandalous reputation, Rhianna," explained Liya needlessly, her own eyes alight with intrigue, and my sluggish recognition coalesced.

"Hush, Rhianna," said Ezirae, though I had yet to speak a word. "He is coming near."

Lord Grisk halted his unheeded flirtations and scowled glumly at the man who approached. Yldana smiled bewitchingly and lowered her voice to its sultriest pitch. If she were angry—as Ezirae's ruminations made seem likely—she contained it well. "My dear Lord Arineuil," she drawled. "The ladies of Ven must be indeed enticing to have occupied you so long."

"Not one is so enticing as you, Yldana," answered the gentleman smoothly. He saw me then, and I stifled a nervous laugh at his quickly covered startlement.

Yldana regarded him from lowered lashes. "My brother's new bride, Lady Liya, will be visiting us for a brief while," she said, misjudging the cause of Lord Arineuil's stare. My sister added, as an afterthought meant, I suspected, to distract Lord Arineuil from Liya's charming blush, "My sister, Rhianna, will remain longer—if Lord Grisk has his way." Yldana beamed at Grisk consolingly.

Ineuil had recovered his wit; he turned an innocent gaze to me as if he had not previously observed my silent presence. "Must your sister depend on such grievous company?" he asked. Grisk's fists tightened. Ineuil prattled, "You are still mourning Tilla, are you not, Grisk? I should not like Lady Rhianna to meet Tulea from such an odious perspective." Ineuil bowed to me with a faint, conspiratorial grin.

"You are not in a position to cast aspersions, Arineuil," growled Grisk.

"Nor should I ever do so," answered Ineuil, guilelessly hurt, but his green eyes danced, "Especially toward someone of such scintillating refinement as yourself, Lord Grisk. I congratulate you on your excellent taste in brides once again. I did congratulate you the last time, did I not?"

"Arineuil," chided Yldana without particular fervor, "You ought not to remind Lord Grisk of his tragic loss."

"Have I done?" asked Ineuil. "I am sorry, Grisk. I do keep transgressing. Perhaps that little parlor maid—Nora?—can console you. She did so well the day Tilla died. Not a soul could have guessed of your bereavement that very afternoon. It was an inspirational display of fortitude, Grisk." Grisk had risen, and Ineuil gave the Niveallan's shoulder a hearty pat. Grisk jerked his heavy arm and swung it with violent intent, but Ineuil dodged nimbly aside. "Yldana," declared Ineuil gleefully, "it was too unkind of you to have kept your lovely sister hidden all these years." Yldana's gaze hardened. I experienced a fervent wish to box Ineuil's ears. Yldana would never forgive me for attracting the attention of one of her interests, and I could hardly explain my prior acquaintance with Lord Arineuil without aggravating a very delicate situation further.

"Rhianna does not frequent your circles, Lord Arineuil," said Yldana with a petulant turn of her lips. "She does not understand your foolish persiflage. If you must break new hearts, please constrain yourself to more worthy opponents than my unfortunate little sister. Your protracted absence from court cannot have deprived you so quickly of selective discernment."

"To the distress of my revered family, my appreciation of the finer things never wanes, nor does my diligence in the pursuit of such treasures as I espy. I could hardly neglect a sister of yours, Yldana. You will excuse us, Grisk? I should not like to interrupt your conversation further. Yldana and Lady Liya appeared so engrossed when I arrived. Lady Ezirae, your embroidery skill never falters." Ineuil gripped my reluctant hand implacably, pulled me to my feet, and removed me from the party before the astonished eyes of every nearby participant. I winced at the flurry of whispers which followed us to the stand of trees that rimmed the park.

"Do you realize how much trouble you are bestowing upon me, Lord Arineuil?" I sighed when we had escaped the range of curious observers.

"You once doubted the sincerity of my suit, dear Rani, implying that I attended you only for lack of other female company. I could not permit your misapprehension to continue."

"You choose an awkward way of proving your point."

"Nonsense! I shall have you know that my attention is considered a commodity of exceptional value. You will be the most celebrated lady of the court for days to come."

"Notoriety is not on my list of desirable attributes."

"You are not very appreciative of my discretion. I could have supplied you with a far more interesting reputation by mentioning our lengthy liaison. How would Lord Grisk react to that information, I wonder? He is a very jealous man, your future husband."

"Our common journey, Lord Arineuil, was scarcely a romantic frolic."

"The truth would incriminate us both with far more serious consequences, my dear sorceress."

"Then please forbear to address me by that ridiculous title," I countered sharply.

Ineuil answered more contritely than I might have expected. "Forgive my thoughtless tongue, Rani. I am not really so free with secrets as you may believe."

My spurt of sincere panic assuaged, I returned calmly, "You evidently keep your own well enough. Do the ladies of Ven never communicate with those of Tulea?"

"Ven women are legendary for their discretion," he said seriously; then he grinned openly. "A gift exceeded only in Tyntagel, I surmise."

"You are a rogue, Lord Arineuil, albeit less irresponsible than you pretend."

Laughing, he draped his arm about my shoulders. "My Lady Rhianna, you know me far too well, which is a humbling admission for a man of my repute. It is a pity to waste you on Grisk."

"I did not come to Tulea to wed Lord Grisk."

"Yldana seems to differ with you." We had wandered near to the upper edge of the wooded glen, and the windowless mass of Ceallagh's Tower loomed starkly before us. "Have you seen him yet?" asked Ineuil, markedly casual.

I did not bother to dissemble. "I have just barely arrived. In any case, the youngest daughter of Tyntagel does not frequent the Infortiare's circle."

"You will be presented to the royal family and its chief adviser soon enough; you are the daughter of a First House." He added with deliberation, "I rather thought, however, that Kaedric might have sought you."

"I served Lord Venkarel's purpose for a brief time, but he has no cause to seek me."

Ineuil took my shoulders to turn me, and he studied me closely. I met his gaze, wondering how much he had descried of the Taormin's tricks. "You did come to Tulea to find him?" demanded Ineuil with abrupt insistence.

I answered tersely, "Yes."

A moment's pause: Ineuil continued lightly, "I know of a very romantic villa where we can together watch the sun set into the Seriin Sea."

I smiled and responded without rancor, "You do spout the most ridiculous nonsense at times, Lord Arineuil." Ineuil was still the most handsome and charming man of my acquaintance, but I knew in that moment that I was immune to his unquestionable attractions. The realization made me feel vaguely invincible and obviated any regret I had at rediscovering the ease I felt in Ineuil's company, despite the trouble which the association would likely cost me. "I am nearly minded to accept your offer just to watch the agility of your retraction."

"Cruel Rhianna, your honesty wounds me. Your acceptance would delight me immeasurably, though I admit that the villa must wait upon the completion of certain business transactions which bind me to Tulea at present."

"Your unflagging devotion to duty is inspirational, my Lord Arineuil. I am sure that my sister appreciates your constant diligence as well."

"Yldana is a luscious vixen," mused Ineuil with a self-deprecating smile, "But the first time I find myself envying Amgor, I shall flee the vicinity until sanity returns."

"Amgor considers himself remarkably blessed."

"Amgor is a weak fool, and Yldana drives him to distraction. He spends so much time suffering pangs of jealous anguish that he has lost any semblance of intelligence that he may once have possessed." Ineuil squarely faced the distant sea. "Serii suffers such a surplus of his kind these days that even such an irresponsible rascal as I must exert myself against the consequences. We are sinking into the sort of self-destructive madness which claimed Hrgh."

I spilled a portion of my troubled thoughts. "Lord Hrgh has wrought such calamity as few could match."

"I am not unaware of the magnitude of the force which Hrgh released," answered Ineuil grimly. "The ramifications of Hrgh's folly may be more pervasive, but the ignorant conceits of Hrgh's counterparts can as easily destroy us. Kaedric's battles have not ended. Consider that before you seek him."

His vehemence startled me, recalling me from my fire-shrined phantasms. "Surely King Astorn must be aware of such an epidemic among Serii's noble Houses," I said tentatively.

"King Astorn manages well such civil cases and trade agreements as have promoted our prosperity for so long, but the line of Tul is as afflicted by indolence as the rest of Serii."

"A trait from which the House of Ven is immune?"

"Very far from it. My uncle advanced in the forefront of ineffectiveness, which is why my cousin rules a decimated domain." He plucked a leaf and began to shred it meticulously. "If my uncle had enforced his laws, there would have been no abused slave-child to ignite a city."

"Kaedric," I whispered.

"Lord Venkarel," amended Ineuil icily. He tossed the leaf's shorn skeleton to the draft which fell from the mountains. "The Infortiare who makes us choose now between himself and a deathless Sorcerer King." Ineuil sighed. "King Astorn still supports the traditional rights of Ixaxis, but he is not strong in spreading that loyalty. The movement against Ixaxis and the Infortiare's influence mounts daily, now that we can least afford it. The fools have even begun to gather at court."

"My father has come to Tulea after an absence of at least a dozen years," I admitted.

"And Lord Baerod dur Tyntagel is vociferous in his hatred of wizardry. He must find your abilities awkward to explain."

"He has never acknowledged them."

"Typical. Lord Grisk incidentally shares your father's antipathies." Ineuil issued a sudden, wicked grin. "I must say to your father's credit, however, that he excels in his production of daughters. He named you aptly, as well."

"My mother named me," I said absently. "How long has this movement against Ixaxis been brewing?"

"Since the first sorcerer exercised his Power. Envy builds hatred, and even those who care nothing for magic and its consequences jealously observe the wizards' longevity. Why should Ixaxins live five times longer than those of us without the Power of wizardry? Because it is their nature; because they are superiorly designed, and the price they pay is not commonly recognized beyond Ixaxis' cliffs; because they are not entirely human: the best of the reasons do not sit well with Seriin nobles, who consider themselves more individually important than any Ixaxin. The less educated Seriins rely on basic superstition for their hatred of wizardry."

"Serii has survived that sort of prejudice since its inception. My father's father hated Ixaxis, but he never tried to overthrow the Infortiare."

"Lord Alobar was an inoffensive little man who never exercised the Infortiare's authority. Hrgh had a popular appeal despite his Power. Perhaps it is merely Kaedric whom the anti-Ixaxins especially hate; he does not have a particularly warm and winning personality. You know how grudgingly I serve his cause, and I know far more of the pertinent facts than do most. You want to know why matters foment more severely now than they have in all the millennia since Serii's birth, and I have no better answer than: Kaedric himself. It is an incomplete answer at best."

We walked silently then, following a winding path against the mountain. A clear and icy stream leaped in and out of a stone bound passage to feed the ponds and fountains of the royal gardens. We stopped beside a waterfall, a narrow splash of silver against the mossy emerald and black-veined ferns. The pool at its base mirrored soft fanned fronds and sheer heights, which glistened with damp slivers of light and violet shadow.

"This path continues to the vale of Tul's forked peaks," said Ineuil, "But the way is rough and seldom used. The wind through the pass is fierce, and the rewards of braving it are meager. Ceallagh's tomb lies there, but it is a simple monument eroded by the years and rather disappointing on the whole."

I cupped cold water in my hand and watched it trickle through my fingers. Another mote of sunlight was lost to shadow. A light blinked to brightness atop the wizard's dark tower. I stared fixedly at the glow. "I must return," I said.

"This makes an admirably secluded location for an evening tryst," suggested Ineuil with a resurgence of his courtier's flippancy.

"Then we had best leave before we interrupt one. I have committed enough improprieties for one day. Yldana will be furious as it is, and I left the party without even meeting the hostess, let alone thanking her."

"Veiga rarely bothers to attend these things. She will not hold your omission against you. You know, I suppose, that she is Hrgh's sister," he added with a sidelong glance.

"No, I did not know," I answered soberly. "She must strongly support Lord Venkarel's foes."

"Veiga's sympathies are difficult to fathom. The Dolr'hans are a clannish lot, but Veiga at one time cultivated Kaedric quite openly. She is a very shrewd and ambitious woman."

"You sound disapproving. Is she so very unattractive?" I asked sardonically, shrugging off my very genuine curiosity.

"How shallow you make me sound. In point of fact, Lady Rhianna, Veiga Dolr'han is an exceptionally beautiful woman whose brother was once my greatest friend, but I have never been able to overcome an intense dislike of her."

"She spurned you?"

Ineuil scowled at me terribly before he laughed. "I confess that may have been a factor. I am too unimportant for Veiga's ambition, and I am not sufficiently exotic for her prurient tastes."

"You make me glad to miss her acquaintance."

"Not miss it—merely delay it a while."

The sun sang a final, amber chord, heightening textures and shedding shadows on Ineuil's silken finery. There were new creases in his brow imperceptible in kinder light. "You appear very healthy for a man recalled from death," I said with a memory of his figure tossed limply in Horlach's hall.

"Abbot Medwyn is an effective medic, and my injuries, unlike yours, resulted from the weak, incidental chaff of that Power struggle. When last I saw you, even Medwyn doubted your survival."

"As you say, Abbot Medwyn's cures are effective," I concurred wistfully.

"The abbot serves body and soul, but it requires wizardry to bring back the mind from where you walked."

"How fortunate for me that such aid was available," I said uncertainly.

"Yes, very fortunate," stated Ineuil flatly.

The garden party had ended in twilight by the time we returned and I never learned whether or not Lady Veiga had attended it. I reached the castle spoke which formed Tyntagel Hall and found fortune had favored me: the men of the household remained absent and were not expected to return until very late. Ezirae had retired for the evening, which left only Liya to fend off with my imperfect explanations.

Liya's somber introspection over Lord Grisk had yielded to her natural ebullience. She arrived at my room almost as I did, plopped herself upon my bed, and beseeched me in a breathless rush for the details of my afternoon. Liya made my answer easy; she did not wait to hear it.

"It is just so romantic," she gushed. "Imagine captivating Lord Arineuil himself. Rhianna, I am so happy for you."

"We only walked about the park, Liya."

"Well, I did not suppose he had proposed yet. But he is interested, and that is what counts at this stage. It is just so romantic," she repeated. Thoughtfully, she added, "Yldana was not pleased, though. I should have thought she would be."

I restrained a cynical retort. I would not contribute to Liya's disillusionment by dispelling her notions of Yldana's generosity. Liya's precious innocence seemed destined to suffer enough without my help.

"Liya, my dear sister-in-law, Lord Arineuil is a very charming man and very pleasant company, but we are not the least bit romantically inclined toward one another." Liya smiled knowingly. She did not believe my protestations, but I did at last manage to send her to her own chamber. She remained certain that I had not revealed all that had transpired with Ineuil, which was quite true, but her substitute suppositions seemed so harmlessly preposterous that I gave them little more thought. I did not take into account Ezirae's position of authority among the ranks of court gossip mongers.

My first inkling of the impact of my imprudent excursion came two mornings later. Two of Ezirae's nieces, Ziva and Flava, had been consigned to their aunt's care; Ezirae's own children were grown and gone, and the halls of Hamley overflowed with any willing relations. Neither Ziva nor Flava displayed particular interest in Ezirae's strained attempts at youthful rapport, but giggling animation sparked in them at my entrance. Their excitement in their private exchange of thoughts trebled and Ezirae's eyes brightened attentively, as a manservant announced both luncheon and Lord Grisk, an unfortunate combination.

The unpalatable Lord Grisk swaggered into view upon the servant's heels. Bowing minimally to Ezirae, he greeted me with a disconcerting enthusiasm. "Good day to you, my Lady Rhianna. That is a very becoming color you wear. Green, is it?"

"So I have heard it called," I answered dryly. I decided that Lord Grisk grew more repellent with every meeting.

Lord Grisk looked at me uncertainly, resolved his dilemma of re-action by a hesitant laugh, and then patted my arm as if I had ut-tered a witticism of astonishing cleverness. I suppressed a shudder as Grisk's spatulate thumb rubbed my sleeve. "Let me lead you in-side, my lady. So much sun cannot be comfortable for a delicate complexion."

I regarded my unfashionably browned hands critically, but I could not escape Grisk's proffered escort from the courtyard. He minced his steps awkwardly, as if suspecting me of partial paraly-sis. My father displayed rare emotion in his surprise at Lord Grisk's sudden attachment to me. I could see the calculating reap-praisal of my worth in bride price.

It was a ghastly luncheon. Grisk attempted charm with bludg-eoning tact. Ziva and Flava tittered constantly. Liya shrank against Dayn and would not speak a word. Ezirae injected my attributes into the general conversation at inopportune intervals. My father and Uncle Dhavod conspired in speculative undertones. I toyed with a bit of fish and counted minutes.

A fortuitously timed message summoned Lord Grisk soon after the meal's completion. He made much of the secrecy of the cause which claimed him, hinting broadly at lofty matters of vital impor-tance to King Astorn and Serii. He found me disappointingly de-void of awe. Undaunted, he managed a few more words between us.

"I hope you did not take my teasing seriously, Rhianna. I never meant to imply that I found you undesirable. You obviously wished to make the point clear by your little demonstration with Lord Arineuil, but now that we understand each other better, I am sure that you will not feel the need to repeat such unsuitable antics. We shall speak more of this when I am free of my duties, and I am sure you will find my apology most acceptable." I snatched my hand from his with a disgust which I tried, for diplomacy's sake, to conceal.

I had not recovered from my distress at Lord Grisk's sudden change in attitude when a liveried messenger brought me a missive sealed with the gull-wing crest of Esmar. Across fully seven sheets of vellum spread a singular outpouring of amorous avowals. The signature of Lord Joret dur Esmar conveyed nothing to me, save for a dubious image of a rather ardent young man who had briefly spoken to Yldana at the garden party. Lord Joret had obviously never seen me, since his flowing paeans to my beauty displayed exceptional inaccuracy in every specific. He closed with a windy sentence to the effect that he would never have risked my reputation by whisking me away as had Lord Arineuil, however great the temptation. I found the letter unspeakably funny, even as I rued the validity of Ineuil's prophecy of my notoriety.

Liya delighted in the ensuing plague of pleas for my company over the next few days, while I retired to the depths of Tyntagel Hall lest I actually encounter one of the prolific gallants. Liya chided me for my timidity, Ezirae speculated gleefully, and my father stared at me as if I had sprouted leaves. I personally suspected, despite my hesitation to put the matter to test, that my admirers would be universally disillusioned if any ever met me; even blessed by Lord Arineuil's tacit approval, ardor could not easily withstand the reality of a rather aloof and unremarkable young woman.

I held to my room and its window's view. I enjoyed the sun only in the inner courtyards. I withstood the sporadic company of Grisk by adopting the full measure of Tyntagellian puritanism, ensuring that we were never without chaperon. He accepted my prudery grudgingly, invariably recalling to me an afternoon with Lord Arineuil, but I gradually mitigated Grisk's suspicions of my deception by currying the belief that my refusal to emerge from Tyntagel Hall was due to my wish to avoid the scandalous lord of Ven. Neaped by events, I awaited the returning tide.

Chapter 5

Heat grows. The yellow crackle of a consuming energy snarls at my flesh. There is a spiderweb of light, and it is blue-hot and deadly. There is dark emptiness gaping where the fires clash. I am caught by the fire. It carries me, and it sears my mind. There is only fire, and I am lost.

My nights were uneasy. The dreams which the abbey had partially stilled were returned to me in their fullest measure. I awoke in the night too frightened to scream. I felt my arms, expecting to find the skin shriveled and hard. I opened my eyes to test the world, and I lay motionless in the fragile relief from horror, counting heart's beats of peace and normalcy.

My eyes traveled the white-walled room, clung to the heavy gold drapes, and slid to the window relentlessly. There was no light by which to see the Tower. There had been no light in the Anxian tavern.

Day's glow took hold, and I lived in the world of my family: a Seriin lady of no obligations save duty to her liege. Liya had begun to love the social pattern, or at least she emulated the enjoyment of it well. She was ever with Yldana or Ezirae's gossipy friends. Dayn was seldom with his wife; he journeyed much on missions of which he would not speak. My father and uncle spent many hours locked in conference with messengers. Lord Brant joined them often, as did Amgor. There was a grim air to all these proceedings except when Yldana appeared. She would laugh and tease, and all their faces would brighten. Then she would flit to another party, another excursion, and Tyntagel Hall would become solemn again, save for Ezirae's chattering.

Grisk visited us too frequently for my taste, but he vanished on unspoken errands as often as did Dayn. My own days were so filled with the inconsequential essentials of my gender and class that I at times forgot that I had once escaped, lived another life and learned a darker history. Even glimpses of Ineuil (we had not spoken again) did not suffice to make real the Venture and that time of hardness. My memories seemed surreal, but when the dreams came in the night, I knew that I was entrapped.

It was inevitable that I would see him eventually: the Infortiare. One who lived in the King's castle must eventually encounter those others who shared that privilege. There would come some festive foolishness of my rank at which my nightmares would invade my saner life. I would meet him again and learn if I could bear his presence.

"Are you not the least bit excited, Rhianna?" asked Liya with such wistfulness that I regretted my inability to empathize with her enjoyment. Having been too young for formal presentation to King Astorn and Queen Alamai of Serii on her previous visit to Tulea, Liya's eagerness now was an obsession of anxiety. My own nerves tingled but not with delight.

"I shall be as pleased as anyone here to see Their Majesties arrive." We had been waiting for over an hour, standing uncomfortably motionless in tightly molded shoes, endeavoring to maintain the requisite illusion of perfection. Though I had been interested when we arrived, now I merely chafed to see the discomforts of protocol ended. I twisted my head very slightly, just enough to see the line of other newcomers to King Astorn's court. One young boy fidgeted cautiously; several pairs of shoulders had sagged from their earlier upright postures.

A large and plump man with black eyes and pasty complexion waddled into view from the curtained recess behind the dais. A steward loudly announced the man's name: Lord Borgor dur Sandoral, Adjutant to His Majesty, King Astorn. The husband of the elusive Lady Veiga ambled gracelessly past the line awaiting presentation. I had expected a more prepossessing figure for the Lady Veiga's husband, but Liin's arrogance had an obvious price; Liin's elitism made selectivity difficult. Lord Borgor paused once, briefly inspecting a blushing Liya, and took a seat near the edge of the dais. A taboret similiar to Lord Borgor's remained empty; it was placed on the opposite side of the royal dais, slightly higher than that of the Adjutant.

We waited several minutes more before the symbolic clash of stone against silver heralded the royal family of Serii. King Astorn and Queen Alamai grandly preceded their children, the heirs following in order of rank. Prince Orlin, a tall, handsome boy who greatly favored his father, beamed with the confidence of his assured place as future ruler of a vast and prosperous kingdom. The Princess Joli, who followed Prince Orlin, marred the procession's dignity with an innocent stumble. The princess recovered quickly but her lapse sent her four young sisters into a fit of muffled snickers and giggles; the Princesses Henzela, Alza, Phoebe and Leytia lost their composure to such an extent that Queen Alamai gestured peremptorily, and a gray-haired governess ushered the four youngest children from the room.

The King and Queen of Serii made an attractive couple, impressive in their costly finery, but I could not deny feeling a hint of disappointment. By the time the royal pair had progressed down the line of their subjects to me, the lovely Queen Alamai's attention had obviously tired of the whole proceedings; she contemplated an emerald which her fine finger hefted awkwardly. King Astorn greeted each individual with a remarkable cordiality, but I could not honestly assess him as a forceful or particularly intelligent man. I dropped a curtsy of respect, recalling even as I did the concern Ineuil had expressed over the present state of Seriin authority.

I could feel no more sanguine over the prospect of Serii's royal heirs. Prince Orlin looked the part of a regal scion with his wavy brown hair and gold-flecked eyes, but I thought my own brothers displayed more signs of the leader's gift than he. I watched as the prince waited petulantly for a servitor to adjust the royal chair to a new position. The four youngest daughters were not so young that they should have abandoned discipline for so slight and unworthy a cause as their sister's distress. Princess Joli glared sullenly throughout the remainder of the proceedings, disfiguring herself far more severely than did the scarlet birthmark which crossed her face. Only Princess Joli lacked the perfection of royal features, and her attitude was devoid of the most marginal civility; it disheartened me that her truculence provided the only evidence of spirit among the royal lot.

The King and Queen of Serii, flanked by their eldest children, took their places on the dais. Lord Borgor offered some preliminary paeans to the heirs of Tul. King Astorn spoke some inconsequential words of welcome, which apparently held his audience enthralled. My own attention was diverted as a tall, spare figure appeared from the recess through which the royal family had emerged. King Astorn himself glanced distractedly at the newcomer, aborted his speech with an absent wave, and yielded the proceedings to Lord Borgor.

I never heard Lord Borgor's speech. Lord Venkarel departed after only a moment of converse with the king, but he remained in my thoughts throughout the rest of the ceremony. The emblem of his office had hung from the fine gold chain around his neck, the gold starkly prominent against the formal black silk of the Infortiare. The man was so familiar to me that I could bring memories from his past into my mind, but the Infortiare of Serii stirred awed humility in me, as my King did not. I saw the clear ice of well-remembered eyes, but Lord Venkarel did not look beyond the royal dais.

I stood as one entranced through the exit of the royal family. Liya nudged me urgently, else I would not have filed out as required. She fortunately mistook my abstraction for deep emotion at my presentation to the king. When we had escaped the King's Hall, she linked her arm in mine as if we were sisters in truth. She gave me the silence for contemplation I wished, and I mentally applauded my brother's choice of bride.

Dayn and Ezirae met us upon our return to Tyntagel Hall. Dayn frowned slightly at sight of his wife's friendliness toward me, but Liya ran to him gaily and his expression cleared. Ezirae burst forth with questions, asking about every detail of pomp and attire. Her own life had been spent almost exclusively at the king's court, yet she never tired of further stories.

"Then His Majesty suddenly stopped speaking," recounted Liya, "and Lord Borgor continued, while King Astorn conversed with the tall man in private."

"Lord Venkarel," asserted Ezirae, bobbing her head up and down decisively.

"The Infortiare," breathed Liya. "Do you really think it was he? Imagine, Rhianna, the King and the Infortiare could have been deciding the fate of Serii as we watched."

"Lord Venkarel had no business interrupting His Majesty," mumbled Dayn.

Sensitive to her husband's mood, Liya swerved to a less controversial topic. "Now that we have been presented, Rhianna, we are eligible to attend the royal ball next week. Shall I wear the pink satin, Dayn, with the Bethiin pearls you gave me? Or does the pink make me look too childish?" Dayn touched his wife's hair fondly, and I retreated, glad to escape.

There were plots and counterplots around us. A man who could destroy Tulea with a thought lived among us, and he had deadly enemies. I wondered how many of the bright courtiers around me recognized the falseness of court life, how many believed it; how many merely played the game. Certainly the promise of a royal ball featured prominently in every conversation I heard for a week of days.

Most of the castle's inhabitants had been planning for the king's ball for several weeks, and Liya seemed determined to compensate for lost time by going into a whirlwind of preparation. My influx of cards and missives began to include pleas for dances, as well as requests for more substantial favors; the line of court gossip still celebrated me unreasonably. From Ineuil I received no word; after plunging me into the role of fashionable desirability, my notorious acquaintance had remained conspicuously absent.

Tyntagel Hall seethed with such frenzied activity that I took to escaping the social madness at dawn, exploring the castle gardens from rill to rocky peak in glorious solitude. The enjoyment which I derived from those stolen hours mingled with an ache for the rapport I had felt with my Tyntagel woodlands. I could hear the trees as clearly as I had ever been able to do but they would not welcome me freely. More than mere strangeness of unknown gardens, I suspected the cause stemmed from the changes I had undergone in the maze of the Taormin. I had lost the easy intimacy with the wild which had long been my solace, and the realization hurt me. I added to my list another claim against the Infortiare of Serii.

I climbed through a tangle of undergrowth, which betrayed the disuse of the path I trod, and found myself again at the waterfall glade to which Ineuil had brought me by a more orthodox route. Around the bole of a white pine were wrapped the arms of a spindly-limbed girl weeping heavily into the mossy bark. On the verge of retreat, I saw her push away from the tree and beat against it blindly. She lifted her face, and the violent stain of the birthmark from cheek to chin confirmed her identity. "Stupid tree," she cried, "you probably hate me too."

I hesitated, torn by her despair, and the young princess saw me. She scrambled to her feet, shouting imperiously, "How dare you spy on me? I shall order you thrown into the castle dungeons." She stood even shorter than I did. Her eyes red with tears and with a twig dangling from her chaotic brown hair, she could not achieve a very intimidating pose, despite the blazoned emblem of Tul upon her wrinkled frock.

"Forgive me, Your Royal Highness," I answered solemnly. "I did not mean to interrupt you. I came to speak with my friend."

"Is someone else coming?" shouted the princess wildly.

Tentatively, I tried to soothe her as if she were a trapped bird or a frightened flower. Aloud, I answered as reassuringly as I could, "It seems most unlikely, Your Royal Highness. The friend to whom I referred is the pine beside you. He really is a fine, stout fellow, though he does tend to be a trifle stuffy and self-important at times. He certainly does not hate you."

The disheveled Princess Joli regarded me suspiciously. "How would you know?" she asked. At least she did not again threaten me with imprisonment in a dungeon which did not exist.

"I asked him," I returned calmly. "He sorrows for you and would comfort you more if you would accept him."

She sniffed contemptuously. "I suppose you think I am stupid because I am ugly. Do you know who I am?"

"You are the Princess Joli an Astorn yn Alamai dur Tulea y Serii. I consider Your Royal Highness to be neither ugly nor stupid."

"You are a liar. Everyone knows about the stupid, ugly Princess Joli. I shame my family. Princesses ought to be beautiful. My sisters are beautiful: even Leytia, who is only seven, and my brother is handsome. I am the misfit. I am also impossible."

"Then we have much in common, Your Royal Highness. I also have a very beautiful sister, and my two brothers are quite handsome. I am generally considered to be entirely impossible."

Princess Joli dropped to the ground ungracefully. "Are you impossible?"

"I never thought so."

"I am," she declared proudly. "I never do anything I am told, and I never see anyone I dislike."

"Does not constant rebellion grow rather tiresome, Your Royal Highness?"

"If you try to lecture me, I shall banish you. Why do they think you are impossible?"

"I tend to talk to trees. It is considered an unsuitable pastime."

Wide eyes of amber peered at me intently. "Are you a wizardess?" demanded Princess Joli.

"No, Your Royal Highness." I equivocated. "My mother was a sorceress of Alvenhame, and I inherited a few small skills from her."

"I thought all Tyntagellians disapproved of sorcery." She congratulated herself with a smile, saying, "You thought I did not recognize you. You are the Lady Rhianna dur Tyntagel, and you were presented to me last week. You are going to marry Lord Grisk dur Niveal, though the betrothal has not yet been formalized. Servants know everything that happens in the castle, and I can hear everything from my room if I hold my ear against the wall in just the right place. You also had a scandalous rendezvous with Lord Arineuil. What is the pine saying now?"

"He is pleased to see you smile," I answered, disconcerted by the princess' rendition of my life.

"Can you understand any tree?"

"I have not found an exception as yet."

She rose with exuberant alacrity, grabbed my hand, and began to pull me with her. "You will tell me what all the trees in the park are thinking, or I shall tell everyone that you are a sorceress."

"Your Royal Highness, the park contains a great many trees," I protested, astonished by the princess' transformation of mood.

She considered, absently prying the twig free of her tangled hair.

"We shall start with the special ones. What is that one thinking?" She pointed to a gnarled spruce.

"She thinks you are an outrageous imp."

Princess Joli gave me a scathing look. "It is no good at all unless you tell me the truth."

"The spruce revels in your joy; it is a tonic to her weathered soul. I think you are an outrageous imp."

Princess Joli gleamed, and her elation did fill the trees as surely as had her earlier depression. She drew me in an undignified run from tree to tree of the garden's less frequented regions, and we stopped only when the encroaching afternoon sun wilted even Princess Joli's enthusiastic energy. She said no good-bye but threw her arms around me, then dashed away in an unladylike scramble. She stopped for just a moment and called back to me, "I really never meant to banish you or anything like that." She disappeared into the royal enclave. I shook my head, exhausted but oddly charmed by the princess with a capacity for trouble worthy of an army of pestilent demons. I did not mention my morning excursion to my family. Though my tardy return elicited some initial questions, the more enticing subject of the incipient ball maintained its sway and spared me.

Chapter 6

I finally achieved the grudging approval of Mistress Tamar, though the accolades of Liya tended to accord the credit to Tamar's artistic touch. In sapphire sea-silk and silver, I felt foolishly self-pleased by a reflection almost as fair as the imaginary subject of Lord Joret's fanciful prose. I actually partook of sufficient eagerness to satisfy Liya's impatient anticipation of the ball, as we awaited Ezirae in my room.

"What a lovely pendant, Rhianna!" said Ezirae, appearing at last as Tamar adjusted about my neck the chain on which I had hung the Lady Varina's gift.

"It is lovely," said Liya, herself exquisite in rose silk and gold lace. "What is it, Rhianna? I think I have never seen such a stone before."

The stone, my sole contribution to my attire, did seem to glow more brightly than I had remembered. It recalled the stars of Nimal's crafting. I began to regret my impulsive choice of jewelry, despite its loveliness. "I really have no idea what it is," I answered vaguely. "I have had it for some time. We ought to go downstairs before father sends a search party for us."

We were very late, and the men of the household had begun a predictable discussion of our lack of punctuality. Lord Grisk had arrived; the widening of his eyes as he beheld me disturbed me, though it did in some measure please my vanity. I had not expected his escort to begin at Tyntagel Hall, and my hopes of eluding him in the crush of the ball vanished. I accepted his arm grudgingly. Liya refused to look at him; she clung determinedly to Dayn.

Painfully self-conscious, I approached the royal ballroom with Grisk still at my side. Before we had even left the arched entry to the King's Hall, Lord Brant met us, along with Grisk's brother, Egar, a brusque and bearded bear who towed along a timid wife. My father greeted the Niveallans with a hearty clasp of arms.

I distrusted this gathering of Niveal, an atavistic fear of conspiring predators rising within me. My distress mounted when Liya wheedled Dayn away to the ballroom proper, and Ezirae deserted us for a clutch of her Hamley cousins.

Amgor came to us through the crowd of gilded celebrants, his black hair sleek and his waistcoat scarlet satin. "My Lord Baerod," he said tensely, giving me no notice, "Master Ruy has been awaiting your arrival."

"Then direct him to us, Amgor," ordered my father impatiently. Tyntagel's ruling lord presented an imposing air in his finery, and the chronically nervous Amgor shuffled his finely shod feet. "Lords of Serii do not dance attendance on Caruillan message-boys," added my father with ill humor.

"Arku Ruy represents King Cor himself, Baerod," interposed Lord Brant. "We do not want to offend him by arguing points of etiquette."

"The man assumes too much," retorted my father, tapping his fingers together ominously.

"He is less presumptuous—and far more palatable—than that common villain, Venkarel," growled Grisk, gaining nods from his kin and from my uncle. Amgor glanced guiltily about the room and its indifferent throngs.

A lovely vision in amber tissue floated over to us with chiding words. "My incorrigible father," said Yldana, "you are corrupting my husband by working him at a royal gala. I will not have it."

Amgor gazed at his wife pitiably. His shy uncertainty toward the woman he had wed reduced the lord of Amlach to a figure of ridiculous weakness. I saw Amgor's desperate expression when Ineuil joined us. Amgor was a handsome man, but his wife overshadowed him and made him insignificant. Ineuil was rare, for he held his own share of attention, complemented by my sister and enhancing her. Ineuil placed his arm around Yldana's waist quite naturally, and he beamed innocently at Amgor. "You are a sly man, Amgor, to have captured this woman before the rest of us could come to our senses from shock at her beauty and charm. And you, Grisk, appear determined to repeat the crime against those of us less quick to act. Lady Rhianna, you do look exceptionally lovely this evening."

"You are most gracious, my lord," I answered with an effort at proper sobriety. My father was frowning intensely, and Ineuil's bland indifference amused me disproportionately.

"It is amazing, is it not," purred Yldana, "How a few formal trappings can transform even the plainest of women? Your maid, Rhianna, truly has worked wonders today."

"She spent long enough at it," grumbled Dhavod, for Ezirae had embellished the account of my preparations so as to excuse her own tardiness.

"I find the merit of frills and furbelows seriously overrated," answered Ineuil with overly emphatic solemnity. "A beautiful woman shines in any setting—to the eye of a connoisseur."

"It is good to know that the lord of Ven had honed his skills in some respect," said Lord Brant with little grace.

"Lord Arineuil certainly strives to ensure an ampleness of experience," sneered Grisk.

"Even irresponsible fools must occupy themselves somehow," added my father with a contemptuous stare which would have withered most men. Ineuil smiled broadly and brought my hand to his lips, his other arm still around Yldana.

"So long as Lord Arineuil does not occupy himself with my future wife," warned Grisk, jerking me ungently away from Ineuil.

Yldana interrupted with ominously oozing sweetness. "Why Rhianna, how *very* naughty of you not to have told me. I am so pleased for you. And I must commend you as well, Grisk. Have you begun the wedding plans, father? You *will* let me help? I can *hardly* wait to tell simply everyone that my own little sister is going to marry the handsome Lord Grisk dur Niveal. Rhianna, you should be proclaiming the wonderful news to all of Tulea instead of standing here with these gloomy folk." Yldana clucked and cast lidded glances at our father and Lord Brant, inviting them to join her cheerful censure. "I, at least, shall see to it that the news is spread sufficiently to forestall unwelcome interruptions of the two of you tonight. I am hopelessly jealous, Rhianna, and my dear Amgor is too devoted to his other duties to be able to comfort me." Amgor essayed a denial, but Yldana waved away his protestations. "It is quite all right, Amgor. I understand that Amlach and Serii must take precedence over your silly wife's fancies. I am sure that Lord Arineuil will take pity on a poor, respectable matron and accompany her in a waltz."

Ineuil had been watching me with peculiar abstraction, but he answered Yldana quickly and brightly. "If the other matrons of Serii looked like you, Yldana, the incidents of marital infidelity would diminish by half. Or perhaps they would double. It rather depends on one's perspective. You have considerable experience in infidelity, Grisk. What do you think?"

Grisk had begun to seethe anew, but a look from his father stopped his nearly violent response. "The opinion of a dandy who can forget his family's murder does not merit notice, Grisk," stated Lord Brant with contempt.

Ineuil's facile grin hardened, but he spoke almost merrily. "You would have me call out the Infortiare? A fascinating notion, Lord Brant. If I won, I should hang for treason. But why should I allow that eventuality to concern me, since I assuredly would not win?"

"There is such a thing as family honor," pronounced my father coldly.

Ineuil's arm tightened around Yldana. I marveled anew at my sister's infallible ability to avoid censure; had I stood as near Ineuil as she did before our father's face, I would have paid for the impropriety for many months. Ineuil murmured, "I am sorry to disappoint you, gentlemen, but suicide holds no appeal for me. If the matter of Ven's honor concerns you so deeply, I should be delighted to relinquish the privilege of vengeance to you."

"Please excuse us, Lord Baerod," said Grisk, ignoring Ineuil with an effort. "Rhianna will dance with me now."

My father and Lord Brant nodded in joint approval, stiffly disregarding Ineuil's taunt as deliberately as Grisk had. Ineuil shrugged, grinned at me crookedly, and took Yldana's arm to lead her to the floor of the ballroom. I followed unwillingly with Lord Grisk.

I did thereafter achieve better opportunity to observe the king's ballroom than I had in the press at the entrance. Tiered crystal crowns of candles hung from a high vaulted ceiling set with golden mosaic, and the walls mirrored the flames to infinity. The gilded royal dais loomed dimly at the far end of the polished floor of ebony-dark marble. A colonnade of alabaster lined the length of the hall; beyond it the moon glinted on fountains of diamond and light. The patrons of the gala clustered and whirled like bright butterflies.

That which had appeared to be a chaotic throng displayed on closer inspection the full, segregated structure of Seriin snobberies and suballiances. No First House member associated with the lesser ranks of nobles, and the Houses of Liin and Sandoral were gathered nearest to the royal family. I could see Lord Borgor speaking to Queen Alamai. A beautiful titian-haired woman laughed with King Astorn. Better matched to the king than to the plain and portly Borgor, the woman fulfilled Ezirae's most glowing descriptions of the Lady Veiga dur Liin duri Sandoral. Another man joined them, and his chilling resemblance to Lord Hrgh snatched at my throat in a constricting grasp. Then I realized that the man was Hrgh's brother, Lord Gorng Dolr'han, heir to Liin since Lord Hrgh's abdication.

My father stood glumly sour, arrogantly upright. He defied the general gaiety to affect him or those he ruled; Grisk at least spared me that sorry company. I later saw my father sequestered in a curtained alcove with Brant, Amgor and an oily little man in barbaric garb whom I took to be Arku Ruy of Caruil. I only glimpsed them, but the Caruillan unsettled me; I realized that he exuded a low aura of sorcerous Power. On consideration, the revelation was not extraordinary. Minor sorcerers were not so very uncommon. I watched the man, however, as best I could without revealing my interest to Grisk, and I regretted my inability to hear the conversation which transpired in the alcove. After a few minutes a pass of the dance revealed the alcove empty. Arku Ruy and the representatives of my extended family had left, and I did not espy any of them again that evening.

I was left with the inauspicious prospect of an entire evening of Grisk's dismal anecdotes and crude innuendo. I glimpsed Liya and Dayn occasionally, but they were completely engrossed in one another. Arm firmly entwined with Ineuil's, Yldana apparently fulfilled her intent to dispense news of my supposed betrothal, discouraging any possible savior. I saw her whisper confidingly to many; those few who missed or disregarded the warning drew no nearer than the reach of Grisk's threatening glare.

After more than an hour of incessant dancing, I began to despair that Lord Grisk would ever release me. I had lost any hope in the courage of my supposedly enamored swains. Ineuil had not again approached; Yldana occupied his full interest. Grisk persistently drew me closer, and the reek of stale liquor banished any lingering illusion of Niveallan gentility. I bore his touch by a mental withdrawal which left him partnered with a witless mannequin. My inattention passed unnoticed amid his tales of hunting's bloody fervor, with which recounted escapades he apparently thought to impress me.

I actually sighed aloud with relief when Grisk edged me toward the colonnade and freed me from the dance. I paid little heed to where he led me, glad only to escape from the noise and chaos inside, until we reached an untenanted portico near the rugged bones of Tul mountain, which the castle abutted. The enclosed passage from the king's castle to Ceallagh's Tower gaped and shimmered at the end of the walkway we trod.

I mustered my voice with difficulty. "I think we ought to return to the ballroom, my Lord Grisk. This is not a fit place for light conversation." I could feel the power of the Tower's shielded entry, and I could feel the greater Power beyond it. I blinked rapidly; tongues of fire crossed my vision.

"It is not for conversation that I brought you here, Rhianna," sneered Grisk. "As we are to be married, it is fitting that you learn to please me. I have given you the mincing dances you women enjoy. Now the night is mine to dictate."

I pulled my eyes from the Tower entrance to this new danger. "I am not yours to command, Grisk," I answered hotly.

"You must learn first to drop these pretenses, Rhianna. You are not so innocent as to have withheld your favors from Arineuil."

"You are an unbelievable fool, Grisk," I said in disgust.

Grisk gripped me, and he was strong. I tried to pull away; he shook me viciously. I clenched my teeth, but with each jarring impact, the sight of Grisk's unwholesome gloat mingled more ineluctably with my fiery nightmares. The scream I tried to suppress tore with fire from my mind.

Chapter 7

Varina's stone throbbed achingly cool against my breast. Ten paces from where I stood, Lord Grisk struggled to rise from the tiled flooring. A lengthy shadow stretched across him.

Grisk cursed profusely; blood trickled from his mouth. His most civilized words amounted to, "Bastard son of a whore—Venkarel, you will regret this."

"You are scarcely in a position to cast either threats or aspersions, Lord Grisk. You have intruded upon His Majesty's private quarters." The precise voice of the Infortiare, my erstwhile Venture Leader, rang scornfully against the cold stone.

Grisk regained his feet inelegantly. He tugged his coat into sorry order; it had been ripped in his fall. He glared. "Come with me, Rhianna," he demanded with confident disdain.

"Lady Rhianna will remain," countered Lord Venkarel calmly.

Grisk snarled, "Do you expect me to leave my betrothed wife with *you?*"

Musingly, Lord Venkarel said, "You really are a detestable slug, Grisk. I strongly recommend that you leave my sight before my regret at sparing you mounts further."

Fear wrestled visibly with arrogance, and Grisk wisely reconsidered the danger of arguing with the Infortiare. The Infortiare began to walk toward the lord of Niveal; Grisk scurried into the dark without another glance at me, running with panic's haste not to the ballroom but into the shadowy gardens. I closed my eyes to stifle the nausea roiling within me.

When my eyes reopened, the view I faced had drastically altered. Before me curved a wall: the lower half was paneled in polished burl, the upper portion paned in exceptionally clear glass, beyond which the dark expanse of Tulea spread a flickering tapestry to the lower valleys and the sea beyond. To my left and slightly downward, the castle shone with candle glow, and the lilt of distant music could be heard. It occurred to me that I was developing a habit of leaving court functions abruptly. I shifted in the chair of well-worn fleece.

The wall opposite the windows stretched straight between a pair of heavy wooden doors. Books lined the wall entirely; as the room was large, the number of volumes was considerable, and many were fragile tomes of great antiquity. What furniture the room boasted showed the craftsmanship of quality worn smooth and haggard through an age of usage. Motley manuscripts, maps and missives were strewn on every desk and table and on every chair save two.

The chair which my Lord Venkarel occupied appeared to have once matched the one in which I sat, but a haphazard application of velvet to its upholstered parts had defaced it. The sorry chairs struck me as inordinately mundane and unimpressive attributes to Ceallagh's Tower. History surrounded me, but it was tired.

"Do you often dissuade unwelcome suitors by attempting murder, Lady Rhianna?' asked Kaedric sardonically. Legs stretched before him, he lounged at ease, as remote as he had been in the Anxian tavern.

"I attempted nothing of the sort," I protested indignantly. My head wanted to crack into a score of splinters.

"You not only attempted it, you very nearly succeeded." Blue eyes narrowed. "I expected the wretched Grisk to attribute the attack to me, but you should be capable of distinguishing your own handiwork."

"Thank you for your intervention," I murmured ungraciously, belatedly adding, "my lord." I had forgotten how coldly he attacked, whether with Power or word. The Taormin had distorted my perspective, giving me memories of the child's vulnerability, which the man had destroyed. I wished desperately that my head would clear and that Kaedric would not badger me. I had felt such a compulsion to seek him. I knew the gladness of achieving the necessary, but I could not recollect the questions which had seemed so vital. I pressed my fingers to my temples. "Why did you stop me?"

"I could hardly allow you to fling Power indiscriminately on His Majesty's doorstep, though curtailing a lovers' quarrel is a novel application of the Infortiare's authority." A trifle less harshly, he added, "I also rather suspected that you did not intend to kill."

"How should I have thought to intend the impossible?" I asked bitterly.

Kaedric considered me over tented fingers. "You blame me for the destructive turn of your Power. I seem to recall warning you repeatedly against my company for fear that something of the sort would occur. Since you patently disregarded my advice, I cannot feel excessively guilty about your current plight."

I shook my head, too weary to spar. "My lord, I wish only to learn if the change can be reversed."

"Not by any method I know."

"Then I must live with the risk of destroying those around me at any moment?"

"I trust you have more sense than that. Power can be controlled by mental discipline; you must learn the techniques."

My senses had begun to return. I smoothed my sapphire skirts, shyly feeling again the wonder which had touched me at the royal presentation: this man was the legatee of Ceallagh, the Infortiare of Serii and every land in the Alliance. I had traveled with him for many leagues, but I had not known him then. Tardily, I assumed the formal deference due the Lord Venkarel dur Ixaxis. "My lord, I shall obey such commands as you see fit to give me." I lifted my eyes to his cool regard. "But my father would never permit me Ixaxin training."

"Tyntagel has yet to secede from Serii. As it happens, my lady, I outrank your father."

"My father has many allies, my lord, and he acquiesces easily to no one."

"I recognize Lord Baerod's influence, Lady Rhianna, but I think you know that I could counter it. However, I do not intend to press the lords of Serii for the sake of your education." Blue eyes flickered. "In point: you must learn sufficient safeguards of Power; such learning must transpire without your father's knowledge. I presume you intend to remain in Tulea with your affianced husband."

I did not bother to deny commitment to Grisk. "I shall remain in Tulea as long as cause exists."

"Then I shall teach you myself."

I stiffened, unsure of my reaction. I could exercise a certain freedom within the castle enclave, so the suggestion was reasonably practical. I argued weakly, "My lord, I am unworthy of your time." The lamp flared, and the windows revealed our reflections: a frightened lady in blue silk and silver, attired for a frivolous court occasion and not a wizard's study; the man of dark adamant who watched her. The lamp grew ordinary and dim; the world beyond the glass returned.

"My lady, you preserved my life," answered Kaedric with a grim smile. "It is a dubious honor but a singular one."

"I deserve no credit for the outcome, my lord. It was a reaction not of my planning."

"Whatever your intentions may have been, you did supply the necessary margin to counter Horlach for the nonce. Horlach has awakened now and is gathering forces from every corner of the Alliance and even stirring the old troubles with Caruil, but you prevented the war from ending with the first battle."

"There was a Caruillan named Arku Ruy at the ball," I said, embarrassed by thanks I did not merit. "He was a sorcerer, but my father met with him."

Kaedric cocked his head. The Infortiare's medallion gleamed. He studied me. "Arku Ruy's Power is insignificant, but he has mastered the rudiments of disguising it more effectively than most of his ilk. With some training, my lady, your empathic capabilities should make you a most efficient monitor."

"I am not so gifted at rapport as I once was, my lord," I answered with a careful dearth of emotion. I remembered with hurt the remoteness which had restricted my level of contact with the trees of the King's gardens.

"And I am more so. The Taormin seems to effect interesting exchanges. The polarities have shifted, while we have each gained in total Power. The ramifications would make a fascinating study." He elaborated dryly, "You surely realized that the 'contamination' was not one-sided." He paused, but I gave no response; the past had ensnared me.

"Keep the kid in your sight tonight, Pru. I have important customers coming who need my attention," warned the fat man. He pushed a very small boy at a youngish woman, insufficiently covered by a tawdry robe of yellow chintz.

"Do I look like a nanny to you, Doshk?" complained the woman peevishly.

"You work for me. You do as I say," shouted Doshk. "I paid for the boy, and I don't let go of what is mine. Which you'd best remember, Pru," he added significantly. The woman rolled her eyes at a stale but sincere threat. The boy watched the two adults from a cautious corner of the dingy room.

"I earn my way, Doshk," said the woman crossly, "And I can earn it in other quarters as well as yours." Doshk's florid features reddened, and Pru wisely recanted, "I'll keep him, but you'll pay me a full night for this, Doshk."

"Where's your charity, Pru?" sneered Doshk.

"In the sewer with yours, Doshk," snapped the woman. "You only want the boy because you couldn't have the mother."

"He'll bring good money in a few years," retorted Doshk.

"If he lives, and if he takes after Fylla. You're going head-soft, Doshk. He's a rotten risk."

"Shut up, you worthless slut," snarled Doshk. "You've not been bringing them in so fast lately. If the kid runs, it's from your pretty hide I'll take the price." He slammed the door behind him, and the thin walls shuddered.

Giving Doshk's back a rude gesture, Pru squatted inelegantly before the boy. "You won't give any trouble now, will you, Kaed?" she said assertively. "Because you'll be as sorry as your dead ma if you do." The child continued to stare blankly from his very blue eyes. Pru snorted, "You don't understand a word, do you? Well, at least you won't be telling stories about Pru's little vices." Pru withdrew a vial from her ample bodice and waved it before the child. "Doshk wouldn't much care to know I had this out of his own supply." She giggled ridiculously, as she contemplated her cleverness in stealing the drug. She reached for the boy's hand, and he pressed himself against the paint-peeled wall, unable to retreat further. Pru smiled. The boy relaxed, and Pru slapped him, grabbing him and shoving him into the room's tiny wardrobe. She locked the wardrobe door, thumped herself onto the lumpy mattress, and extracted the stopper from the vial.

The child in the closet cried very quietly.

I reached for the child who suffered, snatching back my hand as I recognized the man whom my hand had nearly touched. "We ought to begin your training immediately," said the Infortiare slowly, "But your thinking is muddled tonight. I suggest you avoid your enchanting Grisk for the moment. I shall expect you here in the morning." He rose abruptly and strode to the far door.

"My lord," I called, needing to detain him whom I wished I had never known. "My lord, I cannot command my time reliably," I whispered, a weak excuse for halting the Infortiare.

Kaedríc answered with acrid irony, "I shall trust your ingenuity to overcome the obstacles of a Seriin lady's burdensome existence."

Feeling ridiculous, I interrupted his exit once more. "My lord, might you direct my return to the castle before you leave?"

"First lesson, my Lady Rhianna," he said distinctly and dangerously. "It is better to pursue your instincts than to question a wizard over nonessentials. Take any path you like, so long as you do not enter *this* door." So saying, he closed the forbidden portal behind him with resounding emphasis.

"My Lord Venkarel, you are not a gentleman," I said to myself, contemplating the room in which I found myself alone, reluctant to depart. The room bore the blurred imprint of many owners, no one most dominant, as if the current tenant had kept his own personality carefully absent. I idly perused a few of the myriad documents which covered the furnishings beside me. Most bore the angular scratches of a hasty and purposeful hand. The languages varied, and unfamiliar symbols covered several sheaves.

I turned to the nearest door, that which Kaedric had obliquely recommended. I found behind it a descending stair; I was very near the Tower's summit. I closed the door carefully and gathered my skirts above my ankles.

Two levels down I found the passage to the king's halls. The moon still dusted the loggia, but moonlight's shadows had shifted with the hour. I bypassed the obvious exit, too appalled by the prospect of returning to the ball. Another five flights of stairs: a door opened onto the lower gardens.

From the castle rang the merry laughter and dizzy whirls of music. Against my heated pulse, the cacophony pounded imperiously. I heard each whisper of night wind, each breath of grass and leaf as if it were a raucous shout. I began to run, heedless of my fragile attire. I shadowed to reach my room unseen, bolted my door, and crumpled, shaking, against the flimsy barricade. I could not say what I feared just then: the force of Kaedric, the dark, impending fury of Horlach, or the fire in my own veins. I sobbed silently, weeping in huddled despair. I fell to sleep clenched in midnight's black solitude.

Chapter 8

The lesser gray of dawn roused me. My twisted muscles ached a peevish protest, and I stretched them painfully. A hound whined in the distance, but no other creature-sound marred the stillness. The revels of the royal ball had delayed the castle's morning.

The clear, cool light revived me, and cold water restored me to some coherence. I had survived my dreaded reunion with the Lord of Ixaxis, and he had offered me, in his dauntingly impersonal manner, an anchor of hope. I put aside my tears and my rumpled silks, donned a smock of coarse cotton, and slipped down the stairs. I hastened, for my family might well question me when they arose, and they could thereby curtail my freedom to depart. My Lord Venkarel had commanded me to return in the morning; I intended to comply.

I crossed the dew-decked lawns and climbed the wooded slopes below the Tower. I opened the gate in the low stone wall which encircled the Infortiare's residence, an obstacle which I had penetrated blindly during the night. The Tower seemed to rise unbroken from the hills, polished basalt etched unnaturally straight against velvet blue and lilac mountain shadows. I could not see the windows which encircled it, nor the portal through which I had left it. I closed my eyes and reached for the door, hoping my actions were not as absurd as they seemed. My hand met the latch; the door was unlocked. I grimaced and entered the smoothly paneled circular vestíbule.

I climbed the seven levels, wishing at about the third that Lord Venkarel had selected a lower floor for his study. Carved doors of intricate design hid the Tower's lower regions from view. Curiosity nearly bid me open one, though most displayed the dust of long disuse. I had been effectively granted permission the previous night, but I decided not to risk a needless offense.

The door to the study stood open. The daylight view sprawled spectacularly. Distance made orderly the teeming of Tulea's streets, and the circles and spokes of the city's planning showed clearly. To the west lay thick forests; the eastern slopes rippled in bands of ocher crags. The sea, rimmed by the cloudless sky, painted the distance dark and bright; inlets etched deep blue streaks. Intervening hills hid the nearer shores, but the isolated island of Ixaxis stood freely visible.

"From the standpoint of wizardry," greeted Kaedric without preamble, "three classes of elements exist: matter, energy and infinity. That which distinguishes wizards and sorcerers—the appellations are interchangeable for theoretical purposes—from the so-called mortals is the ability to manipulate energies as well as matter." He spoke from behind the most heavily laden desk, addressing me without raising his head from the documents before him. I whispered a sigh, recalling my legions of tutors. The latest was certainly the most daunting. "If a mortal wishes to access energy," he continued, "he must do so by material means; he strikes a flint to light a fire. A wizard handles the energy directly." The candle near his hand tossed sudden blue fire from its wick. "As the mortal uses energy, so the wizard can use infinity, but any form of indirect usage entails a degree of hazard concomitant with the magnitude of desired effect, making infinity a very intimidating tool. That is an oversimplification of a very intricate subject, but it should suffice to introduce you to Zerus." He stood and handed me a faded tome which I could barely heft. "Zerus covers the basic operations of action, conversion and commutation along with their properties and essential postulates. You may use Lord Amberle's desk: the enameled monstrosity beside the denuded plinth." He left me, withdrawing through the door I had entered, and the room felt of ghosts and not of life.

I toted the book to the indicated desk, an object of craft inordinately detailed and ghastly. It had been newly cleared; the dust drew imprints of the literary stacks now settled on the floor beside it. I brushed at the dust with my kerchief, which brightened the desk's designs but did not improve their character.

As morning strengthened into day, I studied alone in the Infortiare's library. It was my familiar life returned, and I cared little that I might be missed and less that Zerus' symbolisms and derivations seemed to offer minimal practical significance. It required no depth of wizards' lore to accept that action could affect a book or a table. That Lord Venkarel could spin fire from air appeared evident; if Master Zerus wished to call the operation "conversion" and name the result "commutation," I felt no inclination to quibble. It was more difficult to accept the mortal actions which impacted energy. The cited examples did not accord with any mortal effects I recognized, making the correlations to infinity's manipulation largely unreadable. I could, however, tolerate Master Zerus cheerfully, because he distracted me from a world quite as complex but all too real.

I returned to Tyntagel Hall just short of midday. I had assumed a substantial delay of normal activity after the night's festivities. My prediction proved well founded. I reached my room and changed to a luncheon gown before the chambermaid appeared. Yielding my room to her ministrations, I joined my family in the dining hall.

Only my Uncle Dhavod had preceded me. He greeted me solemnly, inquiring after my enjoyment of the ball with courteous disinterest. "It is perhaps unfortunate," he continued, "that the announcement of your engagement occurred so informally, but it does save considerable bother." He added more generously, "Though I suppose you women like that sort of fuss. I am sure your father will ensure you a substantial wedding ceremony. Ezirae can provide you with considerable advice on the subject. She personally supervised the weddings of each of our five daughters." I murmured a noncommittal response, having altogether forgotten Yldana's carefully fomented acknowledgment of my betrothal. My uncle and I sat in awkward silence until Liya joined us, her eyes as shiningly bright as her buttercup dress.

"Good morning, Lord Dhavod," said Liya cheerfully. "Good

morning, Rhianna. Is no one else to take luncheon? But of course," she recalled, dramatically clapping her hand to her brow, "Lord Baerod is with Dayn. It is so unfair that they should have to rise early after such a lovely evening. Will Lady Ezirae join us at least?"

"Ezirae is indisposed," contributed Dhavod stiltedly. "She will take her meals in her chamber."

"The poor dear," said Liya contritely, though I could not imagine why Liya should feel apologetic over Ezirae's condition, an infallible result of the Hamley tendency to overindulge. Lord Dhavod strongly disapproved of his wife's weakness, but he had never succeeded in curtailing her habit. The result was a tacitly acknowledged family secret known throughout Tulea's social enclave.

"Rhianna, I nearly forgot," bubbled Liya suddenly. "Yldana has invited us to join her afternoon gatherings. All of her closest friends attend, even the Lady Veiga duri Sandoral. It is quite a social honor. We would have told you last night, but we could not find you." Liya's sentence trailed uncertainly at the end. More firmly, she added, "We could attend in Amlach Hall this very day. You will come?"

I looked at Liya's eager face, hating to disappoint her, but the thought of enduring Yldana's taunts weighed more heavily. "Perhaps tomorrow I shall feel more ready for witty converse," I temporized. "The excitement of the ball has quite fatigued me. Indeed, I think I shall retire to my room as soon as luncheon ends. Do you mind very much, Liya?"

She did, but she answered bravely, "Certainly not."

"You might go yourself," I tried.

"Nonsense. Court society will just have to await us a little longer."

Feeling wretchedly guilty for my lie to Liya, I locked my chamber door and left Tyntagel Hall for Ceallagh's Tower by the window of my room and a helpful elm outside it. I had stubbornly determined to master the text which Kaedric had given me, however useless its contents might seem, and my luncheon had been only an impatient interlude. I did not know how to study by half measures.

I blithely intended to regain the mood of secure unreality which had warmly enwrapped my morning, but the door to the Infortiare's study was firmly closed. I could feel Kaedric's Power beyond it, and I knocked tentatively, regretting my haste in returning. I found the Infortiare again at his desk, inspecting a document on which the ostentatious seal of Caruil showed prominently. "Your devotion to study is laudable," he remarked and continued working.

I moved slowly to the desk he had allotted to me. I opened the text of Master Zerus carefully. It was essentially a mathematical treatise, fine for distracting mind-games but insufficient to compete with the intense occupant of the room. Head bowed over the vellum on which he wrote, Kaedric frowned and impatiently brushed an errant black lock from his eyes. Memory taxed me remorselessly. I concentrated on Zerus' postulates. The page blurred; I reread it, achieving no greater understanding the second time or the third. I pressed my nails into my hands, cutting the skin. The freezing winds of Ven intensified the hurt.

"I don't pay you boys to loll," said the fat man, lending emphasis to his words with a kick at the nearest of the three children. The boys quickened their strokes, chopping the wood for the inn with frenzied energy. The innkeeper was fat and lazy but strong and quick with a blade, and the boys feared him utterly. They knew by the reek of the man's filthy tunic that he watched them still, though they dared not face him. After a critical moment, the man moved inside to escape the bitter cold.

"You don't pay us at all," muttered one boy, taller and broader than the other two. He dropped the axe into the snow with disgust. "But you'll pay me one day, Master Doshk, or greet the Ven-Lord's gallows."

"You do talk grand, Deev," mocked the red-haired boy beside him. "Are you going to tell your story to the constable personal? Or maybe you're minded to talk to the Ven-Lord himself? He'd be mighty pleased to talk with a flea-wracked piece like you."

Deev snorted and gestured rudely. "There's plenty who'd like a glimpse at Doshk's private larder."

"And I suppose Doshk is going to tell you where it is because he likes you so much," said the red-haired boy. Only the third boy, black-haired and thin to emaciation, continued to work.

"Maybe Doshk doesn't have to tell me," said Deev mysteriously. The redhead leaped at Deev and grappled for the larger boy's throat. "You slimy beggar, if you know where it is, you'll tell me or wish you had." The redhead tightened his fingers around Deev's neck.

"All right," croaked Deev. The redhead eased his grip slightly, and Deev struck hard. The red-haired boy doubled in anguish. Deev kicked him, an unconscious imitation of Master Doshk.

"You little nothing, Ag. I'd as soon tell garbage boy there." Deev threw a heavy piece of kindling at the black-haired boy, who ducked it indifferently and persisted in hewing the wood.

The wayward stick struck a burly man just entering the inn. Cursing, he spotted the three boys at the woodpile. Deev and Ag ran behind the inn, shoving the black-haired boy to the snow in the process. The stick's angry victim grabbed the fallen boy and beat him into unconsciousness.

The impact of snow thrown into his face and a rough nudge brought the black-haired boy to his feet in practiced haste. Arms akimbo, the blubbery Doshk glared at the boy. "You're a worthless brat," said Doshk disgustedly. "I'd give you to a Caruillan slaver for an iron kesne. Your mother knew what she was about when she sold you, you lazy runt. Get back to work." Doshk hit the boy hard with the flat of a hefty knife.

Moving stiffly, the boy regained the axe he had dropped. Deev and Ag were making a great show of effort for Doshk's benefit. The black-haired boy winced as he resumed his labor; the angry man had cracked three of his ribs.

"What's the matter, Kaed?" sneered Deev, after Doshk had left. "Don't you like honest work?"

"That sailor who came today isn't going to admire those bruises, Kaed," said Ag. "You'd better cover them by tonight, or Doshk will cook you for sure."

"That's right, Kaed. You know how Doshk likes to satisfy his paying customers, and you've not been too popular anyhow since you shivved old Brodae."

The black-haired boy did not answer. He raised the axe and brought it down on the log with vicious deliberation. His blue eyes burned.

The snatch of vision hurt and embarrassed me. I suffered very personally for the boy, Kaed, but I could not equate him with the

Ixaxin liege who stared at me so arrogantly. "You are not going to master the laws of wizardry by watching me, Lady Rhianna," said Kaedric coldly.

"No, my lord. With your permission, my lord, I shall take my leave now."

"That was a remarkably short lesson."

"I have recalled a conflicting appointment."

Kaedric knew that I lied, but he waved his arm indifferently. I closed Zerus' text firmly. It would beckon me again, but escape comprised my present need. Memory's flood rebuilds old sorrow if the memory is sharp and anguished; if the memory comes newly to the mind, it has no cushion of familiarity to soften its pain. For now, I could not hold myself free of Kaed so long as Kaedric faced me. Whether it was my mood or simply fatigue, it was inexorable. A sharp rap on the door made me jump.

"Your taste in company has certainly improved, Kaedric," announced Ineuil grandly. He bowed to me, his fair hair gleaming. "Lady Rhianna, I assumed you had forsaken the realm of sorcery in favor of a more traditional role as lady of Niveal." Ineuil intoned the title with the pomposity of Lord Borgor. "You have heard, O Great Infortiare, that our fair sorceress is to be the next bride of that infamous paragon, Lord Grisk?"

Kaedric had raised his head. He fingered a slim red leather volume lettered in faded gold. He answered, "If that is all you came to tell me, Lord Arineuil, you may return the way you came."

"It is not, but I thought the tidbit interesting." Ineuil considered me thoughtfully. "I should not personally have considered Grisk a likely choice for any sorceress."

"I must be going," I murmured swiftly, still eager to escape Kaedric, more eager now to escape Ineuil's scrutiny and the chance that he would discover my infernal binding to the Infortiare. Neither man stopped me.

I did not at once return to Tyntagel Hall. I sought the garden corner farthest removed from the Tower of the Infortiare, hoping to discover some measure of the tranquility that had once been mine with my Tyntagel oaks. The touch of tree and earth did soothe me, but it could not erase the truth of what I had seen.

I could not escape my own mind, and there was a canker in it. Whether I faced the Infortiare or fled to far Ardasia, his Power

would taunt me; the memories which had twisted him would follow me. The fractured images of a life not mine would continue to
coalesce, filling me, until I should be in memory's darkness the
murderer of Ven.

Selfishly and fervently, I rued the creation of the Taormin in that
hour. I hated the Sorcerer King Horlach quite personally with a
recognition of the wrong his tool had inflicted upon me. I rubbed
Varina's stone and hated the pain he had given that lady's world. I
thought of Hamar and Lord Hrgh Dolr'han and the miserable
dead-alive creatures who still guarded the castle of their ancient
tormentor: victims, along with many others whose names in the
history tomes had never greatly affected me. I railed against fate's
instruments: Lord Brant, Lord Grisk, and my liege-father who had
driven me to a desperate decision in a tavern in Anx. Perhaps I was
unjustly bitter, but I was growing to doubt my ability to survive
Kaedric's resurging past.

By eventide, I had grown calmer. I could not alter that which
had been done; anger bought me nothing. My father had not sent
me to Anx. Lord Grisk had not forced me to a mad attempt at healing the Infortiare of Serii. If any cure for my sorcerous ailment
could be derived, it was the Infortiare who must lead me to it. I
would return to Zerus, because the alternative was madness.

Chapter 9

My days assumed a pattern, and the mastery of the wizardry I had previously shunned grew to occupy my mind if not my heart. I had become slightly less apprehensive around Kaedric, for I had experienced no recurrence of involuntary, empathic memory. In truth, I saw him seldom, considering how many hours I spent in his library; the king and the cares of Serii occupied him, taking him beyond the Tower confines. Never did he fail, however, to antici-pate my need for further materials to study.

History lessons had joined the theoretical material, and the his-tory taught by Ixaxis did not always agree with the legends I had learned in Tyntagel. The practice of wizardry I still regarded with ambivalence, but I could no longer question the superiority of Ix-axin scholarship. Their histories, their philosophies formed cohe-sive wholes. Most important, Ixaxis remembered.

I had mastered the symbolic machinations of Zerus by forcing my mind along new pathways of thought and perception. After several texts of a similar nature, the strange mode of thought which they promoted no longer seemed so unnatural, but I tried to curtail its intrusion into my other life. My mind kept a precarious balance. Even my vaguely projected wedding, which only I con-sidered less than inevitable, demanded little of my time. Having presumably assured himself of his bride, Grisk appeared content to defer the marriage for as long as Lord Brant would condone. Grisk cited frequent business in Sandoral, but I privately considered the cause to be a combination of pride still pained by sorcerous encounter, the obvious ebb of Lord Arineuil's attentions to me, and the rumored addition of a comely young parlormaid to the staff of Niveal Hall.

I was uneasy but too occupied to be ill-content. It was Liya whom I began to pity, for she had not ceased to seek the rarefied social sphere of her imagination. It did not exist; the castle inhabitants were men and women, as good or bad as any others. Liya had coerced me to attend a very few of Yldana's afternoon confabulations, and each had bored me to distraction.

"Worm-silk lasts to a tedium, Ritsa."

"But sea-silk simply will not take the range of colors."

"*I* could never want for any hue more pure than sea-silk's natural gold."

"I found the most perfect lavender silk the other day."

I could not comprehend how the noblewomen of Serii could devote so much time to debating the relative merits of silk from a worm or a mollusk. The other conversations to which I had marginally attended lacked any greater substance. I had come to Yldana's little gathering to appease Liya, who was animatedly expounding about lacquerwork dolls to a portly lady of Esmar. Yldana was displaying her latest gem acquisitions, and I was endeavoring to find a quiet corner in which to retreat.

I sidled through the clusters of shrill gossipers toward the salon's ornate doors and the library beyond them. I blessed the silence as I slipped through the doors, but I was not the first to escape. The woman at the library window stood motionless and remote. She was exquisitely gowned, and rubies coiled in her titian hair. She turned suddenly, and she was as beautiful as my sister, but her manner was icy told.

"Even the library is crowded," she remarked caustically.

"I did not intend to interrupt your privacy, my lady," I returned, appalled by her rudeness. "My sister's guests seldom frequent the library."

A faint smile curled her lips. "So you are Yldana's little sister," she murmured. "The sorceress' child."

I recognized the oddness about her then: she has Power, I

thought with shock, and she knows the use of it. "I did not realize that my sister included wizardesses among her acquaintances."

"I am not an Ixaxin," retorted the woman with cutting disdain. "A Dolr'han does not bow to a Venkarel. A Venkarel serves only to amuse us."

Her attitude frightened me, recalling to me the calamity which her brother's arrogance had wrought. "I meant no offense, Lady Veiga," I said with all the contrition I could feign.

"You are merely inept, then. How common." She left without further comment. I could hear my sister greet her with an enthusiasm undiminished by Lady Veiga's haughty responses. I could not remember ever meeting a woman I liked less than the Lady Veiga dur Liin duri Sandoral, though she did fulfill Ezirae's ebullient descriptions of elite, sophisticated perfection. Despite the prestige and influence of Lady Veiga's heritage, I could not comprehend her popularity among court circles, unless it was her Power which gained it. Lady Veiga had the Power of a wizardess—I had begun to appreciate the distinctions by which Ixaxins measured their fellows—but her Power was difficult to perceive clearly. Even Ineuil, who was otherwise so well-informed, seemed unaware that Veiga shared her brother's ability. I wondered how Lady Veiga had come to befriend my sister, a lady merely of Tyntagel and Amlach, and I remembered with peculiar distaste Ineuil's linking of Lady Veiga with the Infortiare. I began to develop an unwise curiosity about the sister of Lord Hrgh Dolr'han, but it was days before I humored it.

"You are late today, Lady Rhianna," said the Infortiare as I entered.

I had slowed at sight of him, though I had run much of the way from Tyntagel Hall. "I was detained, my lord. My family begins to wonder why I am so often absent of late."

"Does your Niveallan lord suspect you of illicit trysts?" asked Kaedric with crisp sarcasm.

"Lord Grisk has been much away from Tulea," I answered stiffly. "My kindred are concerned lest I disappear from them as I once did."

"That would be notably difficult from the king's castle without recourse to your Power, which your family denies exists."

"That is why I have been allowed such unprecedented freedom, my lord. My family believes that my time is spent in the king's gardens, and they consider me both well betrothed and well guarded against departure."

He answered acidly, "Then you should have no difficulty in attending your studies promptly."

"They still question me, my lord," I retorted defensively.

"Discourage their questions. You have sufficient Power."

"I am not accustomed to the use of Power as a weapon, my lord," I said sharply. I lamented the words as I spoke them.

"As I am?" asked Kaedric with biting precision. "The Infortiare does not attack without provocation, my lady, nor does he otherwise defy Ceallagh's laws. I suggest you reread those laws if you cannot recognize the difference between 'discouragement' and 'aggression.' "

"Yes, my lord," I answered meekly.

"Lady Rhianna, I distrust you most when you are so dutifully humble and compliant. You have honed that particular illusion too well."

I regarded him with genuine surprise, but I flushed before his mocking gaze. "Perhaps you would prefer that I emulate Dolr'han hauteur, my lord," I said.

"It would not suit you, and it would be equally transparent."

"A Dolr'han's qualities *are* doubtless too rarefied for a lowly lady of Tyntagel," I returned.

"As I am only a Venkarel," responded Kaedric in like tone, "I am doubtless too inferior to appreciate either noble species."

"Including the Lady Veiga? She has Power."

"Veiga prefers to turn her talents in other directions than wizardry." He blocked me from a rush of his recollections before I could even see their general form. He cannot prevent my sharing his memories of Ven any more than I can, I thought wonderingly, but Ixaxis is shielded from me save for fleeting and irrelevant images.

"I am pleased to know that a choice is given to some," I said tartly.

"But not to us, my lady." I regretted my sharpness for that instant of unexpected sympathy, but he proceeded with irritatingly obscure irony. "I doubt, in any event, that you share Veiga's tastes. What prompts this sudden interest in Veiga Dolr'han?"

"She is my sister's friend," I answered diffidently.

"Do all of your sister's friends incur such fascination on your part?"

"No, my lord." His ice-blue eyes had narrowed. He distrusts me, I realized with shock; he tests me for motives and schemes against him. What does he think I could possibly do that he could not easily counter?

"My lord," I began, trying to convey something of my curiosity's motives, because I loathed being suspected unjustly. "I never truly met Lord Hrgh Dolr'han. I thought his sister might be like him."

Kaedric nodded very slightly, a grudging admission that my explanation was tenable. He answered me with deliberation, "Veiga is more ambitious and possibly more intelligent than Hrgh, but she has less Power. Veiga allowed Ixaxis to bind her Power a number of years ago, when she opted for the mortal path and Lord Borgor."

"How could she be more ambitious than a brother who would steal the Taormin?"

"Hrgh's bane was arrogance. He believed he could master the Taormin, and that belief opened him to Horlach's influence. Hrgh would not have awakened Horlach intentionally."

"Whereas Lady Veiga would have done so deliberately?" I asked incredulously.

"In like circumstances, presuming the perfect Power which Hrgh believed himself to possess, Veiga would use any means to further her personal goals—including the awakening of Horlach." He spoke with detachment, but he measured his words carefully.

"You state your suppositions, my lord, with great assurance. You must know the Dolr'hans well." I felt cautiously for his reaction.

"My own history will not further enlighten you regarding Lord Hrgh Dolr'han. I suggest you resume your studies and permit me to continue mine." He spoke to me no more, and I did not try to question him again that day, but several times I found him observing me as I read. It was an expressionless regard which I could not fathom, for he had retreated entirely from my mind's awareness. He understands only distrust, I thought, because he has never himself been trusted. But how could anyone trust such Power as his?

Chapter 10

"Rhianna!" called Liya, excitedly waving a sea-tossed find for my inspection. With her skirts tied above her knees and her hair flying free, Liya looked no older than Ziva and Flava. The three of them ran across the sand with bubbling laughter, daring the waves to catch them. Liya paused to steal another shell from the churning water; she raced to regain the dry dunes before the waves could drench her.

I had resisted the outing, grudging a day of idle shopping and meaningless chatter. Protests disregarded, I had been summarily sent forth with Ezirae, Liya, Ziva and Flava. We had indeed passed most of the day in pursuits as tedious as I had anticipated; lengthy discussions with sea-silk purveyors over the weave suitable for my bridal gown struck me as singularly fatuous, since I privately intended that no marriage would occur. Our day's excursion had led us, however, to the edge of Tulea, and the young Hamley sisters had pressed for permission to visit the shore. Ezirae had clucked about the encroachment of twilight, but Liya's added blandishments had overcome objections.

I had seldom visited the sea, and I had never before trod the warmth-washed southern beaches. The inlet which approaches Tulea is largely protected, and the waves which reach that far lose most of their force and majesty in the effort. We none of us minded the lack. Even Ezirae removed her stockings and stepped a few gingerly paces across the sand. Liya and the giggling sisters explored the length of the cove, discovering caves and corners with the supreme delight of innocence. I laughed with them, but though I did not, like Ezirae, sit sedately on the safer heights, I could not find the freedom of joy which the young trio showed. I lingered near the water's edge, gazed at the glimmering sea, and studied the distant island in its midst.

Ixaxis did not draw me. The force which held me to the wizards' path dwelt not on that island. I could feel Ixaxis, nonetheless, through its shields of strength more formidable than its looming cliffs. I could visualize the path which climbed to the school itself. I could see the columned buildings and the twisted pines which, clinging to precipitous rock, gave shelter from the cutting winds. I could see the gray-robed students, the scholars in white and gold, members all of a guild whose origins stretched back to time's beginning. By its own accounts, the Ixaxin guild predated the rise of sorcery, stemming from a time of magics more remote from my concepts than the wizardry of the Infortiare. Those very ancient histories bewildered me more than any feat of a Sorcerer King. The records of Ixaxis, though more complete than any others, acknowledged their own inadequacy regarding the lives and events predating the rise of Horlach.

The people of that early time, having attained both plenty and leisure, had refined all energies into the single goal of personal longevity. Some experimenter finally derived a successful means of prolonging life, but the price of the gift was sanity. The first "Immortals" were destroyed, for they were murderous in their violent outbursts. Those few who proved controllable were confined and allowed to exist for the purpose of further experiments. By the time the creators of these aberrations realized the extent of the change which had been wrought, the Immortals had used their new Power to effect escape.

Naming themselves Sorcerers, the immortals destroyed the civilization which had reared them and began to remold the world to their own liking. They bred and raised children to take from the world as they pleased. They fought among themselves, and many died violently whom the passing years could not otherwise touch.

Of the first Immortals, none survived to verify their natural longevity. Rhianna of Dwaelin was believed to be of the third generation. Horlach may have been son or grandson of the first; his lifespan appeared never to have been matched or fully measured, but he had exerted absolute rule for at least ten millennia. He destroyed his most potent foes, thus weakening the Immortal strain. The blood of mortals further diluted the sorcerous gifts over generations, but the loss brought forth the tempering of sorcery with compassion.

After ages of sorcerous reign, many of the Immortals' heirs still sought their kingdoms of tyranny, but some began to seek a restoration of justice and knowledge. Those few began to gather at Ixaxis, an isolated school which had preserved some meager part of pre-sorcerous lore by maintaining a constant aura of insignificance. This final bastion of mortal science became the womb from which formalized wizardry was born.

It was a quelling thought: much of the world I knew had been molded by lunacy. The heir of Power was the heir of madness. The scions of Power stood sentinel against themselves.

I heard Ezirae call a reminder of the passing time. Liya returned reluctantly with Ziva and Flava. We restored our skirts and our hair to a reasonably presentable state, but a trail of sand and our dangling slippers betrayed us. Master Stev, the coachman, resumed his post lazily; the footman helped us into the carriage with a somewhat scandalized air.

We bounced over rough roads for some miles, the road smoothing only as we regained more civilized routes. We were admiring Liya's trove of flotsam and a fisherman's float found by Flava, when the carriage jerked and then settled askew. Ezirae fainted with a melodramatic flair. Ziva and Flava promptly began to scream.

"Hush, sillies," chided Liya. "We have only tilted into a ditch. Rhianna, can you see what has happened?" I left to Liya the unenviable task of calming the Hamley contingent, while I clambered from the vehicle.

"There has been an accident, my lady," apologized the footman, a burly fellow who seemed overly mature for his occupation.

"Obviously," I answered dryly. The left front wheel of the carriage had half vanished in thick mud at the road's edge. Master Stev was staring at it as if it might at any moment leap free of its own accord. "I assume, Master Stev, that you would like the carriage emptied so as to clear the wheel," I prompted. "We would like to reach the castle before nightfall."

Master Stev pursed his thin lips and shook his head slowly. He looked at the wide road, the horses and the carriage wheel. He straightened his hat, and I thought I would shake him if he did not speak soon. Just as my patience was failing me completely, Master Stev decided to answer me. "There is an inn just beyond the far hedge, my lady. We cannot leave before morning."

"Master Stev, if you require assistance from the inn, by all means obtain it. The suggestion of remaining here until morning is not at all satisfactory."

"It is a very pleasant inn, my lady," offered the footman helpfully.

"It may be a veritable palace, but I have no intention of staying there because of a misguided carriage. A wheel in the mud cannot be so complicated as to require more than an hour's effort. Place a plank beneath the wheel and let the horses draw us free," I concluded in exasperation.

Liya asked from the coach, "What is the trouble, Rhianna?" Disgusted by Master Stev and his cohort, I stalked to the side of the carriage from which Liya leaned. Irritably, I said to her, "Master Stev seems determined to afflict us with a night at the local inn, an establishment most probably operated by his relatives, judging by his insistence."

"Is the carriage damaged?" asked Ezirae, who had revived on her own when sympathy was not forthcoming.

"Not a whit," I returned. "I find it incredibly convenient for our previously competent driver that the one intractable ditch in Serii should coincide with such a well-favored inn."

"Rhianna, you are too suspicious," rebuked Liya mildly. "We are not in such a hurry. A country inn might make for a very pleasant evening. Your father even suggested that we stay away for the night. It really is rather exciting."

"It really is too thrilling," said Flava in a poor imitation of Liya's enthusiastic style. Ziva tossed her braids and forgot her hysteria with a giggle. Outnumbered again, I abandoned any further objections. I could hardly admit that the return for which I chafed was to Ceallagh's Tower and not to Tyntagel Hall.

The inn was indeed a pleasant establishment, clean and pros-

perous and well-trafficked. The innkeeper welcomed us, and his effusive wife cooed with all the sympathy even Ezirae could desire.
They managed to find three choice rooms for us and a space in the
rear for our servants. Had I been the affluent merchant turned
away for lack of quarters just as we arrived, I should have
protested the injustice heartily. I made no mention of my observation that our arrival seemed to have been anticipated, deeming further protest pointless.

"Just wait until you see the new bonnet Stev bought me, Ylath,"
said Inda proudly. The second floor chambermaid of Tyntagel Hall
had few opportunities to boast to her third floor counterpart. Ylath
was well wed, and Inda still waited for Stev to decide himself.

"It cannot have cost more than a copper kelne if Stev gave it to
you," retorted Ylath with a disparaging wag of her white-capped
head. "He has not had more than that in his pocket since his old ma
quit keeping him away from the taverns."

Inda preened and crowed, "It happens Stev did a bit of service
for His Lordship lately. His Lordship can be very generous when
he has a mind."

A skeptical Ylath laughed. "What could Stev do that His Lordship much cares about?"

Inda answered mysteriously, "That, Mistress Ylath, is none of
your concern!"

Chapter 11

I wandered in the garden near the walls of Tul a moon after the protracted shopping excursion. A queer, nostalgic notion had bidden me don an approximation of my old travel garb and imagine myself again the hopeful suppliant of the Dwaelin Wood. Of late I had grown too far apart from my old friends due to more than my changed Power. I still could not merge with them as once I had, but I no longer minded so keenly that slim distinction. I could speak to them still and heal their sorrows. I coaxed a sapling to survive that afternoon, and the effort gladdened my own heart as well.

When first I heard the woman calling, I was too far removed from human speech to understand her. Her persistence led me finally to focus on her words. "Your Royal Highness," she cried plaintively. "You must present yourself before the Caruillan emissary. Your Royal Highness!"

I let my awareness explore, and I followed it to a tangled thicket. "You are being summoned, Your Royal Highness," I whispered to the princess hidden in its midst.

I heard a startled rustle. "Lady Rhianna? Please do not tell her where I am," pleaded Princess Joli. "Caruillans always remind me of bloated spiders, and they are worse now that Liin and Sandoral have supported their suit to join the Alliance. I will not smile and simper for another one of them."

The approach of the governess silenced Joli. Espying me, the harried woman began, "Have you seen. . . ." I might have revealed the errant princess if the question had been completed. The governess, however, assessed my unprepossessing attire, categorized me, and assumed a pompous manner. "Her Royal Highness may be in this vicinity. You will search for her," she demanded firmly.

The governess' self-important manners irritated me. Even if I had been the servant for whom she mistook me, I should have expected some element of courtesy. I drew on my loftiest demeanor as I retorted, "Mistress, if Her Royal Highness were nearby, she would undoubtedly censure your insolence. Your incompetence in assuring Her Royal Highness' familiarity with significant appointments is solely your responsibility to remedy. Your arrogance offends me."

I evidently spoke to better effect than I anticipated. Quite deflated, the governess mouthed a servile, "Forgive me, my lady. I did not recognize you. I was distraught." She fussed nervously and hastily retreated toward the castle with another muttered apology.

The princess' voice rose again from the thicket when the governess had gone. "Lady Rhianna, that was wonderful," Her Royal Highness whispered. "I knew that you would not betray me."

"Your Royal Highness, I shall remain pleased to have aided you if you justify my trust by appearing before the Caruillan emissary. However much you may dislike Caruillano, you can hardly avoid official functions on the basis of prejudice." I filled the final word with distaste, feeling somewhat hypocritical, since my own uncharitable feelings toward the people of Caruil were largely unsupported by personal encounter. I had known only one Caruillan, a bitter warrior-Venturer who had been unpleasant but not without honor.

"I do not trust Arku Ruy," sulked Joli.

"Your distrust may serve Serii," I answered impulsively.

The thicket rustled, and a tousled head appeared. "I could help if anyone would listen to me," said Princess Joli seriously.

"Then prove yourself. Accept the responsibilities of your position. Show that you are the heiress of Tul, who alone of mortals dared join Ceallagh against King Horlach."

Princess Joli neither moved nor spoke. I scarcely breathed, sensing great import in the moment. A bird warbled evensong.

The princess cocked her head and grinned impishly. "Mistress Amila will look foolish when I appear of my own accord," she said with ungenerous relish.

"I suppose she might," I responded. Assuming Mistress Amila to be the haughty governess, I could not help but sympathize with Joli's observation. I made a poor oracle of advice on duty and decorum.

In her hasty fashion, Princess Joli dashed to her father's castle. Disproportionately pleased with myself, I curtseyed to the thicket. "I think we have done well, my friend," I said and made my own way toward the castle.

On my return to Tyntagel Hall, I found Liya seeking me urgently. "Thank goodness. I thought you had vanished from the earth," she spewed in a breathless rush. "We are due at Amlach Hall within the hour."

"What social obligation besets us now?" I responded with no more anticipatory delight than Princess Joli had given to her Caruillan encounter.

"We are to spend the night as Yldana's guests."

"That is a cause for urgency?" I asked with a laugh.

"Your father ordered it, Rhianna," answered Liya, and my sister-in-law finally conveyed to me her sincere distress.

"Liya, what troubles you? Yldana's hospitality is not that grim."

"You and I are to stay with Yldana," said Liya with a threatening tear. "Ezirae has gone to Hamley Hall. That is all we need to know."

"Are those Dayn's words?"

"Yes," she returned as the tear fell. "It is only for a night."

Any quarrel with Dayn could set Liya crying, but a sudden coincidence struck me. "It was only a day's outing a month ago. Liya, in what have my father and Dayn become involved?"

"Rhianna, I vow I do not know anything about it. Please hurry."

"It pertains to the Caruillan to whom they spoke at the ball," I prompted unmercifully.

"Caruil wants to join the Alliance. It is natural that the emissary should speak to the members of a First House."

"In a secretive manner which upsets you so visibly?"

"I never learned to hide my feelings like you Tyntagellians," said Liya with a depth of bitterness that silenced me.

Ezirae entered propitiously, bubbling with delight at the prospect of a night amid her comfortable Hamley kin. Her chatter hid the stilted coolness of those of us doomed to an occasion of less blissful camaraderie. Liya's mood seemed likely to alienate any scion of Lord Baerod's House, and Yldana and I had never savored one another's company.

With Yldana, Liya and I spent an uncomfortable evening dwarfed by the exaggerated formality of Amlach Hall's ornate decor. Yldana may have even regretted the petty snobbery for the sake of which she and Amgor had segregated their portion of Amlach Hall from that of Amgor's score of cousins. Subdued by our solemnity, Yldana toyed idly with her supper. Liya might have been ages absent. Without even Amgor's attendance, the enjoyment of baiting me offered insufficient enticement to Yldana's denigrating wit. We three who ought to have shared the camaraderie of sisters found only discomfiture in common. I was least betrayed by fate, for I could find the joy in loneliness as well as the torture.

With the clearing of the last trace of the barely sampled meal, we ceased to feign the fondness of familial friends. Liya withdrew to the room allotted her. Yldana took to her own lavish chambers. I sought the Amlach library, though my memory linked it unpleasantly with the Lady Veiga Dolr'han.

The clan of Amlach took little stock in literary pursuits, and I had never been in accord with Yldana's taste for novels about exaggeratedly impassioned females. I selected a nonsensical romance of more promise than the bulk, but it proved too predictably mindless for distraction. After an hour of struggling, I yielded with a sigh of resignation to my dangerous curiosity. Shadowed against servants' eyes, I left the Amlach library for the dappled starlight and the ward of Tyntagel Hall.

The lawns were damply cold and soaked my slippers. I thought myself into a measure of warmth as I watched my father's Hall. I was not alone in surreptitious nocturnal wanderings. Cloaked and quiet figures converged, very gradually, very naturally. Only a steady, careful observation combined with preconceived suspicions would have questioned the influx. I observed Lord Brant with Grisk arrive openly; they were customary visitors. Others whom I could not identify were muffled and tended toward the lee of shrub and wall. The waddling strut of Lord Borgor betrayed him; I followed the king's adjutant, Lady Veiga's influential husband, into my father's assembly room.

I never learn the value of ignorance; I could have wished to witness less that night. It was Lord Borgor who nominally led them, these conspirators from every major House of Serii. I saw my father and Dayn, Dhavod and Amgor, Brant, Egar and Grisk: they heeded the words of Borgor; they lauded the Caruillan, Arku Ruy, who spoke fervently against the influence of Ixaxis. Arku Ruy curried favor for Caruil by denouncing the Ixaxins as the sole cause of Caruil's exclusion from the Alliance. He omitted any mention of Caruil's lawless approach to sorcery as the original source of the rift; Caruil had provided a haven to every renegade, sorcerous or otherwise, for uncounted years. Dayn, at least, ought to have recalled Caruil's history as well as I; we had learned it from the same stern tutor.

I winced at Arku Ruy's slippery platitudes and the murmurs of approval rising from the honorable lords of Serii. "As you know," said the Caruillan, "King Astorn has taken our plea into serious consideration. Hours ago, His Majesty informed me that he may soon undertake a journey to Bethii to discuss the matter with Queen Marylne and the other rulers of the Alliance. King Cor regards this as an auspicious sign for the unity of our peoples, but my king is concerned, as I am, that the Infortiare will not accept a decision in our favor. We must be vigilant in our defense against treachery. The time of proof against Ixaxis comes, and our long efforts will be vindicated!"

Cheers of fanatical zeal chorused his emotional words. Lord Borgor stilled the crowd with tolerant patience and proceeded to recite the chronicle of traitorous conspiracy. "An unfortunate lapse on the part of our Pithliin operative has been referred to Lord Morgh dur Liin for amendment. Lord Morgh assures us that the Ixaxin representative in Pithlii will be successfully eliminated by month's end.

"Regarding the Ixaxin agent discovered in Coru: it has become apparent that an elderly woman witnessed the execution and was permitted to survive on the basis of her age, gender and social insignificance. The situation is an expensive reminder of the folly of maudlin self-indulgence in a cause as dangerously vital as our own. The alcoholic drudge proved to be an englamored wizardess working with the dead agent. It became necessary to dispose of our own hireling so as to protect our operation against discovery. We cannot afford such incidents! The Infortiare is a cunning foe, who will use our every weakness. If we are to remove the evil canker from our society, we must proceed with caution and intelligence— and as little mercy as the Infortiare himself would show.

"A personal note: Arku Ruy informs us that King Cor recently welcomed to his court Lord Hrgh Dolr'han. I am sure that many of you join me in rejoicing at this news. We have all been deeply con- cerned for the worthy young man who first awakened us to that dangerous villain in our midst, the wizard who calls himself Lord Venkarel. Lord Hrgh is still troubled by the realization of Ixaxin du- plicity, but he is well and establishing himself rapidly in Caruil as a man of influence and sound judgment."

I could not listen to further insanities. I moved to depart, think- ing to exit through my father's office rather than the now-crowded portal by which I had entered. My mind turned toward my goal, and I felt the darkness.

It was the full burning pain of memory which I had thought vanquished by the gentle peace of Benthen Abbey. Serpents writhed in bleeding ribbons across my mind, opened charred fis- sures which my thoughts could not traverse. Careful walls of Ix- axin discipline, which I had not consciously realized I had built, crumbled helplessly, but recognition of the toppling barriers an chored my escape.

I coiled within a deep recess where oak trees grew and sunlight brushed the age from weathered stone. I breathed of a sculptor's love for his lady lost in a nacreous whorl. I recited Zerus' symbolic litanies, and I held to the image of a man of black hair and eyes of ice who had carried me from the flames once before.

The fire retreated to a waiting, deadly ember of dark menace. It searched for me still, hidden from my sight by the door of my fa- ther's office. The crowd at the outer door no longer daunted me. I brushed aside the blind fools of Seriin noblesse, eluding their no- tice with a thought. King Astorn himself could not have stopped my flight from the shade of the Sorcerer King.

I inhaled deeply of the garden's chill air, gratefully absorbing autumnal cold until I ached and shivered. I strove to expel all trace of the malignance which hovered unbearably near. I did not know the form it currently wore, but I knew that it and not Lord Borgor led the mad conspiracy. I was tormented by the knowledge that the illusory break from sorcerous dominance would be led by Horlach, the deathless Sorcerer King, and that my family served him.

An impractical impulse urged me to run and cower childishly within the shield of the Infortiare's will. I caviled at the impropriety of paying midnight visits to any man, but it was outright fear of further embroilment in the conflict of wizards which actually restrained me. I rationalized that the news I bore would be no more than Lord Venkarel already knew.

I reentered Amlach Hall in the bleak company of guilt and worry. Silence cast soft echoes from my slippered feet. Pale light fell from Yldana's door across the darkened hall. A diaphanous silken cloud haloed her silhouette as she slipped with the ease of practiced intimacy into the arms of the man she greeted. She drew him warmly into the candle glow of her room. That Yldana amused herself in Amgor's absence did not surprise me, though her openness when Liya slept across the passage annoyed me. Nor could I claim particular shock that Yldana's favor had enticed the profligate Lord Arineuil dur Ven. The assignation did shed a cynical light on Ineuil's disparagement of Amgor; while Amgor conspired with the other pawns of Horlach, Ineuil did not exactly occupy himself with the salvation of Serii. I was only surprised at how greatly the discovery aggravated my sepulchral mood.

Chapter 12

Dawn brought high clouds and frigid winds, signs of autumn's onset. Leaves, tenacious beyond their time, withered slowly. One stubborn rose still budded in the king's gardens, but the other canes were barren. Skeletal stalks became sere and brittle in the fields.

In Cuira, a man died, purportedly of a wizardess' theriac. A child of Esmar espied armed men in Caruillan colors entering her liege lord's hold. Fire claimed an inn in Malka; a stranger welcomed there the previous night had commented on the queer effect of moonlight on the chalky cliffs of Ixaxis.

I watched Yldana sweetly greet her husband, mocking him subtly with a hypocrisy which cloyed. Liya met Dayn with no less canting an embrace. With frozen distaste, I accepted Lord Grisk's encircling arm, and my father nodded righteous approval. I envied Ezirae's naive delight in the blithe social facade surrounding Tyntagel Hall, but Ezirae had indulged heavily in her own crutch; her reddened eyes were blurred. The essence of Horlach had left my father's House, but the taint remained in all of us.

Another full day elapsed before I enacted the inevitable betrayal of my family. My decision had progressed beyond choice when I felt Horlach stain Tyntagel Hall, but still I did not want to be Ixaxin, and I did not want to choose Ixaxis' Lord above my own.

I found him with the dusk amid a litter of texts and tattered documents. Kaedric met my eyes, demanding with a trace of exasperation, "Have you any idea how little information exists regarding Horlach, the man? Legends abound of his evil reign. His victims are legion. But of substantiated personal history, virtually nothing can be found. The Taormin is worse. Horlach did not create it; he merely warped it to his own schemes. The Taormin's original purpose and the methods of its making are buried beneath an eon of superstition." He rubbed his brow wearily. "Forgive my pedantry, my lady. I have just spent a day reciting history to a king who will not heed the lessons of his ancestors. He prefers the patent nonsense of a Caruillan sycophant."

"Most of the lords of Serii echo His Majesty's sympathies, my lord. They conspire against you, and Horlach leads them."

Kaedric's compelling eyes narrowed slightly, and they held me. "My lady, you are become astonishingly well informed."

"The conspirators met in my father's Hall the night ere last," I answered, feeling traitorous myself, though it was treachery I betrayed. Kaedric had frowned, and I knew his mood. I burst forth unthinkingly, "I feel sufficiently wretched without you constantly distrusting me and examining my every word for subtle intentions against you. I have betrayed my liege and my family to you, my lord; you might at least *pretend* to believe me."

"Was Horlach among the conspirators?" demanded Kaedric after a pause.

"Yes, my lord, but I could not identify his host. I am sorry, my lord. I ought to have realized the importance of such an identification and probed farther."

Kaedric's expression had softened, though there was puzzlement in it. "I can hardly blame you for the omission, my lady. I have myself encountered Horlach twice of late, and neither time did I linger beyond necessity."

"I evidently bring you no new information," I responded glumly. My agonizing decision had not even been necessary.

Faint humor touched Kaedric's eyes. "In fact, my lady, your 'betrayal,' as you call it, is itself a most astonishing disclosure." He touched the sorry velvet of his chair. "I have given you little but grief and trouble, Lady Rhianna," he said hesitantly. "I merit neither your loyalty nor your trust, but if you are willing, I should like to hear a more detailed account of this conspiratorial meeting."

I recounted the scene I had witnessed, hiding the embarrassment which invariably beset me on the rare occasions of Kaedric's gentler moods. He listened to me intently, nodding occasionally and clenching his right hand tightly as I told of the Ixaxin murdered in Coru. He continued to watch me for some moments after I had finished. "Thank you, Lady Rhianna," he said at last.

"I hope the information is of use, my lord." I could feel his memories pull at me. I spoke to break their grasp. "Shall I resume my studies, my lord?"

"Only if you are irredeemably enthralled by Telmar's *Treatise on Metaphysical Foundations*. Personally, I have had quite enough for one day both of scholarship and intrigues of state. I am even tired of this room, inconceivable as I should once have found such a thought."

I looked at the vast room with its limitless view. "With Ceallagh's Tower at your disposal, my lord, you hardly seem constrained in your surroundings."

"The exploration of my immediate domain is an indulgence vanquished by a sea of ceaseless crises. When I was named Infortiare, I thought the function's sole redeeming feature was the opportunity it provided to leisurely excavate the Tower's recesses. Ceallagh himself lived here, as well as every succeeding Infortiare, and a great many of their possessions have never been removed. The historical wealth never interested Alobar. I had grandiose ideas about the forgotten secrets I might uncover among the dusty relics of my predecessors. I have lived here for five years, my lady, and I have yet to enter any room beneath this floor." He laughed in self-mockery.

"You did not wish to be Infortiare," I said, bemused by his sudden communicativeness.

"I have no heroic ambitions, Lady Rhianna. The choice of the Ixaxin Council devastated me as much as it did Hrgh."

"Could you not have refused the honor?"

"I was persuaded, reluctantly, that Lord Hrgh was too unpredictable for the post. I could not name another candidate who would accept. Every other significant Power of my acquaintance sat on the Council which had chosen me! I still wonder whether Hrgh would have been a better choice."

"Lord Hrgh surely demonstrated his unsuitability by taking the

Taormin. Even Lord Arineuil, who was Lord Hrgh's friend, recognized that act for madness."

"Yes, Hrgh Dolr'han is quite unsuitable now, if he even lives (which I doubt, despite Lord Borgor's pretty story). I ensured that Hrgh could never be Infortiare when I defeated him in his formal challenge. In a perverse way, I am responsible for the awakening of Horlach."

"Lord Hrgh ought never to have challenged you at all. He should have respected the Council's decision, whatever his private misgivings."

"The Infortiare should be, by Ceallagh's decree, the member of the Ixaxin Guild who holds the greatest Power at the time of selection. The Council's choice is not infallible, since few of us ever exercise the limits of our Powers. Hrgh sincerely believed himself to be best qualified, and I would never have willingly told him otherwise."

"You defend Lord Hrgh more fervently than does Ineuil," I observed.

"And Ineuil, as we all know, despises me for destroying most of his family and his domain. Did he tell you that he actually tried to kill me once? I defeated him, of course, but not with wizardry or even blade. I suggested to him that his family's indolent neglect of their duties had produced me and the miserable hole which I finally purged. I reminded him that as my liege lord, his uncle had been legally responsible for my enslavement and its unsavory conditions. Ineuil's sporadic allegiance to me owes as much to misplaced guilt as to anything."

Diffidently, I asked, "Did your mother actually sell you?"

Kaedric appeared not to object, though he did start perceptibly. "I must remember that the Taormin exchanges more than talents: how much of my history did you acquire? No," he said firmly, halting my response. "Perhaps you had best not answer that.

"As far as I know," he continued, "my mother sold me shortly before one of her less satisfied customers slit her delicate throat. Having no conscious recollection of the event myself, I can only trust to the dubious word of Master Doshk, who thereafter owned me."

The clear depths of dangerous eyes met mine, and my own gaze fell. "You did not know that you were a sorcerer?" I asked softly.

"The only sorcerers I knew were charlatans and potion ped-dlers. I never realized that Power actually existed, until Doshk and circumstances pushed me that inch too far. I incinerated him and nearly everything else within reach, and I spent the next few days staring at the horror of ash and rubble I had created. I was not par-ticularly repentant, but Doshk's world I had at least understood."

"How old were you, my lord?" I did not tell him that I knew he had regretted his unintentional act of retribution deeply and im-mediately.

"Fourteen or fifteen, I suppose. My age is one of those many un-certainties in my life. Is your curiosity satisfied, my lady?"

I answered hurriedly, "I did not mean to pry, my lord."

"Obviously no one informed you that Lord Venkarel does not discuss his past," said Kaedric dryly. "Since I have said so much, however, I shall add one more note. I do not merit your sympathy for my childhood misfortunes. If that is the basis of your choice to serve my cause, then return to Tyntagel before you are disap-pointed. My detractors do not apply their vivid epithets without a measure of justification. The pretentious mask of an Ixaxin scholar does not eradicate my unsavory origins, and the slums of Ven do not yield men of gentlemanly honor."

He spoke with sarcastic indifference, but the words hurt him and I felt his pain. I said nothing, fearing to injure further this man whom I had thought invincible. "Blast your empathy," he said sud-denly, rising and turning away from me.

Indecisive, I remained as I stood. The depths of long-held bit-terness stirred in me the need to heal, and I ached to touch the dark sorrow away. I would have gone to him at a breath of acceptance.

When the gray-robed woman spoke, both Kaedric and I must have whirled to her with the speed of guilt. "Dear me," she mur-mured mildly, combing knotted fingers through unruly white hair. "I thought the ghost of Lady Erian had surely claimed you both." She extended her hand to me and announced bluntly, "My name is Marga. You are not what I expected to find in this stolid hive." She projected her focus beyond me. "You have been keeping secrets from me, Kaedric."

"The Lady Rhianna dur Tyntagel is my student, Marga."

"You teach unusual classes," she retorted, stepping back to ap-praise me critically.

"I learned the art from you, Mistress Marga," answered Kaedric. "I do not, however, recall a lesson on impugning one's host after an uninvited entrance."

"I could not have my student surpass me in everything," grumbled Marga indignantly.

"An eventuality which you need never fear. If your donning of student gray is a subtle attempt to prod my humility, rest assured: my pride has suffered several setbacks already tonight."

Marga raised an eyebrow. "Perhaps I ought to have insisted that you take a student years ago. Teaching can be a humbling experience." Mistress Marga winked at me, but I found her frightening. "In fact," she explained to me, "I wear gray because the white robes of a scholar are so confoundedly impractical. I formed the habit of entering here unannounced because it used to shock Alobar, and Kaedric has never reformed me of the practice. Dear Alobar always reacted to my arrival as if he suspected me of the most indiscreet ulterior motives. I hope you give Kaedric a great deal of trouble, Rhianna. He was by far the most difficult student Ixaxis ever suffered."

"Must you disillusion her completely, Marga?"

"It is only just. You caused me enough inconvenience. Are you going to welcome me properly, Kaedric, or are you too addled by your lovely student to remember courtesy?" Kaedric bent and solemnly kissed Marga's proffered cheek, while I wished myself in farthest Ardasia. Mistress Marga might sound disarmingly direct, but she conveyed unsettling insinuations.

"With your permission, my lord," I said a trifle stiffly, "I shall take my leave." Mistress Marga smiled with irritating complacency. Kaedric started to speak but, instead, nodded curtly.

Chapter 13

When next we met, Kaedric accorded me a careful formality which I did nothing to dispel. I adhered to my lesson rigidly and exchanged with the Infortiare only minimal conversation. I did not see Mistress Marga again; I assumed that she had departed as abruptly as she had appeared.

The days were growing colder, and inclement weather curtailed my garden visits, making my absences from my family more difficult to explain. Tyntagel Hall had become increasingly dismal. Liya and Dayn bickered constantly. My father's temper had deteriorated to such a point that even the servants avoided him: Arku Ruy had departed for Bethii, and King Astorn's promise to follow had yet to be enacted. Lord Grisk had become a frequent visitor, and Dhavod and Ezirae could speak in accord of nothing but my impending marriage.

When Abbot Medwyn arrived at Tyntagel Hall, my delight nearly overwhelmed him, and I did not even pause to question his unlikely appearance in my family's vestibule. He clucked mirthfully as I hugged him. "The lot of an elderly priest has certainly improved, Rhianna, when he merits such a welcome."

"I am so pleased to see you, Abbot," I responded sincerely.

"And I you, Rhianna, but you need not strangle me to prove it. The exhibition is delightful but most undignified," he added with a wink which creased his whole face.

"Is all well at the Abbey?"

Abbot Medwyn frowned fleetingly, and my warmth of pleasure froze. Grisk, from whose tedious company I had been summoned to greet the abbot, approached us, and Abbot Medwyn inquired politely, "Is this one of your kin, Rhianna?"

I tried to suppress a grimace as Grisk placed his hand on my shoulder possessively. I responded with restrained distaste, "Abbot Medwyn, this is Lord Grisk dur Niveal."

"Lady Rhianna is to be my wife," announced Grisk firmly, eying the abbot with suspicion.

Abbot Medwyn nodded once. "My congratulations, Lord Grisk. I know you will forgive an old man for his dearth of social grace, but it is so seldom I can discuss old friends when I leave the Abbey. The conversation would bore you, so I shall briefly steal your intended bride. May we stroll in the garden, Rhianna? These noble manors rather daunt me." Abbot Medwyn smiled like a cherubim as he maneuvered me to the door.

Grisk let us go with little grace. Having been told the acknowledged story of my lengthy stay at Benthen Abbey, Lord Grisk quite thoroughly disapproved of my association with Benthen's abbot. Grisk would have liked the truth far less. I sighed with relief when we had left him.

"You do not seem to have gained any fondness for your betrothed, Rhianna," said Abbot Medwyn gently.

"I wish I could tell you otherwise, Abbot Medwyn."

"A wizardess cannot be coerced into marriage, Rhianna."

My glance dropped guiltily, and I countered the accusation with a query. "You did not answer my question about the Abbey. Is something wrong? I am sure you did not journey to Tulea to visit a Tyntagellian lady who once burdened your charity."

"You were not a burden, Rhianna," said the abbot kindly. He frowned. "A great many things are wrong these days, Rhianna. Benthen Abbey is not immune." Our footsteps fell on sand. "Kaedric tells me that you have been studying wizardry."

"You came to Tulea to speak with Lord Venkarel?" I asked, already certain of the answer.

"Another attempt was made to steal the Taormin, Rhianna."

"But it failed," I insisted urgently.

Abbot Medwyn agreed hesitantly. "It failed," he answered carefully. "Master Gart was slightly injured, but no other harm was done." I started; I had nearly suppressed all recollection of Master Gart, inextricably linked as he was with Hamar and Horlach's undying guardians. "Master Gart agreed to remain with the Abbey after the Venture," explained the abbot, "though he holds generally to himself. Kaedric suspected another attack would be forthcoming, and he deemed the protection of a warrior's steel an advisable precaution. Master Gart was a compromise between a contingent of the Seriin army and the Abbey's traditional reliance on faith and peace."

"I am glad that Master Gart has found a place of refuge," I returned truthfully.

"Yes, age does not make the loss of friends any easier: Hamar and Gart traveled together for many years." We walked some minutes in easy silence, which made me rather wistfully recall the secure sanctity of Benthen Abbey. I walked with the holy man rather than the Venturer; with the holy man I felt at peace.

"In many ways, Abbot Medwyn, I envy you your calling."

"It would not suit you, Rhianna, even were you not possessed of that other Power. Your faith lies in the creatures of the earth and not in Him who made them."

"Is the difference so great?"

"Perhaps not." Abbot Medwyn smiled. "Let not my fellow clergymen hear me say that. They already consider me quite eccentric because of my dealings with Ixaxins." He added suddenly, "Your family—and Lord Grisk—support the movement against Ixaxis."

It was not a question, but I responded with acerbic precision, "The attitude of my kin regarding wizardry is not well hidden."

"When are you going to make your choice, Rhianna?"

I looked at Abbot Medwyn in surprise. "Having already betrayed my own father's plotting to Lord Venkarel, I should think my decision clear," I answered defensively, "but I suppose Lord Venkarel did not mention the incident; I told him little he did not already know."

"Kaedric told me of the meeting in your father's Hall. He has made good use of the information. My question, however, remains. You have assuredly served the Infortiare more than once, but you still regard your father as your liege lord. You are also promised in marriage to Lord Grisk, who would hardly approve of your association with Kaedric. Lord Grisk does not even approve of a harmless old abbot. You cannot forever maintain such contradictory allegiances, Rhianna."

"I am not eager to dissolve all ties with my family, Abbot. That does not mean that I agree with politics."

"You do not agree with them, but it is easier to acquiesce to the dictates of your heritage. Thus far you have accepted the easy route: running from a family decision you disliked, appeasing your family by apparent agreement when flight proved an unpalatable alternative. You have helped the Infortiare when it was convenient for you or you had no other option. If I asked you to take a deliberate step in this battle we wage, would you take it despite the possible cost?"

I disliked the truth of his words. I answered gravely, "I have no great fount of courage or strength, Abbot Medwyn. I should like to say I would not hesitate before the wrath of Horlach: we have so very much at stake." I could not face him as I finished, "I am neither Ceallagh nor Tul. I am the very unimportant daughter of Lord Baerod and a wife he despised. I do not know what answer I should give you."

"Rhianna," said Abbot Medwyn with deliberation, "the Taormin was not taken from the Abbey, because it was not there to be found. Kaedric did not return it to us."

I turned to him with deeply felt dread. A shaft of sunlight blinded me. "Abbot Medwyn, what do you imply?"

"Rhianna, I think perhaps you alone, save Kaedric himself, know truly what transpired in Horlach's castle last winter. I have tried to discuss it with Kaedric." At my expression of protest, Abbot Medwyn continued quickly, "Kaedric has ever been reticent. Perhaps it is only that which keeps him silent, but he will not reveal the Taormin's whereabouts to me or to the Ixaxin Council."

"He would not conceal the Taormin without cause, Abbot Medwyn, and he would not take it for his own use," I insisted with less assurance than I would have wished.

"So I believe, also, but I feel some responsibility for it and for Kaedric as well. Talk to him, Rhianna. You were with him when he used it first. You have the best chance of learning from him whether he has used it again."

"Abbot Medwyn, I have not the right to question the Infortiare."

"You defied him openly to join a Venture."

"I did not know whom I defied, Abbot Medwyn."

Abbot Medwyn smiled at me sorrowfully. "I know, Rhianna." He did not need to add that he had strongly dissuaded me from that defiance at the time.

"Surely the Ixaxin Council would be better suited to such a task as you suggest."

"I have already spoken to the representative of the Ixaxin Council. Mistress Marga agrees with me that you are best qualified to approach the subject."

I thought of the forceful little woman who had taught wizardry to the Infortiare. The absurdity of Abbot Medwyn's suggestion struck me fully even as I caviled, "If Lord Venkarel refuses to answer both you and Mistress Marga, he will consign my questions to ridicule."

"We ask only that you try, Rhianna."

"He would not take the Taormin for himself."

"I would believe him if he said it. In his own way, Kaedric is as stubbornly proud as a Dolr'han."

We had nearly circled back to Tyntagel Hall. Grisk watched us from the entryway. "I make you no promise, Abbot. Lord Venkarel frightens me nearly as much as does Horlach."

Abbot Medwyn merely nodded thoughtfully.

Chapter 14

I waited in the Tower library, unable to concentrate on any task but the confrontation which Abbot Medwyn had beseeched of me. I paced the room nervously, touched the gilt and leather spines of carefully tended volumes, and realized that the books were the only items in the room that had seen any significant recent attention. I brushed a corner chair and rubbed a cobweb from my fingers with distaste.

"Traditional dread of Ceallagh's Tower makes housekeepers an elusive commodity," commented Kaedric from the door. "One of my predecessors, a Lord Pareth, grew so desperately offended by the pervading grime that he devoted the better part of his tenure to a search for a dust-cure. His contributions to Seriin government lapsed accordingly."

"It is a pity that he failed," I murmured uncertainly. Kaedric wore the formal black silk and gold of the Infortiare, and I thought it unfair that he should so resemble the ageless Sorcerer Kings of legend. He began to examine the stack of letters on his desk. He had already spared me more converse than he had done in a fortnight.

I began tentatively, "I spoke with Abbot Medwyn this morning."

The Infortiare answered absently, "He mentioned an intention to see you."

"Is he staying in the Tower, my lord?" I asked, though I knew the answer.

"He prefers the local manse of Parul," responded Kaedric, still studying the papers he held.

With headlong decisiveness, I embarked. "Abbot Medwyn said that an attempt was made to steal the Taormin. He also said that the attempt failed, because you had never returned the Taormin to the Abbey."

I had gained the Infortiare's attention. His eyes had hardened. He enunciated dangerously, "What further bits of wisdom did the good abbot impart?"

"He is concerned for you, my lord."

"Ergo, he announces my business to the world. Medwyn's tongue has grown heedless."

"Mistress Marga shares his concern, my lord." Slowly, Kaedric straightened the letters in their stack. "Do you have the Taormin, my lord?" I pleaded.

"You presume too much, Lady Rhianna," he responded tightly.

Privately I agreed with him. I moved nearer to him; I sat on the edge of the too-cluttered chair facing his. His muscles were tensed, his hands' slight motions exhaustively controlled. "Lord Venkarel, I have walked with you in the Taormin's world. I am afflicted by it with some shade of your Power and your memories. If you use it, I shall know."

With a rapid movement, his hand gripped mine across the wood desk. His fingers were hard, and they pressed into my bones.

He could have touched the walls on any side: the flat, gray planes which did not end. The prison above was the bloated face of Doshk, a drunken, drug-mad Doshk from whom prosperity had turned her favor. Doshk giggled, an obscene sound spilling from an evil humor. The boy wanted to cry, but he had forgotten the way of it.

Doshk was large, too strong and tall. The boy was very thin, stretched by recent, undernourished growth; he was still small for his age, but he was not quite as much a child as he had been a month before. Doshk reached a huge, rough hand toward the boy, and there was no escape.

Doshk simpered, "You're not going anywhere, Kaed." Doshk

rubbed his hand across the boy's chest, and the boy stiffened, assessing the chances of survival if he struck at the offending hand. Deev never had retreated from the intrusive touching of Master Doshk, but Deev had died of greed. Ag had finally struck, and Ag lay downstairs in a pool of blood widening from his crushed red head.

"You're growing, Kaed," said Doshk with a rough, abusive caress. "You'll favor your mother. I've told you about Fylla, haven't I, Kaed? She was a slut, your mother, who thought she was too good for Doshk. You're not too good, are you, Kaed? You'll do just as Doshk says, won't you?"

The boy knew: what Doshk wanted of him; what Doshk could do to him; that Doshk would kill if defied; that a sober Doshk was difficult to elude, and a drunken Doshk was relentlessly powerful. The boy wished for the knife which had been taken from him a year ago, when Doshk had realized that the boy's skill had begun to compensate for physical weakness. The boy tried to stand immobile as Doshk ran heavy hands across him, but pain and disgust made him gag and jerk free of his owner. Doshk glared from reddened eyes. Doshk hit the boy, the heavy metal studs at Doshk's wrist raising oozing welts across the boy's back.

The boy relaxed determinedly, and Doshk bared his yellowed teeth in approval. "That's better. Be smarter than your mother and maybe you'll live to a happier age." Doshk giggled again and began to wheeze. "She sold you, Fylla did, and only Doshk would take you." A clatter sounded through the floorboards.

"You've a customer, Master Doshk," answered the boy. He spoke so rarely that even Doshk was startled, but the words made no impact. Doshk was entirely focused on his drug-spawned dreams. He fondled; he struck. The boy bled and hated. The thief below the stairs found the body of Ag, stepped around it indifferently, and proceeded with his petty pilfering of the little that remained in Doshk's crumbling inn.

With deft and practiced fingers, the boy lifted a key from Doshk's waistband. The boy submitted to Doshk's painful touches, but he patiently worked toward the door. The key turned. The boy tensed, and Doshk's suspicious eyes squinted. The boy moved quickly, pressing open the catch of the door and pushing against Doshk. The big man fell; the boy clambered past him, through the door, down lightless stairs. Doshk sprang on him with a leap, crushing the boy to the grimy floor.

The sharp, sallow face of the thief appeared against the kitchen's yellow light. Distracted from the boy, Doshk eased to a crouch. The boy rolled clear, but he could not stand, for his head throbbed unmercifully. The two men grappled now; their knives were too sullied to shine. The thief's knife gouged Doshk's heavy thigh, but the thief stumbled, tripping over Ag's body and cursing it. Doshk kicked the knife from the thief's grasping hand, and the boy snatched it eagerly.

The boy tasted hope. He sidled carefully around the dark room, avoiding the clutter of tables and limping chairs which might betray him by a sound. The door would open to him soon, and he would be away. Ag and Deev—even Pru—were dead. Doshk's hirelings had deserted when the pay fell short. There remained none to stop the boy but Doshk, and Doshk was methodically hacking the body of the thief to bloody strips.

The door opened. A black-browed mongrel filled the entry. He saw his partner beneath Doshk's butchery; he saw the boy who sought escape. With arms of steel strength, he grasped the boy's neck in a deadly hold, and the boy saw hope depart, as it had always done.

The boy had always been weak in a world which honored only strength and cruelty. He had paid and suffered for his weakness and for his mother's pride. His back was crossed with scars, for he had not fulfilled Doshk's hopes; the boy had been too determinedly cold to bring money to Doshk's larder. The boy had fought to survive, driving himself beyond strength to outlast his fellows. He had absorbed every trick of duplicity, every crumb of knowledge which might help to free him. He had given nothing of himself save the labor which Doshk had beaten from him. He had hoarded hope, and it ate at him from within.

The thief tightened his grip, and the boy choked. The thief would kill him in another instant. It would be easier to acquiesce, thought the boy wistfully, easier than being weak among the strong. The thought angered him, because if he died now, he would never know what it was to be strong. The boy gave a death's-edge scream, and the world caught fire.

The fire spread rapidly. Doshk died in a searing burst. The thief who thought to kill a spindly boy gawked at fires springing wildly from the stale wood room and the bodies on its floor. The black-browed thief felt his arm burn crisp, though the young throat which it encircled did not blister. The thief stepped backward in horror and agony. He watched the boy's still figure, alone in a circle of flame. Like Ag's red blood, the circle widened. The thief beat at his own burning body as he ran; he would be among the few in Ven to survive that day, but he had lost his arm from shoulder down.

The fire, now started, would not stop. It was anger and hatred from years of abuse, bitterness against a mother who had sold her son; it was fueled by memory of all the cruel haranguers who had beaten and used the son of a too-arrogant whore. It was the fear of a child, raised to iniquity, of the lawgiving enemy—the liege—whom he did not know and of the lawless whom he knew too well. He had found a key more potent than Doshk's. Kaed felt the dark and callous minds as he reached through the city, and he purged them, hating them, wanting them gone. He chanted it like a desperate litany, "I hate them. I hate them. I hate them." He trembled from exertion and the terror which pounded from his own mind. "I hate them. I hate them. I hate them." He intended to destroy them all, not knowing that there was kindness or a world beyond Ven's underbelly. "I hate them." His voice trailed into silence.

His mind cooled. He was only a child; he grew tired. He had stricken to fiery death five thousand men and women; each scream stayed screeching in his mind. Some three thousand more would die of the ancillary mortal flames. Tomorrow's dawn would weep.

He freed my hand, and the visions stopped. His eyes defied me to speak again. "You have the Taormin, my lord," I said. I hated his memories and his guilt, for it was mine now, and I would not let it rule me.

He shot stark words at me. "I am the Infortiare, Lady Rhianna."

"I can find the Taormin without your permission if I wish, my lord."

"You could offer it to His Late Majesty, King Horlach, as well," retorted Kaedric sharply. He stood now, and his ice-laden eyes delved within me. "But if Horlach did not destroy you, I would. My lady, you live by my sufferance," he hissed, dropping the shields by which he had learned since Ven to protect those around him from his Power. No more than a selected easing of those perpetual barriers had sent death to a band of brigands in a mountain crevasse. Only once had I seen him actively attack: in the hall of Horlach with a focus of power so narrow that the impact had barely touched my awareness. The Infortiare did not need to attack me; his blatant Power blinded, and I bit my lip to hold to my sanity with the distraction of a physical hurt. I shuddered for the benighted citizens of Ven, even as I ached with personal guilt over their murder.

"By what right," prodded the Infortiare relentlessly, "do you question me, Lady Rhianna dur Tyntagel? If I take the Taormin, or if I choose to use it—have you the knowledge, the wisdom to judge my decision? Would you send the Taormin to your wizard-hating Tyntagellian hypocrites? The very name of Tyntagel was enwrapped with sorcerous legend long before your ancestors took it for their *sorcerous* domain. Did you think your heritage of Power came solely from a woman too frail to survive her twentieth year? Your father is a sorcerer, Lady Rhianna, though he blocks his Power even from himself. You never observed that simple fact, did you? You cannot recognize your own father's Power, you have never realized that the first Lord of Tyntagel was a Sorcerer King, yet you consider yourself qualified to judge me?"

I repeated obdurately, "I entered the Taormin with you, Lord Venkarel."

"By right of which accident you dare dictate to me?" He stood perilously near to me, blazing down at me with the blue of ice and fire. "Return to your Niveallan lord, Lady Rhianna. Raise children to the glory of Grisk! You have learned controls enough to emulate your father in denial. Expect no more of me."

He compelled me to leave, pressing me with his Power down the long flights of stairs. I left the Tower by the garden door; I knew the door would be locked to me if I tried to return. I think I wept like the silent rains of Ven.

Chapter 15

I had succeeded, after a fashion, in attaining Abbot Medwyn's
answer: I knew that Lord Venkarel held the Taormin still, and I
knew that he intended to use it. I had scant cause for the certainty
I felt; for that reason alone, I told myself, I hesitated to reveal my
story to the abbot. Abbot Medwyn visited me twice more in the
next week, but he did not press to know whether I had acceded to
his request. I volunteered no syllable of reference to the Infortiare.
If the abbot knew of our argument, he did not speak of it.

I had grown very accustomed to my hours in Ceallagh's Tower,
and the days seemed long without them. I greeted the news of
King Astorn's departure for Bethii with an approval which nearly
matched my father's though my reasons differed vastly from his.
The festivities attendant to the event would mitigate the boredom.
I was become no better than any jaded courtier, ignoring the
scheming which I knew transpired. I had made my try at bravery
for Abbot Medwyn's sake and had failed miserably.

On the day of King Astorn's departure for Bethii, solemnity vanished from Tulea. Curricles and carriages denied encroaching
clouds, as the parade circled the castle grounds, collecting its bright
array of Seriin nobility. The youngest members of various house-
holds (most especially the numerous Hamleys) dashed and darted
everywhere underfoot. I glimpsed among them Ziva and Flava;
hair ribbons streaming, they blithely disregarded the dignities of

self-proclaimed maturity. They grinned at me as they whirled past in mock flight from an assortment of friends and cousins. I waved at them and thought it a pity that Liya still sequestered herself.

"This is not a day for genteelly observing from afar, Lady Rhianna," mocked Ineuil. He had appeared with Yldana glowing radiantly at his side, her husband not in sight.

"Ezirae and Dhavod have claimed Tyntagel's right to participate in the parade. I am not so privileged," I responded lightly, but I felt uncomfortable with the knowledge of my sister's illicit affair. That her partner was my sometime comrade, Ineuil, made me even more uneasy.

With more friendliness than I should ever have expected from my sister, Yldana said, "Carriages are for old dowagers who have forgotten how to enjoy a festival day, Rhianna. Walk with us to the town and learn what they miss." She bestowed on me one of the enchanting smiles which she used to such advantage. I cynically suspected that she invited me only for the sake of public propriety, but the mere unlikeliness of the offer swayed me.

Somewhat to my surprise, neither Ineuil nor Yldana pierced my chimerical contentment. The two maintained a patter of sharp observations, but their barbs did not cut deeply, and Ineuil firmly encouraged me to join in their laughter. "Your sister is too solemn, Yldana," he twitted. "We must try to corrupt her."

"So long as the efforts stop at a touch of frivolity, Lord Arineuil," returned Yldana admonishingly, but her smile betrayed unlikely confidence in Ineuil's affections. I should not have trusted Ineuil's fidelity to any woman, but I obviously lacked Yldana's perspective.

We sampled sticky buns and meat pasties from colorful stalls. We cast encouraging coins at dancers and minstrels and poets who recited slyly humorous lays. We watched King Astorn, proud and distinguished, ride past us on a horse of pale gold. The fair and fragile Queen Alamai, who would accompany her husband to Bethii, followed him in a golden carriage. Prince Orlin, the young heir who would be regent in his father's absence, rode beside a carriage laden with his brightly bobbing sisters. Princess Joli sat rigidly pressed against the carriage seat between the golden, soft-eyed twins, Alza and Henzela.

A rude jest from the crowd brought the haughty Prince Orlin to a protective stance before his sisters. He flourished his shiny sword ineffectively under the tolerant watch of the official royal guards. I could feel Joli shake her head with disgust, and I could appreciate the uncharitable comment. Prince Orlin was a handsome boy who might one day mature into an acceptable king, but he seemed an insubstantial leader for a troubled Serii. I shivered, recalling the forces who would not cease their scheming while the regent ruled.

"If you are moping over our king's propensity for producing ineffectual heirs," whispered Ineuil mischievously, "At least credit him with proving more prolific than his own sire."

Yldana actually giggled. "King Astorn has not stinted of himself in the servants' halls either," she said in an undertone.

"Do not offend your sister's delicate sensibilities, Yldana," chided Ineuil with sententious sternness belied when he grabbed her wrists and pulled them to his chest.

"Better my influence than yours, rogue," teased Yldana, breaking free of Ineuil's grasp. With a laugh, she took my hand and drew me with her in a dash through the crowded streets, disregarding equally spattered mud and indignant victims of our careening race. Yldana ensured that Ineuil did not lose sight of us, and he took care not to catch us too soon, but I could not help enjoying their delight in the game.

"A fine spectacle we make," said Yldana when, breathless, we stopped. She raised her fine wool skirt enough to reveal the sodden stockings clinging to her ankles. "I shall be taxed even to convince Amgor of my impeccable propriety this day."

"Your persuasive gifts more than equal the task, Yldana," said Ineuil as he joined us. "To enjoy a festival day is a patriotic duty, and we know how highly Amgor regards a duty."

Yldana grimaced, comically twisting her fine-featured face. "Amgor can be such a pompous bore. Now, quit your disapproving glances, Rhianna. Your thoughts regarding Grisk are not so loyal."

"I am not married to Grisk," I answered defensively.

"You are promised to him. It amounts to the same thing," returned my sister.

"My opinion was never requested," I said.

"Do you think mine was?" asked Yldana. "It is the lot of a Seriin lady to wed as her liege commands. We may turn into suffering slaves like Nadira or mope like Liya because our pretty dreams grow sour, or we may find enjoyment as it comes." She exchanged a look with Ineuil which made me suspect that my presence would soon become burdensome. Yldana's words rankled, because I wanted to condemn her, but I could no longer quite manage it. On my own hypocrisy, Yldana and Abbot Medwyn agreed.

"My lovely ladies," said Ineuil, draping an arm around each of us, "This talk grows depressingly familiar. I have a friend nearby who pressures no one to the dismal task of upholding tradition and family honor. He stocks the most tantalizing vintages this side of Mahl, and his rooftop boasts a sensational view of King's Street."

"Your friend doubtless happens to await us?" asked Yldana coyly.

"Master Caylin has keen insight and an even keener sense of profit," intoned Ineuil seriously. "I may have mentioned my possible arrival with Serii's two most exquisite pearls."

"Does Master Caylin flirt as outrageously as you do, Lord Arineuil?" taunted Yldana.

"He practices, but his technique requires some polishing. I thought perhaps Rhianna could lend him some literate quotes from young Joret dur Esmar's outpourings."

"You are remarkably well informed, Lord Arineuil," I answered. Of all my spate of admirers, Lord Joret alone had persisted beyond the official announcement of my betrothal. I had yet to meet him; Lord Joret seemed to thrive on contemplating the unattainable unknown.

Yldana laughed prettily. "Since Arineuil's attention to you at Veiga's little party gained you the admirers, it is unsurprising that Arineuil should be aware of their existence. The reaction is as inevitable as it is fleeting."

"Have you seen Veiga of late?" asked Ineuil too casually.

"I should be jealous of your interest, Lord Arineuil, save that Veiga is too busy manipulating her beastly husband to find time for someone of your frivolous temperament," said Yldana. "Veiga scarcely appears in public anymore." My sister spoke lightly, but she was not pleased with the turn of discussion.

"Borgor never impressed me as such a captivating fellow," remarked Ineuil. "Perhaps I shall have to cultivate the Adjutant more carefully to learn his secret attraction."

"My dear Arineuil, you know quite well that Lord Borgor associates with no one less than the king or the Dolr'hans." Yldana's voice was tight. "He has barely acknowledged his own family since he became Adjutant, and that honor stemmed solely from Veiga's efforts. You may as well try to cultivate the Venkarel."

I listened with care, curious to know the cause of Ineuil's questions regarding Sandoral's loftiest pair, but Ineuil terminated the conversation with a timely arrival at Master Caylin's touted establishment. I had, for a moment, pondered a careful question to the Infortiare as to whether Lord Arineuil served Ixaxin interests with his probes. I recalled with a painful jounce that Lord Venkarel would not hear me. I might have questioned Ineuil directly, but the trouble of seeking him out for private conversation outweighed the dubious rewards.

I had lost some of my defiantly buoyant humor, but Master Caylin proved as fine a host as promised and did his best to please us. He was an unimpressive man of middle age, beset by a myopic squint and stooped shoulders, but he served a savory lunch in simple but substantial style. From the rooftop aerie, we watched the merry folk at holiday below us, while we enjoyed privacy from disapproving peers. As the afternoon progressed, Master Caylin brought forth his colorless wife and two rather unprepossessing children. I feared we might pay for our pleasant meal with a tedium of family tales, but the gifts of Caylin's brood extended beyond the obviously well-stocked cupboard. An adept lutenist, Master Caylin played while his wife's vibrant contralto gave counterpoint to the clear soprano voices of the ungainly boy and his angular little sister. We lingered until shadows overtook the city, and though Yldana leaned indiscreetly close to Ineuil, I might not approve, but I no longer greatly minded.

I wore a strangely surreal mood upon my return to Tyntagel Hall. The festive air of the day had infected even my father, who was as nearly cheerful as his nature allowed. I refused to seek in him the stain of Power with which my Lord Venkarel had derided me.

Though Dayn and Liya remained conspicuously silent, the evening passed easily until the arrival of Lord Brant and Lord Grisk. "Perhaps we have been selfish, Baerod," said Lord Brant with a sly wink at my father, "in delaying the wedding of our children. Eager young lovers should not be forced to bide for the sake of political convenience. We could yet arrange the ceremony for year's end as originally planned."

Ezirae's protest covered my own horror. "Lord Brant," she said primly, "two weeks will not suffice to prepare for a Young Lady's wedding."

"We are not altogether unprepared," said my father. He nodded thoughtfully to Lord Brant. "I shall consider the matter."

To escape such talk, even Grisk's suggested stroll in the courtyard appeared palatable. I let him escort me beneath the cirrus-speckled sky of near-winter Tulea. I stepped away as he reached for me. "Do not paw me, Lord Grisk," I said absently.

"I am losing patience with you, Rhianna."

"Have you tired of your parlormaid?"

"You have not been so chary of your favors yourself."

"You are worse than Joret dur Esmar, building a world upon a conversation I once had with the lord of Ven," I returned with scorn.

"I suppose you just conversed with Lord Venkarel as well. Credit me with some sense, Rhianna. I never mentioned that little incident, but I did not forget it."

"Then you should recall that my favors did not seem to agree with you," I said with sudden fury.

"That meddling bastard, Venkarel, is not here tonight. You are not very selective in your lovers, Rhianna."

I raised my hand to slap him, but Grisk struck my arm. He hit me once more, knocking me back a pace, with a blow that would leave a blue, mottled imprint on my shoulder. Wickedly, Grisk snarled, "You may give more pleasure as a wife than I expected."

I glared at him, holding tight rein on my anger. "I have no intention of marrying you, Grisk." He grabbed at me, but I shook him off with a wisp of Power. He reentered the salon in my wake, docile with puzzlement. Our kin regarded our quick return with surprise.

"My Lord Father, Lord Brant," I announced clearly, "You suffer under the impression that I intend to marry Lord Grisk. I regret that I have not previously made my position clear, but I remedy that remission now: I shall not marry Lord Grisk."

I had shocked them, and I did not await their recovery. I heard my father calling to me angrily, as I took the stairs to my room with deliberate haste. I could hear incoherent snatches of Lord Brant exchanging abuse with his son. Ezirae shrieked pathetic apologies, and the chaos set Liya and Dayn to arguing.

The most disquieting feature of the following morning was its utter normalcy. Tamar awoke me with a firm knock and a piece of new brocade which she consideringly draped across me. She had no sooner departed than Ezirae arrived requesting her. "She promised to do something with Ziva and Flava," said Ezirae fussily. "I do hope she has not forgotten." I began to wonder if I had only dreamed the events of the previous night.

"Good morning, Rhianna," said Liya to me in the hall. "Do you know that Prince Orlin has already planned a dance? It will be small, of course; only the First Houses and the prince's favorites will be invited. But it will be all the better for being exclusive. I am so tired of hearing about nothing but whether or not King Astorn will go to Bethii and whether the Caruillans will join the Alliance! It will be wonderful to have the court normal again. I think I shall wear the silver tissue." She sprinted to her room as gaily as if she had not just spent the last month in sullen withdrawal and bristling defensiveness.

"Good morning, Rhianna," said Dayn courteously as I entered the small dining room reserved for the break of fast. My father nodded curtly and continued to talk to Dhavod of the news that my brother Balev's wife would soon bear another child. Liya and Ezirae joined us, and the atmosphere was nearly cordial.

"I hope you need not leave Tulea until after the dance, Dayn," said Liya.

"I must speak with Lord Morgh before he departs Liin for Caruil. We must agree upon the spring shipments. I would delay it if I could, Liya," said Dayn sincerely. It was the first civil exchange I had heard between the two of them in weeks.

"Dayn will be gone no more than a month, Liya," offered

Dhavod as consolation. "The negotiations should proceed quite quickly, since nullification of the Niveallan agreement virtually demands acceptance of Lord Morgh's terms." My father made no comment, and the conversation strayed to other topics. It was the only reference made to any change of status effected by my declaration of the previous night.

Chapter 16

As Liya predicted, the Solstice Dance of Prince Orlin was a much less extravagant affair than the king's ball. Held in the same enormous hall, the ranks of attendees seemed even smaller than the scant two hundred of Ezirae's estimate, despite the extending illusion of the mirrored walls. The effect apparently satisfied His Royal Highness, who enjoyed the company of the prettiest Seriin ladies of his age. In contrast to the remote splendor of the royal dais the night of King Astorn's gala, the vivacious swarm around Orlin had the impact of a young boy's birthday party supervised from a discreet distance by his elders.

As a result of the youthful takeover of the positions of highest traditional rank, many of the more exalted members of the Seriin court mingled freely among the multitudes. Liya tallied the aristocracy of her dance partners by a ratio involving the number of times she had previously met them and the occasions of their fame; since she had never before met Lord Gorng Dolr'han dur Liin, that gentleman apparently achieved the highest rating. She berated me, during a moment of private discussion, for my inability to name more than three of my own partners. I had danced with Ineuil, Amgor, and Ezirae's brother, Lord Zam; I had danced with a few others, but their faces had faded as well as their names.

"You are hopeless, Rhianna," sighed Liya with a hint of condescending humor.

"And I hoped she might be improving," said Yldana, appearing with the illustrious Veiga. "Perhaps we can endeavor a cure. How has Rhianna failed us, Liya?"

The sight of Lady Veiga had Liya speechlessly entranced by virtue of an astonishing display of rubies, as much as by the lady's own mystique. Lady Veiga obviously enjoyed her effect on the gaping girl. Liya's eyes widened farther as a subtle movement brought the chandeliers' fire to ignite the stones around Veiga's neck.

"Lady Liya seems rather hopelessly uncommunicative," drawled Veiga. "Is the failing congenital among your kin, Yldana?"

Liya blushed in embarrassment. "Rhianna and I were discussing dance partners," said Liya, belatedly answering Yldana's query.

Veiga raised her topaz eyes to the ceiling, commenting, "What a fascinating subject. Tell me, Lady Liya, have you actually discovered anyone of interest in this prepubescent assortment of our regent's delight?"

Yldana responded diplomatically, "Not all of us are so difficult to please, Veiga. Even I have found a few intriguing opportunities tonight."

Lady Veiga scanned the room with blatant boredom, but her inspection narrowed upon a late entrant. "Possibly you are correct, Yldana," she murmured. "Not every interesting man kept to his own Hall tonight."

Following Veiga's gaze, Liya proffered doubtfully, "I suppose he is handsome."

"So are many statues," retorted Yldana in a brittle voice.

Lady Veiga's lips twisted in an arrogant smile. "You disappoint me, Yldana. There is fire beneath that ice for the lady who dares to rouse it."

"Lady Veiga!" remonstrated Liya, shocked into rebuking her idol. "He is the Infortiare!"

"Lady Liya!" mimicked Veiga. "I am a Dolr'han!"

Yldana was uncomfortable. "Veiga, I am sure Liya meant no insult."

"Really, Yldana," sneered the beautiful Veiga, caressing her burning rubies with a spidery hand. "The affair was no great secret. If it offends you less, Lady Liya, you may console yourself in knowing that Lord Venkarel was only an insignificant Ixaxin student when I knew him. At the time, my association with him was considered quite demeaning to *me*, but I happened to be very bored that particular summer."

Liya having been effectively horrified, Veiga left us with an airy smirk. Not quite able to conceal her own dismay, Yldana said brightly, "Veiga enjoys her little jests, Liya. If I am not mistaken, Lord Ghren is trying desperately to attract your attention. Be merciful to the poor man and dance with him." She shooed Liya across the room, then stood immobile and expressionless, watching Lady Veiga stop to bespeak Lord Venkarel.

"It was not a jest, was it, Yldana?" I asked with studied calm.

Yldana had quite forgotten me, and she started when I spoke. "No, of course not," she answered impatiently. "Veiga often amused herself with Hrgh's classmates." Almost angrily, she snapped, "What does it matter to you? You are a sorceress. What a pity for Tyntagel that Father never offered *you* to Hrgh!" Tears gathered in her eyes.

"Yldana," I began, bewildered by this vulnerability from my unassailable sister at a moment when I was myself none too steady. Yldana pushed away from me and fled toward the ladies' chambers. I started to follow, but Yldana would not welcome my sympathy. I made my own escape to the deserted patio in the shadow of the colonnades. Yldana's collapse distressed me—more since I deemed its cause was largely the golden Lord Hrgh. With Lady Veiga I was infuriated; I refused to examine the cause of my excessive ire. I forced myself to unthinking calm as I listened to the nightsong of the trees, merging with the music and the murmurs from the ballroom.

I did not hear his approach, but I felt his presence. "Does a contrite wizard merit a waltz with a lady of Tyntagel?" asked Kaedric softly from behind me. I paused before turning, trying to still a torrent of conflicting reactions. I would not meet his eyes, but I accepted his hand with a silent curtsy.

He held me gently, in his arms and his Power. "You spoke to me truly, my lady. I grow as dangerously arrogant as Hrgh."

"I ought not to have spoken as I did, my lord."

He grinned at me. "It was incautious," he admitted. "I ought to flay Medwyn and Marga for putting you up to it."

"Please do not blame them, my lord," I said with some concern.

"Worry not, my lady of the Dwaelin. I have not allowed my temper to exceed the capacity of my antagonist since Ven." I must have looked doubtful. Kaedric laughed a trifle shamefacedly. "As you so pointedly observed, my lady, we did use the Taormin together. I have a rather good idea of the extent of your Power."

"That is not a particularly comforting thought," I answered dryly, but a part of me exulted.

"It should be; it is the reason Marga supported Medwyn's choice of you as the voice of sanity. If I seriously tried to harm you, my lady, I should be opening myself to equal injury. Marga knows that I am far too selfish to risk that contingency."

I could not credit his words, though he voiced them sincerely. "The only person I seem able to injure is myself, my lord."

"Lord Grisk might differ with that statement, if he were privy to the pertinent facts." After a moment's silence, Kaedric added, "Would it be injudicious to applaud the termination of your engagement?"

"Is there such a thing as a secret in Tulea?" I asked rhetorically, but his innocuous comment affected me disproportionately. For no good reason, I felt it incumbent upon me to explain, "My lord, I never acknowledged my supposed betrothal. I was simply slow in informing my family of their mistake. I expected them to be furious."

"They are not?" asked Kaedric with an intonation between statement and question.

"By appearance at least, they are not," I agreed.

"Lord Baerod finally realizes how foolish it would be to waste you on that Niveallan catastrophe. It may be the first time your father and I are in accord."

"More likely, my father found a better trade agreement and was glad of an excuse to break with Lord Brant." I attempted a lightness I did not feel. The touch of the Infortiare's devastating Power disturbed me less than the unexpected, deep awareness of the dance we shared. I collected my unruly emotions. "But you have certainly analyzed my father's motives in this as in any other act of potential political import."

"Suspicion is a bad habit of mine," conceded Kaedric in a self-deprecating whisper. His fingers gripped mine. He had gathered me against him: I was not sure when we had moved so close; I did not know how long my cheek had brushed his. A tremble would bring my lips to his. I stepped back, fiercely flustered, until only my fingers lay still within Kaedric's.

"May I expect you at the Tower tomorrow, my lady?" asked Kaedric, watching me intensely with his blue crystalline eyes. I drew my hand quickly from his grasp, regretting my panicked retreat as his eyes returned to frost. "Since you have apparently taken an interest in the Taormin, Lady Rhianna, I would discuss it with you. Come or not, as you please. I thank you for the dance."

"Rhianna?" came Liya's tentative whisper. Warily, she glanced from side to side of the desolate patio before joining me. "We are preparing to leave, Rhianna. Your father is looking for you." Hurriedly, she added, "I did not tell him where you were. I was so afraid *he* would still be here."

"You are muddling your pronouns, Liya," I commented.

"I looked for you earlier, Rhianna," said Liya. "I saw you with Lord Venkarel."

"You wanted me to find interesting dance partners."

"He is the Infortiare."

"That obviously did not concern Lady Veiga," I remarked wryly, "whom I thought you so fervently wished to emulate."

"A Dolr'han may do things that are questionable, but you are not a Dolr'han, Rhianna."

I smiled at her a little sadly. "I only danced with the man, Liya. Even my father would not consider that a crime."

She sniffed disapprovingly. "I should not care to be seen dancing that way even with Dayn. You were virtually embracing."

"What nonsense," I answered crisply. "You let the shadows delude you. Even if I were as brazen as you imply, why would the Infortiare take an interest in me? Ixaxis and Tyntagel are not notoriously compatible." I laughed at her crestfallen face. "I believe you are so desperate for a scandal that you have begun concocting them. Ezirae is influencing you badly, Liya." By the time we returned to our family, I had convinced her that her imagination and Lady Veiga's jest had conspired to create delusions.

I nearly persuaded myself as well.

We met not in the Tower library but in a small adjacent room furnished with a single large table and the five mismatched chairs we occupied: Kaedric, Marga, Medwyn, Ineuil and myself. I felt out of place. The feeling mounted as Kaedric explained his reason for summoning us.

"You are each in some sense integrally involved in this decision. My own vote has been made, but I have been reminded that even the Infortiare—or especially the Infortiare—must not make the choice alone. Obviously, I could consult His Royal Highness, Prince Orlin, and the King's Council: they would debate the question, if they considered it at all, for so many months that the point would lose all relevance. We shall not need to locate Horlach via the Taormin once he has begun his attack in earnest."

"Since you have chosen the electors," suggested Ineuil, "it seems that you intend still to make the decision yourself."

"Ineuil's point is well taken, Kaedric," said Abbot Medwyn.

Marga interposed, "Kaedric has been accused at one time or another of nearly everything but stupidity and overwhelming concern for the opinions of others. Be grateful he consults us at all, gentlemen." With a flash of potent spirit, she proceeded, "If either of you considers *me* a spineless sycophant, let me reassure you: I vote against the use of the Taormin." Only Kaedric did not visibly react to Mistress Marga's announcement; he had withdrawn from the discussion to observe. "The rest of you may discuss it as long as it amuses you, but you either agree with Kaedric or not. This business of weighing factors is a procrastinator's pretense."

"Not all of us understand the subject as well as might a member of the Ixaxin Council, Mistress Marga," said Abbot Medwyn. It struck me that the charitable abbot did not much care for Mistress Marga.

"It would be helpful if we at least understood the feasibility of using the Taormin to any advantage," suggested Ineuil carelessly, tilting his chair to a precarious angle.

"Very well," said Marga irritably, "I shall apprise. Kaedric is perfectly capable of using the Taormin."

"I thought Ixaxis considered the Taormin impossible to utilize in these days of diminished Power," inserted Ineuil.

"Do not interrupt me, Lord Arineuil. However, you have made a relevant comment. On the occasion of your brash, youthful masquerade as a latent sorcerer, you apparently absorbed some small amount of sense. At that time, we did teach that the Taormin's secrets were beyond the capacity of current wizardry. Circumstances forced us to amend our assessment as we realized that Kaedric's Power exceeded anything referenced in the annals of Ixaxis since Ceallagh contained Horlach initially. Kaedric can use the Taormin, which is precisely why he must not. We cannot be sure whether Horlach originally warped the Taormin to his schemes or whether it corrupted him."

Ineuil summarized with incongruous jocularity, "All hail, King Venkarel!"

"Horlach knew that the Power of a Sorcerer King was reborn," I said slowly, without thinking. Even Kaedric displayed a flicker of surprise at my words. I had suddenly become the reluctant cynosure.

Pensively, Marga nodded and said with a trace of wonder, "What a thought that is. Hrgh did not awaken Horlach. Horlach was never fully bound; he used Hrgh to draw Kaedric into activating the Taormin."

Abbot Medwyn sighed with regret, "I wish I could disbelieve it. I am sorry, Kaedric. I must vote with Mistress Marga."

"Then the deciding vote belongs to Rhianna," declared Ineuil unexpectedly. "I prefer the possibility of King Venkarel to the certainty of King Horlach." With a shrug, he yielded attention to me.

I had wanted no part of this conference, agreeing to attend only under the combined blandishments of Abbot Medwyn and Kaedric. Uselessly, I wished that Ineuil had not this once opted to concur with the Infortiare's choice of method. I directed my answer to Kaedric, for the decision had been made and he alone mattered. "My lord, if you will accept my presence when you use the Taormin, I shall give my sanction."

With a slight smirk, Marga observed, "Under the circumstances, Rhianna is uniquely qualified to monitor. Your lady appears to be a suitable match for you, Kaedric."

Kaedric did not answer for a moment. "Are you prepared to begin immediately, Lady Rhianna?"

"As you will, my lord."

Chapter 17

The stairs leading upward from the Tower library were much narrower and more tightly coiled than those with which I had grown familiar in the Tower's lower realms. They were paneled in the same dark wood, giving them a claustrophobic impact which chilled me. Kaedric had taken me alone through that door which I had never yet passed. Marga, Medwyn and Ineuil had left us; Marga had agreed with Kaedric that the dangers inherent in the experiment with the Taormin made non-participating observers an inadvisable luxury.

We climbed the stairs to the highest room of Ceallagh's Tower, a room so small in girth that I suspected it had been intended as no more than an observatory. It was a spartan chamber, that which Kaedric had made his own. Despite sense and the weighty cause which brought us, I halted at the threshold in prudish reluctance. Kaedric remarked with some amusement, "Since you intend to enter my mind, Lady Rhianna, entering my chamber ought not to daunt you."

He was quite correct, but Tyntagellian custom had conditioned me. I focused on our goal and its import. "The Taormin is not here," I observed in puzzlement.

"It is accessible from here." Kaedric nodded toward a high window which framed the vale of Ceallagh's tomb. "This is the only window in the Tower from which Tul's peaks are clearly visible."

"The Taormin is unguarded?" I asked incredulously.

"I entrusted it to him most qualified to hold it: Lord Ceallagh. It is far safer than keeping it here or at Benthen Abbey." He moved a fawn rug, which might once have been fine, to an area of the floor from which the tomb could be seen, and he seated himself cross-legged upon it. "For our present purpose, a certain distance from the Taormin itself is desirable. I merely feel more comfortable knowing the thing is in some sense before my eyes. It is probably an unnecessary conceit."

He gestured, and I sat opposite him on the rug, my wine-colored skirts spilling across the smooth wood floor. Kaedric studied the base of the mountain cleft, but I was certain he beheld a thing of amber filigree. I watched his eyes grow distant. With a fatalistic sigh, I reached for him with my mind.

Images of images: the Taormin shed impersonal perspective on a child of Ven, a child of Tyntagel. I saw Master Doshk and the dying Fylla. I saw Mistress Ericka and a gardener's son whom I had not known I knew. I heard words which I could never have consciously recalled to comprehension.

This was not the chaotic scramble fostered by Lord Hrgh. Kaedric drew on the Taormin lightly, probing its intricate tangles with a delicate respect for the patterns' potentials. I could not alone have found any method in the tortuous weave, but I followed Kaedric, and my surety of Power grew with the design.

Kaedric pressed a twist of tangled filament: anger, fear, confusion, and a bitter depth of loathing abetted by shattered pride. It was the larger part of Lord Hrgh Dolr'han, the part which knew that Horlach had condemned him to be a pawn in the struggle for an ill-born, once-slave of Ven. Kaedric smoothed the binding knot of darkness.

"You are as damned as I, Venkarel," stated Hrgh clearly. "Horlach will use you, but it will be your name, not his, that is cursed through the coming ages. You and your infernal Power will live forever, more surely enslaved than you were when you were born."

"I can free you, Hrgh," sighed Kaedric with rending pity for the paragon of whom only hatred remained.

"I want none of your mercy, whoreson," countered Hrgh furiously.

Kaedric stayed the releasing touch. "Have you not paid enough

for the sake of pride, Hrgh?" I marveled that the remorseless Infortiare could find such sympathy for a man who returned only
disdain. Hrgh suffered terribly, but I could feel no compassion for
the lord of Liin, bound as much by his own superciliousness as by
King Horlach.

It was murder, in a sense, which I contemplated. As such, I
would rue it, but Hrgh had already lost the form of man, and he
lacked the strength of Power to walk the Taormin freely. The bindings wracked him. "Lord Hrgh," I said coldly, "you shame the First
Houses of Serii. But my sister loved you." Hrgh stiffened, for he
perceived and knew me then, though we had never truly met. Arrogance poured from him, and he would not bespeak me, but he
raised no will to stop me, for I was a lady of his own rank. I completed the gesture which Kaedric had begun, and Lord Hrgh an
Morgh yn Elga Dolr'han dur Liin received such peace as death
could give him.

Kaedric touched me gently, and we sat again in the Tower room,
the burnished sun of Tulean winter patterning our shadows.
"When first I arrived at Ixaxis," explained Kaedric pensively, "I
considered Hrgh Dolr'han the epitome of everything I had never
known: honor, erudition, refinement. I emulated him, and he tolerated me because I amused his vanity. His patronage eased a time of
very difficult transition for me." Kaedric stood and, offering his
hand, drew me to my feet. "If I attempt any more today," he said
with a slight regretful smile, "My head will throb for a week. The
Taormin apparently requires the exercise of some neglected mental
sinew. Will you forgive me, my lady, if I neglect to escort you out?"

I withheld a faint smile of my own, for such genteel courtesies
had never concerned him previously. "Of course, my lord," I responded very formally. I turned to leave, but Kaedric restrained me
briefly.

"My lady, if you continue to assist me, Horlach will no longer
need me to regain his material life."

"Is that what he seeks of you?" I asked slowly.

"He wants a host able to hold his Power. I doubt the question of
gender will seriously concern him. Be very cautious, my lady."

Ineuil had lingered at the garden access, and he hailed me as I
emerged. "I feared I might be waiting here a day and night or,

worse, that the earth might shatter while I watched. Since neither calamity transpired, shall I assume the experiment proved un-eventful?"

I felt little urge to speak of the past hour, especially to Ineuil. Since I had just sent his erstwhile friend to death, I found answering his cheerful query grimly awkward. Unable to gentle the news, I said directly, "Ineuil, Lord Hrgh is dead."

"I suppose I expected that," he responded soberly. "Still, I kept hoping for some miraculous resurrection of the friend of my youth. Fate is seldom kind to foolish hopes."

"I am sorry," I murmured sincerely.

"It is not of your doing," he said with forced brightness, and I did not correct him. The truth held too much complexity to convey. "Were there any other discoveries of note?" When I shook my head negatively, he continued, "Well, we shall see stirrings soon enough, I warrant. Horlach will not rest idly while Kaedric masters the Taormin. I assume that Horlach knows when the Taormin is used?"

I shrugged my ignorance. "It seems likely. We may only hope that he has no means of reaching it for the present."

Ineuil stared at me strangely. "I wish I could shirk the eerie feeling that I am talking to Kaedric."

I looked at Ineuil with surprise which yielded to disquiet. "Was I quoting him?" I asked brittlely. "I suppose in matters of wizardry I have few other references."

"You have become a model wizardess, infinitely loyal to her Infortiare. I regret to say that I preferred the shy sorceress."

Having accustomed myself to Ineuil's meaningless praise, I found his earnest criticism a stinging reversal. "I serve the Infortiare as you do, Lord Arineuil. That does not make me an Ixaxin."

"You have changed, Rhianna. Even your sister sees it."

"You know my sister far better than I do," I returned caustically.

"I am not the one to blame for your lack of sibling understanding. Yldana envies you devilishly. I once thought she had some cause, but I can only pity a woman who loves Kaedric. Good day to you, Lady Rhianna."

"Good day to you, Lord Arineuil," I responded mechanically, benumbed. The Taormin could mold me to Kaedric's contour if I were incautious, a fact which I had allowed myself to forget. As for the rest, I concluded that Ineuil had devoted himself too long to the pursuit of romantic interludes, shook my head, and followed the path to Tyntagel Hall.

Year of Serii—9008
Liin Keep, Liin, Serii

How like Morgh, thought Dayn uncharitably, to give better to Caruillan sycophants than to a fellow member of a First House. Since I arrived, I have been managing Liin for him virtually unaided, and not a whit of appreciation does he give me; he does not even give solid answer on the trade agreement. This is the first state dinner to which he has invited me, and I only serve here to fill the odd corner by the kitchen.

Dayn stared glumly at the half-naked backs of two bulky Caruillan officers, wondering how the Caruillans kept from freezing in the Seriin climate. The two soldiers comprised Dayn's view of the dining hall. When one of the officers moved to another table, Dayn decided that the expanded view was yet worse. The room seemed a sea of Caruillans, grabbing food indiscriminately and seldom resorting to any proper utensil. The soldiers (Dayn had yet to discern any Caruillan whose function was not primarily military) seemed to spend remarkably little time actually eating; they occupied themselves mainly in pulling at and pinching the comelier serving maids. The result was a chaotic failure of the usual Liin staff efficiency and a great deal of grumbling from the kitchen.

In his neglected corner, Dayn, receiving barely a third of the dinner's courses, retreated farther toward the wall in a vain attempt to avoid the crush of distraught servants, and began to feel even more miserable than he had during the last few depressing days. He tried a gingerly sip of wine, grimaced and settled for another roll. Dry bread seemed more palatable than the richly sauced comestibles. Unhappiness and worry had always tended to take a toll on Dayn's stomach.

Dayn watched the noble men and women of Liin, while his vague feeling of nausea grew. These selfsame silken sophisticates had no use for a younger son of the Tyntagel Lord, but they toasted the king of Caruil and cheered his pirates, because Lord Morgh commanded and Lord Morgh knew where advantage lay. All hail King Cor of Caruil, for he has eradicated a great, terrible hold of schoolchildren. All hail Blood-Talon Cor, who has conquered for us, because he does not share our shrinking cowardice.

Morgh is going to toast Caruil again, decided Dayn, as Liin's liege rose and commanded silence with an imperious gesture, which most of the Caruillans ignored and most of Liin's nobility were too sated and stupefied to comprehend. "To new friends!" declared Morgh grandly. Insipid, thought Dayn; Morgh looks his age and more, despite his tailor's talent for hiding Dolr'han paunch, but need he act so feeble-witted? It is a wonder even these Caruillan savages can abide him.

"To the expansion of the Alliance, and to the strengthening of our united cause!" cried some Dolr'han scion.

"To the death of Ixaxis!" added another Liinite thickly. Do they ever tire of hearing themselves prate, wondered Dayn sourly, and an extra hint of guilt gnawed at his pained internals.

King Cor rose rather slowly, pausing to adjust the gilt scabbard of Caruillan formal wear. The Caruillan men, so far as Dayn had been able to determine, never changed their peculiar attire, nor did each own more than a single set of leather breeches and soiled silk vest. For state occasions, Caruillan dignitaries simply doffed steel arms in favor of painted tin, as Cor had made a great show of explaining on first arriving.

Cor was a swarthy, surprisingly little man with a shrewd eye, a ruthless sense of humor, and a fine instinct for opportunism. "My good friends," announced Cor with such deliberation that Dayn straightened and forgot his discomfort. "The welcome you have shown us is deeply heartening. We are pleased by your city, which makes my next remarks sincerely sorrowful to me." Every Caruillan in the room had grown quiet and attentive. The oblivious voices of Liin arrogance sputtered over incoherent sounds from the city beyond the keep walls, while Blood-Talon Cor displayed his stained and broken teeth in a feral smile.

"When your emissary first approached me, Lord Morgh," continued Cor cheerfully, "I must confess that I thought your ideas of cooperation absurd. We of Caruil are warriors, who take and rule by strength. I had doubt of any benefit you soft-living Seriins could offer us." Morgh's finely pleased expression did not waver, carved from either political practice or too much wine, even when Cor draped his glance appreciatively across the Lady Galea Dolr'han,

Morgh's second cousin and reputed mistress. "We have come to see, however, that your city holds more treasure than we ever realized. It is fortunate, this," said Cor heartily, "for otherwise we might be very unhappy with you for misleading us."

Those nobles of Liin who remained capable of any comprehension began to look puzzled. Dayn struggled to push the clouds from his own senses, for an illogical suspicion had occurred to him. He eyed the wine from which he had briefly sipped and wondered if he imagined the trace of cloudiness in its midst.

Three staccato screams seemed suddenly to drive into Dayn's brain. The bulky soldier in front of him drove his ornamental dagger into the neck of Lord Okhren Dolr'han. Through the nobleman's spurting blood, Dayn watched a ghastly play of treachery begin, and yet he did nothing.

"You promised us the 'unimaginable wealth' of Ixaxis," shouted Cor to a bewildered Morgh, "so we fought the stinking rocks of Ixaxin waters to take the accursed island, and we found nothing! There are no wizards there, and the only treasure is a load of chalk and lies. I do not know what game you thought to play, Morgh, or if you could really be so simple as to believe in the godhood of your damned Infortiare, but I am not a fool to humor you longer. I conquered your dreaded island for you, even if the winds and reefs alone fought back, and I will be paid." Cor had taken a sound sword from his tinseled scabbard, and he sliced Lord Morgh's still bemused head from its neck.

Dayn had risen, but the door from the kitchen had been flung open, pressing his back against the cold, mirrored wall. He heard the shrieking slaughter, and he feared to move. It was his old, deep fear and doubts made real: that in true battle he would be unable to function and would so bring shame upon his father. He had served in the king's army for five years and found no certain answer; he had guarded Serii's vague northern borders diligently, earned (what he considered) unmerited praise for so well securing the northern cities and townships of his jurisdiction, captured and successfully intimidated many of the thugs and robbers who frequented the more desolate lands, but he had never fought a battle that was not wholly weighted in his favor.

Dayn believed himself a coward. The notion had grown in him over the years since he first ran in panic from his sister's sorcery.

He had clung to his older brother's side and opinions, trying to emulate one who did not know this terror of being found weak. His frail baby sister had exploded into an ogre before the eyes of his imagination, and he had never again felt secure in his own abilities.

The sounds of bloodshed retreated from Liin's Great Dining Hall, and Dayn emerged cautiously from his dim corner. He would not look at the carnage which was all that remained of Dolr'han nobility. He would not face the fabulous rooms and passageways which Dolr'han feet had for centuries proudly trod. Dayn slipped around the door and into the kitchen, taking the servants' way, for he felt it suited his shame.

The servants had fared no better than their masters, and bodies slumped against the once spotless white tiles. A woman was crying, and Dayn saw a grinning Caruillan complete the act of rape by stabbing her to death. The Caruillan spotted Dayn and lunged at him with bloodied sword. Dayn dodged and kicked instinctively, knocking the Caruillan against the kitchen's marble table. Dayn ran blindly into the unfamiliar corridors of the servants' wing, but the Caruillan followed in an instant.

It took only a pause before a latched door for Dayn to lose his previous lead. The Caruillan was as huge as most of his countrymen; he slammed Dayn against the door with an effortless force. Dayn tasted warm blood and did not know whether it flowed from the sharp pain in his lip or the ache of a smashed nose. He waited for the searing sharpness of steel to cut his spine. He could only turn around dumbly when the Caruillan's weight sagged and slipped from him.

"That is for what you did to Leisa," cursed a rather pudgy man to his victim; he pulled a hefty knife from the dead Caruillan's back. The man wore servants' clothes, and they had been torn and spattered. "I never butchered anything but dinner before this," added the man a little apologetically, now addressing Dayn. "My name is Targar. Can you use one of these?" he asked, offering Dayn the Caruillan's sword.

Dayn's voice caught, and he could not answer. He settled for a nervous nod and accepted the weapon from Targar's rough hand. Dayn fit his fingers around the sword's hilt with loathing; only a few traces of the deceptive gold paint still clung to the sword's pommel.

Dayn helped Targar to drag the Caruillan away from the door, then meekly followed Targar through the portal. They picked their way through dead men and women who had been dragged from work, ease or slumber. The bodies of the Keep guards had already stiffened, and their cloaks had been stripped from them. All of the bodies were nameless to Dayn, but Targar acknowledged each with a nod of stoic respect.

"There is a stair to the cellars along here," offered Targar. "We can take the cellar route clear to the gate house."

"I cannot leave the keep undefended," said Dayn automatically, though he continued to follow.

"You want to die?" demanded Targar. "You will if you stay here."

"I am a lord of Serii," argued Dayn unreasonably.

Targar cast Dayn a look of utter disgust. "The whole bloody Caruillan army is in Liin, and you lords of Serii brought them here. I am not blaming you personally, mind, but if I were you, I think I might trust to someone else's judgment for a while. Maybe you have not been seeing too clearly who your friends are."

Dayn stared at the plump and very ugly Targar, realizing that he owed his life to a menial from the Liin Keep kitchens. "Mayhap you are correct," conceded Dayn with a sudden sympathy for Targar's resentment. Targar had extended the first generosity Dayn had witnessed in Liin. It irked Dayn, for it forced on him unpalatable ideas.

A pair of Caruillans lurched from a side passage, espied Dayn and Targar, and spilled the bounty of their looting across the floor. Dayn rushed at the larger of the pair, driving his borrowed sword upward through the man's viscera. Targar had tackled the other Caruillan, before the pirate could free himself of his plunder. Dayn hacked off the Caruillan's foot, and Targar's knife found its way into the Caruillan's tattooed hide.

Dayn offered a sword to Targar, who shook his head. "I would as soon use a tool I know," insisted Targar fervently. Dayn nodded; he could understand a need for the familiar, even when the familiar served less well. A clamor echoed from the hall from which the Caruillan attackers had come. Dayn and Targar rose wordlessly and made their way through narrow, less frequented passages. They could hear the Caruillan plague spread loudly around them.

The cellar door was locked, but Targar drew a key from his waist-ring. Targar entered the dark cellar and found candles by touch. Dayn closed and locked the door behind them, softening the grow-ing sounds of the Caruillan raiders.

As they descended into the cool recesses beneath the servants' wing, the sounds ebbed further, until Dayn could almost persuade himself that the whispering cries were the sounds of a normal, busy Keep. The acres of stored goods astonished him. Dayn thought he could never alone have found passage through the maze of root cellars, wine cellars, fur closets, and granaries. Targar led unerringly and only broke the silence after many minutes: "I wonder how long it will take Cor to find his way down here?"

He was answered by a roar which shook the ground, and the dark room they were on the brink of entering became bright before them. Dayn and Targar retreated hurriedly as a portion of the ceil-ing crashed to the floor in flames. "They have set the Keep on fire," exclaimed Targar wonderingly. The fact seemed to dismay him more visibly than the horrors of the carnage they had already ob-served.

"Is there another exit on this side of the Keep?" asked Dayn sharply.

"There is a loading access, but we could never reach the gate from there."

"We shall certainly never reach the gate from here," countered Dayn, shouting to be heard over the flames and cracking timbers.

They were forced to retrace their steps through four rooms. They hastened through four more rooms as the sounds of fire raced behind them; the greater part of Liin Keep had been carved from layered stone, but the servants' wing had been built primarily of wood. When Dayn and Targar had climbed the last stair, Targar hesitated, fumbling overlong with his keys, before opening the door. Dayn did not press him, for he, too, feared to face the cer-tainty of enemies in the courtyard; Dayn did cast uneasy glances at the glow of spreading fire. The flames expanded into fury as they reached the kegs of ale in the next room, and Targar flung open the door with a burst of desperation.

Liin Keep burned spectacularly, though the marble and gold fa-cade of the Dolr'han quarters resisted the assault. In the yard the army of Liin fought, taking better toll of Caruil than Cor might have expected, but the effort could be called no more than feeble. Liin's army had been outfitted for parades and trained in protocol; even Dayn knew more of tactics than Liin's generals. Dayn and Targar shoved themselves through the fray, clinging to each other's company, though they barely knew whether those at whom they slashed were foe or ally. The bright banners, which had been hung in honor of Caruil and Cor, curled and smoked overhead; they would carry the sparks through the city, and the finely carved woods and tapestried walls would shrivel to cinder and ash. Like a wizard's fury, thought Dayn bitterly.

Dayn shut his ears to screams and lingering moans, to the crackle of a city afire, and to the cries of incredulous Liin. He and Targar ran when they could, pressed relentlessly through mobs of fleeing citizens, killed when some persistent Caruillan could not be dodged, and gradually neared the city's edge. There is no honor in survival, thought Dayn, when so many who are innocent die. He wanted to stop, yield to the massacre, but Targar tugged at him and he continued.

Did hours pass? Years could have come and gone, and Dayn would not have known. The mighty Pontneun gate of Liin had crumbled by the time Dayn and Targar reached it; it had been clawed and torn by its own desperate citizenry. With Cor's fleet occupying the harbor, and the eastern half of the city aflame, only a few of the great gates offered exit. Cor's legions had secured the wall early, knowing its strategic advantage, and they held it comfortably, sending Liin's own arrows into the frantic crowds below.

It had become a Caruillan game to let most of those who neared the gate stand safely. The Caruillans rained arrows only on those who sought to pass. The game did allow a few escapes, but the Caruillans enjoyed the sport of baiting still more than easy slaughter. They watched closely the folk who hesitated: it was hard to leave a sanctuary, however temporary and artificial, to face such unpromising odds of survival as awaited those who braved the gateway. Shopkeepers, who had never thought to face such certain danger, wavered, debating their chances. Scrubs and harlots huddled with merchant's wives, united by indecision. Occasionally one figure would start to run, hoping to catch the Caruillan archers unaware, and a flurry of frightened people might follow.

A tow-headed girl ran out the gate alone and died a pace from the wall. A young boy ran next and died a handspan away from her, but a dozen of his comrades continued fleeing. Arrows pursued them, but at least two men kept running, and one survived beyond the archers' range, his example encouraging another rush. Dayn and Targar joined the dash, though Dayn berated himself fiercely; he was quite probably the only lord of Serii left alive in wretched Liin, and duty whispered cruelly that her defeat belonged to his cowardice. Dayn also knew that Targar had been right to counsel escape; Liin, the great, golden hub of Seriin elitism, could not be salvaged by any resource left within her.

Dayn did not see Targar fall, but the serving man with his brave butcher's knife did not reach the haphazard cluster of survivors, who had gathered in exhaustion at the nearest edge of safety. Dayn sat with the others upon the bare earth, watching the smoke of the city hide the stars. The cries were muted from here, indistinguishable if one did not know the source. The tired little knot of survivors shared the silence. Most had lost home and family. All had lost a measure of innocence and hope. All feared that morning would renew the horror, bringing the Caruillan horde spilling across the valley like a spreading disease. Most recognized that the nightmare which had so abruptly shattered their complacent lives had only begun its work.

Chapter 18

Year of Serii—9008
Tyntagel Hail, Tulea

"**H**ave you received any word from Dayn, Liya dear?" asked Ezirae across the table. My father looked at Ezirae irritably, for her supper conversations with Liya invariably managed to cut across his with Dhavod.

Liya did not quite succeed at smiling. "There has been nothing since the first letter, Aunt Ezirae," she said patiently, as she had done each day of the past week. "Dayn told me that he would have little time for writing. Lord Morgh asked him to assist in entertaining the Caruillan guests."

"Caruillans," tutted Ezirae predictably. "My father, may his soul rest freely, always maintained that the only thing less trustworthy than a dyrcat was a Caruillan. He always maintained that."

"I am sure he did," responded Liya gravely.

"I simply cannot understand it," continued Ezirae heedlessly. "Everyone is treating the Caruillans like honored guests these days. Lord Morgh dur Liin caters to them, and King Astorn has gone off to Bethii to discuss giving them trade privileges. A year ago, Caruillans were raiding our coasts. It is all so bewildering."

My father had heard Ezirae make similar comments many times before, but he had disregarded them as he disregarded nearly everything Ezirae said or did. His mood was less charitable tonight. "You need not parade your ignorance for us constantly, Ezirae," he said cuttingly. "We are well aware of your indomitable biases. What is it now?" he demanded impatiently as a commotion arose in the hall.

A stained and disheveled version of my usually impeccable brother pushed past startled servants. With a little cry of horror, Liya ran to him and stopped a pace away, not quite touching his rent and blackened coat. "My Lord Father," said Dayn with the stiffness of exhaustion. Dayn swayed, and Dhavod moved to steady him, guiding my brother with Liya's help to the chair which Liya had occupied. Dayn raised his head slowly, and I could not believe that the bitterness contorting his features belonged to my brother.

"What has happened to you?" demanded our father accusingly. Liya shook her head in protest, but Dayn straightened defensively.

"I failed you, Father," said Dayn with forced tightness. "I did not gain your precious trade exchange with Liin. Lord Morgh is dead, and the Caruillans have taken the city."

"What madness is this?" asked my father irritably.

"An ugly man with a knife told me that the madness was ours, my Lord Father. The lords of Serii are all mad." Dayn's voice trailed, then surged harshly. "I thought to spend no more than a few idle days in Liin, merely formalizing a trade agreement on which all interested parties had already concurred, but Lord Morgh requested my assistance in a matter of 'local diplomacy.' Lord Morgh intimated that I could alleviate the painful vacancy left by the banishment of his son. Lord Morgh needed me to manage Liin's mundane affairs, while the Dolr'hans celebrated their Caruillan guests."

"Why ever would Lord Morgh associate with such barbarians?" asked Ezirae. "I really cannot understand what the Caruillans have to offer which could possibly outweigh their disgusting personal habits."

Dayn laughed acidly. "They offered to attack Ixaxis for us, Aunt Ezirae. We lacked the stomach to do it ourselves."

Our father interposed with a quick frown, "Dayn, you are rambling."

Dayn struck the table an impatient blow which rattled the crystal. "It is not a secret any longer, Father. By the morrow, the word will have spread all over Tulea, and the rest of Serii will know before the week ends. It is the Caruillan battle cry; they laugh it in our faces." Dayn turned to Liya, who gazed at him possessively. "We have kept the secret overlong, alienating even those we love for the sake of conspiracy. Lord Morgh was not the only Seriin Lord bewitched by Caruil." Dayn looked meaningfully at our iron-willed father, who only fractionally dropped his gaze before my bedraggled brother's censure. "The result of the Caruillan foray against Ixaxis is not altogether clear, Father, since we have only King Cor's rendition on which to rely. The Caruillans claim that they took Ixaxis unchallenged. They fought the island's natural defenses, scaled the chalky cliffs, and found nothing: no treasures, no pillage for their coffers, and not a wizard, scholar, or beardless boy.

" 'You offered us a city, Lord Morgh,' said Cor, 'but your choice did not impress us. We have decided, however, to be generous and accept as substitute the city of Liin.'

"I am not sure Lord Morgh ever really comprehended Cor's words. Cor drew a very genuine sword from his decorative scabbard and decapitated the Lord of Liin."

Dhavod had turned ashen; Ezirae stared without comprehension. Liya had buried her face against Dayn's trembling knee. My father had closed his eyes and bowed his head toward the goblet in his hand. "How many others escaped?" asked my father with the faintest trace of a quaver.

Dayn shook his head. "From Liin Keep, perhaps a few servants. There were more survivors from the city itself, but not as many as there should have been." Dayn's voice cracked. Liya's hand crept into that of her husband, and his fingers tightened around hers.

"You are free of it now, Dayn," she reassured him quietly.

"You never saw Liin, did you, Liya? One could deride the Dolr'han snobbery, but they were right to be proud of their domain." Dayn stared beyond us. "A serving man named Targar used a butcher's knife to save my life. We fought our way free together through the whole accursed city, and Targar died at the gate." Dayn choked at the memory.

"Did the Caruillans use sorcery?" I asked fearfully. My own mind echoed Dayn's account with the chaotic horror of a dying Ven.

Dayn explained to me with care, as if I had no wit to understand, "It was to abolish wizardry that we approached Caruil initially. Caruillans do use minor sorcery, but they are not wizards to fight with Power." Dayn twisted around toward our grim-faced father. "I think now that such wizards do not exist at all. We have sacrificed Liin, Father, out of fear of a phantasm."

"Venkarel exists," returned our father thinly.

"He is one man," countered Dayn, almost shouting. "We have dreaded to act openly against him for fear of what his guild might do to retaliate. We have listened to Cor and Arku Ruy and Borgor, but what miracle have we ever seen an Ixaxin do? The wizards we fear do not exist. The Ixaxins are a handful of men and women who have built their influence out of myths, and Caruil has made good use of our credulity."

Dhavod answered, "I saw Lord Hrgh fall before Venkarel, Dayn."

"But Hrgh was not harmed," argued Dayn.

"Venkarel destroyed most of Ven," insisted my uncle.

"So the rumors would have us believe," said my brother in response, "but fires start in many ways, and no special Power is needed for their making. The Ixaxins are expert at implying enormous capability without providing any real evidence. They manipulate us! We pour our resources against them, and we achieve nothing. Our supposed allies turn against us, and Venkarel sits in his damnable Tower and laughs at our naiveté."

"Venkarel must have paid Cor richly to betray us," mused our father, unshaken in his confidence. Lord Baerod dur Tyntagel did not show the strain of shock which suddenly painted Dhavod with age. Dhavod lacked the strength of a sorcerous heritage.

"The name of your enemy is not Venkarel," I asserted scornfully. Dayn and my father fastened their attention on me. There was an element almost of contrition in Dayn's eyes, but my father showed suspicion and open loathing. I said firmly, "You have been hurt, Dayn. Take him upstairs, Liya. I shall come shortly to tend him."

Liya obeyed without question, and Dayn was too weary to object. Ezirae hovered helplessly, but a glance at her liege lord's set expression made her decide to follow Liya. My father issued an order to Dhavod with all the natural authority of Tyntagel's Lord: "Bear word to His Royal Highness. The Council must convene." Dhavod bowed and complied, patently relieved to yield to his brother's command. I awaited the confrontation I knew must come.

"What do you know of this matter, Rhianna?" demanded my father. His voice condemned me, blaming me unquestioningly.

"Caruil has started war upon us, and you accuse me?" I asked incredulously.

"I am not altogether blind to your acquaintance with Lord Venkarel, Rhianna. If you know something of his involvement in the attack on Liin, I demand that you reveal it."

"Are you not confusing the names of Caruil's conspiratorial allies, my Lord Father?" I asked, wondering whether Grisk had spoken or my father himself had actually discovered my visits to Ceallagh's Tower.

"The Caruillans have proven their own treachery; they have not exonerated the Infortiare. The story of a deserted Ixaxis is patently absurd. It is far more likely that the Infortiare merely offered the Caruillans a substantial incentive to alter their target to Liin." He reiterated his theory to himself more than to me. "How does one fight the devil?" he growled.

"Why would Lord Venkarel wish to destroy Liin?" I prompted, desolately impressed by my father's unfailing faith in his prejudices.

"Attend your brother, Rhianna. You clearly know nothing of import."

I responded with the meekness expected, "Yes, my Lord Father," feeling helpless against his obduracy. I could not combat my liege. Abbot Medwyn was correct: I could not choose definitively.

Chapter 19

Dayn's physical hurts were not deep. I cleansed them and gave him an infusion of valerian, which would heal Dayn's ragged nerves more than it would his rent skin. I left him to Liya's solicitous care and sped to Ceallagh's Tower, but my delay had given others time to act; Prince Orlin had indeed convened the King's Council, and Kaedric had been summoned to it.

I waited in the Infortiare's library, reading, studying and pacing. My Ixaxin lord would come eventually. Kaedric would not give me comfort, but he would understand my fears. He would recognize the specter which I dreaded more than any Caruillan.

"Your father does have a flair for narrative, my lady," remarked Kaedric as he entered, accepting my presence without question, "but I could wish he had expounded less on his peripheral theories regarding the sack of Liin. Is your brother faring well?"

"Only exhaustion seriously plagues him, my lord. I think Dayn has slept little since fleeing Liin."

"I shouldn't wonder; the death of a city is a nightmarish business. I suppose you await my report," he added with a rather twisted smile. I wanted to tell him that I sought reassurance rather than uncomfortable truths, but I held silent. "And you need not bother with the protest that you have no right to question the Infortiare, since that is presumably why you are here in despite of your Tyntagel proprieties. Very well, I report: Prince Orlin convened the King's Council at your father's behest. After a prolonged dissection of your brother's story, with which I assume you are already acquainted, Prince Orlin has decided to ride forth with a detachment of the Tulean guard to rout King Cor and the Caruillan scavengers. The members of His Royal Highness' select troop will be young gallants who know nothing of actual warfare, but enthusiasm recognizes no damping logic."

"His Royal Highness will not listen to you," I observed resignedly.

"His Royal Highness quakes like an aspen when I address him. In any case, the Adjutant presides over decisions of soldiery, and Lord Borgor encourages His Royal Highness to take immediate military retribution. Since the Caruillans used no obvious sorcery in their attack, I have no lawful jurisdiction save what the regent allows me."

"What of King Cor's allegations regarding Ixaxis?"

"His Royal Highness has been 'persuaded to disbelieve the Caruillan account, but the matter is of secondary importance.' In point of fact, Lord Borgor has convinced His Royal Highness to accept your father's theories, but Prince Orlin is not about to tackle me with an outright accusation. Hence, he shelves the subject and pursues his vision of glorious combat."

"Is the Caruillan account true, my lord?" I persisted.

"I suspect King Cor is incapable of telling the complete truth on any subject."

"My lord, you have a most provoking way of eluding questions."

"My lady, I have had a great deal of practice." I met his mocking glance. The Taormin had made him a part of me, yet I agreed with Ineuil that the woman who loved Lord Venkarel would earn no envy. With more irritation than I had a right to feel, I rose to leave. Kaedric stopped me with a gesture. "By my order, Lady Rhianna, the island of Ixaxis was evacuated over a month ago. I so informed the Council, but the Seriin lords devoted themselves to doubting me rather than assessing the implications of my statement. I did not inform the Council that the Ixaxin Guild members are now dispersed throughout Serii, while most of the Ixaxin artifacts remain concealed on the island."

"Ixaxis had become an obvious target," I mused, focusing on the dark patch amid the phosphorescent sea.

"And a demonstration of wizardly defense, while effective, would only heighten the animosity which we wish to dispel. Unfortunately, I did not account for the Caruillans' peculiar persistence; otherwise, I should not have left Liin so vulnerable, despite Lord Morgh's efforts to counter me."

"Did Horlach direct the Caruillans?"

"I wish I knew the answer to that conundrum, my lady. Horlach certainly merits a share of the blame, but the degree of his involvement is as elusive as his precise location. I spend each Council session inspecting the Seriin lords for Horlach's taint, but I find no madness but their own. Have I assuaged your curiosity sufficiently?"

I had received more information than I had anticipated. "I have been presumptuous again," I said apologetically.

"Where should I find so sympathetic an audience if you were not?" Kaedric rubbed his neck and grimaced. "With the lords of Serii and a Sorcerer King intent upon my demise, words from anyone not bent on my immediate destruction are warmly welcome. I begin to wish that Medwyn had left me in the ashes of Ven. It would have made for a much simpler life."

My mind moved involuntarily to soothe him. It was a reflex as direct as a shift to ease a cramped position. It was the habit of an empath enhanced by the Taormin's patterning. In my mind, Kaedric met me, touched me and withdrew. I recalled that I had feared his touch; I had more cause now, for I comprehended his Power and its ability to change me.

"My lady, I recommend that you depart summarily, lest I harm you more than I have already done." It was a superfluous warning. I had run to the stairs in spontaneous retreat, and his caveat sounded only to my Power.

Chapter 20

Prince Orlin led a brave, bright troop. In crisp crimson, they rode forth proudly; the golden horses, the famed breed raised in Viste, stepped daintily. It was a fine parade: young men well-favored and eager, personally selected by His Royal Highness, the prince regent. His Royal Highness scorned to note the occasional jibe which followed him through Tulea's streets. His troop shone too boldly to be diminished by a few soured soldiers whose scarred maturity did not accord with His Royal Highness' concept of a suitable army of vengeance. When the genial troop had passed, Tulea seemed betrayed into unkindly age and cynicism. The citizens placidly resumed routine, but unwonted stillness created a mournful pall.

Winter held us: Tulean winter, made mild by ocean gentling but gray and somber, nonetheless. Whispers rose: that Ixaxin wizards had joined the legions of Blood-Talon Cor, and they wrung from Liin such despair as would cry to the winds for eternity. The threads of unrest twisted around Tulea and caught in her heart. In the marketplace in full daylight, a merchant fell upon the impoverished carcass of a self-styled witch for the thieving of a skin of spirits from his stall. The witch's comrade in poverty intervened to spare the woman from the bane of imprisonment, but mischance struck the merchant to his death upon the cobbles. The cry arose against sorcerous intrusion: the bewildered witch in her grimy rags became a conniving wizardess, her comrade a Caruillan spy. By the time the Tulean guard arrived to suppress the riotous mob, the conflagration of irrationality had claimed some thirty lives. Sanity returned with the timidity of shame, but the specter of distrust had been raised.

Ezirae's nieces had been returned to Hamley amid protesting squeals of social deprivation. Ziva and Flava were not alone among the noble young to find themselves suddenly banished from their accustomed court haunts. The growing exodus exceeded any usual seasonal variations in Tulea's castle populace and left a hollow dearth of joyful chatter. Even the most stalwart supporters of Prince Orlin's foray did not expect quick redemption from Serii's troubles.

With the diminishing population of the castle, the Hall of my father lost something of the excessive gloom engendered by unfavorable comparison. Tyntagel's meager contingent among court nobility had not dwindled; indeed, Amgor and Yldana now joined us as often as not, for the despised Amlach cousins all had fled, and Amlach Hall echoed dolefully. Little gaiety could be found among us, but stiff and leaded silence grasped Tyntagel Hall no more firmly than it did the larger part of Tulea.

Kaedric had essayed the Taormin a ten of times, discerning with each effort new strata of complexity, but Horlach had made no overt, betraying move. Orlin had been gone a tenday, and rumors that the prince regent had liberated Liin met with skeptical indifference. "I have an uneasy suspicion that Lord Borgor's couriers bear us biased news," said Kaedric. "I have neglected His Royal Highness in searching for Horlach. Let us see whether the Taormin can serve to bring us more reliable reports."

Kaedric turned inward, transitioning smoothly to the Taormin's webs, and I accompanied him, more certain of my own path than I could have anticipated a week before. Kaedric had not warned me idly; I could have used the Taormin alone now, and I knew how precariously I should exist were that realization to extend beyond Kaedric and myself. I disliked considering how far the Infortiare's own Power had expanded.

Liin had indeed burned, leaving only a pitiful shell of the once-great city. I had never seen her glory, and it was gone now. Little about her lived, though some survivors had begun to rebuild.

Caruil had left proud Liin sacked and shorn of every beauty. I thought I felt a relict of Dolr'han conceit amid the wrack, but the scion of Tul drew us along another path. Kaedric touched the threads of many minds and many memories, and he took from them a single fading strand. At Kaedric's touch the pale filament glowed and shivered like taut wire. We wrapped ourselves around it and absorbed it.

Prince Orlin observed with a frown that the flag of Tul had slipped; a gust had pulled it from the column, and dew had plastered its silk against the charred ledge where it had caught. The sight depressed him, but the whole of Liin looked very grim now that dawn revealed the sum of her ravages. In the dusky light of yesterday's fog, the city had somehow still seemed glorious to him. And the skirmish at the gate: that had been grand.

Orlin gazed at his injured hand with a touch of pride. True, the nasty little creature who had wounded him had been a Seriin vulture rather than a Caruillan warrior, but the vulture had fought fiercely. When cornered, the awful parasite had actually bitten Orlin's hand, and Orlin had been forced to whack its head with the flat of his sword. It had seemed quite a marvelous battle at the time.

Really, this gray mood which was taking hold of him was most annoying. Victory had been wonderful: riding staunchly into Liin and watching the scavengers scatter before the crimson wave of Orlin's handsome troop. They had arrested quite a large number of looters, driven off many more, and rescued one screaming woman from a villain whom they had summarily executed. The only Caruillans they had seen had been dead or dying, but Orlin's men had quickly dispatched the few survivors. No doubt Blood-Talon Cor had observed Orlin's approach and launched his ships in hasty retreat. Perhaps Orlin would plan a retaliatory attack on Caruil.

It really was too maddening that he should feel so depressed. He had deliberately established camp in the quayside portion of the city, which had been thoroughly leveled by fire and lay upwind of all those dead citizens in the less devastated districts, so as to avoid the contaminating touch of disease; Orlin had been quite proud of that decision. Of course, thought Orlin sourly, I suppose we ought to effect some more permanent protection by disposing of the bodies altogether.

This was not turning out as Orlin had anticipated. Disposing of the dead and arresting looters were not the stuff of great sagas. The more Orlin considered his mood, the more he decided that it was all the fault of that man, Mots, who had spent a considerable portion of the night berating Orlin quite unjustly. Orlin's men had saved Mots' life, freeing him from beneath a timber Mots could never have budged alone, fed the man a hearty supper and made him welcome in their camp; all Mots could do was sneer just like the fools in Tulea, who were only jealous of Orlin's youth, after all. Orlin wished Lord Borgor were with him. Somehow Borgor always managed to explain things so clearly, eradicating Orlin's self-doubts with a deftly knowing gem of advice. Borgor would certainly dismiss Mots' theories that Cor only savored his conquest, tarrying on his ships until the next attack: the attack on Tulea.

It is strange that we have seen so few Caruillans, nor even a distant vessel on the sea. I assumed yesterday that the fog hid Cor's retreating fleet, but the fog has cleared, and the wind has been poor; no ship ought to have been able to travel yet so far in such weather. Maybe it is true that Caruillans use sorcery to speed their vessels. Orlin shunned that final thought.

When the day had lengthened, and Orlin's spirits had not improved, he gathered his officers around him. The prince thought their bright, patrician faces and good humor would cheer him, and he felt a vague need to plan something or do something now that his goal of reclaiming Liin had apparently been achieved. Orlin's officers displayed little enthusiasm for talk of scouring Liin into some sad respectability, but the hesitant suggestion of a foray against Caruil did excite them. Orlin felt no better than before.

The fog had returned: a thick, yellow cloud which Orlin found unsettling. If only Borgor were here, thought Orlin again. He would tell me that this pressure I feel constricting my lungs is only from sour smoke. Borgor would assure me that my head reels with victory and not with the echoes of the restless dead. Borgor would tell me that I feel cold and hot at once only because of a slight chill and fever, and he would send me immediately to bed.

Orlin's officers were laughing, building and rebuilding every story of capture or chase, comparing and concocting amusing anecdotes about this prisoner or that capture. Lord Joret's tales had a particularly imaginative flair. How can they be so carefree amid the rubble of so much ruined beauty, wondered Orlin enviously. Why can I not set aside Liin's tragedy and rejoice instead in my own good fortunes, as they do?

Orlin felt his head begin to pound. He noticed that several of his officers had fallen silent, their faces pinched and strained. Across the camp the horses had begun to whinny in an off-key tone which Orlin could have sworn held panic. Lord Chath dur Viste, Orlin's second-in-command, made a restless, awkward attempt to rise, but he fell back, choking horribly.

All the young officers tried simultaneously to reach him. They succeeded only in creating a scramble of utter confusion and incoherent apologies. Feeling absurdly sickened by his comrades' useless gentilities, Orlin took hard hold of Lord Drimon and ordered him very fiercely to fetch the medic. "Clear away, for lords' sake!" shouted Orlin roughly, and he did not care that they stared with more astonished concern at him than at pitiable Chath. Chath's coughing had grown deep, and the young officer's hands came blood-smeared away from his face. A terrible contortion racked the Viste lord, and he struck Orlin in a mindless spasm. Chath jerked violently on the ground, his back arched horribly and cracked, and Chath lay still and colorless.

Lord Joniax had started shaking heavily. Lord Rosh had turned pale, and he clutched at his throat. Orlin's own breath had grown more labored, and his tongue felt like fire. He looked across the camp, and the fog had parted. The ships of Caruil loomed in the harbor, and Blood-Talon Cor laughed from the nearest bow. At Cor's side, three spidery women in black veils and silver robes waved their arms and moaned.

Ixaxins spurn such melodrama, thought Orlin wildly. These are sorcerers not wizards, but, lords, they have Power. Relying on an instinct he had never tested, Orlin commanded, threatened, and physically pushed his men, coercing as many as could move to mount the horses. It was a nightmarish effort, for each of them was suffering from the attack, and no armor did they have against Power, no weapon with which to retaliate. A number of the horses had fallen, too, but somehow, some few of Orlin's troop struggled enough to mount and ride. Orlin headed his steed toward Tulea, following a figure who might have been Joret. It mattered only that they distance themselves from the harbor of Liin and the sorcerers of Cor. Orlin could not quite remember if distance greatly affected Power, but he knew no other escape to try. Orlin had never listened well to lessons of wizards' history.

The horses carried them, the bright young men who so recently had planned to conquer their world. No Seriin-troop shall make foray without escort by a representative of the Infortiare, Orlin recalled with horror. No battle shall be waged without Ixaxis' aid. Precaution, said Ceallagh's laws, can forestall catastrophe, and only Power can defend against Power.

The sting of hot acid racked Orlin's throat and lungs. It spread to his eyes, and he could not see. All sound and sense, save pain, had failed him. The horse ran erratically, torn by its own demons until it dropped, its fine bones shattered. The prince regent landed heavily in the filth of a ditch, and he could only dimly suspect that the horse no longer bore him. *Venkarel,* cried Orlin in his failing mind, *why did I never listen?*

Then the Venkarel was there, like a vision of death. "Venkarel," croaked the young, dying prince. "Stop them," Orlin pleaded. A feeling had come upon Orlin that there was something that the Venkarel needed to know. It was a strange feeling, for it raised in Orlin an odd sense of kinship with the long dead Tul: not for Tul the warrior, whom Orlin had hoped to emulate in battle, but for the mortal Tul who had dared to defy a Sorcerer King. "What a pompous fool I have been," said Orlin to himself.

"You have served Serii honorably, Your Royal Highness," said the Venkarel with a gentleness of understanding which struck Orlin as remarkable. "That is a claim as great as any man should wish to make."

Tied to Kaedric's will, I could not recoil at the litter of shriveled skin and fallow pelts. I could not turn away from Prince Orlin's death. "Caruillan sorcerers do not have such Power," I protested to Kaedric alone.

"Evidently, their abilities have been altered," he answered, and he added, "they will turn toward us soon. Orlin's few surviving followers should reach the city by this evening. We ought to have a brace of days before the Caruillans reach us." Kaedric had grown very grim, and hard lines of tension crossed his face. "I had best inform Lord Borgor that a siege is imminent and let the Council begin its panic gently."

"Prince Orlin was young to pay such a price for folly," I murmured.

"Horlach is no respecter of age or its lack."

"Benthen Abbey will despair of me soon if I continue to devote all my energies to laical issues," jested Abbot Medwyn. "Young priests are allowed to be vagabonds and meddlers in secular affairs, but an abbot is expected to tend his abbey."

"At least your vocation is not threatened with extinction," said Marga sourly. "Another day of playing stolid merchant's widow in a dingy Tulean flat will leave me as mad as Nimal. I am going to frizzle Wal Seris and plant myself on Kaedric's doorstep."

"You know that you are always welcome, Marga," said Kaedric as he entered, "though even Ceallagh's Tower cannot very well accommodate all the wizards of Ixaxis. Who is Wal Seris?"

"An oaf of a sea-silk merchant who thinks himself a very fine marital catch indeed."

Ineuil commented mischievously, "Perhaps you should not scorn your suitor, Mistress Marga, until the future of your profession grows brighter." Marga glared, and Abbot Medwyn choked back a laugh.

"I did not call this meeting to discuss Marga's marriage prospects," interrupted Kaedric, though he had also suppressed a fleeting grin at Marga's indignant ire. "We are about to be attacked by the forces of Caruil, led ostensibly by Blood-Talon Cor but certainly abetted by Horlach. And, Prince Orlin is dead."

"That little monster Joli is regent?" exclaimed Marga. "Lords help us, Orlin was bad enough."

"His Majesty's Council was not pleased either," said Kaedric, "though Borgor already schemes to seize another puppet. Borgor will manipulate himself into control of a realm that will no longer exist."

"I hope King Astorn is enjoying Bethii," observed Ineuil morosely.

"Did Prince Orlin's troop share his fate?" asked Medwyn.

"Some few were permitted to escape," said Kaedric in answer.

"Once they reach Tulea with their tale, anarchy will ensue, and that miserable witch in the marketplace will not want for company. King Cor did not exercise mercy in allowing survivors."

"So we must prepare to keep discipline now," said Ineuil. "If we start conscripting our defenders against Caruil immediately, they will be too busy grumbling at mortal troubles to think about distant sorcery."

"You may have trouble convincing Borgor to authorize official mobilization," suggested Kaedric doubtfully. "Whether or not Borgor has become Horlach's direct tool, Serii's Adjutant appears intent upon serving Horlach's interests."

"By the time Borgor realizes that I am using his name in vain, we shall have the persuasive presence of Cor on our doorstep. My tavern acquaintance with Tulean soldiery will give me credence— as will the talent of an excellent forger I know." Ineuil smiled wanly. "I was trained for the military role; it is the part tradition dictates for lesser noblemen. I have avoided its official bonds for years, and now I tie the noose myself."

"Console yourself with your forged authority," recommended Kaedric dryly.

"I fully intend to do so. You just keep me clear of sorcerous interference, O Infortiare, and I shall remind King Cor of the justifiable renown of Tulean—and Seriin—indomitability."

"There ought to be enough of us in Tulea to form an effective Wizards' Circle," mused Marga. "That would leave Lord Arineuil free to form his army. I do wish you had allowed more of us to come to Tulea, Kaedric."

"The first business of Ixaxis is education, Marga," returned Kaedric wearily. "We must not destroy the seeds of future hope in our focus on the present war."

"I am certainly not going to call on you to inspire our army, Lord Venkarel," reproved Ineuil with black humor.

"I should rather hope not!" agreed Marga fervently. "Really Kaedric, we are not defeated yet. We are, in fact, quite a formidable group."

"You are not alone in this battle, Kaedric," added Abbot Medwyn carefully.

"I am simply another cog," rejoined Kaedric with light mockery. "Well enough—I am assuredly no warrior. Lord Arineuil, the army is yours to command. Mistress Marga's Circle should be able to counter the Caruillan sorcerers to a large degree. Abbot Medwyn, the cares of the inevitable wounded are yours. Lady Rhianna and I shall do what we can to mitigate Horlach's meddling. Let fortune favor us if she will."

Chapter 21

"**M**y lady," said Kaedric when the others had gone, "I am going to seal the Taormin against remote usage. I should like to seal it altogether, but I suspect that can only be done from within, and I am not so noble as to imprison myself in amber filigree on the chance."

"You no longer think it can be used against Horlach."

"I think it cannot be used further to find Horlach. Our searching has in a sense served its purpose; it has pressed Horlach into action at a time not altogether of his choosing. Beyond that, the Taormin's aid becomes double-edged. Horlach knows it too well."

"That has ever been true."

"Yes." Kaedric laughed shortly. "Perhaps my nerve is weakening." He shrugged. "My decision is not irrevocable. We know where the Taormin lies, and physical proximity will release it to us again."

"You implied to the others that we would continue to search for Horlach's presence."

"You and I have formed our own Wizards' Circle, my lady. We no longer need the Taormin for work at the monitors' level."

"How much more effectively could Mistress Marga's Circle operate if its members were enhanced by the Taormin?"

"If any of them survived the experience, they could probably shake Serii to the bone. The qualifying question is significant, however."

"I survived it, my lord, and I am no wizardess."

"Hrgh was a full wizard, and he did not survive." Kaedric grinned ruefully as he added, "And no matter what you may once have been, you are quite decidedly a wizardess now. You have the Infortiare's word on it."

The ragged, wounded remnants of Prince Orlin's glorious troop limped into Tulea on half-dead horses in a silent hour of the night. Abbot Medwyn met them and, as silently as the city, he gathered them into the ward of Parul Church. A young cleric was dispatched to the king's castle: to summon the Infortiare and to inform the princess regent that her brother's death had been confirmed by his erstwhile followers.

I awakened to the distant ring of matins and a flustered Tamar shaking me urgently. She wore a flannel wrap, and curling papers twisted her hair alarmingly. "You would never allow me to leave my room looking like that, Mistress Tamar," I commented sleepily.

"My lady, there is a royal messenger demanding you," persisted Tamar. "You must get dressed, my lady."

"A royal messenger?" I asked, honestly bewildered. "His Majesty does not even know me," I began. But King Astorn was in far Bethii, and the regent in his stead was an impulsive girl with whom I did, after a fashion, share an acquaintance. "Tell the messenger that I shall come presently, Tamar."

Princess Joli appeared singularly humble for the titular head of Serii, dwarfed by her magnificent room and lacking the bravado she had occasionally shown. Princess Joli dismissed her attendants when I arrived, and they departed reluctantly, awkwardly bemused by the elevated status of their royal charge. Mistress Amila, the governess against whom I had unintentionally conspired with Her Royal Highness, eyed me suspiciously as she left.

"They all blame me for everything," lamented Joli without preamble. "I never asked to be regent. How could papa leave us like this? How could he leave Orlin in charge of anything? Orlin had to show how great and brave and clever he was, and all he did was make a mess of everything. What am I going to do, Rhianna?"

I could sympathize with Joli's confusion. I found her beseeching plea for my advice more than a little daunting. Having thoroughly embroiled myself in the Infortiare's concerns, I knew what answer

I must give, but the giving of it immured me with the guilt of my own partisanship. I compromised. "Your Royal Highness must seek the counsel of those best qualified to give it."

"Lord Borgor is a weasely toad," responded Her Royal Highness. "Look what his advice did for stupid Orlin," she added disparagingly, but her voice caught on her brother's name.

"The chief adviser to the sovereign of Serii is the Infortiare, not the Adjutant," I returned.

"Everyone tells me to depose Lord Venkarel. He even makes papa nervous. Lord Borgor says that Lord Venkarel has made a pact with King Cor and is just waiting to take Serii for himself."

"As Your Royal Highness mentioned, Lord Borgor's advice has not proven very sound."

"Lord Borgor is not the only one to say it," grumbled Joli, but she watched me keenly. "Do you recommend the Infortiare because you are a sorceress?"

With impulsive honesty, I replied, "I am a wizardess, Your Royal Highness, and I serve the Infortiare, but I also serve you and Serii. You are an intelligent observer, Your Royal Highness. Do you believe it is Lord Venkarel who conspires with Caruil?"

"Arku Ruy could have been pretending to conspire with Lord Borgor as a diplomatic artifice to cover Ixaxin intrigues. Arku Ruy did not *like* Lord Venkarel, but neither does anybody else."

I blinked at Joli's unexpectedly intricate analysis. "As it happens, Your Royal Highness, I like Lord Venkarel very much, though he does not exert himself to acquire friends. I also trust him. I cannot expect you to share that trust on my testament, when our own acquaintance is scarcely substantial. I submit, however, that Lord Venkarel has no cause to make pacts with King Cor. If Lord Venkarel wished to control Serii or Caruil or the entire Alliance, he could reach and take his desire unaided."

The princess regent hugged herself in tight contemplation. She wore a pale pink robe trimmed with pink and white flowers. Her hair hung lankly. "I was only nine when Lord Alobar died," said Joli slowly. "He was a nice old man who used to tell me stories and make me paper stars that glowed yellow when I held them." I failed completely in an attempt to visualize saturnine Lord Venkarel similarly entertaining a little girl with paper baubles. "He told me he was going to die," said Joli with retrospective sadness.

"He was not very old for a wizard. He told me not to be afraid of Lord Venkarel, because Lord Venkarel could not help being Powerful any more than I could help being a princess." Joli raised her head. "Will you bring Lord Venkarel to me, Rhianna?"

"I believe he is at the Parul Church, Your Royal Highness. I shall bear your summons to him," I answered, aching for both the princess and the Ven slave whom fate had laden with responsibilities neither could eschew.

I had not traversed Tulea or any other burg unescorted since my Venturing sojourn and an almost forgotten sense of liberty stirred in me. The temptation to stray from my errand grew, but I could not give in to it. I knew the location of Parul only vaguely; it was Kaedric's presence there which marked it unmistakably.

The tiny hospital which the Parul priests maintained had been overburdened. Abbot Medwyn had converted a wing of the Parul parish classrooms into added wards, and such physicians were gathered as could be recruited to the cause. Most of the cots in these rooms were still empty (filled only by Orlin's few survivors), but their number held a gloomy promise. A solemn Sister directed me through the waiting rows of starkly linened pallets. A half-dozen beds held muffled forms; a low whimper drew me to a boy whose delicately featured face had escaped the ravages which marred those of his comrades. The Sister who tended him brushed his fine, dark hair from his feverish brow and teased him with a smile.

"My handsome young lord," she said cheerfully, "if you must toss about and disturb those dressings over which I labored so carefully, you should not be surprised by a little discomfort."

"I only wanted to see how badly scarred I shall be," apologized the lordling with great contrition. "I could never face my lady if I were maimed."

"Your lady will be nothing but proud of you, my lord. Is she your betrothed?"

"Oh, no!" responded the young man. A fit of deep coughing wracked him, and it was a few moments before he continued. "She is the finest, the most beautiful lady of Serii. She does not know that I exist," he finished despondently.

"Come, she probably thinks you the finest, handsomest man in Serii and just bides in hope that you will bespeak her."

"Do you think she might?" asked the boy with almost religious awe. "I shall be healed soon, shall I not? I must defeat the Caruillans for my lady."

"You will have time enough to think of battle after you nap."

"I am not a child," complained the young lord. The Sister gazed at him sternly, and he continued meekly, "At least bring me some paper that I might write to my lady first."

"You have already written her a score of pages," laughed the Sister, but at the boy's crestfallen expression, she relented. "One more sheet of vellum, my lord. Our supplies are not infinite, and you need your rest."

"One more sheet, and I promise I shall behave. Thank you, Sister," gushed the boy.

The Sister espied me. "I am here to see Abbot Medwyn," I said, unwilling to advertise Kaedric's presence more than necessary.

The Sister smiled. "Of course, my lady. I am headed that way myself. I shall be pleased to guide you."

She led me into a warren of cells, and I commented idly, "You seem to have conquered that young lord's intransigence easily. You have nursed before."

"I have had some experience," she agreed. "A religious must tend the folk too poor or too wise to trust an untried medic's filthy leeches." She sighed heavily. "Not that anyone can likely help or hinder that poor boy you saw."

"He suffered no great pain," I asserted with troubled surety.

"He has been very heavily drugged. It is unlikely he will live to serve his adored lady in battle or anything else. Abbot Medwyn," said the Sister in curt announcement, "there is a lady here to see you."

"Thank you, Sister Adri," answered the abbot, and the Sister left us. "Rhianna, I would feel more sanguine about this visit if you did not look so woeful."

"Forgive me, Abbot Medwyn. Sister Adri and I were discussing one of your patients. I actually bear a summons for Lord Venkarel from Her Royal Highness, Princess Joli."

"You reveal the most unlikely connections, my lady," said Kaedric, emerging from shadow. "When did you become Princess Joli's emissary?"

"Her Royal Highness asked for me this morning. We share a

common interest in trees. My lord, I am not sure how long her resolve to trust me will persist."

"If it lasts long enough to gain me an exclusive audience with
the regent, I shall throw the wealth of the Infortiare at your feet.
Medwyn," he said with a shrug, "You know better than I how to
administer a hospital." Kaedric ushered me from the room, remarking as we walked, "Lady Rhianna, it might be best if you were
not seen accompanying me back to the castle."

"It might be best if I did not wander Tulea at all, my lord, but I
must obey the princess regent's orders. I promised to bring, not
send, you to Her Royal Highness."

"Are you supposed to guard Her Royal Highness from the evil
machinations of the Infortiare?"

"Princess Joli does not blindly oppose wizardry, my lord. She
was very fond of Lord Alobar."

"Lord Alobar was a poor wizard but a good man." We had
reached the occupied ward, and Kaedric grew silent. Sister Adri
had returned to the young, besotted lord, but she drew the linen
pall over his face. "How many will die before we are done?" asked
Kaedric with a sigh.

"I wonder who he was," I said sorrowfully.

Kaedric answered absently, "Lord Joret dur Esmar," and I closed
my eyes, willing denial. In one of those ridiculous, effusive paeans
to which I had paid so little heed, Lord Joret had written that he
would make himself worthy of me. He had not specified how, and
I had not until now missed the daily letters which had ceased with
Prince Orlin's celebrated, sorry foray. The tragic, wasted death
roiled in my heart: another dram of guilt.

Chapter 22

The most influential gathering in Serii, the King's Council, numbered nearly half a hundred of the most prestigious representatives of Serii's nobility. I felt woefully misplaced and exceptionally conspicuous entering at Princess Joli's side, but Her Royal Highness had pleaded with me, and her desperation had persuaded me more than a direct command would have done. I think few of the councillors actually gave me notice, intent as they were on observing the previously disregarded princess who had imperiously summoned them. I saw my father start at sight of me, but he betrayed by no other sign that he recognized my existence. The less impenetrable Lord Brant dur Niveal scowled openly and often.

Lord Borgor spared me a brief, unflattering glance before convening the assembly. Joli proceeded to the chair of Tul with laudable dignity in light of her shaky condition moments before entering. Kaedric already occupied the place at her right. I stood behind Joli's chair in the region between the regent and the Infortiare.

Lord Borgor took his position on Joli's left, saying to her in a placating voice which managed to carry across the room, "It is customary for your father to state the purpose of the meeting at this juncture. If Your Royal Highness will inform me of the cause of your concern, I shall be pleased to announce it to the members of His Majesty's Council."

"I am quite able to speak for myself, Lord Borgor," said Joli regally. "Please recall that I am the regent, and you serve me." She continued more loudly, "It would be well if each of you recalled that Lord Borgor's is not the voice of Tul and Serii." She did not quaver now. "Serii has stood firm against many tides of trouble and dishonor since Ceallagh crowned my great-sire. Serii is the first and the greatest member of that Alliance which restored peace and prosperity to the tortured world shaped by the Sorcerer Kings. We are a single kingdom in that Alliance, but we are much more, for it was from Serii that freedom spread through the aid of the Ixaxin wizards, who give us allegiance.

"My lords, Serii is beset. The pirates of King Cor of Caruil have committed heinous treachery, defiling the fair city of Liin where they were welcomed, and even now they approach Tulea. The might of Serii can counter Cor's barbaric brigands, unless we allow our own self-seeking elements to overcome us. Serii's strength is the unity of Tul and Ceallagh, the cohesion of mortal sinew and wizard's Power. I have called you here to demand of you an answer: do you, the lords of the Seriin domains, support the realm of Tul and Ceallagh? If you affirm your faith, then we shall fight the battle before us with the sure strength of millennia. If you will not trust to the heirs of Tul and Ceallagh, then the battle is already ended in defeat, for Serii exists no more. Let those who believe still in Serii pledge their loyalty aloud: to the Regent of Tul and to the Infortiare of Ixaxis.

"Lord Sieg dur Aesir, what is your answer?"

I had heard Joli's speech before, the joint product of Kaedric, Ineuil and Joli herself, but Joli was a surprisingly compelling orator. The initial spatter of poorly suppressed laughter among the councillors had faded quickly in face of Her Royal Highness' persuasive determination to exert her proper authority. The hapless Lord Sieg dur Aesir, whom alphabetical honors afflicted, shifted nervously, helplessly beseeching Lord Borgor with an eloquent glance for some guidance in handling the recalcitrant child who presently held the crown of Serii.

"Your Royal Highness," said Lord Borgor smoothly, as clearly pleased by Lord Sieg's deference as he was disgruntled by his intended puppet's refusal to be tied to his strings. "Surely you cannot doubt that every rightful," he smiled in a superior manner at

Kaedric, "Lord of Serii supports your father, King Astorn, un-equivocably." Kaedric returned Borgor's scathing sneers with cool austerity. Encouraged by a lack of argument, Lord Borgor turned a patronizing tone against Joli. "We understand, Your Royal Highness, that your brother's tragic death has upset you overwhelmingly. Naturally, you seek reassurance at this time of distress, but the Council Hall is perhaps inappropriate for personal pleas. Your handmaiden," he said with a slight gesture toward me, "can doubtless reassure you more effectively than a room full of dour old men. With your permission, Your Royal Highness, the Council will proceed to the topics which press us. Lord Sieg, you may be seated."

"Lord Sieg," announced Princess Joli indomitably, "you have not yet given your response to me, and you shall stand until I declare the answer satisfactorily clear." Lord Sieg halted in an awkward half-seated position. "As for you, Lord Borgor, I understand and acknowledge your refusal to pledge your loyalty to me and to the Infortiare. Your resignation is accepted. Lord Arineuil dur Ven, you are the new Adjutant. Lord Borgor, please relinquish your position to Lord Arineuil and depart this Council."

It was difficult to equate this assured young regent with the hysterical girl who had hidden in a shrub from her governess and berated an inoffensive pine. Even Lord Borgor was shaken. He began to splutter an incredulous protest, echoes of which flickered through the hall, but Kaedric's piercing attention quickly cured Lord Borgor's hesitation: Lord Borgor blanched and obeyed Her Royal Highness' dictate without another word. With admirable calm considering the derogatory whispers which followed him, Ineuil assumed the Adjutant's vacated place of honor. He looked a query at Joli, and she nodded her very royal permission. "Lord Sieg dur Aesir," demanded Ineuil, "how do you vote?"

With an uncertain quaver, Lord Sieg replied, "I support the Princess Joli dur Tulea, regent of His Majesty, King Astorn."

"And the Infortiare, Lord Venkarel dur Ixaxis," insisted Ineuil.

Lord Sieg looked coldly at Kaedric but bowed his head and affirmed, "And I support the Infortiare, Lord Venkarel dur Ixaxis."

There were no refusals to comply with Joli's ultimatum after the example of Lord Borgor. The sincerity of the pledges could be termed dubious under the circumstances, but the circuitous ethics of the nobility would be stalled in rebellion by the tether of a witnessed oath. My father's compliance was not gracious, but the stiffest response of all issued from Lord Gorng dur Liin, the younger brother of Hrgh and Veiga, the man on whom Cor's treachery had just bestowed liegedom. I could not altogether blame the councillors for their grudging acceptance. Not one of them doubted that Lord Venkarel had just assumed virtually unfettered control of Serii.

"Do you think they will really obey me, Rhianna?" asked the princess regent of Serii, shivering with reaction now that her councillors had left to perform the tasks of defense allotted them by the Infortiare and the new Adjutant.

I answered briskly, hoping that I sounded reassuringly confident, "They will at least cooperate for the moment and weigh carefully any thought of rebellion. They will respect your leadership, Your Royal Highness, because you give it, and for all their gesturing, very few of them know how to issue a decisive command."

"Your Royal Highness," said Ineuil with enchanting fervor, "If you will speak to your soldiers as eloquently as you have favored your Council, you will have an army of such loyalty as you have never seen."

Joli's amber eyes sparked with shy delight, and I reflected that Ineuil would some day regret his habit of instinctive conquest. The princess regent of Serii was both vulnerable and tempestuous, and Ineuil's flirtation in that quarter could garner him some severe repercussions. If it gave Joli the moment's confidence which she needed, I was forced to admit that the deception might profit us all; I resolved to ensure, however, that Princess Joli suffer no whit of anguish over Ineuil's transient attentions, even if it cost Serii the services of her Adjutant. Before Ineuil could whisk the princess to the fore of her burgeoning troops, I whispered to him sharply, "If you cause Her Royal Highness any sorrow by your intemperate flattery, Ineuil, my sister will lack for a lover."

"Rhianna, I am quite reformed of frivolous pastimes," he scolded with an unrepentant grin. "I am the Adjutant now." He turned to Joli and very respectfully offered his arm. She accepted it timidly, almost lustrous with pleasure. I left them to pursue their plans for proselytizing and departed the castle.

Late afternoon sun washed the terrace; Kaedric stood at the

balustrade, surveying the city which still held an illusory peace. Prince Orlin had died, as had absurd, idealistic Lord Joret. A war was almost upon us, but it still felt quite remote. Kaedric had sealed the Taormin, and the curbing of its turbulent force in my awareness increased in me the deceptive sense of calm. Even the Infortiare himself no longer gave me terror; I had lost somewhere in the Taormin's coils that dread of him to which I had clung so long. I had told Princess Joli that I liked him, unapproachable though he strove to be. I had spoken truly.

Attuned by the Taormin and with no mist of fear and awe to blind me, I could see uncertainty in him. The harsh stain of slavery had left him hard and unnaturally lean, as scarred by sorrow as by the lash of Master Doshk across his back. I knew he stretched the physical scars into deliberate pain as he clenched his long fingers upon the unyielding rail. He was worn, though he wore the indefinably ageless youth which was the purest legacy of Power. I thought how fair he was with his startling eyes and black hair; even that gift had cost him by making him appealing to the merciless clients of Doshk. He was a man inconceivably gifted with all the inherent attributes which men desire, and by his gifts he was accursed. Ineuil had accused me rightly: I had grown to love the Infortiare of Serii.

I did not bespeak him, leery of his ridicule if he recognized the most honest source of my devotion to his cause. At the least, the perception would disconcert him, and he had enough serious concerns to occupy him without my contribution to confound him. I left the terrace, girding myself to confront my father instead.

Chapter 23

I was destined to discover quickly that my presence at Princess Joli's side had attracted greater notice than I had realized. Lord Artos dur Endor made a point of greeting me whom he had never deigned to observe before. Lord Misch dur Vedma acknowledged me with a nod, Lord Gorng dur Liin with a glare of withering vitriol. Yldana intercepted me before I reached Tyntagel Hall.

"You have made rather a sensation, Rhianna dear," said my sister with aloof grandeur. "You have been a very busy girl to make such influential friends in five months." Yldana's mood was not the best, and I suspected that I would be wise to escape her before her evident strain of temper erupted into venom. I shrugged noncommittally, unable to devise any safer response.

As Yldana continued, I gleaned a glimmer of the envious cause for her irritation. "Veiga would like you to join us at a small supper this evening." She added very sweetly, "Do bring an escort, if you can find one."

An intimate dinner with Lord Borgor and Lady Veiga did not rank high on my roster of desirable occupations, however covetous a prize my sister might find it. I thought cynically that Lord Borgor wasted no time in seeking substitute puppets. "I am sorry, Yldana," I murmured insincerely. "Could you convey my regret to Lady Veiga? I am otherwise committed."

With gratuitous relief, Yldana replied, "Of course, Rhianna."

She added with a knowing smile, "Do give my love to father when you see him." I returned her smile blandly, realizing as well as she did that my reception at Tyntagel Hall threatened to be a stormy one.

My father had left word with the staff to escort me to his office immediately upon my arrival. Liya watched me gravely from the stair as I passed; she retreated quickly when she discerned my glance upon her. My father awaited me, enthroned in a tapestried chair and drumming his desk with impatient fingers.

"You wished to see me, father."

His eyes beneath his menacing brows sought to pierce me. His signet winked rhythmically. "What is your part in this Ixaxin contrivance?" he demanded sternly, and I did tremble inwardly through the conditioning of long habit. My father's neglect in punishing me for my denial of Grisk had given me a baseless hope of his softening.

I answered with apparent poise, "Ixaxis did not contrive Her Royal Highness' Council meeting, father, if that is the subject to which you refer."

My father snapped, "You know quite well to what subject I refer."

"Princess Joli determined the content of the meeting, father. She chose to support the Infortiare and Ixaxis without coercion of any kind. I applaud her decision, and I am very proud that the Princess Joli considers me her friend."

"It is interesting to note that Her Royal Highness' choice of Adjutant should coincide with a name unfortunately linked with yours."

"Lord Arineuil dur Ven brings to the post of Adjutant much more substantial military experience than his recent predecessors."

"He is an amoral wastrel," said my father with disgust.

"He is an educated and intelligent man, who may possibly preserve Serii from the attempted assassination abetted by men whom you have professed to admire."

My father stared at me coldly through the whole of a minute. "You insinuate to me, your liege lord, that I am a traitor. You laud Her Royal Highness for demanding fealty of her rightful subjects. I give you then the selfsame opportunity: affirm to me your loyalty, or confess yourself Tyntagellian no longer and leave my House."

"My lord father," I said woodenly, wounded by the formal ostracism I ought to have expected and had always felt, "I esteem you as my sire, but I shall not serve you more." I had finally freed my father of his responsibility to me, and I think it was the only gladness I had ever given him.

I devoted my evening to consoling Joli over her newly discovered potentials and listening to her issue infatuated sighs over her new Adjutant. The occupation kept me from my own distress and so served us both. I had strayed from her once only in mind: a flare of brutal fire in Tulean outlands met the reassuring control of Marga's Circle. Cor's army approached.

Joli recounted her quavering apprehension as she beseeched the people of her city to unite with her against the Caruillans. Later, in the Infortiare's library, Ineuil described to me the remarkable effectiveness of her entreaties. "She has the full charisma of the line of Tul when she elects to use it," he told me, and he sounded sincerely impressed. "Who would ever have expected it from the ghastly little delinquent? She even had the Tulean rabble cheering the Infortiare! We have had volunteers flocking to us; most are not experienced soldiers, but they know of their city's natural defenses, and they are inspired. If we parade Her Royal Highness before them periodically, we may actually be able to keep them in patriotic fervor."

"It is a terrible burden for her, Ineuil," I said. "Do not push her to the point of snapping."

"My lovely wizardess, I shall accord Her Royal Highness all the delicate handling possible. She is one of our most valuable assets!"

"Can she keep the lords of the Council in tow?"

"Not on the basis of an emotional appeal. They are a cold lot, His Majesty's councillors."

"You number among them, I believe."

"A result of unkind fate and insufficient brethren, not to mention the thoroughness of Our Infortiare's revenge on my improvident kin." Kaedric, who was intently composing for Ineuil various (authentic) letters of authority by which to enlist Tulea-dwelling Ixaxins, gave no sign of having heard the taunt, but I wished it unsaid, nonetheless. I gave Ineuil a quelling look; he proceeded glibly, "Has war erupted yet in Tyntagel Hall?"

I forced a careless smile. "Erupted and ended: exit one Lady Rhianna. I am banished."

"Awkward for you," clucked Ineuil.

Without raising his head from his scribing, Kaedric offered distantly, "Ceallagh's Tower suffers no dearth of lodging."

"Thank you, my lord," I answered, caught by the knowledge that Kaedric was fully aware of our conversation. I caught Ineuil's amused glance and decided that increased responsibility made Lord Arineuil increasingly annoying.

Chapter 24

The army of Cor flung itself against Tulean battlements five nights after the death of Orlin. They had tarried, reckoning the defense they faced, but they had the might and the insidious guidance of Horlach to drive them. Marga's Circle, augmented now by independent wizards whose bonds with Ixaxis had otherwise ebbed, gripped Tulea and cradled her from the sorcerous onslaught.

Against those unversed in the workings of arcane Power, the Caruillans poured forth a legion of murderers and mercenaries. Their ships occupied every inlet, and the vessels spewed forth hordes. Such farms and settlements as surrounded the borders of Tulea proper had been ordered vacated, but the Caruillans destroyed wantonly, defiling against future use and slaughtering those who had refused to leave their family homes. Tulea was fully besieged; the flux of trade and travel which sustained her ceased.

Ineuil's hastily gathered army struck intermittently at the legions of Cor, attacking under the command of Tulea's few experienced warriors and retreating again to the city before the Caruillans could fully organize their might. In discipline, both forces suffered equal inadequacies. Tulea held the more strategic position (so long as her ample storehouses did not fail), and the brief clashes had so far taken a slightly greater toll from Caruil. Still, Abbot Medwyn's improvised hospital filled, as did the Parul gravesites, and King Cor held the advantage of time. Not only would Tulean supplies ebb, but the enhanced sorcerers of Caruil would not tire as quickly as Marga's woefully small Circle.

One of Marga's number, a wizened wizard, Achmyr, who had schooled in Ixaxis with Lord Alobar, had already taken his death blow. He had grown fatigued, and the Caruillans had focused upon him to destroy him. Lesser sorcerers, whom Marga had lately recruited, could battle for only the shortest of durations before becoming too weak for useful contribution to the sorcerous defense; they could not replace Achmyr. Kaedric fed his Power to the whole of the Circle, sustaining every member far beyond normal endurance, but he had battles of his own besides the general defense. I think he never rested in those days, for Horlach had begun a sourceless, wearing attack against the Infortiare. I had been recruited for Marga's Circle and so did not realize for some time how severely Kaedric was beleaguered.

Much of the individual mischief which Cor's sorcerers wrought gave more inconvenience than serious tribulation, but the number of loci of the disturbances began to exceed the level of minor irritation. Thatch and timber in the heart of the city suddenly caught fire; Abbot Medwyn's supply of medicinal potions attracted an untoward number of destructive accidents. Abraded tempers began to erode Tulean unity, and it became incumbent upon Joli to appeal incessantly to her subjects merely to maintain a shadow of their initial spirit. Joli's own frame of mind remained remarkably firm. The afflictions which wearied the rest of us seemed to give her a strength of purpose, which carried her far beyond anticipated measure.

Marga's Circle lacked the clarity of individual identity which I had felt with Kaedric in the Taormin, but like Joli, the Circle had a strength yielded by cohesion of purpose. Horlach expended energy holding the Caruillans together despite their innate distrust of one another; I could feel his filtered taint. The energies surged and swayed, Tulea and Caruil stirring the infinities, while mortal men spent blood, and their women wept.

The ruling Lords of Serii began at last to relent and lend their own resources to the battle, as the spur of personal hazard reached them. Some still demurred and debated, but others had sent word to their own domains. At least one message had successfully

passed the Caruillan blockade, for a small troop from Elt appeared
to taunt the Caruillans from the rear. The Elt contingent offered a
reassuring hope that Serii had not forgotten her king's city, but the
passing days brought no further forces, and the aid from Elt dwindled with death.

There was much death, and there was the hollow emptiness left
by the parting of soul from frail flesh. There was pain and the ache
of those tears which bleed into the heart. There was sorrow and ancient, bitter reckoning of dreams' glory lost, the end of hope and
the beginning of futility. We died in the Circle with every thrust of
sword, wept with every desolate, bereaved child. There was no
dawn, no sun of clearer seasons; there was night and a dusky, darkling cloud of despair. There was nothing, and there was a heritage
nearly forgotten yet newly restored. We should have lost, but failure was too hard a foe.

Horlach waited, watching, pulling at the weak and entwining
the strong in webs of helplessness. Marga held her Circle firm, disciplined by her command. When Marga weakened, the sorcery of
Caruil wrought horrors and havoc.

Though no more greatly gifted with Power than many lesser
wizards, Mistress Marga had indomitably instructed Ixaxins for
more than a century. She had the gift of great teachers to kindle the
best in her charges. She brought that force to the Circle, pressing
even the most unruly individuals into fruitful cooperation; as one
of that errant number, I found Marga's lessons often humbling but
cogent. Though others among us, both younger and more puissant,
had failed before the steadiness of the Caruillan onslaught,
Marga's collapse shocked us into a moment of blindness to the battle we waged. In that moment, Caruil took a toll from which Tulea
would not recover, gaining holds in dangerous places due to our
inattention. A double dozen of Blood-Talon Cor's most aggressive
partisans breached the Tulean gate, and we could not afterward as-
certain how many of them escaped into the city to work their clan-
destine terrorism. The sorcerous holds they took were more subtle
and more insidious still.

Medwyn ascribed Marga's condition to the inevitable result of
protracted exhaustion and confined her to a room in the king's castle. Joli had provided both the chamber and the attendants, for
Marga required care unavailable in Ceallagh's Tower. Marga

would have rebelled vehemently over the fuss, but she did not rouse enough to realize her condition. The Ixaxin master who took her place as Circle leader was a skilled wizard named Macoll, but he lacked Marga's ability to unite our efforts, and the Caruillans tightened and took hold as sedulously as a bramble.

"How, Rhianna?" asked the child of Tul, "How do I keep on being strong? I want to run away from all of it. I cannot keep pretending to be brave and sure of everyone. I have nothing left to give them."

"There is no one else, Your Royal Highness," I answered, my own heart aching in echo.

"I cannot keep on like this," quavered Joli.

"I know. But you will."

"How?"

I shook my head helplessly. "There is nothing else you can do.

Chapter 25

The winter mist covered me and set me shivering, but I had need of solitude and the comforting persistence of the trees. I had been sent from the Circle to seek a few hours' sleep; I suspected that troubled dreams would provide less of a restorative than imperturbable old friends. Having accepted at last that my Tyntagel oaks were as lost to me as Rhianna's Dwaelin Wood, the gardens of the castle had grown increasingly dear. I should never again know the trees as deeply, closely as I had done, but I savored these avidly. They were the trees of Tul, and Horlach threatened them.

I wandered near to Tyntagel Hall and espied Ezirae waving erratically from her parlor window. I returned the remote greeting, feeling more distanced from her than if I had not seen her at all. I had met Yldana a few times of late; she continually beseeched me to visit Lord Borgor and Lady Veiga, while maintaining ambivalent relief that I did not comply. I knew that Dayn had accepted a captaincy under Ineuil's command, but I had not seen my brother nor my other kin since my severance from my father's rule. When Ezirae came bobbing across the lawn to beckon me under the arbor, I felt as displaced from her in time as from the Lady Varina dur Castor whose stone I now wore.

Poor Ezirae stopped several paces away from me, plainly leery of too near an approach. She flicked her heavy cloak nervously, as if she could remove unpleasant circumstances with the drizzle of rain. "You should not walk about in this weather with your head uncovered, Rhianna," said my aunt automatically.

I hid a smile and answered demurely, "I am sorry, Aunt Ezirae."

"Your father would be most unhappy if he knew I spoke to you, Rhianna. He has given very specific orders."

"I did defy him very thoroughly this time," I answered, touched by Ezirae's own rare defiance.

Ezirae wagged her head assertively. "You must apologize to him, Rhianna. He will forgive you."

"I have other obligations now."

"It is not at all seemly, Rhianna," said my aunt with a worried cluck.

"We are at war, Ezirae," I responded gently.

"It is all so very distressing." Ezirae drew herself up primly. "What good will come out of defeating the barbaric Caruillans if we all become barbarians ourselves in the process? Your behavior has been most improper, Rhianna. I must insist that you return to your family."

"Aunt Ezirae, I cannot."

With a blush of effort, my aunt persevered, "You cannot continue to defy convention without repercussions, Rhianna. You have a proud heritage, but you are making yourself quite unmarriage-able. I have actually heard that you live in the Infortiare's Tower."

"I am a wizardess, Aunt Ezirae. Lord Venkarel is my liege lord."

Ezirae involuntarily stepped back another pace, but she was resolute in her well-meant intentions. She frowned and fretted, "It is so difficult. I simply do not understand Baerod, moping in his office and allowing a young girl to make these decisions for herself. First you and then Liya."

"Liya?" I asked, startled.

"Liya has gone to work with that abbot as some sort of a nurse, if you can imagine." Abbot Medwyn had gathered a number of volunteers, but he had not told me that my brother's wife was among them; we had neither of us had, of course, a great deal of time for idle chatter recently. I felt a pleasure of pride in my diminutive sister-in-law. Ezirae resumed her purposeful critique: "Lord Venkarel does not even keep a suitable retinue, and after all those dreadful stories about Lady Veiga—well, it is most im-

proper." Ezirae paused as if an astonishing revelation had just
come to her and mused, "Dear me, I wonder if that is why Lady
Veiga has become so peculiarly interested in you recently. No
wonder Lord Borgor is so displeased." The prospect of new gossip
excited Ezirae into forgetting her careful distance and her disapproval. She said conspiratorially, "They have had nothing but
troubles between them since he was replaced as Adjutant. One
understands disappointment, naturally, but Lady Veiga is positively contemptuous when she even notices him or anything else."
I did not point out that Lady Veiga appeared to share the Dolr'han
failing of chronic contempt; I was sufficiently puzzled by the inti-
mation that Yldana's persistent conveyal of invitations had indeed
been instigated by the lady of Sandoral and not the lord. I could
not share Ezirae's belief that jealousy spurred the arrogant Lady
Veiga.

A blow of discordant sorcery rippled through the Circle of wizards and very briefly disoriented me. Too much damage was
wrought, and I reckoned my remaining respite would soon end.
"What manner of interest in me does the Lady Veiga express?" I
asked directly.

Ezirae opened her eyes very wide, bewildered as she always
was when anyone attempted to redirect her from a scandalous
speculation. She did gather her wits to form a reasonable answer
without excessive delay. "She seems to ask about everything. what
you studied as a child, where you have traveled, what you usually
do for amusement. She has spent a simply outrageous amount of
time with Lord Grisk. She has even been asking about your
mother, though I do think she has had the sense not to speak of the
subject to Baerod. Yldana is becoming quite irritated with Lady
Veiga's obsessive conversation, and I must say I am beginning to
agree. All of this war foolishness is bad enough without Lady
Veiga dun Sandoral constantly hinting that you are somehow tied
up in it. I wish these awful Caruillans would go away so we could
get back to normal."

My head had begun to throb with fatigue and the echo of another Caruillan attack. The rain had begun to pound heavily. "I
really must leave you now, Aunt Ezirae. I am very grateful for your
concern about me." I kissed her cheek before she could jump away,
and I think she was pleased, though it could have been only relief

at surviving the experience of conversing with me. I could hear her tutting dolefully as I crossed the saturated lawns to Ceallagh's Tower.

I did sleep for several hours, spared the early Circle summons I had anticipated. The sun had fallen before I woke, and I could only vaguely guess the time as I studied the shadows shrouding the bedchamber I had borrowed from a long forgotten wizardess. The striving flux of Power was muted; evidently, even the Caruillans had begun to feel the need of rest. I climbed the stairs to the library, knowing I should find Kaedric there.

He occupied the worn velvet armchair, his eyes lidded, though his mind remained rigidly awake. He spoke to me lazily. "Your eccentric choice of conversational locales appears to be a Tyntagellian trait, though I should have thought Lady Ezirae's Hamley practicality would have proved stronger. The soldiers of Tulea and Caruil are daunted, but Tyntagellian ladies deem freezing rain ideally suited for an afternoon chat." Kaedric opened his clear blue eyes. "I saw you from Marga's window."

"Has Mistress Marga roused?"

"She has not stirred, but she is disquietingly busy on some level. Perhaps you could visit her later; you might have more success than I in reaching her."

Checking a selfish sigh at the omnipresent demands of duty, I offered meekly, "I have been remiss not to have visited her earlier. I shall go at once, my lord." My Power protested its weariness.

"At this hour, you would probably frighten her attendants into hysteria, and another night's delay will not disturb Marga. That, at least, is my rationalization for keeping you here instead. Tell me something simple and commonplace, my lady: something not weighted with the cares of the Infortiare. What occupies the Lady Ezirae duri Tyntagel? Is she ferreting new court scandals from the foundering fulcrum of our society?"

"She is concerned that Sandoral Hall suffers a lack of marital bliss," I said lightly but hesitantly, ambiguously motivated in discussing Lady Veiga with Lord Venkarel.

"That is very stale information. Veiga and Borgor share only a rapacious taste for power—of any kind. Your aunt's perspicacity wanes if she has only now discovered disharmony in Sandoral.

Surely mere war cannot have caused Lady Ezirae's repertoire to grow so meager."

"Lady Ezirae is enormously upset by the state of her kindred. Lady Liya has begun to tend wounded soldiers in Abbot Medwyn's wards, I have forsworn my father for the Infortiare, and my father does nothing to stop either of us from such vastly improper behavior."

"Lady Ezirae suffers qualms for your moral character?" asked Kaedric with a cautious smile. "I suppose she dislikes your association with me nearly as much as does your father."

I replied with a trace of wistful humor for my aunt's particular perspective, "I believe my aunt considers the crime of wizardry less heinous than that of inhabiting Ceallagh's Tower."

"Alone with me," finished Kaedric wryly. "On the verge of calamity, your aunt quotes court etiquette." Meticulously, he traced with his finger the crease of velvet across the arm of his chair. "I doubt that Lord Baerod can be appeased by any act in which I am involved, but we might remedy the impropriety which so disturbs Lady Ezirae."

"I shall inquire of Her Royal Highness for other lodgings, my lord," I answered woodenly. Under less demanding external circumstances, I should not have expected the Infortiare to tolerate my precarious status as houseguest as long as he had. Mistress Marga had commented upon it slyly, for Kaedric's aversion to permanent visitors was well known by Ixaxins.

"That was not my meaning, but you might prefer it to the alternative." He was very firmly barriered, and I could read nothing from the stringent tone he took or the precise, expressionless set of his gaze. With extraordinary diffidence, he continued, "I thought you might consider marrying me, though I have an awful nerve to ask it under the circumstances," and I could not believe that I had heard him correctly. Kaedric proceeded in an uncharacteristic rush, which gave me no chance to speak, "Lords, I wish I had Ineuil's glib tongue just now. I should like to make some extravagant speech to tell you that you are the only meaning I have ever found in this world, you are become the faith which Medwyn despaired of ever instilling in me, and you have shown me the wizards' infinity, which I thought a theoretician's device until I felt you enter that unlikely Anxian tavern. Courtiers learn to say such things without sounding ridiculous, but I am not a courtier. I think you know what I am. I wish I could offer you better." Kaedric fell silent abruptly, and I caught my breath with an uncertain laugh.

"I shall be a difficult wife, my lord."

We were wed in the Parul chapel by Abbot Medwyn, while the cries of the wounded sang a strange marriage hymn. Kaedric had dragged Ineuil from the midst of a violent morning's skirmish by means which I preferred not to consider. Princess Joli had espied me leaving Mistress Marga's room in the castle and insisted on accompanying me, once she had by persistent badgering extracted my intent. Liya stood beside me also, though she had at first demurred from coming so near to the Infortiare, and her concession gave me much pleasure.

It was a very short and peculiar ceremony: Abbot Medwyn and Liya carrying the faint scent of the dying and the astringent odor of healers, Ineuil blood-stained and sporting a sword of battle, the princess regent of Serii acting as acolyte. Midway through the service, a messenger arrived from the castle with an urgent summons for Kaedric from Mistress Marga's nurse. We hastened through the final words, sealing the vows as Caruil hurled a virulent wave of destruction against Tulea, a blow which shattered irrevocably the Wizards' Circle which had been our chief defense.

"Go to Marga for me, my Rhianna," said Kaedric with a rueful sigh. "Ineuil, the Caruillans have breached the city gates; you and I had best see what we can do to stem the influx. Your Royal Highness should return to the castle before the fighting traverses the city."

"I can be more useful here," declared Joli determinedly, donning again her regal presence and certainty of command, "If only by aiding morale. Lady Liya, you will direct me, please." Liya smiled at me slightly without quite managing to look at Kaedric; then she followed Joli and a subdued Abbot Medwyn to the makeshift hospital. Ineuil coughed discreetly, Kaedric kissed me lightly, and both were gone.

Chapter 26

"Where is your sister, Yldana?" demanded Veiga fiercely. "We have asked you many times to bring her, and still you disappoint us."

"I have no influence with Rhianna," answered Yldana irritably. "I never did." Can Veiga talk to me of nothing else, she thought. And where has she been? I have awaited her for nearly an hour. "Did I misunderstand the hour of your invitation this morning, Veiga dear?"

Veiga withdrew her attention, and Yldana watched the change uncomfortably. This was the second time that Yldana had witnessed Veiga's shift into impossibly intense abstraction, and the last occasion had not ended well. Yldana had grown truly concerned that Veiga suffered a physical ailment, for Veiga's eyes were utterly distant and her skin was clammy and cold. Veiga had raved as well, and Yldana had sought Borgor's aid. Borgor had refused to come to his wife, and he would not speak of her. He had closed his study door in Yldana's face, and he had refused to emerge. When Yldana had returned to Veiga with a drafted servant, the lady of Sandoral had regained her normal aspect. She had derided Yldana, denying that the troubling incident had transpired. Now, it was recurring, and Yldana feared to an unreasonable degree.

The Lady Veiga dur Liin duri Sandoral laughed in private triumph. "He has kept it in our very reach, my Liege, defying us to find it. Even the wizardess did not know how close to our hands it lay."

Yldana regarded her friend with growing disquiet. "Veiga, to whom do you speak? Borgor is in his chambers." The two women stood alone in the enclosed garden of Sandoral Hall. The heroic figures amid the formal plantings stared at Yldana with mocking, marble eyes.

"Borgor is a weak fool," said Lady Veiga, but she still gazed beyond the world in which Yldana stood trembling. "An insignificant threat from Venkarel made him crumble. The wizardess is stronger, but she is not the one. The one who took Hrgh, my King? Yes, the one who aided the Venkarel. It must be the other. The Lady Rhianna? Yes, we must see her dead."

"Veiga," cried a very frightened Yldana. "What are you saying?"

"Your sister must die as must the wizardess," responded Veiga in her own controlled, scornful tones. "She destroyed my brother, Yldana, and we cannot let her go unpunished."

"Rhianna never knew Hrgh," pleaded Yldana with bewildered dismay.

Veiga had returned to her inward sight. "But the Taormin is first. We have shattered the Ixaxin Circle and found it while the Venkarel's mind was elsewhere. Kill the wizardess who still fights us, Veiga, and it will be ours to claim. The Venkarel will be too besieged to stop us from taking it—and him. Then the tree-witch will be yours, Veiga, and your brother will be avenged. Yes, my King, I shall kill the Tyntagel witch, and my brother will be avenged." Lady Veiga's words trailed into silence, and the titian-haired sorceress stiffened into a death-image trance. Yldana touched her tentatively; Veiga did not react, and Veiga's flesh was as cold as the rubies around her neck. Yldana ran from Sandoral Hall, too horrified to care that servants watched her with dubious stares.

Marga was dying. Her distraught attendants reiterated their innocence of her failing condition until I nearly screamed at them to keep silent. The bewildered nurse was little better, apologizing endlessly for a situation she could not explain, and I finally dismissed them all in desperation for some peace. I had left Marga a few hours before, unawakened but at no apparent hazard for eventual recovery. I studied Marga's ashen face, as faded as her eternally uncooperative hair, and I knew that Kaedric would not see her alive again.

I tried to reach the obstinate spark of the wizardess which yet lingered. I could so nearly touch her mind; Marga strove to meet me. I ought not to have been so riven from her, but something had altered her in a fashion which frightened me. She was dying in body; in mind, she was already largely gone.

The forceful little wizardess died with my hand brushing her brow. Her passing shook me, and Kaedric would suffer it more keenly by far. I had failed to find the cause of Marga's unnatural decline, and I had failed to learn what activity Kaedric had felt her somnolently pursue. It was not pleasing news which I must bear unto my husband.

I felt impatient and aggravated by the nervous grief which had replaced my morning's precious euphoria. Yldana hailed me before I could escape the castle, and I met my sister with fractious asperity. "I am available for no luncheons, dinners, or other social functions in the foreseeable future, and you may so inform Veiga Dolr'han in whatever words please you. I am in rather a hurry, Yldana."

"Listen to me, Rhianna!" said my sister without any of her usual composure. She pressed my arm urgently. "The wizardess is dead, is it not so?"

I stopped abruptly and stared at my sister. Her jet hair was imperfectly coifed. Her brown eyes held worry rather than enticement. "If you mean Mistress Marga, yes; she died moments ago."

Yldana nodded nervously. "It was Veiga."

"What?"

"Veiga killed her. Veiga intends death for you as well," said Yldana fervently, and I could feel in her words the horror of truth. "Please believe me, Rhianna: I would never have helped her if I had realized what she planned. I knew she wanted vengeance against Lord Venkarel for Hrgh's sake, but she blames you also, though you never even met Hrgh. I think I no longer know Veiga. I think she is no longer sane."

"Yldana, what does she say of Hrgh?" I asked with the calm of unbearable dread.

Yldana wrung her restless hands and turned her eyes away from me. "Hrgh has been hidden in Tulea for the past year. He looks so much the same, but his mind is—gone."

"You have seen Hrgh?" I demanded, trying to persuade myself that I had not in fact killed the lord of Liin. I wanted to believe that Veiga could have learned of my part against her brother from the soulless husk, which was all that could now remain of Hrgh Dolr'han.

"Yes, I have seen him," burst my sister in despair, "And I thought I should do anything to see him avenged. I spied for her, Rhianna, on you, on Ineuil on anyone Veiga claimed would bring us closer to the Infortiare. I even stole private missives from father, though I never knew why Veiga wanted them. I thought I did it for Hrgh. I did love him, Rhianna. Veiga knew, and she used me."

"Where is she, Yldana?" I asked with cold certainty. I had set my mind to search already, and I had found Kaedric on the Mountain of Tul, while Cor's sorcerers wrought unchecked havoc at the city gate.

"I left her in Sandoral Hall an hour ago," answered my sister. "She was fey, speaking in two voices and two minds. She said she would see you dead, Rhianna. I never meant that you be harmed."

I stared at the path to Ceallagh's tomb, a pale and twisting snake against the mountain above us. A shaft of sun through angry clouds caught a crimson speck of shining. "Veiga wears the Dolr'han rubies," I said, and Yldana nodded a startled agreement. "Yldana," I insisted urgently, "send word to Ineuil and to Princess Joli at the Parul wards that we have found Horlach." Yldana regarded me dubiously, but my Power and near-panic united to persuade her. "Tell them that Kaedric goes to face him in the Taormin. Ineuil must use Horlach's distraction to destroy Cor's sorcerers by mortal means; we may have little time. Please, Yldana," I begged. My sister nodded rigidly; I fled to the trail of Tul.

I could feel the changing: we were losing the constancy of life and history which our world had known for so many ages. We had always known that there were other times. We had always known that there were other, turbulent forces locked beneath our rules and solid customs. Did I enact this rending upon myself? I did not rouse Horlach. I had run from gilt imprisonment, but I did not stir the fires which I found. I did not seek Kaedric; I did not know that he could exist. The fires would have burned without my intervention, but I felt guilt. I felt that I had overthrown more lives than mine with my small rebellion, and I felt my husband's guilt of rebellion against Ven. I wished deeply that the turmoil could be undone, that the rip could be repaired; but how could we two not have acted as we had done?

I ran the path as far as I was able, seeing nothing of the beauty or dizzying view. I felt the journey endless in my desperate haste. I drew heedlessly to myself the strength of the earth and trees, gathering such forces as I could muster, knowing I would spend the dearest of them for the cause of my lord and husband. My feet began to stumble and slow, but the inner vistas grew clear and close. When Kaedric furled his fingers around the Taormin's layered shell, I stood in sight of him, though my physical shell still labored up the rock-wracked incline.

They were three: my gaunt and perilous lord; the dim, avaricious image of the Lady Veiga Dolr'han; and a confusion of forms which rippled over a man of ordinary proportions, a man who wore the crown and barbed wreath of the Sorcerer King. "You must realize by now that you cannot defeat me, Venkarel," said Horlach. "We understand the laws of wizardry, you and I, better than the unimaginative Zerus who purported to codify them. Zerus neglected the orders of infinity shamefully: infinity commutes all things. You are merely matter and energy, while I am energy and infinity. You cannot overcome the basic laws of existence."

Kaedric answered with a comparable detachment, "You have not forsworn matter, Horlach. You persistently seek its restrictions; hence, you abrogate the advantage which you claim."

"You are an interesting foe, Venkarel. You make a point which I had not considered. Nonetheless, I shall take you now that I have found the Taormin again. You tricked me once, Venkarel, with your tree-witch, but I was not ready then. You will not repeat your small triumph. You have made the inevitable error of a relatively superior intellect in judging all others by the paltry standards to which you are accustomed. You try to use the Taormin against me, deeming yourself more exceptional than the multitude preceding you. You will fail as they did; I have held the Taormin longer than you even imagine."

"Yield to us, Kaedric," whispered Veiga seductively, "and you and I shall rule for eternity."

"With your chosen lord, Horlach, manipulating my every breath?" returned Kaedric grimly. "You were never that enticing,

Veiga. Or do you forget that I refused such an offer even when you gave it to me honestly?" Veiga lashed out a coil of acid spite, which Kaedric blandly parried. Horlach chuckled indulgently, seemed to darken and coalesce, and exuded with a breath a throbbing wave of Power which pulsed into a semblance of the Taormin's whorls.

With a wand of inner light, Kaedric culled the angry nodes, smoothing the menacing webs. I moved beside him, lending my own will and Power as I had in less treacherous walks. He accepted me without pause, for we had become too closely bound to be distinguishable.

The sparks of baneful fire began to course. Kaedric moved to alter the weaving's pattern, and Veiga retreated in alarm, while Horlach implacably gathered the changes and rewarped them. The issuance from the Sorcerer King came faster, and there was no time for the care of certain study. We were well into the Taormin now, treading tortuous paths which I knew that Kaedric had not explored. We glimpsed souls caught within the twines, but they were lost, and we evaded them. Horlach did know his holding well, and it flexed and ebbed too easily to his command.

The fires stirred and sputtered into elusive furies. I knew peripherally that I had overtaken a foot-weary Veiga on Tul Mountain's merciless heights; Horlach's leaping essence had not needed of her the extra steps to Ceallagh's tomb. I continued to climb, and the stresses and taunts of Horlach and Kaedric waxed vaster, while the unwary and weak who stumbled in the path of the warring pair burned in acid and fire. Victims perished haphazardly in Tulea, Tyntagel, Ven, Caruil, Ardasia, and Mahl; the geography of the Taormin cared nothing for material rationality. Horlach's dead-alive were roused, and the gargoyles of his ancient gate spewed forth into innocent lands. Evil things stirred in the Dwaelin Wood, which had been stilled of any major sorcery for long ages, and the barrier-wall of Anx rippled and took flame. Horrors stirred lakes, and travesties of life crawled from forgotten crypts: the neglected toys of the Sorcerer Kings were revived in animus by the rending play of energies tearing magma from the Taormin. Horlach had taken his world thus; he had only to patiently persist, and any mortal would fall to him, who had no precious runnels of blood to protect.

"You never took the final step, Horlach," said Kaedric coldly, as he absorbed another spear of dark fire with a pain which he determinedly denied. "Despite your contrary contentions, you remained essentially energy and, so, mortal." The darkness which was Horlach hardened. He is alarmed, I thought; he fears my husband, whom he waited so long to use.

"You cannot go beyond me," insisted Horlach persuasively. Horlach paused and laughed cruelly. "You bluff well, Venkarel. You essay to push me into rashness. You would like to see me leave this domain to you, would you not?"

Kaedric responded slowly, "I shall not emulate you, Horlach. I do not wish to be a Sorcerer King."

Horlach emitted derisive fury. "You are a fool, after all," said the dark, undying king, as he wove destruction across the world. "What have your pathetic mortals given you that you should serve them so far?"

"They have given me fear and hatred, Horlach, and I have had a surfeit of both."

"I shall take you," promised Horlach. The darkness pressed against us with lethal skill.

"I cannot surrender to him, Rhianna," breathed my husband to me in his mortal voice; I had reached him at last in physical presence, and we stood alone to reasoning sight before the dull gray stone which marked the dusty bones of Ceallagh. Kaedric held the Taormin lightly, a strong and delicate grasp of a mechanical thing of twisting wires and mineral fragments. I could see its glow press light from his fingers; I could see the press of his fingers twisting light from Horlach's tangles. We stood in two worlds, and both were real and terrible.

The breeze carried the scent of rain. I touched my husband's hand and brushed his lips with tears. He held me softly, fiercely, and the beating fire of him filled me. "You shall not leave me, Kaedric," I whispered in return.

"We must lose this world, beloved."

"We have the other, and it will not end."

He parted from me slowly, and I had no recourse but to let him go. I watched him feverishly, remembering, though he would remain to me in mind. I recalled how cold I had thought his eyes, as the blue turned to gold with the fire which claimed his form.

Kaedric took the Taormin, wrenching it piecemeal from Horlach's grasp. Horlach's layered faces faded: a sallow, unimpressive little man remained. "You cannot defeat me," insisted Horlach.

"I can save Serii from you, Horlach, and from myself." Blue fire burst outward, and the darkness melted before it. "I release you, Horlach," whispered my husband, and the darkness died.

I stood alone atop Tul Mountain. I gathered the fallen Taormin from the hard ground and cradled it against my breast. The filigree was cloaked by ash, and I pressed it to me tightly.

I bit my lip, and the salt of blood mingled with silent weeping. "You had best return to the castle, beloved," said my husband gently. "Cor's forces will scatter without the insistent drive of Horlach, but there remains much work of recovery. You are the Infortiare now."

I shook my head, though the gesture had little meaning. "You are not dead, my husband."

With a sardonic humor which I well knew, Kaedric replied, "Even Ixaxis is unlikely to follow a ghost."

"I am little more without you. Let me join you now; I am your wife."

"And difficult, as you promised," said Kaedric with a shaken laugh. "We have unleashed years of turmoil this day, and we must effect a laborious remedy, my Rhianna. I can no longer act upon the world of matter save through you. I would I had not burdened you with this."

I essayed a smile and succeeded to a measure. "But I did bring it upon myself, my lord and love. Very well, I shall fulfill our obligations in this plane, but it is a delay only. You have accepted immortality, Kaedric; your wife must share it with you." I paused. "Kaedric, can you hear the trees?"

"Dimly, but as well as I ever could."

"I am glad," I said and turned my eyes and feet toward my city.

VI
THE EMBER

Year of Serii—9009
Tulea, Serii

King Astorn will return tomorrow, and Joli will relinquish the regency. Our king will not like what he finds, though word by now has reached him of the worst of it. His prized son is gone, and most of his councillors not dead have retired, like my father and my uncle, to domains which will not remember their traitorous follies. Joli has forged a new Council, and she has done well. I shall see that His Majesty heeds his daughter's words, for she has proven wiser than he; she will be a strong queen.

Horlach's futile war claimed so many: irascible, irreplaceable Mistress Marga of Ixaxis; the brash piratical king of Caruil, Blood-Talon Cor; the sadly unlamented scion of Niveal, Lord Grisk. Amgor is among the dead, victim of a festered wound. He failed steadily, despite Abbot Medwyn's efforts to save him. I think Amgor could not face the guilty truth of his part in conspiracy any more than he ever accepted the fact that his wife would never love him. Yldana was kind to him at the end at least; though grief has subdued her lustrous spirit, it has taught her mercy. Ineuil, I think, will wed her when her mourning time is done. He knows she worked with Veiga to use him, but Ineuil is not himself blameless of deceit. They seem to understand each other well, my sister and the errant lord of Ven.

Abbot Medwyn frets for me, delaying anew his return to Benthen Abbey, though Master Gart has come to escort him on a now uncertain journey. I have told Medwyn vainly that he has no cause for his deep concern over me, I have Liya to attend me in Tulea, for Dayn has assumed Tyntagel's place on the Council. Joli comes also to see me, and there are ever visitors from Ixaxis. I do not try to explain that other sustaining presence; I should be adjudged as mad as the pitiable Veiga.

Abbot Medwyn knows that I bear Kaedric's child. The priest in him disapproves, for he realizes that Kaedric most truly wed me with the asking, but Medwyn remembers too clearly an intense young boy in a ruined, smoking city. Abbot Medwyn will welcome my son for Kaedric's sake.

I stand beside a sapling oak on the Mountain of Tul. The island which has made itself my domain catches sunset from its chalky walls. Dusk stains the castle below me, and the Tower is shadowed black. I feel the hearts of Serii, the throngs of Tulea, the bright glow of Ixaxis, and the solemn strength of Tyntagel oaks; I feel the lives across the seas and in the earth. There are more troubles in Serii now, and Ventures have been called to begin the healing of them.

I rub the stone of Varina of the bittersweet sorrow. He whom I love holds me next to him in that other world we share. I know that I must soon return to the castle, for Abbot Medwyn worries greatly when he deems me alone. He does not know.

FIRE LORD

I.

Let (X,T) be a topological space.
Let S be a subset of X.
The union of S and all of its limit points is called the *closure* of S.

CLOSURE

Chapter 1

Disjointed words tumbled across the screen. As though burned, Beth snatched her hand from the smooth membrane of the keypad. The surge of data ebbed into a silent, mocking glow:

LIFE EXTENSION PROJECT
STATUS REPORT #7
GENETIC RESEARCH CENTER,
IX AXIS REPUBLIC

Beth's fingers hovered above the keys which would delete the unbidden file. "A fine psychic researcher you make," she chided herself, "shuddering like a superstitious crone." She relaxed her hand deliberately and steeled herself to read the document. The brutal details of the descriptions appalled her. No such information regarding the Immortals' predecessors had emerged at the trial or appeared in any published records. The GRC personnel had exerted great care to ensure the thorough destruction of those peculiarly talented children.

Beth tapped the keypad delicately, and the flat display became blank. She brought her hands together slowly, folded her manicured fingers, and pondered the eerily pertinent data. The initial gifts of anonymous information had fascinated her, augmenting her thesis invaluably. She had attributed the data to Dr. Jonet; she had eventually dismissed her initial assessment. Jonet could not possibly anticipate her paths of research so accurately, nor could his sources be so uncannily complete. Beth considered the subject of her research and the unsettling conclusions that coalesced from her analyses. Beth Shafer Terry began to fear, and a young and cunning man, who was something nearly human, smiled viciously in the city of Sereia.

Jon Terry grumbled to himself as he emerged from transfer, evaded an overly zealous young woman who tried to direct him to the off-world queue, and entered the DI security scanner. His identity flashed coldly on the guard's screen; the security guard stared at the flashing name, stared at Jon, and requested a second scan. "Welcome back, Dr. Terry," said the guard stiffly, as he confirmed the computer release of the dome's exit barrier.

"Officious cretin," muttered Jon sullenly, annoyed by the unnecessary delay of dual scans. Awaiting the tram, he ignored the flustered whispers of the DI personnel who rushed around him. He studied the DI complex with its peculiar use of structural texture and color; Jon reaffirmed his loathing of that sterile gaudiness, as the tram lifted him from the port dome to the upper entry of DI technical headquarters.

"Dr. Terry, how good of you to join us." The immaculately clad man who greeted Jon looked young, which meant that he might be any age between twenty-five and eighty. "I am Derek Coggins, senior relational specialist."

"I am only here because Network threatened to terminate my research grants unless I cooperated," replied Jon bluntly.

Coggins abandoned his strained smile. "I did not favor your inclusion on the Crisis Committee, Dr, Terry." A rumpled figure shambled across the crimson lobby and tapped Coggins' shoulder. Coggins tried to recover his bland courtesy. "You know Dr. Davison?"

Jon smiled at Davison, a man of peculiarly imperfect appearance in a world dominated by genetic uniformity. "The reclusive Tom Davison emerges just to welcome me? How have you been, Tom?"

"Terrible," answered Davison, and Coggins shuffled uncomfortably. "Come talk to me after your meeting, Jon."

"Same office?"

"Have I quit yet?" retorted Davison.

Coggins interrupted crisply, "The other members of the Committee will be waiting, Dr. Terry." Davison retreated without a word to Derek Coggins. Jon stared after Davison, wondering for the first time if a crisis might actually exist.

"We are no longer able to complete transfer to Aleph 2C7."

Only a purist like Weywood would bother with the cumbersome Aleph designations. "Is that Floral Park?" asked Jon innocently. "What happened to that lawsuit they brought against DI?"

Pained expressions acknowledged Jon's bleak irony. Helen Martines, another reluctant DI recruit, replied evenly, "Network arbitrators suggested a sizable settlement in favor of Floral Park, citing the precedent of Terry versus DI."

Weywood never faltered. "Aleph 2C7 corresponds to Smithson's Well. We have been forced to reroute through Aleph F8."

"Our transfer monitors perceive Smithson's Well as topologically nonexistent," said Coggins, glaring askance at Jon. "The Smithson's Well monitors report nothing extraordinary, except that DI central no longer responds to their contacts."

"The topological flaw is obviously local," commented Dr. Martines.

"So it appears," conceded Weywood.

"You have run all of the customary tests, Dr. Weywood?" asked a dark, nervous man whose sesquipedalian name Jon had forgotten.

"The DI central monitor verifies that our equipment is functioning flawlessly."

"A flaw could exist in your verification procedures," suggested Jon.

"I designed those procedures myself," returned Weywood coldly.

Terrific, thought Jon, wondering how many other members of the Crisis Committee resented him. He slumped a little farther in his chair, bored and distinctly unimpressed with the meeting, the committee, and the few facts that had emerged in the past two hours. The eager experts like Weywood could transform even a simple problem into a subject of endless debate. Marliss and Eaton had contributed nothing intelligent; Landsian had droned interminably on about the vital need to protect the public from awareness of the crisis, which he also paradoxically insisted did not exist.

Wade and Martines had asked some pertinent questions, but Coggins had waylaid every answer with a reminder of DI's technical supremacy in topological systems.

If your systems are so perfect, Jon wanted to ask, why have a few minor transfer disturbances thrown you into such a frenzy? Jon did not voice his question, because he had promised himself to maintain some small degree of diplomacy where technical issues were concerned. At the first opportunity, Jon abandoned the meeting. His marginal diplomatic restraint had worn very thin.

Tom Davison's office wallowed beneath an impressive array of technical archives and quasi-historical trash. "You escaped your committee," remarked Tom from his computer console.

"I doubt they'll miss me. I seem to have been inflicted upon an unreceptive audience."

"DI loyalists have never forgiven you. A lot of heads rolled on your account."

"Punishment of the innocent."

"Honors for the nonparticipants." Tom moved his hands over the vast control grid, which had been elaborately redesigned to his specifications. The computer responded with a scaled holographic image of the DI transfer ports. "I made this recording last night. Watch that couple enter the Culver port."

Jon sank into the chair beside Tom and leaned forward with his chin in his hands. The DI node intersected an exceptional number of Network sets, making it one of the busiest ports in connected space. Tom's matrix displayed only a small portion of the terminal building, but Jon still spent several moments distinguishing the Culver port among the opalescent arc from which radiated endless queues of travelers.

A very modish couple approached the Culver port with the indifferent confidence of habitual travelers. They stepped through the light curtain, that nonfunctional aspect of transfer mechanization which protected the untrained eye from the mind-confounding sight of topological space distortion, and they remained visible. They strode two meters into the central field, which should have been unattainable via three-dimensional passage, before disappearing into spatial distortion. The holographic image faded.

"The couple reached their destination safely," said Tom. "They fortunately asked a minimum of questions."

"Transfer ports cannot spatially translate of their own accord. Someone has altered the configuration."

Tom adjusted the projection to produce the controller in a highly magnified rendition. The intricate arrays resembled orderly golden lace trapped in pale amber. Tom increased the magnification, and the resonator webs became distinguishable. "See any signs of tampering?"

Jon frowned. "I haven't looked at a resonator in thirty years," he began, but something about the maze of circuitry stopped him. "Has anyone modified the portal structures?"

"No one but you ever understood the DI portal structures well enough to try. You created a thing of genius, and nobody has ever found a way to improve on your design."

"That is not my logic."

"DI central insists otherwise."

Jon shook his head stubbornly. "That is not my logic," he repeated, and Tom nodded. "You're not surprised?"

"No other answer made sense to me, but I wanted to hear it from you."

"The controller adapts to natural changes," mused Jon. "But the basal structure cannot vary without a major upheaval in the projected physics of the associated set. I think we would have noticed if gravity had changed direction." Tom grunted in laughter. "Wait." Jon closed his eyes, retreating into the infinite-dimensional realm which defied physical representation. He opened his eyes just long enough to assimilate the images registered in Tom's computer; he reconstructed the mental gyrations which had produced DI's original transfer port controller. "That reflects an incipiently unstable system," he concluded with a dawning of concern. "I'm surprised that the transfer ports are functioning at all."

"They are not working very well, even within the Taormina set."

"Weywood only recounted two incidents which sounded like anything more than coordinate errors."

"Most of the facts have been declared DI-proprietary." Tom gave Jon a lugubrious glance. "You are still cleared; I verified it before I submitted your name for the Crisis Committee."

"Preservation of my clearances was one of the few concessions my lawyers gained for me."

Tom grunted. "I'd been tracking inexplicable quantum phenomena for a month when this transference problem surfaced. Seven of the ports have now stopped mapping completely. Twelve others have shifted focus. New Loring and Thess have cross-mapped. The Governor of Thess missed his birthday gala due to transfer port error, and you can believe he let DI know about it." Tom allowed the viewing matrix to fade. "We have real trouble."

Jon tapped the arm of his chair. The chair reconfigured very slowly to his straightened posture. "You need a new chair," he commented. "This one is going inflexible."

"Supply center has been promising me one for a year." The two men studied the emptiness of the viewing matrix. "If we inform Coggins and company that the controller is defective, they'll order immediate development of a replacement."

"Without analyzing the cause of the first failure."

"They'll use this incident to press funding of redundant units."

"Expensive and pointless in this type of system. Topologically connected systems must fail equivalently, and the controller of a given space must be topologically connected to any other mechanism of equivalent control. Otherwise, the system is unstable."

"What happens if an unstable system is perpetuated?"

"Cataclysm. I can see why your transfer port quanta are misbehaving."

"The problem is not localized around the transfer ports. My team has measured erratic data on a planetwide scale, extending into the upper ionosphere."

"I haven't noticed any unusual interference."

"The most severe disruptions have centered over the Axis Republics. Let me show you something else." Tom touched the view grid, and the display matrix became a two-dimensional screen. "The first column reflects occurrences of energy transfer aberrations. The second column represents incidents of abnormally high electron counts in the ionosphere."

"One-to-one correspondence?"

"Yes. My quantum aberrations follow the pattern as well."

"That's actually reassuring. As long as the energy fields react consistently, my faith in the physical laws can remain intact. We have an anomalous force in play which we haven't yet identified."

Tom murmured with uncharacteristic diffidence. "I have one more list to show you: a correlation that Weywood and the DI central system failed to check."

"The thoroughness of DI central must have deteriorated since I left here."

"Not really. They still enter new scientific developments almost as soon as they emerge, scrutinize them via the latest in intelligent algorithms, and apply extensive consistency thresholds to the resultant statistics. Unsubstantiated theories migrate to a holding file, and elements of pseudoscience are automatically purged." Tom touched the grid again, and a third list of dates appeared beside the first two. "Did you ever hear about the GRC scandal sixty-some years ago? A social worker claimed that the geneticists had illegally created and subsequently abused a group of experimental children. The Ninth Axis Governor fined the Genetic Research Center and would have prosecuted the project's administrators, except that everyone involved in the project died before the court could complete its investigation."

"Of course. The case of the 'Battered Immortals,' as the more imaginative media types called it. The GRC trial evidence is central to Beth's doctoral thesis."

"I'd forgotten: she's a psychic researcher, isn't she?" Tom became pensive for a long moment. "Well, my boy, Rob, adopted the plight of these 'forlorn' victims as evidence of the immorality of the scientific community. Rob is an anarchist at the moment. He was lecturing me on the sins of my profession and praising these 'Immortals' for their rebellion."

"I assume this discussion is leading somewhere pertinent?"

"I decided to gather some facts on my own and give Rob a good debate. I had the DI computer attach the data base of the sensationalist news media, some of which have pursued the Immortals to this day with pretty wild accusations. As soon as I attached the new data, my computer registered the third correlation to the transfer port anomalies." With quick motions across the grid, Tom added brief event descriptions to the columns of dates. "The timing of every port anomaly corresponds to an act of aggression by one of these Immortals."

"I thought the sensationalists reported such acts on the hour. How many of those aggressive actions have been authenticated?"

"All of them measure at least ninety-five percent probable. None of the other reported actions show a verification probability greater than fifty percent. Don't ask me why the legitimate news sources haven't picked up any of this."

Jon leaned back, and the chair reluctantly adapted to support him. "Maybe the Immortals perceive quantum variations as we perceive ultrasonics: with a headache. A little physical discomfort can inspire a lot of aggression."

"Maybe. Or maybe the Immortals really are bringing us to Armageddon, as the doomsayers of the anti-genetics movement would have us believe." Tom Davison's round face and tilted features always gave his expressions a puckish cast, but something woeful dominated that face today. "You want to hear how paranoid I've become? I think that the Immortals are changing the universal topologies, energy patterns, material world, and who knows what else. I think those GRC geniuses accidentally tapped a motherlode of the kind of mental powers that inspired supernatural legends throughout history. None of the original Immortals ever showed much interest in anything beyond themselves, but these later ones may have begun to look beyond private insanity and family squabbles. Don't say it, Jon—I sound as mad as an Immortal myself."

"It is quite a theory," murmured Jon vaguely. He would have ridiculed anyone but Tom Davison for proposing anything so preposterous. Tom had always been an unusually stable and sensible member of one of the most esoteric of scientific communities. "Beth did mention some peculiarity of the Immortals' projected energy. I suppose that a correlation could exist, though I have trouble believing that it poses the danger you suggest."

"If anyone can rigorously prove or disprove the topological cohesion of my theory, it s you."

Jon grimaced. "Thanks a lot for the confidence. What do you intend to do while I study aberrant psychology?"

"Prepare a closure of the transfer ports, just in case you decide to agree with me."

Jon wondered for a shocked moment if Tom Davison had spent too many years working among overly educated eccentrics.

"Maybe you had better downplay your intentions, if anyone else asks."

"Don't I know it." The puckish face grew sadder.

"I shall need more data on these Immortals," said Jon slowly. "I don't suppose that anyone else has addressed their peculiarities from a topological perspective."

"The DI computer has nothing on them except the garbled media garbage I attached last week."

"I'll talk to Beth."

"You should appease your committee first."

"And waste the day talking in circles," grumbled Jon. Though Tom might sound crazy, he was not boring company. Jon sulked all the way to the meeting room, while topological improbabilities rattled his nerves.

Chapter 2

"**H**ow far do you believe the allegations regarding these Immortals you've been studying, Beth?"

"Don't tell me you're developing an interest in my work, Jon Terry. I could never stand the competition." The dog ran yapping through the room, followed closely by Kitri and her brother. "Kitri, Michael, don't run in the house!"

"What sort of data do you have on them?"

Beth became peculiarly still. "How much do you want to hear?"

Jon tilted his head, pondering his wife's sudden change of mood. He said slowly, "Everything." Beth's obvious distress bewildered him; he had not yet told her of the day's events.

"Of the original seventeen Immortals," began Beth didactically, "only two are still thought to be alive. 'Immortals' is clearly a misnomer, though the subjects' potential longevity has certainly been enhanced. The Immortals are remarkably resilient to injury and impervious to most diseases. The characteristics which enhance their longevity appear to breed true. Unfortunately, the mental instability has also been perpetuated, a situation doubtless aggravated by inbreeding."

"The mental instability is balanced by unusual mental strengths in select areas?"

"All of the original subjects demonstrated exceptional intelligence, countered by acute paranoia and (in five cases) schizophrenia. All seventeen produced consistent indications of active psychic abilities." Beth became fervent. "The problem with psychic research has always been the intermittency of the data. These bizarre products of a misguided experiment seem to offer incontrovertible evidence of the human mind's potential power. If the GRC administrators in charge of the Immortals project had concentrated less on concealing their crime, we might have learned enormously from these people while they were still manageable."

"Before all the administrators and technical personnel died."

"The apparent causes of the deaths ranged from heart failure to a freak fire in a laboratory. All of the deaths were explicable, albeit oddly coincidental in light of the allegations of the GRC administrators. Even the social worker who had rescued the children began to question the children's stories. Most of my data was gathered at that time, but the study was never completed. The Immortals were psychiatrically treated and released after the aborted GRC trial, and the matter was officially closed. Since the GRC administrators had been discredited on an ethical basis, it seems that no one gave their findings much analysis."

In the next room, Kitri shrieked at Michael. The children dissolved into giggles. Beth stared at the connecting door, but she made no move toward it. She continued her recital restlessly, "According to the GRC personnel associated with the Immortals project, the children demonstrated psychic talents closer to witchcraft than to any scientific category, at least in appearance. When tested, the Immortals displayed no telepathic capabilities, though subsequent events suggest that the Immortals can indeed influence the thoughts of others. They do not appear to be clairvoyant. Some psycho-kinetic ability has been cited, but it appears to be an incidental result of the actual psychic intent."

"Which is?"

"Manipulation of energy sources. At least, that is the theory on which I have based my thesis. The records regarding the Immortals' effects on GRC's atmospheric control center are extraordinary." Beth hesitated. "And a little frightening." Beth leaned forward and placed her hand on Jon's. "What happened at DI today?"

"Tom Davison thinks that these Immortals of yours are altering the topological structure of this world. I need access to whatever information you have." Beth's lovely face, the result of genetic control at its best, became solemnly pensive.

"The Immortals were given only standard testing when they were contained at GRC," explained Beth. "The geneticists were not equipped to run full psychic analyses. Once the children were declared psychologically cured, they had the right to refuse further testing, which they did. They matured into class C functional citizens, which meant that they could live on their own with only the most sporadic, limited supervision. Inbreeding should never have been allowed. However, the city of Sereia, where the Immortals were assigned after their creators' trial, is ridiculously protective of its citizenry."

"The Immortals don't seem to merit much protection, whatever their past misfortunes might have been."

"They are cruel, ruthless, and exceedingly dangerous. All of the deaths among them have been attributed to conflicts among themselves, and a good many would-be interviewers have disappeared over the past fifty years."

Jon nodded soberly, his fingers nervously tapping the computer console. In an explosive movement, Jon applied another test to his wife's data, hoping to see his previous results contradicted. The pattern remained uncannily consistent.

Beth said gently, "You have been running tests all night. Do you expect the answer to change?"

Jon shook his head reluctantly. "How did you acquire your initial data, Beth?"

Beth smoothed her blonde hair, recently cropped short after the fashion of the year. "Someone sent it to me anonymously."

"Do you have any idea of your benefactor's indentity?"

"Yes." Beth slid from the console. She walked to the window-wall, which currently displayed a wintry mountain scene, subdued for the waning night. "I have avoided the obvious answer."

"That you have been fed this information, just as the social worker who originally 'rescued' the Immortals from GRC received anonymous information about the Immortals' plight."

"I consider it unlikely that these genetic abominations would send their psychic histories to an insignificant doctoral student on the far side of the planet, unless they intended that I convey the information to my extraordinarily famous husband."

"Maybe so," Jon agreed, finding the ramifications distasteful in the extreme. "If these Immortals can alter physical topology at will, they could destroy all connected space."

"And they want you to know their power."

"A deliberate taunt."

"It would be psychologically congruous to their profiles."·

"My God." The facts were consistent. The conclusions were inescapable. "Class C citizens do not have transfer privileges. So far, the Immortals are confined to this world." Jon drummed his fingers pensively. "Take Kitri and Michael to Inulaii. Leave this morning, while the ports are still functional. I shall try to join you this afternoon. We are not likely to return, so take whatever is most important. Take the stupid dog."

Beth did not even protest his disparagement of her prized puppy. She watched Jon transfer the night's work to light disk and erase it from the central memory. "Where are you going?" she asked him tightly.

"To DI. I need to see Tom about closing the ports."

Chapter 3

"**S**omeone is playing games," growled Tom. He struck the view grid irritably, and an image appeared, suspended in the center of the display matrix: ⋈ "I've lost thirty files since I talked to you yesterday. Each emptied of everything but this symbol." Tom looked at Jon. "Did you find anything in Beth's data?"

"Yes. Courtesy of your gameplayer. I sent Beth and the kids to Inulaii."

"Eleanor is visiting her sister on New Athens. Rob refuses to go anywhere, if only because I suggested it."

"Too bad. This world could become a very unpleasant place to live."

"Are we overreacting?"

"No. We can't allow the gameplayer to define the rules."

"I have configured a closure mechanism. It's basically the same device we use to inhibit travel to inimicable habitats and previously tenanted spaces."

"Can you gain me access to the controller?"

"That depends on the reason."

Jon smiled wanly. "We cannot entrust reconfiguration to DI central, since the gameplayer has apparently claimed our computer networks."

"Can you ensure permanence of the closure?"

"I can rearrange the universe, if you can give me environmental isolation from the controller's energy fields."

"With the controller in node, I can only guarantee you about ten minutes. After that the operational distortions will begin to alter your molecular contiguity. The process does not promote longevity."

"Ten minutes should suffice to tangle a few connectors."

"We are condemning a lot of people. Maybe we should consult Coggins and company."

"We cannot wait for these Immortals to master topological transport. If we allow them to spread beyond local space, we could jeopardize the entire Network."

"You want me to implement the closure device while you sabotage the controller?"

"Yes." Listen to us, thought Jon, matter-of-factly condemning our home world to eternal isolation. Even if those we strand should revive conventional space travel, there is not a benign planet within practical reach. Neither Tom nor I have any close frends at risk, but Tom will lose a stepson, and I shall lose my home. I know a lot of people on this world, even if Beth does call me antisocial.

"The planet is self-sufficient," mused Tom, as if in answer to Jon's own doubts. "It's one of the most agreeable worlds we ever discovered. We cannot possibly evacuate the whole planet anyway. Our gameplaying friend won't wait for us to debate about who should be saved."

"We may eventually discover another solution and be able to rescue this place from whatever it has become."

Tom turned his head back to his computer. "You believe that?" he asked curiously.

"No. When I've finished with the controller, not even DI's technical wizards will be able to reassemble the open structure."

Beth and the kids still waited in the line for Inulaii. Beth was forcing cheerfulness, and Michael had adopted his mother's enthusiasm. Kitri looked bewildered, muddled between Michael's exuberant teasing and the strangeness of sudden change.

Jon did not speak to them. Beth saw him, but she averted her eyes quickly. Beth knew that her husband had no legal authority to close the Culver port for maintenance inspection. She kept the children's attention on the light curtain ahead of them and the window-wall simulation of Inulaii's tropical beaches beside them.

Jon felt a yank at an internal tension when he saw his family disappear through the Inulaii port. He released a tightly held breath when the controller signaled a normal transfer. He activated the entry barrier, isolating Culver port from the rest of the DI sights and sounds.

Tom had disengaged the light curtain, and he was removing his closure device from the maintenance unit that he and Jon had appropriated. Jon walked gingerly toward the dark, rippling distortion of air, which encompassed the shifted Culver port. He half expected to pass the marked entry and find himself on Culver, but the synthetic floor beneath him did not change to otherworld metal. He stepped around the Culver port, feeling queasy as he did it. The ports should have formed a continuous sphere surrounding the controller, extending even to the nulls beneath the dome's smooth floor. Walking around a disjointed port, as idly as if circling a piece of furniture, should have been impossible.

"Ten minutes, Jon." Tom was not as engrossed in setting his mechanism as he appeared.

Jon activated the protective field which was part of the maintenance uniform he had taken. The field had not been designed to defeat the controller's direct energies, but Tom had made some delicate changes. The changes, Tom had warned with disheartening candor, would almost certainly destroy the mechanism after one usage, if they lasted that long.

Jon entered the controller space, feeling decidedly relieved when his monitor's readings remained level. He walked toward the cylindrical extrusion which housed the node. Jon knew the controller's theory intimately; he was accustomed to seeing the controller itself in magnified versions, as represented on view matrices. He had seldom interacted with his creation physically. The reality of the controller was no bigger than his fist.

He breathed deeply three times to achieve some sort of steadiness, reached out his protected hand, and lifted the controller from its energy nest. He could not hear anything beyond the ports, but he could imagine the confusion which was resulting from the sudden failure of transfers all over the world. A dozen DI officials would descend on the maintenance consoles in a few minutes; it would take them some additional time to focus on the controller.

Jon inserted the force probe through the controller's outer network, adjusted the intensity and registered the coordinates that were to be fused. He extracted the probe, reversed it, plunged it back into the controller for the required instant, and restored the controller to its nest. The fields began to operate again, warping the air across the ports.

The controller had never been designed to emulate a personality, but its complexity had necessitated a synthetic intelligence. The intricacy of the controller's fail-safe mechanisms made it self-teaching and almost capable of original thought, so carefully had it been programmed to preserve universal integrity. It certainly comprehended the alteration Jon was inflicting. Jon felt like a murderer.

"I am sorry," he whispered to the controller, the prototype for all of the topological controllers on all the Network worlds. He was beginning to feel sick. He checked his watch: seven minutes. He turned to circle again around the Culver port, but the port had shifted. It had returned to its proper location, locking him into the controller's distorted space.

A short, fidgety young man stood beside the controller. Jon tried to recall how many seconds a man could survive unprotected beside the controller-in-node. "Which port were you entering?" demanded Jon hurriedly, even as he set his monitor to scan.

"I had hoped that you would offer me more of a challenge, Dr. Terry," replied the young man sadly. "Sabotage is such a childish effort." The young man directed his fingers toward the controller with a respectful care. His fingers shifted and blurred as they neared it.

"Don't try to touch it!" cried Jon instinctively. The monitor on his wrist was recording energy contortions of alarming magnitude surrounding the young man. The controller's fields were being impaired, and the implant had not had time to complete implosion. Tom would hesitate to implement the external closure until Jon reappeared. Damn.

The young man had paused, apparently unable to touch the controller's lacy surface. "It repels unprotected flesh," recalled Jon aloud, feeling a momentary smugness for that precautionary tactic.

The young man's sharp gaze became angry and supercilious.

"How little you understand, Dr. Terry. Bereft of your technological trappings, you mortals are a very primitive people," he remarked. "I mean to improve this sterile society of yours. Your controller and every world it touches will be mine, despite your feeble attempts to thwart me."

The controller space shuddered, and the energies roared. A strange expression nudged the confidence from the Immortal's face: shock and recognition. Fear surged in Jon, who knew that an explosion of energy so near the node could dismantle the controller's hold on dimensional continuity.

Another shifted port rippled beside the controller node. Too close to the controller to be safe, thought Jon, but he edged toward it. Jon watched the Immortal carefully, but that impervious young man had concentrated all of his desperate attention on the controller. Jon calculated the odds of surviving a leap through the tantalizing port, finding them low but better than any other chance of escape. He wondered where the port would take him; he wished that he could signal Tom, but the controller's interference would overwhelm the maintenance uniform's transmitter.

Jon readied himself to risk transfer, when the port's directional reading registered negative on his monitor. "Damn, damn, damn!" he muttered, but the newcomer had already emerged: a young man whose perfect, chiseled features suggested genetic manipulation of the most elaborate kind. The newcomer was holding the controller. The controller remained in its proper place, beneath the gaze of a startled Immortal.

Jon smacked his wrist monitor, hoping to jar its readings into sense. "The DI controller has never been duplicated," he told himself, but he queried the monitor further: unidentified program overlays stabilized the active coexistence of the DI controller with a time-shift of the Taormina set. "Time transference is a cataclysmic mapping," he informed the monitor sharply, while the monitor blandly reiterated its message. "A future-shift of twenty-two thousand years?" murmured Jon, staring in wonder at the flawlessly handsome man who was the future node of the DI controller.

The Immortal cried with sudden shrill defiance. He dropped his hands upon the present controller, claiming it and tearing it from its node. Jon imagined he could hear the controller scream at the agony of strange reconfiguration inflicted by the merciless Immortal. In a shuddering of violated space, the Immortal and the captive controller vanished. Waves of topologically sundered energies stormed the stability of a broken node.

Shock destroyed the protective field of Jon's uniform. His monitor registered the commencement of molecular disruption; warning lights flashed with indifferent efficiency. The twisting and churning pulled and mutilated the fragile working mechanism of a mortal body. Jon's legs buckled. Something harsh and fiery thrust itself through Jon's head.

"Recall the pattern," commanded a compelling, sourceless voice.

The dimmed ports rekindled, skewed from their proper space. They existed here, now, and they existed there, then. *Now* was being shredded by dismembered control. Jon had a foggy view of ports rippling across waves of terrified, bewildered travelers and DI personnel. The fortunate were fully caught; others were severed by partial transfer. Nothing remained stable, except the oddly anachronistic young man who held the strands of a thousand infinities in his unprotected hand.

Jon closed his eyes against the onslaught of a world's death condemning him, a mortal who had failed at an Immortal's game. "Recall the pattern," repeated the relentless voice in his head.

Jon could see nothing but dark, broken space shot with fires of blue, gold, and green. He found himself on his feet with no recollection of how he had achieved that position. He reeled, took a step forward and tripped. Arms caught him: soft arms wearing a scent he recognized.

"Jon," whispered Beth, relief and concern flowing from her.

"We nearly lost you, despite your emergency signal," said a shaken port official, observing Jon's singed maintenance uniform with puzzlement. "What's wrong with your transfer port?"

"Everything," muttered Jon, clutching at Beth to feel her reality. He focused on the monitor grid, near which Kitri and Michael stood in uncertain silence. Jon laughed a little hysterically to see the stupid dog wrap its leash around Kitri's legs.

Jon tugged at Beth, and she steadied him as he hurried to the monitor. The monitoring personnel argued as he shoved them aside and ran his hands over their console. "Step away from the grid, sir." One of the monitor officials had run to summon the guards. The others hesitated, deferring instinctively to Jon's purloined uniform. "You have no authority on this world, sir."

Jon moved his hands once more. The view matrix became entirely dark. He took Beth's hand in his. "I think you'll find that DI transfers have become inoperable," he announced calmly.

He began to walk away from the ports. Beth held to his right arm; Michael and Kitri vied for his left. The dog strained its leash to speed their pace. Guards were gathering at the doors. There would be many questions.

"Tom's closure seems to have worked," he told Beth tersely.

"Where is Tom?"

"I don't think he transferred. The node was disconnected prematurely, which would have nullified the delay mechanism, effecting suffocation on instant of closure. Atmospheres are peculiarly sensitive to disruptions of topological spaces."

"You're rambling, Jon," said Beth with slow, taut fear. Jon squeezed her arm and fell silent, as the guards surrounded them.

RENDING

Chapter 1

She returned alone from Ceallagh's Tomb on the Day of Rending. Her gray eyes were cold and intense with the Power she bore. Only her hands retained any softness, as they clasped a spindle-shaped thing of amber and gold filigree. "The war is ended," she said.

"Where is Kaedric?" Abbot Medwyn asked her cautiously. The abbot's face strained for the faithful brightness which minimized his true age.

The woman delicately stroked the spindle before responding. "He destroyed Horlach." She added rather bitterly, "He conquered the unconquerable, deathless Sorcerer King to save the mortals who hate him." She lifted her eyes to meet the abbot's, and he saw for the first time how distanced her vision had grown. "No mortal host could contain that much Power."

"He is dead?" whispered the woman's dark-haired sister hopefully. Kinship had snared her in a pattern she did not understand. She blamed Lord Venkarel, as would others, and she welcomed the possibility of his death.

The golden woman with the amber spindle did not answer. She opened the hand which had been clutching the spindle most tightly, and her hand was bleeding where the filigree had cut it. She swayed slightly, and the fair-haired man who was King Astorn's Adjutant steadied her with perceptible concern. "Let me take you back to the castle, Rhianna," he urged softly. His own hand shook, for he had fought many sleepless hours against the mortal tools of their Immortal foe.

The golden woman responded clearly and firmly, "You and I have yet much work to do, Ineuil. The patterns have been Rent. Serii is no longer as it was. The mortal world is no longer as it was."

The King's Adjutant studied her oddly, then gave a slow nod. "Of course," he murmured to himself, "the wizard of greatest Power at time of selection—you will become the Infortiare now."

The golden woman remained silent. Her sister stared, fascination and lingering shock making her dark eyes wide. The sisters had never been friends, but it is hard to watch the familiar become strange.

"I must go pray for him," said the abbot painfully. He turned his face toward the rough path which climbed the Mountain of Tul to Ceallagh's Tomb. The path was long and very steep.

The golden woman removed her open hand from the spindle. Very fine, gray dust covered her bleeding fingers where they had rested against the spindle's surface. She pressed the fingers to her taut lips before responding, "I think the prayer will be quite as effective, Medwyn, from here."

He scanned his surroundings closely. He assessed the patterns, cleansing those he recognized, sorting those he mistrusted. "Energy and infinity," he said softly, mocking himself. "I begin to understand you, Horlach, and your obsession with mortality."

He moved carefully, for he had not lost mortal caution. Suspicion was instinctive in him, bred and trained. He had come to know himself strong in a mortal world. He accepted no such certainty in this strange environment.

The Taormin had let him glimpse the deeper Powers. It had not prepared him for the sense of personal infinity. He had not, like Horlach, prepared himself for centuries.

The patterns extended farther and deeper than he had known. His own pattern impressed him quietly, but still he did not trust his strength. He would test new Power cautiously, as had ever been his way. So he had learned Ixaxis; Ixaxis had been new to him once.

"Ixaxis plays a child's game," said a voice he knew.

"You survive," he remarked, knowing the comment idle and unin-

spired. He was unsurprised by the voice, but neither had he anticipated this moment. He berated himself, yet asked smoothly, "Whom can our contest serve now?"

"As ever, Venkarel, it will serve the victor."

"What do you hope to gain?" mused the Venkarel. "I eliminated your last bond to the mortal world by destroying my own physical shell." The Venkarel revised his infinite conceptions. There were other patterns at work here; immediate analysis was imperative.

The dark, little man chuckled gleefully. The Venkarel's anger coiled within itself; the Venkarel would not yield the satisfaction of its emergence to his foe. "An interesting maneuver," remarked the Venkarel very mildly. "Commuting mortal fear and anger into energies which perpetuate themselves at mortal expense."

"As you say, it is an interesting maneuver, but is it mine?" taunted Horlach. The Venkarel knew an unaccustomed sensation: inability to grasp the fullest meanings in an opponent's words. The sensation made him deeply uneasy. "Do you know your foe, Venkarel, as well as you believe?"

"Defeat has not humbled you," commented the Venkarel dryly. "You are conquered, Horlach. I have bound you from yourself."

"You have Rent the mortal world in the process. You have freed energies older than mine so as to thwart me."

"Your sudden concern for mortal kind is most laudable."

"Mock me now, Venkarel, but you will need my aid. You said it to me: by clinging to mortality, I abrogated the advantages of infinity. You have eliminated my flaw, and you were correct. Much has become clear which I did not see before. You will begin to understand soon. You will know that you need me to complete the pattern."

"The Taormin's pattern," murmured the Venkarel, testing his answer, uncertain still of the ramifications and wary of his own doubts.

"The pattern of control," responded Horlach cryptically. "Consider it, Venkarel. I shall be waiting."

Chapter 2

Fifth Month, Year of Rending
Tulea, Serii

The King's Councillors recovered their arrogance rapidly, thought Rhianna with wry distaste. Five months of humility evidently satisfied their sense of collective guilt over Liin and the Caruillan War. It was regrettable that Princess Joli had yet to achieve legal age; she was far more adept than her father at manipulating the Council's temper.

"His Majesty recognizes Lord Aesir," announced Ineuil stiffly. It entertained Rhianna to watch Ineuil squirm in the role of peacetime Adjutant. It amused her equally to observe the grating reluctance of the Council to acknowledge the notorious Lord Arineuil dur Ven as Serii's Adjutant; wartime heroics provided dubious atonement for prior scandals.

Lord Aesir reached his point abruptly: "There have been at least a dozen more reports of these night attacks since yesterday. What do we intend to do about it?" He looked directly at Rhianna, but he was answered from all sides.

"Fables!" shouted Lord Davril. "Are we superstitious peasants?"

"Fables do not murder men and women by the score!" That was Lord Sian, a young and fiery replacement for Lord Cail, dead in the war's last hour.

"Men murder men! There must be three hundred Caruillans still in our lands."

"Caruillans cannot account for deaths in Serii's farthest corners. There is not a man here who has not received reports of these strange deaths and disappearances from his domain." Do they exclude me unintentionally, wondered Rhianna, because I am the only woman among them, or have they realized that Ixaxis is immune to the Rending wraiths? "These deaths are foul deeds. Bodies are found dismembered and brutalized. Whole families have been rendered mindless."

"Servants and villagers begin to fear the night. Have you tried recently to find an inn with its doors open past dusk? Our people are being terrorized."

"It seems that the 'servants and villagers' are not alone," commented Ineuil. Rhianna noted with acrid interest the sudden silence in the room. "How many of you gentlemen have hired guards in the past month? I have heard that some members of the assassins' guild have begun to guarantee safe night passage, and they have more business than they can handle at any price."

"Certainly, we have hired extra guards. Our families are frightened." Was that Sian again? Sian's voice was not distinctive, and Rhianna could not consistently see him past the gloomy figure of her brother, Lord Dayn dur Tyntagel.

"Frightened enough to traffic openly with K'shai assassins?" demanded Ineuil.

Lord Aesir answered impatiently, "The K'shai are the only ones willing to face the night these days."

"Except for the Ixaxins," growled Dayn. It would be Dayn, sighed Rhianna to herself; of all the antagonistic Councillors, only Dayn fully acknowledged her as the Infortiare, and his belief was born chiefly of childhood fears.

"Ixaxis, too, has been visited by these creatures," responded Rhianna carefully. She had not wanted to address this subject until she better understood her data. "We have been fortunate in that the attacks have had no serious consequence among us."

Aesir shouted triumphantly, "Finally, someone admits that they are 'creatures' and not looters or stranded Caruillans."

"Of course they are 'creatures,' " seconded someone from the room's rear. "Have you not read the reports of wraiths who move without sound and appear without warning? Nothing can stop them."

"They are never seen during the day."

"Myths!"

"What of the night? The creatures penetrate a pane of glass as easily as light."

"K'shai can stop them."

"The things cannot pass through a wall of stone or a shutter of sound wood."

"There have been no incidents reported in a solid house sealed for the night."

"What does Ixaxis call these creatures?" demanded Dayn, loudly enough to dominate his fellow noblemen. He stared across the room at his sister: the deceptively frail woman who was liege of Ixaxis.

Rhianna responded reluctantly, "Creatures of the Rending. They are the legacy of Horlach—his parting gift to the mortal world."

"They are things of wizardry?" asked Sian with a trace of accusatory horror.

Why do you pretend surprise? wondered Rhianna grimly. It is the answer you have each whispered since the Rending. "They are constructs of Power abused," Rhianna countered. "They are the tools of a dead Sorcerer King."

"Tools of the cursed Venkarel," murmured someone indistinctly. Rhianna could guess the speaker's name without probing for it: Lord Gorng dur Liin, whose brother's envy had first betrayed them all to Horlach.

"You are much more open in your slander of Lord Venkarel now that he is dead," remarked Ineuil. Only Rhianna smiled appreciatively at his irony—and his support, which she suspected was on her behalf and not her husband's.

"It matters not who caused the creatures of the Rending. How do we combat them?" Dayn must have given this matter much thought, mused Rhianna; his statements sounded rehearsed.

Then she sighed in resignation, realizing it was again for her to answer. She wished she had a clever answer to give. "Accustom yourselves to a changed world," she suggested evenly.

"Is that the best that Ixaxis can recommend?" This complaint issued from several sources.

"The mortal world," said Rhianna in a soft voice, which yet penetrated the din of grumbling, "has been Rent." She was tempted to blame them: these sanctimonious men who had forced her beloved Kaedric to combat a Sorcerer King unaided. If Kaedric's weapon had been more than the mortal world could bear, it was no more than this thankless lot deserved. "Be grateful that the Rending has left anything intact. As for the Rending creatures, lock your doors, shutter your windows, and remain in your Halls at night." She was angry; she was furious. Every man in the room gave blame for the Rending to Kaedric, Lord Venkarel, who had saved all of their lives.

Rhianna saw the King's page following her at a wary distance when the Council session adjourned. The boy was one she had met, and he had not seemed a particularly fearful lad. Still, none of the pages approached the Infortiare without hesitation.

"Someone finds you daunting, my dear Infortiare," murmured Ineuil.

"I mistrust messages delivered formally."

"Perhaps our great King Astorn, having succumbed (like others we know) to your incomparable charms, seeks a discreet rendezvous."

"Your suggestion, Lord Arineuil, is as appalling as it is treasonous," she responded. They both smiled engagingly at Lord Davril, who acknowledged them in passing with a suspicious nod. "I suppose the lad's message must be accepted. It is likely another report of death or disappearance from some inexplicable cause."

"Another fat farmer carried away by Rendies?"

"Do not be so flippant about the Rending creatures, Ineuil. They pose a serious problem." A wave of dizziness possessed her, but she remained upright by dint of will.

"So I continually hear, but I stare at the stars by the hour, and I have yet to encounter worse than a chill breeze."

Rhianna's feeling of illness deepened, but she beckoned to the page and smiled at him as she accepted the parchment from his tremulous hands. A cursory glance confirmed her gloomy expectations; incidents had occurred in every domain of Serii, and reports from throughout the Alliance indicated that the Rending had spared no corner of the world. "I should think you might already have contended with enough foes beyond your measure," she told Ineuil, trying to return her attention to painless conversation.

"My dear Infortiare, your lack of confidence devastates me. My battle record compares quite impressively with that of any man but Kaedric, who can hardly be counted. If these ragtag assassins can combat your Rending creatures, then assuredly I can do as well."

"The K'shai scarcely qualify as 'ragtag.' I do concede that you could very likely stop a Rending creature, but please, Ineuil, do not test the matter needlessly. I have already lost my husband to hero-ics. I should rather not lose you as well." Her head was spinning with the effort to stifle the sickness rising within her.

"You look as white as the snow on Mindar."

"Do I? I cannot think why." She adjusted her energies subtly, so the signs of her weakness would be concealed.

"You are a poor liar, Rhianna."

She touched his arm with a tentative gentleness which silenced him. "Come and talk to me this evening, Ineuil. There is something I would discuss with you." She was away from him quickly.

Ineuil would have pursued her, but a trio of Council members waylaid him with yet another demand for military action against the Rending creatures. Their arguments were absurd, but they were as difficult to elude as Rhianna was difficult to hold.

Chapter 3

Her head was bowed. A twist of the golden strands of her hair fell free of confinement; she smoothed it back into its knot. She finished reading the most recent report from Ixaxis and replaced it on her desk with meticulous care. She rose in a rush which carried her to the window. Her purpose seemed to falter, for she only stood and watched the fog. All distant views were hidden.

The glass of the wide windows was smooth and very cold. She leaned her face against the pane, then straightened guiltily and used her full sleeve to rub the mist of her breath from the glass. Mistress Amye, whose job it was to maintain the Infortiare's quarters, had labored lengthily to make the vast windows spotless. The task was largely a futile one, since the Tower stood free to absorb all of Serii's buffeting winds. Nonetheless, Rhianna was too grateful for Mistress Amye's service to criticize excessive zeal.

Mistress Amye entered just as her Lady stepped away from the window. Amye was of an age to retire to a cottage at royal expense, but she had accepted the Infortiare's service as an alternative to leaving the castle enclave. Her children thought her daft with age.

"Will there be anything else this evening, my lady?" Amye was quartered with the King's servants, which still seemed odd to her, since she was not rightly one of them any longer; but it was the Lady Rhianna's wish. Amye dismissed her children's notions that Rendies frequented the Tower at night.

"No. Thank you, Amye." The Infortiare smiled graciously.

At least, thought Amye, the Lady Rhianna is a lady born, not like *him*, her predecessor. The Lord Venkarel's origins had been nothing short of unsavory. It was birth rank that counted, right enough. See what that Venkarel person did to us. Imagine calling a man like that a Lord, indeed.

"Unbolt the lower door as you leave," commanded the Lady sharply. "I am expecting Lord Arineuil soon." The Infortiare's sudden sternness puzzled Amye a bit, but it did not do to question the moods of the nobility.

"Yes, my lady. Would you not like me to stay and escort him to you?" Amye could not sound eager. She was tired and ready for a nice cup of tea in her own room.

"That will not be necessary, Amye. Lord Arineuil is quite able to find me on his own." The Lady Rhianna's expression had a sardonic twist to it. She was such a delicate wisp of a woman that her occasional hardness always startled Amye. Perhaps, considered Amye sagely, the child is beginning to make its presence known in uncomfortable ways.

Amye had begun to suspect her Lady's state some weeks back. To Amye the pregnancy was now obvious, even though the Lady wrapped herself in voluminous black robes. It was not Amye's place to wonder about the father of the Lady Rhianna's child. Still, Lord Arineuil had certainly come and gone frequently all winter, and he had a reputation, that one, below stairs and above. There were, of course, the whispers about the Lady Rhianna and that Venkarel person, and the Lady certainly did seem to mourn his death, goodness knows why. She seemed such a polite, respectable Lady. Although, pondered Amye, she was Infortiare, and that was a queer enough thing of itself.

Muttering, Amye left the Tower. It was an odd service, she admitted to herself, tending the rooms of so nearly mythical a personage as the Infortiare. But the Tower largely tended itself; the water ran freely with never the problems of the castle proper; the lamps never sputtered and died (there was something odd about the clarity of the Infortiare's lamps, but Amye spared little thought to that sort of thing). It was an odd service, but the Lady was fair and rarely harsh.

Will she want me to tend the child? wondered Amye. Surely the
father could not be the Venkarel. Surely not.

A moment's doubt made Amye shiver. She shook her head free
of the bleak images of fear which she associated irresistibly with
the Venkarel. A terrible man, he had been: dark and terrifying with
those cold-ice eyes of his. Amye hastened from the Tower.

Chapter 4

"**Y**ou have acquired too many of the devil's traits," commented Ineuil from the door of the Infortiare's study. As was usual when he alluded to the late Lord Venkarel, Ineuil spoke with a mixture of cautious disapproval and regret. The disapproval had commenced years before; the caution stemmed merely from prudence. The regret mildly puzzled even him.

"Occasional abstraction in study is scarcely a trait unique to Kaedric." Rhianna shook herself free of indignation. "I need no more quarrels, Ineuil. I spent most of the afternoon listening to Lord Gorng demand Ixaxin aid in the reconstruction of Liin."

"Demanding assistance from his family's intended victim? Gorng always did have nerve." Ineuil perched on the corner of the Infortiare's desk. "You are certainly solemn this evening."

"I am a widow, and widows mourn." Her voice was clipped, her emotions tightly bound.

Ineuil's nod was noncommittal. He leaned forward to take hold of Varina's stone, the milky pendant that Rhianna had made her badge of office. Kaedric's Power had destroyed the medallion of gold which had been the emblem of the Infortiare since Ceallagh's day. "I remember the day you found this," said Ineuil, eliciting clear surprise from Rhianna. Ineuil smiled a trifle smugly. "I caught you studying it, just as Kaedric saw you and you hid it. You, of course, could see only Kaedric." Ineuil laughed and let fall Varina's stone. It struck Rhianna's breast dully, and she clutched at the familiar weight. "I could hardly blame you for the distraction. Kaedric so rarely looked at you openly in those days that he astonished even me. I already knew that you fascinated him, but that day was when I first realized that Kaedric was actually beginning to feel love for you."

"You did not believe him capable of any warm emotion, Ineuil," Rhianna mocked. "Hindsight, I think, has contributed much to your memory."

"Then say, if you prefer, that I had concluded that Kaedric felt for you a fiercely obsessive passion. Did you know that he forbade me to see you while you healed from that battle for the Taormin? Kaedric sat with you day and night at Benthen Abbey, scarcely even allowing Abbot Medwyn to approach. Kaedric would emerge (looking like death himself), snatch a few minutes of sleep, and sequester himself with you again, never speaking a word."

"Benthen Abbey maintains vows of silence," returned Rhianna automatically.

Ineuil shrugged away her comment. "Kaedric did not mind breaking the silence when he learned your rank. He treated me to an unprecedented quantity of speech then: trying to pump me dry of information regarding the noble family of Tyntagel."

"He never told me of that," said Rhianna with the wistful gentleness she reserved for Kaedric.

"It would have been entirely uncharacteristic of him to have confessed to such a very mortal weakness as awe of the nobility."

"I think you did not hate him, Ineuil, nearly so much as you pretend."

Ineuil's grin twisted. "I care for you, my lovely Rhianna, and you possessed him from the day you found that stone." An element of bitterness appeared furtively in Ineuil's handsome face, but he recovered his careful facade of levity to ask, "You wanted to speak to me about something?"

"I am going to have a child, Ineuil." She sounded calm.

Too calm, thought Ineuil, wondering that he could still feel such envy for a dead man. "Kaedric's, of course," responded Ineuil phlegmatically.

"You take the news calmly."

"My dear Infortiare, bemoaning accomplished facts is far too tedious a pastime to tantalize my jaded senses." As ever, dearest Rhianna, you perceive everything and nothing at all. I am seething with jealousy.

"I wish I might expect as indifferent a reaction in other quarters." There was a hesitation in her voice: fear?

Ineuil let his expression grow pensive. "I see what you mean. Very few of Kaedric's enemies ever dared attack him openly, because dread of his Power restrained them. The same protective mechanism will not apply to his child. The fear will be all for what the child might become if allowed to mature into Power."

"And I, as Infortiare, cannot directly defend my own child without defying the laws that I am sworn to protect."

"You have a dilemma."

Rhianna's delicate features tightened. "I hoped for a more useful comment."

"Even a deceptive one, which might not be in keeping with your laws of Ceallagh and your maternal wishes?" She is admitting a need for me, thought Ineuil with twisted self-deprecation; I should be ecstatic. "Very well. My advice: tell no one that the child is Kaedric's, for a start. Few know that you married him. Attribute the guilt of fatherhood to me, if you like. You certainly cannot damage my reputation." Rhianna blushed, which made Ineuil want to laugh. "Then foster the child in some remote domain where Kaedric never made his endearing qualities known."

"Is there anywhere so remote?" asked Rhianna ruefully.

Not bloody likely, snarled Ineuil to himself. "The 'Venkarel' may be cursed across the nine continents, but not a hundred (living) men beyond Tulea and Ixaxis ever met or saw him with knowledge of who he truly was."

"It is not any physical resemblance which concerns me."

"Power? Send the child to Ixaxis. The novelty of rearing an infant might stir some stodginess from the place."

"Do you think that Ixaxis would be any safer a haven for my son than the King's castle?" There was angry bitterness in the storm-gray eyes. The black silk of her widow's gown emphasized her lack of color, making her skin seem pale as the milky stone which hung from a fine silver chain about her neck. Only her hair retained any warm color: fallow gold which seemed to gleam with a light of its own.

She is so damnably beautiful, thought Ineuil with a silent curse. Why did the confounded fates bind her to the devil? "You are the Infortiare. You command the Ixaxin Council."

"Ixaxis understands the Rending just well enough to know that Kaedric did cause it, though Horlach fashioned its evil. The same laws that forced Ixaxis to elect me will convince them to destroy a child whose Power could produce another such calamity."

"Possibly," said Ineuil with great care, "they judge rightly." He watched Rhianna very closely, knowing better than most that her anger could be as lethal as her dead husband's.

She betrayed no sign of reaction. "Kaedric grew to manhood alone," she said at last. "Unguided save by hatred."

"Ixaxis did train him."

"As best they could, which was far short of what he needed. My son will fare better."

"And become even more dangerous?"

Rhianna smiled at him brilliantly. Does she think to hide her anguish? wondered Ineuil. She is breaking apart before my eyes. "Will you arrange the fostering for me, Ineuil? You know the way of such things, having fostered a few of your own."

It was not a difficult discovery to have made, but it irritated Ineuil that Rhianna remarked on it so coolly. "Confounded wizardess," he grumbled only half lightly, "can I hold no secrets from you?"

"Not from me, Ineuil, but I pray that you will hold one for me." Her eyes held him, or her Power did; Ineuil was never sure how much she used her wizardry to effect her will.

"Have I ever been able to deny you, Rhianna?" His tone was dry.

"I rather suspect that you have, but I think you would never betray me."

She manipulates me so well, he thought. Yldana is not the only enchantress in the family, but Rhianna is more subtle. Ineuil slid from the desk and ambled across the room. "Do you know the 'Excursis Santii'?" He pulled a book from the shelves. "It was a favorite of my Ixaxin proctor. The Santii says, 'The young hope, but the wise remember.' 'Walk through life as through the garden of your enemy.' " He flipped a few pages idly. " 'Obsession's great madness is truth.' "

"Your proctor's taste in literature enchanted you?"

"Sporadically." He tapped the book's cover with respect.

"That particular volume is an obsolete almanac, I believe, but your gesture is a nicely theatrical one. Has it some significance?"

" 'To give love is to withhold nothing.' " He nudged the book back into its place on the shelf and so did not see the Infortiare blush for a second time that evening. "I shall assist you, Rhianna, in whatever mad scheme you concoct."

"Thank you, Ineuil," she whispered in a small voice.

He only nodded at her with a self-mocking grimace, before he left her to her Tower alone.

Chapter 5

Tenth Month, Year of Rending
Tulea, Serii

How did I let Yldana connive me into this? wondered Ineuil. He appraised his dark-haired bride, busily enthralling her usual host of admirers. She is exquisite, of course, he mused, and she will never expect monogamy of me; the very concept of fidelity is foreign to her. Effectively, our relationship should be no different from what it has been: physically satisfying, emotionally uncomplicated. Marriage will appease my family and hers. The whole practical business makes me feel conventional, ordinary, and old.

Since Serii's Adjutant despised chronic pessimism, he began to tally extraordinary features of his wedding. Few weddings, save of royalty, were celebrated in the castle's grand ballroom. As Adjutant, he had been able to insist that the royal ballroom would best appease all tempers: his own and Lord Baerod's being of most personal concern. Ineuil had insisted that Rhianna attend. Lord Baerod had refused to admit Rhianna to Tyntagel Hall, where the wedding festivities would normally have been celebrated. Lord Dayn, who represented Lord Baerod in Tulea, had argued rather surprisingly on Rhianna's behalf, but Baerod possessed an incredible talent for obduracy. Fortunately, Baerod favored Yldana enough to overlook her choice of husband. Or perhaps, thought Ineuil with cynical insight, comparison to Rhianna's selected husband makes my merely scandalous flaws seem insignificant.

Ineuil assessed the elegant crowd. It included virtually every prominent Seriin noble. It was a pity, he thought, that the ballroom could no longer be kept open to the portico after the sun had set. Without the breezes from the harbor, the ballroom became stifling. The moonlit colonnade had always offered such a useful retreat as well. The creatures of the Rending had played havoc with romantic evenings.

A servant passed, bearing a tray of replenishments for the refreshment table. Ineuil deftly exchanged his empty goblet for a filled one. He sidled away from the congratulatory crowd around Yldana, glad that wedding celebrations centered on the bride. Ineuil generally enjoyed the tribute of attention, but he would be expected to speak and think only of Yldana tonight. He had imbibed too many goblets of wine to trust his tongue to feign fidelity.

Ineuil espied Lady Liya, animatedly conversing with a portly dowager from Cam. Rhianna had been clinging to her brother's young wife for most of the evening. Ineuil displaced several conversational exchanges with an insincerely cheerful smile, so as to reach Liya's side. He was forced nearly to shout in her ear to make himself heard above the clamor. "Where is Rhianna?" he asked her, and he had to repeat his question to make himself understood.

Liya looked around abstractedly, puzzlement creasing her pretty face. She cannot possibly be so engrossed, thought Ineuil, in a conversation she cannot possibly hear. He pulled her toward a curtained wall, where the sound was somewhat muffled. He was not particularly pleased when the persistent dowager accompanied them.

"I last saw her speaking to Her Royal Highness," replied Liya, trying to balance a frown at Ineuil with an apologetic smile for the neglected dowager.

"She is not there now," contributed the dowager helpfully.

I can see that much for myself, thought Ineuil impatiently. "Lady Ruith, I am glad I found you! Yldana is so eager to thank you for your gift. Do go speak to her." He prodded the bewildered dowager into a maelstrom of milling guests.

"Arineuil, that was not Lady Ruith," amended Liya with faint concern.

"Just as well. Yldana despises Lady Ruith. Rhianna did intend to congratulate me, I trust?"

"I am sure that Rhianna is here somewhere. She cannot have

gone anywhere very quickly." Liya was frowning at him more sternly. "You are not supposed to worry so much about your sister-in-law on your wedding night."

Ineuil grinned at Liya amiably and left her. He appreciated Liya's good-hearted intentions, but the Lady Liya was a trifle too proper for his tastes. Rhianna's disappearance had begun to worry him; she had appeared well enough earlier, but the child was over-due.

Ineuil edged his way across the room, successfully assuring himself that Rhianna no longer remained among the celebrants. Numerous guests accosted him, but he escaped them with glib un-truths of random inspiration. A man was expected to be preoccu-pied on his wedding eve.

With a guileless smile, Ineuil trespassed on the royal quarters to reach the royal entrance to the Infortiare's Tower. The King's guards answered to him, after all. They might wonder at his rea-sons for deserting his guests, but they would not stop him.

Rhianna maintained no shimmering wizard's barrier to block the King's Way. Ineuil knocked firmly upon the stout door and was answered by a sallow slip of a girl. "My Lord Adjutant," she ac-knowledged him archly.

"I have an important matter to discuss with Lady Rhianna," re-turned Ineuil with lofty self-assurance. He had not seen the girl be-fore, and he felt disinclined to flatter himself into her good graces. She was certainly an ugly little obstacle. It was like Rhianna to choose for staff a charmless misfit. Ineuil put his hand to the door, pressed, and met unrelenting resistance. He pondered the girl through the narrow opening: not a servant but a wizardess. "It is a matter of considerable urgency," he told her firmly.

"Lady Rhianna has retired for the evening."

"The matter cannot wait."

"I am sorry, my lord." Ineuil inserted his arm between the door and the jamb. Ceallagh's laws would hopefully prevent her from closing the door on his arm. "Please, my lord, step away. Lady Rhi-anna will not receive you."

"She will when she knows why I come," insisted Ineuil, trying to believe in a nonexistent cause so that the wizardess would not perceive his lie. "Kindly use some sense, young Mistress. Would I pay a social visit on my wedding night?" What kind of visit is it?

Ineuil asked himself quizzically, but he suppressed the inner questioning quickly. He knew that few wizards could penetrate his carefully practiced techniques of deception, unless his concentration on the lie began to waver. He needed to persuade the girl, for her Power could deter him indefinitely.

"My Lord Adjutant, I was given strict instructions." Good, thought Ineuil, she begins to make excuses. She is beginning to believe me.

"If you do not let me enter immediately, you will answer both to me and to the Infortiare." Will I anger Rhianna too far if I badger this girl further? "Open the door!"

The girl lost the confidence of her stance. Her Power wavered. Ineuil's continued pressure against the door suddenly served to slam the door open. The metal bolt clanged against the wall as the girl jumped hastily aside. The door had struck her forcibly, but Ineuil did not concern himself about any lasting damage to a wizardess. Ixaxins could not be sorely hurt so simply.

The study door was ajar, but the room was empty of life. Ineuil began to retreat, intending to seek Rhianna's private room two floors down. A scream stopped him, shaking him deeply. The sound came from above him, where there was only one tiny room, the room which Rhianna seldom used, though it had been Kaedric's. Ineuil flung himself at the stairs and began to climb two at a time. It was a precarious mode of ascent, for the stairs were narrow and often treacherous.

"Come no closer, Ineuil!" commanded Rhianna. Her pain and panic drove into his mind, making his own muscles contract against the echo of agony. He clutched the stair's rail to keep from hurtling backward in recoil from the will which had stopped him.

A crack of light appeared above him, and a woman's silhouette filled the gap, but it was an old woman with hair of white. Another sound of incoherent pain tore through the darkness and made him shudder. "You must not stay so near to me, Ineuil," pleaded Rhianna in some shadowy recess of his head. "You are too open to my feelings." She dictated his descent with precise and absolute control, though her dreadful suffering beat against him.

She released him when he reached the study, and the sense of shared pain left him. Ineuil slumped into a chair, drained by the contact with Power desperate for ease.

"Rhianna, blast you, what is happening?" he murmured softly, but he shouted it at her in his thoughts. He felt infuriatingly helpless. It must be the child, he realized: Kaedric's child, he thought with a forceful resurgence of envy. "Lords, Kaedric, can you not spare her this? Have you not hurt her enough?"

Ineuil settled deeply into the velvet recesses of the chair. He expended several minutes in wishing that he owned more than a useless taste of Power. With such concentration as his wish could muster, he imagined Rhianna and tried to will a lessening of her anguish.

Chapter 6

Ineuil awakened near dawn, finding himself stiff from the chair's inflexible contours. He noted with a certain sour amusement that it was Kaedric's chair which he had absently selected for his fretful waiting. The old serving woman, whose entry had interrupted his restless sleep, observed him with some surprise. Her hesitation became alarm when he reached toward her, grabbed her firmly and demanded, "How is she?" with the force of fury.

The woman cringed, fear widening her pallid eyes. "Ineuil, let her go," chided a faint voice from the narrow stairs. "You are terrifying her."

Ineuil looked upon a golden-haired wraith, leaning heavily against a rather worn and twisted stair rail. She was wan in her widow's black, her fair hair lay damp and tangled around her shoulders, and her smoky eyes seemed deeply sunken in her thin face. "My beautiful Infortiare," he whispered to her. "Sight of you gives greater gladness to my impenetrable heart than you will ever credit."

Rhianna smile at him crookedly, but the slight gesture filled him with the warmth of its issuance. He became aware that he still gripped an indignant serving woman. He released her with a rueful grin, and she fled upstairs past her mistress.

"You are a stubborn woman, Rhianna, and a remarkably durable one. I hardly expected you to survive the night, let alone start the morning by berating Serii's Adjutant."

"Even my stubbornness will not much longer keep me standing." She raised her thin hand to her face in a gesture of exhaustion and suffering. "You have made the arrangements?"

Ineuil frowned. Slowly he nodded. "A wet nurse, K'shai as escort, even a genuinely dead infant." He added hurriedly, "There are always too many who really do die at birth. Are you still certain that this is what you want?"

A reedy wail floated down from the Tower's upper chamber, and Rhianna winced. "It is the only course possible," she murmured thickly. "He must be away from here tonight. I cannot conceal him from the King for more than a day."

"I shall arrange it. Your serving woman is discreet, I trust."

"Amye is a simple and honest woman. She will know that the child died, and she will be believed."

Ineuil whistled soundlessly. "Altering a mortal's memories?" But to himself: why not? Rhianna was defying Ceallagh's laws merely by bearing Kaedric's child.

"I have too much at stake to quibble over the finer points of the Ixaxin ethos," snapped Rhianna. She made an effort to straighten but ended up sinking to the stair. Ineuil reached to help her, but she glared at him dangerously.

Ineuil glowered at her in return. "There is also a young wizardess guarding your door," he reminded her. "You cannot alter her memories without tackling the entire Ixaxin Council."

"There will be no need. Lizbet is young and believes implicitly in her Infortiare." Rhianna's wryness echoed Kaedric with uncanny accuracy.

"No one else is in the Tower?"

"Only yourself, my friend." Rhianna's laugh was hurtful. "Yldana will be furious with you." Another cry sounded.

Ineuil knelt to take the Infortiare's hand gently, and this time she did not stop him. "You have an infant to tend—at least until I return."

"You married me only because you could not have Rhianna!" accused Yldana furiously. "Even on our wedding night, you run to her."

"I was concerned about her," replied Ineuil evenly.

"You obviously were not concerned about me."

"You were not in labor."

"You are not a midwife."

"I am her friend, and she has few."

"Do not try to make me feel guilty for neglecting my little sister. She has made it very clear that she does not need help from me."

"You have never demonstrated particular eagerness to offer help."

"I was the one who warned her against Veiga's treachery. I probably saved Rhianna's life."

You probably caused her to witness her husband's death, thought Ineuil, and how much other pain have you given her? "You are a model of sisterly devotion, Yldana. You can stitch a shroud for her dead baby."

"I am not happy that she lost the child."

"Are you not?" asked Ineuil with sudden weariness. "Are you not pleased that the Venkarel's child is dead? Does it not make everything very much simpler for all of us mortal survivors?"

Yldana's anger wavered. Her face resumed the softness which could entice and deceive, but there was simple hurt in her beautiful eyes. Ineuil did not see, and the hurt in her deepened. Because it was her instinct to strike at a source of pain, Yldana remarked with cool disdain, "I have never loved any man but Hrgh, but I understood that his Power would never let him love me. Accept the second-best, Arineuil, as I have." She laughed with the shivery magic which was only mortal witchery.

What momentary madness possessed me to marry this vixen? wondered Ineuil. She is right, however. Is it some great cosmic jest which uses us? Hrgh is dead, and Rhianna might be, so obsessed she remains with Kaedric. And Yldana and I tear at each other like dyrcats, because we can neither of us have what we want.

Ineuil grinned easily. "You and I are not made for eternal devotion, Yldana, and that is the kind of love an Immortal requires. You and I will not shake history by our loves or loathings. If we are faithless to one another, it is at most a peccadillo in time."

"And we shall be faithless, Arineuil. Do not ever expect me to plead for constancy or to give it: not after this. But we do have appearances to consider."

"Rhianna is not likely to bear another child," drawled Ineuil mockingly. Rhianna remains too stubbornly loyal to a ghost, he added with silent bitterness.

"Nor shall we have another wedding night from which you can so indifferently abstain."

"I doubt that our guests were sufficiently sober to note that we left at different hours."

"Father noticed."

"Your father already despises me."

"If you were his subject, he would have you flayed for your behavior."

Ineuil shrugged. "Then I must thank whatever deity exists that I am not a Tyntagellian."

Chapter 7

He was born, and he had potent enemies, but those who would have destroyed him did not know that he existed. They believed that the Venkarel had died without heirs, and those who knew a little truth of the Rending sighed in ignorant relief at one problem's resolution in the midst of so much other calamity. Those who knew only the chaos of the Rending's effect were too occupied with new hazards to care about any but their own kin. Those very few who knew nearly the full truth, even those who had reluctantly supported the Venkarel in the final days, felt very much safer for the Venkarel's death. They would not welcome any remembrance of the Venkarel's overwhelming Power, least of all an heir.

The child was born, and he would have quickly died had the mortal enemies of his Immortal father known that he existed. The mortal world in ignorance of his nature did not choke him from itself; an infant was a weak thing, a thing perhaps to be protected, never feared. Other energies were less kind, but they would not seek death for their own. They had laid their patterns about him, and they would await him.

In the tiny chamber at the apex of the Infortiare's Tower, a weary, golden-haired woman clutched her infant and wept with guilt. The child is unnaturally quiet, she thought. It is as if he already condemns me for betrayal.

*   *   *

The messenger mercilessly crushed and cracked the autumn leaves beneath his boots. Serii's Crown Princess hated him for destroying so carelessly all that remained of a lost spring, though she recognized the injustice of directing the blame so narrowly.

"Word has come from the Infortiare's servant, Your Majesty," said the messenger distinctly. "The Infortiare's child was born dead." The King sighed his relief, and echoes sounded from his staff.

"Send condolences to the Lady Rhianna," ordered King Astorn.

"Hypocrite," breathed the Princess Joli, and she alone shed tears.

THOSE WHO GO MAD

Chapter 1

Tenth Month, Year 7 of Rending
Tyntagel, Serii

Tyntagel is dreary in the fall. The sky's dark clouds spill watery souls upon the drenched and muddy earth. Leaves sag and fall into slippery splotches on cobbles and clay bricks. The clinging mists conspire to conceal the reassuring truths of solid land and stable township. When the sighs and creaks of soggy branchlets penetrate the sound of rain, careless imaginings conjure the creatures of the Rending. It is hard to be brave when the mist hides the truth, and sometimes the truth holds all the chill horror of the fears.

The night things do come. They rarely harm the cautious: those who bar their doors and shutter their windows between the dusk and dawn. This is the first lesson a toddler learns: never see a night sky. The Rending stole the stars from mortals. The night belongs to the creatures of the Rending, and they will devour your soul and body. Three kinds of people survive the Rendies' stars: wizards, K'shai, and those who go mad in the night of seeing.

My mother told me many tales of the night and the horror of Rendies. She used to read me moral lessons each evening before I slept. I always thought it unfair that I received such an inundation of those moral lessons, which were usually unpleasant, when my sister, Ylsa, received few. I was hardly a model child, but Ylsa was not much better. I blamed the discrimination on gender. Boys were always accused of wrongdoing. I only knew one boy who could dodge suspicion as well as a girl, and he was Arvard, of course.

I met Arvard shortly after my sixth birthday. I was at that time pathetically undersized, excruciatingly shy, and absolutely terrified of a bully named Miff who delighted in tormenting me because of my appearance: I was pretty, a loathsome situation for a young boy. Every adult visitor to the Tyntagel Keep school avowed that Nori and I were by far the prettiest children in Tyntagel. Nori savored every morsel of the adulation. The attention embarrassed me to a painful degree. I cringed as cooing mothers extolled the fineness of my features, the richness of my hair, or the quickly shifting color of my eyes. Several times I hacked at the black curls I hated, but I received no less teasing with ragged hair, and my mother beat me until I could not sit. By age six, I had developed a thoroughly cynical perspective on life.

They were waiting for me again. I knew they lurked just beyond the toolshed, though I could not yet see them. I knew even before I heard their broken whispers. I could return to the classroom, giving Mistress Caroianne some excuse of a forgotten paper, but Miff would only be the harder on me for the delay. I wished there were another way, but there was none, so I walked forward.

Miff emerged first, taunting me with a grin on his freckled face. Denni jumped from behind the cistern to jab at my back. "Where are you going, Evaric?" asked Denni.

"Answer him, Evaric," said Miff. "Little girls should be polite and answer their betters."

"Say something, Evaric," said Nik.

"Can you speak, Evaric?"

Nik tried to grab me, but I wriggled free and ran. My tormentors would not let me run toward home and momentary safety. They herded me, pressing me along the road through the dry maple wood. The Keep wall and a gully overgrown with briars imprisoned me. I might have twisted my way through the briars, but I had heard that dyrcats laired beyond the gully. I did know better than to choose a dyrcat over Miff and his pranks.

Miff caught my arms and dragged me to the ground. He held me against the dirt and gravel, while Denni methodically ripped the pages from my workbook, shredding those pages to which I had devoted hours of tedious effort. I sacrificed the dubious privilege of watching Denni, so as to protect my eyes from Nik's barrage of acorns and pebbles. As I turned my face, I caught a glimpse of straw-colored hair rising from the gully.

Nik landed near me on the ground, and I saw my workbook tumble into the brush. Miff loosened his grip, and I rolled free. The owner of the straw-colored hair was pounding Miff with an efficient strength I envied. Nik helped Denni to rise, and the two of them raced after Miff, who had ducked his assailant and taken undignified flight.

"You've a share of enemies," commented my straw-haired savior, sucking his abraded knuckle.

He had a strange, strong accent. "You are not local," I observed, which expressed nothing of the gratitude I felt.

"Near enough. You from the village?"

"The Keep." My savior was a little taller than Miff, shorter than Denni, and heroic to my innocent eyes.

"Ta." I could not discern if disbelief, disgust, or awe prompted the boy's suddenly cautious expression, but he was plainly diffident now, which made me feel as if I had betrayed a trust. "You'd better watch yourself with those three."

"Thanks."

"Don't mention it to anyone else."

"No, I never would. Miff would deny it if I did." I stared at my own uselessly small, scratched hands, folded too tightly and nearly hidden by the woolen sleeves of a too-large sweater. Comparing them to my savior's strong fists, I began to feel the worship which would carry me along for many years. "No one ever frightened Miff before."

"My sister could fight better than those three," replied this remarkable boy disparagingly, but the praise clearly pleased him. "Of course, I've frightened better fighters than them. Just a moon ago, I frightened ten of the biggest, meanest bears you ever saw— in that very wood over there."

For a fraction of a second, I believed him. I was not usually so gullible, but the boy had impressed me deeply. When I appreciated his exaggeration, my respect only increased. I smiled hesitantly. "Did they have teeth as long as daggers?" I asked, trying to win my savior's approval by imitating his wit.

My savior grinned broadly, and I was delighted. "Longer, and their claws were as sharp as a cat's."

"Were the bears as tall as that oak?"

"Much taller. When they walked the ground shook, and all the buds shrank back into their branches, hiding until the bears passed. How old are you?"

"Six," I replied, unconcerned by his redirection.

"So am I," responded my savior, surprising me, for he looked and acted older.

Wheels creaked, warning of an approaching cart. The face of my straw-haired savior closed into caution. "Maybe I'll see you around here again," he said, already sliding down the gully's edge. That is my first memory of Arvard: a straw-haired, six-year-old hero who saved me and slipped away from Master Cormagon's dairy cart.

We next met near the old bridge to the wild, northern woods. Arvard was looking for me, which flattered me immensely. "Anybody bother you recently?" he asked me.

I shrugged, unwilling to admit that Miff harassed me more incessantly than ever. "Miff visits my sister sometimes." Ylsa longed for Miff's approval and achieved it best by teasing me.

Arvard nodded, as if he understood my problem. Some sound of wood and wind caused him to duck beneath the bridge, but he reappeared quickly with a large, straight stick in his hand. "I'll slay your enemies with my sword," he said, brandishing the stick. He surveyed the road closely before beckoning to me. When I approached him, he informed me in a conspiratorial whisper, "The evil King Gill wants to capture me because I'm the rightful heir to the crown he stole. Do you want to be my devoted servant, who followed me into exile?"

"Exile from where?"

"The Great Kingdom, of course. You need a sword." He pried a stick from a bedraggled bush and offered it to me with solemn grandeur. "It's not as large as mine, because mine is magical, but yours is also a jeweled treasure from one of our glorious battles."

I accepted the stick uncertainly. "I think I need to hone it," I said, breaking a twig from its length.

"Good idea," agreed Arvard soberly. "I have some honing tools over here."

"Beyond the bridge?"

"It's not far," he promised me, and I trusted him implicitly. After all, he was the Lost Prince of the Great Kingdom, and I was his loyal retainer, who would follow him to the death.

We fashioned dragons from a breath of wind, and mystical cities from a beam of sunlight on a stream. We rode magical steeds, and we conquered evil Sorcerer Kings and Queens. We performed great, valorous deeds and won the gratitude of vast civilizations, but always some enemy would strike in treachery, and the Lost Prince and his servant would resume their endless journey, reliant only upon each other.

Most of my childhood years have blurred now. Most of my images of Arvard have been tainted by later memories. Only rarely can my mind recapture the unsullied innocence of those early dreams. For an instant, I am six again and Arvard is my truest friend and hero. Then my recollections race beyond those first two years, and I see the fragments of the design in which Arvard and I were already entrapped.

Chapter 2

Ninth Month, Year 9 of Rending
Mindar Wilderness, Tyntagel Domain

"**A**rvard! Get the wood in here! The cook fire is nearly out!" The girl who shouted was thin and gangly. She wore an undyed dress which had been made and remade several times as she grew. Even the recent addition of an odd, uneven flounce had left it too short by several inches.

She shaded her eyes from a beam of sun piercing the thick clouds and thicker trees, and she scanned the woodsy clearing for the boy. Arvard had disappeared again. "Drat him," mumbled the girl. She tied her mismatched skirt around her waist, which left only a bit of the flounce dangling taillike over her pantaloons. She crossed the yard and clambered down into the gully where the tree had fallen the previous winter. Several of the logs were already twisted with ivy, but she pulled away the stubborn tendrils, ripping bark from the wood. She gathered a bundle of logs against her bony chest. She pulled herself from the gully using her one free hand on the protruding roots of trees she recognized but could never have named.

She mumbled to herself continuously as she carried the logs to the house, which was almost indistinguishable from the trees around it. One of the trees even leaned across it, and rats sometimes dropped to the roof that way. Pa had been talking for a year about cutting away that big limb, but it hid the house so well that he would probably delay until he thought the limb a bigger danger than unfriendly eyes.

The structure of the house was wood, but ivy had fastened into every crack. The door was almost lost amid the new growth. The house was no more than thirty-five years old, for it had been built by refugees from the Venkarel's destruction of Ven, but the Mindar wilderness had made the house a part of its timeless, ancient self. The house had only two rooms: the main room, which was used for sleeping and living, and the kitchen, which was always smoky from a half-clogged chimney.

A woman, who looked older than she was, knelt before the stone fireplace in the kitchen, trying to stir the dying fire into life. "Here, Ma," said the girl, dropping the logs onto the hearth.

"The bread will be heavy as lard," muttered the old-looking woman. "Where is Arvard? He promised to stock the wood closet."

"He's off again. Likely spying on the village folk."

"Useless whelp. We ought to have left him where we found him."

The girl threw a log onto the fire. She watched flames burst from a dried leaf still holding to its shriveled stem. "Arvard's all right most of the time." She never liked to think of finding Arvard. She had not been the one to lift him from the tangle of his dead mother's torn body, but it was she who had first found that litter of Rendie victims.

She had brought her Pa. He had shown her how to leave no trace when searching for valuables, but she had not wanted to touch the mutilated bodies. The Rendies had not left much of the two men, but Pa had taken a fine sword from one and two nice daggers from the other. There had been a brand on the man with the sword, which Pa said was a K'shai assassin's marking. Pa had hacked at the brand to make it unidentifiable. No one would notice the extra damage, Pa said, considering what Rendies had already done, and it was better not to be caught stealing from dead K'shai.

Not many K'shai were caught by Rendies. Maybe, Ma had said, somebody wanted the attack to look like Rendie work. A few armed men could work as much mischief as any Rendie if circumstances were right. That was why Ma had made Pa sell the takings for so little. It was too bad; there had been a pretty necklace on the dead woman, and not much nice jewelry ever came their way. Too bad, but Ma wanted no visible ties to those dead travelers. So nothing had been kept but Arvard.

Sometimes Arvard was a nuisance, thought the girl, but he was just so full of grand plans that he forgot the simple things like stoking the fire. Arvard was clever. The girl wished she were as clever as the boy, who was not even as old as the Rending. Arvard understood things. He could make her understand things, too, when he bothered; like how to watch the moon to know when her times would come; or how to make Mitshch look at her.

She wondered if Mitshch would come with the other men tonight after the hunting. If the men had been successful, there would be good meat, and maybe Pa would dole out some of his Tonic. The Tonic would make everyone warm and friendly, and maybe Mitshch would be friendly with her.

Ma had locked Arvard in the wood closet, so he would remember his duties next time. The girl felt a little sorry for the boy, so she smuggled him a bit of venison. Everyone else was enjoying the Tonic in the main room, and Ma never noticed her sneaking off to the kitchen.

She lifted the iron hook to free the door. Arvard was huddled among the logs he had spent the afternoon carrying. His knees were tucked under his chin. Even so, there was hardly enough room for him to sit. "I brought you some supper, Arvard," whispered the girl.

"Thanks, Nel," he whispered in return. His face and yellow hair were all smudged by the dust from the logs, but he still looked neat and proud. "Ma hasn't forgiven me yet?"

"Give her time for another mug of the Tonic, and she'll be holding no more grudges against anyone."

"Another hour maybe?"

"Maybe. I'll let you know. I'll leave the latch undone, but I've got to close the door again. Sorry."

"That's all right, Nel. It gives me a chance to think."

Nel pushed her lank hair over her ear. She hoped Mitshch would finish talking to Pa before she returned to the main room. "What do you think about, Arvard?"

"Things. Like how to sell Con's leather pieces in the village, where they'd bring a proper price."

"We can't go to the village. The Lord's taxers would catch us for sure."

"That's why I have to think." Arvard was always patient with her, but sometimes Nel knew he was thinking her stupid. She did not mind. She knew she could never be as clever as Arvard. "Quit fussing with your hair, Nel, and twist your skirt right way around. You want Mitshch to think you're still a baby who can't keep herself straight?"

Nel adjusted her skirt in a hurry. She clasped her hands together so she could leave her hair be. "Do I look right?"

"Mitshch will think so." Arvard fastidiously cleaned his fingers of the venison's grease by wiping them on the old kerchief he always carried for that sort of purpose. He never forgot to clean that kerchief. He never forgot the tasks that mattered to him.

Nel smiled nervously. She closed the door; it stuck, and she had to push it. "Later, Arvard," she whispered against the wood. She could not hear his answer over the sounds of her father's laughter in the other room.

Arvard tried to shift. The wood closet allowed no comfortable position, but Arvard did not mind a punishment he had anticipated and earned. He had freely made the choice to spend the extra hour with his Keep friend. He did not regret his decision.

It was strange to have a friend who occupied such a different world. Pa would never understand how Arvard could enjoy the company of anyone so weak, timid, and naive. Arvard could never have explained to Pa, Wilard, Con, Ols, or Kite that imagination could matter as much to a boy as an ability to fight, hunt, and make a good taking from an unwary traveler. Arvard's foster family and their friends would despise Evaric, and Arvard agreed with them in many respects. Arvard was sure that Evaric would not have survived a moon's time in the wild lands; Evaric could not even hold his own with the puny Keep brats.

Evaric was weak, but no one listened the way Evaric did. No one else understood the things that mattered. Sometimes Arvard envied Evaric a little, because imagining and questioning were a Keep brat's privileges, rights denied to a boy like Arvard whose life consisted chiefly of struggle. The wilds' families had no time for any learning that did not contribute directly to the subjugation of a relentlessly antagonistic environment.

Arvard sighed. The closet really was uncomfortable. He wished that Nel would return.

Ma was telling a story. It was a bawdy one. Maybe Arvard would not need to wait long for Ma to forgive him.

Mitshch was looking at Nel. Nel blushed because her brothers were laughing at her. Nel was the youngest—save for Arvard, who was different—and she was the only girl. With four older brothers, she took a lot of teasing.

"Nel's looking pretty, Mitshch," said Ols slyly.

Mitshch was beginning to blush himself, which made Nel feel tingly and fine. Wilard handed her a mug, and the sip of Tonic gave the tingle an embarrassing warmth. Mitshch shifted on the bench so she could sit beside him, and she felt dizzy and hot and fine. Everything was *fine.*

A loud crash interrupted Ma's story. Ols went to check the kitchen, while everybody else sat breathless. "Nothing there," said Ols on returning.

"Must be that rotten branch breaking," said Pa. "Knew I should've trimmed it." He was trying to sound cheery about it, but everyone could see that it worried him. The limb hung over the house. Nel snuggled closer to Mitshch, who put his arm around her protectively.

"Wilard, go fetch Arvard from the kitchen," ordered Pa, and then Nel knew how worried Pa really was. Pa thought the limb would fall through the kitchen roof, and then the house would be open to the night.

"It'll be fine, Nel," Mitshch told her, and Nel began to feel better, but she kept thinking about the way the kitchen door sagged and never wanted to close soundly.

There was another great cracking and a crash of smashed and broken timbers. Wilard yelled. Mitshch ran to help him. Pa and Kite dragged the great table across the floor so as to seal off the kitchen more effectively.

Something already occupied the kitchen doorway. It was neither Wilard nor Arvard. It was gray and misty, and it was reaching for

Mitshch. Nel screamed, and Ma screamed, and Pa was bleeding, and Mitshch was gone.

Everything around Nel was gray. Everything was cold and hot, and it hurt, and she was screaming at the Rendies, but it did no good. They were eating her and hurting her, and nothing was fine anymore. Nothing would ever be fine again.

Chapter 3

Keep Enclave, Tyntagel

The day had cleared despite the morning's damp promise. The wind had risen, hurtling across the snowy Mountains of Mindar, dispersing the clouds but bringing bitter cold. The wind had carried away the little snow that had fallen. The barrenness of the earth enhanced the illusion of a desolate summer heath, making our heavy woolen garb appear incongruous.

Ylsa kept searching the road and the trees, doubtless hoping that Miff would appear. I watched with equal care, hoping that Ylsa would be disappointed. "I can reach that tree before you," said Ylsa suddenly. I began to race toward the maple. "Hey," called Ylsa plaintively, but she saved the rest of her protest.

I slammed into the tree just an instant before Ylsa, despite my head start. "Cheat," Ylsa snapped at me. "Runt," she added meanly.

"Sore loser," I accused.

"Runt," repeated Ylsa. "No real boy would need to cheat against a girl."

I ran ahead of Ylsa, not wanting her to see how her accusation embarrassed me. I was still running when I heard the voice crying for help. I stopped abruptly, and Ylsa ran into me.

"Evaric is a girl," taunted Ylsa again.

"Hush!"

Ylsa frowned at me. "What?"

"Listen."

"There is nothing to hear."

"Listen!"

The wind softened. No clearer sound breathed for a full minute. The wind gathered itself in a rush which could have carried a faint cry, but it was a less tangible voice I heard. "What is it?" asked Ylsa restlessly, impatient with me, as usual.

I ignored her. I still do not know if Arvard actually called to me that day, or if imagination fulfilled itself by driving me to find him. I cast a cautious glance at the lengthening shadows. The thickets across the ravine held menacing circles of darkness, but the road lay clear of shade or specter. I headed for the old bridge, even though the day approached its end.

"Evaric," called Ylsa angrily. She gave the path toward Miff's house a wistful look, but she knew that our mother would be angry if Ylsa let me wander too far alone. Ylsa chased after me, grumbling, "Unless you come with me now, Evaric, I shall leave you."

"Then go."

"Mother will beat you if you come home late."

Some terrible trouble had assaulted my great, secret friend, and Ylsa pestered me with threats of punishment from our mother. "Will you be silent, Ylsa!" I shouted, stunning her into compliance. "Arvard!" I cried in my head, for his danger reached inside of me. I heard the screaming, felt the cold fire, and tasted misty death. There was a figure before me, but it was a man.

I stopped, for the man stood squarely in front of me. "What are you?" he demanded, staring at me fiercely. My fear became all for myself. I retreated a pace, but the stranger restrained me with a hand on my shoulder.

"Let go of my brother," said Ylsa, suddenly protective.

"I shall not harm you," said the man earnestly, and Ylsa became oddly silent. When I looked at her, she did not seem aware of me. "What domain is this?" asked the stranger, though he could not have come so near the Keep unchallenged.

Ylsa answered him woodenly, "It is Tyntagel, Master."

The man's furrowed brow cleared. "Of course," he said. "The patterns would be strong where She originated."

"You know someone in Tyntagel, sir?" asked Ylsa courteously.

"Know someone?" The stranger winced, and his next words

were whiny. "I was happy as a cobbler. I was never strong enough
to serve in such a circle, but they said that I was needed. The Power
of the Infortiare burned through us, and then he left us, and the
world writhed in anguish at the parting." His Power pushed his
emotion upon me. He endangered me, and I hated him. The man
stiffened. "I am mad now," he acknowledged calmly, "for I was
weak, and I must now walk the Rendies' world in blindness, pursuing their paths of fear, reft of the illuminating fire of him who
was Infortiare. I thought that I sensed him here, but he is dead, as
I should be. Some thickening of the pattern deluded me into hope."
Solemnly, the man admonished, "You really ought not to be outside at night, little Mistress, but I shall protect you this time."

I sensed deep wrongness in the wizard, a crippling more severe
than any physical deformity. I wanted the wizard gone. Something
sinuous began to form near the wizard. It reached toward the wizard and shuddered. "I want him gone," I whispered. Mist became
thick.

"Come away," pleaded an urgent voice, which was oddly thick
with accent. "He's bespelling you." I felt a tugging on my arm. The
wizard rambled on obliviously of War, cobbling, and the uselessness
of fire-fused hands. "Please, come away. It's very dangerous here."

"I can save you, little Mistress," promised the wizard.

"The Rendies are gathering," said the voice urgently.

"I want the wizard gone," I insisted.

"No," argued the wizard. "I am not the one who wants to hurt
him." I observed that something very peculiar was occurring to the
wizard's face. It had begun to bleed.

"Come away."

Several pieces of the wizard's face seemed to be missing now. It
was hard to tell, for the regions not covered in blood had become
foggy. Maybe I was the one who was becoming blurred.

"When did it become dark?" I demanded. Darkness spread
above me, though it was less black than my room at night. The sky
was dusty with lights: stars, I supposed. Adults made much of the
stars. Perhaps they had some cause.

The stars awoke me from the wizard's trance. The wizard stood
amid a cloud of Rendies. Ylsa's gaze began to drift from the wizard
to the wraiths. "Ylsa," I said sharply, "do not look at them." I did
not know why I voiced the warning.

"Evaric, come away from there." Arvard crept a little farther from the brush, warily watching the cloud of Rendies wrestle for the mad wizard. Matted with leaves, Arvard's hair still shone in the dimness. He tried to coax Ylsa into moving. "In here," ordered Arvard, looking greatly relieved when I nodded. We ducked under twisted limbs and into a hollow of tangled brush. Arvard dragged Ylsa, and she sat stiffly where he placed her. "We will survive," Arvard assured me. "The Rendies have a wizard, and that must be a rare treat to them."

Arvard settled among the damp grasses and leaves. I could see him more clearly than I would have expected. Could the moon be so bright? I wondered, recalling grown-up reminiscences. I shifted my head, and I could see the brilliant orb through the brush. "You stayed and watched us even though night came," I remarked dreamily, knowing that such a decision was indeed worthy of the noble, exiled prince who Arvard was to me.

"I couldn't tackle a wizard like he was some stupid Keep brat," snapped Arvard, and he immediately muttered an abashed, incoherent apology. I knew that he considered me a Keep brat, but I also recognized the depth and worth of his singular friendship.

"You called for help earlier," I said.

"I didn't."

A loud wailing trill made us both cover our ears, though the gesture did little good. Smoky, tenuous ribbons snaked through the trees and into the brush. A lacy tendril brushed my back. It stung frightfully. The tendril blackened, becoming opaque and stiff.

"You burn!" accused the Rendie, as the wailing sank to a low moan. The Rendie enclosed its injured member in a hastily gathered veil of frost, which it tore from its own pulsing body. The wraith's color deepened to a steady russet, and discord made its keening voice feel harsh. "You are cruel, and I have killed for you," lamented the Rendie.

"Fire-child," sighed a second Rendie in what sounded queerly like a plea, "why do you burn your own?"

I had never heard that Rendies talked. I did not relish the privilege of their conversation. "Think about something else," suggested Arvard.

"You hear them, too?" I asked him curiously.

"I don't listen to Rendies. You shouldn't either."

"Son of the Taormin," cried a Rendie softly, "come to us."

I tried to disregard the Rendie's unsettling voice. "What happened, Arvard?"

"The Rendies came," answered Arvard tersely.

"They killed your family?" Arvard and I had rarely discussed our families, for our own world of danger and great deeds had always been more real to us.

"Yah. I thought I could reach the village before dark came again, but I guess I started later than I thought."

"Fire-child," sighed an echo through my head.

I tried to shake free of the haunting voice. "Do you know anyone in the village?" I asked, clinging to the sense of my friend, someone alive, strong and familiar.

"Nah. We were a secret." Arvard's laugh was a little off-key. "Pa never wanted to tithe to the Lord, so he hid us away on the edge of the wild regions."

"Fire-child, come to us. We are not your enemy."

"You're listening to them again," accused Arvard sharply.

"No!" I retorted, but it was impossible not to listen. I touched Ylsa's cold face where a drop of the wizard's blood had hardened. I shivered.

"That's only the wizard's spell holding her a while," Arvard assured me knowledgeably; I suspected that he had become the Lost Prince again. "She's lucky. She'll not hear the Rendies through that."

I wrapped myself more tightly in my cloak. "Are you cold?" I asked Arvard, whose leather coat looked worn and thin.

Arvard shrugged. A wraith dashed through the brush in a pattern of shreds. Arvard shrank from the trailing mists.

"Only three kinds of people survive the night: wizards, K'shai, and those who go mad." I recited the warning, though I did not yet know the meaning of Rendie madness.

"Maybe wizards and K'shai know better than to listen to Rendies," replied Arvard staunchly. Arvard did not intend to let me think about fear. "The Rendies won't hurt us. The wizard satisfied them. We'll survive the night, and nobody will ever know that we saw Rendies."

I nodded, more to placate Arvard than to concur. I closed my eyes as a wraith swept past me, crying enticingly. "You can stay with us," I promised Arvard.

"Me live in a Keep house? Your family won't want my kind. The liege'll place me somewhere." The Lost Prince preferred noble exile.

"You will stay with us," I repeated firmly. I became aware that the Rendie voices in my head had stopped. The keening continued, but it circled warily. "They are leaving."

"About time," grumbled Arvard. He did not like this game of Rendies and reality. He snuggled down among the leaves. "I feel like I've been awake forever."

"You intend to sleep out here?"

"Where can we go? Your sister's not going anywhere tonight, unless you want to try carrying her, and she'll be dyrcat-bait if we leave her."

"What could you and I do against a dyrcat?" I asked, which seemed to me a reasonable question; a dyrcat would not respect an imaginary sword. Arvard began to snore softly. I lay down, covered my face with my cloak, and slept uncomfortably.

In my nightmare, I could feel the cold presence of a wounded Rendie in limping pursuit. The Rendie's attenuated limbs twisted restlessly, constantly shifting in both color and amorphous form. The face was difficult to define; I caught glimpses which appeared variously to be a single silver eye, a multifaceted expanse like the eye of an enlarged insect, and a flash of green as deadly bright as a dyrcat's stare. The Rendie exhaled its coldness into a web, which stretched toward me. The atmosphere grew thick and strange.

The Rendie's voice trilled with an odd, melodic disharmony. "I have tasted you now, and I know you. I shall remember, as will you. It must be, for it was. Look at me," said the Rendie, and it wore the face of Arvard. The Rendie/Arvard felt pain from the burned and blackened limb, and the pain became mine. I reached for some offering within myself to ease the creature's pain. The Rendie/Arvard howled with heightened agony.

As the dream wavered, I recognized its deceptions, but it carried me on relentlessly. It was the first of many nightmares, and it was mild, though it horrified me at the time. I had survived the night, and I was neither wizard nor K'shai.

I awoke to the piercing sound of Ylsa's screams. Arvard was shaking her to rouse her, when the searchers burst upon us. The sun had crept above the trees, and the searchers were the familiar folk of Tyntagel.

"We have found them!" called someone triumphantly, and in a moment the hollow of brush became crowded.

Mother gathered Ylsa and me into her arms in a rush, but Father saw Arvard and stopped, obviously puzzled. I extricated myself from my mother's embrace with some embarrassment. "This is Arvard," I said. "He helped us last night." I would not admit to our secret friendship. "I told him he could stay with us." I poised myself for defiance. "His family was killed by Rendies."

Mother raised her head slowly from cradling Ylsa. She exchanged with Father a forbidding look composed of the night's dreadful worry. She had regained her children; she was too exhausted to deal with further complications. I took advantage of my mother's momentary weakness; I knew that my father could not deny me.

"He can stay with us," I insisted, pressing my point with a fierce determination which was rare for me in those days. "He is my friend, and he has no one else."

"We shall discuss it later, Evaric," said my father absently. Arvard gave me a guarded shrug. I took my father's hand and tugged it until he looked at me. "Arvard may come with us for now," conceded my father weakly, and I knew that I had won.

My mother's expression began to reproach Father's weakness, but Ylsa stirred. "How did you two stray so far from home?" clucked our mother, postponing the inevitable argument with our father. "You know what I told you about staying nearby."

"Mother?" asked Ylsa in bewilderment. "Where is the wizard?"

The friends and neighbors who had assisted in the search became very silent. "What wizard, Ylsa?" asked our mother cautiously.

"I saw no wizard," volunteered Arvard promptly. "Did you, Evaric?"

"Ylsa must have been dreaming, Mother. We met no one but Arvard." Both Arvard and I gazed at Mother with solemn sincerity.

"Mother," Ylsa begged, "my head hurts awfully. I cannot remember. What happened to me?"

"You have learned a lesson, I hope. The night comes quickly in the autumn," answered our mother brusquely. She watched me whisper a reassurance to Arvard, and I fell silent beneath her inspection. I think she suspected our conspiracy of silence even then, but she knew nothing of the Rendies. She thought that Arvard and I had somehow left Ylsa to face the night alone. Ylsa worried her, but she still considered me sane.

Two weeks later, the Ixaxins came to give the annual testing to all children of school age. I had never minded the testing, but an unaccountable sense of dread overcame me as I left the schoolroom. I stayed close to Arvard, who watched me with puzzled concern. Arvard was called early, for he had never previously been tested. I could not remain among my classmates without Arvard to defend me. I left the schoolyard, deliberately disobeying Mistress Carolanne's instructions.

I ducked inside the toolshed, closed the door, and pressed myself against its rough surface. My arms began to shake. I felt the cold heat of a Rendie's breath. I could feel the wraith's hunger, and feeling it made it mine. I felt soiled and evil, and I loathed myself for sharing in the Rendie violence.

I wanted to hurt them. I wanted to hurt myself, for I was part of them. I pressed the point of a nail into the flesh of my thigh and felt the heat of welling blood. The pain inflamed me.

"Fire-child," I laughed hysterically, but it was the echo of Rendie voices which made me long to crawl away like the ants into the soil. I shook for long minutes, beseeching myself to stop. A spasm of pain sprang through my skull, and I cried aloud. After a moment, the deep pain passed. Lights beat against my eyes with aching pressure, but they faded one by one. "Lords of Serii," I whispered hoarsely, wondering what horrible legacy I had reaped from my view of the night sky.

"Evaric?" called Arvard into the dark shed. "Are you in there?" Arvard peered into the shed, but I had crawled into the shadows, so he could not see me.

"Yes," I answered tightly. I clenched my teeth to keep them from chattering. I covered the bleeding wound with my hand, feeling shame for my weakness in yielding to the voices. Arvard was here; the Rendies could not claim me.

"Your name has been called, little brother. The Ixaxins want to test you next."

Lords, no. Ixaxins could not see me like this. They would see the Rendie sickness in my mind. They would know my guilt. Everyone would know my guilt.

"Get me out of it, Arvard. Make an excuse for me. Please."

"Are you sick?"

"Yes." Lords, yes.

"You want anything?" Arvard was concerned. Arvard was coming closer. I could see his silhouette against the light.

"No. Nothing. I cannot face the Ixaxins, Arvard."

"All right. Don't worry, Evaric. I'll take care of it."

I smiled a little wanly in the darkness. Arvard would take care of me again. I removed my hand from where it rested on my leg. There was no wound. There was no hurt. Even the fabric was whole. I laughed with relief. "Only three kinds of people survive the seeing of the Rendies' stars," I recited aloud, though only my own ears heard. "Wizards, K'shai, and those who go mad in the night of seeing." I did not wonder that Arvard had apparently survived unscathed; heroes were not susceptible to the afflictions of the rest of us.

"Arvard, where is Evaric?"

Arvard answered with a fine semblance of surprise. "He has gone home, Mistress Carolanne. He has already been tested."

Carolanne's surprise was not feigned. "His name is next on the list, Arvard. I thought you went to fetch him."

"Mistress Carolanne, he has already been tested. He failed and was dismissed."

"Mistress Carolanne," demanded one of the Ixaxins, appearing at the vestibule door. "We are waiting for the next candidate."

Carolanne fumbled with her papers, recalling how ashen Evaric had looked when he left the classroom. Arvard had certainly devoted himself to Evaric's protection; she wondered if Arvard realized that lying to Ixaxis was a treasonous crime. "I apologize, Master Tain. I lost my place for a moment. Arvard, will you please bring Quin to be tested." Carolanne held her breath, waiting for the Ixaxin to perceive her falsehood.

Arvard nodded agreeably, his expression frank and cheerful. Carolanne placed a check beside Quin's name, indicating that he

had been called. The Ixaxin retreated into the classroom. Beside
Evaric's name, Carolanne placed the check which indicated failure
of the Ixaxin test. She felt only the faintest of qualms and did not
even wonder at her own calm compliance with deception. Arvard
was very persuasive.

Chapter 4

Seventh Month, Year 18 of Rending

Arvard stayed, of course, and became my foster brother. He never quite lost his status as affable guest of long duration in our house, something like an orphaned cousin accepted out of family duty. He was brother to me, though not to Ylsa, and he was never son to my parents. Mother, at least, came to respect his abilities, if not his glib excuses for evading chores and due punishments. Father never gave Arvard much attention of any sort, but Father never knew how to deal with any of his children; Father was even uncomfortable with me, and he overtly favored me over Ylsa.

Arvard excelled, and I took pride in him. He won every school honor, and he claimed every festival prize without apparent effort. He protected me from Miff and the others. I protected him from criticism and loneliness. That much of the old dream persisted: we were two against the world.

When the Rendie madness claimed me, as it did too often throughout those years, Arvard lied and manipulated to conceal my ailment. Arvard succeeded, and no one guessed my affliction. My parents considered me merely weak and prone to illness; others considered me a malingerer. Only Arvard knew the truth: I spent as much of those ten years in the Rendies' world as in my own. A few teachers tried to encourage me, sure that I performed far below my capabilities; most despaired over my inattention.

They were good years, despite the Rendies. Arvard's enthusiasm for life infected me, though I viewed everything but Arvard with unalloyed cynicism. I often wondered how I managed to retain Arvard's devotion for so long, because we had never shared any trait but a taste for adventurous sagas.

Arvard and I viewed the world too incongruously to retain forever a bond as close as ours had become. My tastes were simple ones; I craved peace from madness and little else. Arvard's ambitions had no bounds. Tyntagel could not contain him, as I should have realized long before he actually departed. I suppose he stayed for my sake. When our differences finally became obvious, his cause for remaining vanished along with his old ideals.

The argument began in a small way, three years before it matured. While searching our room for some forgotten article that Arvard had borrowed from me, I discovered a letter that he had wedged between the bureau drawers. We had both begun our apprenticeship on the Keep staff that year, and Arvard had already been promoted twice. When I found the letter, I began to perceive the method of Arvard's astonishing advancement.

"Just you watch me, Evaric," gloated Arvard with a wide grin across his face. He jumped to reach the barn's loft and lifted himself to straddle the stout support beam. "I shall have Chul's own position in a year."

I never doubted that Arvard could do just as he claimed. Arvard always achieved his goals. "And after you replace Master Chul, will you seek Father's post?" I asked sardonically.

Arvard twisted his expressive face into comical disgust. "You make a little ambition sound like patricide."

I frowned into my fist. I sat amid the new hay on the barn floor. The Keep's smaller barns, such as this one, were used mostly to store feed for the Lord's horses in the adjacent mews. Arvard had selected this barn as a private retreat from the other members of the Keep staff, most of whom lunched together in a room designated for that purpose. Arvard preferred not to socialize with the other staff apprentices. He intended to direct that staff soon, and he generally behaved as if his superior rank were accomplished fact.

Arvard leaped from the beam and landed in the hay near enough to me to make me jump. He took a sandwich from the parcel that our mother had packed for our lunch. "What is the matter with you anyway? You act as gloomy as Father Guiarde. Did Nori refuse to go to the festival with you?"

"She could not refuse what was never asked of her."

"You're afraid of her."

"I dislike her."

Arvard continued as if I had not spoken. "You can't go through life believing that the things you want are unattainable." Arvard gestured emphatically, orating to a vast, unseen audience. "Decide what you want, and take it. If you want Nori, conquer her and be done with the matter. Moping never solved anything."

"I am not moping."

"You need to set goals for yourself, then pursue them. A man can claim a kingdom if he sets himself to it and works for it."

"Kingship does not appeal to me."

"After I become Keeper of Records, I shall pursue a position with access to Lord Baerod. I'll have real influence then. I can carry you with me, little brother, but you have to quit accommodating everyone. Even the pages take advantage of you."

"Should I resort to blackmail, too? I found the letter, Arvard." I withdrew it from my shirt. Arvard snatched it from my hand.

"It's my duty to reveal corruption when I find it," said Arvard defensively. "You don't think I'd actually try to profit from Irrn's misdoings."

"Why did you hide the letter?"

"I wanted to be sure before I said anything. Evaric, I found the letter by chance. What would you have had me do?"

I wanted to trust Arvard. Irrn's corruption did not dismay me; corruption inhabited every corner of the Keep. I did not want to believe that Arvard could be contaminated. "You must not use that letter."

"Why can't you ever sound so implacable at the Keep?" asked Arvard with a humorless laugh. He grimaced and offered me the incriminating missive. I tore it into shreds. Arvard muttered, "Irrn is too slippery to let such flimsy evidence bother him anyway." I did not like the wistfulness in Arvard's remark.

The bits of torn paper drifted from my hand. I began to shudder, and Arvard redirected his concern. "The Rendies?" asked Arvard quietly. I barely managed a nod. Arvard touched me cautiously. "I'll cover for you at the Keep," Arvard promised.

I did not try to answer. The madness carried me far from the familiar barn to a place of mists and horror. There were voices, anger, and hunger. There were Rendies, and they desired my soul.

Arvard gathered the remains of the lunch we had shared. His eyes shunned sight of me, caught in the Rendie spell that never quite ended. Arvard left the barn, returning to the Keep to tell more lies on my behalf. If I had accompanied him, it would have been I who performed the minor errand for Master Garnett; it would have been I who met Mistress Giena, an insignificant serving woman who had come with Lady Yldana from Tulea for the summer.

When my agony finally ebbed, I left the barn and walked without any particular goal. I was overdue at the Keep, but I could not face the connivery and hypocrisy with my nerves still raw from Rendie visions and Arvard's suspiciously un-heroic schemes. I tried to brush the sun's heat from my neck and smiled at my own useless gesture. The early summer had made its presence felt throughout both Keep and village. I was both fortunate and unusual for Tyntagel, for the sun never burned me.

The clash of swords startled me, until I realized that I had approached the practice yard. I drew closer from idle disinterest in anything more pressing. Lord Buern, the noble recipient of the lesson, struck an unenthused pose opposite the swordmaster, Master Conierighm, a large man with thinning hair. They argued, and Conierighm prodded Buern into sparring. I leaned for a moment against the fence rail to observe them.

The swordmaster drove his blunted sword against his student's chest. Buern staggered, though the blow had been light by my inexpert reckoning. "Carelessness like that will cost you dearly," commented Conierighm with cool contempt.

Buern straightened. "As your arrogance will cost you, Master Conierighm."

"I teach fighting skills, not manners. I suggest that you cultivate the latter and return when you have mastered respect."

Lord Buern threw the dull practice sword at the sword-master's feet. He left the practice ground proudly, but Conierighm shook his head in disgust. I retreated a pace to let the oak shadows better conceal me; the dry fence rail creaked. Conierighm's head lifted.

"Come here," commanded Conierighm.

"Master Conierighm," I acknowledged, trying to imitate Arvard's confidence, and failing. I left the oak shadows reluctantly. I had no reason to fear the swordmaster, I reminded myself, but I was not convinced. I was a coward for good reason; I was a Rendiemad young man of no particular distinction except the friendship of a remarkable brother.

I did feel surprise that I could meet the swordmaster's narrowed eyes with a level gaze. Master Conierighm had always seemed such a hugely imposing figure. I had gained my own height so recently and so rapidly that I had yet to accustom myself to the sudden diminishment of the world. After so many years of craning to see my classmates, I had not merely grown to ordinary height; I had surpassed Arvard, a transformation that I found both unexpected and disconcerting.

"I have seen you previously." Conierighm made the statement an accusation, but he was appraising me closely. I knew the look and accepted it with patience: the long hesitation as Conierighm associated a formidably tall, overly lean young man with a small, spindly boy of features so softly delicate as to appear feminine. "You are the clerk's son: the one who never leaves his brother's shadow. I suppose your brother had the wit to escape before I caught you."

"Master Conierighm, I merely paused to observe his lordship's lesson."

"Did you learn anything?" snapped Conierighm.

Some shade of Conierighm's contempt struck me as too fatuous for credibility, and my fear of him evaporated. "Not from Lord Buern," I returned wryly. I had too recently faced the demons of my mind; Conierighm's efforts to intimidate could not compete.

Conierighm almost smiled. His thin lips stretched. Appraisal, calculation: I wondered if he expected to see me crumble back into fear. "You are so eager a student," said Conierighm. "Let us see what you have learned." In a single fluid motion, he tossed me a blunted sword and he attacked.

I accepted the hurled sword from the air without thinking. Conierighm's blunt blade hit my chest and forced the breath from me. I sparred (badly), because Conierighm's blows struck uncomfortably.

Conierighm pursued me the length of the practice yard. The

match was absurdly one-sided; the only sword I had ever held before that day was Arvard's ragged stick. Another of Conierighm's
blows struck my shoulder heavily. I managed to block a second
from my head. "Do you find great sport in beating an apprentice
clerk?" I asked in as scathing a tone as I could manage between the
gasps which Conierighm's blows elicited.

"A clerk would be at his duties now," retorted Conierighm.

I could hardly tell Conierighm that a spell of Rendie madness
had kept me from my work. "I never claimed to be a diligent
clerk." I had begun to parry a few of Conierighm's thrusts, which
pleased me disproportionately. Conierighm's game bore unfavorable resemblance to Miff's bullying, but Miff had never inspired an
urge to retaliate in kind. I had always shunned competition, leaving the contests to Arvard.

My incipient self-satisfaction died quickly. With a quick play of
feint and stroke, the swordmaster tore the student's weapon from
my hand. Conierighm's lips again narrowed into an unappealing
smile. He raised his sword and lowered it with rigorous formality.
"Return tomorrow," ordered Conierighm, retrieving the fallen
sword as he retired to the armory.

I stared at the swordmaster's retreating back. I felt hot and
abysmally sore. I felt harshly aware of the burning sun, the hard
earth, and the air I labored to absorb. This was Arvard's game
made real; this was solid and true, not misty with Rendie madness.
The wielding of a weapon conveyed an amazing sensation of
strength; slow as I was to recognize my new height, I was slower
still to realize that I had matured in other ways as well. "Two hours
past noon?" I called across the yard. If I raced through my mindless duties at the Keep, I felt sure that I could escape for a time
without attracting notice, even without Arvard's help.

"Satisfactory," replied Conierighm without turning.

Arvard would never understand. He had virtually forgotten the
game that he had invented, for he had become a man with a man's
ambitions. I was still in many ways a boy, trying to cling to old
dreams. Playing at swords now, when I was already apprenticed to
the Keep staff, was ludicrous. Deliberately shirking Keep duties
was not the route to Arvard's much-vaunted Success.

Arvard would not approve, but Arvard need not know. It was a
small secret to keep from Arvard, though it was the first. I suppose

that I was trying to repay Arvard in kind for the secret that he had attempted to keep from me. Arvard's was a solemn game of the kind he had just begun to master, but I saw only that he played it without me. I was certain that Conierighm would never sustain this whim to teach a clerk for more than a single lesson. When the sword lesson ended, I fully intended to let Arvard know of it. Arvard had disappointed me, and a gesture of my own independence was the hardest punishment I could consciously give him.

Conierighm surprised me. Rather than teaching me a lesson in humility, as I expected him to do, he actually instructed me in combat, and he did not begin with the sword. He insisted that I must first learn to defend myself unarmed; I must develop the strength, control, and agility to counter even a superior opponent. He gave me assignments to perform on my own, and Conierighm would not hear any protest that my apprenticeship would interfere. He scorned my function as merely another of Lord Baerod's numerous apprentice clerks; inasmuch as I agreed with him, I began gradually to give priority to Conierighm's demands. My apprenticeship deteriorated, but I was viewed as merely inefficient, lazy, and irresponsible. Not even Arvard seemed to notice that I had redirected my energy, for Arvard's ambitions consumed his full interest, and I practiced with Conierighm at obscure times and places.

The Rendie madness ebbed to an affliction only of the night; I still heard Rendie voices as I slept, but the true dreams had never taken the toll of the waking terror. I was slow to correlate my improved mental state with the swordmaster's lessons. Conierighm had very subtly commenced my training as a K'shai.

By the time I realized Conierighm's intentions, I had proceeded too far to stop. I lied to myself instead, assuring myself that Conierighm's teaching would never make me an assassin, whatever Conierighm might plan. I refused to believe the truth that Conierighm would kill me himself rather than let his investment of time be wasted by my recalcitrance. He owed a favor to the K'shai, and he recruited for them as payment. In later years I came to understand why Conierighm devoted himself so thoroughly to my mastery of swordsmanship and those other skills he taught; I was the only viable candidate with whom he could hope to appease the K'shai. If he failed to please them again, as he had done several times in the years prior to my training, the K'shai had promised him death. Not even Conierighm dared contradict a K'shai.

For the sake of easing the Rendies' grasp upon me, I might have accepted Conierighm's way even if I had known what I would become. My parents ought to have apprenticed me to a butcher so as to educate me appropriately and give me warning. Death was unreal to me. I would become death's instrument before I would understand that tearing of soul from body which comprised it.

Chapter 5

Third Day, Seventh Month
Year 21 of Rending

Master Irrn sat at his great polished desk with his head low and his hands interlaced before him. His assistant, glancing through the door, thought that Master Irrn had drifted off to sleep. Master Irrn was an old man, thought the young assistant with callous satisfaction. Master Irrn would need replacement soon, and the young assistant considered himself quite the most likely candidate for the position.

Irrn watched his assistant through narrowed eyes. Irrn had a very good idea of the young man's aspirations, but Irrn was unconcerned by that sort of feeble competition. Irrn was a shrewd man. He had advised Lord Baerod on judicial matters for many years, and Irrn did not intend to relinquish that privilege.

The young assistant was of no concern, but this Arvard who had replaced Chul was another matter. Chul had never been careless, but this boy had produced enough incriminating evidence to undo years of Chul's good service, and the boy had used the data well. This Arvard had handled the matter with a delicacy worthy of Irrn himself—and Arvard had become Keeper of Records at the inconceivable age of twenty.

Irrn sighed. Thirty years ago he might have made good use of Arvard, but such an ambitious young man presented too much of a threat to an aging retainer. It was time to put a stop to Master Arvard's advancement through the Keep ranks.

Weaknesses: everyone had weaknesses. What were Arvard's flaws? Irrn had been collecting data for several months. The basic facts were not difficult to obtain. Arvard was the foster son of that ridiculous idealist, Evram, whom Lord Baerod perversely insisted on admiring; there could be no more impeccable a family in Tyntagel, even if the wife did have a reputation as a shrew. The daughter was insignificant. The natural son was more interesting; imagine that too-beautiful young man a swordsman! But swordsmanship, even practiced in secret, was an insufficient aberration for Irrn's purposes. The entire family was despicably innocuous. There was no hold to be gained in that direction.

This letter, now, was more promising. It said nothing overtly incriminating, but Mistress Giena was obviously attempting to blackmail the slippery Master Arvard. She knew or hoped she knew something which Master Arvard would not want made public. It would be interesting to observe the young man's reaction to the letter. Unfortunately, Irrn could not effect such an observation without admitting guilt over the letter's interception. No matter. Any of Irrn's agents could extract information from a perfidious serving woman in the Lady Yldana's employ. Irrn would see to it that one of his men carried Lord Baerod's messages to Tulea this month: perhaps Jorame. Jorame had always performed effectively for an adequate price. The man was more greedy than loyal, but Master Arvard was not so significant as to tempt Jorame into betrayal. Yes, Jorame would serve the purpose nicely.

Chapter 6

Eleventh Month, Year 21 of Rending

The air felt chill, though the sun burned brightly through the scattered clouds. Arvard tucked his hands into the pockets of his coat. He saw only his own feet taking strides across the ground, for his head was low in contemplation. Jorame had died in Tulea by a K'shai hand: an inconsequential event to Arvard, but Master Irrn, of all people, seemed to think that Arvard knew something of the circumstances. The lofty Master Irrn had become ridiculously, improbably accommodating; why? Mistress Giena had not responded to the last communication; why? Arvard's Power refused to appear; why?

Arvard felt a muscle twitch at his eye. He tried to smooth away the tic with his hand, but it persisted. The sense of panic had begun in small ways over the months since Arvard realized, thanks to Mistress Giena's cupidity, the truth of his heritage. The knowledge should have made him stronger; it had certainly delighted him initially. Imagine how proud Evaric would be to know that his foster brother was the only son of Lord Venkarel. Perhaps it was the need for silence that had corroded Arvard's spirit. He had not dared tell even Evaric the truth. Without mature, usable Power, even the son of Lord Venkarel was vulnerable.

Arvard could recognize his own dangerously emotional state, but he could not control it. The growing inability to master his emotions frightened him further. A wizard cannot panic, screamed

Arvard in his mind. Without control, Power comprises absolute destruction. A Power which cannot be controlled must be destroyed. That is Ceallagh's law. That is the Infortiare's justice.

I need to find Evaric, thought Arvard wildly. I shall remain strong because Evaric believes that I am strong. I have always been the strong one. I have always been the one to protect my little brother. Evaric understands. I must find Evaric.

Inquisitive whispers pursued Arvard as he stumbled from his office and the Keep. Let them think me ill, he prayed. Let them not stop and ask me why I leave my work at mid-morning. Let Evaric be at Fielding's office or at home and not running errands to farmers and tenants beyond the village. Let me find Evaric quickly. Evaric will listen.

"Ai, Evaric," called Nori with zealous brightness. I conceded that she was a very pretty girl. I could hardly blame her for unfortunate childhood comparisons between us. I could blame her for her long allegiance to Miff, but Miff had left Tyntagel over a year ago, seeking his dubious fortune. "Are you walking to town, Evaric?" asked Nori coyly.

Since the path connected only my family's home and Nori's to the village, the question was absurd. I answered stiffly, "Master Fielding asked me to collect some papers from Master Sodaii." I glanced at the thickly growing evergreens lining the path, wondering who was hiding, waiting to see Nori make a fool of me.

I began to move more quickly, but Nori matched my pace, though it must have been uncomfortably rapid for her. "Whom are you taking to the next festival, Evaric?"

"No one."

Nori place her hand on my arm. "You cannot go to a festival alone, Evaric."

"My family will be there." I tried to disregard Nori's unsettling proximity. I did not trust her. I did not particularly like her.

"Arvard has asked Vina."

Because Vina's mother was Lady Nadira's confidante, I thought cynically. "Yes."

"Did you never think about asking a girl yourself?"

"Not really."

"Evaric." Nori stepped in front of me, forcing me either to stop or bowl her over; I stopped. I stared over her head, until her hands began to draw patterns on my chest. I looked down at her reluctantly. Her smooth chestnut hair was gathered by ribbons which drifted over her shoulders. Warmth, softness, and the scent of lavender: she was obvious in her approach, but she was difficult to ignore. "Your arms are strong," she said, as if awed. She traced the muscles.

"Arvard is stronger," I said, which was untrue.

"Arvard never makes me tremble."

I knew that I should walk away from her. I was certain that she meant only to bait me. I was entirely innocent, for I had always been too shy to court a girl formally, and the advantages of less chaste pursuits had not yet occurred to me.

"You make me tremble, Evaric."

I did desire her; the realization surprised me mildly, for I was backward in such interests. Conquer her and be done with the matter; that had been Arvard's advice, considerably in advance of any inclinations of my own. I grabbed her clumsily, having little idea of the ways of seduction. I expected resistance, which would spare me the embarrassment of trying to proceed beyond an awkward embrace. I felt her press tightly to me. She guided me, leading me to the thick autumn grasses hidden by the trees. The ground was uneven and rough. I tried to protect her from the twigs and pebbles, but she directed my hands in other ways. She had lain with other men, I decided: hardly a difficult conclusion but an astonishing revelation to me. Her lips tasted of ale, which also shocked me.

"What have you done!"

I rolled to a crouch, while Nori tried to cover herself with her shift. Arvard was not looking at her but at me. I had never seen Arvard so angry.

"How could you soil yourself with this slut!" shouted Arvard. His eyes held a wildness I did not recognize.

"Arvard . . ."

"Betrayer!" Arvard turned sharply and ran toward the village. A jutting branch tore across his cheek, leaving blood in its wake, and he did not seem to feel it.

Nori began to laugh, a sharp, shrill sound which reminded me of mockingbirds. "Your brother is jealous of me."

I stared at her, disgusted with her, with myself, and with Arvard. I retrieved my coat, while Nori pouted at me. I left her struggling to refasten her skirt.

I had lost all interest in the errands I had begun. I retraced my steps toward home, feeling ashamed and angry. I hoped to find the house empty, but my mother stood at the gate. "Bother," I sighed, a much milder expletive than my emotions reflected. My mother was hardly the person I wished to see at that moment.

She met me with a frown, but she did not speak to me. She walked beside me, taunting me with silence, until I stopped and faced her. "Master Fielding released me for the rest of the day," I said more defensively than I had intended. Lying did not come easily to me, though I had practiced a fair amount of it to keep secret both my madness and my lessons with Conierighm.

"Then you will be free later to accompany your father to the Ratquer mill. You can load the barley while your father discusses the discrepancy he found in the last accounting with Master Ratquer."

"Ratquer's son can load the barley. We pay them enough for it," I replied mechanically, though I thought the physical effort might eliminate some uncomfortable tension.

"Siahan works hard, as does his father. They earn their prices." My mother puckered her face: she did not believe my lie. Master Fielding would not release me from duties too often shirked. "You might do well to spend some time at the mill, Evaric. Not everyone lives as easily as we do."

"I am fortunate. My brother succeeds enough for both of us, however dubious his methods."

"You are not Arvard's shadow. He dominates you only because you encourage it," said my mother slowly. I had never previously criticized Arvard aloud, and my mother was clearly astonished.

"Domination is Arvard's life and sanity, but it is a madness in itself. Arvard calls it ambition."

"Arvard understands poverty. He does not want to face it again."

"I know," I said tersely, wanting only to end this discussion. I could still taste Nori. I could still see Arvard's shock and anger. "The patch on the roof has slipped. I had better fix it." Master Fielding would not tolerate another neglected assignment; he would terminate my apprenticeship.

I went to cut the new shingles. My mother watched me with a troubled expression. She entered the house just long enough to find her shawl and change to her walking shoes. I did not ask her destination.

She returned some two hours later. I was in the kitchen, sanding the edge of a door that had sagged and begun to stick. My mother observed me for a time in silence. I let her think I did not know that she had come. "You already finished the roof?" she asked me, though she must have seen the evidence of my work.

"You said that I should learn about working hard," I reminded her, indulging myself in a strong dose of self-pity. "Arvard wants me to abet him in his boundless ambitions. Father frowns and says nothing, and Ylsa says nothing constructive. Roofs and kitchens would seem the safest place for me to occupy myself, since none of you approves of anything I choose for myself."

"I want what is best for you, Evaric."

"Thank you, Mother. I appreciate your concern."

The bitter edge to my voice must have made her wonder. She must have known that Arvard and I would reach this point of schism eventually. She must always have expected it. "Arvard wants only to see you succeed. I think you are the only person who actually matters to him."

"So I am, Mother: the only person who matters to him, except himself. Arvard would never hurt me. Arvard is always so capable, so much in control of everyone and every situation. Since I met him, I have wanted to be like him."

My mother hesitated. She placed her roughened hand on my shoulder. "You and Arvard are very different people. It is time you found separate interests."

She put her arms around me and hugged me to her tightly. I reacted stiffly at first. My mother was so rarely demonstrative that I was startled. I grinned at her apologetically, warmed by the sympathy I did not deserve.

"You do know how to smile like an angel when you want," said my mother, pulling back to study me. "That smile could break hearts more surely than any of Arvard's schemes." She whispered, "That smile could break my heart." I did not understand her comment at the time.

"What a charming domestic scene," drawled Arvard from the entry.

My mother dropped her arms to her side, looking absurdly guilty. "What are you doing here at this hour?" she demanded of Arvard.

"It appears to be the place to gather. You are here, Mother, when I was sure I saw you entering the village church not an hour ago. My dear little brother is here, when he should be running errands for Master Fielding. Surely, at any moment, Ylsa and my honored, honorable foster father will enter as well, and the entire, tightly respectable little family will be together." Arvard's jaw was tensed. His yellow hair stood at stiff angles.

I sensed a deeper disturbance than his recent anger. Something had altered in Arvard. Perhaps it owed to his shock at seeing me with Nori; perhaps I had stopped gilding him with my own ideals. I asked him tentatively, "Did something happen at the Keep?"

Arvard answered very clearly, "Nothing happened at the Keep, little brother. Nothing happened anywhere. Nothing is all that happens." Arvard kissed our mother's forehead lightly, which made her start. "I am going to my room, dear Mother, so that you and Evaric may continue your family discussion without further interruption from the fosterling." Arvard kicked the flowered throw rug into a huddle.

Mother allowed me to follow Arvard alone up the stairs to the attic room we shared. "Are you drunk, Arvard?"

"No, little brother, I'm not drunk. Not very. I should be much more drunk than this." Arvard flung open the door to the room, and the door's handle slammed another indentation into the wall. "Where is Nori? I thought surely you would have smuggled her into your bed. Or did she tire of you already? Is she off telling stories about you to her other lovers? Can't you ever learn not to be a victim?"

I should have been kinder, but I was annoyed. I replied dryly, which aggravated Arvard the more. "Nori did not exactly attack me, Arvard."

"She degraded you, which is worse." The light caught something on the table, drawing Arvard's attention, impatiently at first; then he stared as if nothing else existed in the room. I looked to see what had distracted him, but I could see only my brother's back. "The acknowledgment has finally come," said Arvard wonderingly. "The waiting has ended."

He reached, and I saw his object of desire winking past his hand. It was crystalline, pale violet, faceted and exquisite. It did not resemble the sort of prosaic items one might expect to find in the room of any commoner. "No!" I shouted. I leaped across the narrow room, striking Arvard with a force which carried us both to the floor.

"How do you dare to touch me with the stain of a whore still on your hands?" snarled Arvard.

"Did you touch it?" I shouted urgently, too concerned by my question to notice Arvard's mood.

Arvard closed his broad hands around my throat. He seemed to savor my shock. I tried to pry his fingers loose, but Arvard tightened his grip relentlessly. "No more games," said Arvard coldly. "No more pretense. You made your choice. You shame the aspirations I would have shared with you. You have dragged at me long enough, holding me to a nothing's destiny."

I drove my fingers deeply into Arvard's side. Arvard choked and doubled, his hands releasing their hold. His eyes watered. I was on my feet, breathing hard and glaring down at my brother, "You just tried to kill me, Arvard." Arvard groaned, unable to speak or move; that was the way of the movement I had used against him. "Do you realize that I saved your life an instant ago? That elegant bauble is yadovitii, an assassin's tool." I slowed my breath but not my anger. Arvard shifted laboriously to see the crystal cluster he had mistaken for a noble gift.

"What?" Arvard was fuzzy, confused.

I informed him stiffly, "Yadovitii is one of the more exotic weapons of a K'shai, but it can be very effective when properly utilized. The crystals resemble razors in their sharpness, and they splinter very easily. The K'shai coat them with an oily, penetrating poison, which requires very minimal contact with the bloodstream to kill. I do not know what you have been doing to advance yourself to glory. I do not want to know. But you have offended someone badly—someone who can afford to hire a K'shai to eliminate you."

With a bleak abruptness, I extended my hand to Arvard, who

struggled to rise from the wooden floor. It was my strength which lifted Arvard and led him to the bed; I did not like seeing Arvard helpless and uncoordinated.

"I shall go downstairs to find something to wrap around the yadovitii," I said. "Then I shall burn the poison from it, smash the crystals, and bury the shards. I suggest that you ensure that no one touches the yadovitii in my absence."

"Of course," agreed Arvard meekly. Sobriety was slowly asserting itself. He managed to roll onto his side, and he stared at me. "Miff should try to harass you now," he remarked with pallid humor.

I left him, went to the kitchen, and selected several empty grain sacks. Mother watched me curiously, as she heated water for the laundry. "Tell your brother to save the sporting practice for out-of-doors."

I answered tonelessly, "I shall tell him." She knew that Arvard and I had argued. I wondered what she would think if she knew how seriously we had fought.

"I'm sorry, little brother," said Arvard as I returned to our attic room.

"If you know who has named you as target, I suggest that you try to placate him or her. I also suggest that you request your own lodgings, since your presence here would appear to endanger all of us." I kept my voice devoid of emotion.

"I need your help, little brother."

"You have considerable authority on the staff, as you so often tell me. You might even manage to obtain a room in the Keep itself."

"I never intended to hurt you."

I wrapped the yadovitii with delicate respect. I had brought oil and rags to clean the wood of the table. I dropped the cleaning materials on the bed beside Arvard. "I am gathering the loose splinters, but be cautious when you clean. Wrap your hands, and let none of the oil soak through to your skin."

"Listen to me, Evaric."

I turned from the table. I looked not at Arvard but at a point on the wall above Arvard's head. A nail protruded; unadorned for years, it had held a wreath of leaves, until the leaves had turned to dust. Arvard and I had jointly won the wreath as a school prize not long after Arvard had become my foster brother. "I am listening, Arvard. I always listen to you. You are the one who cannot hear above the sound of your ambitions."

"Our goals differ. That does not make either of us wrong."

"Someone wants to kill you, Arvard."

"Not for anything I have done, little brother. I swear it."

"Then you do know who is responsible for this attack."

"Not who, but I think I know why." Arvard paused dramatically. "Someone has learned that I am Lord Venkarel's son."

I categorized his statement as another claim of the Lost Prince. I barely raised one brow, a lack of reaction that must have tantalized the raw violence that Arvard had suppressed. "That would explain why you continue to request Ixaxin testing at every opportunity. I assume that your startling discovery occurred approximately three years ago. Prior to that time, your interest in Power was resignedly wistful. Since then, you have devoured Ixaxin texts, when you thought I would not notice, and you have pursued every reference to Power that has been made in your hearing." I shook my head, exasperated by Arvard's latest fantasy. "You do not need to build yourself false histories to impress me or anyone else."

"I did not concoct this story, Evaric." Arvard hoisted himself upright.

"You told me once before that your father was a farmer." And I suspected strongly that he had been not a farmer but a thief and cutthroat.

"Pa was not my father. Without your help, Evaric, Lord Venkarel's enemies will have me assassinated, as they have tried to do today."

"Your imagination has always favored extravagance, Arvard. You obviously have an enemy, but you are scarcely a wizard."

"Not yet."

"Not ever." I began to gather up the bag which contained the yadovitii.

"Don't you understand, Evaric? My Power has been bound."

"I should not have thought that binding could take effect against any kin of the Venkarel's."

"Not if normal means were applied." Arvard gave his words urgency. " 'Son of the Taormin.' Do you remember, Evaric?"

I stiffened. I answered coldly, "The Rendies' chant."

"Yes!" hissed Arvard eagerly. "The Taormin binds me."

I hated the subject of Rendies. I loathed the brightness that it now brought to Arvard's face and manner. "I do not recall that the Rendies addressed you in particular."

"You did not understand them as I did," replied Arvard hurriedly. "Evaric, the Taormin is a tool of tremendous Power. I've read about it. It was the key to Horlach's dominion. That is the binding that has been used against me!"

"Arvard, we have both listened to Rendies more than anyone's sanity can fully accept." Arvard shook his head at me and laughed, though the movement was rigid and the laugh was hoarse. "I have nightmares, and you have this delusion . . ."

"It is not a delusion."

"This delusion that you are something other than what you are. You do not need to manufacture skills or strengths. You can do anything, achieve anything, become anything you wish. Can you not be satisfied with your own excellence in everything you try?"

"It is too much for you to believe, isn't it, little brother?" Arvard sounded compassionate now, as if he deeply regretted my failing.

I tried to shut away the sympathy that Arvard exuded. I tried equally to evade the pity that I felt in return. I did not want to pity Arvard, my faithful and invincible friend. Arvard had tried to choke the life from me, but I understood the potency of Rendie lies too well to withhold forgiveness. I had combated the Rendies every night and nearly as many days since that first fateful night. I knew that Rendies had corrupted my own mind and soul. I had once thought Arvard immune, but the hero had failed me in more ways than one.

"You want me to leave this house, little brother? Very well. Perhaps you're right. I have stayed too long."

"I spoke in anger."

"I know, but you were correct. I am endangering you by remaining. I can work my way to Tulea. I shall go to Ixaxis, and I shall learn everything there is to know about Rendies, wizardry, and the Taormin. I shall master my Power, and I'll find a cure for your Rendie madness. I'll prove myself to you, little brother."

I watched a squirrel steal an acorn from the tree beyond the window. I dropped my glance to the wrapped yadovitii. "How do you expect to live once your money is spent on inns and tariffs? You can hardly afford to hire K'shai Protection, and your travel will be slow and circuitous without it. Caravans are notoriously ponderous and costly."

"You might come with me," said Arvard cunningly. "You could provide Protection."

"I am not a K'shai," I replied, startled.

"You're nearly one." Arvard smirked, supremely pleased with himself. "I know that Conierighm has been teaching you. I've seen you. You're better than he'll ever be."

"That does not qualify me to fight Rending wraiths." I was not pleased that Arvard knew my secret, though I could not feel particularly surprised. I disliked his calm assumption that I intended to fulfill Conierighm's expectations. "No matter how unbearably the Rendies haunt me, I do not intend to become an assassin simply to learn the K'shai methods of surviving the night."

Arvard leaned back on the bed. "You refuse to accompany me," he said quietly.

A quality of such loneliness shrouded Arvard that I winced. "I understand Rendie madness, Arvard. I know how real it seems, but the Rendies will destroy you if you heed them. You have no Power; you have been tested repeatedly. Only Rendie illusion makes you believe that some sorcerous conspiracy has deprived you of your heritage."

"It is not Rendie madness but truth."

"Was it truth that made you want to kill me?"

"No. I didn't. You don't understand." Arvard pushed himself along the edge of the bed and forced himself to stand. "I must go, little brother, not just from this house. You do understand that much?"

"I suppose I do." Rendie lies were inescapable.

"I shall succeed. I've finally realized what must be done."

"What shall I tell Mother and Father?"

"Nothing. Or tell them that the liege has sent me on some needful journey. It's better if no one else knows the truth. There has already been one attempt on my life. I don't want to be followed from here. You must not tell anyone what I've told you today, little brother. Promise me."

"As you wish." I felt as if part of my life were being ripped away from me.

"We'll always be brothers, Evaric. Whatever happens." Arvard reached for my arm, and I met the gesture, knowing that it signified an ending. The Rendies had claimed the Lost Prince.

Chapter 7

Arvard wasted no time. He gathered his possessions, gave me various letters of deception to deliver to the Keep, and counted his silver at least a dozen times. He sorted that which he would hide from that which he would need to pay for the first step of his intended journey, a step which would carry him farther from his destination. He meant to misdirect any pursuit by starting toward Cam and turning aside as soon as he passed the Tyntagel border.

A caravan for Cam had just left the village when Arvard bought his passage. Rather than wait a month for another caravan, Arvard chose to catch this one at the crossroads. He took the shorter route through the dense woods, a route seldom traveled, for it boasted no proper road. I accompanied Arvard, running beside him until he could grab a berth on the last wagon. I watched until the caravan disappeared beyond the trees, and I continued to watch when nothing remained to be seen.

The road was darkly ruddy with streaks of late afternoon sun through stormy clouds when I finally began my return to home. I did not have the road to myself. Another traveler was approaching from the east, though the hour had grown late and inns would soon be sealing their doors for the night. The man was large but not extraordinary. Taxes were due from the Gellan district; many strangers came to the village for a day or two, citizens who lived far from the Keep. I often passed such men on the country roads without thought, but this one attracted my notice. Wrapped in a ragged brown cloak though he was, he exuded a confidence near bravado in his gait. The man's hands were hidden in the folds of his cloak, but I did not need to see them. He was K'shai: an assassin. He had attempted to kill Arvard. Because of this man, Arvard had gone.

The conclusion filled me with a strangely secure calm. I had no doubt of the man's identity. I had no question of what I must do. I approached the man with a smile so warm that he looked startled. The K'shai was reaching within his cloak; he reached, I was certain, for a weapon. A sword broke free of the cloak and sliced the air that my neck had occupied a moment earlier.

I had ducked and kicked, catching the K'shai behind the knees before the sword could complete its stroke. The K'shai staggered and recovered. I knew that he meant to throw his dagger while I avoided the sword. I dodged the dagger before it left my opponent's hand.

I had fastened my eyes on the K'shai brand. The brand had not been cleanly made; the sword was barely identifiable, but the significance of the seared skin was unmistakable. The brand moved quickly as the K'shai attacked, but I frustrated his deft moves.

I could feel the man change from cool professionalism to aggravated bewilderment. I could follow his thoughts as if they issued from my own mind. Every quick, strongly directed K'shai action found the target absent. The K'shai thought uneasily that it was like fighting wraiths. The killer had never faced such an elusive opponent of human kind. For a wraith, the K'shai would have known the proper forms to follow, as he knew the way to kill a man efficiently. This youth was neither one nor the other. This spindly youth, smiling so uncannily, began to alarm the powerful K'shai.

My foe's disquiet fed my calm. This game required less concentration than sparring with Conierighm, for the K'shai's intentions shone so abrasively clear to me. I found myself slowing deliberately, allowing the K'shai's blade to cut close to me, testing my own precision of evasion. It was a game: an exhilarating game. This K'shai had tried to kill Arvard; this K'shai would die.

"Feed on him, Fire-child." The voices in my head sang of

blood's sweet fire. "His energy is fear, and his fear will make you strong." The K'shai lay dead with his own short sword buried in his heart. The freed energy flowed into me, expanding into heady strength, but the madness faded with the act of killing. A man's hacked flesh lay bleeding at my feet, and I had stolen the life and soul from it.

Evening would come before anyone else took this path. The Rendies would consume the assassin's remains, for they would protect their Fire-child. Only the Rendies and I would know that the voices in my head had learned to destroy.

"He tried to kill Arvard," I reminded myself, but I had lost my certainty. I wiped blood from my hand; I had murdered a man, and the man's final, agonizing incredulity would now haunt me as surely as the Rendies. I had killed, and the worst guilt of all lay in the fierce joy that I had derived from the killing. Conierighm had trained me well; the Rendies had trained me better.

"You understand," said the little man.

Grim laughter was the answer of he who had been known as the Venkarel.

The little man felt annoyance. "You require me, Venkarel."

"Your motives are so pure," responded Kaedric.

"I am selfish. I do not deny it."

"You excel at both selfishness and cruelty."

"You are arrogant."

"Shall we scatter a few more epithets across infinity, Horlach? How very productive we are become."

"We are both necessary to the stabilization of the system."

"The process which will preserve you."

"And you, Venkarel. And your precious mortal world. You must yield him to me. I am the only one who can direct what must be."

The image of Kaedric smiled with feral coldness. "You are a very accomplished deceiver, Horlach."

"You cannot exclude me, Venkarel. See what the mere attempt has done to your world."

"It has opened a gate."

"The wrong gate!"

"By your choosing."

The little man's voice became hard and deliberate. "The cause is irrel-

evant. The remedy is necessary. Release him to me, or nothing will sur-
vive. This is truth."

"Truth, Horlach? Half-truth at best, I think."

"You have recognized the instability. You understand that it cannot last."

"Yes, Horlach, I understand. I also understand your treacherous na-
ture. Any remedies must be of my own devising."

"You lack the necessary knowledge."

"You lack the necessary Power."

The little man, who had been a Sorcerer King for twenty thousand
years, shrieked.

"Do try to behave, Horlach, until I need you. As you have said, we are
both necessary to the process." The shade of Kaedric vanished.

"Your arrogance, Venkarel, could easily destroy us," murmured Hor-
lach in his own mind, but he felt no personal anger against his too-
perceptive foe. The Venkarel was worthy.

It was the other toward whom Horlach's darkest anger burned, and the
other was long dead and dust upon another world. "Wretched mortal,"
snarled Horlach, "you dared condemn us all." Jonathan Terry was fortu-
nate to be dimensions removed from the little man's reach.

PATTERNS

Chapter 1

"**I** wrote to Ixaxis." Evram raised his head from Lord Baerod's accounts. "I wrote to Ixaxis," reiterated Terrell calmly. "I told them that our son is a latent sorcerer."

Evram blinked several times. "After all these years," asked Evram woodenly, "how could you betray him?"

"It is not I who betray him. I love him—for himself and not for memory of a Tyntagel witch. He deserves more than we can offer him."

"She will send for him when the time comes."

"How long does she intend to wait?"

"Time passes differently for Immortals."

Terrell sniffed disdainfully. "Her son has become a man, and she has not seen him since his birth. We cannot keep him forever hidden from anyone who might recognize him as the son of the Venkarel."

"Do not speak that name again!" hissed Evram furiously. He added more quietly, "Would you undo all our years of silence?"

"I am not so afraid of the Venkarel's enemies as you."

"Then you are thrice a fool." Evram rubbed his brow. "I must send word to Rhianna. Perhaps I can rectify at least a part of your mischief." Evram clenched his fists, the only sign he gave of the depth of his fury and concern. He left the room with a jerky stride, as if even motion had been stunned in him.

"It is not often I promote such strong emotion in you, Evram," said Terrell to the smooth walls of whitewashed boards. "I almost wish you would strike me. We might then understand each other a little better." She rubbed her aching hands roughly on her apron, as if the argument had soiled them irreparably. She looked up to find Ylsa watching her.

"Are you all right, Mother?" asked Ylsa hesitantly.

"Why should I be?" snapped Terrell. Ylsa's eyes acquired the glaze of tolerant hurt which made them so like Evram's and so annoying to Terrell.

"I did not mean to upset you, Mother." Ylsa withdrew softly, holding her drab green skirts close about her to keep them from rustling in any disturbing manner. She tries so hard to be a nonentity, thought Terrell. I wish she did not succeed so well.

Terrell began to clean: anything, everything. She needed distraction, because she felt less confident than she wanted to believe. She actually feared the Ixaxins far more than did Evram, because Evram's imagination did not encompass the inhumanity of Power. He had always adored his Lady Rhianna, but he respected her birth-status more than her position as Infortiare of Serii. Terrell felt nothing for the Lady Rhianna dur Tyntagel; she dreaded the Lady Rhianna dur Ixaxis. More, Terrell feared that darker shade who had also visited them on the night of choice over twenty years past. She had never confessed that strange interchange. She occasionally wondered if even the Lady Rhianna knew of it.

The Lady Rhianna had appeared first: the silvery, fragile enigma Terrell remembered. Evram had seen nothing else, for he could not bend his attention from the Lady who constituted his only dream, even when the Lady's image was only a projection of the wizardry in which Evram disbelieved. Terrell had not so much seen as sensed the other. She had faced the dark one rather than watch the blatant worship in her husband's eyes. The darkness had blurred and reformed.

She had seen the man with his ice-cold eyes and known that he appraised her. She had felt him coolly probe and categorize; she had felt her soul dissected and reconstructed in some complex file in his awareness. She had felt the danger of him. Even to her unflaggingly prosaic person, the contact had brought a nearly sensual enticement, the irredeemable fascination of the unimaginably remote.

Terrell knew the man's identity: he was Lord Venkarel. Terrell knew, as did all her world, that Lord Venkarel had died in the Rending. Terrell knew, as the rest of her world apparently did not, that the truest part of Lord Venkarel had not died. Almost, she could forgive Evram his obsession with the Lady of Ixaxis. Terrell had felt a hint of its like when the Ixaxin Lord had confronted her.

Terrell had tried to confess to Father Guiarde that the dark wizard obsessed her. She had needed to tell someone that the perilous wizard had come again. She could not speak of the matter to Evram, and to no one else could she speak. When she reached the priest, she realized that the long years of silence prevented her from trusting the church, also.

Almost a month ago, the wizard had returned in the night. Terrell and Evram had argued that evening, as they often did: herself shrill, Evram calmly reasonable but more infuriating to her because of his impenetrability. Ylsa had eaten silently, pitifully attempting to smile her parents into peace; her efforts failed. Arvard had observed them with that detached amusement of his. Evaric's comment had constituted the only unusual factor.

"Why can you never argue honestly, Father," Evaric had asked calmly, "instead of pretending that Mother originates all of your differences? We all know that you detest one another equally."

The idle remark, patently valid though Terrell found it, had caused Evram's color to drain in shock. Arvard had laughed outright, and Ylsa had looked miserable. Evram had later blamed Terrell fiercely for corrupting their son's perceptions. Terrell had laughed at the man who could ever consider Evaric innocent or incapable of penetrating the simplistic deceptions of others.

"For all his meek facade," Terrell had chuckled in sincere amusement, "he is his father's son." She had clarified wryly, "Lord Venkarel's son," and Evram had stoically marched from the room, reverting to his customary policy of avoiding unpleasantness.

Terrell had scarcely blinked (she thought) at Evram's retreating back, when the silhouette had stretched and reversed direction. Evram did not return; the figure who approached was considerably taller and leaner, more finely cast, and far more graceful of movement. His hair was dark, and his clothing carried the somber gleam of black silk. His eyes were intensely blue, but they were deeply cold.

"My Lord Venkarel," she had murmured both in horror and in awe.

"Applicability of the title has ever been questionable, but the appellation will serve." He had smiled austerely, some trace of a daunting humor stirring in the frosty eyes. "You shall write a letter, Mistress Terrell, to Ixaxis. You shall petition Master Ertivel, who currently presides as headmaster, on behalf of my son. You shall affirm that the boy displays evidence of Power, and you shall offer your sworn testimony with full acknowledgment of the penalties accrued by perjury."

"I would be lying, my lord," she had whispered. "Your son displays no Power, and he was yearly tested by the Ixaxin representatives, as law demands for any child."

"I do comprehend Ceallagh's laws, Mistress Terrell. I yielded the greater part of my mortal life so as to preserve their hold."

"Are you not suggesting that I defy them?" Terrell had asked, accepting the impossible conversation as a nightmare's gift.

"Do not mistake my 'suggestion' for a subject of debate. You shall write the letter that I dictate."

In the nightmare, Terrell had written it without further question. She awoke in the morning with a throbbing head and a lingering thrill of terror from her dream. She had found the letter on her bureau; the hand was hers, but the formal intricacies of its legal wording had not issued from her knowledge. She recognized his precision of style and shivered. She had quickly hired a messenger to bear the letter to Ixaxis.

Chapter 2

"The lords of Serii are a rough lot," murmured the voice in her mind.

"The impenetrability of bureaucracy outweighs the aggravation of mere individuals," complained Rhianna to the voice. "I despise councils and conspiracies. I loathe enforcing my will by virtue of this Power which accident inflicted upon me. I practice deception and domination for the good of our world, as if I were some omniscient authority on what the populace of the Seriin Alliance needs and wants."

"Omniscience—or the pretence thereof—is the lot of the Infortiare."

"Perhaps Ceallagh was omniscient. I am not. I feel wretched." The usual frustrations of fools and foolish customs had grated on her severely that day. She read a missive which had been left for her and laughed bitterly. "The Ixaxin holdings in Caruil have been attacked again. Several recent recruits have deserted us."

"Infortiares have tried to tame Caruillan sorcerers for centuries, Rhianna. You have made far more progress than your predecessors."

"You effectively shredded such primitive unity as they possessed, dear husband," she returned glumly. "A sound defeat is generally quite persuasive."

"You have no intention of being consoled, have you?"

"Not the slightest." She quit her pacing and sank into the chair which her husband had once favored. It had been badly worn at that time, over twenty years ago, when she had first entered Ceallagh's Tower. It was dreadful now, but she could not bear to replace it, though she had renovated most of the more dilapidated furnishings.

"You are the most confoundly obstinate woman." His unpredictable temper flared. "You have been as touchy as a dyrcat for a week, but you stubbornly pretend that a very predictable mote of political turmoil is all that concerns you. Must I coerce the truth from you?"

Rhianna smiled wanly. "Could Serii survive such an argument between us?"

He did not lighten his focus. "Not if it were a direct conflagration. We could attempt a circuitous contest in hopes of sparing the mortal world, or you might condescend to think honestly for a while."

"I need to keep some thoughts my own rather than yours," she countered a bit sharply.

"Your independence does not seem to have flagged severely in the twenty-one years since you married me," retorted her husband. The coils of his consciousness gathered, twisting and probing at her. It was a sting of rapidly directed Power. "Our son," he concluded ponderously.

"Of course, our son! He is our son, or he was once. I see him now, and he belongs wholly to Evram and Terrell." Admission deepened her depression. "Terrell has written a letter to Ixaxis." She had read it repeatedly, but she could not explain its existence. "She has sworn that Evaric is a sorcerer."

"Then you can hardly defend the claim that 'he belongs wholly to Evram and Terrell.' "

"Evaric has evidenced no Power. Terrell has perjured herself."

"Only in a technical sense," answered her husband in detached tones. "Evaric has not displayed any Power which Mistress Terrell could clearly identify, but she knows his heritage."

"He has no active Power, Kaedric. Do you think I would not have reclaimed him if he did? How can I subject him to Ixaxis— and your unforgiving enemies—when he has no defense?"

"I recall that Ineuil endured Ixaxis for almost a year, and he had neither Power nor the promise of it."

"Ineuil is a marvelous pretender, and he was obsessed with vengeance against you."

"I meant merely to remind you, dearest Rhianna, that precedence exists for the Ixaxin acceptance of a student without Power."

"Not when Ixaxis knows for certain of the student's lack."

"You own no such certainty about Evaric." Kaedric's response held an untraceable element which touched Rhianna oddly. "Evaric conceals his Power, as does your father, even from himself."

"Evaric was tested, as my father never was. It was you who instructed me that Ixaxin tests are infallible." Rhianna assessed her husband's lack of response. "Or did you lead me to that conclusion by letting me read and hear from others that such tests could not lie? Did you want me to accept that which you do not credit?"

Kaedric's amusement tingled with the pleasure of being discovered. (He had ever been so, building puzzles around that which he sincerely wished hidden, while genuinely hoping that someone would pierce the clues to his deviousness.) "I possibly distorted the truth, but it was a slight deception. Ixaxin testing is virtually infallible. I know of only two individuals who have defeated it."

"You hypothesize the second," Rhianna suggested dryly. "I assume that you were the first."

The image of Kaedric grinned wickedly in her mind. "I cheated regularly during my early days on Ixaxis. Marga suspected, I think, but she could never catch me at it."

"You wanted your Power to appear less than it was."

"Naturally."

"It did you little good," Rhianna murmured sweetly. Kaedric could still infuriate her with his unnecessary secrets.

Kaedric's specter grimaced. "I overestimated the average performance."

"If you suspected Evaric of concealing Power, why did you not tell me until now? He must be trained."

"He will be trained."

"So you assured me at his birth. Yet I must wait to be informed by Terrell that he has Power!"

"I could have been wrong," shrugged Kaedric.

Rhianna stared at her shadow-image of Kaedric with his twisted smile and perceptive crystalline eyes. She was certain that Kaedric knew his own abilities too well to doubt his judgment of Power.

The coldness of a forgotten fear began to instill its icy core within her. She knew that he was deceiving her, and she had no idea of how or why. "If you—and Terrell—are correct," said Rhianna coolly, though doubts of many kinds twisted mercilessly within her, "our son could be an untrained Power waiting to explode across Tyntagel." Rhianna shuddered at a muddled vision of Tyntagel oaks caught by the fires of Yen's destruction.

"Evaric is not likely to find himself in my circumstances."

"But you consider the danger sufficient to send him to Ixaxis."

"Not at all. Our son will certainly not go meekly to Ixaxis on his 'mother's' whim. He will demand explanation, and he will weigh it against the K'shai."

"The K'shai are too practical to court Ixaxin displeasure."

Kaedric murmured wryly, "The K'shai pride themselves on developing their nearly supernatural abilities out of purely mortal strength. It might be amusing to watch them discover a major Power in their midst."

"As your Infortiare, my love, I must inform you that you are displaying a complete dearth of conscience. Lord Ceallagh would not approve." Nor would she have done had she believed him serious in contemplation of creating a sorcerous assassin of their son. She implicitly trusted her husband's self-imposed, unyielding rules, which he insisted knew no moral base. She trusted enough that though she could feel him manipulating her, she did not forcibly analyze his motives as she would have done with any true opponent.

"Dear, proper Rhianna, you have always attributed too much honor to me. It is probably as well for our marriage that carnal sins are beyond my ability."

"The only major sin to which your instincts incline you, my Kaedric, is murder. It is hardly an honorable tendency, but your capacity for destruction remains undimmed and unrivaled. I certainly should never fret over the specter of infidelity. No other woman would tolerate you."

The image formed clearly: dark, expressive eyebrows raised over blue-ice eyes; lips quirked in mingled irritation and amusement; lean elegance deceptively relaxed. "I do love you unconscionably."

"What can the child of our love become," sighed Rhianna, for she desperately loved and sometimes hated Kaedric as well, "save a dangerous aberration?"

"Like his father," added Kaedric evenly. His wife touched him and his terrible burning Power gently. "Dear Rhianna, would you have loved me if the Taormin had not forced my life upon you? You never had much of a chance to choose your own way, being flung from your father to me. Is that why you endeavor so fixedly to defend Evaric from my influence?"

Rhianna protested, "It is not from you that I defend him, Kaedric, but from your enemies and mine. It was you who chose the course we have taken for him."

"When he was a child, there was cause. Now, he is nearly a man; by mortal reckoning, he is a man already. You scarcely speak of him, but you watch him secretly. You want desperately to see him without the veil of your Power, but you leave your Evram believing that you have forgotten your son."

"Our son," she amended absently.

"Our son," agreed Kaedric. His voice held an emotion that Rhianna could not name. "Evaric begins to need more than Tyntagel can give him. Even Mistress Terrell recognizes that he outgrows his fosterage. You still hesitate to interfere, though you know that continued restraint could press Evaric into the K'shai, a group of whom you deeply disapprove. Ergo, you view the alternative to restraint as the greater evil. The alternative is, of course, the environment of major Power: Evaric's, yours, and mine." Kaedric's voice sharpened critically. "You cannot prevent the eventual manifestation of Evaric's Power. You condemned him, if you choose to consider it as such, when you elected to bear my child." He added, "Do not protest falsely to spare my feelings," in anticipation of her response. "You never wanted Power beyond the bespeaking of trees, hounds, and squirrels. You gauge Evaric's feelings by your own, discounting the fact that he may not share your disdain for the trappings of authority. Darling Rhianna, I leveled half a city to escape the clutch of poverty and ignobility. You pity my childhood. You form excuses for me out of love, despite the legion of curses which enshroud my name. Almost, my dear, you have made a decent man of me by your faith, but for Evaric's sake, I must impress upon you the inaccuracies in your image of me."

"Kaedric, do you think I love only an illusion?"

"I think you do not admit that the man whom you (astonishingly enough) love is very nearly the devil his detractors paint him. I am dangerously ambitious for Power—arrogant, ruthless, conceited, and quite amoral. The Ixaxins call me a revert: a Sorcerer King born to a later age by calamity of breeding. They are half right: I am more than a Sorcerer King. My Power exceeds that of any member of our ancestral race of madmen. Their greatest flaws, however, are mine. It was purely by accident of fate that I did not destroy more than Ven. Had I matured more fully before rebelling, my outburst might well have eradicated the mortal world." He enunciated with acuter emphasis, "Though he does not yet know it, Evaric is like me, Rhianna, and like Horlach."

For a moment of utter silence, Rhianna sat altogether alone in the Infortiare's Tower. She could see the ordinary sights: the view of Tulea, the Queen's exquisitely impressive castle, the distant white blossom of Ixaxis against the blue-violet sea. Her own thin hands were spread before her on the desk which had been her husband's. The ancient books, the walls, the burnished wood had been restored since the days of his tenure, but they had known his touch more often than she. In such still moments, she missed him most deeply. Her heart and body mourned him, though her mind and Power denied that he had ever died. She could not bear to let such moments linger. She forced the tactile world to fade, and she touched her husband desperately. He took her hand with a queer deliberation and pressed to it a kiss of mist and longing. Too late, she perceived his intention. She screamed his name, but she was battering a wall which no longer barred her way.

He withdrew from her each fiber and fiery tendril of sensed spirit of himself, emptying quarters of her soul which she had not even known were his. The frozen chill curled her into herself like a sorely wounded animal. She cried his name again, and Ixaxis might have trembled had they understood her Power's desperation. For the first time since Kaedric's Power had tested her in an obscure Anxian tavern, no trace of him stirred in her deepest senses. Rhianna was again alone, as she had been until she met him. She thought of how much more alone Kaedric was, and she was horrified.

"Dear God, why?" Rhianna heard her own small voice and scarcely knew it. She clasped her hands together, for they were icy and stiff. She could feel the silence. The room smelled of ashes years gone. How many widows, she wondered, must feel their husbands die a second time?

Of all the futures, this one she had not foreseen. She could have seen him turn from her in anger; she could have seen herself despised. She could not have believed they could be parted so completely.

Analysis was imperative. She must understand. "Whatever plan you have concocted," she whispered, "I shall be part of it, Kaedric." Nonetheless, she was torn; she had a son as well. "My Kaedric, what have you done to me?"

The little man frowned: something odd was occurring. The Venkarel had always been a clever opportunist, but where was the reason in using a tool like this wretched Terrell? Puzzlement disturbed the little man greatly.

He reviewed his analyses with adamant care. A few uncertainties were inevitable given the subject's nature, but the analytical weaknesses were exceedingly minor. The central pattern was strong, for it had been developed over centuries, and the little man had woven his own design near to the focus. He knew the outcome, for he had lived it once before. It was unfortunate that he had been so young and impatient. If he had been less quick to escape with his stolen prize, the uncertainties might have been eliminated.

The little man gathered darkness like a cloak and pondered the Venkarel's moves. "Distraction?" he mused. That would be almost too childish, for it served no purpose. Did it?

A vivid joke struck the little man, and he roared appreciatively, "Distraction!" It was sensible; it was clever. It was tortuous and like the Venkarel..It was directed against another!

The little man frowned again. "Against her?" he demanded dubiously. His puzzlement doubled; so also grew his doubts.

Chapter 3

Mountains of Mindar, Serii

The rocks had tumbled recently. The cliff still wore the red scars of wounding. The man who cursed the stones matched his stony, scarred surroundings. He limped across the littered path and sat heavily upon a flat boulder.

He drank deeply from his flask, corked it carefully, and wiped the damp residue from his mouth with a dusty sleeve. The brand on the back of his hand showed through the dirt of travel: it represented in primitive form a bloodied sword, the hilt upon his wrist, the blade extending up the middle finger, the blood dripping along the sword's length. The man was K'shai. His K'shai name was Fog, for he could assassinate and escape as elusively as his namesake.

Fog was old for an active K'shai. He had been K'shai before the Rending. He could have retired in luxury if he had ever learned to curb his drinking and his gambling, but Fog did not crave respectability. He belonged to the old K'shai. Fog was strictly an assassin. He took no partner. He fought Rendies only for the practicality of his own defense.

Fog shaded his eyes to study the landslide. Part of the path had fallen away from the mountain. He would be forced to retrace his steps. "Blasted Mindar fangs," he muttered. His quarry could be in Alvenhame before he found passage around Dwaelin. He had lost too much time in Anx. He was growing old.

He massaged his knee. The rough passage had made it sore. He had torn it years ago, but it had only begun to trouble him again lately. He tried to straighten it where he sat; the knee cracked and argued.

He heard a faint keening. As it grew louder, Fog began to grumble anew. "Blast Gnarl, he told me all the gargoyles had retreated north."

It was a nightmarish beast that flew at him in attack. Fog had fought gargoyles before. The bloated, taloned beast could not suffocate the K'shai with fear, and Fog knew its vulnerability. He knew the proper K'shai pattern. He began his sword dance stiffly, but the rhythm of it smoothed as he fended against grasping claws and slavering teeth. His sword sliced cleanly through the barbed tail.

Fog stepped aside to consider the fallen gargoyle as it gasped for death. He did not try to finish it, for he had given the lethal blow. Any further butchery would only spread the acid ichor, and severed pieces would die no more quickly than the gargoyle's writhing tail.

Fog left the creature thrashing among the rocks. He wiped his sword in the first soft dust he found. A few bits of dried grass shriveled when the ichor touched them. Fog did not sheathe his sword until he had removed all taint of the gargoyle from it.

"Worse nuisance than Rendies," he snarled as he buried the traces. He looked at the painted sky, which soon would shine with stars. He grunted and decided that it was too late to return to level ground before nightfall. The narrow cliff path would be a poor place to fight Rendies, but the gargoyle had left him too winded to succeed against a Rendie unless he had some rest. He would just have to hope that no wraiths came this night. He was growing too old, he thought again. He settled himself among the rocks.

Fog awoke from sleep before midnight, knowing the chill forewarning of a Rendie visit. He flexed his stiff knee gingerly. He folded and packed his blanket neatly, chose a stable space on which to stand, and waited with his sword and a sigh. He had fought too many Rendies not to know their habits of timing.

Two wraiths began to form, and Fog resigned himself to his final battle. He might have managed to combat one. He was too sore and tired to master both. He had grown old in his profession.

Fog began the sword dance mechanically. The knowledge that

he would fail succumbed to the hypnotic rhythms of the familiar. He moved automatically, and the Rendies did not exist. It was the secret of the patter; it denied the Rendies even while it fought them.

A stone caught Fog's foot, and his traitorous knee buckled beneath him. His sword flew from his hand, and his mind forgot the pattern. He saw a Rendie open itself into a lightless maw. He could feel it snatch pieces of his mind. Defeated, Fog crawled to his feet and ran, knowing flight was a desperate and unlikely hope. He misjudged his direction, but he realized his mistake only as his feet slipped across the cliffs crumbling edge. He wondered idly whether he would be smashed to his death before the Rendie could devour him.

The rocks seemed to spread throughout his body. Fog felt punctured and broken. He opened one eye; the other was swollen shut. He lay upon his back at the bottom of the cliff, and there were no Rendies. Fog grinned as he spat out a broken tooth. Miraculously, he had survived. It was very hard to kill a K'shai.

Fog's satisfaction ebbed when he tried to move. He tried to shift his legs and found that they responded no more readily than the rocks which seemed to cover him. He could not lift his arms. He craned his head, expecting to see himself at least half buried. A single dagger of stone jutted from his side. The remainder of his body was skewed upon the moon-dusted dirt.

Fog's head fell back hard against the ground, but he felt little pain from the shock. He tried to wet his lips and realized that his mouth was parched. He cursed himself for botching his own death. He had always taken pride in executing his victims cleanly and quickly.

By morning the ravens began to gather. Fog shouted at them, until his voice cracked like their own. They circled him steadily, awaiting his death.

By evening, his sight had failed him. He could hear only a steady roaring, which he knew meant failure of his ears. The pain had faded, but Fog did not welcome the easing. He knew it was a precursor of death, and resentment against death had been building in him during his paralyzed hours.

"*I can preserve you.*" The voice filled his head, and no other senses remained to distract from it.

"What are you?" whispered Fog. He saw death as an absolute, an inevitable prospect, especially for a man of his profession, but it was a phenomenon he found exceedingly disagreeable. He did not believe in salvation of any kind, but Fog would bargain with God or devil to save himself. He began to feel eager.

"*Immortal,*" answered the voice.

"You will preserve my life?" demanded Fog. "What does it cost me?" There was a price on everything.

"*Your soul, of course,*" replied the voice dryly.

"Preserve me!" said Fog with nearly a laugh. He had no qualms about bargaining away a thing in which he disbelieved.

"*You will be physically whole. The world will generally perceive no change in you, but you will not be as you have been. From time to time,*" warned the voice carefully, "*you will become an extension of myself.*"

"Word the contract as you will."

"*Your choice will not be irrevocable,*" said the voice slowly. "*True death will remain an option.*"

"What are you? A devil with a conscience?"

The voice chuckled softly. "*Something of the sort.*"

"I am dying, blast you. Quit wasting time."

The voice did not respond, and Fog began to despair. He began to curse himself for believing his own nightmare, and he cursed the nightmare for being unreal. He cursed his body for failing him at last. He cursed the dead gargoyle, who had exhausted him, and the Rendies, who had driven him to fall. With a final gasp, Fog cursed the Rending which had released both Rendies and gargoyles into the inhabited lands. Fog's heart stopped, sputtered, and began to beat strongly again. The body of the K'shai called Fog began to heal.

"*Venkarel has deceived you from the beginning,*" whispered a dim, nearly unnoticed voice in her mind.

Rhianna stiffened. Her Power flared. She scanned for other Power and found no source. She found nothing, and the voice did not return. Slowly, she relaxed into her chair, but her eyes were troubled and her Power wary.

Chapter 4

Tyntagel

I lay in my bed and stared at the fastened shutters, the solid walls, the heavy door of oak, which in any case led only to the rest of the well-sealed house. I feared to move, feared to seek my parents or my sister, feared to know or not to know what I might or might not find. Rendies had entered, despite the solidity of walls and wood. Arvard had gone, and nothing remained to divide me from the bitter night.

I arose and dressed slowly. I took from the bureau the small knife that Arvard had given me five years before. I had no better reason for taking it than the fact that it comforted me.

I opened the room's door and met the prosaic aroma of bacon. Ylsa yelled from the kitchen, "Evaric, are you planning to eat breakfast?"

I walked down the stairs, employing all of Conierighm's lessons in cautious, silent movement. I trusted nothing I saw and nothing I felt. I paused at the base of the stairs, studying the walls, rugs, and chairs. Grimly, I inspected the charcoal sketches of Tyntagel Keep, which hung in oak frames upon the wall. Suspiciously, I searched them for some skewed image which would betray them as imposters, visions of a Rendie dream from which I might yet wake.

I entered the kitchen. My breakfast sat cooling on the table. All other places had been cleared. "I thought you had decided to sleep all day," grumbled Ylsa, who was scrubbing the tiles of the floor.

"Father has already gone to the Keep, and Mother went early to the market."

I lifted a piece of cold bacon from my waiting plate and stared at it. I replaced it carefully. I could not eat. Not after yesterday. Not after last night.

"Mother wants you to fix that loose fence rail before you go to the Keep this morning," said Ylsa as she worked.

I nodded without hearing her. "Do you ever have nightmares, Ylsa?"

Ylsa stopped moving. "Sometimes," she conceded wanly. She began to scrub again at a furious pace. "You had better hurry if you intend to eat your breakfast, finish your chores, and reach the Keep on time for work. Father will not plead with Master Fielding for you again."

"I misplaced my appetite." I opened the door and breathed slowly of the cold air.

"Will you close the door before you freeze me!"

"Sorry, Ylsa." I stepped outside into the drizzle and closed the door behind me.

"Your performance disappoints me," said Conierighm with disdain. He withdrew his weapon from its position at my throat, deliberately drawing the blade across my jaw.

I blinked at the unexpected cut, annoyed by Conierighm's ruthless disregard for any hurt that did not kill or maim me. "Your point, Master Conierighm," I replied stiffly.

"The winning point, Master Evaric." Conierighm's thin smiled reappeared. "At least you accept the unpleasant consequences of inattention."

Conierighm had developed an unfortunate tendency to gloat each time he scored against me. I told him coldly, "I could have killed you a dozen times today."

"Generosity does not constitute victory." Conierighm forestalled my wordless retreat. "There is a man you must meet. He will be here tonight. Come after sunset."

I answered over my shoulder, "I have no interest in your nameless strangers, Master Conierighm."

"The K'shai need not explain themselves to insolent little boys," sneered Conierighm. "Or perhaps it is the night that you fear to face?"

I regarded Conierighm without response. I had faced the night before, and Conierighm knew it; Conierighm knew nothing near the whole of it. I vaulted over the low fence rather than elbow past Conierighm to reach the gate.

For two hours I sorted records, carried Master Fielding's ledgers as he made his rounds, transcribed the lists of taxes paid and owed, and wondered if I looked to be a murderer. I received a few questions regarding Arvard's sudden errand; I lied consistently, saying that I knew nothing of his mission's nature, and no one troubled to question me twice.

For three hours I updated family rolls with the recent birth and death reports. I carried boxes for Master Croft, fetched ink for Master Ban, and listened to a recital of Master Garnett's health complaints. Master Fielding berated me at some length for inattentiveness, while I wondered if anyone had actually died yesterday on a lonely road at dusk; I was not sure if Rendie madness had goaded me to slay a man, or if Rendie madness had merely made me believe that the murder had been done. I smiled, apologized to Master Fielding, and took orders. Arvard had gone, and I had killed, and Rendies had entered a solid, sealed room, but the people of Tyntagel Keep saw only that Evaric was dreaming again and never would amount to anything. I left early.

I walked home slowly, berating myself for allowing Arvard to depart. Arvard had supported me through years of harassment and Rendie madness. I had abandoned him the first time he asked for my help.

Someone had again knocked the loose rail from the fence, and I replaced it, absently recalling that my mother had asked me to repair it more permanently. I glanced at the ground near me, searching for a suitable wedge to keep the rail in place. I knelt and dug my fingers into the soil, bringing up nothing but recollection of the last digging I had done. "Why trouble to use yadovitii against someone as unprotected as Arvard?" It rankled me that I had no palatable answer. There was no sense in attempting a yadovitii kill, unless the assassin had good reason to maintain distance from the victim. Someone considered Arvard a dangerous target.

Arvard might win every festival contest in Tyntagel, but he could not present a threat to a K'shai. Someone thought otherwise.

Someone believed Arvard's fantastic theory. Someone believed that Arvard was the son of a dead Infortiare.

I entered the house diffidently, preparing myself for confrontation and more lies about Arvard's errand. I strode directly to the kitchen, peered into the laundry room, and frowned because my mother was not at her usual tasks. I went to my father's study and found it empty as well. It was early yet for Ylsa to be home from the Keep, but I checked her room mechanically. Save for myself, the house was empty.

I had no reason to expect to find my father or sister at home. My mother could be in the town on one of the ladies' errands. Too many explanations contended, and none of them deserved disquiet. It was only the shadow of last night's dream, I thought uneasily, and the troublesome uncertainties about yesterday. I curled my fingers restlessly, wishing for one of Conierighm's swords.

"You do not need a weapon, Master Evaric."

I wheeled at the voice, furious with myself for not having heard the speaker approach. Recalling Conierighm's lessons with deliberation, I gathered my energies into the center of myself, relaxing and subtly readying muscles for attack.

"Master Conierighm has trained you well." The speaker smiled slightly. He was a thin man of indeterminate age. The sharp-featured face was pale; the hands were empty, and no blade hung at his side. I stared and wondered, speculatively appraising the potential hazard.

"You were not sent by Master Conierighm."

"No, indeed." The man paused. "You do not know who I am?" he asked slowly.

I felt oddly suspicious that the question contained a test: not Conierighm's test; not the test of a K'shai. It was another kind of test, a darker one. "I do not know you, nor do I know why I find you alone in my parents' house." I filled my voice with the sort of bellicose indignation that Miff had often favored. The man's cheek tightened infinitesimally. I felt my own tension ease, knowing that I had failed the man's examination.

The man became direct. "My name is Ragon. Your mother sent for me. I gather that she did not tell you."

"Where is she?" I demanded.

"Elsewhere. I prefer to meet candidates alone."

"Candidates for what?" I asked with heavy irony, refusing to accept the truth I sensed but did not understand. "Or is that something else which I am supposed already to know?"

"It is all a part of the same." Ragon's scrutiny became puzzled. "I must admit that you present me with a novel—and rather awkward—situation. It might be best to await your parents' return. Still . . ." Ragon appeared intense but increasingly dubious. "You have truly no idea of my identity."

The Rendie dreams had always been worst before the Ixaxins came. "I suggest that you consider your plottings more carefully if you intend to make a habit of this sort of unexplained intrusion. I have another engagement." I needed to escape before the Rendie madness overtook my careful control. I did not trust my marginal sanity in the presence of an Ixaxin, especially after yesterday's events.

I could not depart. I frowned, feeling more irritated than angry. I could not direct my limbs to carry me.

"It saves trouble," commented Ragon evenly, "which your ignorance might bring upon both of us." Ragon seated himself in the chair which was customarily my father's. "As you must finally have begun to realize, I am a wizard. Currently, I am assigned to escort recruits to Ixaxis. I generally take groups of five or six, but I made a special journey for you." Ragon's voice held a trace of disapproval. "You apparently earned attention from someone of importance."

Lords, I thought, he has confused me with Arvard. It was not my own madness that the Ixaxins pursued but Arvard's. "I am not a wizard, Master Ragon."

"Obviously, you are not a wizard. You are untrained. Therefore, you are at best a sorcerer. Evidently, you are also a latent. Surprising," mused Ragon. "The Scholars do not generally exert such effort to recruit latents."

"I have no Power, latent or otherwise."

"You are the son of Evram and Terrell, liege-bound to Lord Baerod dur Tyntagel?" It was not voiced as a serious question, and I did not answer it. "Your mother has sworn that you show Power. Do you say that she perjured herself?"

It was my mother who answered, arriving at the door and meeting my incredulous glance with defiant implacability. "You have arrived much earlier than I expected, wizard. I have had no opportunity to discuss this matter with my son."

"I hope, Mistress Terrell, that you have not brought me here without just cause," warned Ragon. "The Infortiare does not treat deception lightly." Ragon stood, a solemn, menacing symbol of a guild more deadly than the K'shai. He said curtly, as he left, "Discuss quickly, Mistress Terrell. Your son and I have a journey before us, and I should prefer to leave before night." The door closed softly.

I breathed slowly, wondering why I alone seemed unable to accept Arvard as a sorcerer. "What have you done?"

"What was necessary," answered my mother tersely. She was unsteady; the wizard's appearance had obviously frightened her.

"Necessary for whom? For Arvard? Did he tell you that he had Power?" If Ixaxis believed, then the Venkarel's enemies would be certain; Arvard would be the target of more than one K'shai attack. Arvard would need more Protection than he could afford, and he would be unprepared and overly confident. "You sent Ixaxis a letter of lies."

"Forget about Arvard for once."

I would not listen; I did not want to hear what she was telling me. "Forget? Arvard is my brother, and I intend to Protect him against Ixaxis, against you, against whatever enemies he may accrue." I grew harsh. "Arvard may have gone to Ixaxis already, but I want any talk about his specious Power ended here. Such talk has already made him a target of attack. I shall tell the wizard that a mistake was made. He believes that I am the sorcerer; I shall tell him that I deceived you, never expecting my joke to carry so far. I shall tell him anything to be rid of him, but I shall not let Arvard's delusion return with Master Ragon to Ixaxis. You see, Mother, Arvard asked for my help, and I shall give it to him, albeit belatedly."

"You will not hold to your intentions," said my mother sternly. "Your father will not allow it."

I laughed. Because, of course, I did not yet realize that the father of whom she spoke was not Evram of Tyntagel Keep.

Strange, thought Ragon, the candidate shows no sign of Power. Yet, the orders came, quite clearly; Master Amardi even intimated that the Infortiare herself had confirmed the candidacy. There is something odd about that young man, but I should not have considered him a likely Ixaxin.

Ragon stared thoughtfully at the cloudy sky and the massed green of Tyntagel's ever-present oaks. Ragon belonged still to the student class himself, though he had devoted many years to Ixaxin studies. He no longer expected to win a Scholar's white robes; his Power sufficed only for the level he had reached. Unlike many others of his ilk, Ragon had not left Ixaxis upon realizing that he could advance no further in the ranks of the Wizards' Guild. Ixaxis was home. Ixaxis was the only home for Ragon, for Ragon had been born in Ven.

He had come from a wealthy family, though they had no claim to noble kinship. Ragon had visited them once yearly during the first fifteen years of his Ixaxin education, an extravagance of time and travel in which few of his fellow students indulged. Ragon's mother had been enormously proud when he gained senior status, though wizardry had not been popular among her circle. Ragon's father had smiled and nodded, as if no doubt could have ever existed that Ragon would pass the senior level examination.

Ragon missed them: his parents, his sisters, his cousins, uncles and aunts. He wondered why thought of them had suddenly come to him so keenly. The greatest part of his sorrow had surely faded with the passing years, and he seldom thought of it now. Tyntagel affected him badly; even the trees brood here, he thought. He recited a silent litany of control to still his disquiet.

He turned to find the candidate, Evaric, approaching him. The mother stood clearly visible at the window, but she did not follow her son. "Master Ragon," said the young man distinctly. Why is his voice familiar? wondered the wizard. "Unless you intend to take residence here, I suggest that you return to your Guild and inform them that I am not what they seek."

The youth is too confident, thought Ragon; Ixaxis will teach him humility at least. Ragon contemplated holding the candidate again by Power, but the feeling crossed him that another demonstration of strength would only antagonize the candidate further. As Evaric started down the road toward the village, Ragon fell into place beside him.

The candidate seemed unconcerned. "This is not the route to Ixaxis," he remarked. Ragon merely smiled.

* * *

The wizard would not leave me. I was doubly dismayed by the unwelcome company and the concern that someone might mention Arvard in the wizard's hearing. I deliberately led Ragon to a disreputable tavern, where a member of the Keep staff would not likely be acknowledged.

I drank little, but I forced myself to linger over the tavern's bitter ale. My pose of a brashly indifferent youth, annoyed by an old man's company, demanded effort and concentration. The unpleasant ale helped my focus, as did a mildly vindictive enjoyment of the wizard's evident distaste for his environs. The wizard did not speak, and I did not encourage him. My mind was busy with schemes; Arvard would be proud, I thought wryly.

Observing the oddly unresponsive candidate, Ragon felt strangely apprehensive. There was something icily inhuman, Ragon decided, about the unconcerned way this young man courted the danger of a wizard's anger. The candidate seemed too intelligent for bravado. Something troubled was stirring in the young man's silver-gray eyes, and Ragon doubted it was merely superstitious fear of a wizard's mild disfavor.

Conierighm's cottage masqueraded as a peaceful, stonewalled haven from the encroaching night. Warm light spilled from the window, not yet shuttered against darkness. The gardener had trimmed the hedges into well-ordered boxes; no stray limbs cast those inexplicably active shadows.

The pair of us who silently approached the house did not suffer from the delusion of peace. I knew better what to expect from the visit, but Ragon held the imperturbability of trained Power. I rapped sharply upon the moss-green door.

Conierighm pursed his lips in a vain attempt to conceal his satisfaction at seeing me on his doorstep. I entered without invitation, and Conierighm closed the door without remarking that I seemed to cast dual shadows. Conierighm placed a sword in my hand and motioned me to enter the salon alone.

The salon was stark, for Conierighm had stripped it of its plaster moldings and flowered rugs, and he had painted even the plank floor with untempered white. He had left intact only the iron candelabrum suspended from the far wall. The K'shai stood before it, his face shadowed, his back protected, his sword lightly held but readied. He was a professional.

The sword rose to meet mine in salute. We both began to move in a careful arc, neither presenting to the other more access than required. Our swords met first with slow, deliberate grace. They met again and rang clearly, for they were true, hammered steel, and they were deadly. I moved to meet the K'shai's swift lunge. I parried and attacked. The K'shai circled and feinted. I countered.

We proceeded carefully through the first form. It was a practiced pattern and a relatively simple one, but absolute precision of execution was mandatory for acceptance. The next form followed; the motions grew more complex. With the sixth form, the steps began to quicken into a flickering of motion. The tenth form incorporated the element of unexpectedness. The subtleties and surprises of the twelfth form generally killed those candidates who lacked such concentration as could defeat a Rendie. Only twelve forms were required for acceptance. We completed fifteen; no higher form was taught to one who was not K'shai.

A final ringing of swords: I began to feel again. "You are not unworthy," commented the K'shai, and he waited for me to speak the ritual plea. I could feel Conierighm's triumph—and his envy. He fancied himself superior to a K'shai in skills of arms: he would never admit that he feared the night.

I feared more than Conierighm ever would comprehend, but my fears were no worse beneath the stars than behind my bedroom walls. If I became K'shai, I would confound the wizard who trailed me. I could Protect Arvard, as I deemed necessary, even against Ixaxis. Perhaps I would be freed of dreams. I need not be assassin, I assured myself; I could not be assassin.

"My worth cannot yet be measured," I said, cursing my own weak words.

"I hear," the K'shai answered evenly. "Seek us before the year passes, and we shall hear you again."

The K'shai's expression became guarded. His sword aimed at a dark, detached shadow. "Face us, wizard," ordered the K'shai, and his voice coarsened, reft of stiff formulas. "You have no place here."

Conierighm entered the room slowly, cautiously inspecting the corner toward which the K'shai addressed himself. Ragon did not stand among us, and then his gray figure became clearly present. "I do not often meet K'shai," remarked Ragon mildly.

"We are not fond of wizards."

"You have offered your Choice to one who is promised to us."

The K'shai's attention broadened to encompass me. "Is this a true claim? Are you a sorcerer?"

Conierighm and I replied in unison, "No."

"Yes!" asserted Ragon, though he looked doubtful. "His sword burns more brightly than yours, K'shai." Ragon seemed bewildered by his own words. "It is an extension of his Power."

The sword I held began to glow dimly. It brightened, blue fire coiling vividly along its length. The nimbus appeared to radiate from my fingers. I raised the hand so as to better observe the illusion. The sword-light streamed from my blade, flickering in a sardonic mockery of the fifteenth form of the K'shai.

The fire began to touch the room. Across the walls, the twining tracery began to etch fiery runnels. Both Conierighm and the K'shai began to beat at the sparks, which appeared to relish the conflict: an army of malicious imps with a potent sting.

"You are a madman," said the K'shai to Ragon fiercely. "What do you hope to prove by your tricks?"

"This is not my Power," Ragon answered weakly, but only I believed him. "Would I wear student gray if I could control something like this?" The wizard shouted at me, "Sheathe the sword before you destroy us!"

I lowered my arm and concealed the blade to its hilt. The fire faded. The room cooled, as if a winter's draft had suddenly chilled it.

The K'shai spoke into the silence. "To what weapons have you trained your apprentice, Conierighm?"

I pushed past Conierighm. The swordmaster grabbed my arm and walked with me, whispering sharp words which I did not hear. I jerked away from Conierighm's clutching questions. Though it was fully night, I drew the bolt from the heavy door and flung myself from the house. I threw Conierighm's sword beneath the manicured shrubs.

The K'shai and the wizard faced each other in the empty white room. "Do you realize how much Power it takes to control fire in that manner?" whispered Ragon. "Not just to start it—any novice can do that—but to mold it, color it, pattern it, investing every spark with apparently independent will? Only once before have I seen anything like this done, save by Rendies, and that was an act of him who became Infortiare."

"Venkarel?" demanded the K'shai gruffly.

Ragon assented. "I was a student with him. He rarely used his Power openly in those days, but I saw him angered once."

"I saw him defeat Lord Hrgh dur Liin at the Challenge," commented the K'shai, as if he understood Ragon's allusion fully. If he witnessed the Challenge, thought Ragon, he probably does.

I followed the road away from the Keep and the Keep enclave. Above me, darker branches bowed against the dark sky. Nothing else moved. Tyntagel had withdrawn for the night behind its stout shutters and strong barriers of wood and stone. I let my long strides turn into a loping run.

Something dimly visible drifted beside me, but I disregarded it. It floated before me, and I circled to avoid it. It coalesced into a thing of weaving limbs and amorphous tendrils. "Come with me, Fire-child," it begged.

"Damn you!" I cried at it.

Another joined the first wraith, adding its mellifluous singing to the other's plea. "Son of the Taormin," whispered a third into my ear. I brushed it away angrily: a useless gesture against a thing of no substance.

"Come with us, Fire-child."

"You belong with us, Fire-child. You are the son of the Taormin, and one world cannot contain you."

"I am the son of Evram and Terrell!"

"You are the son of the Taormin. Come with us. You will have greatness among us, for we can teach you the way of your gift."

"I want nothing among you or from you. I want none of your tricks to help me. You tainted my sword with your spells, you damnable creatures of hell."

"You belong with us, Fire-child."

"Come with us, and we shall have all worlds and all energies. You are the Taormin's son. Come with us, and understand. Feed with us, and be strong."

"Come with us. Come with us."

"Away from me!" I roared. The wraiths shrieked and winked from sight. They were not usually so accommodating.

"Nuisances, nothing but nuisances." I wheeled to face the latest speaker. I saw a man with a sword, assorted knives, and leather armor. The man raised his fist in a haphazard greeting; the back of his hand had been branded with the bloodied-sword emblem of the K'shai. "Rendies bother you often?"

"Only at night," I responded flatly.

The K'shai croaked a chuckle. "The problem is you listen to them. Never listen to a Rendie. Never look at them. Never acknowledge them."

"Only fight them?"

"Only follow the patterns. If you follow the patterns, the Rendies do not exist."

"Who are you?"

The man considered. "Call me Fog."

"You are K'shai."

"I am your instructor."

"As what?"

"K'shai." Fog squinted at me through the darkness. "You are the one who wanted to be K'shai?"

K'shai did not read minds; that was a wizard's trick. One K'shai tested and offered. Another claimed. Was that their method? I had already declined to give answer once.

"The assassination attempt was not directed at your foster brother."

"How did you know of the attack?" I snapped. Fool, I told myself, he knew because he was K'shai.

"I never use yadovitti myself—too unpredictable." Fog's voice thickened, but it became sharp again. "But Stone always was lazy about research. He did not expect you to recognize the yadovitii. A K'shai should never underestimate a target, especially when the target has been labeled dangerous. The attack was aimed at you, of course."

"At me?"

"A man of Tyntagel, a Master Jorame, was sent to Tulea to learn something about your foster brother. Master Jorame tried to market the knowledge he acquired to Lord Gorng dur Liin."

"Jorame is dead." Fog's smile was chill and informative. "What kind of knowledge?"

"That the Venkarel had a son, who lived in Tyntagel as the son of Evram and Terrell."

Arvard actually was Lord Venkarel's son. It was impossible. It did not matter. "Jorame did not specify which son?"

"There was some confusion," agreed Fog. "You are the target."

"If I believe you . . ."

"You do."

Yes, I believed him, though I had no sound reason to do so. "If I believe you," I repeated carefully, "then I cannot accept your offer of training. A target cannot become K'shai."

"If a target eliminates the assassin, then he is no longer a target. You did eliminate him?"

Did I? "I intended to Protect my brother."

"You will not help anyone by remaining here, performing menial chores for Lord Baerod's clerical staff. We should leave before dawn."

He gave me no true choice; he had maneuvered me too effectively to the brink of madness, that I might know the threat and resist it. I repeated my internal debate on the subject of K'shai, but I could have saved myself the effort. Either I accompanied Fog, or I acquiesced to the Rendies' way. "I must deliver a message."

"Delays can be costly."

"It will not take long."

Fog nodded. He matched my pace easily. "Fire," he said: slowly, as if tasting the word.

"What?"

"Fire: it is a good name. It will be your K'shai name."

I accorded him a sharp look of sudden suspicion. "I thought you said never to listen to Rendies."

"Rendies?" he asked, his scarred face becoming innocent and stupid. "What have Rendies to do with your name?"

"Nothing," I replied gruffly. "I think I might prefer another name."

"No. You get no choice of name. You need never use it." Fog shook his head. "It is a good name, though. I knew a K'shai named Spit. He had cause to hate the name. Always used it. Most do. Pride. It is not easy to earn your name." I stopped before my parents' home. "Nice," commented Fog.

"I shall need only a few minutes."

Fog sat against the fence, which creaked reluctantly at the weight. "Bring a better coat, if you have one. Too bad you threw away the sword. We shall have to find you another."

I exhaled through clenched teeth, but I only muttered, "Right," and entered my home for the last time.

I studied my sister's sleeping face by the light of the single candle I carried. Her face had been with me always: square, a little sad, only rarely pretty. I lifted a stray brown tendril from her forehead and laid it gently in place.

Ylsa stirred and gasped when she realized she was not alone. "What do you want?" she asked me roughly. She drew away from me and set her jaw in mulish distrust.

I smiled tightly. "I want two favors."

"In the middle of the night?"

"First, I want you to tell our parents that I have left. I am K'shai."

"K'shai!" I had shocked Ylsa into a moment of concern, but she recovered quickly. She did not yet believe me.

"Tell them yourself," she growled sleepily. "Father is likely still at work downstairs. He never sleeps much anymore."

"I know. But he might try to delay me."

"Write him a note."

"I prefer that you tell him."

"Why?"

Because a note was too impersonal, and I could not face the crushing disappointment and horror in my parents' eyes. "Because it fulfills the proper order of things," I said evenly. "You will rejoice to see me gone. I am offering you a chance to participate in gaining your wish."

Ylsa narrowed her eyes, probably suspecting some jest of Arvard's planning played at her expense. "What is the second favor?"

"I want you to memorize a message for Arvard. If he returns, you will repeat it to him—only to him—exactly as I tell it to you. You have always had a knack for reciting."

"If he returns?"

"He may not."

Ylsa twisted her dark braid contemplatively, then she raised her head sharply. "You really mean to leave? Without waiting to see Arvard yourself?"

"Yes."

Ylsa stared at me. Arvard and I had always been too close, excluding Ylsa and making her bitter against us, but she was my sister. Worry had snagged her. "You cannot leave in the middle of the night anyway. Why not go to sleep now? We can talk about this in the morning."

"I am K'shai, Ylsa." I am not sure why I wanted Ylsa to believe; perhaps I still resented old taunts. I forced Ylsa to see me as K'shai; Conierighm had taught me the tricks of attitude, and I had a few less tanglible resources as well.

"Tell me the message," said Ylsa slowly, and I knew that I had made her fear me, whose weakness she had always despised.

"That which we buried between us came for me. The sender will leave with me. A wizard named Rogan is similarly misinformed about the son of Evram and Terrell, but you must make your own decision about him and his kind. Be cautious, Arvard. Be well."

Chapter 5

L ike the namesake of my self-proclaimed K'shai instructor, I
faded from Tyntagel and into a K'shai's world of chill Rendies
and remorseless death. As I would tell Lyriel years later, none of
my K'shai indoctrination seemed to constitute reality. I walked too
close to the core of a vast design, and proximity made me blind.

The dawn in Tyntagel came cold and damp. Conierighm sat
alone in bitter, resentful despair; he had not slept, for he had failed
again to fulfill a pledge to the K'shai, and no one escaped K'shai revenge. Evram sat alone in his study, reproaching himself for failure. Ylsa stood at her window, feeling guilty for her sense of
freedom and of gladness; she wondered if it were too late for her to
become a person, released at last from the shadows of her exceptional brothers.

Terrell kissed the worn jacket that Evaric had laid across a
kitchen chair. She carried it to the attic room that Evaric had shared
with Arvard. She closed the door, gently touching the gouged wall.
She had never cured either boy of opening that door too energeti-
cally.

The wizard, Ragon, walked the empty roads of the early morning at a somber pace. He passed the Tyntagel outer wall by the
main gate; the guards nodded curtly at his letter of passage. Less
than a mile from the gate, a man broke fast beside the road.

"The journey to Ixaxis must be long and lonely," remarked the man. He was the K'shai who had tested Evaric's sword.

"You travel alone," returned Ragon.

"I am K'shai." The man raised his branded fist, then lowered his open hand. "I had a partner, but he died recently."

"I am a wizard," answered Ragon, "and accustomed to solitude." Ragon glanced at the K'shai, who shrugged indifferently. "But your company is welcome. Not," added Ragon, "on a paid basis, of course. A poor wizard can scarcely afford the services of a K'shai."

"I am called Summer," volunteered the K'shai gruffly.

"Ragon. Why Summer?"

"We do not explain."

"Sorry."

"You did not help the boy?" asked Summer after a moment.

"I did nothing," answered Ragon, willingly sharing his uneasiness.

"Was it the boy himself?"

"Someone thinks he has Power. Important people want him in Ixaxis."

"He cannot be K'shai then."

"He has refused to be Ixaxin."

They sat for some minutes in a mutually acceptable silence. "I wonder where he went," mused Summer.

"I cannot sense a trace of him."

"He is a dangerous swordsman."

"He may be dangerous in other ways as well."

"He could have become a superior K'shai."

I wonder, thought Ragon glumly, if Ixaxis will as easily accept the loss of its candidate.

Chapter 6

Fourth Month, Year 22 of Rending
Benthen Abbey, Serii

Rhianna entered the aged gate of Benthen Abbey and grew wistful at the sight of the orderly gardens in which she once had worked. The silent figures in brown robes and heavy cowls could have been the same as those she remembered. The gardens had not changed. The seedlings of spring emerged shyly from the soil, and Rhianna longed to go and whisper encouragement to them. She chastised a rabbit for coveting the new growth. The rabbit fled in terror; Rhianna had not meant to frighten him so deeply.

Twenty years had wrought too much of a transformation. Rhianna had become Infortiare, and those whom she had briefly known as fond friends perceived her now as the symbol of a discordant order. Rhianna had altered inwardly, while they had aged in body. She had joined a species apart. She had become Kaedric.

Rhianna curtailed a familiar cycle of painful memory, but her contentment had escaped her. Power disrupted peace. Benthen Abbey could not welcome a wizardess. Only for Medwyn had they admitted her. Abbot Medwyn was dying.

He was so frail! All the strength of life within her could not help him. His hair had lost all color. His cheeks were sunken, and his eyes were shadowed. He smiled when he saw Rhianna, and she smiled in return, but bright tears clouded her sight.

"How lovely you look, Rhianna," he told her, for the vows of silence did not bind the abbot.

"I am travel-worn and tousled."

"You did not journey all the way from Tulea just to see a feeble-witted old man?"

"Feeble-witted? I wish that certain Lords of Serii had wits as stout as yours."

"That could be a twisted compliment."

"You are quite right, dear Medwyn. Too many members of our nobility have no wits at all. Yours, however, are as sturdy as the stone of these walls."

"Unlike the rest of me."

"You abuse yourself with overwork," Rhianna accused him sternly, though she knew that he had been completely invalided for over two months.

"I do hate being coddled."

"It is justice, Medwyn, for all of the unpalatable cures you have inflicted on others."

His eyes twinkled almost as of old. "Did you come here to insult my cures?"

"Never. They are too successful. I simply wanted to see you. We have had so little time to visit in recent years."

"Your duties have kept you busy, Rhianna."

"Even the Infortiare deserves an occasional holiday with old friends."

Medwyn grew suddenly solemn, and the awful gray of his face seemed the more pernicious. "Old friends," he mused. "I have had the oddest notion, Rhianna," he said slowly, but his eyes held a trace of their old bright perception. "I have thought several times that Kaedric was here—not as memory or even spirit of the dead—but as a living man. I have felt that terrible force of him as keenly as the day he stood beside me in the rubble of Ven, and I have heard him speak." The weakness of Medwyn's smile bit deeply into Rhianna's heart. "Do I sound feeble-witted now?" he asked lightly, despite the effort speech cost him.

Rhianna shook her head jerkily, before she could bring herself to answer. "Never you, dear Medwyn. You always see more clearly than those of us who think in suspicious circles." She touched his hand gently, feeling the veins pulse erratically.

"Then tell me the truth now, Rhianna." Medwyn's hand returned her grip weakly.

I might conquer kings or change a world, thought Rhianna desperately, but I cannot keep a good and gentle man from the gate of
death. "Kaedric lives," she said simply, though she was not certain
that she spoke truthfully.

Some tautness left Medwyn's wrinkled face, and his hand relaxed. "I felt it rightly then."

Rhianna finished quietly, "His son lives, also."

Medwyn's eyes sought hers. He murmured, "No, that had not
occurred to me. I had not thought you would lie to me about that."

"I never wished to lie to you," insisted Rhianna emphatically,
but her fierceness faded quickly. "Not to you. Not to anyone. He is
my son also, whom I held only for the briefest of days. I sometimes
forget that he is mine as well as Kaedric's, because it is as Kaedric's
son that he is both endangered and dangerous."

"You are hardly insignificant in your own right, Rhianna."

"I am only Kaedric's echo, Medwyn." Guiltily, she set aside the
haze of her private tauntings. "Well enough, you have the truth
now: all my awful secrets "

"I could wish you had confessed it earlier. I am asea with questions, and I can barely whisper a one of them." He spoke through
a wheeze of labored breath. He shifted as if to rise.

Rhianna's concern sharpened, and she stilled him. "You ought
to be sleeping. I shall be here in the morning, and questions kept so
long will keep a little longer."

"Rhianna, dear child, I may not wake again."

"It has been many years since anyone called me 'child,' " she
told him with a laugh, but she considered him soberly. She knew
that he indeed would sleep but once more.

"Tell me, Rhianna, for yourself if not for me."

"My child has been raised as the son of other, safer parents. He
knows nothing of me or of his father, and the ignorance has allowed him a childhood I could never have provided him." Rhianna
tried to soften Medwyn's disquiet, but Power had no place in Benthen Abbey, and she had forgotten any other way.

"There is more to tell."

"He has shown no trace of Power."

"Is it possible that he has none?"

"Even a latent generally displays some trace by this age, and he
has been tested thoroughly." She did not consider her response a

falsehood; her own misgivings were built not of fact but of speculation and Kaedric's misleading truths.

"It is time you reclaimed him, Rhianna."

"I am rather a lot to inflict upon anyone without warning." And
I fear him and what he will think of me.

Medwyn barely managed to smile. "The child of such parents
should be strong enough for the shock." He hesitated. "What of
Kaedric?"

"I have lost him. He chose me once, but he never learned to
trust."

"Did you, Rhianna?"

She did not answer, and then there was no need. Medwyn died
so gently. Between one breath and the next, his deeply good spirit
escaped her. "Dear Medwyn," she whispered. She kissed his parchment cheek. She no longer had reason to hide her tears, but they
could only well within her. She had hidden so much for so long.

Chapter 7

Tyntagel

How absurd it all seemed in retrospect, thought Rhianna sadly. Could I have ever been so innocent? What an overly educated idiot I was, and what a blindly obstinate fool was my liege-father, sanctimoniously playing censor to the laws of King and Ceallagh! Yet, if her father's coldness had not pressed her into rebellion, she might never have known Kaedric. Horlach would have claimed his prey. Or Kaedric would have won and lost humanity. In either outcome, a Sorcerer King would now command Serii.

Instead, Serii had acquired an incipient Sorcerer Queen pining for her ghostly liege and consort. She struggled harder daily to remember that greater Power did not convey greater wisdom. I am Rhianna still, she reminded herself, though I can mold minds and destinies according to my whim. I am no more fit to rule a world than was that silly girl who sought seclusion in the Dwaelin Wood.

She had even sundered Evram from his Terrell, never knowing it until her return to Tyntagel after so many years and so much change. In the twenty intervening years, she had reached lightly to her oaks; she had dared risk no nearer observation of her son than the dim sense garnered by the stolid trees. She did not forget that time moved more rapidly for mortal humans, but she did allow the remembrance to slip behind her fear of dislodging the precarious serenity of her son's existence. At her return after so long an absence, fear of her son supplanted even her fear for him.

The Keep had not changed greatly, but the village had spread a bit, and the familiar faces with which her memory still peopled it had gone. Rhianna did not know this place or these people. Which of these Tyntagel strangers would recall the face of their liege-lord's youngest daughter, whom they all had shunned as a suspected sorceress? It had always been easy to tell their eyes not to see, their ears not to hear, their minds not to know. It had ever been easy to walk unobserved in Tyntagel.

Rhianna knew the cottage where her son had been reared. It had belonged to Evram's family, most of whom save Evram and a brother in Hamley had died of a fever years before. The cottage looked quite as pristine as Rhianna recalled it, but it sagged a bit more along the eaves. She recognized with a start the small woman hanging laundry in the yard. This was Terrell, the woman whom her son knew as mother. Terrell looked old to Rhianna, but then Queen Joli had been a child when last Rhianna saw Mistress Terrell.

Terrell had only looked up at her for an instant, and Terrell's politely expectant expression became icy. "My lady," she acknowledged stiffly. "It has been a long time since you deigned to visit us."

"Too long, I know." She daunted Rhianna, this woman who had raised her son.

"You are not what I expected," said Terrell shortly. She sounded disappointed.

"What did you expect?" Rhianna asked.

Terrell shrugged. "You are not that impressive in person. I anticipated more of the Infortiare."

"You knew my appearance."

"Of course. You do not change." Terrell made the accusation a plural, despising all of wizardry.

"Not externally."

"Inside? I would not know of that. I only know you as a woman who cares little for her only son."

"Then you know nothing," retorted Rhianna sharply. "I am sorry," she apologized after a pause.

"You need not be. I have long wanted to meet you again. How old were you when we last met in flesh?"

"Twenty-three."

"So, we are the same age. Who would know it to see us? I certainly cannot say that my rival had no cause for victory."

"We have never been rivals."

"I raised your child. My husband loves you." Terrell smirked in self-deprecating fashion. "I know that you never encouraged his love. You did not need his love, only his devotion. Why are you here?"

"I came to see my son."

Terrell's expression tightened. "You come too late. He is gone. The wizard did not tell you?"

"What wizard?" demanded Rhianna, feeling unwanted currents snatch at her.

"Master Ragon: the man your Ixaxins sent for Evaric."

"I never told them of your letter," said Rhianna hollowly. "I gave no order to Ixaxis in Evaric's regard."

"Then you are even less omnipotent than I believed. Your own Guild has secrets from you."

Kaedric, thought Rhianna with a pang, are you manipulating me still? Terrell's words explained so much: why Rhianna had been unable to sense her son since autumn; why Master Ertivel had become so preoccupied of late with the accuracy of testing latents. Terrell's explanations explained nothing. "Evaric accompanied Master Ragon?"

"Evaric went with the K'shai. That is all I know of it." Terrell turned her back to the Infortiare, but she glared over her shoulder to add, "Evram knows nothing more of Evaric than I have told you, but I do not doubt he would be elated to see you."

Rhianna heard nothing beyond the word of abomination: K'shai. "Evaric has become a K'shai assassin?" she whispered, believing only because Terrell's despondency proclaimed the truth with vehemence.

Terrell paused at the gleaming door of her home, a small house which looked warm and innocent; the house hid its secrets well. "Arvard might know more," admitted Terrell stiffly, conceding the information.

"The other boy whom you fostered?"

"Evaric's brother," said Terrell sternly, and Rhianna knew herself chastised. "How can you know so little of us?"

"Where may I find Arvard?"

"He has also gone. I do not know where. But you are the omnipotent one."

Terrell made Rhianna feel insignificant, as she had always felt in
her father's wizard-hating domain. "Do not mock me, Mistress Terrell," said Rhianna coldly. The two women stared at one another: a
tired once-governess and a woman who could raze cities with a
wisp of thought. Terrell's gaze held steadiest.

"Venkarel lied to you, Rhianna."

Rhianna whirled to seek the source of the velvet voice, but only
Terrell's distant figure stood behind her. Rhianna willed herself to
calm. She searched for patterns of Power and found no trace of any
near her but her own. She resumed her course, her expression set
in cold anger.

"Venkarel has stolen your son from you." Rhianna did not pause
nor acknowledge the voice. *"Venkarel persuaded you to forsake your
child, so that Venkarel could mold the boy as tool. Venkarel used you, for
he needed the child that only a wizardess of major Power could provide for
him. It was Venkarel who manipulated Terrell; you sensed it in her, as in
her letter. You know that I speak truly; you recognize his twisted, ruthless
way. Venkarel has used you and discarded you. He will use and discard
your son. Protect your son, Rhianna. Retrieve and protect your son."*

Rhianna stopped, pressed her hands to her ears, and shouted in
her Power, *"Stop!"* The sourceless voice fell silent, but the echo of it
would not fade.

Chapter 8

First Month, Year 23 of Rending
Ixaxis and Tulea

Arvard cursed the retreating ferry beneath his frosted breath. The sea was as gray as the sky, and the two figures on the ferry faded into the general gloom. Even the island appeared dim on that day, and it had never seemed so distant to Arvard.

He had reduced all of his goals to the single determination of attaining Ixaxis. It had not been easy, working his way across the domains, paying for his passage from village to village by hard labor. He still had his small, secret hoard of silver bound close to his skin, but he did not want to spend that fund until all other options had been exhausted. As perhaps was now the case. But he had no more goals toward which to apply either money or effort. He had reached Ixaxis, and Ixaxis had refused him.

Arvard felt quite as much numb shock as hot anger. Despite all the failed Ixaxin tests, he had been so sure that the Ixaxin scholars—not the lesser wizards who traveled to the domains—would recognize him for what he was. When his feet first touched the chalky Ixaxin shore, he had known triumph. A wizard had led him by long stairs up the cliffs. Three other candidates, who had traveled with Arvard on the ferry, were taken by other wizards in other directions.

Arvard had gazed at Ixaxis' white stone buildings with proprietary pride. Gray-robed students had observed him, and he had known himself to be the greatest among them. Arvard's quiet escort had taken him to a simple office filled with ordinary furnishings and extraordinary history. The wizard had indicated one of the room's several chairs, and Arvard had accepted the position with gracious delight.

"Master Arvard," acknowledged a man who wore robes as white as his hair. Arvard had not heard the wizard enter, nor had he seen where the first wizard had gone. Arvard nodded; this silent coming and going was an effective means of conveying superiority. Arvard wondered how many of the carved panels concealed doors; Tyntagel Keep held similar secrets, or so Arvard had always heard.

"I am Arvard. You have read my letter."

The wizard pursed wrinkled lips. "You stated that your parents both were wizards, but you failed to name them."

Arvard spread both of his broad hands apologetically. "It would be indelicate of me to supply such names. Unfortunately, my parents were not wed. I would not make mention of them at all if they were not pertinent to my immediate situation."

"Indeed." The elderly scholar folded his hands and assumed a dignified stance directly before Arvard. Though the wizard, old as he must be to show his age so clearly, was obviously the physical inferior of the young man in the chair, the Ixaxin managed still to convey his own strength.

The mystique of Ixaxis, thought Arvard admiringly, is more than Ixaxin Power. I must cultivate that attitude of invincibility. "I have spent years studying such texts of wizardry as I could obtain," remarked Arvard, establishing a tone of equality with the wizard. Arvard did not mean to begin his Ixaxin career as a subordinate. "I look forward to exploring your library."

"You have no Power, Master Arvard."

Arvard's jaw tightened fractionally. "I explained in my letter to you. My Power was bound, but I have recently begun to feel it growing in me." Arvard had not told the Ixaxins about the Rendies, whose supplicating voices had vanished with the distance to Ixaxis. Let the Ixaxins wonder about the nature of his Power. He would summon Rendies for them when they were ready to understand.

"You have no Power. Master Laning will return you to the ferry." A young wizard emerged from somewhere indefinite and grasped Arvard's arm firmly.

"Please accompany me, Master Arvard."

"You have not even tested me!" said Arvard, abandoning his composure. An irresistible compulsion to depart enveloped him. These wizards dared to use Power against him. Arvard contemplated direly vengeful plots, but he was bitterly unable to resist the decision of Ixaxis. Arvard trailed the young wizard out of the fine, ancient building, back to the cliffs, the beach, and the ferry. The ferryman still waited patient and unsurprised. There was no sign of the other candidates. The ferryman and the young wizard, who had begun to look bored, returned Arvard alone to the mainland.

Arvard's fingers found a piece of Ixaxin chalk in his coat pocket. The passage up the cliff had dislodged many such fragments. Arvard threw it to the earth and ground it into powder with the heel of his boot. He turned his back on the sight of Ixaxis and began the hike to the main road.

There were many carts and carriages on the road, which connected the walled city of the Queen to the main harbor of Tulea. Arvard had bypassed the main city in his haste to reach Ixaxis; he had worked at the docks for over two months, waiting for Ixaxis to grant him an appointment, and impatience had made the time a torment. His urgency was gone with his sense of purpose. He paid a kesne to ride on a wagon loaded with candles. The driver made some desultory attempts at conversation, but Arvard did not encourage the man.

The chandler journeyed only to the inner harbor region. Arvard changed transport twice more to reach the great marketplace of Tulea. From there he walked to the gated enclave of Serii's lower nobility. Guards watched closely to keep him from proceeding farther. Arvard did not stay long near the center of Seriin wealth and authority. A little distance gave a clearer view of the castle and the Infortiare's Tower, if he felt the need for a reminder of what was owed to him and denied him.

Arvard took an inexpensive room and accepted a badly paying job cleaning carriages. He had no resources in Tulea. Return to Tyntagel? There was nothing for him there either, except Evaric, who had disbelieved. Arvard had wanted to return in triumph of which Evaric would be proud.

How could Ixaxis deny him? Arvard studied his distorted reflection in the carriage's brass siding. The Ixaxins were wrong, or they had deliberately lied to him. Either way, the obstacle could be overcome. Anger had made him briefly forget the inevitability of his destiny.

Arvard's resilience began to reassert itself. "Jerk," he told himself sternly, "did you expect it to be easy? You must work for what you want in this world." He laughed at his reflection and began to polish the brass of the carriage with renewed vigor and a satisfied whistle. He would succeed. He would find a way of approaching the Infortiare directly. He could contact that greedy serving woman, Mistress Giena. Arvard would return to Evaric as a man with whom kings reckoned. Arvard did miss Evaric sorely.

"That is a fine rig," remarked a well-dressed man entering the carriage house. "Is it for hire?"

Arvard felt expansive. "Master Fraileen would be the one to see in that regard, but I think you will find that your needs can be accommodated. Would you care to inspect the carriage?"

The man nodded and approached. He began to clamber into the carriage. His foot slipped on the step. Arvard extended his arm to save the man from falling. The shock of a sharp puncture made Arvard recoil from the man's weight. The man's face blurred as it bent over Arvard, and there was darkness.

"Has he not roused yet? If you gave him an excessive dose, Sandhig, your family will mourn."

"He is rousing, my lord."

Lord Gorng dur Liin waved aside the medic and the guardsmen. Lord Gorng had already studied Arvard closely, steeling himself to seek a resemblance to the devil he remembered too well: the devil who had once been his brother's insignificant friend, who had brought death to Gorng's brother and father, who had destroyed Veiga's mind, and whom Gorng would never forget and never forgive for the endless evils inflicted on magnificent, maimed Liin. This yellow-haired young man's cheeks were too bland with flesh, the nose was too wide and the mouth was too full; the body was muscular but too broad. Arvard's eyes fluttered, and Gorng saw the dark hazel of their color; the Lord of Liin began to feel secure again. This was not the Venkarel reborn; this was only a young man, and the might of Liin had nothing to fear.

Gorng waved to the Caruillan sorceress for whose service he

had paid extravagantly. "Test him, Limora," murmured Gorng. "Question him." Gorng would not repeat his siblings' mistake of underestimating the Venkarel; no hint of the Venkarel's taint could be dismissed without investigation and appropriate action.

The sorceress raised her arms dramatically. The fabric of her sleeves made a winglike web of russet shot with blue. The russet matched her hair, which flowed long. She drew her fingers softly along Arvard's face, but her touch left bruises in its wake. Arvard's body shuddered. The sorceress held his mind.

Questions, there were so many questions. Who are you? Why did you travel to Ixaxis? What do you know of a Tulean serving woman named Giena and a Tyntagellian messenger named Jorame? Did you always live in Tyntagel? Did your foster parents ever speak of the Infortiare?

"He does not know that the serving woman is dead, my lord. He does not know that Jorame killed her and sold her information to you. He believes that he is Lord Venkarel's son. He has no Power, but Power has touched him. The stain of it is deep and buried beneath confusion and misinformation. I shall injure him permanently if I probe to identify the source of the Power."

"Probe, Mistress Limora. His value lies only in the information he can supply."

"As you command, my lord." She spread her hands one atop the other and laid them both across Arvard's face. She pressed, and the skin of his face rippled from the force. She spoke distantly. "Infants. Two of them. One suckles at his mother's breast. The one who is apart reaches for warmth and touches the infant who is not his kin. All are parted, but Power does not forget."

Her voice became shrill. "Rendies are everywhere, stealing my soul. Nel, is that you? Run from them. Find the brightness, the warmth, the safety. Help me, please, Evaric, my little brother." The sorceress gathered her hands into the web of her robe. "That is the key, my lord: the brother, the other infant."

Gorng frowned. "Explain yourself."

"A bonding, built of the brother's latent Power, exists between them. The patterns of their lives are twisted together. This one," said Limora, pointing at Arvard, "belonged to the wet nurse, who was slain by Rending creatures." A faint furrow appeared on the sorceress' brow. "The other child evidently learned to transfer a large part of his own Power to his brother, as a means of concealing the Power from Ixaxis. Understandably, this one became confused. Until leaving Tyntagel, this one served as his brother's channel." Limora turned to the Lord of Liin. "The other is the Infortiare's son."

Gorng's muscles tightened; his breath seemed to become constricted. "So there was truth in the serving woman's story, albeit misdirected."

"Your investment has not been wasted," returned the sorceress without irony.

Gorng examined Arvard's strained, unconscious face. "Is he still usable?"

"Possibly, if I bind the broken pieces of his mind. He was stronger than I anticipated. Traces of Rendie madness gave him some immunity, as did his delusion of Power. Anyone who knew him, however, will soon recognize that he has been altered."

"Then he must not encounter anyone who knew him, until he can ensnare the devil's whelp and destroy him for me." Gorng pensively fingered the brocade of his vest. "Keep him unconscious for the moment. I must determine the proper influence to place upon him."

The little man asked irritably, "Where do you hide, Venkarel? What is your scheme?" Horlach pulled at a few strands of Power, searching but seeing nothing he did not know. "Concealment avails you nothing. In the end, you will need me. Only I know how to use him, as he must be used."

Chapter 9

**Third Month, Year 28 of Rending
Infortiare's Tower, Tulea**

"Kaedric, what have you wrought!" demanded Rhianna, and it was less a question than an accusation, for she knew that he twined his devious deceptions with relentless purpose. She ran from the Queen's chamber, startling even the Queen's expectations of her. Anger battled hope. After the years of ceaseless searching, Rhianna had ample cause for intense emotion, but she could not explain even to Queen Joli what she had so laboriously sought.

Rhianna sank into the chair which had been his. She whispered to the empty room, "My Kaedric, what have you done?" Seeking her son, she had found an instant of her husband's dreadful force. She had felt the terrible burning by which his Power destroyed. He had shrouded his Power immediately, and now there was again a cold void.

She needed Abbot Medwyn's counsel. She needed advice from the man who had tried to tame the boy, Kaedric, and who had tried to instill a soul in the man, Lord Venkarel. Rhianna missed Medwyn acutely.

She considered seeking Ineuil, but she did not want to see Yldana. Rhianna still envied her sister. She could perceive Yldana more clearly than of old and understood Yldana a little better, but the sisters had never learned to be friends. Rhianna envied her Ineuil, though Rhianna had refused him.

I could have loved Ineuil, thought Rhianna wanly, had I never met Kaedric. Knowing Kaedric, whose lesser weaknesses all were flayed from him in childhood, she could accept no gentler love. She loved Kaedric, as she could never love any other. When she hated him, the emotion seared her.

Rhianna rose and climbed the narrow stairs to the Tower's pinnacle. She seldom entered it anymore. It was the room she had shared with Kaedric for a single night, and it had been his room. It was the room in which Evaric had been born. Rhianna pressed the central stone below the embrasure and twisted the Power she had woven around it. The wall-stone softened into a milky echo of the stone around her neck, and Rhianna drew the light into her hand.

Rhianna had installed the vault herself, carefully expending insignificant Power over months of slow effort. She had not even told the Ixaxin elders of its creation. During the last twenty-five years, she had opened it only once.

The spindle's amber glow never dimmed. Rhianna touched the traces of gray ash on its filigree with tender distress. She had never cleaned the ash from its surface; she had forgotten.

She took the Taormin in her hands with delicate respect, and the old pulsing began immediately. She had never used it alone, though she knew the way of its intricate coils. Always, Kaedric had led her, when it had been Horlach's. When Kaedric took it, the need to use it had gone, and she had hidden it, abetting Kaedric's deception of the world: she had pretended that the Taormin's Power had been destroyed with Horlach and Kaedric himself.

Rhianna sat on the edge of the bed, closed her eyes, and turned inward. The dizzying webs blinded her for a moment, but she eluded their grasp and began to follow the remembered path. The way was smoother than she had recalled, and it was brighter. She could glimpse a few distant, dark corners of the old tangle, but Kaedric had permeated the central domain. The Taormin held more Power than it had ever known with the deathless Sorcerer King who had so long ordered it.

It tempted her. Its enticements had increased with its Power, or Rhianna had grown more vulnerable to the Taormin's peculiar allure. The energy fed her, until she felt almost euphoric with strength. She could have spread herself across its coils and become truly omnipotent.

"It only feels that way in the beginning," commented her husband

calmly. Rhianna focused on him hungrily, while he equably re-called to her the perilous nature of the tool she courted. *"It is the nature of infinity,"* he continued, *"to be always incomplete."*

"Like us?"

"At present."

"You left me," accused Rhianna, and her voice trembled.

"You found me," answered Kaedric with infuriating irony.

"After seven years of searching, and still I cannot reach you. I might be searching yet, had you not scattered your Power across the Alliance."

"I did generate a rather more spectacular display than I had intended. These Rending wruiths are rather a nuisance at times."

"You rattled every sorcerer in Serii."

"I have grown careless."

"Kaedric, why have you raised this wall between us?"

"Now it is you who forget the lessons of the novitiate: do not delve into another wizard's secrets."

"Only you consider secrets so essential."

"You imperil yourself, my dearest." He moved away from her, but Rhianna clung to his Power's pattern.

"You cannot elude me again so easily, my beloved."

"Do not press me, Rhianna."

"Then make me understand."

He denied her firmly, and when she tried to reach him, he threw at her a tangle of the Taormin's web. Such twisting skeins of energy could kill or capture for eternity, but Rhianna took the strands and kept her own pattern. She followed him, though it was a treacherous path, and she did not know why he led her upon it. He could not conceal himself within the whole, for she knew his patterns too well; they were a part of herself.

He wove Rhianna deeply in the Taormin, and all of it spoke of Kaedric. No great knots of Horlach's making existed here, save one. It was a dim but intricate snarl. Intent on Kaedric, Rhianna did not study it until a span of it struck her, and she knew it.

Had Kaedric led her to this choice? He must have recognized, as she did, the image of a major Power bound against itself. He surely knew that she could follow only one pattern: his or the other's.

Rhianna's hesitation sufficed for Kaedric to elude her. Feeling betrayed, she traced the bound pattern deftly, but it extended into a thickened mass of ancient chaos. Was this Horlach's final jest?

The shackles conformed to an unfamiliar design, but it was a potent one.

She could not free Evaric of the devious webs, for they spun into the Taormin's deepest parts. It was a clever trap, even for Horlach. Rhianna could easily become ensnared herself; she retreated very cautiously.

When she again felt the Taormin as only a thing of filigree in her hands, she allowed herself to despair. She hid the tool of terrible Power in her simple vault, hating it. She hated Horlach, for he had maimed her son. Kaedric's secretive schemings angered her nearly as much.

She opened the window, the highest in Tulea, and let the wind from Tul's Mountain chill her. She could visualize Ceallagh's tomb in the pass between the peaks. Horlach had died there; perhaps her husband had died there, also. They had Rent the world between them.

Evaric lived, as Rhianna did. Though Horlach had wrought great mischief, Evaric remained her son. He was not yet a mad Immortal, despite Horlach's intentions and the elusive, other patterns which Rhianna could indefinably sense. Evram and Terrell had reared and loved her son. He was K'shai, but at least he functioned in the mortal world. Rhianna did not know her son, but she would find him. She knew his pattern now.

Chapter 10

Fifth Month, Year 29 of Rending

Ineuil did not age, mused Rhianna. More sorcerous blood stirred in him than he admitted. He remained much as she saw him first in Dwaelin Wood, though responsibilities had clenched their relentless teeth in his careless attitude. He had accepted the position as Adjutant solely because of a desperate time, but he had fulfilled the role well enough. He had appointed deputies to handle all the peacetime tasks he found so tedious. Extreme delegation of authority had afforded him a sense of freedom from work's confining nature, else he would not have so long retained the distinguished post. Nonetheless, his was a marginal acceptance; he was, after all, the ultimate military authority in Serii after the Queen, a position of undeniable responsibility.

Marriage had not greatly affected him. His relationship with Yldana could be termed at best tempestuous, but their marriage had produced four children, three of whom were most probably of Ineuil's siring. Governesses preserved Ineuil and Yldana from the throes of parenthood, allowing them to share a relationship more akin to that of occasional paramours than husband and wife. It appeared to suit them, though Rhianna detected on occasions an underlying discontent beneath the couple's insouciant sophistication.

Ineuil bowed to Rhianna with exaggerated courtesy before draping himself haphazardly over an armchair. "The Infortiare has summoned the Adjutant," he announced grandly "and he is here to serve her." He folded his arms. "What the devil is so important that you officially request my presence?"

Rhianna answered him quietly, "I have located my son.

Ineuil cocked his head. His green eyes gained a contemplative cast. "Where is he?"

"On a ship headed for Ardasia."

Ineuil shook his head. "The land of religious fanatics and barbarians. He could hardly have traveled farther from you if he tried. Or did he try?"

"He still does not know of me."

"Or of Kaedric?" Rhianna answered with silence. Ineuil said cynically, "I have no official jurisdiction in Ardasia, my dearest Rhianna, and your own influence in that country is at best insubstantial."

"Official methods have no place in my intentions, Ineuil. I shall not lose my son again." As I may have lost Kaedric, she thought with a stab of hurt, unless my most tenuous suspicions prove true. "I am going to Ardasia."

"It will be a lengthy journey."

"I am not so very indispensable at court these days." And there may be vital need for me beside my son, if I have analyzed correctly.

"Does Her Majesty know?"

"She will agree."

Ineuil grimaced, frowned, and darted at Rhianna, "Why is he bound for Ardasia? If you tell me that he has become a pilgrim, I shall know that he is not Kaedric's offspring."

"K'shai often journey to Ardasia. That country employs many Protectors."

"And many assassins. I shall never accustom myself to the concept of an Immortal K'shai."

"I should not like to be entirely alone in Ardasia," continued Rhianna, studiously avoiding further comment about the abhorred K'shai. "The marriage of Princess Lilyan to Prince Stal would provide you with a reasonable cause for the journey."

"And you?

"I shall travel in my own way."

"Yldana will still suspect indiscretion." Ineuil remarked dryly. "But I have been respectable far too long. Do you realize, my lovely Infortiare, that we have not traveled together since the Venture?"

"I have rarely left Tulea, save for visits to Ixaxis, in the past three decades." She sounded wistful. "Between duty and bondage first to Tyntagel and then to Ixaxis, I have traveled little."

"You did not particularly savor your journeying, as I recall."

"It was the freest time I have ever known."

"Following Kaedric?" scoffed Ineuil. "He owned you from the moment you joined the Venture."

"He owned me before that," admitted Rhianna wanly. The imprisonment had been of her own choice. She did not try to explain to Ineuil; she wished that she had told Kaedric.

"You have some plan beyond merely sailing to Ardasia?" demanded Ineuil, suddenly cheerful. "It is a sizable continent, I believe."

"It is largely uninhabitable, however."

"So are Serii's northern reaches, but I should not like to search their entirety."

"You are not the one who will be searching."

"And you are less constrained than most by mortal probabilities?"

"Knowledge is itself a potent weapon against chance."

"Quoting Kaedric again," he remarked idly. Rhianna frowned slightly, but the accusation was true. "Ah, well," Ineuil continued briskly, "at least you are planning with your brain and not your despair."

"Concentrate on your own rusty skills, Lord Arineuil," returned Rhianna tartly.

"Is that the command of a Venture Leader?"

"I fear the Rending creatures have rendered Ventures nearly obsolete. The K'shai claim to be the only mortals who master the night."

"Do you think the K'shai might try to recruit me if they knew I had survived Rendies?" asked Ineuil impishly.

Rhianna shook her head at him sternly, but she was subtly pleased: the prospect of adventure had ensnared him. She had not wanted to use other persuasion. "It will require considerable effort to make of you a credible pilgrim."

"You are not a likely candidate yourself, my dear Infortiare."

Rhianna took a dark shawl from the chair and pulled it close about her face. She cast her gaze to the floor and let her posture soften into something humble and timid. "Have you never met such a pilgrim? Who would know me from one?"

Ineuil studied her critically. "Possible, I suppose, but do you intend to prate of the holy Shrine and the end of our evil world? I might manage it," he mused, "but I think you are too sincerely religious to vilify your faith."

"I shall be a reticent pilgrim."

"A nonexistent breed!"

"No longer," retorted Rhianna firmly. Ineuil merely smirked.

Chapter 11

Tenth Month, Year 29 of Rending
Serii and Ardasia

Rhianna dressed in somber gray and black robes of sturdy, common cotton, as befit a pilgrim woman of limited means. She had packed her satchel carefully, ensuring that nothing in it betokened too much of wealth or proud origin. She studied her reflection critically, adjusting her demeanor and her bearing until the image became a stranger: someone helpless, someone mortal. By Power she could alter the visions others gleaned of her, but her act demanded that she fix in her mind a solid personality that she could wear like a reliable cloak.

"If I am wrong," she whispered to the image in her mirror. She closed her eyes, unwilling to complete the thought. If she erred, she betrayed her love, the son she did not know, and the world she feared to know too well. She waited for the silent voice, both frightened and relieved that it did not come. "Your chosen path is not an easy one to follow, my Kaedric."

She checked her desk for the hundredth time. She had left complete instructions for every conceivable crisis, and Master Amardi was well qualified to attend the more ordinary matters of Power. Queen Joli had assured her (with mischievous persistence) that Serii could survive a few months without its Infortiare. Ineuil had taken ship to Ardasia over a month ago. There remained no more justification for delay. There were no more excuses.

"Let it be the right answer," she prayed. She took her satchel in one hand and clasped an amber spindle in the other. Had anyone been present to observe the Infortiare in her Tower, a brief rippling glow might have been seen where she had stood and then vanished.

Idle blue-green swells lapped at the ship and docks, the water's noise unheard above the human din. Fruits and fish of kinds not seen beyond Ardasia's rich coast spread bright colors, making mosaics of the open-air shops beneath the breeze-blown sky. Clay brick dwellings, adorned with bits of colored glass and anarchic images, lined the sandy streets. Sultry heat discouraged most daily traffic from any roof more substantial than a square of colored canvas, but the night demanded walls even in Ardas.

Men and women jostled and cheated one another with equable good humor. Only the very youngest children decked the open schools, squares of land distinguished by rough benches and the gathering of youth; the marketplace taught the subjects of greatest interest to Ardasians, who generally cared more for a clever bargain than for the easy life purportedly promised by formal education. Even the Ardasian clothing shouted strangeness to the foreigners spilling from the ships, for there were men uncovered above the waist, and there were women with arms and ankles bare.

Rhianna tasted the strangely rich, hot moisture of Ardasian summer. The trees feel me, she mused, though they have not met my like before. The newness held a thrill of unanticipated clarity, but it told her the full strangeness of this place. Those who were natives knew no Power here, neither as sincere memory nor as buried truth. No seeds of Power lingered in the Ardasians who were pure of lineage. Rhianna understood now the frustration of those Ixaxins whom she had stationed here. How eerie was the feeling of this matter-minded country! Wella, she thought determinedly, it is time Ardasia learned to face the world.

II.

Let (X,T) be a topological space.
Let p be an element of the set X.
Let S be a subset of X.
If each open set containing p intersects S in at least one point distinct from p, then p is a *limit point* of S with respect to the topological space (X,T).

LYRIEL

Chapter 1

Tenth Month, Year 29 of Rending
Ardas, Ardasia

Rubi's Troupe made no claims to any particular prosperity; they roved and performed throughout the three seasons, and they struggled to survive each summer in the seaport city of Ardas, when Ardasia's summer heat made inland travel impractical. Traveling companies such as Rubi's Troupe had been common during Rubi's youth; the cost of travel had grown high since the Rending. Only the K'shai would guarantee traveling Protection with any certainty, and their monopoly enabled the K'shai to command outrageous prices. Very few wanderers owned Rubi's will to persevere. Very few K'shai could be coaxed as easily as Key into an attitude akin to loyalty.

Worry furrowed Rubi's brow; she shook her head with aggravation at her own concern. "Denz!" Rubi gestured wildly at a bit of dropped scenery. Denz retrieved it with a grumble. "Denz!" she called again. This time she waved at him to collar the two boys who were trying for a glimpse at Alisa: Beauteous Alisa, the posters proclaimed her. Exasperating Alisa, amended Rubi to herself: pretending that Rubi's requests conflicted with Alisa's lofty standards, when it was only laziness that prevented Alisa from complying. Troupe of thieves, Alisa said, flinging names like a blasted pilgrim. If anyone else could be paid as erratically to draw customers so well, the Alisa would learn a lesson or two in respect. It really was too bad that Lyriel had displayed so little inclination to perform regularly since Silf left.

"We need more money for the jerked beef, Rubi," said Taf, a spare man near Rubi's age, who had inspired Rubi to create the Troupe all those years ago. Once, Rubi had hoped that Taf would love her for providing him a focus for his talents. Rubi had hoped to pry Taf from his precious Silf.

Well, thought Rubi ruefully, Silf had gone. After years of jealousy and contention, Rubi had seen her rival vanquished, and nothing had changed. The old Silf, the dancer who had drawn more adulation than Alisa, the Silf whom a reckless and defiantly optimistic young conjuror named Taf had loved sincerely, still held the tired Taf who now remained. If Taf felt nothing for the coldly righteous Silf, shipbuilder's wife in Diarmon, the fact held no consolation for Rubi.

Taf loves only the past, thought Rubi sourly. He loves the Silf who was warm and free and forgiving. He pines for the naive preRending Ardasia that did not weigh a conjuror against bearers of Power and the creatures of the night. He rues the Taf who expected good from the world. Taf has the past, and I have the Troupe, and neither of us remembers how to care deeply for anything.

"I thought you found a deal," Rubi muttered to him, as she ransacked her purse.

"A pilgrim company interrupted the bargaining. They claimed the lot was stolen property." Taf shrugged.

"You let a few pilgrims best you? Taf, you are growing soft. Why do I pay you?"

"You do not pay me, Rubi dear. Haggling in the marketplace is purely a gesture of my good heart, and pilgrims make it no great pleasure. This latest Shrine Keeper of theirs has bought every supply and service in Ardas."

"This whole city is pilgrim-mad. Any luck replacing Kaya?"

"Let the Alisa do the stitching," retorted Taf. "She does little enough else."

"There must be an unemployed seamstress somewhere in Ardas."

"Not one who is willing to travel with a barely solvent troupe of players. They can earn more from the temples, stitching pilgrim robes and Shrine cloths, and it costs them a fraction of the effort."

"If the task were easy, I would not need your skills to accomplish it." Rubi let her hand rub tentatively against Taf's narrow shoulders. Taf grunted, and Rubi allowed her hand to fall to her side. "If you cannot find a seamstress for us," snapped Rubi, "how shall I expect you to find us new K'shai?"

"Rubi dear," said Taf with his usual gloom, "am I arguing with you?"

"So." Rubi wished she could forget: about Silf, about Taf, about Key's death and the urgent need to replace the dead K'shai. "So either find us a seamstress or persuade your daughter to add another duty to her list." Rubi stabbed her finger toward the darkly graceful young woman who so hauntingly resembled Silf.

Taf snorted. "You have seen Lyriel's stitchery."

"She can benefit from the practice," retorted Rubi sharply, but she felt a bit of guilt for the jab at Lyriel. The daughter did not merit the legacy of Silf's effect on Rubi. Rubi recalled Taf and Lyriel on the day of Silf's departure, father and daughter turning pain to fury: each had blamed the other for the loss they shared, and neither had ever relented enough to apologize. They rarely acknowledged their kinship now, and they argued almost every time they talked. Still, the bond was there, unspoken; neither would desert the other. Like Taf and me, thought Rubi, dependent upon one another but too proud or too embarrassed to allow ourselves the solace of mutually acknowledged weaknesses.

"A seamstress," grumbled Taf to himself. "Why do we need a seamstress, Rubi dear, when we have no K'shai?" Taf had not asked the question of Rubi; she could not confront the prospect of the Troupe's ending. She preferred to pretend that no problem existed. Taf's own gloomy expectations would only anger her.

"Do you think, Rubi dear, that I mind less than you the thought of disbanding your precious Troupe?" What did Rubi think he would do without the Troupe? Settle in Diarmon with Silf and her jealous shipbuilder? A fine place that would be for an embittered conjuror, whose peculiarly Ardasian art had been essentially obsolete for a quarter of a century. "Ask Lyriel the likelihood of my choosing such a course," snapped Taf. Lyriel had never spared him the fire of her opinions on his "abandonment" of Silf.

"Our daughter has a temper in her," mused Taf absently, as if Silf were returned to hear him. "She scolds me more than ever you did, Silf girl. She thinks she must take your place in protecting me from myself. Well, she is young—as young as we ever allowed her to be.

"You had reason enough to leave me, Silf girl. I could never blame you for wanting to be free of me. But how could you leave Lyriel? You knew she could not stay with you in Diarmon; you knew she would feel obliged to come with me, to save me (as she thinks) from too much self-destruction. Silf girl, you consigned your daughter to all the things you hate. You consigned her to Rubi, who makes a slave of her. You consigned her to my thieving ways. Lyriel deserves better. She has always deserved better than you and I could give her." Taf frowned at himself for straying too near to emotions he had interred the day Silf left. "Past is past and best forgotten," he muttered.

Taf espied his goal and relaxed his scowl. The temple's tiny garden constituted one of the few shaded, uncrowded retreats in Ardas. Since the pilgrims seldom used it, Taf had claimed it as a refuge of his own. He squeezed through the iron fence surrounding it. (He would never have considered entering by the gate.) The garden held a prior occupant: a pilgrim woman too lost in some private and desolate sorrow to notice Taf. She occupied the half-rotted bench beneath the bao tree. She sat motionless, her satchel tucked neatly beside her.

Taf's scowl returned, but the delicious coolness of the shade enticed him to remain. The woman gazed into the leaves above her, as if to find within them some long-departed, secretive happiness. Something in her unspoken pain appealed to a deep empathy buried beneath any normal awareness Taf might have acknowledged.

A history for her seemed to rush at him. Raised in some tight little village, the sort where everyone knew every shadow and scandal of every other life, she had spent her pitifully hoarded funds on the sea voyage to Ardas, not realizing that the Shrine lay many miles from the coast. Like so many naive pilgrims, she had nothing left to her once a few Ardasian merchants had cheated her, and she had not come within leagues of her goal. She would be lucky to earn enough for her return voyage. Even if she knew enough to plead for temple charity, she might wait months before the temple bureaucracy could attend her case.

Taf scratched his head and indulged in a momentary hesitation.

He felt reluctant to believe his fabricated history, but the woman did have the meager look of poverty. A woman in such miserable circumstances might be grateful for any employment of honest kind, and she would not know what wages to expect. If she stitched even as badly as Lyriel, she would satisfy Rubi. Taf absorbed her despairing posture and felt a qualm, but he rarely allowed conscience to interfere with business.

Taf circled the bao tree, approached and sat near the woman as if unaware of her existence. He heaved an overtly emphatic sigh; he had long ago concluded that few of these pilgrims, stupid innocents that they were, could be expected to discern a subtle approach. He muttered quite distinctly, "Good copper to pay, and none to earn it." Taf's second sigh contained a substantial dose of distress.

After a long and silent minute, Taf ventured to raise his head and look about him dolefully. The woman was gazing at him without much expression. Dull-witted, thought Taf regretfully, but what does Rubi expect with the little she is willing to expend? Rubi ought to be glad if I find a seamstress at all, even a dim one. "Hello," said Taf with enough awkwardness to convey embarrassment. "I had not realized anyone else was here. I thought I knew everyone who used this garden. Are you newly come to Ardas?"

Taf had barely hoped for a response. When the woman spoke, her voice surprised him: Though her manner reeked of timidity, something almost compelling underlay her cautious whisper. "I arrived two days ago."

The woman sounded younger than Taf had expected. All that ridiculous yardage concealed her age effectively. "Bound for the Shrine, are you?"

The woman did not smile, but the sorrow about her retreated a pace behind interest. "It is a costly journey," she remarked. She fixed on Taf a gaze of certain intensity. She had remarkable eyes. She might be rather beautiful, observed Taf impersonally, if she donned something less grim than pilgrim drab.

Taf groaned with sympathy. "Between the K'shai and the supply merchants' extortion, even those of us who have been making the journey for years find it more difficult to manage every season."

Perhaps the woman reached some obscure judgment, for she became as innocently eager as Taf could wish. "You have been to the

Shrine?" she demanded with such persuasive awe that Taf nearly forgot his own cynical view of pseudo-religious folderol. "If you knew how I have dreamed of attaining it! I have traveled so far, only to be defeated at the last. When I bought pilgrimage, I never imagined that my purchase would leave me so far from my goal."

To his amazement, Taf found himself almost bemused by the mousy pilgrim woman in her black and somber draperies. The deep sorrow he had imagined in her had been vanquished or veiled, if it had existed at all. Taf knew a moment's suspicion, but the woman was a foreigner and a pilgrim as well. No pilgrim could decently feign a feeling or disguise it. No foreigner ever matched an Ardasian in the business of deception. "Indeed, I have seen the Shrine. I am employed by a traveling troupe of players, and our itinerary takes us to D'hai each year."

"Each year?" breathed the woman. "How wondrous for you!"

Taf fixed his gaze on the woman's gray eyes as an artful ploy, but he found himself so fascinated by the storm-dark depths that he garbled his intended lines, demanding simply, "Do you sew?"

The woman blushed lightly, though Taf imagined for a moment that the light itself grew rose-colored around her. "My needlecraft is no less fair than another woman's."

"Our troupe needs a seamstress. You could travel to D'hai with us. Our troupe is known, and I with it, if you would verify my sincerity of intention." Not that any Ardasian who knows us would give the truth to a pilgrim, thought Taf, but the claim of sincerity generally gives a good impression.

Have I spoken too quickly and befuddled her? wondered Taf, but the woman replied, "I shall bring you answer, Master Taf, this evening."

She gathered her satchel, rose, and disappeared into the arbor which led to the temple, leaving Taf to stare agape. "What an odd bird she is," he muttered. He felt outwitted, for his mark had escaped him, and he had not even anticipated the attempt. He disregarded her final promise; it was just the sort of equivocation he expected of a pilgrim, who never would give a forthright refusal if a lie would serve. No Ardasian would use a lie to so little purpose.

Taf grumbled to himself as he left the garden, the pleasures of which had for the moment been destroyed for him. "It was not even a good lie," he grunted under his breath, "for she never let me tell her where to find me again. She never asked the wages!" The final consideration seemed almost an affront to Taf's basic tenets. He laid the crime against the whole of foreign interlopers, none of whom had ever mastered the rudiments of decent business dealings. Having once again justified to himself his loathing for humanity, especially in its non-Ardasian form, Taf began to whistle a soundless tune of contentment, as he jostled through the heated crowd and returned to Rubi's Troupe.

Chapter 2

Same day, a few hours earlier

Occasionally, in lonely moods, I weigh the future against the past, and I wonder that a jealous scheme against my mother should have come to shape my life. I remember the Troupe as Rubi first formed it. We numbered ten: Rubi, Taf, Silf and I, Kays and Vila, Diafe, Lu, Bin, and Arious. Taf and Silf had partnered with Rubi (and Broh, who left us) for three years or more, when Rubi discovered the six unemployed performers who would join us to become the first Rubi's Troupe.

Pitiful survivors of a once-prosperous company, the six had been rendered nearly witless by the calamity of a Rendie attack. Rubi extolled the potential of the Rendie-broken company to Taf and Silf, as I sat quietly forgotten in the corner, celebrating my fifth birthday with sand-cakes and Sanston, my sole childhood friend. I recall the evening clearly, for Diafe arrived to introduce me to the terrible Rendie madness that had warped him and his companions. The morbid fears of those half-mad players exacerbated all the terrors that a child's imagination could produce.

From the first, the players talked volubly to me, whom they regarded with the intermittently tolerant amusement of childless adults. They assumed that I did not understand, because I answered their more dire tales with the solemn promise that Sanston could protect them if they asked. I believed in Sanston utterly; perhaps I did imagine him, but I can visualize him still, though he left me years ago and relinquished my Protection to the K'shai.

All things change: Key never yielded to me a more sensible nugget from the K'shai philosophy. I would have had the words scribed above his grave, but K'shai do not mark their tombs. I found it tragically ironic that a man who had defeated scores of Rendies should die of the bite of a tiny, timid wind-snake. As Key had said, all things change; death comprised simply another transition. Nonetheless, I missed him. For a K'shai, Key had been an exceptionally decent man.

Rate abandoned us, of course, to seek a new K'shai partner and a more lucrative contract. The new Shrine Keeper had established a policy of so overpaying for services that we Ardasians could scarcely compete. Rate had never shared Key's unlikely sense of loyalty to the Troupe.

I paused to kick a stone. The back streets of early dawn stood empty, else my stone would have struck an argument. I almost regretted the lack of a human target. My nervous temper wanted an outlet badly, and Taf had been too preoccupied for weeks to listen to me rant; I never dared speak freely to anyone else in the Troupe, for Rubi expected me to appease the Troupe members, not befriend them.

I twisted through the alleys to the warehouse that we leased. I could hear the dim rattle of vendors staking their posts in the market. I considered detouring through their midst for distraction, but Rubi's Troupe awaited too many uncertain exchanges; we had placed large orders to supply the Troupe, and the time of payment and receipt approached quickly. Taf would devise a way of reneging, if he could not resolve our lack of K'shai, but we would retain few friends among the merchants. Too many of our suppliers already suspected our intentions.

I stopped at sight of a long and unfamiliar shadow. The hour was too early for the debt collectors to ply their humorless work, and Taf had not committed any recent thefts, so far as I knew. Nonetheless, I poised my hand on the knife at my waist, and I waited in uneasy silence.

The shadow's source turned the corner suddenly; a brightly polished sword extended from his hand as easily as if the blade comprised a natural appendage. The young man scanned me in an instant, and his caution melted into a smile so beguiling that I scarcely noticed his arsenal of weapons or the foreign cut of his leather coat. I did manage to recognize that his skin was too fair and fine, his hair too uniformly dark to have survived life-long beneath Ardasian sun.

I leaned against the wall in the pose that Rubi calls sultry. I volunteered, "If you are seeking the marketplace, go through that alley, right twice and left." Foreigners often strayed among the streets of Ardas, and I seldom wasted courtesy on them; few of them would acknowledge an Ardasian woman for any moral purpose. Very few of them proffered smiles of overwhelming warmth and vividness.

"I appreciate the directions," he said in a clear voice, richly colored with the elegance of a Seriin accent. He studied me with a softly curious gaze, while I concluded that I had never seen a more handsome man. "I am actually seeking a woman rather than a marketplace." I raised my brows at him, and he flushed. "A Mistress Rubi," he explained hastily. "Do you by any chance know which warehouse she leases?"

"Indeed, I know it." Yielding unnecessary information to a stranger can bring trouble, but the potential value to the Troupe of such a man merited the risk. "I am Lyriel; I work for her. Are you an actor?"

"No," he laughed with a peculiar acerbity. He raised his left arm, bent and taut, the hand clenched, the brand at my eye level. "I am K'shai," he murmured with some embarrassment, presumably augmented by my dumbfounded stare; I had never before failed to recognize a K'shai. "I am truly K'shai," he assured me, as if I could doubt him; no sane man would forge a K'shai's bloodied sword from wrist to fingertip.

"Of course," I answered hollowly. I might mourn Key, who had Protected me for most of my life, but I categorized all other K'shai as somewhat less estimable than the fungus which rotted the wall beside me.

"I am older than I appear." He sounded apologetic, which was absurd. I wondered wildly if he also apologized to those whom he slaughtered in his vile profession.

I straightened, and I fingered my knife. I responded coldly, "If you want employment, our terms are these: Protection for the duration of our season, fall through spring, at the rate of eleven silvers a week plus room, keep, and performance passes. The value of the total exceeds standard, and our schedule will allow you considerable free time during our city-stays."

"Actually," he remarked with more embarrassment, "the Guild's current rate for Protection is seventeen silvers a week, exclusive of other benefits. You will not hire K'shai for less, and you are not likely to hire others at all just now. The Shrine Keeper offers thirty silvers a week for pilgrim Protection."

"Then why are you not escorting pilgrims?" I snapped. I did not need to hear from him about the Shrine Keeper's offer.

His smile twisted ruefully. "I have reasons to avoid the Shrine Keeper's employ."

"If you plan to fulfill an assassin's contract while Protecting, look elsewhere for your customers."

"I have no contracts pending," he assured me. He exuded sincerity and the rare sort of strength that inspires implicit confidence. I remained wise enough to recognize the potential hazard of his charm and gain caution from it; however, I could not concoct any reasonable argument against him nor any good reason to seek one. This unlikely K'shai offered life itself, though I hoped he did not know the Troupe's desperation.

"You have a partner?" I asked him.

"His name is Fog."

"You have not yet told me your name. We shall require references."

"Captain Tarl of the *Sea Dancer* will supply whatever information you need. I use my birth name, Evaric."

His eyes resembled the shadows on the shifting ocean: dark and light and elusive. His smile might seem open and warm, but the eyes evaded me. I looked at the branded hand and again at the secretive eyes. "You do have a K'shai name?"

"Naturally," he replied with undaunted coolness. I continued to gaze at him expectantly, and he admitted with a grimace, "Fire. The name tends to convey wrong impressions when called loudly, and I prefer to avoid causing unnecessary panic."

"Reasonable," I conceded, still a little suspicious; no one has ever accused me of susceptibility to casual influence, however appealing. "I shall take you to Rubi," I told him rigidly.

"I did not mean to inconvenience you, Mistress Lyriel."

His Seriin courtesy disconcerted me. Taf had taught me to equate such gentle speech with either hypocrisy or foreign weakness, and I could not mold either characteristic to the form of an assassin. "It is not a favor, K'shai." I began to feel grateful, after all, that he was K'shai and displayed his iniquitous nature openly. "How many assassinations have you completed?" I asked him chattily. He regarded me very oddly, as well he might, and he did not answer, which was just as well. Had I received any response short of mass genocide, I might have forgiven him even for being K'shai.

Chapter 3

The grand procession of a royal wedding through the streets of Ardas made the crowded city all the more congested. The members of the procession enjoyed the protection of their guards and servants, but onlookers faced considerable risk. Ardas' usual noise and furor turned to chaos, and thieves emerged to ply their eager trade with near impunity. Other questionable professions derived equal advantage from the occasion.

Serii's Adjutant enjoyed a prominent position in the festivities, but at some point between the palace and the cathedral, those regal visitors who had ridden behind him observed that Lord Arineuil dur Ven had evidently shifted his position in the train. Since Lord Arineuil had already caused his Ardasian hosts enormous consternation by refusing to comply with set schedules and safe itineraries, his disappearance from the parade generated limited concern. Lord Arineuil had exasperated his hosts, and they considered him deserving of any misfortune he accrued by his disregard of prudent warnings.

"These wretched bumpkins have the most tiresome conceit," complained Ineuil from the garden bench of the Ardas villa he had let. "Inasmuch as I am Seriin, they assure me that I could not survive for an instant unescorted in their city. They speak for me, act for me, watch me like a jealous lover—I am quite sure that they would attempt to think for me, as well, if they could discover any means by which to manage it. What are you trying to do to that tree, Rhianna? It languishes hopelessly beyond aesthetic redemption even by you."

Rhianna withdrew her hand from the strange Ardasian tree that seemed to grow indiscriminately with no sensible design of trunk and branch. "I am trying, Ineuil, to understand it. The Ardasian people are not the country's only living things to feel an insular disdain for other sorts."

"How anyone could take pride in anything in this beastly climate, I shall never comprehend."

Rhianna gazed at the vivid aqua ocean; it met the cliff below her in streaks of snowy foam. "The weather will grow milder soon."

Ineuil folded his arms to sulk, but he abandoned the pose quickly and reached for the fan of plaited palm. He waved the fan in restless affectation. "Have you made any progress in your search?" he asked her idly. Rhianna did not answer. Ineuil snapped into stillness heavy as the humid air, "You have found him."

"I have found him."

"Where?"

"At an inn, one of those dreadful native places in the city's central district. A traveling company of players has employed him for Protection."

"Have you spoken to him?"

"Not yet. I have only glimpsed him once, as he entered the inn with the young woman who hired him. I have sensed him, though. That barrier has gone. I wonder why . . ." She fell silent again, gazing inward. When she continued, her voice retained a whisper's hush. "He is haunted."

"By you?" asked Ineuil with a cynic's whimsy.

"By me, by his own Power, by Rendies, by . . . too many things of dire kind. I carried him when I stood beside Kaedric at the Rending's broken gate, and Evaric was tangled like the Rending creatures in a place that is neither this world nor any other. By that dormant Power in him, he is as much a Rending creature as any chill wraith. Ineuil, he is a lethal promise waiting for its time. He frightens me."

Considerate of you to join the rest of us, thought Ineuil, now that regret can serve no purpose. "Do you mean to speak to him or not?" demanded Ineuil with some impatience.

Rhianna looked sharply at the lounging lord of Ven. "I shall observe him for a time. I shall accompany the troupe with which he travels. I shall not hold you here, Ineuil." She finished meekly, "If you wish to return to Serii now, I shall not stop you."

"My lovely, temperamental wizardess, I have no intention of sitting idly among my stuffy peers, while you gallivant across the world. I resigned myself long ago to an absolute dread of your infant prodigy, just as I accepted dread of his father as the normal course for my life. Some men like to shun the objects of their greatest fear; I prefer to watch those objects closely."

Rhianna inclined her head. A breeze caught at her hair. "The company that has hired Evaric is known as Rubi's Troupe. Their route is well established. You should have no trouble in pursuing them."

Lords, thought Ineuil, cursing his own credulity. She never doubted that I would remain. She has been manipulating me this past hour. Is she even conscious of the spell she weaves? "Kaedric's shadow," murmured Ineuil bitterly, quoting Rhianna's own description of herself. Rhianna closed her eyes but did not reply. "I begin to feel a considerable sympathy for these awful Ardasians after all."

Chapter 4

Rubi allowed me little leisure during the summer's final flurry; we had delayed too many tasks, until K'shai were found. Exhaustion claimed me. Of all the Troupe members, only Noryne offered to help me, and against my better judgment, I accepted. Fatigue would make me sharp, and Noryne was far too sensitive. She would make me feel guilty.

We sat together in the warehouse, sorting costumes and props. Noryne's red-gold hair had been braided tightly and pinned close to her head for rehearsal, making her look even younger than usual. She held one of the oldest gowns, shook it cautiously, and wrinkled her freckled nose at the resultant cloud of dust. "Have you ever seen a Rendie, Lyriel?"

I dropped a skirt into a pool of wrinkles. "Yes." I felt cold, though the heat made incense of our perfumes. "So have you. Do you not remember?" Few of us did remember the Rendies' visitations and the mesmerizing battle/dance of the K'shai. Key had told me once that my facility for recalling Rendies, augmented by my dancer's training, could make me a promising candidate for the K'shai. The intended compliment had appalled me, and I had not liked discussing my ability since then.

"I always remember," murmured Noryne, surprising me a little. Her eyes were wide and serious. "The memory frightens me even in daylight: I expect every swirl of smoke to become a wraith's breath seeking me. I can better understand a man who lives by killing men than a man who can face a Rendie unafraid. You know about so many things, Lyriel, more than anyone else I ever met. Are the K'shai human, do you think?"

"They are not lizards, Noryne, though they may be equally quick and unpredictable. Key died just as painfully as any other victim of wind-snake venom."

Noryne flushed, hurt by my careless acknowledgment of Key's death, and I felt guilty once again, though I had mourned Key more than any K'shai deserved. Noryne said softly, "They say a wizard can die, too, if he is stricken unaware. But wizards are not quite human, are they?"

"I would not know about wizards. I never met one."

"There is an Ixaxin school here in Ardas."

"Foreigners."

"Not always."

"Always," I answered impatiently. "Any Ardasian who traffics willingly with foreigners, whether they are wizards, pilgrims, or K'shai, has no right to claim his citizenship."

Noryne bowed her head meekly. "You are angry with me now. I am sorry I made you angry. I used always to anger my foster mother with my questions, and she used to tell me that Rendies would seek me for angering her."

"I am not angry," I insisted, but Noryne would not look at me. "Anyway," I continued, trying for conciliation, "you have K'shai to Protect you, whether you anger me or not."

"They are new K'shai, strange K'shai. Why did Key die?"

"It was his time. It was his privilege."

Noryne stared at me long and curiously. "Privilege of death," she mused, as if she had never thought before of death as gift. "Is it kinder than the gift of life?"

"That depends on the life and how it has been used."

"What of a life not yet given?"

I shrugged. "That depends largely on the giver."

Noryne inhaled deeply. "I carry a life in me, Lyriel," she whispered in a hurried breath, "I carry Zakari's child."

"Zakari is pledged to Alisa," I replied blankly, stunned not by Zakari's infidelity but by Noryne's concession to it.

"Alisa hurts him so much," said Noryne, pleading for the forgiveness she could not give herself. She continued with such misery in her voice that I cringed, "I have not told him. I have not told Rubi either. Will she be angry?"

"Noryne," I said despairingly, wondering what I could possibly tell her that would not hurt her the more. "How can you even consider raising a child, when you can barely support yourself? Zakari will not help you, and Rubi is not a great believer in charity."

"She lets Solomai's children travel with us, and you were raised in the Troupe."

"Solomai's children are performers in their own rights, and Solomai is a wagoner with much more time to spare for them than you could give. Rubi tolerated me only for Taf's sake, and I was born into a simpler world: Ardasia did not yet understand the Venkarel's Rendies." I was saying too much but my tongue raced ahead of my more sensible thoughts. "You fear Rendies even in a darkened room, Noryne. How could you condemn your child to face the night with only a wagon's flimsy canvas for visible defense?" Noryne had begun to cry. I handed her a scrap of linen from the fabric supply. She rubbed it across her damp cheeks, achieving little good.

"Tell me what to do, Lyriel," she pleaded.

I rubbed my temples. "Let me think about it." Rubi would not be easily swayed, much as she preferred to leave matters of the Troupe's personnel to my judgment. "Rubi will explode." She would call me sentimental and pilgrim-hearted, and I would be forced to threaten, deceive, and cajole her.

Noryne smiled amid her tears. "You will calm her. She respects you, Lyriel, and she values you, as I value you. I never thought to have such a friend as you." I grimaced at her.

After Noryne departed, I spent a discouraging hour trying various solutions in my mind and abandoning all of them. The suggestion of a new burden on the Troupe could have been better timed. Key's death and the aggressive policies of the new Shrine Keeper had left us barely solvent.

I did not hear the K'shai enter. "Mistress Lyriel?" he called, emerging like a wraith from the dusky shadows of stacked crates and shrouded furnishings.

I jumped and spilled an open tin of beads across the floor. The beads clattered to a stop, leaving an awkward silence. I realized that I was staring at him, so I knelt to gather the worthless, tarnished beads. "Blast," I muttered, as one of the beads skittered away from me.

Evaric retrieved it, offering it to me courteously. "I apologize for startling you."

I snatched the bead from his hand. "You wanted something, K'shai?"

The openness in his expression vanished. His smile tightened and twisted. The transformation was unsettling, for it made him look like a truc K'shai: a man who would do murder with remorseless efficiency for anyone who could afford his price. "Mistress Rubi indicated that you maintain the lists of inventory and personnel," he said with strict formality. "I should like copies of each. Fog and I like to establish the specifics of our responsibilities, so as to eliminate possible misunderstandings."

I stood and studied him squarely; it was a mistake, for close inspection only made him look better and just as dangerous. "Do you write?" I demanded, determined not to yield unnecessary advantage. Few literate K'shai sought work from impoverished Ardasian troupes.

"I write, Mistress Lyriel," he assured me very solemnly. A trace of laughter sparked in his shimmery eyes for just an instant.

"Then the lists are yours, as soon as you write them. Personally, I have never seen much purpose in wasting paper on such fleeting facts, and I am trained to memorize." I explained deliberately, "Lines and such for the plays."

"Tell me," he said shortly, and he leaned against a cracked bureau as if anticipating a lengthy stay. He elaborated too carefully, "I shall, of course, require your signature—or whatever mark you use for legal documents."

I did not dignify his cynical witticism with a reply. I returned to my task of sorting costumes and began to recite, "As of today, Rubi's Troupe consists of thirteen players—sixteen if you count Solomai's children—eight wagoners, one cook, one master of property, Taf, Rubi, myself, and two K'shai. . . ."

I was forced to credit the K'shai yet again. He listened attentively. When he returned with the promised list, written in a strong, swift script, it was complete to the last packet of pins.

Evaric placed the document before me. I set it aside deliberately after a single glance. "I shall attend to it later, K'shai," I remarked without looking at him. I had progressed from the costumes to the scripts, and I meant to finish my task before dusk demanded my return to the inn. I wanted this K'shai to understand that I would not rush to do his bidding.

"Tomorrow will suffice," he asserted calmly, managing to sound only quietly polite.

I could not even dent his Seriin chivalry, which, perversely, discouraged me. I sat and glowered after he had gone. The Troupe had not promised a more troublesome season since Broh deserted Rubi. "If you had any sense," I told myself, "you would follow Broh's example."

Taf looked as glum as I felt when we met in the dying light of day. We entered the inn together and the innkeeper growled at us as he bolted the vestibule's inner door against the night. Taf helped himself to the tankards of ale, and I claimed a table in the corner farthest from Alisa and her following. Noryne was not in sight, nor was Rubi, and the rest of the Troupe sojourned elsewhere. Taf brought the ale; the innkeeper's boy brought us fruit and twice-cooked beef, and for a time we devoted ourselves to the meal.

"Luck with the seamstress?" I asked when we had finished all but the ale.

Taf grunted, which usually meant no. "Pilgrim," he snarled.

"Poor Taf," I murmured. "Can she sew decently?"

"Should I know? She could not fare worse with a needle than you."

"When should I have studied stitchery? During performances? While persuading Denz to work another season on half pay? While writing plays that we can perform between licenses? While bribing some Tanist's minion to ignore your latest thieving?"

"Trouble with Alisa?" asked Taf glumly.

"Not yet," I grumbled in return. Alisa and Zakari were playing draughts in seemingly good humor. Judging by Miria's giggles, Alisa appeared to be winning, likely with Zakari's cooperation. Alisa was distractedly twisting a long curl around her finger. She was pretty, and her dearth of any concept of financial sense let us keep her in the Troupe by guile, when she could have achieved much more success elsewhere; she was lazy and temperamental, and I disliked her heartily. "Have you talked to the K'shai yet?"

"I discussed our route with Fog. He seems a sensible man."

From Taf, sensibleness amounted to high praise. "What of the other one?"

Taf shrugged. "Foreign."

"So is Fog," I suggested wryly, but I understood the distinction: Taf approved of Fog; Taf disapproved of Evaric. Since Taf disapproves of nearly everyone, the latter comment signified very little.

Taf nodded toward the stair, and I turned my head to follow his glance. "Mistress Anni, the pilgrim," he explained.

Not very distinctive. Why is she staying here?"

"Coincidence."

"This is an odd place for a pilgrim to choose."

"Odd," grunted Taf, rolling his eyes.

I looked at Taf sharply. "Are you sure about her?"

"No."

The pilgrim woman was trying unsuccessfully to attract the attention of the innkeeper. "What does Rubi think of her?"

"You know Rubi: The Troupe is All."

I darted another glance. "Only a pilgrim would suffocate willingly in all those depressing draperies. What do you suspect of her?"

Taf's hands rippled, and he cradled a kesne in his palm. The engraved wreath of the Alliance gleamed brightly on it. Taf tightened and released his fingers, and the copper coin lay dull and twisted.

"Balmy?" I asked.

"At least," he answered.

"Harmlessly so, I trust."

"She looks weaker than water," he muttered.

"She looks helpless." The innkeeper maintained a deliberate preoccupation with other customers, and the pilgrim woman had yet to gain supper. "Invite her over here, Taf," I suggested, "or she may starve before the season starts." I held no fondness for foreigners, especially pilgrims, but I tried to know the Troupe members.

Taf's expression said that I was as daft as the seamstress if I thought to make him share table with a pilgrim, but he did rise to rescue the hapless woman. When he returned with her, he wore his poorest imitation of amiability. "Mistress Anni," I said with suffi-cient warmth to compensate for Taf's sullenness. "I am Lyriel. Taf tells me that you have agreed to be our seamstress. We are pleased to have you with us." I disliked the way her hood shielded her eyes; I like to measure honesty from a full expression.

"It is gracious of you to say it," murmured Mistress Anni pre-cisely. She was a mild, gray-shrouded figure of indeterminate age and nondescript character. She was pleasant, polite and so self-effacing that she almost failed to exist. Why did she disturb me? I answered myself: because she is not a whole person. I could not quite decide what my conclusion meant, but it seemed appropriate to her.

Taf muttered something about finding the woman some supper, and he left us. Taf has never been one to waste effort in cultivating people to no profit; deceptions of character, which he enacts excep-tionally well when he wishes, do not amuse him. I did not expect to see him again that evening.

"Have you been long in Ardasia?" I asked the seamstress, ob-serving the delicacy with which she seated herself on the bench.

"Not long," she replied. The innkeeper's boy brought her a bowl of the stew's dregs, let it thud upon the table and splatter her, and slapped a broken loaf upon the board beside the bowl. "Thank you, young Master," said the woman graciously.

"The service here is not always dependable," I murmured, qui-etly conspiratorial in my lie. The service simply reflected the preva-lent Ardasian attitude toward foreign clientele.

"I have encountered worse," responded the seamstress with a faint smile.

"Tulean hospitality must be worse than I had thought."

"You have an excellent ear for accents."

"Training," I answered confidently, though I had done little more than guess the seamstress' origin.

"You serve Mistress Rubi's Troupe as actress?" Most pilgrims disparaged our profession as frivolous and licentious, but Mistress Anni's question was respectful; my opinion of her increased.

"I am nominally a dancer, but I serve the Troupe as needed. I seem to find fewer opportunities to perform with every season. Other obligations have a way of taking precedence."

"Then you have traveled with Mistress Rubi's Troupe previously."

"All my life."

"The night has never troubled you?"

She intoned the question oddly, though she did not appear to be affected personally by the prospect. She reflected the pilgrim folly that holy pilgrimage granted immunity from Rendies. Most pilgrims professed it; few believed it enough to travel the night alone. "We have K'shai to Protect us," I responded evenly.

"Of course." She seemed a decent sort for a pilgrim. Taf's comment about her peculiar character appeared excessive; she struck me as simply misplaced. She did not belong in Ardasia; no pilgrim ever really did belong here. I began to regale Mistress Anni with inconsequential chatter, while she consumed the stew with poorly disguised distaste.

I forgot the pilgrim woman momentarily when Evaric arrived. The Alisa rose, gushed, and drew him directly to her side. It was no great surprise that the K'shai displayed a ready appreciation for Alisa's welcome. I could see Zakari seethe, as Alisa and Miria both frothed with enthusiasm. The potential development of another complication disturbed me.

Mistress Anni had followed the direction of my stare, and she studied the vivacious group fixedly. I realized with some amusement that the seamstress watched only the K'shai. "Alisa is fierce competition for us mortal women," I remarked, nodding toward the group. Anni returned her steady gaze to me with the slow reluctance of thick honey. "The curly-headed blonde," I explained, "who is deftly sinking her claws into our new K'shai, is touted professionally as the Beauteous Alisa. She is our Troupe's leading actress. The rather handsome man sulking beside her is Zakari, our leading actor, and the fidgety woman with the child-fine, auburn hair is Miria, another of our actresses. The bored young men just leaving are two more actors: Minaro and Rayn. The K'shai calls himself Evaric. It is not a K'shai name." I shrugged. "But he does not seem concerned by that fact."

"Some men need not the artifice of a thing's name to mitigate evidence of humanity." Her comment was odd; something intense in her way of speaking it nearly rendered me speechless—no easy task. Anni proceeded quite naturally, "I merely hypothesize. K'shai do take such pride in appearing uncanny."

I laughed a little awkwardly. "You sound like Noryne, another of our actresses. She also suspects K'shai of being inhuman."

"You disagree?" asked Anni softly.

"Not altogether. They do live by killing."

"The assassin's trade is reprehensible but quite human."

"You are the one who spoke of K'shai mitigating humanity."

"By selecting names of artifice. It is pretense, illusion: That is the K'shai way."

"They do not slay Rendies by illusion," I insisted.

"On the contrary, illusion is precisely what the K'shai wield. The true K'shai survive the night because they are as remote from the creatures of the Rending as is a street-witch from a major Power."

She was certainly Seriin, I thought; they are all obsessed with their Ixaxin wizards. "Is there such a thing as a K'shai who is not true?" I mocked.

"He has no K'shai name."

Had we been discussing Evaric all this time? "He does not use a K'shai name, but he is certainly K'shai. Look at his hand!"

"A brand marks the skin, not the man."

"What do you think he is, if not K'shai?" Why did I expect anything sensible from a pilgrim?

"I do wish that I knew," she murmured almost wistfully. So, I thought with a certain sympathy, he affected even a pilgrim woman; the familiarity of Anni's reaction made me feel more kindly toward her.

Rubi summoned me to the upper floor with a shout, distinctive and loud even above the din of the common room. "Rubi has ways of making her wishes known," I muttered to Anni. A summons at this hour would surely mean a late night of working. "If anyone gives you trouble, Anni, refer them to me."

"Thank you, Mistress Lyriel. You are kind." Perhaps Anni's courtesy was mechanical, but I felt suddenly sure that she meant it warmly. I smiled at her as I left, deciding that Taf's comment about her oddness merely reflected Taf's usual surliness.

Anni remained alone at the table, observing the K'shai. I glimpsed her still there two hours later, and I think she had not moved at all. Miria had gone, and Zakari sulked by the wall. Alisa entertained Evaric to the apparent exclusion of the world. I grumbled a few unpleasant thoughts and returned to Rubi and Taf.

Chapter 5

"What do we still need?" demanded Rubi.

I gave her my tally. "Sandals, gilt paint, oats, dried fish." Taf made a terrible face; he loathes fish, which is why we always ran short of it. "A cooking pot to replace the one Solomai threw at the sand wolf last spring, another load of flour."

"How much flour can you possibly need?" complained Taf.

"Weevils infested the last two bags we opened."

"We have made do with worse."

"Not if I had a choice about it!"

"You think the flour comes to us for free?"

"Rubi asked what we need, and we need flour."

"It will only become infested like the other."

"Buy the flour, Taf," ordered Rubi.

I continued my interrupted recital, while Taf grumbled. "Paper, a new harness. We could use some nails."

"Denz again."

"He wants more than nails."

"Better iron prices inland." I only shrugged at that: Taf was probably right.

Rubi slapped her hands onto the broad plank table between us. "We are in fair shape."

"We leave in two days," commented Taf with a severely dampening humor.

"Will there be a problem?" asked Rubi. She has always excelled at portraying ingenuousness; the ploy relates to her fleshy, soft face and the trick she has of smoothing any intelligence from her expression.

"A problem?" demanded Taf indignantly. When Rubi continued to exude blankness, Taf sank into gloom. "I suppose I can manage, if Lyriel procures the fish and flour."

I took my turn at indignation. "I have enough to occupy me already, thank you."

"You want the supplies."

"We need the supplies."

"Then help acquire them."

"In two days? At the prices we can pay?"

"You expect me to obtain them for you!" Taf was gloating now.

"You are the conjurer, Taf." And if he were not kept busy during the remaining two days, he would certainly manage to cause some sort of trouble. Taf liked to depart Ardas each year with a flair, which meant that we spent each spring bribing our way back into the city's good graces.

"Give him the help he asks, Lyriel," commanded Rubi.

"Blasted conjurer," I growled. Taf came close to looking smug.

I was still grumbling when I reached the fish market a good two hours into the morning. The leering Bethiin sailor who lurked everywhere I turned did not improve my mood. He was not shopping for fish. Several of the merchants who knew me snickered and made snide comments. I snapped back at them.

"Taf has you doing the buying again?" commented Kikula, a vendor with whom I have dealt frequently. She is a rotund woman with a temper nearly as notorious as mine.

"You know how Taf feels about dried fish."

"Good for me that Rubi disagrees with him. Your Troupe brings some of my biggest sales," laughed Kikula, and we began the serious bargaining. Since we knew each other's measure well, we completed a sound exchange in little more than an hour. To my intense irritation, the Bethiin had not left.

"You belong to Rubi's Troupe?" he asked. Kikula and I had made no secret of our delivery arrangements.

I remarked mildly, "Not interested, Bethiin."

Kikula laughed uproariously at the Bethiin's blush. He persisted, "Your Troupe hired the K'shai from our ship."

He had acquired a portion of my interest. "Why did you replace them?" The Bethiin carried enough salt and herbs to equip a ship fully, which meant a return voyage soon. A lengthy voyage would require K'shai.

The Bethiin looked so eager when I addressed him that I nearly pitied him. "Oh," he stammered. "No choice. They left us." He confirmed the story I had heard from the ship's captain. I dismissed him again. "I could tell you about them," he offered uncertainly, when I continued to ignore him. He obviously lacked experience in the type of transaction he hoped to complete, and his approach was accordingly clumsy.

"Still not interested," I replied firmly. These foreigners cherished persistent misconceptions about Ardasian morality.

"There are things you ought to know before you travel with them," insisted the Bethiin nuisance. He came closer to me than I liked. "Some of us were glad to see the last of those K'shai."

"Why?" I asked him sharply.

Kikula mumbled under her breath, "I would be glad to see the last of all foreigners," and I approved her sentiment heartily, as the Bethiin pushed his unappealing face close to my ear.

I pondered the advantages of driving my sandal's heel hard upon his bare toes. He whispered nervously, "They are not like any K'shai I ever met before."

"You have doubtless established a large acquaintance among K'shai during your extensive career as a common galley boy," I suggested scornfully.

He backed up a pace to a more comfortable distance, which constituted his most sensible action so far. "Maybe I am a galley boy," he sulked, "but I know wrongness when I see it. Even a K'shai does not talk to Rendies."

"What did you say?"

The Bethiin smirked. "He talked to the accursed Rendies—conversed with them—a dozen of us heard it. Ask Captain Tarl of the *Sea Dancer* if you doubt me."

"Captain Tarl said the K'shai gave excellent service." Why did I waste my time on this fool of a foreigner, who only wanted attention?

"So they did. But we never saw more Rendies than this trip brought. They came in dozens every night. K'shai fight Rendies. This pair attracts them like flies to carrion." A spitefulness in the Bethiin's voice might have represented envy. "Captain feared to tell you the whole of it, for dread of what those two would do to him."

Fear of K'shai was plausible, even likely, but no one talked to Rendies. Few even recalled their coming. The Bethiin was a fool seeking attention via a farfetched story. Kikula pointed at the young pest with one of the dried eels that she usually waves at customers. "He does tell a good yarn," she said to me with an approving nod.

"Ask anyone from the ship," persisted the Bethiin, "or ask the K'shai why soot covered the deck the morning after a storm. What sort of fire burns in the rain?" His voice had grown loud, gaining him an audience.

"Rendies assume odd forms."

"Other incidents occurred. I saw . . ." He began to cough. When he stopped, he only stared at Kikula's strings of fish.

"What did you see?" I did wonder, even if the man was an obvious fool.

"How much do you want for the dried salt tuna?" he asked equably.

I hushed Kikula with a peremptory wave. "What did you see the K'shai do?"

"Could I see the third string from the end, please?"

He refused to acknowledge me again. Kikula shrugged at me and began to haggle with him. By that time, I felt inclined to scar the man's back with my dagger, but I decided he did not merit the trouble. At least he had stopped following me, so I could buy the flour without further annoyance.

Fog reached for his glass, found it empty, and shouted at the tavern keeper. "I told you to keep my glass filled!" The tavern keeper looked fearfully at Fog and Evaric.

Evaric said quietly, "I asked him not to serve you any more."

Fog's hand reached for his partner's throat. Evaric did not evade the larger man's attack, and Fog allowed his hand to fall. "You are a good partner, boy."

"Come outside with me, Fog. You need the fresh air."

Fog shuddered. "Did I tell you I was dead once?"

"You are alive now, and we have a job of Protection to fulfill."

"You saw what happened on the ship. The Rendies killed me again, and I burned them. How can a man burn the blasted Rendies?"

How? wondered Evaric, but he severed the questioning thought. The Rendies had nearly claimed him that time, and Fog had saved his life and soul—again. "Outside, Fog," persisted Evaric gently. "You will feel better when you are sober." Because K'shai control would suppress this talk of death and devils. Sober, Fog would again become an ordinary K'shai: like me, thought Evaric, a man who denies his haunts.

Evaric watched his partner and wondered grimly if he saw his own tormented future. Not even a K'shai could deny haunts forever.

Chapter 6

Afternoon arrived in all its heat before I returned to the inn, where nearly half of Ardas' constabulary awaited me. One of the least popular men in Ardas demanded, "Mistress Lyriel?" as if we had never met.

"You know my name, Harbing," I replied with dry discouragement. Taf, could you not have waited until tomorrow? By tomorrow, of course, the fish would have been delivered, and Taf hates fish.

Harbing's partner, Shober, scuffed at the sand and said, "We need to talk to you, Mistress Lyriel."

"You have a charge against me?"

"I could find a dozen," grunted Harbing, exaggerating by at least a factor of three.

"About your father," continued Shober, as if he had never been interrupted.

One of the constables shouted, for Taf had appeared briefly at the end of the twisting street; most of the officials deserted me. Harbing ought to have known better than to waste energy on one of Taf's meticulously unlawful jests; Harbing had failed repeatedly to hold Taf on any number of charges.

"What did he do this time?" I muttered to Shober.

"He snatched the purses of three Seriin nobles, directly in view of their private guards." Shober nodded in appreciation. "I never saw a cleaner bit of work. Taf is an artist, Lyriel."

"Then why do you detect him so often?" Taf's remarkable talents no longer enraptured me. I had paid too many officials (including Shober) too dearly and too often for the privilege of Taf's continued freedom; too many of the officials preferred a more personal currency than copper or silver.

"You know how Taf enjoys an audience. He warned us in advance."

"I pay you to tell me such things before half of Ardas is on his trail. You owe me, Shober."

"Complain to Taf, not to me. He informed Harbing directly. What could I do?"

"Make it right, Shober, or I shall tell Harbing a few facts about you." I left Shober glowering and ran to find Rubi. I yelled, "Harbing," at her and continued my hasty course.

Locating the K'shai entailed a deal more persistence. One of the innkeeper's sons finally directed me to a tavern (a common commodity in Ardas) with solid walls (an exceedingly uncommon encumbrance for an Ardas establishment with no sleeping rooms). The tavern's owner catered to foreigners, who knew no better than to bake indoors while the sun heated the day. I had expected more sense from Master Evaric.

The stifling tavern held only three customers: a drunken pilgrim preaching to an empty chair, and at a table in the far corner, Evaric and a man whom I presumed to be Fog. The two K'shai conferred softly, but I would have wagered that they argued.

"We must leave now," I told them tersely.

I drew them both from some distant realm. Evaric nodded without expression. Fog informed me with care, "You ought not to have come here." He spoke with peculiar precision for a man who sat amid so many emptied tankards.

"It is her city," remarked Evaric with sardonic wisdom. "This is Mistress Lyriel, Fog, the young woman of whom I told you."

"I recall," mused Fog. "She persuaded you to accept K'shai minimum." I had not thought his eyes were pale when I looked at him initially, but old fires and older vices had veiled the room with deceptive smoke. "The heiress of the mortal strain fulfills the pattern: how poetically appropriate." I wondered if Fog had encountered too many Rendies to keep his sanity. "She has arrived prematurely, however." Fog's remote assurance rang like a dire warning.

"A day early," I agreed. "Circumstances have advanced our schedule. Please come immediately."

Fog ignored my injunction, though he stared at me with disquieting care. Fog appeared old for an active K'shai; he looked as battle-scarred as any K'shai I had ever seen. When he spoke again, his voice slurred: "Careful, girl. The devil has taken note of you!" An uncanny expression stole across his battered face: calculating, sardonic, and rueful all at once. For an instant, Fog resembled an extremely wealthy and powerful Tanist I had once met; both men shared an element of unspoken assurance that made my skin crawl.

Everything about the conversation struck me as peculiar. In the bar's dim interior, I convinced myself that Fog's eyes were a very pale blue in his scarred brown face. In the daylight, the eyes looked dark, almost black. Fog's voice coarsened and I began to think that he might actually be as drunk as I had expected initially.

The sunlight warmed Evaric's smile. He smiled so easily; his eyes remained hard and secretive. "Pay no mind to Fog, Mistress Lyriel. He does enjoy your Ardasian liquors." Evaric's effortless charm nearly succeeded in allaying my suspicions, until I concluded that distraction was his intention. I was not sure exactly what I should suspect of these K'shai, but they certainly constituted an unconventional pair, whether they talked to Rendies, affected sporadic madness, or merely made a fool of me.

I left the K'shai to Rubi's frantic orders. The single constable we passed ignored us; he was Shober's man. I headed for the stable in search of Solomai. The voices of the Troupe's preparations for departure reached me dimly. "Solomai!" I called, hearing movement from the stable's darkness. I received no answer. I turned my back to the row of lightless stalls, most of which loomed empty this time of day.

My shoulder felt the clench of harsh fingers from behind me. I tried to reach my knife, but the man gripped my wrist. His hand wore the bloodied-sword brand. "Be calm, Mistress," he hissed, "I only mean to speak to you."

"What do you want, K'shai?" I whispered hoarsely.

"You require Protection. I seek to serve you."

Why? I demanded in silent alarm; a month ago, we could not

hire K'shai at any price. Aloud, I said, "We have already hired Protection. You may have seen them. We passed this way together a few minutes ago. Let me call them. They will speak for themselves."

"You need Protection."

"We have already hired K'shai," I repeated in frustration. "We require no others. We cannot afford more."

"I am called Straw. You will remember me." I nodded stiffly.

"We cannot pay you."

"You need Protection."

Are you a Protector, Straw, or an assassin? Whom have you been hired to kill? And why are you talking to me? "When we need new Protection, I shall remember you, Straw." The noncommittal concession seemed to appease him. He relaxed his grasp.

"I shall be near," he promised me ominously.

"Thank you," I murmured, because I feared to offend him. Straw stared at me. I would have welcomed even Harbing's appearance at that moment. "I must go now," I said, and I moved very slowly toward the stable door. Straw did not speak; neither did he stop me.

The Troupe departed Ardas within the hour. Taf met us beyond the city's edge. I did not tell him of my strange K'shai encounter. Taf was too busy gloating over the artistry of his thieving escapade. At least Solomai had managed to load the dried fish.

Chapter 7

The freedom of early autumn was a glorious release after the long summer of Ardas crowds and cacophony. The villages along the northern coasts smelled of uniformity (in a literal sense: they all reeked of rotting fish), but we stayed in none long enough to become unduly bored. We arrived, the sun rose, we performed, the sun set, we traveled and slept; by the next day another shore village welcomed us. The inland times were easier on the mules and the wagoners, and they did spare us from the nightly stars, but even a week in a single city left me restless and anxious to depart.

Diarmon saw the first of our protracted stays. We would remain for a full week, preparing for the journey inland. Equipped with several resident troupes, Diarmon did not encourage us to provide multiple performances. Rubi accepted the burden of the Troupe's own keep in Diarmon, as in no other city but Ardas, for two reasons: Diarmon preceded one of the most arduous stretches of our season's journey, and Taf insisted that I spend some time each year with Silf. It was his sole quirk of fatherly concern, and Rubi hated it. My obligatory visit to Silf's shipbuilder did not particularly enchant me either, but dread of it comprised a healthier obsession than Rendies or K'shai.

Anticipation of renewing old wounds made me too restless to sit through our first day's play. I abandoned my privileged position in the audience, and a dozen less fortunate viewers crowded forward to vie for my tree-shaded bench. I aggravated two rows of the audience unnecessarily, simply to avoid Rubi. She was frowning fiercely at the play's weak rendition; its leading members blossomed with apathy. I would rewrite the roles, but I refused to entrap myself intentionally in the midst of Rubi's fury, Alisa's inevitable tantrum, and Zakari's self-pitying whines.

Evaric leaned near the theater gate, apparently observing play, players, and passersby with equal allotments of amused equanimity. The dappled shadow and light danced around him. Even the hot Ardasian sun adored him, gleaming off golden arms below rolled sleeves. I wondered cynically if he practiced posing, like an actor.

"Walking out on a performance?" he asked me with a studied smile. "What will Mistress Rubi say?"

"That the Alisa demonstrates the professionalism of a cabbage. That you are goading Zakari into a jealous frenzy, which has made him forget acting altogether."

The smile disappeared. "I am goading Zakari?"

"That the three of you had better come to an agreement soon, or I shall revise the script to eliminate both Alisa and Zakari, and I shall charge the loss of revenue against your contract."

One dark brow rose curiously. "You wrote the play?" Not a word did he give about placating Zakari or settling his position with Alisa one way or another.

"Of course I wrote the play," I snapped at him. "It saves on performance fees, and we must save all we can so as to hire K'shai Protection." I swept close past him. He moved so nimbly that his unaffected elegance did not suffer. He ought to have been on the stage. He could have drawn audiences without uttering a line.

I selected a suitably tasteless costume for my visit to Silf and her shipbuilder. Since the shipbuilder's family chose to perceive the members of Rubi's Troupe as brassy and ignorant, I cultivated the expected attitude to emphasize every difference between the shipbuilder's world and my own. If the ploy failed to jeopardize Silf's own position with the shipbuilder, it still underlined her alienism to Diarmon. I wanted her to remember.

The shipbuilder's manservant frowned when I arrived, but he knew me. He escorted me to the parlor and into the disappointing presence of the shipbuilder's two pale, prim, and myopic daughters. Both girls affected the high-collared, voluminously encompassing gowns of foreign fashion, ridiculous in the Ardasian climate. The girls differed a few years in age, but I never bothered to distinguish them by names.

"Your mother will return soon," announced the first very properly. The inspection she gave me was less gracious.

"Father and she are visiting Tanist Melhar," added the other with a trace of deliberate snobbery. "We are pleased to see you again, Lyriel." I flashed an insincere smile and said nothing; the best enjoyment I ever derived from the sisters came of letting them squirm in my company.

The younger girl asked, "Did you see the royal visitors when you were in Ardas?"

"No." I had been unable to see past the crowds in front of me, save for a brief glimpse of Serii's Adjutant escaping the parade, but I felt no inclination to elaborate for the sake of the shipbuilder's daughters.

"I heard that the procession was wonderfully elaborate. Queen Marylne sent the finest of everything for her daughter's entourage."

"Stal must be terribly pleased. All of the Bethiin princesses are reputed to be quite stunning, and Lilyan is supposed to be by far the prettiest." The sisters scattered royal names like familiar friends I doubted they addressed even their dear Tanist so intimately in his presence. The foreign custom of formal speech had so far eluded the sisters' mastery.

"Did you hear that King Nion has authorized five more Ixaxin schools? Father expects one of the schools to be established in Diarmon."

"Have you ever visited an Ixaxin school, Lyriel?" asked the oldest sister, but she did not await a response. I have never understood why the shipbuilder's daughters consider me sheltered as well as ignorant, since I am far more traveled than anyone else they are likely to meet, save Silf. "An Ixaxin visited Tanist Melhar last winter. The Ixaxin actually took the farrier's son away to Ardas."

"Surely the farrier's son cannot be a sorcerer. He is such an untidy boy."

"Even Ixaxins must make mistakes."

Boredom made me murmur, "They made one at least: They named the Venkarel as Infortiare, which brought the Rending upon us. Had Ixaxis elected Lord Hrgh dur Liin, as anticipated, we might not need assassins to escort us through the night." The sisters were staring at me as if a none-too-clever parrot had suddenly mastered its first word. "Of course, the present Infortiare insists that the Venkarel curbed the Rending's effect from the total destruction that might have resulted, but Lady Rhianna does have a vested interest in preserving the illusion of her position's inviolability."

Since the shipbuilder's daughters could not possibly acknowledge that I knew something more than they of history, they settled on expressions of tolerant disbelief. Silf and her shipbuilder arrived in the midst of the reciprocated disparagement. "A united family," beamed the shipbuilder, "is a reverence to a man's proud little kingdom." The shipbuilder's impromptu speeches unflaggingly betrayed him as a fool.

His daughters pecked his papery cheeks. He offered me the same opportunity, doubtless thinking his gesture a generous one; I pretended not to understand. I had no intention of according him the coy tribute he expected of a daughter. Silf knew my reluctance. She came to me, sweeping forward in her unwieldy skirts with a grace that broke my heart. She took my hands and held them. I wanted to beg her to leave with me on the instant, return to Taf and me and the world in which we three belonged. "Rubi sends her regards," I told her cruelly.

Silf blinked, her long, dark lashes rising slowly. "How is your father?" she asked a little hoarsely. The shipbuilder and his daughters retreated discreetly, closing the door on us to give us privacy and a dearth of breathable air.

"As well as ever," I returned stiffly. "You could see him."

"Taf would not wish it," she answered, releasing me with a sigh. She had coiled her beautiful black hair in a tightly bound knot, and the effect aged her.

"You mean that your shipbuilder would not wish it."

"His name is Marlund," amended Silf wearily. "He is a good man, Lyriel."

"He is a fool."

"Because he does not know how to steal, cheat, and lie as deftly as Taf?"

"You never minded when you loved Taf."

"I knew nothing else, I have taken most of a lifetime to realize that there is a better way to live: an honest way among honest, open people."

"Honesty is an overrated commodity."

Silf shook her head delicately. "I wish you would stay here long enough to understand what you scorn. Marlund would welcome you as a daughter. Peliia and Olna would be your sisters and your friends if you would accept them. You could be free of the scrounging and starving and wondering when your father will be caught and hanged."

"No one catches Taf unless he wishes it," I remarked, as I inspected the dozens of dusty little porcelain dolls cluttering the tea table. Every one of them bore the mark of an importer, the shipbuilder's daughters liked exotic toys.

"Even Taf will slip some day. Someone will catch him, or someone will catch you concealing his crimes and Rubi's. You have a right to a life of your own, Lyriel."

"With you and your shipbuilder?" I scoffed.

"You could be schooled properly instead of snatching at any morsel of neglected lore you find. You would meet good, intelligent people. I know how you detest the stupidity of those you coddle for the sake of 'The Troupe.' "

"Your shipbuilder exudes intellect." The ridiculous sleeve of my costume slipped from my shoulder, and I replaced it irritably. Silf and I no longer shared anything but a frustrated yearning to make each other understand. I began to count the room's baubles so as to stifle my unruly temper. "I think I had better leave."

"Will you not dine with us?" asked Silf, now hurt and desperate.

"I must discuss some revisions with Rubi."

"Tomorrow?"

"I do not belong here, Silf. Neither do you."

"Rubi is consuming your soul as surely as a Rendie," Silf muttered bitterly. "Like Taf: you become empty and cold."

"Rubi did not steal Taf from you. You threw him at her—and me with him." I flung open the door and nearly choked on the influx of cooler air. The shipbuilder and his daughters shuffled awkwardly in their own entry hall, every inch of which had contributed to some foreigner's profits. I waved at them flippantly, disregarded Silf's attempts to detain me, and stormed outside just as the disapproving manservant reached the door with undignified haste.

I scattered venomous thoughts against the shipbuilder's sprawling lawns. Staffs of servants pumped water endlessly, but the lawns wore a parched look. Such lawns were a Seriin fashion. They had no place in Ardasian soil and climate.

Even the newly cobbled street discouraged me, though it represented a more practical affectation of foreign ways. Hard dirt and sand had always served Diarmon well. The heavy rainstorms, which churned the streets to mud, came rarely.

I felt easier when I reached the older, less reputable section of town. The stained beggar who accosted me carried a strong, unpleasant reek, but he was thoroughly Ardasian. I flipped him an iron kesne out of respect for the tradition of his trade. I ignored the flock of other beggars who materialized at my gesture, reaching out their hands in supplication and trying to grab at my arms. Respect for tradition did not make me a fool; the beggars likely enjoyed more wealth than I would ever achieve.

Chapter 8

The man who shuffled through the crowd did not belong among the Troupe's performers or admirers. He pressed uncomfortably between the enthused youths who cast petals before the Beauteous Alisa. The man's age lay between the old and the young. He wore a comfortable paunch. His face glistened from exertion in the sun. He was soft, unaccustomed to the streets.

Lyriel saw him briefly and knew him for one of the shipbuilder's ilk. She wondered why he walked alone in the dusty streets around Diarmon's oldest inn; he was misplaced, making him an obvious target for a clever pickpocket. Taf could easily have freed him of the bulging purse which showed a faint outline beneath his tunic. Lyriel could have stolen it herself, but neither she nor Taf stole in Diarmon out of deference to Silf.

The man moved away from the Troupe, and Lyriel lost sight of him. Near the inn's entry, the man saw the two K'shai, whose presence discouraged trouble far more effectively than did the constables with their bright, brass-decorated scabbards. Dark leather concealed the K'shai weapons, but K'shai hands brandished fiercer blades.

The man hesitated near the K'shai. When he was beside them he dropped his gaze and began to turn away. When he looked again into the milling crowd, he reconsidered. He mumbled his words to the K'shai. "I need to talk to you."

"Then talk," suggested Fog easily.

"Not here!" returned the man, appalled.

Evaric's silver-blue eyes became vaguely disdainful. Fog snarled, "Inside, south hall, third door."

"Five minutes," added Evaric. The man sputtered an agreement.

"I can pay whatever you ask," said the man.

"What is the job?"

"There is a man who has wronged me."

"You want him killed," commented Evaric mildly.

The man could not complete a nod, but all K'shai were accustomed to such uncertain customers, who were laden equally with vindictiveness and guilt. "I can tell you where to find him," offered the man. " 'In the early morning, there is no one near. . . ."

"When we accept a job, it is we who decide how to execute it," said Evaric quellingly.

The man fingered his collar. "I only meant. . . ."

"To help," finished Evaric sardonically.

"Perhaps I . . . I should begin again. My name is. . . ."

"We do not need your name," interrupted Fog. "Why did you come to us? We are already employed."

"What?" The man was growing ever more frightened. "Your Guild-mate sent me to you. He said that you. . . ."

"Which Guild-mate?" asked Evaric.

"A scarred man. He came to me. I thought you would. . . ."

"What name did he give you?"

"What name?" asked the man helplessly. "Straw. Yes, that was it: Straw."

Evaric said pensively, "I have no interest in the contract." To Fog, he added, "It is yours, if you want it."

"Empty your purse," Fog ordered the man.

With shaking hands, the man obeyed. Evaric inspected the mound of silver which the man poured upon the table. Evaric sorted from it the few small coppers. He dropped the coppers back into the man's leather purse and pushed the silver across the table to Fog. "Describe the target," Fog said shortly, "in detail."

"You accept the commission?" The man was looking at his silver, unsure now of the worth of his jealousy.

"I shall take this," Fog said, spreading his fingers across the sil-

ver, "as retainer for my trouble. If, upon assessing the target, I elect
to decline, then I shall return to you one half of this sum. If, however, I decide to complete the contract, then I shall expect twice this
much again. Are the terms agreeable?" .

"Twice again as much? That is more than a year's savings!"

"Are the terms agreeable?" repeated Fog patiently.

"I cannot afford so much."

"Then why do you waste my time?"

"Accept or decline," said Evaric sharply, "K'shai do not dicker
over trifles."

The man gave the silver another hungry glance, but his eyes
were caught instead by the branded sword on Evaric's hand. "The
man, the target, is young," he began, nodding shakily toward
Evaric, "about your age. . . ."

"How many K'shai have you killed without telling me, Fog?
How many times have you forestalled my death at the hands of our
Guild-mates?"

"A man Protects his partner."

"Against his own Guild? The K'shai do not accept me, Fog,
though they branded me, took my vows, and claimed my soul.
What am I, Fog?"

"K'shai. You have sworn it."

"Straw is challenging us," said Evaric hollowly.

"Then we shall accept his challenge," replied Fog evenly.

"By assassinating some pathetic youth, whose misfortune it is to
be disliked by a man of wealth?"

"The youth sounds noxious from all descriptions."

"Is that why you accepted the contract?"

"The price is good."

"Of course, the price is good." Evaric rubbed at his eyes. "And
we are K'shai, and K'shai accept contracts, and refusal to accept a
good contract is impossible for any good K'shai. Straw has certainly become a generous benefactor. How long shall we let him
live, Fog? If we kill him in Diarmon, we could bury him with Coal;
the grave would still be soft. Is that a practical, K'shai solution to
the problem, Fog?"

"Go to sleep, boy. The nights will grow long soon enough."

*   *   *

The stars shone. The wind sighed warning. A man and woman stood in the lee of Diarmon's oldest inn. "This is a desolate, uncivilized place," murmured the man, who was the more restless of the pair.

"There is a beauty to it," returned the woman softly.

"Can you actually approve of a place with such a paucity of trees?"

The woman smiled, though her expression was difficult to discern in the darkness. "The country has a beauty of its own, but I would not choose it for myself."

"You seem to have adapted well: the little pilgrim seamstress, all in gray, earning her pittance, striving to attain the Shrine. You do know that they are cheating you unconscionably?"

Reminded of her role, she began to gather her hood around her face, but she stopped and shook it free. "I do not need their gold," she replied a bit pridefully.

"Copper, darling Rhianna. You must quit thinking in such affluent terms."

"Or I shall be discovered? Ineuil, these people would not recognize Power if it consumed them. They are more blind than Tyntagellians."

"What about your son?" Ineuil asked darkly.

"He does not see me."

"By your choice?"

"I have not used Power."

"Neither have you made yourself known to him."

"He is not an easily approachable young man. He has become very much a K'shai."

"You traveled halfway around the world to find him."

"And I have inflicted a like journey upon you."

"I have admittedly visited more hospitable climes: cleaner ones, at any rate." Serii's Adjutant stirred the ubiquitous dust with his foot. "How long do you intend to maintain this charade of yours?"

"Until I understand what I must do." She raised a supplicating hand. "Can you bear with me a bit longer, Ineuil?"

Ineuil took her hand and kissed it gently. "Since you ask me, yes. I can bear your pilgrimage, even if I am bound to the company of the most tedious, uneducated, unimaginative assortment of individuals ever inflicted upon my patience."

Rhianna's lips twitched in amusement. "Are they all men?"

"I am portraying a pilgrim, my dear Rhianna, in which tiresome species Ardasian women have no interest."

"You are a far better friend than I deserve, making such sacrifices for me."

"But pilgrimages end in D'hai," continued Ineuil with scarcely a pause. "If you have not acted by that time, then you may as well resign yourself to eternal indecision."

She pulled her hand from his, for he had held it throughout his speech. She stood straight and regal, and she answered him evenly, "I shall not leave D'hai without resolving my position with my son."

"Then we shall meet again before the Shrine."

"You are leaving?" Fear and questioning spilled from her, even as she waved and a Rendie fled in terror.

Ineuil shivered inadvertently at the wraith's wake of fear, though he had defeated enough Rendies himself to impress a K'shai. "I can shadow you inconspicuously along the coast, where I may travel alone, but to journey inland I need Ardasians who know the land. I have paid a fortune in bribes just to join a merchant train, which travels faster than pilgrims. Unless you have reconsidered letting me accompany your little Troupe. . . ."

"No. I become myself too quickly when you are with me." She looked away and back to him reluctantly, "It is better, as you propose, that we meet in D'hai. Then I shall have the time I need."

"He is your son, Rhianna."

"He resembles Kaedric greatly," she said wistfully.

"That should not daunt you." Ineuil was sardonic.

"He is both lighter and darker than Kaedric. He has been twisted."

"If you tell me that he is more a fiend than his father, then I shall never sleep peacefully again." Ineuil took both of her hands and kissed them. "I shall await you breathlessly, my lovely Infortiare."

"Hush!"

"In D'hai," he finished.

"In D'hai," she echoed distantly.

Chapter 9

The rare luxury of a morning without urgency helped revive me. I stayed late abed more for reason of conscious self-indulgence than for any need of extra rest. I left the inn with a sigh of pleasure for the thought of immersing my sorrows in the Archives, Diarmon's chief redeeming feature. The Archives purportedly contain every scrap of Ardasian lore extant. They actually lack a few governing documents, which are held by the king in Ardas, but I have never minded the gap.

Tabok waved to me as I passed the marketplace. Taf stood with him, haggling over the price of dried beans, but Taf does not acknowledge extraneous events when a bargain is to be made. I paused to pursue some idle bargaining of my own. I began to denigrate an opaline brooch, though it was a beautiful piece and far beyond my means. The proprietor retaliated with enthusiasm.

A distinctively familiar hand dropped a ridiculous sum of silver on the proprietor's counter. Evaric grabbed both the brooch and my arm, and he wafted me along the street in complete disregard for my very vocal protest. It would have served him right if I had screamed for help, but I thought better of the notion. Even constables tend to give wide berth to a man with sword both at his side and emblazoned on his hand.

"What do you think you are doing?" I asked him indignantly.

"Accelerating your shopping," he returned evenly. He had

abandoned his Seriin jerkin in favor of a light tunic. He could have been Ardasian, save for the arsenal of blades he wore and the brand, which nothing could disguise. "You Ardasians waste an unconscionable amount of time."

"You paid five times what the brooch is worth," I informed him coldly.

"I paid less than a tenth of the marked price," he protested. I sniffed contemptuously; foreigners had no sense for business. Evaric shook his head, remarking, "I must remember to take you with me the next time I need to make a purchase in this extortionate country of yours."

"Were you listening to us?" I demanded suspiciously. I did not like being spied upon by a K'shai, even an unorthodox one. It reminded me too keenly of a stable in Ardas and a menacing man called Straw.

"I cannot assume credit for such a miracle of attentiveness. Ardasian bargaining far exceeds the comprehension of a mere Seriin." He drew me into the shade of a cafe's striped awning. The tables all were occupied, until Evaric smiled meaningfully at a pair of youths who lingered over an emptied carafe. The boys departed hastily, and Evaric pushed me into one of the vacated chairs. He seated himself in the other. When he had commanded wine for us both, he continued his remarks as if they had not been interrupted. "I did not listen to your bargaining, but I did watch you—a much more rewarding pastime."

"Save your Seriin chivalry for Alisa." I was becoming somewhat less exasperated. The wine was both expensive and good. The flattery did not hurt. I was still not pleased with the K'shai's insolence, but his attention was headier than the wine. "What do you want?" I asked him.

"Entry to the Archives," he responded succinctly. "You are a licensed playwright, which means that you have access privileges."

"Any temple can give you the history of the Shrine, and that is all the Ardasian history any foreigner needs." The cafe's proprietor was watching us and whispering to the serving girl. If they recognized me from previous visits, they might well lodge a complaint against Rubi's Troupe, for the obvious presence of a K'shai was steadily driving away the customers.

"The temples do not sate a harmless appetite for ancient records.

Respectful admittance to the greatest of Ardasian libraries is surely not an excessive request."

"You are a foreigner," I stated. A very curious foreigner, I added to myself; why should a K'shai wish to see the Archives?

"Your license permits you an escort."

"Does it?"

"Yes. It does. As I am sure you already know." He was suppressing annoyance with an effort. "Naturally, I shall recompense you for your trouble."

"What makes you think you can afford me?"

"What makes you think that I cannot?" His branded hand gripped my wrist. With his other hand, he counted twenty kelni into my palm. The coins felt hot from his handling. "I could buy my own license for less, but bribing Ardasians tries my patience." His eyes, which looked gray today, criticized me. "I shall not try to bargain with you," he said, as if bargaining were an indecent occupation.

"Just as well. I bargain only for what I desire."

He spread his branded hand flat against the marble table, which was not a very subtle way of reminding me of what he represented. "Is admittance to the Archives really so much to ask?"

"From a foreigner, yes."

"You sound like Taf, despising anyone who is not Ardasian."

"I am a dutiful daughter."

"Taf is your father," said Evaric with the rigid cadence of revelation.

"You thought I was his Toy?"

Evaric began to shake his head, then resorted to a shrug, "I could not identify the relationship as an emotional one."

"The mistake is common." I never discussed Taf with anyone. Stop it, Lyriel, before you make a fool of yourself over a blasted K'shai. I finished weakly, "Taf and I actually have very little in common."

Evaric volunteered quietly, "I never had much in common with my parents either."

"I always pictured K'shai as disgruntled orphans."

"Perhaps disgruntled," he replied with half a smile, "but not necessarily as a result of childhood deprivation. You would be pressed to find a more sound and stable family than mine."

"All the worse," I snapped, angry again; he did not even attempt to make excuse for his profession. I tried to leave the table, but Evaric pushed me back into place almost before I moved.

"Mistress Lyriel," he said very seriously, "I am attempting to declare a truce."

"Are we at war?"

"So it would appear, though I am unsure of the cause."

"How many men have you assassinated?"

"Is that your reason for snarling at me constantly?"

"Do I need a better one?"

"Since you employ me as Protection, yes. There are many reasons for a man to become K'shai. Inasmuch as you know nothing of mine, I think your judgment against me is rather premature."

"A K'shai kills. There is nothing else to understand."

"Seven."

"What?" I did not want to hear him; I did not want to know him. I could not avert my eyes from him.

"I have assassinated seven men. I have rejected a hundred contracts. I became K'shai because of a nightmare involving Rendies."

"You commit murder professionally for the sake of a nightmare? What sort of reason is that? You are not the first to have nightmares about Rendies. The rest of us do not become assassins."

"I have only killed those who allowed me no choice."

"By whose judgment? Yours alone?"

"Yes. Mine alone." For a moment, he gave me the oddest impression of explosively conflicting forces tightly bound, and then he was only a rueful man of unconscious charm who was trying very hard to be patient with me. "Mistress Lyriel, will you please permit me to enter the Archives with you?"

The shriveled woman who tends the Archives always looks as dusty as her charge. She knows me, but she never acknowledges our acquaintance save by admitting me without question. I think she resents the rare intrusions upon her isolation; not many Ardasians read well, and visitors to the Archives are accordingly few. The woman had fought my first entrance to her domain bitterly; admittedly, few five-year-olds own licenses to anything. I had pleaded for mine, until Taf procured it in a card game. My license had become more extensive and more legitimate since that time, but it was recorded still in its original format: Lyriel, Silf's daughter, of Ardas.

The woman opened the great door to me grudgingly. When she noticed Evaric, she tried to push the door closed again. Evaric forestalled her with an effortless motion. "He accompanies me," I assured the woman firmly. When she failed to alter her defensive stance, I added impatiently, "License twenty-six. The record of it occupies the third drawer in the second cabinet, fifth aisle from the south wall."

"He is K'shai," argued the woman in a papery voice.

"He is in my employ, and I choose to authorize his admittance in my company. The sooner we enter, the sooner we shall depart." She considered my words, and Evaric smiled at her. She let us enter, shuffled into her office, and slammed the door loudly.

Evaric gave a low whistle, which was not for the benefit of the caretaker. "Is there any method to all of this?" he asked me.

"Not much," I responded truthfully. The enormity of the Archives made research among them a highly experimental art. Rows of polished marble shelves contained the random contributions of crates dispatched through the years from the king's palace. Great chests of rusting iron cluttered the aisles, enhancing the impression of total chaos. I had no idea of how one would begin efficiently to seek a particular topic, but that was Evaric's problem and not mine.

While Evaric inspected an upper shelf of one of the few hardwood cabinets, I headed for one of my favorite corners. I pried open the shutters to air the room. I doubted they had been open since my last visit. The overturned crate, which I sometimes used as a stepladder, lay beneath the window, as I had left it two years earlier. The Archives changed so little. They belonged to me more than anything I actually owned.

Several minutes elapsed before Evaric found me. "What do you charge for a clue?" he asked me dryly. The bindings of leather and old cloth muffled his clear, soft voice. I enjoyed seeing him at a loss. I think he did not share my appreciation.

"In what regard?" I replied innocently.

"In regard to this random maze of Ardasian illogic."

"Sorry K'shai. I cannot help you." I turned a page idly. "Unless you tell me what you are trying to find."

He hesitated longer than my simple statement of fact warranted. I abandoned my abstracted pose to verify that he had not evaporated into K'shai illusion. "I have an interest in ancient history," he breathed slowly.

"Choose any tome that crumbles," I suggested.

"Your advice falls short of adequate."

"So also does your stated objective. 'Ancient history' covers nearly everything in this room."

"If I did provide you with a more specific topic, could you find its reference in all of this?"

"Why must you K'shai convert everything into a mystery? If you tell me the topic, I shall tell you whether I can help you."

He walked a few paces away from me and melted into a long shadow. I shaded my eyes from the window's light so as to see him. He scanned the spines of a row of assorted diaries, several of which I had found useful, none of which bore any title or other identifying mark. He answered me over his shoulder. "There was a thing which came to Serii some few thousands of years ago. One tale reports that it originated in Ardasia."

"Has this thing a name?"

"Taormin." He threw the word at me as if it carried a vile flavor.

"You do mean ancient history."

His stare struck me even from the shadow. He tilted his head so that his black shock of hair brushed the pale frost-blue of his embroidered collar. "You know of it?"

"The Taormin was taken from Ardasia by the Sorcerer King of Serii. We never forget a thief nor that which has been stolen from us." I replied tartly, but I was pondering uneasily how I might extricate myself from a K'shai's anger. The colorless intensity of Evaric's eyes reminded me of wraith-glow.

He asked carefully, "What else do you know of this thing?"

"Why do you care? It was stolen millennia ago."

"I have reasons."

"K'shai secrets?"

"Personal reasons."

"Why should I abet a K'shai's furtive intrigue?"

His laugh cut short my question. Something quiet fell from him. The K'shai's long fingers curled into the flesh of my shoulders. He twisted me and held me; I waited for my bones to snap. He whispered to me, "I could persuade you, Mistress Lyriel." He released me. I whirled across the room and faced him with my dagger in my hand. "What do you intend to do with *that?*" he asked reasonably.

It was a fair question to which I had no satisfactory answer. "I am leaving, Seriin. Find someone else to guide you through the Archives."

"And you will never know why a K'shai cares enough about ancient Ardasian history to travel halfway across the world, seek a contract to Protect at half of what he could earn from pilgrims, and tolerate more outright rudeness from a bad-tempered dancer/ playwright than anyone should sensibly accept."

I sheathed my dagger, keeping suspicious watch over the maddening K'shai. "If you intended to answer me, what was the purpose of your K'shai coercion?"

"You may consider it a whim."

"You are the most aggravating man I have ever met."

"The adjective is mutually applicable," he said amiably. I did not trust his change of mood. I kept my responding smile cautious and cynical. "I have a foster brother." He was selecting his words very carefully, which made me wonder how much truth he intended to impart. "We have been separated for a number of years. I believe he may have come to Ardasia so as to research the Taormin. If I study it equally, I may be able to locate him."

"Why does your brother care about the Taormin?"

"Rendie madness often results in inexplicable obsessions."

"Your brother survived a Rendie attack?"

"Yes, when he was very young." I would have given much to read Evaric's thoughts at that moment.

"You were separated when you became K'shai?"

"Before that."

I was accomplishing nothing by prolonging Evaric's tense evasion of total truth. More pertinently, he was hurting, and a particularly foolish notion had begun to tell me that I might enjoy comforting him. "Enough," I said. "I have better things to do than pry your family history from you word by word." I led him to a cache of rejected relics from the king's own collection. "Workbooks of the royal children," I explained. "Be forewarned: Ardasian rulers have never achieved note for scholastic excellence." I selected one of the more intact books and handed another to Evaric. He be-

stowed a doubtful inspection on both the book and me, but he
began to scan the mildewed pages.

An hour's perusal of the exercises of our king's ancestors
taught me chiefly to appreciate the Archive's cool walls. "What
event signified the end of the Ardasian Republic?" Evaric asked
me unexpectedly.

I accorded him a suitably unenthused response, "The first
drought of spring."

"An equally irrelevant answer did not amuse the tutor of this
young prince. The tutor wrote a scathing commentary on the student's inattentiveness to lessons. He also wrote an answer to the
question I just quoted: 'The Ardasian Republic dissolved when the
theft of the D'hai Control by the Sorcerer King of Serii made the Ardasian interior uninhabitable.' "

"That makes no sense," I argued. "The Ardasian interior is as it
has always been: inhospitable but bearable."

"An Ardasian never forgets that which has been stolen from
him," Evaric reminded me. I would not have wagered my coppers
on the truth of his leap of logic, but he made his conclusion sound
like a well-established fact. "How many significant items did a Sorcerer King of Serii steal from Ardasia?" he asked defensively,
though I had not expressed my doubts.

"One, two, perhaps a hundred. The Taormin's theft occurred ten
thousand years ago or more."

"Much more like twenty thousand years, I think, but the prince
and tutor who scribed this parchment lived in this millennium.
They still remembered the theft."

"So the Taormin may once have controlled something in D'hai.
What do you intend," I asked with what I considered rather saintly
patience, "to do with this wealth of information? Pray at the Shrine
for enlightenment?"

His shell of quiet reserve hardened. "How long have pilgrims
journeyed to D'hai?"

"The Rending inspired them in droves. Before the Rending, the
journey was too easy to feel holy. No one traveled to D'hai but a
few 'inspired' lunatics and the usual assortment of merchants."

"Pilgrims claim that the Shrine is ancient."

"It is probably as old as they claim. An ancient, ruined city lies
not far from inhabited D'hai."

"You have never heard anything else connecting D'hai with a Sorcerer King's theft?" He continued before I could vent my exasperation, "No, I realize that you have already answered. Perhaps I shall find something more in these awful workbooks." He grimaced, then bestowed on me one of his devastating smiles. "Thank you, Lyriel."

I wished that he had not dropped his Seriin-incessant honorific from my name. The suggestion of familiarity gave me a dizzy sensation. "It is no more than I would do for anyone who offered to cripple me," I said sweetly.

He had the decency to look abashed at the reminder. "I do apologize for alarming you."

"May I consider myself safe from further K'shai whim?"

"For the moment," he returned soberly. He might have reassured me more.

Chapter 10

"The young woman who admitted him to the Archives: Who is she?"

"The caretaker records her as Lyriel, Silf's daughter."

"You followed her." Of course.

"She is a member of the troupe of traveling players whom the target contracted to Protect."

"Their association is not solely professional?"

"The target was seen to buy her a gift of some value. She is attractive, and the target appears interested."

The first man became contemplative. "You have more data?"

"A Guild-mate, a man named Coal, requested verification of a Seriin K'shai, recently operating in Ardasia."

A frown appeared. "Coal knows of the target?"

"No." The answer came uncertainly. "No," said the K'shai more strongly. "Coal questioned the authenticity of the other, the target's partner."

"Why?"

"Unknown."

"Discover the reasons."

"I tried. Coal was to meet me in Ardas. He never arrived. His partner could provide only limited information: Coal had been negotiating a Protection contract with a Captain Tarl of the *Sea Dancer*, the Bethiin ship that brought the target to Ardasia. Coal has disappeared."

Deliberation, puzzlement, and suspicion vied. "Is the disappearance related?"

"Highly probable. Coal had no significant local enemies, and his disappearance would not be the first in connection with the target. The target is a dangerous man. So is his partner."

"You assured me, Circle, that you could handle them both. You claimed to be your Guild's finest assassin."

"I can handle them. I shall handle them. I am more cautious than an ordinary Protector like Coal. I am also better informed."

"Thanks to the Shrine Keeper. Remember that."

"Of course." Nods were exchanged between the two professionals, each adept in his field and fully aware of his own strengths and lacks. The K'shai killed; the Shrine priest arranged Shrine miracles. Each man garnered a most satisfactory livelihood from his expertise. "The woman?" asked the K'shai shortly.

"I do not want the target attached to any natives. These people are clannish. It could provide complications."

"I prefer that she survive, until I understand her significance to the target. It will be easy to eliminate her."

"As you wish." The hesitation was brief. "It is unfortunate that Coal did not convey to you his source of doubt. I dislike unknowns."

"Where one is falsely K'shai . . ."

"The other also? No." The slightest of superior smiles appeared. "You did not wish to believe that even one man could be falsely K'shai. Would you suspect another? And beyond him, another still who gave training to a false K'shai? Would you suspect your whole Guild?"

"'No!" The K'shai's response was fierce and vicious.

The Shrine priest gave a placating flutter of his white hand. "Fog is known to your Guild. His description has been authenticated by the Shrine Keeper's Seriin sponsor. Fog is K'shai: the false one's tool, but true K'shai, nonetheless."

"Why does your Shrine Keeper interest himself in K'shai justice?"

"As I have told you, the Shrine Keeper serves justice in all things."

"And this great Seriin Lord who finances the Shrine Keeper's contracts?"

"The devoted are many."

* * *

The seamstress gazed beseechingly over the load of fabrics in her arms, as she struggled to reach the handle of the door to the attic workroom. The innkeeper's youngest daughter moved to open the door for her. "They never do give you a bit of rest, do they?" asked the girl in sympathy. The Troupe players intimidated the girl, but the seamstress was both foreign and subservient. The girl felt easy with her.

"I never knew a single garment could be altered so many times," replied the seamstress with a rueful sigh.

The innkeeper's daughter, bored with her own chores, leaned against the door jamb and settled herself eagerly to gossip of the rarefied beings who were Actors and Actresses with Rubi's Troupe. The girl enjoyed a lengthy talk. She would be puzzled, however, when she realized later that she could not recall the precise subject of the conversation, nor could she seem to recall where and when the conversation had occurred.

Rhianna closed the workroom door, having set a misty dream upon the troublesome daughter of the innkeeper. Rhianna spread the fabrics on the large table that Taf had commandeered for her. She frowned, and fabric fell from the lines that she drew upon it with her mind. She sighed, and the threads twisted and rewove themselves to her orders. She held her hands before her, and bleeding marks as of a needle's too frequent imprint appeared to mar her fine fingers; she fastened the illusion in her mind and then released it.

She sat and drew from a purse against her skin a potent thing of filigree and amber. She barriered the tiny workroom with a web of burning Power. She closed her eyes and walked into another realm.

She walked the Taormin's ways more surely now. She could see the vistas beyond the central pattern. She could see the veil of darkness where the vistas ended unnaturally. She could see the rent in the veil.

She stood on a path of fire, staring at the tortuous tangle of energy that crossed the rent. The fiercest part of the tangle extended beyond the bleak curtain; the tangle's bright fibers blurred the broken edges of the dark and tattered veil.

"*I did not cause this thing,*" said the little man, who came to stand behind her.

"*Horlach?*" she asked quietly.

The little man inclined his head. "*At your service, Lady Rhianna.*"

Rhianna smiled crookedly. "*I doubt that very much,*" she murmured. She nodded toward the dark veil. "*The curtain does not conform to the patterns. What is it?*"

"*It was called a closure by the mortal who configured it. It is the imprisoner of our world.*"

"*And of my son,*" added Rhianna dryly. "*A mortal constructed it?*"

"*A mortal,*" agreed Horlach. "*He created the Taormin.*"

"*A most remarkable mortal,*" Rhianna mused.

With care and great caution, she freed a single fiery fragment of the tangle. Released, the strand snapped free of the rent. The rent shifted, and a trickle of inky darkness spilled into the Taormin's bright plain. Rhianna recoiled. The little man laughed, but he, too, felt fear. "*You perceive,*" said the little man, "*that the problem is not a simple one. The son you carried at the instant of Rending has become the Taormin's single stabilizing force, but he is himself unstable.*"

"*Where is Kaedric?*" asked Rhianna, hating the need to ask, hating especially to ask of this dark and evil being.

"*If you do not know, how should I? I am weak now. My great Power has been stripped from me.*"

"*You still walk this world freely.*"

"*By Venkarel's leave. He is too cunning to discard a tool while he has yet a use for it.*"

"*I doubt the value of so treacherous a tool as yourself, Horlach.*"

Horlach gestured again to the tangle and the veil. "*This was not my doing,*" he repeated.

"*You wield even honesty as a weapon of deceit,*" said Rhianna with scorn.

The little man spread his hands. "*Why should I deceive you now? I am vanquished and helpless.*"

"*Why else should you have sought me here, save in hope of some gain for yourself?*"

"*I am trapped in this desolate place between worlds, perhaps for eternity. Is it so hard for you to believe that I am lonely?*"

"*You have chosen to remain. You fear to abdicate control of your spirit. Do not expect me to pity you for refusing death.*"

"*You understand little, Lady Rhianna. I cannot choose; the Venkarel has chosen for me. It is he who has sacrificed his natural life for the sake of his ambition. I assure you: I would never have chosen to abandon my mortal bonds for any cause. You know how I fought to regain that life, though achieving it would have cost me the greatest part of my Power. It is the Venkarel who has chosen Power over life."*

"You allowed him no alternative," said Rhianna tightly.

"For the instant only: Yes, for that instant of Rending, he required more than flesh could hold. But he has gained such Power now as you do not comprehend. He could resume his mortal life: the Power for it is within him."

"He would not steal another's life, as you would have done."

"He would do and will do exactly as he wishes. He plays his game alone, as always, and supremacy of his own strength is all that matters to him. You know him. You know his own fear: that he might be weak and used again as in his childhood. You know that he would do anything to ensure his own protection. For all his Power, he remains the frightened, lethal child of Ven, and his fear will destroy you, your son, and your world. I speak truly, Lady Rhianna; your Power knows."

"Stop!" commanded Rhianna sharply. She averted her sight from Horlach, the veil, and the tangle; she stared fixedly at the pattern she had woven for herself. *"I shall not heed such nonsense."* It was too hard to disbelieve that Kaedric had abandoned her, when she felt so dreadfully alone.

"Only I can help you save your son," said Horlach avidly. *"Lend me your Power, and I shall free him now. I shall not betray you. Now, Rhianna! Reach to me that I may save him."*

Rhianna tore herself free of the Taormin's world, racing through the deadly maze of energies. She threw herself into the saner world, the simpler world, where only one pattern ruled while day's light shone. She breathed heavily, as if she had run in truth, and she wrapped the Taormin into its silken shroud with trembling fingers.

She gathered the costumes into her arms. She draped herself in gray illusions. Her exhaustion was not feigned.

Chapter 11

I visited Silf once more before we left Diarmon. "Where is your shipbuilder?" I asked her caustically. I wanted only to assure myself that he would not enter unannounced.

Silf, knowing the purpose of my question, still answered carefully, "Marlund is with his cousin. The poor woman has lost her eldest son."

"How careless of her."

Silf rebuked me, "The boy is dead, Lyriel."

"So is the brother I never met, but I cannot mourn him very deeply."

"You are callous, Lyriel." I could see Silf's indignant pose hesitate and ebb. She became conspiratorial. "The boy was involved with Janeb's wife, and Janeb is a jealous man." Silf would never have made such a remark in her shipbuilder's hearing, for he disapproved of gossip. Our conversation became suddenly easy, as it had been of old.

"You think this Janeb killed the boy?" I did not care about strangers, but if Silf (my Silf) knew them, then they mattered.

"Janeb?" Silf laughed a little scornfully. "He could not kill a calf, if it were not tied and held for him. This job was a professional one: very clean and quick."

"K'shai," I whispered, my heart feeling leaden for no good reason at all.

Silf caught my mood. "The boy was no great loss. He would have been hanged before this if his father had been less wealthy." Silf paused. "He collected nasty secrets against people."

"You?" I demanded, startled out of my gloom.

"He tried. Once." She smiled wickedly—like Silf of old, who could stand up to anyone—and I loved her, but our brief rapport tumbled back into silence.

"We are leaving tomorrow," I told her, feeling terrible.

"I have scarcely seen you," she said wistfully.

"You could come with us." I was pleading, which was foolish. I knew her answer would only hurt me.

"No, Lyriel."

"You could at least come and speak with Taf."

"Lyriel, let us not argue."

"What else are you willing to do but argue?" I asked her. "You will not even try to understand Taf."

"Has Taf ever tried to understand me? Have you? I am your mother, Lyriel, not an ogre. Have you forgotten how we used to laugh together? We used to enjoy just talking to one another."

"I remember." All of the porcelain dolls were smiling. I wanted to smash their mocking happiness.

"Will you stay for supper?" She knew I would decline.

"I have too much to do before departing."

Silf shook her head at my feeble excuse. "I hope you have a prosperous season," she remarked distantly.

"Thank you. Please, do not summon that beastly servant. I prefer to open doors for myself." We did not embrace on parting. Neither of us wanted to face the other's useless tears.

I never allow the Troupe to see me cry. I walked for two hours, arriving late at the beach south of the Diarmon harbor. I would be caught by the night if I did not hurry, but I was not ready to face anyone who knew me. Some outskirt family could profit by my carelessness tonight. I sat on the sand and let the tide creep to my feet. The waves were mild. If they covered me, they would feel gentle and warm.

I paid for a night's shelter with a family of six who shared a crowded cottage. They were poor enough to welcome my coppers, if not my presence. I slept on the bare sand floor between the two youngest daughters, one of whom snored. I heard no Rendies wail outside the heavy, plaited frond shutters. It was the soundest night's sleep I had known since Ardas, even if I did dream about a lover who became a Rendie in my arms.

"Where have you been?" Rubi screeched at me in welcome the next morning. "We were ready to leave an hour ago!"

The Troupe members were still rushing to check final loads, so I knew that Rubi exaggerated. I waved her an acknowledgment and went to clear my room. "Rubi is frothing," whispered Noryne to me in hasty passing on the stairs.

"You know the schedule," growled Taf when he saw me.

"I set the blasted schedule," I informed him in retort. "I can change it." We traveled mostly at night in any case, for the inland sun could be brutal between oases, and night travel was more efficient between villages. "We have ten days before we are due in Samth," I shouted through my room's door. "We need only six days to cross the Aadi by the Merchants' Route. You can spare me one miserable hour. If you were not such a stubborn, accursed fool, Taf, you would go see Silf yourself. But no, she left, and far be it from you ever to go and tell her that you miss her. Are you listening to me, Taf?" I was beginning to cry again. I raised my head to see Evaric at my door, looking startled. "What do you want?" I asked him gruffly, dropping my head quickly when I realized that he could see my tears. Crying twice in two days: blast Taf and Silf both.

"Mistress Rubi," said Evaric tonelessly, "asked me to carry your trunk to the wagon."

Blast Rubi, she would choose to send the K'shai. "I know how to call someone to load a trunk," I yelled at him.

"Perhaps I should return when you finish packing." He was looking at my ill-fitting costume with a sort of quirkily sympathetic expression, which made me want to scream.

Anyone less quick than a K'shai would have been struck by the door when I slammed it. I promised myself to strangle the Alisa if I discovered she had told Evaric about Silf. When it occurred to me that I had just shouted a great many of my private concerns across the inn, I began to curse myself.

I changed my clothes, threw the costume into my trunk with

loathing, opened the door, and found the K'shai waiting quietly, leaning against the wall as if altogether unconcerned by all the flurry of last minute rushing around him. "Take it," I ordered him sharply.

He was clever enough not to speak or even show his confoundedly charming smile. If he had done either, I really would have screamed. He lifted the awkward trunk lightly and followed me to the wagon without word or expression of any kind.

We left Diarmon over twenty minutes later. Rubi had forgotten to pay one of her young men. I failed pointedly to accuse her of delaying us.

We followed a shorter, quicker route than pilgrims used to reach the southern cities; it was a desolate way. We gave no performances between Diarmon and Samth, for no intervening settlements existed. Nothing substantial survived long in that barren land, called the Aadi.

The Aadi deserved the night. Stars emblazoned the sky, and the sand's slow dunes stretched against the wind. The trails shifted with the sand; not a hundred Ardasians knew the secret ways of crossing. Where Taf learned, I never heard, but he had taught me all the songs he knew of the Aadi and the ancient markers. I would never be lost on the Aadi, which spared me from the greatest fear the Aadi could convey. Occasionally, I even made a point of riding alone past some ridge of sand and standing free from sight or sound of any person; I danced for the joy of solitude, imagining for a time that I owed no one any debt of love or caring, imagining that I could be as free and starkly pure as the ageless, empty sand. I never stayed alone in the desert for long.

Three days from Diarmon, we encountered a train of merchants out of Samth. We spent an awkward day together, crossing tempers at the single well, but conflicts ebbed with the waning afternoon. Tabok and the merchants' cook began to prepare something of a feast. Rubi dismissed the players from rehearsal, and all of us began to gather around the three large fires, where bubbling stews and grain cakes scented the desert air.

I supped with the merchant father, a man named Chalas, because Rubi had told me to entertain him and keep Taf from robbing him too obviously. She had taken charge of the son, who looked like he might have preferred to be left to the attentions of his Toy, a pretty girl with a vacuous expression. Chalas was not bad company, until something started him on the topic of his standing in the cotton market. I applauded inwardly when Rayn brought out his gitar and sent Solomai's youngest boy to draw me into a dance.

At barely eight years old, Zel could not manage the traditional partner dances, but we improvised our own and seemed to please our audience. Miria and Tana joined us, and we began a simple round. When Zakari and Minaro joined, the dance became more serious. Zel yielded his place to Kodelh, and Silvia dragged Jaon into the circle. Kriisa began to dance with her brother, Lotin, though she watched my partner more than her own; Kriisa had developed a youthful passion for Kodelh, much to Solomai's dismay.

"We need a sixth couple, Eolh!" Eolh was the only male player not yet dancing or playing an instrument.

"Alisa," I called cheerfully.

Alisa gave a smooth imitation of eagerness as she rose with Eolh; it was her best performance of the season. She had always danced poorly. The audience of merchants and half-drunk wagoners would never notice points of skill, but Alisa and I knew her lack. I enjoyed an unkind hope that a handsome K'shai might recognize her inadequacy as well.

"May your eyes rot," Alisa whispered to me as we spun past each other in the intricate steps.

I could not retort, because the dance carried me away. Kodelh was not much older than Lotin, but he was strong enough to lift me, and he controlled his energy in easy cadence with Rayn's staccato strings, Sama's drum, and Bethali's chimes. We began a more exotic dance, which required deeper concentration.

The light turned ruddy, but we who danced did not notice. The flame spread unnatural fingers, searching angrily for better fuel than a ring of timber. The fire caught the Toy's flimsy skirt, and her merchant patron battered at the flame with hasty surprise.

The ache of cold wraith-glow pierced us, who had forgotten that night approached. We stopped abruptly in the dance. Kodelh's hands still gripped my waist. The merchants' K'shai had already begun their own dance: slow, fierce, and very different from our frivolous act.

Most of the expressions around me already grew blank. Kodelh's hand slipped from me as he sank to the ground. I sat beside him, compelled not by Rendie spell but by longing for the reassurance of mortal warmth.

We had no time to reach the wagons with their false suggestions of safety. No wagon of sufficient substance to deter a Rendie could be drawn practicably across the sands and rough roads of Ardasia, but even insubstantial canvas gave better comfort than the smallness of the K'shai steel that saved us. The K'shai themselves seemed tiny against the wraith things they fought.

A Rendie's loose form coalesced from blurred nothingness and drifted around one of the merchants' K'shai. A second wraith gathered its undulating limbs around the merchants' other K'shai, a man only a fraction less massive than his partner but dwarfed by his terrible foe. The K'shai dance neared lightning's likeness; the Rendies spun deeper into the pattern's tight circle. Sometimes a Rendie would vanish on the touch of a K'shai's silvered sword, though not even the sharpest steel should have reasonably injured a phantasm; a K'shai must believe that he can kill, Key had told me, despite any contradiction imparted by logic. A fractional doubt would open the K'shai to Rendie soul-stealing. To kill a Rendie, said Key, demanded no more than perfect strength, quickness, endurance, concentration, and good fortune; I had never gauged the weight of truth in Key's facetious comment.

A cloud of Rendies barred my view of Evaric, for they swirled around him thickly. I had never seen so many Rendies gathered at one place and time, and I had seen the chilling K'shai game too frequently. Fog stood apart, observing the cloud with an air of almost detached appraisal. He strolled into the Rendies' midst, and the wraith things stretched away from him and from Evaric. Evaric's sword flashed briefly, striking sparks and erasing an entire Rendie sphere; the Rendies' shrieks might have curdled the sand.

Evaric saluted Fog with an ironic flourish. Fog raised his own sword in bland response. Our two K'shai commenced a more orthodox pattern, but I had the feeling that theirs was a performance no more real than my seduction of Kodelh in the dance. The Rendies wove in dreadful cycles against the merchants' K'shai. They floated away from Fog as if his proximity terrified them. They spun around Evaric as if his presence tantalized them. I shuddered and pressed closer to Kodelh, but I could not feel him. I could not feel anything.

Those of us whom the K'shai had Protected stirred from trance and shook to discover the sky still dark. The aftermath of the Rendie contact had left me with an aching at the base of my skull and a burning blur of vision. I saw Alisa rouse herself, fling herself upon Evaric, and burrow into his grasp. Since Alisa was one who never recalled anything past a Rendie's first appearance, I found her urgent trembling for her Protector's arms irritatingly opportunistic. I rather wished that her ploy had occurred to me.

Rhianna stood before the Taormin's rent, observing the bleak trickle of dark energy that emerged. The trickle had increased; it was a slight change, but she did not doubt its existence or its source.

"*You see,*" remarked Horlach, "*how fragile is the fabric. The Taormin amplifies Power; it also magnifies the repercussions of ignorance.*"

In some small, unwary corner of herself, Rhianna derived a faint gladness of Horlach's presence. He was evil: vile and rotted. He repulsed her, but he represented kindred in a sense that only Kaedric might have understood entirely. "*I wonder, Horlach, if you know the Taormin as well as you pretend. Kaedric did take it from you.*"

"*He has also left it to me—and to you. Lady Rhianna. He has left it and you and all ties to your mortal world. He has defined his own infinity elsewhere; I shall not pretend to any knowledge akin to his in that arena. I do suggest that any remedy for the Rending must be yours and mine to devise, for only you and I now walk here, where the rent is tangible. You cannot depend upon your Venkarel to resolve this battle for you; he has gone from your very universe, and he will not return.*"

"*Do not think to lure me into trusting you above him, Horlach. If Kaedric has left me irrevocably, he had good reason, and I love him no whit less for it.*"

"*I vie not for your love, Lady Rhianna, but for your understanding of the magnitude of the horror that approaches us.*"

"*Persuade me of your trustworthiness,*" Rhianna said dryly.

"*How shall I overcome this prejudice you have against me? By some token word of honesty? I have told you the only crucial truth: aid me with your Power, or nothing will survive.*"

"A 'token word' would be more likely to allay my doubts than blatant lies and shifting 'truths.' I am not so mesmerized by the Taormin that I grow witless within it."

"You maintain your pattern well, Lady Rhianna, as I should expect of one trained by the Venkarel. Hence, I shall grant you your token: the greatest present danger to your son is that very guild with which he affiliates himself. The K'shai deal with Rending creatures by denying fear, that substance for which a Rending creature hungers above all else. The K'shai are served well by their simplistic conceit, but your son is menaced by it. In denying his fear, he taps the subtle harmony between himself and those he fights. He facilitates the Rending creatures' entry into the mortal world. He accelerates the coming of catastrophe."

"How would you propose that I discourage my son in his vocation?"

"Remove his K'shai partner, and other, more imminent interests will take precedence."

"Remove Fog?" mocked Rhianna. "You mean, I suppose, that I should murder him by my Power."

"He is himself a murderer, and he destroys your son."

"I am not an executioner."

"You are the Infortiare, whose duty it is to preserve the mortal world from the destructive use of Power. Your son is a sorcerer, and the K'shai encourage him to be destructive. Which do you rank most highly, Lady Rhianna: your duty as Infortiare or the pretty sensibilities of your sheltered rearing? The survival of your world and all its peoples? Or the survival of a coarse, ignorant brute whose sole purpose is to kill and spend the profit on his base and fleshly pleasures?"

"You weary me, Horlach, with your pious talk, when you are the chief destroyer of these many ages. Your token truth is like you, and it merits nothing." Rhianna spoke with stern grandeur and authority, and Horlach fled from her wrath.

Alone, Rhianna felt small again. Surreptitiously, she turned her Power to a study of Fog, but the K'shai was shallow and unenlightening; a deeper probe would injure him. With a sigh of resignation, Rhianna departed the Taormin and returned to the Aadi by night. When she noted that the Rending creatures had attacked the Troupe viciously in her Power's absence, she berated herself soundly for losing time to Horlach's practiced sophistry.

Chapter 12

Arahinos had few visitors, being largely overlooked in favor of the larger cities, Samth and Destin to the north and Mikolaii to the west. Only the Arahinos copper mine kept the supply merchants coming year after year. The houses lined a single street, if the erratic path among the houses merited such a name. The houses were all stone, for wood was scarce, and the doors and shutters were beaten out of the native copper. We presented our play at the Gathering Place, a ring of stone benches surrounding a patch of desert. Our portable stage always looked its grandest in Arahinos.

We had performed annually in Arahinos for as long as we had been a troupe. The citizens of Arahinos could not pay us as well as some of our patrons, but they always greeted our arrival with enthusiasm. They opened their best houses to us, since Arahinos lacked an inn to accommodate us, and the residents scattered with their relatives for the duration of our stay.

We had true friends in Arahinos. My own favorite was Grenz, an old and nearly crippled miner, who was much the canniest inhabitant of the town. He sought me when we arrived, and I ran to greet him eagerly, but he remained unwontedly solemn. "You have new K'shai," he remarked.

I followed the direction of his glance. Fog had emerged from one of the houses near the Gathering Place. Fog evidently sensed my contemplation, for he turned abruptly and faced me. Fog's wearily sardonic expression never varied greatly, but I fancied it held something near to an amused challenge. For a hurried, shadowy instant, I could have sworn that his eyes glowed as they had that one time in Ardas. I answered Grenz absently, "Yes. Key met a wind-snake outside Patricum."

"Nasty things, wind-snakes," muttered Grenz. After a moment, he added, "Are you in trouble, girl?"

"No," I replied, startled. "Why?"

"Someone in your company is a target."

"Not possible," I murmured, as I tried to set aside my horror and assess Grenz' statement calmly. "You think Rubi and Taf attract the caliber of enemies who can finance K'shai retaliation? Now, if you start seeing irate merchants from Ardas, let me know without delay."

"I never would worry about you holding your own against any merchant."

"Did you ever know me to involve myself in any trouble I could not handle?"

Grenz grunted, and he grinned very briefly. "You have a slippery way with you, girl, and I never doubted it, but a K'shai, all armed for killing, is not the kind of trouble to be avoided by clever words and quick wits. The K'shai earn their fees, and this one has been watching the road from the bluffs for the last week. No one in Arahinos ever afforded a K'shai." Having made his inarguable statement, Grenz left me. My eyes returned reluctantly to Fog, who was now studying the Gathering Place for some obscure purpose of his own.

"My partner interests you, Mistress Lyriel?" Blast him, he moved so quietly.

"I have no interest in any K'shai, Master Evaric." I mocked his Seriin formal tone.

"You have made that very clear, Mistress Lyriel."

Looking up at him, at his smoky blue-silver eyes, was like staring too long at the sun-bright sea. When I blinked and found him gone, the rest of the world was dark and dull by comparison.

"Kriisa's red dress in the first act is too bold," shouted Rubi into my distraction. "Have the seamstress make her something more in keeping with the character. We need it by morning."

I responded automatically, "Anni is already altering the costumes for the chorus of serving women. Which takes precedence?"

"All of them—and tell her to replace the braid on Minaro's cloak. It should be gold not gray."

"She is new at costuming, Rubi."

"If she cannot handle the job, hire someone else!" Rubi could reduce tea with a Tanist to a trivial accomplishment, so long as the deed was another's. I abandoned my useless fretting over K'shai and cryptic warnings as I went to assign Anni an impossible task.

By the time night had fallen, all of my suppressed worry had reemerged in full, and I could not sleep. I shifted uneasily, trying to find some comfortable position. My bed was but a thin mattress laid flat on the stone floor. The mattress was filled with straw, and the straw had been packed into lumps. Every lump seemed to prod me with fiendish ingenuity.

I almost fell off the mattress' edge when I heard the door creak. It was only a door to the rest of the small house, I reminded myself firmly; the girl whose room I occupied had been very proud of that door, for interior rooms in Arahinos were generally divided by no more than curtains. This house boasted true rooms: four of them, built of stone and furnished with copper wares and straw-stuffed cushions. It was the most substantial house in Arahinos, which was why Rubi had claimed one of the rooms for herself.

The door creaked again. A midnight inspiration to change a script had probably claimed Rubi's small sense of courtesy. The uncertain construction of the house could have caused the door to shift on its own. Any number of harmless reasons existed for a sound of copper hinges whining.

And footsteps. Blast, there were footsteps. I should open my eyes instead of cowering under a linen sheet which had failed even to hide the mattress lumps. Rubi would have spoken by now; Taf would never wake me in the night save in emergency. Who occupied the fourth room? I could not think. The footsteps were dragging, and a sound of raspy, labored breathing accompanied them.

Who else had stayed in this house? The fourth room was the kitchen. Rubi had assigned someone to it: the seamstress? The pilgrim woman would never enter my room uninvited.

Why had I laid my dagger on the table across the room? It was a tiny room, but I could not reach the table in a single move. I occupied an insignificant room with a stone floor being crossed by someone who had entered the house from the night: someone who had not feared Rendies. Would a K'shai kill quickly?

"Lyriel?" The voice was hesitant and soft. It exuded pain.

I threw the sheet from my head and sat upright rapidly.

"Sands of the Aadi, Noryne, you scared ten years from me. I heard the raggedness of her breath more clearly. What are you doing here?" She had been assigned to a house on the other side of town, and it was night. "How did you come here?" I fumbled for the oil lamp, found it and dropped the match. "Blast."

"I was with Zakari." Who was quartered across the street. And it was night.

I found and lit the match and wished I had not retrieved it. Noryne's wrist dangled limply. Her skirt was streaked and spattered with blood. "Zakari did this to you?" I asked her softly. The bloodstain on her skirt was still spreading, I jerked at the sheet to free myself.

"Alisa has left him." Noryne held remarkably steady, but I tried to support her. Her poor hand was dark with suffused bleeding. The bones were awry, jutting against the skin.

"So he beats you." I could too easily picture Zakari hitting her once in anger, hitting again in frustration, continuing because Noryne would not stop him. She would weep inwardly and cherish the pain along with her guilt over things she imagined to be wrong. She had been beaten often before she left her pilgrim fostering.

I made her lie on the bed. She winced at trying to sink down to the level of it. The lumpy mattress must have been cruel to those bruises. I studied the streaks of blood and her injured hand. "I am going to bring Anni here." I hoped it really was Anni in the kitchen, and I hoped that Anni knew more of healing than how to prepare an herbal restorative, such as she had made for several members of the Troupe. Maybe she could only be kind, but that alone would be better help than Rubi could give. "Stay put!"

All of the rooms opened to a single hall. Noryne's arrival would not have penetrated Taf's drunken depression, and Rubi sleeps like the dead unless she is inspired. I found Anni awake, seated on a braided sleeping rug, leaning against the kitchen's inner wall. She was much more composed about midnight intrusions than I.

"How much do you know of healing?" I asked her.

"I have assisted healers many times." She reached for her cloak. Pilgrim prudery, I thought with irritation. "Take me to her, Lyriel."

Noryne whispered as we entered. "He was so lonely. He was so unhappy. He needed to talk to someone. I only meant to listen. I only wanted to help him."

Anni had moved to the tiny copper table, where she used water from the ewer to concoct an acridly odorous paste. "Keep her quiet," said the seamstress firmly, which was good advice but a difficult act to implement.

Noryne cried restlessly. "He said that Alisa had betrayed him. He asked me if I knew what it was like to love someone so much that nothing else mattered, not truth, not life, not even happiness. I told him that I did understand. I told him that I loved him. He struck me."

Anni brought the paste and a goblet of herbed wine. She coaxed the goblet to Noryne's swollen lips. "No more talk, Noryne," ordered Anni gently.

"I have lost my child," continued Noryne despite the order.

"You cannot lose what you never had," I grumbled, thinking that the child's loss was the only good to come of this night's doings. The look that Anni gave me scorched the words from my tongue.

Anni's murmur to Noryne was all gentleness. "I shall set your wrist, Noryne. I shall hold the pain away from you, but you must try to help me. You must remain still and quiet. The procedure will take only a moment, and then you will sleep." While she spoke, Anni wrenched Noryne's protruding bones into their proper places. She bound the wrist with a splint and a layer of her herbal paste.

"Brainless little fool," I muttered at Noryne, who fell into a heavy slumber even as Anni had promised.

"For loving the wrong man? Or for wanting his child?"

"Both."

"She does not regret the love."

"She is a fool."

Anni and I shared the floor of the tiny room through the remainder of the night. Noryne stirred only once. She called to me.

"Lyriel, you will not blame him, will you? Promise me that you will not blame Zakari."

She would not be silenced until I gave her my promise, though it goaded me to do it. When Noryne had extracted a like promise from Anni, she pleaded with us not to let Rubi know of Zakari's part in the night's events. Only after we had both agreed did Noryne sink again into uncannily silent sleep.

"How badly is she hurt?" I asked Anni in a muffled breath full of thwarted anger and pity.

"Badly, but she will mend. It is not easy to do lasting damage to a sorceress."

"A sorceress?" I hissed.

"Her Power is suppressed and immature, but she has begun to recognize it. She needs training, before her uncontrolled empathy causes her to repeat her folly with Master Zakari or another." Anni turned her face to me thoughtfully. The dim lamplight made an aura of her hair. Without the concealing pilgrim hood, she looked both younger and older.

I recalled Taf's perception of oddness about Anni. "You are a sorceress."

She did not speak at first. When she did respond, she spoke with a sigh. "I am a wizardess, Lyriel. My presence has certainly contributed to the awakening of Noryne's Power. That is the way of Power. It acts upon its own kind, often forcibly. I suspect that Noryne has been largely sheltered from Power's influence until recently."

"Noryne asked me about Ixaxins before we left Ardas." And I had told her that Ixaxin schools were for foreigners and not for Ardasians to consider; some day I might learn not to issue my opinions so indiscriminately.

"Perhaps other Power than mine affected her in Ardas. It is a populous city." Anni was distant.

I had never met an Ixaxin previously, as far as I knew. I felt vaguely that I should hate Anni for her unusual, unsuspected talent; resentment, at the least, composed the conventional attitude. Foreigners described Ixaxins as monstrous, but this was Anni, who was kind. She also sewed superbly, and I could no more match her stitchery than I could do—whatever a wizardess did. I could not seem to envy her either skill.

Her admission did augment my interest in her. A hundred questions jostled in my head. "Rendies avoid you who have Power?"

"The Rending creatures find Power unpalatable. It has a corrosive effect on them, but it also fascinates them. They do not avoid it; they avoid direct contact with it."

For a moment, I was too busy observing Anni to respond. A certain bright, hard depth of clarity, which was new, emerged from her. Something soft and humble, expected of a pilgrim, had gone from her. She was very finely boned and delicate, quite lovely in an oddly esoteric way. I usually noticed such things immediately. Anni wore a stone around her neck; it was almost a moonstone, such as were sometimes found on shores near Diarmon, but her stone was larger and more changeable in the light. I had the suspicion that I was seeing a part of what a wizardess was: whatever she chose to appear to be. "Power fascinates the Rendies?" I mused curiously. "Do you mean that it might actually attract them?"

"Incidents have been recorded."

My next question formed itself, for I was not aware of thinking it. "Can a sorcerer become K'shai?"

The lamp flickered, flared, and subsided. The flame cast darting shadows across Anni's face. She did not want to answer me. All of her visible emotion over Noryne closed in upon itself, and she became cold. I had never seen anyone more thoroughly controlled. I derived a rather horrible and incomprehensible satisfaction from the transformation.

"A man is born to Power, or he is not," replied Anni rigidly. "He may choose to become K'shai, or he may not. By Ceallagh's law, a sorcerer of any significant Power must be trained and made a wizard. The K'shai Guild would not knowingly accept such a man. No one in your Troupe's employ has utilized active Power since I joined you, Lyriel." Noryne moved again. "We are disturbing her with our talk," said Anni.

"It must be nearly morning."

"Soon."

"Not soon enough," I muttered. I closed my eyes, but I did not sleep.

Rhianna's anger made her Power burn; it seared the Taormin's plain, and the patterns near her shifted in alarm. *"Hear me, Hor-*

lach," she cried across the plain. *"I recognize your handiwork. 'Can a sorcerer become K'shai?' indeed. I do thank you for the warning: I had not considered the value you might place on such a tool as Lyriel. I have sealed her from you now. If I find that you have wrought your mischief in other quarters, I shall be less forgiving. I can punish you, Horlach, in a most unpleasant manner."*

"Threats are unbecoming, Lady Rhianna. Why do you blame me for the girl's words? Would I risk your anger for the trivial amusement of prodding the girl's subconscious doubts into expression?"

"She was influenced. She does not comprehend Power sufficiently well to formulate the connection for herself."

"I did not influence her, Lady Rhianna. You blame me unjustly. Test me. You will sense truth in me."

Rhianna hesitated before the confident taunt, but she issued the probe of Power. *"So,"* she acknowledged stiffly. *"I have wronged you. I apologize."* Horlach thanked her graciously. Rhianna trusted him less than ever.

Chapter 13

Too many worries beset me. After informing Rubi firmly that the cause of Noryne's accident had best remain unspecified, I went in search of our young K'shai. Since Arahinos could not stable all of our animals, our K'shai would have spent the night Protecting. Evaric would not have slept yet, which I hoped would make him more vulnerable and not more difficult. I could not sit and sensibly await his convenience.

I did feel briefly guilty when I found him quartered near the Gathering Place, condemned to seek sleep while two loudly enthused Arahinos matrons gossiped in the kitchen. The women became more excited when I appeared, but I only nodded to them. I tried each of the curtained alcoves before locating Evaric. He jumped to his feet as I entered, looking abruptly relieved when he identified his visitor. I wondered whom he had expected; his sword was in his hand.

He raised the sword. "I ought to use this on you for waking me." To my relief, he laid the sword carefully on the stone ledge which served as table. "I have not had a pleasant night, Mistress Lyriel. Please forgive my brusqueness."

"Are you a target?" I asked him bluntly.

"Yes," he replied with a directness that disarmed me completely.

"Why did you not warn us when we hired you?" I had not wanted it to sound like a plea.

Evaric regarded me soberly. "You asked only if I sought to complete any conflicting contracts while in service to you. You did not ask if I were the subject of any such contracts."

"You quibble over semantics," I retorted.

"If I had told you, would it have mattered? You needed K'shai desperately. You would have hired anyone at that point."

I could lose myself just in watching him. "K'shai do not hunt K'shai," I said. He began to reach toward me and stopped. I could not remember what I had meant to say. "Branded with fire," I murmured, staring fixedly at his strong and slender hand. "K'shai initiation must be painful."

He rubbed at the brand with his other hand and shrugged. "I barely remember. None of it seemed very real."

"How long ago?"

"Seven years." The outer door slammed. I could hear Minaro offering arrogant advice on acting. "It seemed a small enough sacrifice at the time, all considered."

"And now?"

"Perspectives change." He was rueful.

"You are an assassin." I was shouting it at myself. "Whether you have killed seven men or seven hundred."

"Eight. As of last night. Fog is burying him. Master Straw, I believe: the K'shai who pursued me from Ardas. Reveal that to your Troupe, if you like." Only cynical bitterness remained in his smile now.

And I had worried about Evaric. I left him hurriedly, so that he would not see how miserably sickened I felt.

Noryne felt the emptiness within her more keenly than the pain. The quilt still showed the traces of blood, though Lyriel had tried to clean it. The skirt was ruined.

What was the use of anything? Life gave nothing but hurt. It hurt too much. Noryne could not bear more hurt. Please, she prayed, let me die now; let me go into nothingness.

It would hurt to take the knife and run it across her wrists. But that was the way it was done; she had heard of it from the pilgrims, who called it sin. But all that she had done was sin. This sin would end the rest. It would be better to die than to live more evils.

The knife was not very sharp. It would hurt a little more, but it would yield the end of hurting. She had only to place it so—she could scarcely feel the blade's edge. When she pressed it, the blood would spill. She should cover the rug with her shawl.

Noryne placed the knife on the table with reverent care. It was kind of Lyriel to have brought Noryne's trunk here; Lyriel had always been kind. Noryne smiled faintly. She selected the oldest shawl first, then replaced it in favor of the newer one. She touched the finely woven fabric, remembering how proud she had been to wear it. The colors were soft and muted like the sands in shadow. She folded the fingers of her sound hand around the handle of the knife.

"Stop it!" commanded Lyriel from the door. She snatched the knife from Noryne's grasp. "What are you trying to do?" shouted Lyriel angrily, her dark eyes brimming with frightened tears. "Condemn me to play your roles for the rest of the season?"

"Please, Lyriel." Noryne shared Lyriel's fear, and the anguish spread. "Please," whispered Noryne. She reached weakly for the knife; it came to her hand.

"No!" Lyriel strode to the door. "Anni!" she called urgently.

Anni appeared, wrapped in pilgrim gray but looking golden. "She will survive, Lyriel. Power will not allow her any other course." Anni touched Lyriel's arm, and Lyriel's terrible urgency ebbed into a quiet echo of Anni's calm. "My satchel is in the kitchen. Please bring it to me." Lyriel obeyed without hesitation. "She fears for you, Noryne," said Anni. "She thinks you meant to use the knife against yourself."

"I did, Anni. I must."

"You cannot. You must understand that death solves nothing. It is not an end but a gate, and whatever sorrows or joys you bear will follow you. Your Power lets you see the lesser gates and comprehend them. There does exist a final gate of peace, but you will not reach it by your suicide."

"I cannot escape." The beautiful promise of endless darkness ran from her.

"You will heal, Noryne. I shall teach you."

Noryne felt Anni's deep strength and thought of trees; it was a strange comparison for a daughter of the desert to make. Noryne felt Lyriel's more distant worry. She tried to feel Zakari, and she felt nothing.

"He is hollow, Noryne. You love an illusion."

"I have lost my child. I have only illusion left."

"You have Power, Noryne. You have permitted it to use you by accepting its contradictory advice. You must not trust your Power blindly. Your Power will seek madness. Master it, Noryne!"

Noryne twisted the lovely, soft shawl. The knife clattered on the floor.

Chapter 14

Taf has never liked Tanists. They are wealthy, and Taf considers them miserly for failing to convey their wealth to him. The Tanist of Mikolaii is particularly wealthy, which alone should have warned Rubi against performing in that city.

I knew as soon as I saw the Tanist's servants carting the workers' wages to the Tanist's mill. All of that lovely, shiny silver parading past the theater: no wonder Taf had disappeared before the second act. "Taf is at his art again," I whispered to Solomai. "Tell Rubi to plan accordingly."

I raced along the sandy street toward the Tanist's mill. I reached the wage cart in time to see Taf, pretending intoxication, stumble in front of it. The cart's drivers stopped and cursed him, but he sat in the road and cooed absurdly at their mules. One of the cart's guards dismounted, grumbling, and pulled Taf from the cart's path. Taf tripped and struck the side of the cart.

"I wonder how much silver you claimed with that little maneuver," I muttered to myself, wondering how I could prevent him from claiming more. I walked toward Taf and the guards. "So there you are," I said with loud disgust. "Drunk again," I grumbled, taking Taf's arm. Taf glared at me as I stole a full pouch of silver from his coat; replacing it on the cart would be difficult, because Taf would not cooperate.

"Let go of me," snapped Taf, which was warning. "Who are you, girl?" Sands, I thought, he had done it again: notified the constables of his own impending crime.

They arrived before I could react. The pouch of silver felt suddenly heavy, held tightly beneath my arm and hidden chiefly by misdirection. I backed away from Taf. It was I who had possession of the silver and the guilt by implication; explanations would achieve only the amusement of the constables and guards. I exchanged one desperate glance with Taf and ran. Taf would maintain his role of innocent drunk, and no evidence existed by which to detain him, so long as they did not catch me with the silver.

I ran through the streets. The constables pursued me. I could outpace them for a time, for I could choose the path to suit myself, and I could slip through cracks and holes that they must circumvent.

I wished I were more familiar with Mikolaii. I had no safe goal. I stashed the silver beneath a scrubby weed, for I expected to be caught. I dodged into an alley and faced a high block wall. I turned, and two winded constables stood determinedly before me.

I gave them my most dazzling smile. "Lovely day for a run," I remarked brightly. They did not appear to be amused.

A barbed, black disk spun through the air in a deadly whir and embedded itself in the wall beside the oldest constable's neck. Both constables ducked, as a second disk flew between them. I dodged the disks and darted between the men, gambling that the source of the disks had aimed to miss. I was inexpressibly relieved to see Evaric.

He jerked me behind the wall that had concealed him. "Meet me at the stables at dusk," he told me hurriedly. "We can leave the city by night and rejoin the Troupe in Walier." He cast another disk; it cut the shoulder of the constable who had come nearest. "Go!" Evaric hissed at me, and I obeyed.

I did not dare approach any member of the Troupe too closely. I did reach the wagon that I shared with Taf, and I folded the spare canvas in the fashion that signaled my status. I spent the remainder of the afternoon hiding inside an empty cistern and counting the silver, which I had retrieved. The silver did not constitute enough to merit the risk that Taf had taken; as usual, it was the hazard of the undertaking that had enticed him.

Near dusk, I emerged cautiously. I could see the stables and a few straggling visitors confining their steeds for the night. I waited. The shadows of evening stretched. The stable doors had been closed and barred, and all sensible folk were safely hidden behind solid walls. I crossed the stable yard and found no Evaric. I tried the stable door, but the bar had been locked in place, and I had no tools with which to breach the lock. I leaned against the stable wall and watched the sun vanish.

Something darted across the darkened sky, and I almost screamed from fright. I shut my eyes very tightly, wondering with a pang how K'shai first learned to abide the night. I began silently to recite all the roles of our most current play; I visualized every gesture, and I forced the emotions of the characters to dominate my own stark terror. The knot within me loosened, and I dared to re-open my outer senses.

Evaric had strung my dappled mare behind his roan. He was leading them from the stable. The horses were not eager, but my mare nuzzled me for reassurance and reward. She politely accepted a bit of dried apple from Evaric.

Evaric handed me the reins of his roan, while he resecured the stable door behind him. "I was beginning to think you had forgotten me," I told him a bit indignantly.

"I have had you in sight since the sun set," he replied, sounding distinctly less than pleased.

"Did you tell Rubi that we would meet the Troupe in Walier?"

"Yes." He was curt.

"Thank you for your assistance earlier. How did you happen to find me?"

"I sensed you," he answered, and since I did not understand, I abandoned talk and attended my horse.

The air stung me with unusual cold as we rode. The sky burned clear, and the stars were so numerous that they blurred into hazy bands. The moon rose after midnight, and its brilliance cast eerie patterns in our way. The clatter of hooves sputtered loudly across the road's broken paving.

Near dawn, we passed the dry stream bed which marked Miko-laii's boundary. The lands between domains are subject to any law that cares to enter them, but we had run the horses most of the night. We had little shelter but a good five hours' margin against pursuit. Evaric allowed a rest of half that time, then he forced us to travel again.

"I hardly think that Mikolaii's constabulary will bother to chase me this far," I grumbled.

"My job, Mistress Lyriel, is to Protect you," answered Evaric coolly. "I intend to employ all reasonable precautions." He still rode bare-headed, though the sun had begun to sear the morning. His dark hair looked fiery where the light touched it, and his expression suggested an inner drive exceeding K'shai duty to Protect. His leanness and K'shai grace would certainly make him compelling on the stage. I caught myself; I did not intend to fall again into the trap of forgetting what he represented.

"Sorry to inconvenience you this way," I tried.

He shrugged indifferently. "I am well paid for it."

Indeed you are, I thought. "Alisa will be desolate without you," I said irritably. I disliked being treated like unpleasant portage.

"Probably," he returned with detached arrogance. I attempted no more conversation; I did not require the approbation of a K'shai.

We stopped for brief intervals throughout the day, but Evaric pressed us to a rapid pace. In late afternoon, I rebelled. The sweltering sun alone would have deterred any sane individual, and we had come within sight of Walier's outlying hillocks. We could let the heat of the day pass and still reach Walier before full night. I sat, refusing to budge. Evaric looked inclined to load me onto horseback with the luggage, but he leashed his irritation. Rubi paid him, but I had employed him.

I awoke to a darkness broken by the crackle of firelight. After all his haste to proceed, Evaric had allowed me to sleep into the night. Perhaps, I mused, he was endeavoring to make a point, but I did not intend to be more sparing of criticism for that reason. No decent professional should allow annoyance to supercede sense.

I sat upright rather stiffly. My eyes felt heavy with sleep, as if I had been awakened unnaturally from a deep, long slumber. I could not seem to focus clearly; a milky blur coated the world. I turned my head slightly, for I could see the night peripherally. It was not my eyes which lacked clarity.

The K'shai sat as he had sat before I slept, but the Rendies danced around him. This resembled no K'shai dance; this constituted a gathering, and it was Rendies who designed it. They had surely claimed Evaric's soul, for I had never seen so many Rendies collected. They numbered more than had beset us on the long road from Diarmon, and we had met them then with four K'shai. You will have leisure, my clever instincts informed me, to regret Evaric when you have secured your own escape; still, it hurt to feel the loss of him. Such a pointless waste, I told myself severely.

"Accept your kindred, Fire-child. You belong among us. You cannot close us away, for we are within your essence."

The voice made my pulse freeze, for it was inhuman and seditious. It was relentless and irresistible. It craved a soul.

The Rendies had no interest in me. Other quarry had obsessed them. The Rendies were as besotted as Alisa, who would not care for the character of her rivals.

Evaric was conversing with Rendies, as even a K'shai ought not to be able to do. I apologized inwardly to the Bethiin sailor, who had tried to warn me. I could only comprehend a fraction of the Rendies' meanings, but Evaric's words penetrated indelibly. In fact, he said little, merely cycling through the same words endlessly. "I am of *this* world. I am Evaric, son of Evram and Terrell. My father serves Lord Baerod. I am of Tyntagel. I am of Serii. I am neither wizard nor sorcerer, and I have no Power. I am K'shai, and no world exists but the world of my day."

The Rendies called to him, reached to him, caressed him with vaporous tendrils, though the effect seemed to pain them. They pleaded with him, and he cycled through his litany again. The horrid spectacle enthralled me: before me played a caricature of a Desperate Man.

Less than an hour passed. The Rendies thinned, as if blown by a fanciful wind, and then they vanished. I blinked, expecting Evaric to shift or disappear like his unearthly counterparts. I did not perceive for several moments the violent trembling of the K'shai.

I rose very slowly and approached him cautiously. Even in the fading firelight, I could see that his face had grown as pale as the moon. His ailment did not stir me to pity; his ailment was too wildly fierce and dreadful, like the Rendies or the K'shai himself. I touched his clenched hand gingerly and found it bitterly cold. He looked at me with madness in his deep eyes.

"They have gone?" he demanded tonelessly, but a hard precision in his voice terrified me.

"Yes," I answered with a single drawn nod. He seemed to breathe anew. He continued to shudder. I gathered a blanket from the ground and drew it around his shoulders, feeling helpless and ineffective. Some people find all illness intimidating; I find it daunting only in the strong.

"Lyriel," whispered Evaric questioningly. His strangely silver eyes seemed to search for my face.

"Let me heat some food for you," I offered. He trembled like a man who had starved for a week. Meat might strengthen him.

His quickness of reaction had not suffered impairment. He snatched my arm in an instant and detained me beside him with all of a warrior's unyielding force. "Talk to me," he ordered harshly. I detest being commanded, but desperation still shrouded him.

"Of what?"

"Anything."

"Let go of my arm," I said softly, and he obeyed. I stared into his haunted eyes, trying to think clearly. It was difficult not to be drawn into oblivion by those eyes. "First act," I began, because specific words did not seem to matter. "A small farm. An old man sits beside the fire. His wife enters: 'Has Dreke returned?' she asks. 'Not yet,' answers the old man. Woman: 'Late, late, always late when the harvest nears.' Old man: 'It has ever been so.' "

So I recited, as I can do for endless hours. I played all of the roles: queens, paupers, tarts, and innocents. My career's lengthiest performance had an audience of one, but he was utterly attentive. I recited, until dawn freed my audience from his trance. He closed his eyes and relaxed the stiff posture that he had maintained for hours. I let my tired voice grate into silence.

"We should reach Walier before noon," he remarked heavily. He reopened his eyes and gave me a crooked half-grin. "Which of us is the Protector?"

"The constables of Mikolaii begin to seem a very insignificant sort of foe." Everything had begun to seem insignificant to me, except this man who had shared the night with me.

"Simpler, at least, than my foes." He drew his hands through his dark hair. "I do apologize, Mistress Lyriel, for having subjected you to my private little nightmares. I had hoped I was free of them." He was so very polite, so very remote; he might have been apologizing for a sneeze.

"This has happened to you before?" I demanded, feeling shocked despite my memory of the Bethiin's warning. Evaric had always exuded such self-assured sanity; I could scarcely believe that the Rendies had spoken to him prior to this eerie night. Perhaps I had believed Alisa's exaggerated portrait of him; perhaps I had measured him by the imperfect likes of Zakari. A rapport with Rendies might not qualify as a flaw in character; it seemed more akin to a physical disorder; it did not, however, convey perfection.

"They have not claimed me uncontrollably since I left Tyntagel," he answered at last.

"You have conversed with them often? When did you discover this peculiar talent?"

"We shall not reach Walier before noon if I tell you." He regarded me quizzically, beginning to rebuild his invincible facade.

I took cheese and bread from a saddlebag and offered half to Evaric. He accepted it quietly from my hand; his own hand still trembled very slightly. "Nothing beckons me in Walier," I said, assuming my most receptive manner. I doubted that Evaric trusted me excessively, but those who are troubled deeply seldom require much urging to relate their woes.

"When I was quite young, my sister and I strayed intemperately far from home one evening." He smiled apologetically. "I strayed actually. Ylsa, my sister, was merely endeavoring to dissuade me from straying farther. We encountered a wizard."

Evaric stopped, so I prompted him, "Wizards are not uncommon in Serii, are they?"

"I think wizards are not particularly common anywhere except Ixaxis, but it is true that Serii has more than her share overall. In Tyntagel, however, they are nearly as rare as in Ardasia, because the Lord of Tyntagel disapproves of Power."

"But you and your sister met one."

"He was not much of a wizard. He was quite mad. He held us in the open woodland until nightfall. That was when I discovered my peculiar effect on Rendies."

"That they talk to you?"

He averted his face from me before he answered. "They summon me. They occasionally obey me. They killed the wizard for me."

I had listened to more comforting confessions. "How old were you?" I do not know why his age seemed to matter. I do not particularly favor murder at any age.

"Old enough to know what I was doing." When he smiled, he looked a little bit inhuman, both divinity and fiend combined. "My sister remembers nothing of that night, but she learned to hate me from it."

I could imagine a little girl's reaction to the sight of Rendies devouring a wizard at her brother's behest. I was a grown woman of what could charitably be called worldly character, and the passive company of Rendies had certainly unsettled me. "I suppose she had her reasons," I commented dryly.

"Perhaps she believed the Rendies," returned Evaric with quirky self-mockery. "My brother believed, and he went mad of it."

"What did they say?" I asked pragmatically, recognizing the K'shai's bitter eagerness to shock me. At the same time, I suspected, he must hope that I would accept the admission calmly: there was a hunger in him, which tightened around me, for there was no other visible focus for him but the brilliant sky and the open dunes of sand. Look at me, Alisa, I thought spitefully: your irresistible gentleman friend desires my approval. I presumed that his hunger was not for myself, but I did not care; I held more of his true attention than Alisa had ever achieved.

"They call me kindred, Fire-child, and Rending-born," he said carefully. "They call me son of the Taormin. I asked you of the Taormin, if you recall."

"I recall." My exquisite K'shai, what connection have you to an expensive artifact out of Ardasian legend? "Am I likely to forget an offer to dismantle my person?"

"You might. You apparently garner trouble enough."

"I should have thought so until now, but you exceed my skill, Seriin."

He laughed with a fey abandon that made me shiver. "Until I came to Ardasia, I cherished a sense of mystery about the Taormin. It had been named by Rendies! How could it be a mortal thing? When I asked you of it first, I never thought to hear such answer as you gave: of course you had heard of it. Every educated Ardasian has heard of it, although it has presumably lain in Serii for many thousands of years, and very few Seriins know of its existence."

"We Ardasians have perfected stealing from each other," I remarked with cynical honesty. "We are not accustomed to being outwitted at our own game, even by a Sorcerer King."

"Yet you remember so little more than that: the Taormin was stolen from Ardasia by a Sorcerer King. You do not know what the object was or is. You do not know why it was stolen or from whom. For all you know," said Evaric accusingly, "some Ardasian may well have stolen the Taormin in the first place."

"Likely enough, but I was not the thief," I protested; we were heading for an argument. "What have you to do with the Taormin?" I asked, straining my patience to avoid another clash with him.

"Not a thing more than you already know," he answered irritably. He threw a pebble across the sand as if it were a weapon aimed at an unseen enemy.

"Then the Rendies' words mean nothing," I declared firmly. Evaric did not answer me. He threw another pebble, and it whistled against the air. "You think they do mean something?"

"My brother—my foster brother—devised a theory, which I derided at the time he first told me of it." Evaric said flatly. "Both my brother and I were born just over nine months from the Rending."

"So were many others," I reminded him.

"Others do not speak to Rendies," he continued.

"Perhaps they do and, like you, choose not to admit it freely." Evaric shook his head impatiently. Wrong tactic, I told myself. "Were you ever tested for Power?" I shattered my target completely.

"Every Ixaxin test confirmed that I have no Power," asserted Evaric viciously.

I held no particular opinions about Power, but Evaric's own beliefs fairly shouted at me. "The tests were wrong," I said solemnly.

For a moment, I feared that he might strike me. He clenched his fists and studied me intently, as if he observed me for the first time. "Ixaxin tests never err," he said.

"And the Shrine can heal all the world's ills," I scoffed. His scrutiny might have made me self-conscious, if I were not inured to thorough appraisals of every sort. "Have you ever been troubled by any signs of Power other than the whispers of your night friends?"

"Sometimes I hear other whispers as well: stray thoughts from a stranger, the intentions of an opponent, the life force of an animal or a tree. Conierighm, my swordmaster, used to say that I possessed the swordsman's instincts, because I always fought ahead of his next move. I never told him that my quickness came not from instinct. As we fought, I knew his thoughts. It used to be rare and faint, but lately I have begun to perceive thoughts more frequently." Wonderful notion, I mused ironically: a K'shai who reads minds. The possibilities appalled me, and I put a firm clamp on my reaction. "I only read thoughts when I am under substantial stress," said Evaric with a faint smile, which left me wondering if he had read me.

I knew of very few people who hated me enough to hire an assassin of Evaric's caliber, even if they could afford him, but the errant fear struck me that someone might have hired our own K'shai to wreak some vengeance upon me. I dismissed the idea immediately, disgusted with myself for fashioning phantoms to fear. K'shai, wizards, sorcerers: they are part of the world. Even a windsnake can kill, but fretting over the remote possibility of meeting one wastes energy to no purpose.

"You could always petition the Infortiare for Ixaxin training despite the tests. Cite your conversations with Rendies as due cause," I suggested, because it seemed the obvious recommendation. "You might even discover that Ixaxis considers talking to Rendies a common, curable affliction."

"A sorcerer cannot be K'shai." He stood and began to gather the blankets and utensils into bundles. "Walier awaits us," he added with twisted tightness. I helped him complete the packing, thinking uncomfortably of the question I had asked involuntarily of Anni.

Chapter 15

We reached Walier at a little past noon, the unkindest hour of the day for what is basically a very dirty, very disagreeable waystation for pilgrims. Walier did not come into existence for the purpose of bilking pilgrims, but it had put its strategic location to good use. Walier sat atop the largest subterranean reservoir between Ardas and the Shrine.

The city was crowded with pilgrim tours. The one inn which catered to Ardasian natives did not expect Rubi's Troupe for another two days. I was compelled both to bribe the innkeeper and to assure him that my K'shai escort would view the establishment with displeasure if we were not accommodated. After paying the bribe, I was able to secure only a single room, but it was the room that Rubi generally claimed for herself. It was large, airy, and well furnished, and it nearly compensated for the innkeeper's earlier churlishness.

Evaric returned from stabling the horses and nodded approvingly at the room. "Comfortable," he remarked, planting himself in the armchair to watch me complete my selective unpacking.

"Master Lund is bringing a cot for you," I said coldly, daring his foreign notions to find depravity in common economic sense.

"I had not intended to sleep here, unless your father has antagonized the authorities of Walier as well as Mikolaii. The stables will suit me quite adequately."

His bland amusement made me feel like some idiotically prudish pilgrim. I pondered the cost of replacing the inn's glass pitcher and decided that it was a nominal price for the satisfaction it would afford me. I hefted it toward Evaric's head in a fluid motion. It was a good throw, which deserved to hit its mark. Only a K'shai would be so aggravating as to catch the fragile pitcher midair and not even crush it between his hands.

"Have you always been so even-tempered, Mistress Lyriel?" he asked sardonically. He placed the pitcher on the side table.

"Miserable Seriin."

"Thank you," he returned ironically. "As a K'shai in your employ, I shall naturally stay if that is your wish. However, I should warn you that my nightmares are quite as likely to appear in this room as in the middle of the open desert."

Not even a K'shai should face such nightmares alone. "You are being paid to Protect me, Master Evaric, and you can hardly do that effectively from the stable." I snapped at him, because I did not want him to interpret my demand as either personal concession or desire. He was paid only to Protect me from Rendies, of course, but I saw no point in discussing the contract's specifics.

From the suddenly contemplative way he regarded me, I decided that he knew precisely why I had asked him to remain. His silence made me distinctly uncomfortable. I asked him irritably, "Why are you staring at me?"

"I was wondering why you risk your life to defend him."

"Whom?"

"Your father. He wants to be caught."

"Taf never knows what he wants, except the things he cannot have."

"He does not want to see you punished in his stead."

I stood and straightened my skirt's folds. "I think it must be time for dinner. Master Lund likes to serve early and leave the night for drinking and other pastimes of profit to him."

"Why is it so impossible for you to admit to loving your own father?"

"My feelings are my own, K'shai, and not for you to ponder."

"What you did for me last night," said Evaric slowly, "must have been very difficult for you. I know of no one else who would have done such a thing for me."

"How else should I have reacted? Should I have thrown myself to the Rendies' mercy?"

"You entrusted yourself to my mercy, when I was too lost in Rendie madness to recognize a friend. You faced me, and you faced my nightmares without fear or thought for yourself."

I met his eyes. The shadows made them blue and silver in turn. I forgot the angry words that I had meant to use. "I am not so brave, K'shai, nor so selfless. I assure you that I feared every moment. I acted in unsullied self-interest."

He shook his head in solemn denial. "If you had feared for yourself, the Rendies would have taken you," he assured me. "They spared you, because you were Protecting their Fire-child. Not even my brother ever defended me so valiantly."

"Sands," I muttered from embarrassment. "You make me sound like a holy icon." He smiled. I recited silent lays and did not allow a thought about him to creep into my mind. Those clear eyes appeared uncomfortably keen.

Once the Troupe arrived (with an unrepentant Taf), I evicted Evaric from the spacious room that I henceforth claimed alone. A man who kept company with Rendies could foster notions at least as uncomfortable as Alisa's envy. Evaric had not been revisited by his nightmares to my knowledge, but I was not sure that he had slept either. I had wakened several times to see him in the lamp's dimmed light. He stared sightlessly at the ceiling. I hoped that Fog could Protect him.

Freed of the burden of concern for the safety of myself and my K'shai Protector, I should have felt relief. The unlikely K'shai had terrified me more than once; he nearly always infuriated me. I hoped he did not realize now deeply and remorselessly he affected me. I kept imagining our play with myself as the bewitching heroine and Evaric as the determined suitor. "Addlepated," I told myself and decided to investigate the Taormin.

The temples do not care for Ardasian heathens such as myself, but a properly worded plea for enlightenment disarms them completely. The priests allowed me to enter the reading room, though I attracted several disapproving stares. I had dressed as simply and modestly as I deemed practical and bearable; I could not bring myself to stifle neck, arms, and ankles in stiff, dark cloth merely for the sake of some idly curious research.

Most of the temple books dealt strictly with the Shrine, the purported miracle of its discovery a few centuries before the Rending, and the reawakening of its Believers subsequent to the Rending. The first recorded miracle was the salvation of one Zarid, an exiled lord. Ardasia exiled or executed most of its noble families at about that time, so such displaced lords were not uncommon in our history. Zarid had wandered in the desert until he collapsed from starvation and exhaustion before a white and polished obelisk near the great, ruined city of D'hai. He swore that a vision came to him there, cast upon him a glowing aura, restored him, and showed him Truth. He returned to his former holdings and impressed a fair number of citizens with his new humility before he was again escorted from civilization. Whether Zarid's first followers pursued faith in the miraculous properties of an obelisk or showed habitual loyalty to a former liege, they did follow. The pilgrim scorn of D'hai natives has always amused me, since the ancestors of those D'hai Ardasians made pilgrimage to Zarid's Shrine long before any foreigner thought to do so.

I touched the Shrine once and nearly started a pilgrim riot. It is a rather remarkable structure, though it stands not much taller than twice a man. It withstands all weathers, but its surface yields to gentle pressure: It is neither stone nor metal. Pilgrims cite even the substance of the Shrine as holy, disregarding the fact that an entire city of the same material lies an hour's ride to the east. A few enterprising Ardasians have tried hacking off pieces of the old D'hai, but the stuff cannot be cleanly carved or shaped; it serves no profitable purpose, and the effort is uncomfortable.

The temple books equally deemphasized both the settlers who joined Zarid and the very ancient, very curiously preserved ruins of the oldest D'hai of all. The temples only occasionally acknowledge that three D'hais exist: one peopled by Ardasians, one by pilgrims, and one by imagination's haunts. I had been told that creatures like Rendies populated old D'hai even before the Rending. I could not confirm the story, but ancient D'hai was most assuredly an unsettling place. The temples had never resolved conflicting opinions of D'hai as both unapproachably sacred and irredeemably blasted by retribution for old evils.

In a less impassioned text than most of those that the temple issued, I found some data on the first D'hai. The book's author admitted that the Shrine's origins had been lost, that the Shrine had physical counterparts in the ancient city, and that a cataclysm of enormous proportions had decimated its creators and left the city deserted until Zarid's rediscovery. The author compared the cataclysm to a localized Rending, and he attributed both events to the unbridled Power of wizardry.

It was a reasonably rational, literate text. I paid the temple officer a kelne for its loan, exited the clay brick temple, and found Evaric awaiting me. My heart made itself felt in most disconcerting fashion.

"Have recent events actually turned you religious, Mistress Lyriel?" he asked me sardonically. Pilgrims were staring at him, armed as he was with swords and deadliness. "I fully expected the temple to shatter from shock at your entrance."

"Are you doubting the purity of my soul?"

"Far less than I doubt the purity of your actions. Innocents need not suffer the Protection of a K'shai in daylight."

"Did Rubi tell you to follow me?"

"She expressed a concern that you might repeat your Mikolaii escapade. I volunteered myself as Protector, having some experience in that vocation."

"Considering the nature of your admirers, I think I may be safer alone."

"Each time I think you might be learning civility, you prove me wrong. Mistress Lyriel, what is it about me that so effectively awakens the worst in your temperament?"

"Ask Alisa," I replied sourly. "She surely knows all that there is to know about you by now." With perhaps one crucial exception, I thought: I did not think Alisa would care for visiting Rendies.

"Are you jealous?" asked Evaric quizzically.

I laughed at him, even as I placed my hand on his shoulder and allowed my other hand to travel around his neck. His arms enclosed me with a fierce hunger that made my teasing gesture reel into something much more intense. I allowed his kiss to linger, but when our lips parted, I whispered to him, "Remember this moment, K'shai. It holds the only kiss you shall ever win from me."

"I never expected to win this one," he murmured, and I flushed at realizing how easily I could entice him further. He would be the first man I had loved for myself and not for the sake of saving Taf's neck from the gallows; he would also be by far the most complex man I had ever besotted. I extricated myself from his embrace and resumed my interrupted course. I could not switch affections as lightly as Alisa; I would want this man to stay with me, and how long could service to Rubi's Troupe satisfy a sorcerous K'shai?

"Your sojourn into pilgrim piety did not last long," commented Evaric with only a trace of huskiness beneath his casual tone. "We have thoroughly shocked every pilgrim in sight."

I tried to match his cool demeanor. "All the better cause for them to reform me."

"Lyriel, I do believe that you are beyond any pilgrim salvation. Perhaps that is in part why you appeal to me."

"Only wizards and K'shai are irredeemable, say the pilgrims."

"Then my profession should please you reciprocally."

"A pilgrim might condemn you for both categories," I suggested. His smile tightened. I waved at him the slim book I still carried. "Ancient D'hai."

"I appreciate your taste in literature," he remarked idly enough, but he regarded the book so avidly that I drew him to the first wide, shaded stone of comparable cleanliness. Seated in the dappled protection of an acacia, I opened the book to the section I had begun to read. "It falls somewhat short of complete," he said. Disappointment marked him. " 'Traditional Ardasian lore holds that the ancient city of D'hai fell to the Sorcerer King Horlach, who stole from it that object of unholy Power later called the Taormin, which Horlach subsequently used to conquer many lands.' "

I turned a page. "There is a bit more. 'Despite common opinion, ancient D'hai exhibits no proven evidence of active evil. The theory that the evil of D'hai was consolidated into that single object of Power is supported by the Taormin's violent history and the contrasting holiness of the Shrine.' " I was not so sure of ancient D'hai's innocuousness, but I saw no reason to mention my own opinions in that regard.

"Consolidated evil: I have known a few who labeled me so."

I ignored his self-mockery, since I could not identify its source as either bitter or vain. "A footnote says that the Taormin has been secured in a Seriin abbey since Horlach's demise. Are there any abbeys in Tyntagel?"

"No. The nearest would be Benthen, but that lies miles from where I was born."

"Son of the Taormin," I mused. "No abbess attended your mother at your birth?"

"Benthen is run by an abbot." Evaric caught a falling leaf, which had been gnawed from its bough by a greedy locust. "You are reaching too far for explanations, Lyriel."

"How can you sound so certain? You confessed to not knowing the Rendies' meanings. Do you prefer to find unpleasant explanations? You could rationalize nearly any crime by laying blame on a Rendie's words. Is that what you want? Balm for a guilty conscience?"

"I am not sure I have a conscience any longer." He said it with a searching glance, awaiting my reaction. "I can concoct a fair semblance of apology for expedience, but it is almost always specious. I am an ideal K'shai in that respect. I had to become a K'shai to realize how well the profession actually suits me."

Reorganizing my thinking kept me unresponsive for several minutes. "Many people would envy you," I said, wondering how far I believed him and how far he believed himself. The Sorcerer Kings reputedly suffered—or enjoyed—imperviousness to sense of right or wrong, and I supposed that such a trait could resurface as easily as Power. "You seem to commit few transgressions for a man to whom they do not matter."

"The practicality of reward and punishment still serve, and I frequently experience the pain of those around me."

"Then the opinions of others do matter to you."

"Insofar as they dictate my pleasures and convenience. Your opinions, for instance, are beginning to hold considerable weight."

"Expect no reward," I snapped, but I wondered. "Why do Rendies concern you so much if you cannot feel evil in them? Do they harm you?"

"They offer me adulation, not harm, if I follow them, but their shadowy world does not appeal to me. They are incomplete, as I am, though they do not perceive it. I do not shun them so much for their 'evil' as for their determination to keep me incomplete."

"Hence, you pursue the significance of their ramblings."

"I am very eager to reach D'hai."

"You expect to find your brother there?"

"Perhaps."

"Is he a pilgrim?"

"Of a sort."

"A pilgrim will not acknowledge a K'shai." Evaric shrugged and did not reply. I stirred the dust with my sandal. "The city may disappoint you."

"I think not."

"The Taormin is in Serii."

"No one there acknowledges it."

"What will you do in D'hai?"

"Learn, I hope."

As I lay abed that night, I tried to visualize a mental framework without a conscience to support it. Much as my own inconvenienced me, it did so in a reassuringly constant fashion. I liked to know when I defied my sense of right, imperfectly though my ethos might accord with the moralities of others. I took for granted the awareness of good and its counterpart, even among K'shai. The shades between were malleable, functioning by circumstance, surroundings and suggestion, but I expected everyone to own definitive opinions. Even Zakari had a conscience of a sort, though he had scarcely enough wits to know it. Whatever we did with the knowledge, we were bound together by the innate recognition that some common mores exist. Lack of that shared secret made a man inhuman. Did it make him wrong?

Philosophy made me wakeful. I lit the lamp and opened the borrowed temple book. I read it thoroughly, but it did not comfort me. Too many questions remained unanswered. I had an idea of where I might find answer to some of them.

I burst into Anni's room. "Do Ixaxins understand Rendies?" I asked her. Even at this absurd hour, she was awake, embroidering a tunic, and she did not look up from her work.

"To a certain extent," she responded calmly.

Her coolness deflated my nervous eagerness, leaving me only my urgent fear and hopelessness. I would not be discouraged. "What are the Rendies?"

"Energy. Manifestations of the Power of a tortured man."

"The Venkarel?"

"No!" She cast the tunic from her, rose, and swept across the room. The rush of her pilgrim robes crackled like a fire. She held a storm in her eyes. I am as tall as Anni, but she seemed to stand above me; it was illusion, but it was effective. "The Rending," she informed me quellingly, "resulted from the attack of a Sorcerer King on a man who refused to be a pawn. The Sorcerer King was Horlach. The man was Lord Venkarel. If Lord Venkarel had submitted to Horlach, he would have lived, and this precious, fragile world of ours would have belonged to a Sorcerer King. There is not one man or woman or child upon this world whose life is not owed to that Lord Venkarel whose name you dare to speak with scorn. There has never been a greater man, nor one more unjustly maligned."

Hers was a personal ferocity. She had to be older than she appeared. "Did you know him?" I was sure that she had known him well. How did a wizardess who had known a legend come to be a seamstress for a bedraggled troupe of Ardasian players?

Anni dwindled and became a humble pilgrim all in soft, gray sorrow. "I knew him."

The daughters of Silf's shipbuilder would have asked a thousand impertinent questions, since Anni was only a seamstress and therefore unworthy of privacy in their view. I could not think of one question which was not tainted by ignorance. "Educate me." My request startled her. "Or do Ixaxins hoard knowledge for themselves alone?"

She shook her head faintly. "Most mortals seem to prefer ignorance."

"I do not. Teach me about the Rending."

We both moved warily. We sat opposite each other, distanced by the full length of the room. Anni was softly hesitant. I was leery of her deliberately mysterious Power, and I was tired of treading among secretive, unfamiliar ways. Slowly, Anni began to speak.

"When Ceallagh and Tul conquered Horlach, they destroyed his mortal body. They took his greatest tool of Power, and they bound him from it. They did not—could not—destroy Horlach's Power and essence. They could only confine him and try to ensure that he never regained a means of acting upon the mortal, material world.

"Ceallagh's laws were designed to control Power. Any Power which could not be controlled would be destroyed before maturity."

Gingerly, I said, "I have heard that many Ixaxins think the Venkarel—Lord Venkarel—ought to have been so destroyed."

Anni fingered her odd pendant. "There are some who question the wisdom of preserving him, but there was never a choice to be made. By the time his Power was recognized, Kaedric, Lord Venkarel, was much too strong to be destroyed by Ixaxin will."

"So they named him their Infortiare instead."

"They had no other option. Nor did he." She closed her eyes. "Horlach waited thousands of years for a Power akin to his own to be born. Only such a Power could give him life again in the material world. By its existence, such a Power gave him a beacon to follow back from full binding. Horlach expended many lives to gain that Power for himself. Horlach failed, because Kaedric destroyed his own mortal bonds to thwart him. The Rending was an unavoidable outcome of the direct clash between two Powers of such magnitude."

"The Venkarel committed suicide?"

"In a sense. It was the only way he could preserve this world at all. The Rending was an insignificant thing in comparison to complete cataclysm or complete subjugation."

"Rendies have never seemed insignificant to me."

"They are Horlach's creatures, fashioned after his own fears, drawn to this world by his Power."

"Are they intelligent?"

Anni reopened her haunted eyes. "They are self-aware. They have purpose. Yes, you could call them intelligent."

"So a man could conceivably communicate with them."

"Only if he had great Power and his own pattern resembled theirs to such a degree that he could survive as well in their world as in this one." She stopped mid-sentence and whispered, "Who?"

"It was just an idle question."

"Who inspired the 'idle' question?"

I felt as if a pin were jabbing me inside my head. It was an uncomfortable sensation. "Evaric." The pin was gone. "I had not meant to tell you."

Anni smiled crookedly. "I know, but it is well that you did. Please leave now." She made it sound like an edict.

I bristled, remarking, "You give orders as if you were bred to it."

"I did not intend to sound peremptory, Lyriel. I do require some time alone. For Evaric's sake, I must assess the patterns."

"What does a pilgrim care about a K'shai?" I was not jealous of her interest. Not quite.

"He is endangered. Please go, Lyriel. And tell no one else about Evaric's ability!"

She closed her eyes, and she was gone. I was alone in the room with a half-stitched tunic and an empty chair. At least, I seemed to be alone. These uncomfortable foreigners had me doubting my own senses. "Taf would give a lot to master that trick," I said. I left, because there seemed to be no point in sitting idle in an empty room and conversing with the furniture.

Chapter 16

Pilgrims, unnatural beings of gray shadows and black sorrows, stained the landscape, which should have been as pristine and golden as the sun in the hard sky. I hated D'hai. I hated what pilgrims had made of it. The oldest D'hai loomed as a distant smudge against the hills, a reminder of abominations more pervasive than the pilgrim city.

I could only tolerate Ardasian D'hai by restricting my vision to my immediate surroundings. The Ardasians who made D'hai their home remained privately unhampered by the sober public mores they assumed to trade with pilgrims in the other, newer quarter of the city. "Why must solemnity consume the pious?" I asked rhetorically, as we rode through the outer fringe of the Shrine Keeper's realm.

Anni answered, for I rode beside Solomai's wagon. "You invert the order, Lyriel. It is the solemnity, the deep sorrow, which very often masquerades as religious devotion. That sort of holy calling flares hot and expires. Those of deepest faith are serene and joyful."

"D'hai must attract only the first kind," I returned acridly. I would not have spoken aloud initially if I had recalled the pilgrim seamstress' proximity. I did not want a pilgrim's lecture.

"The truly devout do not need reassurance from the Shrine."

"What? Do you deny the Shrine's miraculous powers?"

"You are a cynic, Lyriel. Since you share your father's agility in using human nature to mislead by implication, your cynicism is not surprising, but there is worth also to be found. I wish you could have known Medwyn," she mused.

"A man whose piety would cheer me immeasurably?" I grumbled. Solomai maintained a stoic study of the mules, but her lips twitched with amusement.

"Perhaps," responded Anni remotely. "He was a very good man, the best I have ever known." More quickly—and with an embarrassed flush—she added, "He was the abbot of Benthen for many years."

"I have heard the name Benthen elsewhere recently," I remarked in absentminded perplexity. When I recalled the elusive origin, I regretted speaking, but I decided that secrets did not sate curiosity. "From Evaric." I wanted to see Anni react; she became devoid of all expression. "He was born near Benthen, I believe."

Solomai asked slyly, "Does Alisa know how much time that K'shai has been spending with you?"

"Not from me," I answered crisply.

"Has he told you much about his childhood?" asked Anni. She looked dreamy and introspective.

"A little," I told her. "He was raised in Tyntagel. Do you know it?"

"I know it," she responded. "I also lived there as a child."

"I thought you came from Tulea."

"Tulea is my home now."

As I formulated a means of interrogating her further, our train of wagons stopped. I rode forward to join Rubi and Taf. A balding and stoop-shouldered temple official led the deputation of pilgrims who had halted us. Rubi silenced me before I could speak a word. "You are Mistress Rubi?" the Shrine priest asked her—quite unnecessarily, since her name and image loomed from great posters at her wagon's sides.

"Are you the Shrine Keeper?" retorted Rubi facetiously.

The fussy little pilgrim who accompanied the priest announced, "The Shrine Keeper does not soil himself with the company of non-believers." I heard some snickering from among the passersby, but the issuer seemed disinclined to be identified.

"Enough, Master Curamon," said the priest; his forehead wrinkled when he talked. "Please understand, Mistress Rubi, that we dislike interfering in the pastimes of the local villagers. However, since tomorrow commemorates the miraculous healing of Lord Zarid, you must delay your performances for a few days."

"Our schedules are fixed," I informed him.

"However," interposed Rubi, "under such exceptional circumstances, we shall alter our plans, of course." I stared at her in wonder.

"I am gratified, Mistress Rubi. Tanist Firo assured me that you would be cooperative. If you would care to join our ceremony, you are welcome." The priest departed as regally as he could manage with his wake of followers bobbing behind him like so many plump ducklings.

"Have you lost your mind?" I asked Rubi. "Accommodating a pilgrim?"

Rubi muttered, "Tanist Firo promised to revoke our license unless we cooperate fully with the Shrine Keeper; I received the message as we entered town."

"I wonder what hold the Shrine Keeper has found," I murmured.

"Any of a hundred would serve with Firo," muttered Taf.

"What does it matter?" asked Rubi impatiently. "We can better afford to bend our schedule than to lose Firo's good will. Tell the players, Lyriel."

Both Rubi and Taf glared at me, as if I had instigated the Shrine Keeper's arrogant authority. "If we are to begin bowing to the Shrine Keeper," I grumbled, "we may as well don black robes and worship the Shrine."

"Lyriel," repeated Rubi sternly, "inform the players."

Chapter 17

The Shrine Keeper's enforced delay of our performances did not please any of us, but we realized quickly that we were not the only ones afflicted. Every native I met grumbled about the Shrine Keeper's arrogance and the presumptuous way he had assumed the rule of D'hai in recent months. The problem was largely self-inflicted: If any of the D'hai natives had been willing to sacrifice the Shrine Keeper's silver, the pilgrim populace could have been rendered entirely helpless. One of the attributes I admired most about Vale, our innkeeper, was his refusal to cater to the pilgrim crowd. He did not suffer greatly for his selectivity, but his token effort counted for something.

I had felt uncertain as to how Vale would respond to Anni's presence among us, but he accepted her indifferently as a member of the Troupe; we were long-established customers. I had also begun to wonder about Anni herself for more reasons than her avowed Power. She had reached D'hai, which must have meant the completion of her long pilgrimage. Though we held her contract for the full season, and we had not paid her nearly enough for her to purchase a return journey to Ardas, a pilgrim had privileges in D'hai. If she chose to desert us, we could do nothing legally to stop her, and the Shrine Keeper's intolerance would make even illegal methods unlikely to succeed. Rubi assured me that our pilgrim seamstress would be too naive to know the methods, and Taf agreed. I did not mention that our pilgrim seamstress was also a wizardess who struck me as anything but naive; Rubi and Taf would have thought me daft.

Anni did visit the Shrine the first day, but her interest struck me as academic rather than religious. Noryne accompanied her, guiding her through the pilgrim D'hai which had once been Noryne's home. D'hai had always depressed Noryne with bitter memories, but no dangerous melancholy appeared to envelop her now. Anni's cures evidently served more than body.

Wrapped in a depression of my own, I left the common room soon after supper. I sought the room that Anni shared with Noryne. I had a vague goal of resuming the conversation that the Shrine Keeper's edict had interrupted, but I wanted chiefly to avoid Evaric, who seemed to muddle me more each time we met.

The seamstress' room was larger than mine, but it was crowded with furniture. Aside from the two beds, the room held a stone-topped worktable, chairs, trunks, and motley odd pieces of broken ceramic. Except when Rubi's Troupe claimed it, Vale used the room for storage and repair. Anni had spread fabric across much of the table. She was pinning facing to the finer fabric. I think her fingers could never be still; they were more restless than Taf's, though to more legitimate purpose. Noryne was engrossed in forming laborious letters on a sheet of yellowed paper.

"How is Alisa's cloak progressing?" I asked Anni, for I had no better excuse for coming.

"It is nearly completed," she responded equably.

I seated myself (without invitation) on the edge of the nearest bed. "Are you writing us a new play, Noryne?"

Noryne shook her head with faint embarrassment. "Anni has been teaching me to read."

I might not have chosen a pilgrim wizardess as the ideal instructor for the impressionable Noryne, but at least Anni had managed to overcome Noryne's confused notion that literacy endangered the soul. "Anni, how do you find the time?"

"Noryne learns quickly." I received the distinct impression that Anni preferred not to speak of Noryne's lessons. "How long do you expect the performances to be delayed?" asked Anni, dodging neatly into one of my least favorite topics of the moment.

"Our obstacle is a pilgrim holiday, not an Ardasian one. You should know the details better than I."

Anni replied vaguely, "I have quite lost track of the days."

"Time is easily forgotten in the desert," whispered Noryne. "When we travel the vast lands, I sometimes wonder if the world will not be centuries removed from us before we see a city again. It must have been terrible for you, Lyriel: crossing the desert without the Troupe." Her eyes held concern for me, and her voice was compassionate. Even if her reasons were wrong, I needed the warmth.

"Evaric kept the desert from me."

"He frightens me." Noryne folded her thin hands on the smooth, cold stone of the table. The scar still showed, but the injured wrist had healed remarkably quickly. "He is more vast and terrible than the desert. He is like the Rendies he fights."

Anni's fingers poised. "What do you sense in him, Noryne?" It was an urgent question, asked with potent calm.

"Danger, conflict, turmoil." Noryne's eyes became eerily distant. I think neither woman recalled that I remained in the room. "Change."

"Change within him or because of him?"

"The first. Or both. I cannot be sure. Must I reach further, Anni? He frightens me so much."

"I do understand, Noryne, but the fear will not fade if you turn from it. You are not endangered. He will not perceive you."

"I cannot sense any more. Something stops me."

"What stops you?"

"A wall. It is dark and very cold." Noryne began to shiver. Her skin actually became white; her freckles took a purplish tinge.

I began to wonder what sort of herbs Anni had used in her treatment of Noryne's ailments, "Noryne," I began. Anni hushed me imperiously. I must have been too stunned to disobey, because argument never occurred to me.

"The wall spreads," continued Noryne, shaking now less steadily but more strongly. "It conceals. There is something within, and it beats against the darkness. It stretches and throbs. It will burst soon and encompass us." She was almost screaming.

"Stop," commanded Anni, and Noryne became still. "Turn from the darkness. What do you see?"

"Fire. Fire everywhere."

"Can you discern its origin?"

"It is everywhere."

"It has an origin." Now Anni was desperately shaken and unsure in her insistence.

"Infinity."

"Infinity, yes." Anni was impatient. "It has a focus. Approach the fire."

"I shall burn!"

"Where is the origin?"

"There is fire, and there is darkness. They meet in distortion. There is nothing more. I am sorry, Anni."

"You are doing well Noryne," said Anni, but she was disappointed. "Can you still sense Evaric?"

"Only through the darkness. He confuses me."

I interrupted, "Confusion is not a crime."

Anni said very slowly, "You defend him?"

"He belongs to the Troupe," I replied.

Noryne murmured from her disquieting trance, "You hold so much love and warmth in you, Lyriel, and you barricade it out of fear of bleeding again from your heart, as Silf's loss made you bleed. The K'shai has sketched a crack in the barricade, and you are terrified that he will break your clever, worldly shell and discover you."

I scoffed, "A K'shai? I would sooner love a sand-hog."

Noryne mused wistfully, "Many of us love unwisely."

"Lyriel is quite right, Noryne," said Anni sternly, but I had the oddest impression that she was weeping for me. "Caring for a K'shai would be sheerest madness."

Noryne's comments had made me scornful. Anni's words made me feel perversely inclined to crumble into tears. A light rap sounded at the door. I rushed to open it, enormously grateful for the interruption.

I expected to find Solomai or Rubi at the door. The sight of a stranger startled me; that he was a pilgrim made me wonder the more. Anni reached past me to draw him into the room.

"You found me quickly," she told him warmly.

"Our days apart have seemed endless enough." He had a strong and vibrant voice.

Noryne asked, "Is this your cousin, Anni?" His attitude did not strike me as cousinly, but Noryne had apparently been better informed than I, for Anni nodded in agreement.

"Circumstances forced us to travel different routes," explained Anni for my benefit.

Anni's cousin bowed. "I am Ineuil," he informed me. He repeated the bow in Noryne's direction. His broad smile seemed more appreciative than pious.

"Lyriel," I answered him tersely. "And this is Noryne." There was something familiar about him. He did not resemble Anni, though he was equally as fair in coloring. His features were sufficiently distinctive that I doubted I could have confused him with any other. No, I had seen him elsewhere. He perturbed me. "You parted ways in Ardas?" I asked him cordially.

"We parted much too long ago," was his insouciant response, which hardly constituted an answer. "I have been touring this country of yours in the company of some most unpleasant gentlemen of the merchanting persuasion. I do think that Anni has had the better arrangement."

"Her 'arrangement' has not ended," I mentioned innocently. "Unless you share your cousin's talent for stitching, Master Ineuil, I fear that it is she who must fulfill the rest of her contract." I said it lightly, as if in jest.

Ineuil answered with equal brightness. "Anni's talents far exceed mine in many subjects, not least of which is her present profession."

Anni offered me a more direct reassurance, "I shall not forsake my obligations to you, Lyriel."

"Anni has always been a great proponent of duty," murmured her cousin. The look she gave him was sharp, which intrigued me.

"Did Vale supply you a room, Master Ineuil?" asked Noryne. If I had not known her guilelessness, I might have thought Noryne deliberately diffusing an argument of wills. I made note to observe Noryne more carefully. Anni had certainly helped her outlook, but I began to wonder how much Anni and Power had altered Noryne's perspectives.

"I have quarters," returned the peculiar pilgrim gentleman.

I could evade an answer better than most, but this Ineuil seemed unable to speak directly at all. He rang even less true as a pilgrim than Anni. He wore the robes, and he was foreign. He was no more a Shrine worshiper than Taf.

*   *   *

"These people have no concept of Power," said Rhianna. "The girl, Noryne, is an obvious sorceress, and no one in this country appears cognizant of the fact. Ignorance has done the girl great harm. I only hope that she has not been permanently impaired."

"What of the other girl who was here earlier?" asked Ineuil pensively.

"Lyriel?" asked Rhianna, startled. "Her heritage is entirely Ardasian, entirely innocent of any Power beyond the fully mortal kinds: a sporadic type of empathy, a limited resistance to the Rending creatures' spells. She is not a sorceress."

"I had thought as much, but I wondered," remarked Ineuil mildly. "I observed her at supper. She could not keep her eyes away from your son."

"Evaric appears to have that effect on many women."

"She appears to have the same effect on him."

Rhianna answered archly, "You should be the first to understand if Evaric enjoys a brief flirtation with a girl as lovely as Lyriel."

"I would indeed understand: Mistress Lyriel is beautiful and obviously infatuated. Your son cannot have encountered too many attractive, intelligent young women who could forgive him his profession for more than the span of an evening."

"State your point, Ineuil, without your courtier's circumlocution."

"In my humble courtier's opinion, your son is a true romantic, confronted by a cunning siren of exceptional determination. She will conquer him."

Rhianna laughed with mordant humor. "Of all the problems confronting my son, Lyriel seems hardly the most menacing."

"You underestimate her, I think."

"And you are the romantic, I think. The differences between Evaric and Lyriel encompass far too vast an array to overcome."

"Your son, however, does not know that the salient difference exists."

"He knows," replied Rhianna. Ineuil raised his brows. "In the heart of him, he knows."

"I still think that you wrong him by withholding the truth."

"It is not yet time."

"Why not? And do not allude obscurely to matters of Power incomprehensible to a mere mortal like myself. I understand, my dear Rhianna, a great deal more than you choose to credit."

Rhianna regarded him with a wrenchingly lonely and wistful expression. "Evaric's Power is tangled with the Rending. Every mote of his self-realization frees him a little and frees the 'Rendies' a little more. Ineuil, I do not know how to free him without destroying this world."

"He will learn his Power eventually and free himself," said Ineuil soberly. "Surely it would be better, however dangerous, if you controlled his learning."

"You are not hearing me: If I free him by telling him his heritage, I give the world irrevocably to the Rending creatures. No slightest chance exists of other outcome."

Ineuil replied sharply, "Forgive me, Rhianna, but your prophecy of certain doom does not persuade me to sit placidly and accept. An alternative must exist."

"Indeed," concurred Rhianna grimly, "an alternative does exist: Horlach has offered to free Evaric if I will 'lend' my Power to the operation."

"Horlach? He still survives?"

"He survives. He is imprisoned in the Taormin, and his Power is nearly null, but he retains his serpent's tongue. I know his legacy of treachery; I know how foully he has behaved throughout his history. I would not listen to him, but all other voices have abandoned me. I say to you: Destruction approaches. You listen, my friend, but you do not comprehend, for you have never walked in that other world. I know, and Horlach knows, and I fear—Ineuil, you cannot imagine how much I fear—that I shall have no other option but to accept my enemy's help."

"Loan Horlach your Power? What insanity has beset you? Did Kaedric and so many others die that you might now surrender to the very foe we dreaded?" Rhianna closed her eyes in pain and would not face Ineuil's incredulous fury. "Rhianna, my fair and wise Infortiare, you have convinced me that Horlach still exists: I recognize this brand of madness, having heard its like before from Hrgh. Horlach is possessing you."

"You cannot understand, Ineuil," she pleaded in a forlorn voice.

"Then summon Ixaxis or the monarchs of the Seriin Alliance.

Summon a Wizards' Circle, or summon Kaedric's ghost, but listen to someone's voice beyond the vile one in your head!"

"Can you know how alone I feel!"

"I know how you terrify me with this talk of yours! You mourn Kaedric: I understand. But do not condemn the world to die because you lost your one great love. Find the options that Horlach hides. You might begin by trusting your own son; he cannot be more a devil than the one you fight within you. Work through the girl, Lyriel, if you cannot face your son yourself."

Rhianna shook her head in silence. Her pale hair caught the light; she wore it like an aureole of heaven. Demon or divinity? mused Ineuil in deep frustration; Kaedric, what have you bequeathed to her and to us all?

"He is here in D'hai."

"You assured me that he could never come so far. I cannot have assassins slaying one another in the holy city."

"Pilgrims do not note the death of a K'shai."

"Those he Protects will take note of it, and that will bring trouble with the locals. I paid your Guild well to eliminate him, and you have failed abominably. I must attend to him myself, which is precisely the situation I wished to avoid."

The K'shai called Circle stiffened. He seldom received criticism of his Guild's efficiency, but he had seldom competed with his own Guild-mates for the death of a pretender. "I must remind you, Shrine Keeper, that your information to us was significantly less than complete. Your contract is not the only one aimed against this man." Too many Guild-mates had accepted contracts against this target; too many of those Guild-mates had underestimated the target and given the target warning.

"I want him dead and proven so. You may collect for the deed all the contracts that you find, but bring the body to me." The Shrine Keeper drove his finger against the K'shai's chest, startling Circle into anger.

"You are a rash man, Shrine Keeper." A blade had appeared in the K'shai's hand, and he laid it against the Shrine Keeper's arm.

The Shrine Keeper closed his hand, smiling lightly. "I am a man of faith."

The K'shai hesitated, impressed despite himself by the coolly confident man who owned D'hai. Many K'shai had served this master's ruthless ambition. Many K'shai had abandoned large fees when asked to assassinate the K'shai imposter, Fire. Circle had never failed in a contract, but neither had Straw until the last.

The Shrine Keeper sat alone. "He knows where to find me," muttered the Shrine Keeper to himself. "Why has he not come? How does he survive every attack thrown against him? Is there no one able to kill him? He must come to me." The Shrine Keeper shook his head, as a shudder coursed through his body. "Leave D'hai before I can kill you, Evaric," he pleaded. The deep pain assaulted him. "No. He must die. He will die, my lord. He is the devil's own son, and he must not live. He has lived too long already and endangers us. I am your servant, my lord, and I obey you." The pain returned and intensified as the Shrine Keeper said tightly, "Damn you, Gorng."

Chapter 18

On the third day after arriving in D'hai, six of us headed bravely from Vale's Inn to give our season's first performance at the amphitheater at the city's edge. One of the Shrine Keeper's overbearing priests accosted us before we had walked half the distance. The priest was a gaunt man, and the gray robes made him look sickly. A dozen lesser officials of the Shrine accompanied him, all of them attired in gray robes and gloom.

Ardasian natives of D'hai, who had populated the street moments before, vanished. Even the constable disappeared. Beyond our little group of brightly hued players, everything and everyone looked gray and ominous.

"Your ways are evil!" declared the priest. "Your women are licentious." He pointed his finger directly at Alisa, which amused me in an acrid way. One of the officials actually jabbed Alisa, and she jumped away from him hastily. Quietly, I told Zel, Solomai's youngest, to find Fog. The old K'shai had accompanied us when we departed the inn, though I could not see him now. Rubi had sent Evaric ahead with Denz to establish our stage.

Someone began to shout in competition with the zealous priest. When I recognized the source as Zakari, leaping to his precious Alisa's defense, vexation made me want to strangle him. "Sands, Zakari," I muttered to myself, "you are only meant to be heroic in the play. Leave reality to those who are better equipped to face it."

Zakari marched toward the Shrine official who had dared to touch Alisa. The man squeaked with indignation when Zakari caught him by the collar. The man flailed helplessly, as Zakari began to beat him. The other Shrine officials watched in disquieting calm. A few pilgrims had gathered to gaze aghast and mutter ineffectual protests. The priest stood grimly straight and triumphant. Alisa looked more stricken than I had ever seen her.

As Rayn and Eolh tried to pry Zakari from the unfortunate Shrine official, a group of unusually substantial pilgrims emerged purposefully from one of the nearby buildings. They drew swords from the folds of their pilgrim robes, and they pressed their swords against Rayn and Eolh as well as Zakari. One sword was aimed toward Alisa and myself, and its wielder lacked even the grace to look apologetic.

The man who seemed to lead the sword-bearing pilgrims addressed us. He resembled a soldier more than a humble pilgrim, despite his pilgrim gray. "The Shrine Keeper wishes you to accompany us."

"We have a play to present," I retorted. "When it is done, we shall be happy to present ourselves to Tanist Firo's delegate."

"The Tanist has conveyed his full authority to us, the Shrine Keeper's Guard. You have caused a disturbance. It is our duty to arrest you."

"There has been a misunderstanding," announced Fog gruffly. The old K'shai came among us calmly, his thumbs tucked into his belt. He studied the swords of the Shrine Keeper's Guard with the detached air of a man appraising a possible purchase. "That man," he said, pointing at Zakari, "will pay the proper fine to the Tanist, as will that man." Fog pointed at the priest, who affected shock. "The rest of these people are blameless, and no one will be detained."

To my astonishment, the representatives of the Shrine Keeper's Guard lowered their swords without perceptible hesitation. They retreated by slow, deliberate steps into the featureless pilgrim building from which they had issued; the priest and his entourage followed, half dragging the battered official, who was nearly unconscious. A K'shai is always menacing but seldom so promptly effective against an army. I had a curious suspicion that Fog's eyes would seem blue, if I could see them.

Fog preceded us through the streets to the amphitheater, and most pilgrims stepped well away from us. The Ardasian inhabitants proceeded about their daily tasks but gave us a wide berth. Only Anni's pilgrim cousin, who hovered near the amphitheater, made no effort to avoid us; he smiled broadly at us and waved exuberantly. I wondered if we would have an audience.

The amphitheater was one of D'hai's numerous oddities. It appeared on cursory glance to be a natural formation, augmented by the mix of stone and wooden benches which lined its tiers. Low, slender trees sprang from an old irrigation canal behind the level circle on which Denz had fastened the pieces of our stage. The amphitheater appeared quite natural in its grandeur, so long as one did not delve beneath the layers of encrusting dirt and discover its impervious foundation: smooth, yellow, and molded into odd circles of irregular, lumpish forms. A few of the lumps resembled proper chairs, but the benches served far better. The dirt smoothed the surface enough to support the benches with only an occasional mishap due to instability.

I leaned against the side of Denz's stage wall, part of the assembly which comprised our portable theater, and watched the play inattentively. An audience had materialized, after all; Taf was counting the profits with a nod of mild satisfaction. Rubi stood near me, oblivious to everything but the play's rendition. Evaric sat just behind me, scarcely visible among the shadows of lacy trees and tall grasses. Something singed the air beside me in a rush of heated fury. Evaric had jerked me to his side before I saw the fire explode from the wooden stage wall.

"Denz!" Rubi was shouting. The members of our audience vied to leave us, treading upon one another in their haste to exit the amphitheater. The wooden benches were old, dry, and flammable, but the panicked departure posed more danger than the fire. Taf and Rayn led the sensible contingent in beating at the fire, curtailing its spread to the first tiers and nearest grasses. The stage itself was not faring well; the wall against which I had leaned was gone, caught quickly by the incendiary substance that had struck it.

I tried to reach Taf, but Evaric dragged me from the area. Most of the crowd had fled toward the rear of the amphitheater, and the Troupe members were all occupied in rescuing what they could of our stage and their personal property. Those who did try to escape through the brush behind the stage kept warily clear of Evaric's sword.

Evaric did not let me stop until we were well into the native quarter. Some of the fleeing audience had begun to spread word of the fire, and many of the curious were now returning to the site so recently abandoned. "Did you see who cast the fire-lamp?"

"No." He sounded angry with himself. "I was watching for intelligent attacks. A fire-lamp is a senselessly destructive weapon."

"Not every attacker has the finesse of a K'shai," I remarked caustically. Evaric might not have heard me; he sheathed his sword, but he remained vibrantly attentive to all that occurred around us. "The Shrine Keeper obviously does not want us in D'hai." When Evaric still did not respond, I added dryly, "Audiences are not usually so dissatisfied as to set us afire."

Evaric answered absently, "Fog will find the miscreant." We had reached Vale's Inn. Evaric inspected the courtyard as well as the common room; he acknowledged Vale evenly, but he studied strangers with a care that made several of them cringe. He held me firmly at his left, carefully keeping his sword hand free from interference. Vale's wife watched us curiously. I greeted her with defiant good cheer.

Evaric did not relax a bit until he had closed the door of my room, which he insisted upon searching. I grumbled at him from the chair in which he had placed me, "What do you expect to find here?"

"There are many weapons, Mistress Lyriel, and not all of them are obvious." He was lifting one of my costumes from its trunk, and I held my breath until he replaced it. "I have too long neglected certain unpleasant possibilities. I shall apologize profusely for invading the privacy of your possessions, but only after assuring myself that you are not endangered by them." He had lifted another costume, when he paused. He laid it aside wordlessly, but his lips were tight.

"Spare me your disapproval, K'shai."

He continued his dispassionate search. "Is the drug Zakari's?" he asked tonelessly. "You need not pretend surprise, Mistress Lyriel. A K'shai's education encompasses many fields of doubtful kind."

I responded sharply, "Without Zakari, we have no marketable play by which to earn enough to pay the exorbitant fees of the K'shai. Without the drug, we have no Zakari. I allow him only enough of his beastly virol to keep him functional."

Apparently satisfied with his search, Evaric brought the room's other chair to a position opposite me. Having done so, he did not occupy it, standing behind it instead, pensively running his hands over the chair's roughly carved back. "You take too many risks, Lyriel—for Taf, for Zakari, for me. One of these days, you may realize that the risks are real. That fire-lamp was thrown at you."

"By the Shrine Keeper himself, I suppose."

He did not react to my cynical interjection. "By someone who means to exchange your safety for my life. You really should be more careful as to whom you kiss on a public road."

I wished he would look at me instead of the chair. I could only focus on his hands and the unnatural brand. "I thought that you eliminated your Guild problems in Arahinos," I said weakly.

"Only one of them."

I tried studying my own hands, but my eyes kept returning to the K'shai. "How many lethal enemies do you have?"

"An unlimited supply, it would seem. They have never previously inconvenienced my clients."

My reactions to this Seriin K'shai conflicted in a drastic and unnerving manner. "Are you K'shai or K'shai target?"

"Both, I think, though the dual status does hold some inherent inconsistencies."

Rubi entered without knocking. "The stage is ruined," she announced in a tragic tone, which was not quite credible. She did look the part of a sufferer: She was sooty and scorched, and her rusty hair stood on end, stiffened by the pasty glop she applies to it. She was enjoying her tragedy.

She snapped at Evaric instead of at me, which pleased me. "How could you permit this to happen?" Her indignation was affecting.

Evaric bestowed a lopsided grimace on me and offered to Rubi the chair he still held. Rubi sank into it grandly, which constituted a difficult gesture in a chair of such intimidating hardness. She pretended to languish in exhaustion and despair. Her fingers betrayed her: She was making a mental tally.

"Your K'shai wages will reflect this disaster," she told Evaric firmly. She watched him, as did I, wondering if she could actually bluff a K'shai into subsidizing the new stage that she had long been wanting.

"I think the perpetrator would be a better choice for reparations," replied Evaric dryly.

"The perpetrator whom you allowed to escape."

"Fog will find him."

"You have great confidence in your partner's abilities."

"Implicit confidence, Mistress Rubi."

"You had best be right."

Or you will do what to him, Rubi dear? I wondered. She was taking advantage of his Seriin courtesy, which was fine if that courtesy actually penetrated beneath the polished surface. I was wishing that Rubi would leave, for there were questions I wanted to ask the K'shai. I wanted to ask if he had found his brother, if he had learned what he hoped to learn in D'hai. I wanted him to stay on any pretext, but he left graciously when Rubi stared at him in obvious dismissal. He seemed to be contrary only with me.

"Taf will need your help in replacing our equipment." Rubi was enjoying remarkably good spirits, all things considered. "I shall want you to present the bill to the Shrine Keeper, since he claims responsibility for all that transpires in D'hai." She was positively glowing now.

"If you wanted to antagonize the Shrine Keeper, why did we delay for his useless holiday?"

"He had not attacked my players then."

"We do not know who instigated the fire, and I thought you blamed me for the other incident. You did say something about my failure to keep Zakari out of trouble?"

"I changed my mind."

"You choose a fine time to become sensitive to my perspective. Do you intend to seek restitution from the K'shai and the Shrine Keeper both?"

"They are not likely to communicate with one another."

Sometimes greed overwhelms Rubi's common sense. "And you complain about me looking for trouble."

Fog brought the silver to Rubi that afternoon. He informed her in a grimly affable way that the former owner had no further need of silver serisni. To questions regarding said owner's identity, Fog simply shrugged, "A pilgrim."

I steadfastly refused to deliver Rubi's demands to the Shrine Keeper. I had almost persuaded her to forget that foolish plan, when Vale informed us that citizens of D'hai had been offered the choice of our patronage or the Shrine Keeper's. "It is not you in particular, Rubi," Vale told her. "The Shrine Keeper wants no one in D'hai whom he cannot control. He is bright enough to know that itinerant players with strong K'shai Protection are not about to worship his kind."

Taf muttered, "I suppose he persuaded Tanist Firo to agree."

"First thing," agreed Vale glumly. "This Shrine Keeper only came to D'hai a couple of years back, but he has taken over the temples, sent the old Shrine Keeper into retirement in Ardas, and garnered the blessing of Tanist, constables, and anyone of influence in the nearest six domains. He speaks, and these pilgrims fall all over themselves to do his holy bidding."

"Sounds like the pilgrims are not the only ones," I suggested.

Vale rubbed his big hands on his apron, delaying his answer. "The Shrine Keeper is a rich man," he said finally, which I suspected was not what he originally intended to say. "You know your business is still welcome here, Rubi." Someone called him to fetch ale to another table, and he left us.

"Without supplies, we cannot replace our stage," said Taf glumly.

"We have managed without such luxury before," retorted Rubi.

"Can we survive without an audience?" I asked.

Rubi frowned, but she raised her head defiantly. "We pack tomorrow," she said briskly. "We leave the following morning."

The packing required little time, for the fire had decimated some of our bulkiest possessions. When Noryne and Anni invited me to observe the Shrine blessing with them, I agreed for no better reason than unaccustomed idleness. Anni's cousin materialized as an overly eager escort, which made me glad that I had chosen to accompany the party; I did not want either Anni or Noryne to desert us due to Master Ineuil's glib tongue.

We had neared the Shrine. We traversed a crowded part of the city, packed with pilgrims, pressing to reach their goal. A cluster of gray figures broke free of the mass, ran, and pushed past us roughly. The shouting began. I felt myself shoved from behind. Noryne gave a startled yelp. Her hand let go of my arm, and she was pulled away from me. I could see neither Anni nor Ineuil. The pressing crowd reached me, and I could not move save by the throes of the bodies squeezed against me from every side.

Faces passed me: hollow cheeks, a drooping jowl, narrow shoulders, a bony neck. Grunting and crying, the mob whisked their many faces past me. I sensed no motion on my own part. The Shrine marched to me, and the crowd seeped away. I saw one face then: pinched lips, a satisfied and smiling face above strong shoulders, darkly clad in a tunic embroidered in white. His breath burned my face. The K'shai brought forward his short sword. He raised it; the edgewise blade looked innocuous.

The blood seemed to well very slowly from his throat, startled by the thin dagger which protruded from it. The dead K'shai's short sword grazed my cheek as its stubborn wielder slumped. Jarred by the fall, the dagger sliced a ragged rent, and the straining blood escaped him into a pool. I winced and averted my eyes.

"How much alike death makes them," remarked Fog with ironic wonder. He stooped to retrieve his dagger. For so coarse and big a man, he moved with unlikely elegance and grace.

"You killed him?" I asked stupidly. "He was K'shai."

"He was K'shai," agreed Fog, "endeavoring to effect a paid obligation. You think he did not deserve death?" The question was impersonally curious.

"I suppose I would not have enjoyed the alternative."

How strangely Fog smiled. "What will a man not offer to survive? If one man will forsake infinity in a mere hope of mortality, surely another should not regret the murder of a wretched tool."

I had no idea what he meant, or if he were even sane. "You view his death as murder?" It seemed an odd judgment from a K'shai.

"Do you not?" He nodded toward the knotted mob, which had ebbed from us. A few members had strayed free of the throng, as had we, and several of these had observed our grisly companion. "We would do well to leave guilty verdicts to uncertain renderings."

We circled behind the Shrine, and Fog found a clear path for our escape. We left, knowing nothing of Noryne, seeing no hint of Anni or her cousin, asking no one about the cause or reason for the initial turmoil. We had given the Shrine a bloody offering, which the pilgrims and their Shrine Keeper could interpret as they wished.

Fog and I did not speak again until we had regained the safer city of Ardasian souls. "Shall I speak of the incident at the Shrine?" I asked him, for it was he who had betrayed K'shai practice by so bloodily preventing his fellow from completion of contract.

"Riots and death go together," replied Fog. "Not much news in them." I took his gruff statement as a suggestion to ignore the death of the K'shai. Fog sounded utterly unlike the calmly calculating executioner at the Shrine: a man no less cavalier about death but less philosophically engrossed by it. I almost felt that my pensive rescuer had been some demonic entity, known to the Fog we paid but entirely distinct from him.

Lyriel, I told myself scathingly, you will soon start buying pilgrim icons and talismans against evil auras if you persist in this vein. It came of mixing with foreigners. Sorcery, wizardry, Rendies: look at them too long, and you begin to imagine them everywhere. Nothing mystical had occurred. A pilgrim riot had separated me from my companions, making me vulnerable to a K'shai who had overestimated my significance to Evaric. The idea was not palatable, but neither was it unnatural. What could be more prosaic than violence, coercion, and misunderstanding? I ought to feel satisfied that the assassin no longer stalked me. I certainly owed a debt of gratitude to Fog.

Anni returned to the inn with her cousin, both of them apparently unmoved by the afternoon's events. Evaric returned Noryne, a little battered but safe. She had been caught and dragged by a man she could not identify. The man had dropped her and fled before Evaric located her. I could have suspected that the man had been paid to draw Protection away from me. I could have believed that the K'shai assassin had concocted the riot; someone had purportedly murdered pilgrims in the crowd. Before the evening hour all D'hai had heard another version of the riot, and I no longer knew what to believe. The pilgrims who had been nearest to the Shrine claimed that Rendies had appeared to them: Rendies in daylight. I was glad that we were to leave D'hai in the morning.

Rhianna studied the wall and the tangle. The trickle of darkness had become a narrow stream. *"We have very little time left to us,"* said Horlach urgently. *"The instability accelerates."* Rhianna did not reply. *"Lend me your Power! You have no other choice."* Rhianna touched the rent, bathing it in healing Power. The tangle stretched, achieving pattern for an instant. The rent recoiled, and the darkness spread.

Chapter 19

I sequestered myself in my room, curled myself in the corner and pondered. I seemed to hold many pieces of a great puzzle without discernible pattern, and my inability to resolve the design frustrated me. I had always understood the intricacies of those clever little Bethiin boxes that fit together so uniquely and so well: a single key piece holds all the rest in place; without it, one holds only random wedges of wood. I could not reconstruct the disassembled design of which I sensed that I was a lesser part. I had identified the key, but I could not define his proper placement in the whole. K'shai, target, or Rendie in the guise of a man: Evaric bewildered me.

"Lyriel, my girl, you are a fool," I told myself severely, "letting a crazy Seriin muddle your head." A rap at the door interrupted my self-recriminations, and I snapped at its unseen issuer, "I am not receiving!"

"Lyriel," said Evaric dimly, "please open the door." I had complied before he finished his request; I did not even pause to brighten the lamp. "I missed you at supper," he remarked prosaically, but he rubbed at the K'shai brand with a nervousness rare in him.

"I ate early. We shall leave before dawn, after all."

"I shall not be leaving D'hai with you," said Evaric slowly. "I told Mistress Rubi that I would follow the Troupe from a distance, so as to preclude any further attacks from D'hai, but I deceived her.

Fog will provide you with Protection to Tayn, and he will ensure that you are well Protected subsequently. I wanted you to know, Lyriel."

"You wanted me to know?" I repeated incredulously. "You mean just to disappear and leave me to inform Rubi that you have broken contract? Is this the way you fulfill your obligations? No wonder your own Guild seeks to eliminate you!" Torn between fury and devastating disappointment, my voice trembled.

"My Guild-mates mistake me for someone else," he replied, his expression resigned and miserable.

"You committed to a full season of Protection," I persisted. "Either complete your contract, K'shai, or I shall hire an assassin to seek you myself!" I fought to keep my tears inside of me. Evaric touched my hair, but I shook free of him and leaned my head heavily against the wall.

Lotin emerged from his mother's room and gave us a bluntly questioning look as he passed. He even turned at the stair to regard us once again before descending. Evaric said very softly, "I wish I could explain to you, Lyriel, but I have no rational reason to give. I could say that I must remain in D'hai to answer questions long sought, but I would be lying: I do not know why I must stay here. I know only that departure is impossible for me."

"Blast all foreigners," I whispered, when he had gone.

We packed the wagons quickly, for the fire had claimed our largest items. I searched for Evaric, but Fog joined us alone. I might have informed Rubi of our young K'shai's desertion, but I could not betray Evaric's implicit trust in me, though I felt sufficiently betrayed myself. Rubi would miss him soon enough.

Beyond D'hai, the desert rose in gentle hills, sparsely dotted with thorn trees and the worn, jutting crags of some ancient shift of the solid earth. The sky bloomed pink with dawn's innocence. I reined my mare and allowed three of the wagons to pass me. Alisa leaned from Chard's wagon, looking bored, and I flung my irritation at her. "You may quit searching for him," I told her sharply. "Zakari's rival has abdicated."

"Rubi!" shouted Taf urgently. I rode forward to join him, leaving Alisa's angrily insistent questions unanswered. Taf, alone in the lead wagon, had just mounted the first high hill beyond D'hai.

"What is it, Taf?" I began to ask, but he did not need to respond. "Sands," I murmured. The lovely pink sky did not brush the top of the next range of hills, for the sky melted into darkness somewhere near where the hills ought to have risen. The line of murky distortion cloaked the horizon. I could not look long into the rippling darkness, because my senses recoiled from the chaos of its twisting motion.

"We can circle back through Walier," announced Rubi, as if we might avoid some ordinary quirk of the landscape.

"Circle what?" muttered Rayn, rubbing pensively at the short bristles of his beard. Most of the Troupe had now gathered atop the hill to stare into bleak oblivion.

"Whatever it is," answered Denz, "I want no closer look."

"We certainly cannot leave D'hai by this route," agreed Taf.

"The Walier road will also be closed by the time you reach it," remarked Anni with unsettling calm. She reached her thin hand to Taf's lead mule, absently quieting the restless animal.

"What is that thing?" I asked her.

"A distortion of energy." Her face became dreamy and remote. "It reaches into infinities beyond me. It spreads itself into a sphere, surrounding that point which touches all infinities."

Noryne added nervously, "We must return to D'hai, before the barrier tightens and catches us."

Anni nodded very slightly. "Yes. There was never any question of leaving D'hai."

The Troupe members had begun to return mutely to their wagons. I detained Anni. "If you anticipated this phenomenon," I said, "you might have warned us."

She regarded me keenly. "Would you have believed me?"

"Perhaps," I replied, but I convinced neither of us. I had not believed Evaric, who had warned me of the obstacle in his own cryptic way. The eerie barrier might imprison us or strangle us, but neither prospect could dismay me. Nothing short of a second Rending could have overpowered my awareness that I was returning to my troublesome K'shai.

Vale accepted our return with equanimity; the mail carrier, who had confronted the obstacle shortly after dawn, had already spread news of the barrier surrounding D'hai's ancient valley. I saw Evaric approach Solomai to help her with the horses. Before I could escape my own efforts to unpack, Alisa had reached the K'shai's side. I saw Zakari throw his load to the ground and stalk into the city; I felt inclined to join him.

The day seemed interminable: we could neither depart nor perform. We could make no purchases, for the Shrine Keeper had forbidden trade with us, nor could we even walk safely in the city. Minaro tried to begin a song in Vale's common room, where most of the Troupe sat dumbly, but the song quickly became dismal.

Rubi had seldom looked more mournful. Anni and Noryne had vanished with Anni's cousin. Taf, more comfortable with despondency than the rest of us, displayed his conjuring skills to an attentive Fog, but I knew the tricks too well to share the K'shai's fascination. When Evaric arrived with Alisa clinging possessively to his arm, my frustration erupted.

I marched purposefully to the door. Rubi demanded, "Lyriel, where are you going?"

"To visit the Shrine Keeper. Since we seem condemned to remain in D'hai, we had best try to resolve our position with him."

"We have enough trouble without you seeking more of it, girl," said Taf.

I glared at him. "Fire me," I told him, and I whirled to leave.

"You are not making my job easier," said Evaric.

"Then Protect Alisa instead," I snapped. He ignored my injunction and followed me, for which I felt much more grateful than I intended ever to let him know.

Chapter 20

The Shrine Keeper discouraged spontaneous visits. He surrounded himself with priests, pious servants, and his ubiquitously menacing Shrine guards. Consternation over the black barrier and the reputed appearance of Rendies in daylight compounded the obstacles: crowds of pilgrims had gathered in the entry yard to plead for enlightenment.

By employing bribery, trickery, and threat of the lean and dangerous K'shai beside me, I managed to procure an audience within a little over three hours. Guards led us to a cold, white room, sparsely furnished. Evaric remained near the entry columns in the shadow of the guards' company, as I strode forward to face the Shrine Keeper, whose cleanly carved stone chair conveyed the arrogant impression of a royal throne. Gray-robed priests bustled about their chosen liege, accomplishing nothing apparent but contributing considerable noise.

A large man of fair coloring and with a strong, square jaw, the Shrine Keeper did exude a potent presence, even in his falsely humble gray robes. "Mistress Lyriel," he commented with a proud, vaguely disdainful air, "you are a very forceful young woman. I seldom speak to those who have been unblessed by the Shrine's truth." His priests murmured approval of his words.

"A truth greater than yours seems determined to keep our Troupe in D'hai despite your diligent efforts to oust us. You have attacked us, threatened us, alienated us from D'hai's rightful citizens, and behaved altogether insufferably. The harassment must stop."

The Shrine Keeper remarked languidly, "You overestimate my interest in your little local squabbles. If D'hai's citizens shun you, the fact derives from troubles you have brought with you. I have always found D'hai to be a quiet city, until your recent arrival brought chaos to us."

I sensed motion behind me, as Evaric emerged from his self-imposed position of obscurity. Evaric said quietly, "You always did excel at eluding blame, Arvard."

The Shrine Keeper's blandly superior gaze darted from me to Evaric. "Lords of Serii," he whispered.

"Shrine Keeper," murmured several priests with varied blends of bewilderment and consternation, for their indomitable Shrine Keeper had begun to tremble like an ailing old man.

The Shrine Keeper commanded imperiously, "Leave us." Some of his devoted entourage hesitated, and the Shrine Keeper shouted, "Leave us!" The priests dispersed through various arched doorways amid a flurry of troubled glances.

I remained firmly immovable; I could feel the chill of the cold stone floor even though my sandals. The Shrine Keeper had forgotten me. He walked toward Evaric and touched the face of my K'shai escort with a tentative gentleness full of wonder. "I had forgotten how you affect me," he said delightedly. He clasped Evaric's arms with an enthusiasm that Evaric did not reciprocate. "I knew Conierighm would make a K'shai of you!"

"I left a message of explanation for you with Ylsa. You would have received it if you had ever returned to Tyntagel."

"I never returned, because I have not yet finished what I began. I sent a message to you that I was leaving Serii."

"I know. I received it only a year ago." Something cynical stirred in Evaric. "I came, as you expected."

Considering my own strongly ambivalent feelings toward the K'shai, I had little right to condemn another's obsession, but I did not consider the Shrine Keeper's fanatically hungry, almost tortured gaze a natural expression. I seated myself on the Shrine Keeper's throne and pondered the two men bemusedly. I resented deeply that Evaric had told me nothing of his acquaintance with the Shrine Keeper. Evaric had made such frantic issue of his night-marish concern with Rendies and ancient artifacts that I had almost persuaded myself of his candor. I had actually begun to trust a K'shai.

"I am near to finding the Taormin, Evaric," said the Shrine Keeper fervently, and I became more attentive. "It is here in D'hai. Together we shall find it. I have missed you, little brother."

I began to laugh, ridiculously affected by thought of the holy Shrine Keeper, the man who had garnered more economical influence in Ardasia than any Tanist, being the elusive brother of my K'shai. The Shrine Keeper turned on me like a fury. "Leave us, Ardasian whore!" he shouted.

Evaric said quietly, "Apologize to her, Arvard."

The Shrine Keeper wilted, which made an odd image from a man so obviously capable and strong. "We don't need her, Evaric. We don't need any of them. We need only each other, just as we always have: the Lost Prince and his devoted servant. We'll have our own world. Nothing can stop us: not these narrow, useless Ardasians, not Ixaxis, not Rendies, not . . ." He stopped and furrowed his face in effort. "Not anyone. I am Immortal, and you are my loyal ally, little brother."

The Shrine Keeper, I thought with the beginning of true uneasiness, was entirely mad: Rendie madness, perhaps, but of a kind more pervasive and deadly than any I had seen. When Evaric came to me and reached for my hand, I gave it to him with alacrity. "Mistress Lyriel is under my Protection, Arvard." Evaric's eyes burned with a starkly silver light that seemed inhumanly bright, and he frightened me, though his anger flared on my behalf. "Do you understand me, Arvard?"

"I shall not harm her," promised the Shrine Keeper meekly.

"Neither you nor your people will harm her."

"My people obey me." The Shrine Keeper offered me a brilliant smile. "Forgive my rudeness, Mistress Lyriel. Let my clerk know your Troupe's needs, and I shall see that you have all you require."

"Thank you." I distrusted the Shrine Keeper. I distrusted the exchange between the two brothers, both of whom seemed to keep secrets well buried.

Evaric drew me toward the main door. He told the Shrine Keeper, "I shall return to talk to you later, Arvard."

"You'll understand, little brother, when I explain what I've learned." The Shrine Keeper looked peculiarly forlorn when we left him.

Evaric did not relinquish my hand as he led me through the crowds of curious pilgrims. He remained forbiddingly silent as we crossed the pilgrim city. I let my own speculative thoughts carry me to the edge of the Ardasian district. "So you came to D'hai to combat a Rendie's whisper about the Taormin," I said archly.

"Yes."

"And you happened to discover that your brother, whom you had heard might possibly be in D'hai, just happens to be the Shrine Keeper, who has acquired more influence in the past year than anyone else in Ardasia."

"Arvard has always been quick to achieve the ambitions he sets for himself."

"Nothing that you told me about your brother was true."

"It was all true, as far as I know. Despite his show of delight and incredulity, Arvard was neither surprised nor pleased to see me."

"Why did you not try to see him before today? You obviously knew where to find him."

"I watched him give the Shrine blessing. That abolished any notions I entertained about discovering the brother I remembered."

"Why did he come here?"

"For the same reasons I came."

"To escape a nightmare?" I asked dryly.

"He came to escape a Rendie's madness. Please, Lyriel, I am not in the mood for an inquisition."

"You might have told me," I muttered.

He kissed the palm of my hand, which silenced me very effectively. My thoughts remained largely incoherent until we reached Vale's Inn. I felt very conscious of Solomai watching us enter together, even more aware of Alisa's unheeded voice calling to Evaric from the common room.

Only when we stood alone at the door of my room did Evaric speak again. "Why do we argue, Lyriel?"

"Because you are impossible."

"Then why do I continue to seek your approval?"

My approval? "Because you are a fool."

"Which of us is the more foolish, Lyriel? Me for seeking, or you for stubbornly refusing to admit approval of anything about me? I think you would do nearly anything for me, except confess that you might not dislike me as much as you pretend."

"If you want to earn my approval, Seriin, you might begin by leaving my room now."

"Yesterday, you cursed me for leaving."

"I cursed you for breaking contract."

"You wept for me."

"You have an active imagination." I tried to shut the door against him, but he would not depart. I turned my back on him and walked to the window. The sky grew dusky; I closed the shutters.

"I nearly asked you to remain in D'hai with me yesterday. When I thought that I might not see you again, I realized how much you have come to matter to me."

"You recovered quickly: I hoped Alisa entertained you with the harrowing tale of our failed foray from D'hai."

"No, but she provided me with some enlightening insight into the differences between Ardasian customs and those with which I was raised."

"Have your interests migrated from ancient history to contemporary cultures?"

"Seriin courtship," he remarked blandly, "consists of elaborate rituals, carefully arranged by the families of the betrothed pair. Ardasians are apparently less regimented, generally pledging themselves to one another without any formal ceremony or public acknowledgment."

I began to feel noticeably warm. "An appreciation of privacy," I replied stiffly, "does not make us immoral."

"I agree, which is why my question emerges so slowly. I want your honest answer, not the product of some misunderstanding based on your father's prejudice against 'Foreigners.' "

I faced him, though I could not meet his eyes. "You Seriins talk in circles," I complained. "What are you asking me?"

"Would you accept my pledge?"

"Your pledge?" I repeated absurdly.

"I ask to love you," he explained patiently. "Lyriel?"

"Close the door," I told him sternly.

"From which side?" asked Evaric wryly.

"From inside, you ridiculous Seriin. Do you think I want everyone in the Troupe to know that I am foolish enough to love a K'shai?"

He laughed against my hair. "Why not? Everyone in your Troupe already suspects it."

I formed a retort, but I never managed to use it. I was otherwise occupied for a considerable number of hours.

"You did know that your brother was the Shrine Keeper."

"Yes. Arvard hired the man who tried to kill me in Ardas, the man who tried to kill me in Samth, the man who tried to kill me in Arahinos, and the man who tried to drive the Troupe from D'hai, so that he might kill me outside of the Shrine Keeper's city."

"Your brother wants to kill you?" The man who had greeted Evaric with devouring eagerness had hardly seemed replete with enmity. "Why?"

"Rendie madness. Or human madness. Something altered Arvard after Ixaxis refused him. A Seriin nobleman—Fog's contacts could not tell me which one, though I believe I know—captured Arvard and evidently enhanced his madness by using illegal sorcery. I spent a good part of five years tracing Arvard to that point. By that time, he had already come to Ardasia and already tried to kill me twice in Serii."

"At this mysterious nobleman's behest?"

"I prefer to believe that Arvard would not otherwise have turned on me so thoroughly." Evaric drew his finger along the line of my cheekbone. "I thought that I became K'shai to protect Arvard. Instead, I defend myself from him."

"Then it is not K'shai rivalry that pursues you. All the attacks and the warnings originate with the Shrine Keeper." I never had trusted pilgrims, I mused.

"Unfortunately, Arvard is not the only issuer of a contract against me. Or perhaps the multiplicity has saved me: Some of my more amateur attackers have destroyed one another in their eagerness to reach me."

"What does Fog do while you fight other assassins?"

"At his best, he protects me and those who matter to me; the K'shai who tried to kill you near the Shrine had pursued me from Walier, trying to fulfill a contract to Lord Borgor dur Sandoral. At

Fog's worst, Fog takes contracts and drinks too much between them."

"You dislike him."

"Sometimes." He grimaced. "Most of the time. Dearest Lyriel, I do understand your dislike for the 'typical' K'shai, because I share it. I never wanted to kill, not even defensively. I never even wanted to kill Rendies, much as they torment me. Something pushes me to it. Every death haunts me, but it is so easy at the moment of killing. A life is such an easy thing to take." His voice ebbed.

I murmured tenderly, "How do you define this 'conscience' that you claim to lack?"

"As something independent of self-interest, which is all that motivates me."

"I think you overestimate the motives of the rest of us." He smiled but did not answer. "Why does this nobleman want to kill you?"

"He seeks vengeance against a man he believes was my true father, and he considers me a danger because of that supposed parentage. His contracts are not the only ones aimed at me, but his wealth makes his efforts the most professional and the most persistent. Fortunately, the very magnitude of the reward keeps assassins competing for me rather than joining forces in any effective manner."

"You told me that your father was a clerk."

"He is an accountant actually, though 'clerk' is commonly used to designate all Tyntagel Staff positions."

"Do Seriin accountants generally make such determined enemies?"

"No." Evaric said nothing for many moments. Voices and the sound of dishes clattered through the floorboards. "Vale's Inn prepares for another day caught between a blackening sky's despair and the futile hope of the Shrine Keeper's theatrics," murmured Evaric. "Arvard has always enjoyed domination. It soothes his insecurity."

"He also searches for the Taormin," I prompted.

"I suppose that part of Arvard still expects to have Power one day. Lord Goring's manipulations did not change that old madness. Or Arvard could be baiting a trap for me by hinting at hidden secrets. He knows how the Rendies torment me. He would expect me to do anything to be free of them."

"Who is your father?"

"In the opinions of Lord Gorng dur Liin and a rather impressive roster of others, my father was Lord Venkarel dur Ixaxis."

Evaric felt warm against me, and nothing else mattered. "What do you believe?"

"Evram and Terrell of Tyntagel raised me, and they are my parents, whether by birth or fostering."

"Did you ever ask them?"

"I would not let them tell me if they tried. What would it change?"

"You are not even curious?"

"About people I have never met or ever will? No. I should like to be free of Rendies, but that is a problem only I can remedy."

"How can you be sure?"

"Because I have never met an Ixaxin whom I could not deceive."

"You are the Venkarel's son," I whispered, staring at him, so close to me.

"Possibly. Does the unlikely chance of it make you regret the love you have given me?"

"Only if it takes you from me."

"Not Rendies, assassins, nor even Arvard's schemes could effect such a schism as *that*, my Lyriel."

Chapter 21

I floated through the morning, so dizzily gleeful that everyone I met gave me looks of doubt, suspicion, or knowingness. Evaric had gone to see his brother, and I danced through busy, aimless chores, waiting for Evaric, listening and watching for him, though he had warned me that he would likely not return until late.

When the Shrine Keeper's Guard arrived to inform Rubi that the Troupe could resume performances until the peculiar barrier around the city dissipated, I positively beamed at the horrid little man. When Rubi screamed orders at me, I smiled and did her bidding without complaint. When Taf endeavored to lecture me on the idiocy of my behavior, I laughed at him, kissed his sour scowl, and pirouetted from the room.

I could not argue with anyone. I wanted to please everyone within reach, because euphoria had entirely conquered my sense of practicality. When Anni asked me to guide her to the old D'hai, I agreed without considering my answer for an instant.

Anni's cousin had readied three horses before Anni and I reached the stable. I ought to have suspected his certainty of my compliance, but I cared only about Evaric and the hours until I would be with him again. Noryne was at the theater, where Rubi had assembled an impromptu audience from the restless, worried populace of D'hai. Even a few pilgrims had paid admission to gain the distraction of the Troupe's performance.

*   *   *

Old D'hai did begin to penetrate my haze of happiness. On the brightest and best of days, old D'hai evoked disquiet. When the sky twisted and seethed from the horizon, old D'hai resembled a piece of pilgrim purgatory.

Three facets of the first, oldest D'hai invariably struck me at initial approach: the darkness, the silence, and the cold. All three impressions faded quickly, for it was chiefly contrast which engendered them. The glare of the open desert, the hurling wind in its uproar, and the burning sun on undefended shoulders folded into the city and failed. When the senses adjusted to old D'hai, the city could be seen as blandly smooth and stark in its pure, chaotic colors. The silence rose only of emptiness. The cold came only of shade. When the senses accepted old D'hai, the mind could begin to wonder and fear.

It lay not far from the newer cities, but old D'hai recalled nothing of the familiar. Old D'hai spread sterile and unbroken, more pure than pilgrim pretension, more impassioned than Ardas at the height of summer's humid heat. The same impervious substance which formed the Shrine coated the ground of old D'hai. Walls rose from the ground in unchanging texture. Color delineated one building from the next by exploiting illusions; the structures stood many times the height of sensible constructions. The first D'hai was at least as foreign as the last.

Horses refused to enter the city, as did every creature with any sense. We tied our mounts to a scrubby tree near the city's edge. For once, I did not worry about losing the animals to thieves, who would be as trapped as the rest of us by unnatural barriers. I hoped that Taf had the sense to restrain his light fingers until the barrier cleared.

"The street absorbs the sound of our steps," observed Ineuil. I could have added that his voice, too, would be absorbed at half a dozen paces distant. A shout would fall silent from one building to the next. "Have you entered any of these?" he asked me, gesturing toward an acridly green facade.

"Do you see any entrances?" I retorted.

"The arches?"

"Lie flush with the buildings, despite appearance. They are painted or dyed—all of one piece like the streets and most of the structures throughout the city." Nervousness had resurrected my sharpness. The city's colors blazed too garishly for calm. The colors offended the landscape, which cried for muted tones or at least for softer blendings. This shouting obtrusion of reds and purples, oranges and greens disturbed the dusty respect of time, making D'hai too bawdy to be dead, too vibrant to be deserted. A city of ghosts should keep to ghostly softness. Pilgrim gray belonged in dead D'hai, just as color should have populated the D'hai of the living.

Anni commented calmly, "You have entered the building to which you are leading us." I did not ask her how she had known my intention; she was a wizardess, and I was beginning to understand the Seriin obsession with the breed.

"The dome is different." I stopped and pointed, for a glimpse of it could be had if one sought it closely. The dome lay straight before us and loomed large enough to be clearly visible, but the towers behind it befuddled the view. Ineuil squinted and shook his head. "You will see it soon enough," I promised him. I have known no one who could discern it from afar before seeing it once closely.

I had first visited the oldest D'hai in the company of a citizen of Ardasian D'hai and a party of that young man's friends. I had been barely beyond childhood, but the youth had been enamored of me and eager to impress me. The prospect of seeing the haunted city had enticed me, especially since it comprised a forbidden pleasure. Taf and Silf had warned me against approaching it, though I suspect that Taf himself had visited it, as I first did, in the company of D'hai youths more daring than intelligent.

I remembered the disappointment of my first visit. Expecting ghostly glimpses, I found deserted desolation and a city which wore its lively color only on the surface. Nothing happened to us, though two of the native girls made a great show of fear for the sake of their swaggering beaux. We had played the games of testing the sounds and silences, trying the false doors and endeavoring (vainly) to inflict some pointless, lasting sign of our presence. The only one of us who felt truly nervous was the one boy who had come for a second time. That was the charm of old D'hai: Its specters multiplied with every glance. The first visit was almost always easy and dull; the second became nervous and peculiar; few visited more than twice. Escorting Anni and her cousin comprised my third.

Uneasiness rubbed my nerves. I sensed the wrongness, though I could not label it any better this time than on either previous occasion. The city's spirit had twisted awry. These were odd perceptions, and I disliked them. I trusted them only because the city was old D'hai, and odd things came to those who trespassed there too often. Rumor said that no one had ever visited old D'hai more than seven times and remained sane. Like Rendie madness, old D'hai was insidious. I concentrated on the recollection of Evaric's touch.

Ineuil struck a violet wall with the pommel of his dagger. "Peculiar," he murmured, which could have described color, form, or substance. I did not ask him to elaborate. The street ended at the wide band of the central circle, and I directed his attention toward it. Anni already studied D'hai's central building, the broken dome.

The dome itself was clear like amber, though its feel was like that of the rest of the city. A web of gold fragmented its base. More than a few trespassers had tried to free a strip of gold from its setting, but the ubiquitous, impenetrable substance of old D'hai encased the gold and made the effort futile.

I swayed with dizziness, and Ineuil steadied me. I shrugged away his concern and his hand. Only the city's ill ease, deepest at its heart, troubled me; I recalled how avidly I had derided such tremors when first I visited old D'hai. Anni watched me attentively.

The road drew us beneath the arch, where darkness faced us. I braced myself for the entry, but the abrupt illumination of those inner walls still startled me. Ineuil released his cloak and drew a sword, a weapon suspiciously reminiscent of those carried by the Shrine Keeper's Guard; those folds of foreign fabric concealed a multitude of possibilities.

"The walls brighten automatically," I remarked with supremely specious nonchalance. Some Ardasians would have added that the broken dome desired and demanded entry; they would have likened the dome to those bright plants of the coastal marshes down whose dew-bedecked throats eager insects march to death.

The interior did not maintain the color of the outer city, though precious ores patterned the building's floor in dizzy convolutions. Everything nonmetallic within the dome had an amber cast. Amber might have been the original hue; it might have been the product of age. When one entered the vast misshapen central chamber, one could easily believe that the amber represented the color of calamity.

Great, solid amber tears dripped from the walls, looking liquid, though they were hard and brittle. Pieces from this one room could be broken, though all pieces of any potential value had long since been taken. "I call this room the stage chamber," I informed my audience of two, "due to the raised area in its center." I pointed to the mass of fused amber and melted metals. Brown streaked the amber near it, and the stage was largely black.

Ineuil accorded my description an ironic smile. "What happened here?"

"Fire."

He replied witheringly, "That much I could deduce for myself. When did the fire occur?"

"Years, maybe millennia ago. If you had ever tried to set fire to anything in old D'hai, you would realize that it was no campfire that burned here."

"Lightning?" suggested Ineuil with a glance at the sundered ceiling, opened to the patch of still-blue sky.

"Maybe." I shivered, wondering how long that cerulean morsel would remain untouched by the bleak and growing darkness. The rippling barrier seemed distressingly appropriate to old D'hai. I dropped my gaze to circle the stage, for treacherous amber bubbles pocked and bloated the floor. "You are a pilgrim. You must have heard the histories."

Ineuil probed the stage pensively with his sword's tip. "A Sorcerer King of Serii, stealing the D'hai Control, would likely wreak some damage. Horlach never was noted for his delicacy."

"Ineuil," reprimanded Anni, "this is neither the time nor the place to summon specters." Her cousin offered her a bland smile with an elegant, rather affected sweep of his hand. Anni's expression softened into forbearance; her cousin swayed her well.

" 'Hot as wizard's fire,' " I quoted dryly. The room had set my nerves to needles, and these two dubious pilgrims did not help. I wished for Evaric. "Is this what you wanted to see?"

"I think it is," replied Anni quietly. She stepped gingerly onto the stage, treading carefully among the jutting golden ridges, which marched in an irregular circle around the central point.

Ineuil had been tapping several of the stage formations with his sword, but he sheathed the weapon when Anni reached the central protuberance. The center was less obviously damaged than the surrounding areas of the room; it retained a distinctly cylindrical form extruding from a bubbling black sea at its base. The top of the cylinder was slightly hollowed and etched in a regular, radiating pattern.

"How long do you mean to stay here?" I asked, just as Anni extended her fine, dexterous fingers to touch the top of the cylinder.

Bright sheaths of light bathed the air around her. They danced and rippled and reached toward the nonexistent ceiling. I jumped toward the room's perimeter; the floor had certainly shifted beneath me. As I looked upward, I thought I saw a Rendie swirl and weave an incipient spell. The strange lights vanished, and the room solidified; Anni had removed her hand from the cylinder.

Anni stared at me as if I were the aberration. I slumped against the amber wall and complained, "Nothing is dull with you Seriins, is it?"

Anni turned from me to Ineuil. "What did you see?" she asked deliberately. Her voice chilled me more than the illusion I had just experienced. Anni seemed to address only her cousin, but her voice crawled into my ears and forced me to reply.

"The city awoke," I said without intending response. "The stage shifted around you. Curtains of light appeared. I think I saw a Rendie."

"Yes," approved Anni tersely. She circled the stage, which had become more regular along its circumference. I noted how carefully she avoided the metallic projections. "A construct existed here, connected by wire and light to other constructs throughout the city."

"And to the Rendies?" I asked uncomfortably.

"No. The Rendies came of subsequent meddling. Yet, they reflect the original function of this place: a place of gates to other worlds. I can still sense the pattern of the ancient energies, though the gates were sealed long ago."

"By Horlach?" asked Ineuil, assessing me as he spoke.

"No." Anni weighed her answer. "The gates were sealed because of him, I think. The Taormin was never meant to be a tool of sorcerous Power. Horlach warped it to that purpose by using it to intensify his own abilities. Because it possessed the faculty to learn, Horlach's example distorted it, even while it used his knowledge toward its own recovery."

"Then it was here that the Taormin originated," mused Ineuil.

"It was here," replied Anni slowly. "Did you doubt my assessment as well as my judgment?" she added with a quickly fleeting bit of arrogant humor. "This is where the Taormin belongs. Its removal effected a Rending far more thorough than the latest. The two Rendings are connected by more than the commonality of Horlach's mischief." Anni's expression veered from placid distraction to painful emotion. "Someone has stood here recently. Someone has touched the patterns, as I have. The energies reverberate still from the echo of great Power."

"Whose?" demanded Ineuil, his supple body shifting into wariness.

"I am unsure." Even I could see that Anni lied, and I could not claim to know her well.

"You are still an abominable liar—Anni," said her cousin with a peculiar, rigid grin. "No matter. Whenever you assume that stubbornly defensive air, I know that you are thinking of Kaedric, and I am wise enough to delve no further. Shall we return to Master Vale's charming establishment, or would you prefer to provide further wonders for the lovely Mistress Lyriel's speculation?" He acknowledged me with a gallant flourish of his sweeping gray cloak.

"She is intrinsic to the pattern, Ineuil," said Anni, as if I could not retort for myself. "You were wiser than I in perceiving her importance. Lyriel is necessary to the restoration, and restoration must be effected soon if we are to preserve this infinity; in that much, Horlach has spoken truly. The barrier of distorted energy forming around D'hai bleeds from the Taormin's tangled realm; it flows from the instability, which is destruction. We have been brought here, Ineuil, all of us. Whatever we thought our reasons might have been, we are here because the pattern demands us."

"I have never liked being manipulated," said Ineuil with a shade of weary exasperation, "especially by Horlach."

Anni shook her head faintly. "Horlach is crippled. The manipulator is not Horlach." She added uncertainly, "Nor even Kaedric. Or perhaps both of them manipulate together. Perhaps the Taormin itself directs us."

I wanted to shake from Anni a great many answers that I thought she might be able to provide. I did not want to ask in the presence of her cousin with his sword and his deceptively innocent charm. I did not want to remain any longer in old D'hai with its haunts of old terror and its empty, silent streets. I felt very ready to return to Vale's Inn.

Chapter 22

Evaric strode easily through the corridors to the Shrine Keeper's rooms, while even his gray-robed escort endeavored to ignore him. The sight of a K'shai walking boldly into the Shrine Keeper's Hall had unsettled many pilgrims. Most of the priests who placated those pilgrims felt at least equally distraught. Only a select few of the priests knew how often K'shai entered the Shrine Keeper's Hall in pilgrim guise. None of the priests had quite dared to ask Evaric to leave his weapons at the entry.

The escort led him to the Shrine Keeper's private suite rather than to the more formal reception room which he had visited with Lyriel. Arvard kept his private rooms sparse of furnishings, as a token of the simplicity befitting the Shrine Keeper, but the rooms opened to a magnificent view of D'hai's golden valley. Arvard entered grandly, newly returned from giving a mass blessing to the hundreds of troubled pilgrims at the Shrine. He dismissed his entourage summarily. He shed his outer robe with a grimace. "I may never adjust to this beastly climate." Arvard slapped Evaric's arm boisterously. "I am glad you came. We have so much to discuss, little brother." Arvard filled a goblet from the decanter on the marble-topped table; the table and eight chairs of wrought iron constituted the room's only furniture. Arvard drank deeply of the potent liquor, made from a small local fruit, before offering a goblet to Evaric.

"No. Thank you." Evaric had not moved since Arvard entered. "Why did you send for me, Arvard? A K'shai brother can only be an embarrassment to you."

"We are brothers who have not seen each other in eight years. Do I need a better reason?" Arvard drank again and began to refill his goblet.

Evaric paced to the window and back, no longer bothering to disguise his restlessness. "We are strangers who were brothers once. I watched you give blessing to your followers: a very spiritual performance from someone who once scorned religion as a crutch for the weak and inadequate."

"And you argued with me," mused Arvard, staring for a moment into the past. He roused himself with a start, shaking his yellow hair. "So we have both changed. But the bond between us is stronger than ideologies or position in the world's affairs. You must work with me, Evaric." Arvard raised his hand in a powerful gesture at once supplicating and inspirational; he had practiced the gesture extensively.

"Assuming for the moment that I believe in your sincerity, toward what goal should we strive so devotedly? Toward the conquest of your troubled followers with this emotional display of false miracles and fanatical ravings that you call religion? These unhappy pilgrims are a sorry substitute for the Ixaxin Guild of Wizards and the Lords of Serii, whom I think you meant to conquer when we parted in Tyntagel. Even the petty intrigues of Tyntagel Keep must have offered you more challenge than these pilgrims, who will believe anything told with fervor, and their Ardasian hosts, who will sell anything if they sense some immediate profit to themselves."

"I comfort the pilgrims, and I pay the Ardasians. All derive satisfaction from the result. Of what can you possibly disapprove, little brother?"

"I disapprove of hypocrisy. Would the Shrine Keeper continue to give so generously of his spiritual largess if his long-vaunted, imaginary Power ever became real?"

Arvard threw his goblet at the wall, smashing the delicate glass and staining the buff wall with the liquor that ran like thin blood. He mastered himself by slow increments, while Evaric wondered how even Rendies and abusive sorcery could have molded Arvard into such a stranger. The tension in this man who was Shrine Keeper made Evaric's own muscles tighten defensively. Even Arvard's voice sounded thick with conflict.

"I want you to come with me to old D'hai, little brother, and then you will see for yourself why I am trapped here. That accursed place holds the key to all that it is my right to be and have. I have come so close to it, and it sits there, mocking me. Look at it." Arvard pointed across the desert toward the barren hills so unlike Serii's splendid mountains. Old D'hai lay between the Shrine Keeper's Hall and the hills; the hills were not far, but only a shimmering of the ancient city could be seen, with blackness rising grimly behind it. "There lies the means to prove my heritage to the Ixaxins who rebuffed me and to the great Infortiare, who refused even to acknowledge her own son. There lies the answer to Rendies, Evaric. The answers to barriers of dark Power and to all a mortal's insurmountable obstacles lie there, if only a man could reach them."

"You have not changed in one thing, Arvard. You still talk more to yourself than to me."

"We can leave for old D'hai immediately. I must show you what I have discovered."

"I have obligations elsewhere, Arvard, and you appear to be very well tended."

Arvard spoke sharply. "I control this city, little brother."

"So I have seen. But you do not control me. That was Lord Gorng's primary mistake in selecting you as his tool of vengeance. He trusted in your mistaken self-confidence. You never controlled me, Arvard, except by my choice."

Arvard took another goblet and poured again from the decanter. His hands shook only slightly, but Evaric observed the sign of weakness with mixed regret. Evaric doubted that Arvard would try to harm him directly in the Shrine Keeper's Hall, but clever K'shai instincts whispered sly words of warning, vying with nostalgic sympathy. The layers of this unfamiliar Arvard's deception made Evaric glad of the sword at his side.

Arvard remarked coldly, "That Ardasian actress of yours is rather pretty in a sultry, primitive way. I am told that these Ardasian women possess a very potent physical allure, if one is susceptible to that sort of blatant sensuality. I had hoped that your standards would have risen higher."

"No, Arvard, you really have not changed." Except, thought Evaric bitterly, to become my attacker instead of my defender. But Gorng did not fabricate your mad jealousy of anyone whom I might love beyond you. The sad, isolated traces of the familiar Arvard made the situation both easier and more difficult to accept.

Evaric touched the carefully balanced door, and it opened soundlessly. Two flustered priests straightened hurriedly from positions suspiciously near to the door. Evaric ignored both the priests and the guards, as well as Arvard's anxious commands to return. Evaric employed his laboriously cultivated, unhurried K'shai grace to depart without approaching any Shrine guard or priest closely. He wanted no further proof of the death of the brother whom he had loved

Arvard slammed both hands flat against the marble table. "Kritz!" he shouted, and a handsome young man in pilgrim robes emerged from the inner chamber. "See that he is watched. I want to know every move he makes."

Kritz bowed low and complied. Arvard seated himself before the table. The needles in his head grew more painful with every thought of his brother. He could not hurt Evaric, he insisted to himself; he could never hurt Evaric. The needles seared him, until his eyes burned and he recanted, begging the unseen Lord whose command drove him. He needed to plan. He needed to act. He needed to destroy Evaric. He could not hurt Evaric. The needles made him shudder with pain.

He had tried to comply, he pleaded. He had done more than any reasonable man could expect of him. The target could not be killed. Evaric could not be killed. Evaric was his brother and his friend.

Arvard tried to forget the needles, and he failed. He had already tried all of the tricks he could devise, and he had always failed. The only solution was compliance. Or Power. But his Power was trapped in the Taormin—in old D'hai. If he could reach the Taormin with Evaric, then the Power could save them both.

The needles intensified. Arvard repented aloud to them, "I shall kill him. I shall kill him in old D'hai." The needles eased just a little to a pain that was merely bearable. Not even the Power of a Caruillan sorceress could quite determine which parts of Arvard's schemes held true to Power's dictates, Rendie madness, or a deep, obstinate loyalty to a brother who had always been special.

"Shrine Keeper?" asked a hesitant priest, when his repeated knocks had failed to elicit response.

Arvard straightened painfully, donning pride which was only a remembered mask. "What is it, Lefner?"

"Another member of that acting group," announced Lefner, "insists upon seeing you, sir. You did ask that we accommodate them." Lefner's stilted disapproval afforded Arvard a sorry amusement. "He is a Master Zakari."

"Permit him to enter, Lefner." Arvard felt exhausted, but that was a feeling to which he had inured himself. He posed himself for his visitor, emulating the cool austerity of the Ixaxin who had destroyed his hopes. Arvard appraised the actor indifferently: a fine looking man, albeit a swaggerer. "Master Zakari," said Arvard with just the right mixture of weariness and forbearance. Zakari's swagger faltered a bit. Lefner retreated with a smirk. "You have something to tell me," prompted Arvard carelessly. The Shrine Keeper had impressed the pathetic, ignorant Ardasian and could afford to become condescendingly gracious.

Zakari spoke clearly. That rich voice would serve well in a Shrine blessing, thought Arvard idly. "I heard that you wanted information about a K'shai named Evaric."

Who had talked to a member of that troupe? "I am a religious leader, Master Zakari. Why should I interest myself in a K'shai?"

Zakari's confidence was reviving. "The reason is your concern. I have my own reasons to wish no good to that K'shai. The word I hear is that you would be glad enough to see the last of this K'shai as well. As a member of the Troupe he Protects, I could assist you. Fifty serisni, and the K'shai is yours."

The needles in Arvard's head retreated, replaced by the pleasure of reward for proper thinking. "Where did you acquire this fantastic notion of yours?"

"Gariman," replied Zakari confidently, and the Shrine Keeper's acknowledging grimace did not disappoint him. Gariman was a reliable reference: a man who dealt in information, such as open kill contracts or illegal drug sources.

"If someone performs a valued service for me, Master Zakari, I can be generous." Circle might well make use of the stupid Ardasian.

"I can deliver him to you."

"No, Master Zakari. You will deliver him to a man named Circle, who will himself apprise you of any further details. Ten serisni will await your success."

"You are a wealthy, important man, Shrine Keeper, and forty serisni would remind me much more effectively to keep silent."

"My word would certainly overcome your unsubstantiated claims. However, twenty serisni would express the level of my gratitude properly."

"Twenty-five."

"Acceptable. Master Lefner will show you to the door." This Zakari does not even bargain well, thought Arvard disparagingly.

"It has been a pleasure, Shrine Keeper."

Arvard grunted to himself, wondering if Master Zakari comprehended even dimly the magnitude of the task he had assumed for such a pittance. Knowing that he needed to keep his own wits sharp, Arvard resolved, nonetheless, to imbibe as much strong liquor as D'hai could supply.

"Turn inward, Noryne. Gather peace unto yourself. Become the softness of the morning, the gentleness of a cool breeze."

"There is so much turmoil, Anni."

"Do not address me! Do not focus on me or on the turmoil but on the calm, clear light within yourself."

Noryne's breathing became smooth and slow. Rhianna allowed herself one wisp of Power by which to verify the young actress' control. Rhianna dared exert no more Power than that wisp, for she did not want her pattern to be associated with Noryne's. She did not want her own pattern to provide the warning by which Kaedric would elude her yet again.

Rhianna said softly, "Study the K'shai, Noryne."

"Evaric frightens me."

"Not Evaric." Not this time. "Sense Fog. Define him to me."

"Dead."

Rhianna caught her breath. She maintained her shell of calm with difficulty. "Fog died?"

"Yes. More than once."

"He was restored."

Noryne answered hesitantly, "Yes. Something veils my sight."

"Do not try to pierce the shadow, Noryne," said Rhianna softly. "You have done well." And you would never dent Kaedric's personal barrier. A stronger, harsher Power than yours could not have approached him even so closely, for he would have perceived the threat and repulsed it, as he has denied me repeatedly. But I analyzed correctly. I understand your scheme now, Kaedric, my obstinate love, and I perceive my proper role at last.

When Noryne roused from her trance of Power, she discovered Anni stitching quietly, as ever. A difference, however, which Noryne could only define distantly, had come: anticipation. Noryne wondered, feeling uncertain, awed and frightened by the patterns she could not quite discern; this Power was an uncomfortable gift.

"You are deceived!" shouted Horlach, but he could not pierce the barrier of Rhianna's Power. He sensed the muted essence of Noryne, but that tentative sort of Power had always eluded him, and Rhianna had added extra shields to thwart him. *"Where are you, Venkarel?"* But only emptiness replied. Horlach tried to reach into the mind of Arvard, but Horlach could not touch a mortal save with pallid, voiceless prods of pain; a Lord of Liin might be manipulated by his own precarious Power, but the laws of Zerus, the sole inescapable truths of Power, forbade Horlach from molding a mortal directly.

Horlach turned to face the flood of darkness cloaking the Taormin's silent plain. The tangle burned both bright and black amid the inky tide. Horlach hesitated, but he stepped into the darkness' midst. His image ebbed and faltered; his twisted pattern blurred and dimmed. *"Rending-born,"* hissed Horlach. The tangle did not stir. *"Fire-child, heed me!"* Horlach's pattern nearly failed, as he dredged all lingering motes of Power from his hidden, faded store: all focused, all desperate, he cast it all into one final, fierce attempt. *"Son of the Taormin, hear me!"*

Something in the tangle moved minutely. Horlach smiled; his pattern firmed; but as he tried to grasp the tangle, a rush of darkness burst from the rest. Horlach leaped free of its path and cursed it; Horlach knew its deadliness. Patiently (for Horlach had learned patience through the millennia of helpless, anguished waiting), Horlach recommenced his search for any means to claim the one, entangled limit point of both the dark world and the light.

Chapter 23

I heard him speak to Fog, though the sound came softly overshadowed by more raucous, careless voices returning to the inn as evening neared. I dropped the scripts in Rubi's lap. I did not care how many watched me. I did not care how many of Vale's customers I aggravated in my effort to reach Evaric. When I located him in the courtyard with Fog, I stopped just to delight in the sight of him.

He felt me watch him, left Fog, and came to me. We stood a pace apart. "I never knew how long a day could be," he said, "until today."

"I thought you would never return."

"I cannot sit across the common room from you through the evening, pretending to enjoy anyone else's company."

"Can you reach my room without being seen?"

"Of course." He smiled his miraculous smile. "I am K'shai."

"I shall meet you there in ten minutes."

"Five minutes."

"Five minutes," I agreed blissfully.

Rendies came to him when he slept. I held to him tightly, calling to him as hungrily as did the Rendies, and he woke to me and not to them. "Lyriel," he whispered again and again, "you are all that I need. The Rendies have no more power over me. All the emptiness and anger within me have become nothing, for I have you, and nothing else matters."

I had been taught from a tender age: never let a man know you need him. The first time the advice applied, I forgot it, all for the sake of a foreigner who was K'shai. "Never let go of me, Evaric."

"Not though all the forces of the world try to part us."

"We could escape your enemies in Ardas. I know every useful official in the city. No one, not the Shrine Keeper, not K'shai, not Seriin lords, not even Rendies, will find us."

His laughter against my skin rippled with warmth. "I am more concerned about keeping my enemies from you, my dear firebrand. I am rather practiced in preserving myself."

"Would you fight your brother?"

".I can manage Arvard without fighting him."

"We need to leave D'hai."

"We have a few obstacles," he said, even as he moved to make me forget them.

"We must concentrate on keeping you alive," I insisted.

"Yes, my lady," he agreed with amused irony.

"There must be a way to leave here. This barrier must be a thing of Power. Anni knew that it existed before we saw it." As Evaric had known, I thought, in his own way. "She must know a way through it."

"Anni?"

"She is an Ixaxin."

Evaric became absolutely still. "Are you certain?"

"I have only her word for it, but I never thought to doubt her claim. She certainly has some odd abilities if she is not a wizardess."

"I never sensed it in her. I have never felt the danger in her."

"Anni is not a danger to you." He was troubled again, in much the same way as the Rendies made him.

"Why is she here?"

"She is a pilgrim."

"No."

"Forget about her, Evaric. She does not matter to us." I should have known not to speak to him of Power during the night, when the Rendie voices still rang in him. "Nothing matters, dearest Evaric, except that you are with me, and we shall never be apart again."

*   *   *

I did not try again until morning to broach with Evaric any plans to escape D'hai. I opened the shutters to reinforce the light; most of the sky was dark with turmoil. "By tomorrow, there will be no sunlight," said Evaric from behind me.

"Will the Rendies come?"

"Probably, though not because the sky is dark. The gate between their world and ours is widening."

"Anni spoke of gates yesterday. I took her and her cousin to old D'hai. She said that the Taormin once controlled gates between worlds." I wrapped my arms around Evaric as I spoke. I felt reassured when my words did not make him flinch.

"Arvard wants me to visit old D'hai with him."

"Will you go?"

"No."

"You did come here to learn about the Taormin, as much as to see your brother. I think Anni may know at least a part of the answers you seek."

"None of it matters any longer. I have found what I need, Lyriel, and it is you."

"Your flattery may turn my head, Seriin."

"My love for you is no more than the truth."

"How are we to leave here, Evaric?"

"We shall find a way." He raised his head from me to gaze at the menacing sky. "I shall take a closer look at that barrier."

"Shall we leave now, or shall we eat first?"

"I shall eat as I ride. You are staying here, my love, until I have a better idea of what we are facing."

I tried to scowl at him, but I failed; I enjoyed the novelty of being protected. "Take Fog with you, at least."

"And leave the Troupe undefended?"

"No one will bother with us. It is you whom everyone trails with malicious intent. In any case, we shall all be at the theater, in clear view of most of D'hai. Impending catastrophe stimulates attendance miraculously. We have recovered all the season's losses and more."

"Try not to take too much advantage of the populace until I return. I should hate to lose you to an irate shopkeeper."

"I have been outmaneuvering merchants and city officials since

I could talk." I felt happier and easier than circumstances warranted, but when Evaric reached the door, I ran to him, stopping him before he could open it. "Be careful, Evaric," I beseeched him. I tried to fix in my mind the sweetness of touching him, knowing him, and feeling his love. I was not prescient; the dangers around us simply mocked me.

Our play sparkled, enthralling our audience, packed five to a bench. The performance of every player exceeded anything we had done all season. It was a fitting cap of glory, a final brightness in the closing darkness. I watched it in silent entrancement with Taf beside me. Taf almost smiled at me when the play was done.

We walked slowly and circuitously together to Vale's Inn. Most of D'hai, Ardasians and pilgrims both, strolled the streets with us, clustered in twos or threes, all of us aware that the slender column of hot sun would not likely bless us beyond this day. Many pilgrims still crowded and moaned their fears at the Shrine, but many more had discovered greater courage in the last day's light. It was an eerily beautiful day.

"You have been with that K'shai," said Taf dourly, just as we approached Vale's courtyard.

"I love him, Taf, as thoroughly as ever you loved Silf."

"You have seen what comes of such love," Taf growled.

"I shall never leave Evaric, whatever he is or does."

"Will he be as constant to you, girl?"

"Yes." I was utterly confident of my love. As I spoke, I saw him, and my joy made me hasten, leaving Taf to trail behind me.

Vale and many of the Troupe members had gathered in the courtyard, and all watched Evaric and the man who cowered before him; no one intervened between a K'shai and his victim. My limbs became leaden. The victim was Zakari, and he pressed himself against the stable wall, shrinking from my K'shai in whose blue-silver eyes fury burned. Evaric hissed, "You placed your filthy drug in the water bag that you knew I would take. How much were you paid for my life, Zakari?"

"Nothing," whimpered Zakari, so terrified that his makeup ran with the tears of his fear. "I did nothing."

"How many virol addicts came to the stable this morning, as I was leaving? You hoped the drug would weaken me too much to fight the assassin with whom you conspired. The plan was excellent. Was it yours? No matter. It failed. Fog exchanged horses with me; Fog drank the tainted water; it was Fog whom the assassin struck through the heart." Evaric gripped Zakari's wrist and squeezed it cruelly. "You did not expect Fog to accompany me today, did you? Not after the quantities and varieties of Ardasian liquor that you encouraged him to imbibe last night."

"Is it a crime to drink with a man?" asked Zakari weakly.

Evaric, I wanted to cry, stop torturing him, but I remained mute with fright. "This is Fog's blood that I wear, Zakari," said Evaric fiercely. "He continues to bleed, and there are no drugs to heal such a wound, even if your wretched virol would allow another drug to take effect. Fog dies, Zakari, but you die first."

The deadliness made a mask of Evaric's perfect face. Zakari tried to break free and run, but Evaric twisted and struck Zakari's neck. Blood began to spurt from Zakari's wrist, where Evaric had crushed it. Zakari wavered and grew limp. Evaric discarded him, releasing Zakari to the courtyard's dirty cobbles. Hard and predatory, Evaric stalked away from his kill. He did not even see me.

Noryne burst from the inn and screamed. She sank to Zakari's side and cradled his head against her breasts. "You cannot leave me, Zakari," she implored him. A deeply violet light flowed along her slender arms and covered him. "You must not die."

"My dear," whispered Zakari so dimly that I barely heard him.

"I am here, Zakari," said Noryne with desperation.

"I only wanted you to be safe from him, my dear," whispered Zakari, and Noryne crooned frantic encouragement. We could not drag her from him, even when he had died. She stroked his fine, tranquil face, and she grieved.

"He thought he spoke to me," said Alisa in a shaken voice.

"He made his own choice," I told her gruffly. I had blamed her often enough for taunting Zakari into folly, but her grief compelled me to console her. "He thought he played the hero's role. He did not understand." He did not know that his rival was not mortal.

"Zakari looks nobly peaceful," Alisa answered vaguely. "He always did enjoy a good death scene." I took Alisa's tiny hand to lead her to the inn. We leaned on one another, both sickened by death.

Rubi hailed me unsteadily. "You had better make it right with the constables," she said, and I nodded. The constables would need bribing to ignore a murder; even a K'shai was expected to pay if his kills were not discreetly done.

"I am sorry, Rubi," I apologized, as if I had killed her lead actor or felt less touched by his death than she.

"Lyriel, no," protested Alisa weakly. It was odd to feel comforted by Alisa.

Rubi grumbled roughly, "At least he died quickly, which is better than the rest of us are likely to do in this unholy place. Taf, make arrangements for the burial as soon as possible." Taf was staring at Anni's cousin, who had pried Noryne from her dead gallant. Ineuil carried Noryne into Vale's Inn, and Noryne wept in his arms like a lost child. Ineuil's expression had grown flat. I wondered where Anni had gone. I wondered the more where Evaric's bitter mood had taken him. I was not sure that I wanted either answer.

Chapter 24

The common room was dark and empty with the night. Alisa sat alone, too cold and forlornly tired to make the journey to her chamber. She heard the outer door open and close. When the inner door opened, she heard no sound of other movement from the K'shai who entered. She could not see him well, though dim lamplight filtered through the curtain from the kitchen.

Alisa began to giggle, a high, loud, erratic sound. "I told Zakari that he could never hope to compete with a man like you."

Evaric responded coolly, "You should get some sleep, Alisa. The hour is late."

"Sleep?" Alisa pushed at her hair, and a blonde curl fell loose across her face. She had not removed the silver pins worn for the role she had played opposite Zakari. When she discovered one of the pins in her hand, she stared at it, as it caught the fragile remnant of light. "There is a very old play, as I remember, which comments lengthily on the elusiveness of sleep among the guilty." Alisa dropped the pin onto the floor, where it clattered and lay still. She composed her face as she watched it fall. When she raised her face to Evaric, she was smiling and seductive.

"Let me take you to your room, Alisa."

"Did you kill Zakari for me, Evaric? Or did I kill him for you?" She did not resist when Evaric drew her to her feet. "I want you, Evaric."

"To forget?" asked Evaric crisply.

"Why not?" demanded Alisa with sudden harshness. She wanted to consume this K'shai with passion and then dismiss him. She wanted to eradicate images of Zakari. She wanted to escape all thought.

The accusations of the Shrine priest kept circling in her head. "You are damned," the priest assured her repeatedly. "You belong to us." No, that was wrong; that was not what the priest had said. "Come with us." Why was her haunt changing his words?

Evaric propelled her toward the stairs. She stumbled. Evaric stopped to help her. She no longer felt him. A chill had replaced him, and the room was empty of all but mist. "You belong to us," sang a thing which was gray and nebulous. "Come with us, Fire-child," whispered a cloud that hung before her and around her.

Something very hot and very cold drew a line across Alisa's throat. She could not speak nor move. The tendrils of a Rendie's form slithered against her, and they burned with cold. A tendril began to twine around her legs. She experienced a sensation of sliding through a ragged gap in the floor. She looked downward. The skirt of her gown had turned dark, and the stiff white fabric clung limply to a shape which resembled her legs. There was something wrong with the image, but she could not identify the problem.

"Time ends soon for this sorry world you claim, Fire-child. Come with us before it is too late to escape the endings."

A piece of trailing cloud stung Alisa's face. She touched her cheek and felt the sticky hollow where flesh had been. She looked at Evaric, standing motionless amid the swirls of terrible mist that lashed at her and hurt her. His eyes did not see her, and he did not respond when she screamed at him. She tried to run from the clouds, but they pursued her. They pressed her to the stairs. She could not climb nor escape.

Her throat was opened to air; she began to gag. The retching turned to torment, as her body tried to evict the sweet, sick taste of Rendie. When something hard and hot touched her, she began to scream aloud. The hardness slapped her, but Alisa refused to stop her screams. She would never stop, for pain would never stop.

The light spilled from above her. "Zakari," Alisa cried, and she croaked his name in a shrill shriek of madness, which she knew would never end.

Chapter 25

I was deeply asleep, dreaming of the previous day's horror. Most of the players enacted simple chorus roles. Minaro upheld his part with a quiet, careless conversation. Zakari was shrieking hysterically, though none of us seemed to notice. He shrieked as he drew a dagger and leaped wildly upon a K'shai. He shrieked while Evaric spun and danced the death blow. Zakari continued shrieking, though he lay dead and staring.

I tossed restlessly, awoke, and heard the shrieking still. "The pitch is too high for Zakari," I muttered to myself, but some sense penetrated. I snatched my cloak, for it came first to hand, and the dry, early dawn air felt cold.

Others had heard also and reacted more quickly. Every door along the hall had opened. The timid peered into the dim hall from behind shields of doors; the more bold had gathered around the room from which the screams emerged.

It was Alisa's room, and Minaro stood at the door trying to keep the curious from entering. He was not succeeding well at the task, for craning heads still sought to see the source of chaos. Taf dispersed the mob with a gesture and a curse. Reluctantly, the onlookers retreated to their room, but few doors were reclosed. Rubi's head emerged from Alisa's room. She saw me and beckoned urgently.

The screams sounded much worse inside the cramped room.

Noryne and Miria stood shivering beside the door, looking starkly frightened. I knelt by Alisa, who was huddled in the corner of the room. She had been dreadfully mauled; she would never heal cleanly. Hers were Rendie wounds, deep and ragged.

I tried speaking her name calmly. Failing to effect any change in noise level by kindness, I shook her very soundly. She choked for a moment but continued at a piercing volume. I shook her repeatedly, until she sobbed herself from screams to loud weeping.

Rubi helped me pull Alisa to her feet, and we saw the wretched state of Alisa's legs. Rubi and I tried to coax her, mostly carrying her, toward the bed. Alisa began to shake her head violently, and we finally settled her into a chair. I dropped my cloak around her, for she seemed to need it more than I. She tugged the heavy fabric close to her skin, and the gesture seemed to calm her slightly.

"I heard her scream," chattered Miria nervously.

"Evaric was carrying her up the stairs," added Noryne. "He brought her here."

"Why did he not Protect her?" demanded Rubi roughly. Her wildly uncombed hair made her look all the more ferocious. "My poor, sweet little girl."

"Alisa," I asked gently, "where is Evaric?" Alisa only shivered, her pretty eyes wide and fixed.

Rubi shouted irritably, "Will somebody find the accursed K'shai and bring him here!" The command received an uneasily dismayed response of silence.

"I shall go, Rubi," I answered calmly, though I could appreciate the general reluctance to leave one another's company and seek a man who left destruction in his wake. Rubi only betrayed approval of my offer by a tight nod and the gesture which sent Noryne scurrying to replace me at Alisa's side. Taf eyed me as if he found my behavior idiotic.

Most of the doors had closed in the face of uncertainty. I headed for my room, intending to pause only long enough to pull a skirt and jacket over my sleeping gown; the sun might have risen, but neither heat nor light could seep well through a barrier of black turmoil. Finding Evaric required no great skill or effort. He awaited me in a chair in my room. "Careless of you to leave your door open," he murmured ironically. "Any sort of monster might enter."

Carefully, I closed the door behind me. Evaric had dropped into solemn silence. I circled around him, gathered some scattered garments and hung them in the armoire; I devoted an excessive number of minutes to inconsequential activities. I seated myself on the end of the bed, forcing Evaric to twist his head in order to see me. "The Rendies paid you another visit tonight," I commented, as if discussing an old friend's social call.

"You have seen Alisa."

"I have seen and heard her. The Rendies attacked her in your presence, I suppose. How else could they have entered a solid building, sealed for the night, save by following the beacon of your presence?"

"I told you that the Rendie gates were widening," retorted Evaric acridly. He rose and began to pace, which irritated me unreasonably.

"Will you settle a moment and let me think!" He settled, and I began to pace instead. "Ardasians might tolerate the killing of a jealous lover, who may have tried to kill you. Pilgrims could scarcely bother to disapprove of the death of an Ardasian actor. But not even your Shrine Keeper brother can manufacture forgiveness for a Rendie lodestone. When Alisa begins to talk, as she will, the very wildness of her accusations will make them insidious. There will be nowhere in Ardasia for us to hide, even if we do escape D'hai."

"Would you like to know what happened tonight?"

"I think I can guess enough," I replied sharply. "The Rendies sought you again. But this time they preferred to dine on Alisa. I was more fortunate than I knew. I assumed that you could Protect even while they spoke to you."

Evaric asked wearily, "Do you want me to leave?"

"We have no Protection now, do we? Nothing exists between us and the Rendies? Even Fog is dead. How long can we survive, Evaric, those of us who are not adored by Rendies but merely devoured by them, merely trapped with them in a city of endless night?"

"I shall not let them harm you, Lyriel."

"Can you stop them if they try?"

He closed his eyes. I wondered what he was trying not to see. "Yes. I can stop them from hurting you."

"You failed to help Alisa. Your brother is Rendie mad; I suppose you failed to help him, too."

"It is not that easy, Lyriel!" His anger felt sharp. His eyes glowed coldly silver, and his jaw was tightly clenched. "I wanted to believe that I could forget everything but you. I was wrong. I am sincerely sorry about Alisa, Zakari, Fog, Arvard, that mad wizard in Tyntagel, and all of the other victims of whatever wrongness makes me Rendie kin. I love you, Lyriel." He left before I could resolve my fear and hurt with my longing for him.

The Shrine Keeper's Guard came for me less than an hour later. They wanted to question me, they said. They wanted me to accompany them.

Rubi started to become indignant about this disruption of our grief and mourning. Vale said nothing, as he continued to polish the tavern glasses, doubtless debating the nature of this latest disturbance to his establishment. I had lost interest in arguing somewhere between my fight with Evaric and my morning visit to Alisa, who lay battered and bandaged in her bed, staring at the ceiling and clinging to Noryne. Noryne had tended her alone; no one had seen Anni since the previous day.

"Give me a moment to fetch my shawl," I told the guards.

"Of course, Mistress," their captain responded politely, but the guards escorted me to my room, waited while I collected my shawl, and did not let me leave their sight. I began to feel like a prisoner, but I did not worry greatly. The Shrine Keeper had promised my safety for his brother's sake. The company of the Shrine Keeper could seem no more menacing than the arms of my lover.

"Where is my brother, Mistress Lyriel?" The Shrine Keeper looked worse than I felt. His face had become haggard and as gray as a pilgrim's robes. His hands shook, and I suspected that the libation he poured from the decanter was not by any means his first of the day.

"You are the man who controls the city. Why ask me?"

"My brother has always had a lamentable weakness for women of your type."

I ignored the typical foreigner's insult. "I do not know where he has gone, Master Arvard. I do know that you paid to have him killed."

"No!" he cried, his square, strong face contorting. "Yes," he said calmly. "He is an enemy of all mortal kind. It is the Shrine's will that he die. Lenzl, bring her."

Three guards came toward me; they caught and took me before I realized their intent. I kicked all three soundly and bit one, but they tied me. I called them several choice names, but I divided the best epithets between the Shrine Keeper and myself.

The guards gagged me when I made a particularly disrespectful comment to their holy Shrine Keeper, whose own reaction was remarkably like approval. The guards dropped a rough sack over my head, and one of the burlier men threw me over his shoulder. I squirmed and struggled as he carried me. When I landed over a horse's rump, I abandoned my futile effort.

I felt furious and frightened. I could do nothing to resolve either emotion. I had the meager consolation that our destination must lie within the D'hai valley, for I expected no miracle of the Shrine to abolish a barrier built of some sorcerous abomination. The guards had not killed me yet. I did not know why they would want me, alive or otherwise, unless I was a pawn to use against Evaric. I did not place the odds in such a contest with the Shrine Keeper, but my own prospects did not seem good.

We paused once, and someone unseen checked my bonds. I tried to strike him, but hands tied tightly behind one's back do not move well. I did inspire a reaction, however. "Hold still," he whispered. "It is hard enough to loosen these surreptitiously."

"Ineuil?" I hissed, though his aristocratic voice was unmistakable. "Hush."

The tightness at my wrists eased, and I felt the prickle of returning circulation. He had barely touched the ropes at my ankles when another voice shouted, "Ho, there. You, come hold this wheel steady." My ankles remained as closely bound as they had begun, but at least I had a chance to free my hands. I began to work slowly at the loosened bonds as the journey resumed. Wherever we were headed, I preferred not to be entirely defenseless. I wished that Anni's cousin had managed to restore my dagger to me; it was too small to help significantly against even one armed professional, but any weapon would have boosted my flagging confidence.

The horse stepped into a hollow, and my nose struck the animal's side with a painful thud. My eyes watered. Only yesterday morning, I had been happy.

Chapter 26

Fog's body failed him. The blood escaped too quickly to be staunched. The lungs rasped. He had grown too old and too tired to maintain the agility and alertness mandatory for a K'shai's survival. Ordinary men had caught him unaware. He had grown too old for his profession.

"Where have you gone, devil?" he demanded.

"I am here, Fog."

"You promised me life."

"I have repaired you three times from death."

"I want my life, devil. That was our bargain."

"I did not promise eternity."

"Save me now!"

"Once more, Fog. I shall not guarantee another healing."

"Heal me!"

When the Ardasian medic returned to the death ward, he discovered the burly K'shai struggling to sit upright. The medic felt astonished that the man still lived. The K'shai had drifted in the coma of death since the younger K'shai had delivered him. The young K'shai had departed in despair; the old K'shai had been pierced through the chest and could not possibly survive.

The medic tried to prevent Fog from rising. "Let go of me, fool man," said Fog gruffly, shaking free of the medic with the ease of

K'shai strength and skill. "Where is my partner?" The boy was a good partner, admitted Fog reluctantly, despite his peculiarities and the devil's attention to him. The boy had almost made Fog regret the stubborn years of working alone.

"We told him that you would not regain consciousness," stammered the medic.

"Fool man," grumbled Fog, but he could not blame the medic for failing to anticipate intervention by the devil. Fog himself believed in the devil only when he was very drunk or nearly dead.

Someone had entered the death ward, which stood empty of patients but for Fog and an elderly, dying man whose heart had been too stressed by the blackening sky. The medic turned from Fog to the intruder. "You ought not to be here, Mistress," said the medic. "No visitors are allowed in this ward."

Fog recognized the Troupe's seamstress and wondered why she should have come to the hospital. He wondered still more when she approached him, disregarding the medic's protests. She stared at Fog, disconcerting him, even as her proximity stirred his renewed body. Pilgrim or no, Fog acknowledged to himself, she was a pretty thing in her own way; she might please him.

Sharp lines of fire ran through his head on the thought. Fog felt his newly healed body waver. The medic jumped away from Fog, as if the man could feel the fire, too.

"Kaedric," whispered Anni uncertainly.

Fog shivered only in his skull, for the devil had taken hold. "No more than the shadow of a shadow, beloved," said the devil through Fog's mouth.

"You cannot evade me this time."

"You are a stubborn woman, Rhianna. You realize what you have brought upon yourself by following me?"

"Yes, my darling. I must hold the Taormin until this pattern ends."

"We must go to the old city."

"He will await us."

"As he must. As must all of the players. *Horlach!*"

A cold breath of bitter age made the medic shiver and flee from the ward. In the minds of the Immortals, a little man spoke. *"Your way will not succeed, Venkarel. You can touch the past, but you cannot recover its pattern. You must use my memory. You must permit me to mold the restoration, or it will surely fail."*

"*If I fail, then we shall adapt to another Rending,*" answered Kaedric dryly, "*of my choosing.*"

"*We shall not fail,*" asserted Rhianna coldly. "*Horlach!*" She extended her mind to the image of a little man who had been old ten thousand years before her birth. He argued with the desperation of sincerity, but she did not listen to his pleas. She absorbed the Sorcerer King and bound him within herself with his ancient knowledge and his terrible, hurtful evils. She learned by stealing pieces of his mind, and she saw the past, which was the future. "Let us hurry, dearest Kaedric. I cannot contain him long without destroying my own sanity."

"We require him only a little longer, my darling. I would not have asked this of you. I hoped you would not discover me so soon."

"Have you still not realized, my omnipotent love, that you cannot protect me from that which manipulates us both?" Her husband laughed with rueful tenderness. The frail pilgrim seamstress and the grizzled K'shai left the hospital with their arms entwined and their hands clasped together.

Chapter 27

We had finally stopped. My hands moved freely within the circles of loose ropes, but I could not run nor even see. Anni's cousin had spoken to me; Ineuil was here. Did he mean to rescue me, or was he merely one of the Shrine's more merciful fanatics?

I could not entrust my fate to a pilgrim. I knew better than to rely on anyone but myself; Silf had taught me that lesson by abandoning me. I yearned to trust Evaric, who had promised to protect me from his enemies. Stop it, Lyriel, I chided myself. Evaric cannot help you now. No one can help you but yourself.

When an unknown guard dragged me from the horse's back, I sank heavily, dropping my head in a futile attempt to free it of the stale-smelling sack. The guard steadied me, and I drooped, clutching at his waist until I found his belt. I grasped his knife while he rumbled with my dragging weight.

I stabbed upward blindly, meeting fleshy resistance. I tore the sack from my head and hacked the ropes from my feet. The guard, a mediocre man of innocuous appearance, had fallen; blood gurgled from a deep gash in his throat.

I had no time to feel squeamish. I tried to leap to the back of the horse, but my feet were numb and uncooperative. I heard shouts. I did not look to identify them. I tried again to mount the horse, and I succeeded. I kicked the animal's sides as hard as my sandals allowed. The horse leaped forward, startled into a gallop. The shouts intensified, but I was free. I jerked the gag from my mouth.

The horse stopped short, skidding on the slick edge of old D'hai's polished road. I clung to his mane and barely kept from being thrown. I might as well have fallen; the guards pulled me from the horse and threw me down on the road. I felt glad of the resiliency of old D'hai, but my eyes overflowed with useless tears.

The guards did not speak to me. Whatever hope I had known dissolved at sight of their number. Guards, priests, and the Shrine Keeper himself, lofty in his fine curricle, opposed me. I could not run from them in old D'hai, where there were only straight lines and no concealing shelters. The guards did not even trouble themselves to tie me again.

The priests wore hoods, as did the guards. I could not identify Ineuil among the Shrine Keeper's entourage, nor could I discern any sympathetic expression. The Shrine Keeper had selected his zealots carefully, or he had paid them well to serve him blindly.

They dragged me to the central building, the broken dome. My fourth visit, I thought: over half the way to insanity. "What can you hope to achieve, Arvard?" I demanded, for my tongue was the only weapon left to me.

"He will come for you. He must come for you." Arvard spoke calmly. He had lost the look of madness, which had overcome him when sight of Evaric brought fever to his eyes; rather, the Shrine Keeper wore the tightly ashen mask of protracted pain or illness. I could not help thinking how remarkably strong and talented he must once have been, before Rendies and unnatural commands from a Seriin Lord overwhelmed him, to have retained such force of presence. He must once have loved Evaric, too. I shivered.

"Why here?" I asked him, though I could guess at many reasons. "You own D'hai. Why must you bring him here to die?"

"Because the Shrine revealed the way to me!" He had designed his emotional statement to impress an audience, and he succeeded; the Shrine Keeper was a fine orator.

His inspired priests jerked my arms in opposing directions. I snapped at them, "How can you listen to this man? You should be working to find away to destroy the barrier that imprisons us, not sitting in a dead city, waiting to fulfill the vengeance of some Seriin nobleman."

"Destroy the K'shai," proclaimed Arvard, "and the barrier falls. The Rendies will be driven from this world."

"It is the Voice of the Shrine," murmured several of the priests.

"It is the voice of a man who would slay his own brother." I poured fervor into my speech; I could rant quite as eloquently as the Shrine Keeper.

"Arvard," called Evaric, and the name echoed beneath the damaged dome. A small part of me rejoiced to hear him, but most of me despaired.

"You have come," announced Arvard. His ragged expression smoothed; the lines of anguish vanished. For an instant, the serenity of his demeanor impressed even me. "I knew that you would come to me, little brother."

Evaric walked through the ranks of Shrine guards, apparently indifferent to the swords poised against him. The guards stepped away from him, but the circle closed behind him. "Release her, Arvard," said Evaric softly. "She has no part in the argument that Lord Gorng has manufactured between us."

"She is the tool of evil," replied the Shrine Keeper soberly. "She taints you, Evaric." He pointed at one of his nearest guards and then at me. "Slay the Rendie daughter," he ordered with placid confidence, "that her evil blood may become pure in the chamber of our salvation."

The guard approached me; brown eyes in a round, smooth face observed me indifferently. He raised his sword to strike me, and I could only stare at the large, dark mole on his wrist at the joining of his sword hand. I continued to watch the mole, as it fell with the hand and the wrist, severed by the bright flash of K'shai steel. Blood spattered me, and the grips that had restrained me jerked, became limp, and released me.

I leaped from the path of the swords that slashed at Evaric, and I raced to the dais. Two guards reached for me, but they tripped on the uneven floor of the stage, and Evaric slew them. Evaric's sword pierced another guard, as the shorter blade in his left hand thwarted a stroke from a source behind him. Six guards lay bleeding in crumpled hillocks, as Evaric moved slowly to my side, and the Shrine Keeper's Guard encircled us cautiously.

"I am the tool of holy destiny," announced Arvard grandly. He spread his arms as if to summon some elemental force to strike us.

His sand-colored hair stood awry, but it seemed to shine like a halo when he spoke. "I shall cleanse the affliction from my brother, and he will be made pure."

The circle of enemies tightened around us, flowing to the Shrine Keeper's command. I retreated a pace involuntarily, and the central cylinder bruised my thigh. The cylinder felt colder than the floor, even colder than my hands. Anni had touched it and summoned the slumbering city; I touched it and felt only the reflection of my own chill dread. I was not prepared to die for a madman's vengeance nor for the holy cause in which most of these deadly men believed. "Touch the cylinder, Evaric," I entreated my perilous love.

"No." He studied each of his enemies, pressing around us from all directions. He watched his brother with a bitter regret and a mournful sorrow. "I cannot touch it, Lyriel." The only fear in him sprang from me and my request. "I shall not touch it," he insisted, though I had not argued with him. He no longer spoke to me. "I am Evaric, son of Evram and Terrell. I am not the one you seek!"

From the darkness of the open dome poured wraiths. Arvard covered his ears with his hands and cried, "Never listen to Rendies, little brother!" Rendie wails captured the chant of the Shrine Keeper's priests, as the Shrine Keeper's guards began to shout and stumble in their haste to flee. "You must kill *him*," wailed the Shrine Keeper, but his vigor fled with his panicked troop. "I cannot kill you, Evaric."

A Shrine guard shook the hood from his golden head. Ineuil seemed taller and finer than I had remembered, or perhaps the difference lay in his manner. "Touch the pillar, Evaric," he implored, "for Lyriel. You must save her."

Evaric turned his gaze from Arvard to Ineuil, and the Rendie hunger lay in Evaric's eyes. I thought that he would hurl his short sword at the pilgrim's throat. A wraith wailed, and the mists passed across my arm, leaving uneven, bloody scores. I cried aloud. Evaric cast both of his weapons to the floor, whirled to the cylinder, and struck it with both hands.

The room groaned and cracked. The floor shook, or the ground beneath it moved. The rocking motion thrust me to my knees. Arvard and his remaining followers scrambled on the rough floor. Rendies broke into frightened fragments. Only Evaric continued to stand, for the room did not shudder beneath him, as beneath the rest of us. All shifted and shuddered around him, who alone remained steady and solid.

The floor began to flow into molten, smoothness. With a roar, a clear blue shell snapped across the open dome and sealed it, severing Rendies. The riven wraiths drifted to the floor, slow and soft as ashes. "Fire-child," they howled forlornly. The air moaned with them, and the light grew red and warped. The circle of enemies became a circle of rippling emptiness encompassing the lonely stage.

I blinked, and Anni stood with us on the dais. Around her neck hung the stone like starlight, and her hair glowed like a pale gold sunrise. In her outstretched hand, she held a spindle: no true tool of spinning but a thing of amber and gold filigree. "You must take it, Evaric," she said gently, and she was crying. "You must return it."

"You have no choice," said Fog, but he was not Fog, for an image overlaid his: an image of a man as fine and dark as Evaric himself, save that Fog's image eyes were as blue as the cold, expensive crystal on Marlund's elegant Diarmon table. Evaric's eyes had lost all trace of color.

Someone took my hand. I blinked to see the room beyond the three figures standing before me. Rendies had dismembered many of the Shrine priests and guards, and Rendies still fed upon the dying. A few priests and guards huddled against the dome wall. Arvard sat hunched upon the floor, clutching at his head as if it pained him terribly.

The insistent hand pulled me. I tried to jerk free of it, for the arm was clothed in gray. The man was strong, and he would not release me. "Movement attracts undesirable attention," he whispered with barely a discernible motion.

"Are you a Shrine guard, Ineuil?"

"Only as an actor, fair Lyriel. It was a convenient pose and an informative one."

The room shuddered again. I felt nothing but Ineuil's rigid grip. The circle of dreadful emptiness sharpened; it resembled the barrier around the city, but it spewed a thicker turbulence. I looked at Anni's golden-haired cousin, trapped with me between the barrier and the stage. His attention was concentrated upon the trio near the cylinder.

"You must be the focus," said Anni and Fog as one. "You are the limit point."

"*It must occur now,*" said another voice, entwined with Anni's but emerging from a wider, less definable source.

"She has bound Horlach within herself," Ineuil informed me, though I think he talked only to disperse his restlessness, "that the necessary knowledge of the Sorcerer King be immediately available to Kaedric. Evaric must be the focus, Kaedric the force, and Rhianna the stabilizing continuity."

The shape of Evaric's hands blurred against the cylinder. The muscles of his arms showed sharply as he pressed; he embedded the cylinder's edges in his flesh. His hands became fire, hot and intangible. Those same unearthly hands had touched me with love.

Evaric raised one arm slowly, and the hand became solid as it separated from the rippling cylinder. I could even discern the brand, as he accepted the spindle that Anni offered him. Evaric's strong, lean hand shook. The brand upon it grew hazy.

My vision doubled, producing two rooms and two cylinders, distinct and superimposed. One was bright and frantic; one was dim and frightened. Patches of shrinking and expanding emptiness dashed around me, consuming what they touched. One caught the Shrine Keeper, and he was gone, wailing his brother's name in utter despair.

A stranger in odd, slick clothing occupied the second dais, addressing a little man beside the second cylinder. The little man, who held a spindle like that in Evaric's grasp, laughed and vanished. The sourceless voice spun from Anni, laughing in crazy echo.

The stranger gazed frantically at a glowing band upon his arm. The stranger's face wore bewilderment and shock, but calculation and intelligence stirred there as well. I could not understand his words, but I could sense his revulsion and his fear.

"Recall the pattern!" commanded Fog's voice, which was everywhere and inescapable.

The stranger slumped to the floor. Softly ringing tones issued from the band at his wrist. Anni crossed to him, knelt and touched him. The healing Power that she poured into him was visible even to me.

"Recall the pattern!" repeated Fog.

Evaric alternately studied the stranger and the spindle. The spindle glowed brilliantly. The shape of light around it shifted each time Evaric looked upon it. The air pulsed with the changes. Everywhere was silence.

Evaric grew pale, and I made a motion toward him. Ineuil restrained me, hissing, "You cannot touch raw Power and survive." His words made the only sound in all of that gaping, empty space.

"I love him," I whispered in a breath of loss.

"He is his father's son." Ineuil added bitterly, "And his mother's."

Anni went to Evaric's side, and Evaric let her arms draw him from the shuddering cylinder; I envied her. "He is not yet finished," declared Fog sternly.

Anni stood as tall and adamant as any queen, defending my love. "He cannot bear more alone, Kaedric. I shall not lose him now, having finally gained him."

The cold and heat of Rendies broke upon me. "*Give him to me,*" pleaded the sourceless voice, "*and I shall save him.*"

"No, Horlach," replied Anni irrevocably. "Your part is played. Your era is ended. I can protect my son now, for you have shown me how to untangle his energies and make him whole. It was never your pattern that bound him; it was the Taormin itself."

Angry lightning exploded from the black barrier that had contracted to this single room's dimensions. The lightning hurled itself at Anni. A crackling of fire burst from Fog and met the lightning. I shut my eyes against the brightness. When I reopened them, the old K'shai had crumpled. Ineuil started when the K'shai's dark shade stepped free of its fallen host. Ineuil whispered with something of wry respect in his voice, "I should have known you could not die, O Immortal Venkarel."

Lord Venkarel spoke, and the sense of him rattled me to the marrow. "Concede to us, Horlach, as you must, and spare me this waste of time. You knew from the day you stole the Taormin that restoration must be made. You have lived this moment before, Horlach, and you know that it is your last."

Evaric stepped free of Anni's arms, and she let him go, though her thin hand drifted after him in a tremulous gesture. Evaric raised the spindle once and lowered it, until it hovered just above the blackened cylinder.

"The wait has grown long," said the sourceless voice, sounding suddenly tired and ancient beyond belief. *"Dr. Terry has the final word, after all. He condemned us, Venkarel. You know only this time and this space. You do not know what he stole from us with his 'topological closure.'"*

"You stole it from yourself, Horlach, by desiring it for yourself alone."

"I yield my kingdom, Venkarel. Not even I—nor you—can cheat the past."

Evaric rammed the spindle into the blackened cylinder before him. The second cylinder exploded with amber light, as a golden fury enveloped Evaric. The doubled images merged. The body of the stranger vanished in a rippling wake of air.

The light expanded in blinding vehemence, and the force of it made me stagger against Ineuil. We clung to each other, as wave upon wave of coldly burning Power buffeted us. Rendie mists tore past us, splattered against the light, and disappeared. The wind of Power roared.

And it ended. The light dimmed. The wind failed. The dais storm returned to calm, and no one remained on the dais at all. Nothing remained on the dais but a silver cylinder, empty light, and motes of quietly drifting dust.

Ineuil dragged me from the dais' edge. The barrier had gone. Everything that mattered to me had gone.

My gaze drooped. I stared at the floor. I took each slow step cautiously, though the surface now extended in a smoothly golden plane beneath me. I waited for the floor to fall from beneath my feet, as my prosaic world had fallen from my expectations.

Ineuil stopped abruptly. A body lay before us: dried, as if an eternity of unkind suns had stolen all its moisture and its life. Ineuil knelt beside it and examined its hollowed clothing gingerly. "Fog," he informed me roughly. "It was the K'shai, Fog."

I quipped with raw brightness, "We two must be sturdier than K'shai. Do you suppose we are the last to live upon the world?"

Ineuil grimaced only a little wanly. "I am reassured, at least, to have a beautiful woman as my sole companion."

The dais drew my desolate eyes. The light had darkened to the smoky haze of shattered crystal, and a rainbow smear within it hid the cylinder. I caught my breath raggedly, for a shadow stirred.

Anni emerged, beautiful and joyful, reft of her veil of sorrow. I did not breathe again until my strange, bewildering Evaric appeared behind her. I ran to him, weeping from my heart, but more than blurry tears made his figure seem ethereal and unreal. He looked emptied of all spirit, as he crossed the once-ruined floor with a dutiful deference to the vanished pocks and furrows.

He approached me cautiously and stared at me lengthily before he seemed to see me. He nodded toward Anni. "She is the Lady Rhianna dur Ixaxis," he remarked softly, "my mother."

"You have a peculiar family," I responded with brittle care, recalling the Venkarel's shade with an unwilling shudder.

"I once deplored the prosaic nature of my parents: a Tyntagel clerk and an embittered former governess." Evaric resembled marble, artfully carved but lifeless. He rubbed his chin; the everyday motion shocked me unreasonably. "It is the queerest feeling," he murmured in a voice both casual and calm. He locked on me his eyes of cold silver, and I saw what he saw: strength extending in all directions, ensnaring the unattainable, capturing all desires. By a careless thought, he could take, create, destroy, and conquer; if this was Power, I wondered that the Sorcerer Kings had ever met defeat. He gave me his wonderful smile, and I wanted to fly to his arms and forget.

I clenched my hands at my sides and did not touch him. His smile tightened painfully, and his Power bathed me in compassionate understanding. I shrank from him, for his Power terrified me. Ineuil caught me as I tried to flee, and I burrowed my head against pilgrim gray.

"We are only mortal," Ineuil told me gently, "and they are not."

"She is not your cousin, is she?"

"Hardly."

The sky had cleared to pristine blue, unmarred by any turbulence. The streets of old D'hai felt empty but warm. Arvard was gone with his priests, Shrine Guard, and tortured, ambivalent schemes. A Lord of Serii had been thwarted in his vengeance; a Sorcerer King had surrendered to his past; and I felt quite sure that no one could harm the Venkarel's son now. Behind us, the broken dome had become whole; it emitted a sound like crackling fire, but its unseen smoke was scented more of sweetness than of death.

"The node renews itself," said Anni, who was Rhianna, Lady of Ix-axis. She moved forward strongly with Evaric at her side.

Ineuil and I followed slowly. We did not speak; we both watched the figures that preceded us. I no longer cared who saw me cry.

OPENING

Chapter 1

Only long lessons would persuade a conditioned world that the night dangers had retreated to their own sealed realm. Not even Taf and Rubi believed me. They had determined that I, like Alisa, who struggled to recover mind and body both, had been unbalanced by events.

Noryne believed, but she had always been too trusting. She had even trusted Zakari. She also had Power. She was becoming a little like Anni—Lady Rhianna.

The weather might convince the skeptics: Rain had fallen each evening of the past week. Weeds of strange, unfamiliar kind had begun to rise in great patches of the Ardasian desert, where nothing had grown for long years. Eventually, the changes would prove themselves. Just as the world adjusted to the Rending, so it would adapt to the Rending's repair. Mortals had regained the night, though most of us remained too bound by old fear to face the stars as yet. The histories would explain the changes badly. Pilgrims already claimed a miracle of the Shrine, achieved by the martyrdom of the Shrine Keeper, Arvard.

At least D'hai had forgotten the crimes of Evaric and the part of Rubi's Troupe in bringing him to the city; we were free again to leave or stay, to trade or perform. True, we had lost our two leading players, for Alisa would not fill any major role for a long while. Rubi had already begun to seek substitutes in local, untapped talent. Rubi despaired aloud, inwardly inspired by the obstacles she cursed.

Rubi never considered that the Troupe's sole surviving K'shai might have lost interest in the mundane business of Protecting a sorry group of struggling players, any more than she recognized that Protection against Rendies had become unnecessary. The fact that her seamstress was the Infortiare of Serii never penetrated Rubi's narrow focus. When Serii's Adjutant, the Lord Arineuil dur Ven, offered Protection to the Troupe in exchange for passage to Ardas, both Rubi and Taf haggled with him lengthily over the precise terms of the arrangement. Titles did not intimidate my Taf, and Rubi remained oblivious to anything but her ailing Troupe.

Lady Rhianna seemed to feel indebted to me, though I knew not why. The good will of the Infortiare could only be considered a rare and priceless boon. I was free of enemies, terrors, and awkward entanglements with mysterious K'shai. I ought to have felt delighted, or I ought to have felt devastated. I felt nothing.

I received sympathy from likely and unlikely sources. Taf fretted for me; even Vale patted my shoulder as he brought my supper to my room. I received offers of a willing ear to listen (though I did not know what I might say) from at least three quarters of the Troupe. I received great kindness; my voice gave thanks. My mind tallied friends and blessings I had never suspected that I owned; I felt nothing.

My skull developed a chronic ache at its base, and I did not care. Vale's wife, Epra, prepared her finest meals for me, but I scarcely ate, because the effort seemed excessive and futile. Sleep eluded me, but I could not settle to any useful task. The feelings that assaulted me huddled deeply within me, afraid to emerge into truth; I could not free them, for I could not find them. I had not thought that I could love a man so much nor miss him so sorely.

In lucid moments, I cried uncontrollably. I sobbed and shivered in fear of the Power that had always existed, but of which I had always been blissfully ignorant. I clung to Taf, and I ached for Silf, and I missed Sanston of my childhood dreams with an anguish that nearly shattered me. I had not despaired when the world threatened to fail and darken; I had not despaired when my proud Ardasia seemed likely to crumble into desolate sand. My fears had never seemed so strong, until I faced them in the eyes of my love.

I had not imagined the horror which eroded my spirit; I had seen the dire, infinite calamity that Evaric had faced and conquered. Anni/Rhianna, her Venkarel, Evaric: they were not human. They could not even perceive that the forces they battled were impossible for the rest of us. My Evaric had never left old D'hai: I did not know the man who rode beside our wagons now and wore my lover's face. Ineuil was right; they were beyond me.

During a midday halt on our long-delayed journey away from D'hai, Ineuil approached me, as I attempted to expunge my despair with furious scribbling. "Does it do you any good?" he asked me.

"It might." I did not pause in my hasty scrawl.

"Have you another quill?"

"In the wagon."

He found the quill and took a scrap of paper from my stack. He sat beside me, using a sand-tumbled stone as table. I never saw what he wrote, nor did he request details of my writing. As the Troupe began to stir for departure, he asked me, "Do you ever wonder, lovely Lyriel, why you are subjected to so much of what wise cynics label 'interesting times?' Do you wonder if the fates have truly embroiled you more deeply in drama than the rest of the world's pathetic masses, or if you only magnify your own perspective? Are we special, fair Lyriel, lucky or unfortunate? Or are we no more than common souls, whose individual trials and triumphs emit no greater sound than any plodder's dirge of life?"

"You are poetic today."

"Discouragement makes me so."

"Discouragement?" I tasted the word. "Is that what you feel?"

"It is less sharp than despair, less sanguine than phlegmatism. Yes, I think it is discouragement."

"Why?"

"They are beyond me. They are Immortal, and I am not. They have worlds to walk which I can never see. They cannot care for me."

"You mean that Rhianna cannot love you."

"Just as I cannot truly love her. I do finally realize my absurdity in hoping otherwise."

"Can you cease to love so easily?"

"Nothing about it has been easy. The effort has taken me half a lifetime, and in the process of learning my painful lesson, I have probably destroyed what love I might have earned from the very beautiful, enchanting woman who is my wife."

"You give me little hope."

"There is none if you think to have Evaric."

I looked toward the farthest wagon, where Evaric sat, listening thoughtfully to Rhianna. Noryne listened also, which made me feel unjustly envious. "I love him, blast you," I said, cursing myself more than Ineuil.

"You love a man who no longer exists. Power has consumed him."

"His own Power."

"Ultimately, yes."

"I loved him though he was K'shai and pursued by Rendies. I loved him without knowing or caring what danger he might bring to me. Why should I stop loving him because he becomes a wizard?"

Ineuil answered dryly, "He could destroy you with a thought."

"But he would never harm me knowingly. He loves me." I added, as if in proof, "He has remained with the Troupe."

"He has inherited his mother's obsession with duty. If you are so certain of him, then go to him. You have not spoken with him since he restored the Taormin, have you?" Ineuil folded the paper on which he had written and concealed it in a recess of his tunic, an Ardasian tunic of green and not of gray. "You will grow old, and he will not age."

"I am not old yet," I snapped, rising in a whirl that scattered my papers to the ground. The Adjutant of Serii saluted me wryly.

Evaric met me before I had crossed half the distance to where he had sat with Rhianna and Noryne. "If I touch you now," I asked him roughly, "will your Power destroy me?"

"No," he answered slowly, "not if I am controlling that Power."

"Are you controlling it?"

"If I were not, you would already be as lost to me as Arvard."

"Sands," I muttered, still terrified despite his ressurance. I felt startled to sense no shock but his own when I encircled him with my arms. I murmured his name repeatedly, holding him and touching him as I had done to combat Rendies for him.

"Lyriel," he whispered with a shade of warning and a shade of hungry hope, "do you understand what I am?"

I placed my hands on each side of his too-perfect face.

"You are a man who loves me and who has pledged himself to me."

"You will not allow me to forget it, will you?" His expression only hinted at the wonderful smile, but the promise had returned.

"Not a chance, Seriin. We Ardasians do not take our pledges lightly."

He still tasted like my Evaric.

Chapter 2

J on Terry spoke suddenly, startling his wife. "I think I understand."

Beth raised her head from her work. "What?"

"The second controller, the man who held it, and the voice in my
head."

Beth searched his eyes for the fever brightness which frightened
her. Jon had closed in upon himself so much since closing the DI
ports, as if he had remained part of that strangely altered world
they had abandoned. Network psychologists acknowledged that
he was troubled, but Jon would not accept their advice to confess
the source of his guilt or seek more specialized treatment. Beth felt
sure that Jon had not told even her the full account of that dreadful
day's events. "Do you feel like telling me, Jon?"

Jon smiled at her, and her hope surged into her throat. He spoke
rapidly, but a very rational excitement marked him. "The controller
performed its primary function of preserving topological integrity
by readjusting the aberrations. It discovered a way to redefine the
nodal limit point." Jon sounded almost giddy with delight. He took
Beth's hands and kissed her solemnity from her face. "I designed
better than I ever guessed."

"You're being a bit incoherent, my dear and brilliant husband."

"The Immortal stole the controller before the destruct sequence
could commence. The closure was effected; all the limit points were

removed from intersecting worlds, including the node, which was the only active limit point at the time. Trapped in a closed world, the controller's function as gatekeeper became meaningless, but it continued to exist because the Immortal impeded the energies of implosion." Jon Terry whistled softly, considering his own statement.

"That must have taken some doing. These Immortals of yours are an impressive people, Beth."

"They are mindlessly destructive, Jon," she reminded him gently.

"Not all of them. Not any longer. The controller escaped its genetically aberrant captor by performing its own genetic manipulation. The Immortal who took it was influenced unconsciously; select individuals within his reach could have been influenced equally: The changes could be subtle, because even a marginally stable system could have been maintained for a few thousand years with a little care. The controller needed only to tap a few of the most basic human instincts to breed its own savior. The Immortal who held the controller was restoring it."

Beth did not want to argue with him and watch him retreat again into his shell of fear. "Your controller managed all that without external keying?" She knew her comment sounded weak and doubtful.

"The controller merely fulfilled its underlying requirement to stabilize."

"Past tense?"

"Past and future both. They—the future Immortals—understood the need for topological correction, but they lacked adequate reference by which to define a stable space. So they returned to the source of the last acceptable topological configuration, absorbed the pattern from me, and rebuilt their world's stability."

"Are you suggesting that our home world has existed for several thousand years during the six months since we left it?"

"During the minute that we left it. If they kept decent histories, they would have known which moment to seek. They connected past and future space with a mapping that some of our Network geniuses would sell their souls to understand. I can prove it, Beth."

"Jon, where are you going?" He had not left the apartment voluntarily since they arrived.

"To my office."

"You are on medical leave."

"I need to reopen the DI ports."

"Reopen!" Beth eyed the security alarm; the guards could arrive in a few seconds; they had observed Jon closely since Tom Davison and a world were lost.

Jon kissed her again. "Don't worry, my Beth, I shall use all the proper channels this time. I know what I'm doing."

"Jon, the Immortals are still there, still a deadly danger."

"But they are not mad any longer, Beth, my darling. They have had twenty thousand years to master their Power. Think of what a thesis you can make of them now. My controller has tamed them!"

Even amid his exhilaration, Jon Terry could hear the echoes of Immortal voices laughing in his head with deep delight.

Definitions

I. Let X be a set. Let T be a collection of subsets of X. T is a *topology* for X if and only if:

　　(1) The null set and X are elements of T;

　　(2) If D and E are elements of T, then the intersection of D and E is an element of T;

　　(3) If U is an arbitrary subcollection of T, then the union of U is an element of T.

II. If T is a topology for X, then (X,T) comprises a *topological space*. A subset S of X is an *open* subset of (X,T) if S is an element of T.

III. If each open set containing an element p of X intersects a subset S of X in at least one point distinct from p, then p is a *limit point* of S with respect to the toplogical space (X,T).

IV. A subset S of X is *closed* if it contains all its limit points. The union of a subset S of X and the set of all its limit points is called the *closure* of S.